The Secret

By Raven Black

Artwork by Raven Black

The Secret Copyright © 2015 Raven Black

Cover Illustration Copyright © 2015 by Raven Black Publications LLC by Raven Black. Book design and production by Raven Black.
Author photograph by Raven Black. Design by Raven Black

ISBN-13: 978-0692830475
ISBN-10: 0692830472

DISCLAIMER

DEDICATION

To my husband Eddie for always believing in me even when I did not believe in myself. To my parents Deb and Dan, for nursing my hidden talents and tolerating my night owl tendencies. Nixy for your never-ending support and love. To my most important man, my son, Connor I will miss you.

DISCLAIMER

This publication is protected under the copyright laws of the United States and other countries throughout the world. Country of first publication: United States of America. Any unauthorized distributed, or transmitted in any form or by any means, including photocopying, recording, or other electronic or mechanical methods, without the prior written permission of the publisher, except in the case of brief quotations embodied in critical reviews and certain other noncommercial uses permitted by copyright law. Failure to comply with copyright law may result in civil liability and criminal prosecution. The story, all names, characters, and incidents portrayed in this publication are fictitious. No identification with actual persons, places, buildings, and products is intended or should be inferred.

Prologue

It started with an electric flash of blue light, dark clouds rolled across an even darker night sky. There was a low rumble at first and then an erupting boom that seemed to shake the earth. Somewhere outside within the storm, hidden among the shadows was a figure with deep brown eyes that watched through an open window. Even the storm would not keep him away. A silver lighter flared to life, the flame of it dancing in those hungry eyes as he lit another cigarette. The smoke curled and then quickly rushed away as another gust of wind rushed by him. Any one else would have felt cold but this man (if he could be called that) did not feel such things. It could be in the negatives outside and he would not be affected by the frigid temperature, he would not even develop frostbite. As he brought the cigarette to his lips again, he felt his canines extend with the insatiable hunger and they flashed their perfect whiteness, challenging the ever present storm. He was unafraid of its power for it was not the only deadly thing trolling through the night with the intent to destroy. Although this evil did not wish to ruin or even harm the beauty before him, he wanted to claim her for his own and to keep her for as long as she amused him. The poor dear thing had no idea what was coming for her, not a clue what was in store for her. This would be the first part of his favorite game. A toothy smile crawled across his features again, exposing those sharp deadly canines. Normally, she only had to worry about vandals trying to break in and rob her, but he was the only predator out tonight. He had been taking care of the neighborhood criminal problem by feeding on them. For once in their miserable lives, they proved themselves more useful.

The rain was beginning to pour down harder and now his once combed black hair hung about his head in wet tousled locks, small beads of water dripped from them, landing on his brown leather jacket. Some of the water ran down the soft caramel, skin of his face before dripping off his jaw and hitting his already wet, black, shirt. With the sounds of the storm to mask his actions, he contemplated claiming his prize, claiming her. After all, as far as he was concerned, she already belonged to him, she just did not know it yet.

There she appeared in the window, only partially aware of the voyeur standing in the yard. How long had he been coming here? Some part of him wondered if she knew or did she just like teasing him? For him, this was all just a game of predator and prey. The act of watching her, only help to quicken his hunger and enliven his lust even more. Another flash of lightening and a boom of thunder rocked the house as the rain began to pour down with ever more violently, seeming to reflect own raging emotions. Still he remained in the yard, his rapidly shrinking jeans beginning to dampen. None of that would deter him, he was the perfect predator. Not something created by nature, man or even god. He could not be certain who was the creator of his kind, but he did know that they were eternal. Even death himself shied away from them when they made their presence known, for they were death incarnate. Almost every one of them could wait out their prey for as long as was necessary. So he would wait for the perfect moment, the perfect time to strike, he was an artist and a master of his craft. Her final moments had to be exacted perfectly because he wished not to shame his coven. They expected him to make it clean and quick. To leave no evidence behind the way some sloppy mortal might. Of course even if he did leave a fingerprint, he was older than their science and they would find no DNA or match to any sign of him. For now he would drink her in, indulge in this moment, savor her innocence until the final second when he took it from her. It was all an act to him, a perfect performance of beast and man.

The night was lit by another set of flashes and as she dropped her t-shirt on the floor, she looked outside. For a brief moment she could swear she saw someone in the yard, his shadowy form illuminated by the lightning. He stepped back out of site into the line of pine trees that lined her yard and snuffed out his cigarette on the wet ground, with his boot. It was not time for her to see him yet, she would glimpse his features soon enough but not now. She was a clever little thing, smarter than the others whom he had hunted in this very same way. Still, she was after all mortal, which meant she was weak and vulnerable. So sure she saw someone she pressed a tank top to her breast as she stared out the window and waited for the lightning to provide her with the necessary light to see. The next flash of lightning lit her entire yard as thunder rumbled across the sky. This time he was hidden among the trees so she did not see him but his reddening eyes could see the blood pumping through her body. From his perfect spot, he even heard her heart racing from the sudden shock of seeing him. He knew she had begun to calm when she did not see him for a second time, the ear shattering thump of her heart slowed back to normal rhythm. Her regrettable mistake was assuming it was her imagination-despite the fact that for a few months now she had felt someone watching her every night. That knowing sensation haunted her even now as she tried to tell herself that it was all stupid paranoia. Even though her gut was screaming at her to double check the doors, to look outside again and that someone was out there. She still did the very human thing and ignored every bit of her instinct.

As she started to pull on a clean pair of boy shorts, the lightning flashed and with the next boom of thunder the power went out. That was his cue to move because in the darkness was where he shined the best. He used this opportunity to sneak around the back side of the house where he would not been seen by passing cars. At this distance he could smell her fear and he felt his body react all at once. An animalistic growl attempted to escape his throat but he stifled it so he could keep his advantage. The beast inside of him was tired of waiting and was now fighting to get out. Still he held back, he had been planning this for a while now and he would not let the natural predator within, ruin his perfect moment. Inside the house she stumbled around in an attempt to find a flash light, tripping over pieces of furniture as she headed toward the kitchen. He moved to his favorite spot in the back yard, waiting for her to fall asleep. It was always better when they were asleep, when they awoke to find him hovering over them, their fear became intoxicatingly strong. That emotion heightened the natural sweet flavor of their blood and made the experience much more pleasurable for him. It was not that the entire process of the kill was not enjoyable. When it came to his favorite prey, he liked to make it memorable for both parties and delighted in the theatrics of it.

There were no working flash lights in the home but he knew this, he had snuck in earlier in the week and removed their batteries. This may be her home, but he had marked his territory, staked his claim and now created the perfect set for the final act. So she searched the kitchen for a candle, opening and closing doors until she found a white taper candle. While his predatory peaked, he reached down and rubbed himself through this jeans. That would not be a problem for long, he would sate all his hungers soon enough. He began to wonder if she was a screamer, it was not a thought that had occurred to him before, but now he wondered. If she did not live in a rural area, he would let her scream because he loved to hear them scream. The more he fantasized about the things he would do to her and her reaction to him, the worse his issues became.

As he continued to watch her, his mind drifted off to thoughts of what he might do to her-cut her off in the hallway, blow out her candle and shove her against the wall so he could yank her panties off. He could just imagine sliding his fingers into her wet folds, the feel of her wetness and heat on his fingers. The sound of her moans in the dark, as he body shook with fear and pleasure from the assault. Then the feel of his teeth as they sank into her flesh and tasted the sweet warm liquid that flowed through her veins. It was almost too much for him to bare, his little fantasy nearly pushed him over the edge. The thunder snapped him back to reality and he realized his jeans were growing tighter. In an effort to calm himself, he had dug his nails into the palms of his hands and now blood ran down between his fingers. He lifted his fists to his face, unclenching them before licking his own blood off so he would leave no evidence behind.

The flicker of the candle flame could be seen as she passed from one window to another, heading toward her room. Then it flickered all the way to the living room. She had decided against sleeping in her room, she only usually did that if it was rainy and humid. But tonight it was rainy and cold outside. Something had prompted her to sleep in the living room, maybe she did not fully believe someone was not outside. Or it could be the simple fact that there was still a fire burning in the fire place and she knew that without it, she would freeze. She set the candle down in the empty cup on the coffee table, she headed over to one of the small windows and cranked it open a little bit, letting in the cool air. The damp air brushed across her legs, sending goose bumps, crawling up her flesh and bringing with it the calming scent of rain. All she wanted was to hear the sound of the rain as it dripped off the overhang. She needed it to help sooth her frayed nerves, someone had been decorating the neighborhood with dead bodies. With what she thought she saw, she was a little paranoid she might be next. Then again, part of her believed that the rumors circulating around were the real reason for her anxiety and they were giving her unnecessary cause for alarm.

The storm-despite the ever booming thunder-was beginning to lull her to sleep. So she blew out the candle flame before throwing a blanket over herself and stretching out on the couch. He watched her through the large bay window on the back side of the house. As the temperature began to drop his breath started to fog when he exhaled. It was not that he needed to breath to survive, it was just one of those mortal learned habits he could not break. With a wanting gaze he watched her sleep-lovely mounds rising and falling, perfect waist and hips hidden under a black fleece blanket. The outline of her long legs could barely be seen under that sheet of fabric. The sight of her like this, only made him want her that much more and he purred deep within his throat at the realization she would soon be his.

After a few moments he decided now was the prefect time and he crossed the yard, glancing around for potential witnesses as he made his way toward the back door of the house. When the next clap of thunder tore through the night sky, he cautiously opened the storm door so its loud creak was hidden within the storms violent rage. He then produced a flat-head screw driver from his pocket and placed its narrow end against the doors lock, then he waited. As the thunder rolled again, he punched the palm of his hand into the plastic handle of the tool, popping the lock on the door. Again he waited for the thunder to rumble across the land before he opened the door.

It was pitch black inside the house, but that was perfect for him because she would not hear or see him coming. The smell of her fear coupled with the sound of her beating heart, was intoxicating. An overwhelming excitement began to course through his body as his internal beast slowly took over. The last few minutes of the hunt were always the most exciting for him. He moved quickly towards the living room, he made no sound as he drifted through the darkness almost as if he was made of shadows. As he moved the rain ran down his leather jacket and beaded on his fingertips before hitting the wooden floor. There she lay sleeping with one hand across her stomach and the other above her head. For now he just watched her sleep, his eyes drinking in her unconscious form. The fabric of his jeans had now shrank to nearly nothing as his lust strained against them. Like a phantom in the night, he stood over her, watching her and waiting for her to awaken. It was much more fun if she woke on her own and saw him standing there in the dark. That look of shock and panic in her eyes was the one thing he loved to remember most of all. He hoped she would beg for her life and beg him to stop because he planned to quell two hungers tonight.

There was water dripping somewhere, she could hear the tap tap as it hit wooden floor. She managed to persuade herself to open her eyes and stop or contain the leak before it took the finish off her floor. When she did wake up, it was not a leak she came face to face with but the silhouette of a man standing over her. Even with the little light still coming in from outside, she could not see his face. At first all she could do was gasp. That was what he was looking for, when all she could do was to stare in horror. Her pupils dilated as they filled with fear and the smell of the emotion began to permeate the air. Finally she found her voice and she let out an ear shattering scream before trying to get off the couch. Her screams were delightful but he could not risk her drawing unwanted attention and ending his fun. So he grabbed her and clasped a hand over her mouth, pulling her to him so he was sitting behind her as he held her there. The feel of her soft form against his made him purr. This would be more enjoyable than he had anticipated. She tried to fight but he pulled a knife and pressed the razor sharp blade against the tender flesh of her throat. There was no need for him to have a knife, he could have just as easily held her down. But without the visible threat of death, his plaything might continue to struggle, not that he minded. It was so much better when they fought, it added to the excitement and it warmed his old blood. As the razor sharp edge pushed against her flesh, she squeezed her eyes shut to keep from crying. From her place on the couch, she could not see him but she could smell the cold leather of his coat and the over powering cigarette smoke hugging the fabric of his clothes. There was also, the unmistakable smell of rain and mud, wafting up from his boots. She could only assume that he had been outside for a while. As she thought back to weeks before this event, she realized that there had been the feeling someone was watching her. Even as she left for work, she felt a set of eyes on her, although she did not see anyone. It was as if he had heard her coming outside and he made a quick exit before she caught him stalking her.

She willed herself to breath very slowly, afraid that any wrong move would set him off and he might kill her. So she inhaled in slow, small gasps of air, trying to will herself to calm down. When he finally spoke she could hear the hint of an accent roll from the tip of his tongue with every word that left his mouth. There was a roughness in his tone as he whispered in her ear. It reminded her of gravel rolling across gravel.

"If you scream...I'll slit your pretty throat. But if you behave I won't hurt you."

Although she desperately wanted to fight, she could tell he was not kidding. This was no petty thief, this man knew what he was doing and had possibly planned this for months. There was no other way to explain how he managed to get into her house so easily and undetected. He had no hesitation in grabbing her and did not fumble with the knife like some amateur. To survive this ordeal, she knew that she would have to do every stupid, grotesque or perverted thing he asked of her. So she nodded obediently.

"There's a good girl."

The moment he let go of her she began to glance around for something to hit him with, eyes darting fearfully back and forth. She waited for him to put the knife away, but he never did. Only an idiot would have done that.

"Kneel." He demanded.

Terrified of what he might do to her, she obeyed, kneeling on the couch nearest the unlit lamp on the side table. The stranger grabbed the top of her boy shorts and she swallowed tears. If she did not act now, this man would rape her, kill her, and dump her body in a ditch somewhere. That was not the plan she had for her life and it would not be the way she would die. Just as he would not hesitate to hurt her, in this moment she knew that she should not hesitate to hurt him. She grabbed the lamp from the side table, spun around and cracked him in the face. The ceramic base shattered, slicing his face in various places before the rest of it crumpled to the floor. She leapt off the couch-convinced she had knocked him out-but he grabbed her ankle, tripping her. Even as they struggled, she could not see his face or the damage she know the lamp had inflicted. It was as if the shadows themselves were working for him and they shielded his identity from her.

A fist entangled in her raven locks and slammed her head into the wooden floor. Her vision danced with a carousel of black and white stars. In her moment of incapacitation, she felt his body weight on top of her before his hand wrapped around her throat. The pressure was just enough to cut the air flow from her lungs and increase her disorientation. That was the instant he decided to yank her into a hard kiss, shoving his tongue violently in her mouth. It tasted harshly of full flavor cigarettes. Even in her traumatized condition, she refused to stop fighting. When the time was right, she bit down on his tongue and tasted his bitter blood. How she hoped that taste would quickly be forgotten. Her assailant pulled back and slapped her hard. Now her vision began to blur with the threat of blackout. That would not subdue her, not today. She patted the floor with her hand, desperately trying to find a large shard of her busted lamp.

"You'll pay for that."

She did not give him the chance to hurt her again. Her fingers grazed a large shard and she grabbed it before driving it deep into the side of his neck. A gurgling sound emitted from the depths of his throat where blood had begun to pool. The stranger reared back away from her, giving her the opportunity she needed. She sprang to her feet and felt his fingers touch the back of her ankles. How was he still conscious and better yet, how was he still able to talk?

"Now you did it! Come here ya little bitch!"

"Don't touch me! Help! Somebody help me!"

In an attempt to get away she kicked him in the face. Her leg grazed the blade of the knife, leaving a considerable gash in her calf. He let go of her long enough for her to run toward the front door. She flung open the door, ran out into the street and began screaming as loud as she could.

"Help! Call the police!"

The storm outside had stopped sometime after the assailant entered the house and apparently someone had heard her cries for help because there was already two police cars pulling up out in front. She ran toward it, pointing toward the house.

"In there! He's in there! He broke in!"

The two oversized officers (one fat, one built) climbed out of their cars and hurried toward the house, guns drawn. Despite her disheveled state, she could not help but notice the odd pair they made. One was orange with spray on tanner and entirely too muscular for it to all be natural. While the other one was dark as charcoal and nearly to big to fit through her front door. They were nearly the human version of Tweedledee and Tweedledum. Without their uniforms and privileged positions, she was sure they would fit in no other place.

"Stay by the car."

It was still cold outside and as she stood on the wet concrete, her toes cooled. The breath from her lungs came out in white flurries of fog and she began to rub her arms to try to keep warm. She was not wearing much of anything and the blood from her leg was starting to crust uncomfortably. While she shivered in the cold they hurried inside and searched the entire house for the man she had claimed attacked her. To her disappointment, there would be no sign of him, no DNA to collect or fingerprints. He was much older than they were and far too smart to be caught by a human. In fact he was so assured of himself that he had wedged his way into the crowd outside and lit up a celebratory cigarette. Although she felt the burning gaze against her back, she could not pick him out among the crowd. Of course he already knew that she would never find him, not if she had a hundred years. As the wind shifted, carrying the smell of her blood with it, he felt his hunger surge. Tonight he would dine on something a little less special but there would always be other nights. One of the officers came back outside, unlocked the trunk to the cop car and wrapped her in a gray blanket before pulling a notebook from his pocket.

From the crowd, a white fanged smile gleamed and still went unnoticed. He nearly laughed at their futile attempt to find him. Then he turned and pulled himself from the crowd as easily as he had come. Her time would come soon enough.

The pudgy black cop with the pig face, held his pin tightly between two thick sausage fingers as if it would disappear at any moment. There was a smell of onion and garlic that radiated from him in over powering waves. It nearly made her vomit. She was already nauseated from the loss of blood and the anxiety of the attack, his rancid odor was only helping push bile further up her throat. If he had not been an officer, she might have commented on how tightly his uniform fit and told him to brush his teeth. But she needed his help, so she stomached the sight of him for the time being and prepared herself for his inevitable questions.

"Miss there was a sign of a struggle and we see where he punched the lock on your back door. Unfortunately, whoever broke in is gone already."

"But look." She pointed to her bloody leg. "Someone did attack me."

The gaping wound on her leg was still bleeding, not bad but just bad enough that blood was coating her ankle in a dark sheen of red. At this angle, she could see the depth of the cut. If he had gone any deeper, she might have never walked again. It would need stitches and she would bare a scar. That scar would serve as a reminder of what happened to her.

"What did he look like?"

"I don't know. I didn't see his face...I never saw his face. But I know his voice," She looked off into the distance as if she was trying to see something. "I think I always will."

"What's your name miss?"

"Sara...Sara King."

Sara King

Chapter 1

The air outside was bitter cold and it nipped at her finger tips, reddening her delicate skin as she pulled more of the toxic smoke into her lungs. It was nearly October and in the early morning air she could smell the icy chill of the coming snow. There was already a thin frost coating the grass and glittering on the leaves as they cascaded down from their many branches. In scent alone, she realized it was going to be a harsher winter this year. It felt to her as if this winter would serve as a reflection for her own emotional state. In some way she felt darker inside, colder even, as if the attack had left an evil deep within her that would never be cleansed from her system. Sara hoped not, she wanted the heavy feeling gone from her chest and stomach. A glance at the house filled her with an over whelming concoction of fear, anxiety and anger. She felt cold and not just because of the temperature outside. The only way she could deal with what had happened to her, the only way to function, was for her to shut down entirely and ignore any passing feelings that arose. Otherwise she would be permanently crippled by the attack and never gain the courage to live again.

As she exhaled she could barely tell where the smoke ended and the fog of her breath began. On a normal day she might have watched the sunrise, but today it was over cast with darkening clouds that threatened to break open without warning. To the South the waning moon was still a white silhouette in the sky, peeking behind the scatter of clouds. Sara could have smoked her cigarette inside but she wanted to feel the cold sting of autumn air on her pale flesh because it had a grounding affect on her frayed nerves. She also wanted to listen to the sound of the leaves and acorns as they fell to the ground. The pine trees were releasing their bloomed, cones and they hit the ground with a soft rustle as they landed on the blanket of pine needles that surrounded their base. Today would be the last day she could enjoy their music because it was her last day in Lafayette. After the attack, she could not bare to sleep in her own bed or to even walk into her own house. She no longer felt safe here and staying in the only hotel in town had not proved to be any help. All over town she thought she saw him or wondered if he was the guy behind her at the supermarket. Even going to the gas station to buy a pack of cigarettes proved to be too much for her to handle. Every time she saw a man in a leather jacket, she panicked and sprinted for her car before breaking down. She would always end up crying and shaking, fighting the urge to call the police every time she thought she saw him. The one thing she still could not understand was, why her? She did not consider herself excessively beautiful. So why did someone decide she was the object of his obsession? At twenty-six Sara King was by society standards a decent looking woman. She stood five feet five inches tall, with long legs, and curves in all the right places. Her eyes were her most prominent feature, they were bright green with sparkling flecks of baby blue. The police had said that it was not a random attack, they found evidence of a prowler around the house. There were several spots of boot prints in the mud between her pine trees and some of them were over a week old. He had been watching her for quite a while before he decided to finally make his move. Still she could not understand why. The police never found the man who had attacked her. Although he left fingerprints all over the house, they did not match anyone in the local or federal database. Even after the installation of a high priced security system and heavy locks on every entrance, Sara still could not sleep. Any little noise in or around the house would set her on edge. After about a week of this frantic behavior, she had decided that enough was enough, she had no choice but to leave.

She tossed the butt of her cigarette to the dirt and snuffed it out with her boot. Then she lifted the earbuds from her shoulders and gently pushed them in her ears. As she spun around on the balls of her feet, she began to bop her head to whatever her mp3 player chose in shuffle mode. Even with her headphones in, Sara made sure she could still hear the noises around her-she was still a more than a little paranoid since the attack. Slowly, cautiously, she made her way toward the back door of the house. Every footstep resembled that of a death row inmate, deliberately taking their time getting to the gallows. When Sara reached the back porch, she paused and looked around the yard. As far as she could tell, it was unoccupied but that was not to say someone was not still watching her from beyond her field of vision. Turning toward the door, she paused, staring at its dark wood as if it might collapse and suck her inside. Everything that once brought her comfort and safety, had turned on her and now made her anxious. Sara reached for the handle, its gold painted metal feeling like a block of ice when she gripped it and finally turned it. The back door creaked on its hinges when she opened it, the sound echoing down its long corridor. Its interior was dark, littered with unnerving shadows that made her heart begin to hammer rapidly inside of her rib cage. Sara swallowed the fear clawing up her throat and exhaled slowly to calm herself.

Her house was primarily empty besides the couple of boxes she had yet to move. Sara gathered up the last of the boxes and as she did she heard the thunder rolling in again. It would rain soon and she really did not want to move cardboard boxes in the rain. So she put her key lanyard around her neck and stacked the first two boxes. This would have been easier if she had let someone come help her move, but there was no time to wait for help. Sara wanted out now. The longer she stayed the more she remembered and when she remembered the cut on her leg-which was still healing-began to throb. Of course the sensation in her cut would spark another flashback. The move was the only therapy that would help her to recover from the experience and begin to live again. She set the boxes down and unlocked the truck with the remote. Then she stuffed them into the trunk before heading back to the house. As she turned around she could hear the storm growl again. The air around her was getting rapidly cooler and it was starting to mist.

"I'm gonna miss this place." She said to herself.

When she started toward the house again, a mocking bird fled from one of the pine trees-crying out in alarm as it went. This gave her reason to pause, her heartbeat racing again as she stared at the trees, removing one headphone so she could hear better. She felt her throat begin to go dry as the fear and panic crept through her body. Was he back? In that moment, it seemed as if time its self had stopped. Sara only started breathing again when the neighbor's cat came prancing out from between the trees.

"Geez Max. Way to give me a heart attack."

The black cat pranced over to her and she knelt to greet him.

As she scratched the cat under his chin and listened to him purr, Sara was unaware of the fact that she was being watched. He stood hidden among the shadows of the pines still dressed the same dark brown leather jacket and dark clothes that he had worn when he attacked her. A toothy grin crossed his features, she was going to be more fun than he had anticipated. She must have already sensed him once because she looked for him in the back yard before heading inside of the house. Or perhaps this mortal had developed paranoia, an emotion he had not experienced in centuries. Either way, nothing would keep him from her. As he watched her he licked his lips, his mouth salivated with hunger for her. He was dying to taste her again and next time to hear her scream. The little blood he had tasted on the blade of his knife, only served to drive his hunger for her. A growing problem pressed firmly against the zipper of his jeans as his hunger for her began to grow in intensity. The urge to smoke a cigarette in an attempt to calm his nerves also became more fervent but he knew the smoke would alert her to his presence. So he stood still, watching her and listening as the rain began to come down a little heavier. As he exhaled he breathed into his sleeve to keep the fog of his breath from being seen but his coat smelled like cigarette smoke and only further irritated him. From the still healing gash on her leg, he could smell the familiar aroma of dried blood and his mouth salivated for another taste.

Sara felt the scar on her leg suddenly began to burn and without realizing it, she lifted her eyes to the tree-line where her stalker once stood. She scanned the trees very slowly, staring hard in an attempt to spot the eyes she could now feel. He was careful not to move, standing in the thickest cluster of trees. So, she was smarter than his average prey, that was good, he needed a challenge. Maybe this one would fight back instead of just cowering in fear and begging for him to stop. It was so much better when they fought, of course the fear heightened the taste of the blood. But when they fought back, their adrenaline kicked up so much higher and the disappointment in their eyes when they lost, was beyond arousing. When she failed to see him, she turned her attention back to the creature at her feet. Sara realized it was beginning to rain harder and she cursed the sky before shooing the cat and running into the house. She grunted as she lifted the other two boxes and ran out to the car.

Sara dropped one of them into the trunk before balancing the other one on her arms and shoving it onto the back seat. Then she slammed the trunk, closed the back door and ran back to the house to lock the door.

When she reached the back door she paused, the feeling of being watched even stronger here than it had been. For a few moments the sound of rain faded away and the cold ceased to bother her. Sara opened the door again and peered into the empty space. There were more shadows cast across the hallway that lead to her bedroom. Somehow the interior of the house had become darker now, impossibly dark. Her mind began to recreate the image of the man as he moved toward the living room. She could hear the sound of water as it dripped from his leather jacket and landed onto the wooden floor. Sara's breathing quickened as she watched him make his way into the living room and she heard herself began screaming. A single tear rolled down her cheek, she knew what was happening in the room beyond her sight. There was a sudden flash of lightening that lit her entire house, shattering her hallucination. Sara blinked, shook her head and slammed the door before locking it. She pulled her hood up around her face and ran back to the car. It would be another dark, rainy, autumn day. She started the car, turned on the headlights and paused when her hand hit the gear shifter. For a moment she thought she saw a figure moving in the tree line on the side of the house. Sara stared fiercely into the shadows of the pine trees and tried to see through their branches. As she did someone or something shifted its' weight. There was someone there, she had not imagined being watched, she knew it now. That was enough to make her throw on the wipers, jam the car into reverse and begin backing out of the driveway as quickly as possible-being careful not to hit the neighbors cat as she went. The tires squealed on the wet pavement as she pressed the accelerator to the floor and they fought to find traction. She jolted back in her seat when they finally gripped and she tore down the street, leaving black streaks in her wake.

He watched her panicked movements and her desperate attempt to escape him. The scent of her fear drifted into his senses and enlivened the predator within. If only she knew that she was not getting away from him at all, she was driving right toward him. The rabbit was jumping into the foxes hole, where she would have no escape. It was all a matter of time before she realized this and that was fine with him, he had time. His brown pools had faded to red, their true color. From his pocket he pulled a small cell phone, dialed a number and pressed send.

"Yeah, she is headed your way."

By the time Sara reached the highway the thunder had stopped and it was barely raining. The raindrops hit the windshield and beaded on its' translucent surface like tiny liquid diamonds, before they ran down to meet the hood of her car. For the first few hours of her drive, she enjoyed the silence which was only mildly interrupted by the soft hiss of heat pouring into the car and the rhythmic beat of her wipers. Taking her lighter from the cup holder and pulling a cigarette - from the pack of Smoothes - with her teeth, she lit her second cigarette of the day. Sara exhaled a majority of the smoke from her lungs, through her nostrils. A cooling sensation filled her lungs and the chemicals in the cigarette helped to calm her nerves. She cracked the window an inch so the smoke drifted out into the rainy highway and she could ash her cigarette. It would be four more hours of driving before she reached her new safe haven in Collins. Sara did not mind the long drive, it meant she was putting distance between her and the nightmare in Lafayette.

The traffic light she was approaching, unexpectedly turned red and she slammed on her breaks causing the car to slide on the black top before finally coming to a complete stop. Her body jolted forward and then hit the seat so hard she nearly dripped her cigarette. For a moment she thought she would not stop. The seat belt strapped around her tightened with her sudden stop and now it was digging into her neck. So she readjusted it as soon as the safety locks on it let lose.

While waiting for the light to change again, she glanced at the clock on her CD player. It was nearly noon and she had forgotten to eat breakfast before she left. 'I'll eat at the next diner.' She thought to herself. As the light changed she glanced at her rear-view mirror at the large truck she heard roaring up behind her. Its' windows were tinted so dark that she was surprised the driver could even see out of them. The truck's paint was peeling and from what she could tell it used to be mostly red but now the primer showed. There were no make and model plates to be seen. They had obviously fallen off a long time ago. Sara was surprised that the truck even started, let alone the fact it could handle the highway. She pressed her foot on the gas, and tried to think if she had seen it before. 'Why in the world would you think that? I don't know.' Why did her mind immediately jump to that train of thought? It was not as if the truck had been behind her for a long time and besides that, she was on a major highway. So there was the chance she would see several of the same vehicles for an extended period. Even if she had never seen it before, the vehicle its self still made her slightly uncomfortable and for whatever reason, her leg began to throb. Something about the truck, or its invisible driver, felt familiar to her, . . and not in a good way. The truck engine roared as it accelerated and passed her. She took another long drag of her cigarette before throwing the butt out the window, she watched in her side mirror, as the cherry bounced down the road, exploding into tiny orange-red sparks when it hit the asphalt.

A few miles from the stop light, she found a dilapidated truck stop diner that sat secluded among a clump of trees. Its' outer frame had once been bright and vibrant, but was now faded in colors of pink, white, and yellow. It seemed slightly sad looking, and she thought to herself, 'this was probably a main stop at one time. But now it has been forgotten, lost in time and the world has moved on.' There were no visible signs to identify the name of the business. Despite its run down appearance, the place still seemed to do good business with the truck drivers. Its' parking lot was littered with several large semis and mini vans, packed with families, their tops adorned with suitcase caddies. As she approached the entrance to the parking lot, she felt the familiar sensation of fear, creeping up into her stomach. Her body was attempting to warn her of something and for a few seconds, she contemplated not stopping to eat. However, she had a feeling that if she did not stop here, she would end up driving another couple of hours before she could stop to eat anything. So she flipped on her turn signal and pulled into the crumbling parking lot. Sara located a spot far away from the large semis.

The loosened chunks of concrete crunched and popped beneath her tires before pinging off the under body of her car. As she stepped out, she zipped her black hooded sweater to cover the green tank top she was wearing. Then she shoved her cigarettes in the right leg pocket of her brown cargo pants, her phone in her hip pocket and then checked for her wallet. It was in the usual pocket and its chain was clipped securely to her front belt loop. With everything in place she headed toward the entrance. Her precision was purposely slow and she kept her eyes on the cracked asphalt beneath her. A shiver crawled up her spine as the wind rushed by her, causing the tops of the many trees surrounding the diner to sway. Sara stopped moving for a moment, something had made her stop and scan the woods behind the lot. She turned on her feet and headed toward the back of the building. On one side of it, there sat a weather worn, wooden sign with paint flakes piled beneath it. The wording on it was long gone but there was a cartoony waitress with roller skates and a tray perched on top of her palm. Just next to it sat a pile of cigarette butts along with discarded pieces of chewed gum and other bits of trash. It was a sad sight to see and she knew that this place had once been someone's dream. Now it sat in ruins. Behind the building she spotted a toy soldier by its large blue dumpster, discarded and left to rot in the muck dripping from the crack in the rusted metal casing. Some little boy at some time had loved that little toy and had left it behind. Sara never stopped to think that perhaps this diner was an omen, a reflection of what her future would hold. She too would be discarded and forgotten about, left to rot in filth.

Sara stopped just at the edge of the parking lot where the grass had over taken the concrete and cracked its edges. With watchful eyes she scanned the darkness between the trees, looking for the source of her fear. On the edge of the trees, she found comfort instead but still could not shake the feeling of need she felt. The need to look through the woods, that reason she had stopped her movement toward the restaurant and headed behind it instead. She could not shake that ever present feeling she was being watched or followed. In that moment she began to wonder to herself why she had never thought to get a gun. To have something on her at all times so she could defend herself. When the consideration had come up, she originally thought it was a ridiculous idea. That man would not follow her all the way out to Collins and he certainly was not going to stop at the same places she did. There was the risk of him being spotted and from the evidence the police had found, it was evident that he had worked so hard not to be spotted. He would not compromise that by following her outside of Lafayette. Even with that knowledge, she still could not shake the uneasy feeling she had and instead of pushing it away, she allowed herself to remember it. Although she doubted she would feel it again, she was no idiot, she had grown cautious.

Sara made her way back around to the front of the building, keeping her eyes glued to the ground in an attempt to hide from the strangers here. Her blue-green pools scanned across the many discarded cigarette butts and several patches of long squished gum that had been blacked by dirty shoes. She raised her head as she gripped the steel handle of the door and pulled it open, causing a set of small bells to tingle at the top of its frame. The smell of freshly brewed coffee and cigarette smoke, tingling her nostrils as she stepped over the threshold. A crowd of eyes scanned over her and she nervously tucked her hair behind her ear. They could tell she was not from this area and it was probably the very reason, that most of the gruff looking men sitting at the breakfast bar, were watching her. At the very same time, she was watching them with all of her senses. Her mind flashed back to the barely visible clothing of her attacker and she executed a quick mental comparison to the clothes of the diner's male patrons. Of course that would do her no good because no one she knew of wore the same clothes twice a week. It had been over a week though. Still he knew all too well the police were looking for him, so it was more likely he would avoid wearing any of the same garments all together. If he was smart (and she assumed he was) then he would have dropped them in a trash bin somewhere.

There was one man who looked at her out of the corner of his eye, never fully turning around to look at her. He seemed to purposely keep his head turned toward the front of the bar as if for some reason he was hiding his face from her. Sara paid closer attention to him. His black hair was hidden under a red truckers cap, a heavy green military coat concealed most of his torso, his blue jeans were spotted with grease and brown, round toe cowboy boots covered his feet. For a second she furrowed her brow and watched him, his mannerisms were somehow familiar but he was hunched over drinking coffee at the diner bar, so she never saw his face.

Sara move to a booth in the corner and settled in, hiding behind a laminated diner menu-continuing to watch the man who had been watching her. A waitresses voice broke her gaze and she lowered the menu to find a middle aged, heavy set woman with a tangle of blonde curls that were tied back by a little white cap. Her age given away by the crows feet that lined her bottom lids on both of her eyes and the frown lines stretching from the corners of her poorly painted lips. Her make-up resembled that of a clown, her mascara was smeared into her wrinkles and her lipstick was painted far to high on her lips. It was obvious that she had been working in this diner, far too long and that life had never been an easy trip for her. The older woman was one of those sad characters who obviously had planned more for their life and the diner was only meant to be temporary. Then life got in the way and all their dreams were crushed into tiny indistinguishable pieces. At some point, everything had gone to pot for this woman and she became complacent. Somehow she maintained a friendly outlook (mentally believing that it would all get better, it had to) and she greeted Sara with the kindness of a grandmother, speaking to one of her grandchildren.

"Good afternoon dear. Name's Marjorie and I'll be serving you today. Can I start you off with something to drink?"

"Hi . . . uh . . . yeah. I'll have coffee and can I get extra sugar for that please?"

"Sure," She replied, scribbling on her order pad. "Do you need a few more minutes to decide on your order?"
"Oh, no," She continued to glance at the man. "I'll have two eggs, over easy" She glanced again. "with wheat toast."

"That comes with another side."

Sara was too busy watching the cowboy (which was the nickname she had given him) who had been watching her, when she was not looking. Every time she glanced his way, he was just turning back to his coffee.

"Honey?"

"Oh...sorry, long day," She laughed nervously.

"No, I'll just have the eggs, toast and coffee."

"All right so I've got coffee, extra sugar and two eggs over easy with wheat toast?" "Yeah." She looked at the stranger   again.

"All right, I'll get that in for ya."

"Thanks."

From the group at the table the man had been talking to, there was an eruption of laughter. Sara found herself starring at the back of his head now and trying to see his face. 'Come on, turn around so I can see your face.' Then she thought about it and she realized, that even if she did see his face, she had never seen the face of the man who attacked her and she had already established that there was no way he would come an hour to attack her. A side from today, she had never been out this way, so this was not the place where he would have become obsessed with her. Still no one could have blamed her for being cautious and borderline paranoid. Still she could swear she heard his familiar voice but she could not be sure because the diner was a mass of noise. The sound of his voice and his words were forever seared into her mind. That much she was sure she would recognize, if she heard it. Then again, a traumatized mind can play tricks and make the victim think they heard or saw something. Before she could listen any harder (or begin to obsess), the waitress came with her order. Sara would have liked her coffee a long time ago, at least it could have provided her some distraction.

"All right, here you are honey." She said, setting down the coffee, extra sugar and plate of food.

"Thanks."

"Anything else?"

"No, I'm good. Thank you."

"Oh," She set her bill down on the table.

"I'll take that whenever you are ready."

"Thank you."

Sara emptied six packs of sugar into her coffee and stirred it before digging into her food. Out of the corner of her eye, she continued to watch that man. She never could see his face because the collar of his coat came up too high and his hat was low enough to help cover it. When she finished her plate, she slid the glass closer and lit a cigarette. A cloud of smoke slowly curled up from her corner of the diner as she stared the man down. No matter how hard she looked at him, she would never see his face and she begin to wonder why she was still trying. Why was she obsessing over him? He was not the man she was attempting to avoid. So why had she made him public enemy number one? The only reasoning she came up with, was because it would have helped her move on if she could place a face with her attacker. However, he remained faceless, just a voice in the darkness that haunted her
nightmares.

Time seemed to slow as she watched him and it became just the two of them in the diner. Sara suddenly had tunnel vision, everything else around her faded out. As she continued to stare at him, she flashed back to the attack. "...you behave, I won't hurt you..." Sara was suddenly back in the dark, kneeling on her couch and he was pulling at the top of her shorts. She practically threw herself from the table and sprinted to the ladies room. From beneath his cap, the stranger watched her lovely form dash across the diner and disappear into the restroom. It was a single stall with stained yellow tile floor, graffiti walls and pale neon lighting which contained at least a years worth of dead flies. Sara leaned against the cool tile wall, trying to catch her breath and trying to calm herself down-this was exactly why she was moving.

The man who attacked her, his voice had an accent to it that she knew she would recognize if she heard it again and she wanted to hear the strangers voice just to make sure. She let her head fall against the wall and sighed. 'Pay your bill and go.' She took a slow calming breath, before pushing herself from the wall and finding the strength in her legs again. Sara headed over to the sink, placing a hand on either side before looking in the mirror at her own reflection. Her features were far paler than they should be. 'Pull yourself together.' Sara placed her left hand on the cold steel door and steadied herself again before taking one last breath and grabbing the door handle. It was ice cold under her hot hands, her whole body had flushed warm with nervous tension but she would not let that stop her from leaving here. With her nerves finally calm, she turned the handle and yanked the door open.

The stranger was leaving as she was stepping from the bathroom, still she only saw his deep brown eyes as he shot her a sideways glance. Sara was determined to catch him, so she tossed two dollars on the table, and shoved money at the girl behind the counter before running out of there. When she finally stepped outside she found the parking lot nearly empty and there was no sign of him. It was as if he just disappeared.

"Damn it!"

She ran her fingers through her hair in frustration and then pulled out her cigarettes. As she surveyed the lot, she lit a cigarette-failing to notice the truck hidden in the corner of the lot and the man tapping on the steering wheel, watching her. Their game of cat and mouse was turning out to be much more fun than he had anticipated. What amused him the most, was that she believed she had escaped him. Too bad she might never figure out, he was the man in the dark and that he always got what he wanted. Also, that she was falling right into his hands.

Sara took a couple drags before heading toward the car, it was getting colder out and starting to rain again. The car lights flashed as she hit the unlock button. Sara climbed inside, started it and pulled back out onto the highway.

"Four more hours. Just stay awake for four more hours."

The rest of her trip was virtually uneventful. A few times though she could swear that she saw that truck again but it was never close enough to her for her to be sure. She could feel road fatigue beginning to set in as the long stretch of pavement lulled her into a hypnotic trance. Sara cracked the window, letting the cold moist air brush across her face and wake her from her exhaustive state. It was not long before she saw the 'Welcome to The Town of Hope' sign and she breathed a sigh of relief.

"Almost there."

The later it got the more nervous she became and the more sinister everything seemed to look. Maybe it was because of the various, creepy, broken down gas stations she had seen or the almost ghost towns she had passed through. Whatever it was, something had caused her stomach to fill with butterflies. At least the rain had stopped, unfortunately it was only fifty degrees outside-according to the Credit Union sign that she just passed. It was late enough that only a few gas stations were still open and she was virtually the only person on the road. Well, her and the lights of the vehicles she had been seeing far off in her rear-view for the past couple hours. The clock in the car read ten o'clock and she still had about an hour drive left.

When she finally saw the sign 'Welcome to Collins', she felt herself relax because she was finally home. As she drove into town she noticed an unnatural stillness about the place, that she had not felt before the first time she drove here. The town, it felt dead tonight, even with the beautifully decorative street lamps and the various little shops. During the daylight hours, there were people littering the sidewalks as they moved from one place to another, getting their daily shopping completed. At night time there was absolutely no one on the street. Perhaps this was the reason the town felt dead to her. As she made her way through town, a cop car passed her driving unusually slow and for a second she worried that he might pull her over. The cop turned down a side street, just a few yards away from her. Again she glanced in her rear-view mirror and found an empty street with no car lights. She turned left down Elsmoor Avenue and drove for four blocks before turning right down Lillie Drive and pulling into the drive way of the large white two story house. On one of the front support beams of the large porch, was a white plastic sign that had the numbers 5102 painted on it in black lettering. Its first floor was lined with large windows, two of which faced the front yard and a solid white railing ran the entire length of the porch.

Sara put the car in park, turned off the lights and then the engine. She climbed out and stretched, cracking her back before looking around. The neighborhood was quiet, no barking dogs, no radios and no other cars on the street. That seemed a little odd to her. With an exhausted sigh, she closed the car door before heading to the house and unlocking the front door. Then she flipped on the porch light and the dining room light before going back out to the car and unloading the boxes. As she set the last box down she hit the button for the car lock and heard the satisfying honk of the horn, signaling to her that the alarm had been armed.

Sara had just locked the door to the house when the rumble of a truck drifted in through the house. By the time she unlocked the door again and yanked it open, the truck was making its' way down one of the other streets. Even if she stepped out onto the porch, she would not be able to see any sign of it. She sighed before closing and re-locking the door. A few days before she had set up almost everything in the house. For now, she would go to bed and worry about unpacking, in the morning. After checking the locks and pulling the curtains shut, she headed upstairs to get some sleep. Unaware of the fact, that a Collins Sheriff had pulled up in front of the house. Her street was so dark, that even with his drivers side window rolled all the way down, the only thing she would have seen was his left thumb as it tapped impatiently against the drivers side door. For a few minutes he sat there, staring at the house. There was no logical reason for him to be there and he knew that. Things were progressing just as they had planned and in due time, she would learn her mistake. The radio in his car sounded, he was being summoned back to the station. With a nod to himself, he pulled away from the only lit house on Lillie Drive. There would be time for her later.

Chapter 2

A black down comforter and piles of blankets protected her small frame from the cold chill that encircled her bed. Although she was tucked safely away within the confines of her bed, Sara would find no comfort or sleep tonight. In her conscious mind she wondered how long she might continue to dream about her faceless attacker. How long would he haunt her memories? The demon had not violated her flesh, at least she had prevented him from doing that. Still, that monster remained a phantom in her life, her reason to look over her shoulder and why she always slept with her door locked. None of the precautions she took, prevented him from getting to her. Every night she lay down to sleep he was there, attacking her all over again. The nightmares fluctuated in their depravity, sometimes she would escape and other times he would succeed in violating her. Sara would wake up screaming. They were creatures all their own, thieves of memory and time, completely resistant to outside influence. It is easy to become trapped by one, swallowed whole by their evanescent masterpieces. One step ahead of you, they always know hot to catch and hold you. Always they wait until you are unaware, stalking you through the dream world before they finally pounce on you and keep you for as long as your tired mind will allow. Sara's nightmares were vicious, unforgiving things, that delighted in her pain and took great pleasure in forcing her to relive the events.

Now she was trapped by one (a spy in her own dream) looking just over the shoulder of a leather coated stranger. In epic horror she watched him slowly ascend her wooden stairs and make his way down the hallway before stepping into her room to stand over her. He gazed down at her as if she was his last meal. Some where in the confines of her mind, she heard herself say: 'this is not how it happened.' The dream version of her was covered in a thin shimmer of sweat and remarkably, unaware of his presence. Her faceless attacker moved closer to her, the sound of his boots against the wooden floor she knew should have woke her already, but the dream version of her did not move. Time was moving much slower than it should have been. The result being that she had to watch this horror go on for much longer than it should.

When she finally realized he was standing over her and she opened her eyes, he placed a hand over Sara's mouth before she could scream. He was stronger this time and she found it nearly impossible to fight him. This nightmare was strong, she could not force herself to wake up and she could feel the steady increase of fear. Sara tried to fight him off, but he climbed on top of her, pinning her to the bed. Again, she could not see his face, but his smile revealed two pearl white canines. The nightmare had reached a new level of sinister. 'Wake up!' Sara was screaming at herself over the shoulder of the man in a desperate attempt to wake up before things got worse. Was there nothing that could stop this depravity? No course of action she could take to shatter this prison? For a second he turned his attention away from the dream version of her and looked at Sara. It was one of those movie moments where the character looks into the camera. That was how she felt right now. The features she glimpsed were not human. A set of two red eyes glared at her from the darkness and a set of sharp canines gleamed in the shadows. There was nothing to illuminate those pearly daggers, so there was no reason she should have been able to see them. Then again, this was the dream realm and in here, logic need not apply.

"Leave her alone!"

She heard herself scream, but the creature standing over her unconscious form, paid her no mind, directing his full attention to her dream body. Without warning, a hand shot out of the darkness and yanked the covers from her lower half, exposing her bare legs and revealing just how little she was wearing. She fought to get him away from her. All her efforts were futile because two more shadowy figures emerged from the ever present darkness to hold her down. One of them yanked her shorts off and exposed her most delicate flesh. Whatever they were (call them demons if it helps) these creatures were cruel lustful beings. They delighted in the pain of others. A voice whispered to her from the dark, mocking her pain.

"Sshh...Sara. If you're good, we won't hurt you."

Her mouth fell open in complete horror as she watched two shadowy hands wrap around her bare thighs. Sara tried to scream at them to stop but when she opened her mouth, no sound came out. It was as if her vocal cords had been removed and she clawed at her throat in desperation. A single tear rolled down her cheek as her eyes widened in horror because she realized there was nothing she could do to stop them. At the same time she could not bare to watch this happen but they were in control and had given her no choice. When at last they (those faceless, nameless things) yanked her legs apart, her physical body finally woke up and sitting straight up in bed she screamed until her throat was raw. Until her lungs hurt from the air suddenly forced out of them, and her ears rang from the echo of her own voice. When her screaming ceased, then the shaking and panting began. Sara was on the verge of tears as she pulled her covers against her body tight. The down comforter and Egyptian cotton sheets were not some magical cloak that would save her. Nevertheless she still felt better. Although she had a white knuckle grip on the mass of fabric as she mentally coaxed herself back to placidity. Her eyes darted frantically about the room in search of any sign to tell her if the nightmare had even been partially real. Sara was panting and shaking, on the verge of tears as she pulled her covers around herself. In one night she had come to understand that there was no escaping the past, it was encoded into every part of her. The feeling of being touched still lingered on her flesh as if threads of spiderweb were stuck to her. A smell of cigarettes lingered in the room. It was not the aroma of fresh smoke but the kind that lingered on the clothes long after the cigarette has been extinguished. The unknown source of the smell gave her even more cause for alarm because she herself had not had a chance to smoke in the house.

For a few minutes, she just sat curled into a ball on the bed trying to come back to reality and calm herself. The smell of the smoke only made her more nervous because she now recognized their scent. Her attacker smelled of the same cigarettes. There was a noticeable chill in the air around her bed as if someone had opened a window or come in, sometime in the night. She scanned the room slowly and could not place the source of her continued uneasiness. 'Had it really all been a dream?' Her fractured mind continued to question and analyze. If she did not modify her conscious soon, her paranoia would chime in to feed an already susceptible mindset. Sara stared out the window, her vision drifting to a blur as she listened to the wind whistle by the gaps around its wooden frame. After a minute she blinked and nodded to herself.

"Bolt locks and window locks."

To anyone else that thought would have seemed random but it was actually something she had been silently contemplating and now she had made her decision. She threw back the covers, grabbed her robe, and wrapped it around herself. As if it would hide her from the violated feeling still tingling on her skin. A shower would be the only thing to get that feeling off. She headed into the bathroom and closed the door in a rather defiant manner, almost as if to say 'fuck you dream' Then she locked the door and yanked the shower curtain closed before turning the only knob all the way to hot. The water sprang to life and she felt a sense of calm pass over her as the sound of running water broke through the ever present silence. With a few quick movements, she disrobed and moved into the stream of hot water. It's nearly scalding heat quickly burning the dream violation far away from her and she scrubbed her skin until it was red. 'This will be our little secret.' That phrase passed effortlessly through her mind as she started to wash her hair.

"Stop it!"

She was yelling at her own mind. An over active mind will easily turn on its owner. When she felt as clean as she ever would, she got out of the shower, twisted her hair in a towel and tossed on her robe. There was a moment of hesitation as she turned toward the bathroom door. For a few seconds she could only stare at the door handle as if her nightmare would kick it from its hinges and take her away. The image even flashed through her head. With a slow sigh, Sara unlocked and opened the door letting the steam pour out into the hallway. A feeling of relief passed over her momentarily when she realized that she was alone. Still, some subconscious part of her must have felt vulnerable because she ran to her room. As she disrobed to dry off and dress, she thought she saw something dash past her open door.

"Shit," She robed herself again. "Who's there?"

This was not a good position for her to be in, so she threw her robe down and dressed as quick as possible. She slipped on a pair of black jeans, a black shirt, her zip up sweater and pulled her wet locks in a ponytail. From one of the many boxes in her room, she grabbed a heavy metal candle stick. Despite the attack, Sara did not like having weapons in the house. Everyone she had told about the assault, had begged her to get something to protect herself but she still did not feel comfortable having a gun in the house.

"Someone better not be screwing around in here! I've got a gun!" She lied.

They did not know she was lying (if there was someone sneaking around) she could very well have a shotgun. Slowly, she moved down the hallway (candle holder perched over her right shoulder) and hit the light switch on the wall, illuminating the empty hallway. She searched the entire house, flipping on lights as she went. When she found no one, she set the holder down on the kitchen counter.

Outside the wind was slowing down, but her heart was not. She swallowed the lump of fear that had been forming in her throat and sighed to calm herself. The silence in the house was deafening and she needed to get out before she completely lost it. Sara grabbed her wallet, keys and cell phone, shoving them in her pockets before heading out to her car. Even the sound of leaves blowing made her jumpy. They scraped the pavement as they drifted across her driveway. An eerie feeling passed through her whole being and she looked around for the source of her discomfort. The neighborhood was a little too quiet for her taste. Her eyes caught sight of a large building that towered over the town. From what she could deduce it was a factory. Its worn brick exterior gave her reason to believe it was currently abandoned. Not too far from it was another factory with white billows of smoke coming out of the three large stacks on its roof. She briefly glanced at it before turning her attention back to the other building. A knot began to form in her belly. Something was very wrong with that place. Sara shuttered before finally climbing in her Taurus and heading into town. There was one church in the town and she assumed one school. It was the sort of place where kids could walk from school and not have to worry about being kidnapped. Where women did not have to carry pepper spray when they went out to their cars at night and everyone knows their neighbor. Most of the businesses closed early and from what she had seen, almost no one worked on Sunday.

As she made her way through town, it occurred to her that the streets and sidewalks were nearly empty. It was Tuesday, where were the daily shoppers? Or the housewives getting their weekly groceries? There was no one headed to work and there were no school buses coming to pick up children. What was going on in this town? Maybe she was being a bit paranoid, but if she was not and it turned out that this town was really this creepy normally, she would move again. For now, she had to get more locks or she would be in for another sleepless night. 'Maybe you should, just get up and go. Move to a bigger city even farther away, several states away in fact.' Sara shook her head, popping a cigarette into her mouth and lighting it. She took a long drag from it before she pulled it from her mouth and ashed it out the window.

On the opposite side of town she found a small hardware store where she hoped she might get the supplies she needed. The small parking lot next to the store was nearly full and she ended up having to park on the very edge of the lot. It was busier in this part of town and she felt a little better because of it. In the morning light, Collins regained some of its small town charm. Its little shops were a bustle with people and they greeted one another as they passed on the sidewalk. As she exited her car, she looked around and felt her paranoia rear its ugly head again, causing her to survey the parking lot for suspicious characters. She cursed herself to stop and closed her car door before heading up to the hardware store. Even though she was feeling slightly less freaked out, she still yanked her hood up to hide her face before tossing the expired cigarette out and shoving her hands in her pockets. On her way through the lot, she spotted a Collins Police car and wondered if there was one cop in this whole town.

"Is that the car from last night?"

Before her imagination could run wild, she shook her head and hurried into the hardware store to get out of the cold. The rush of air from an electric heater mounted just above the door, greeted her chilled skin with a welcome heat. Its interior smelled of sawdust and metal shavings. Every wall was lined with tools of various types and a series of metal shelving units filled up its center. Above each isle hung a green sign with chalk white lettering that listed its contents. The yellow halogen lights mounted to the ceiling cast the an eerie, sick glow on everything inside. Sara glanced once at the signs above, located her isle and headed quickly toward it. She kept her eyes glued to the dirty linoleum floor as she moved about. No one here needed to see her face. Although the parking lot was nearly full, the store its self seemed oddly empty. 'Hmm'

"Bold locks, bold locks...ah!"

She was thinking out loud again. When she finally found them, she picked up three of those before spotting the window locks and grabbing a handful of those. She wanted to get what she needed and get back to her safe zone. Sara knew she had to get over the attack and quit being paranoid. That she at least had to attempt to live again. If that meant she had to lock herself in her house for a few days in order to get over the attack and stop being afraid of everything, then she would. With an armful of locks she hurried toward the end of the isle and almost ran into the officer walking by.

"Oh, whoa. Easy Miss."

"I'm sorry sir."

"Why are you in such a hurry? You are going to pay for those right?"

"Oh...uh..yeah..yes..I just wanna get home and...uh...before the weather gets too bad."

Sara suddenly found herself staring at him, he was not overly handsome but there was something attractive about him. It may have been the uniform or his hypnotic gray-blue eyes that seemed to sparkle with unspoken desire. Just beneath his right eye, she noticed a small barely visible scar that lined his bottom lid. There was a sign of stubble that decorated his upper lip and bottom jaw, where he had not had the time to shave. A mess of dirty blonde hair peeked out from beneath the brim of his hat. As Sara began to move toward the cash register, she caught sight of him licking and chewing slightly on his bottom lip before he finally spoke.

"Expecting trouble," He motioned toward her haul. "that's quite a security system."

She paused in her movements, scanning his dark blue Collins City uniform, for any sign of his badge. In case she had any issued, she wanted to be able to call him by name (especially if he was the issue). She did not trust anyone in this town. His name glimmered at her in engraved lettering, T. Ellis. It took her a moment to realize that she had been so enthralled by him, she forgot he had asked her a question.

"What?" She glanced down at her bundle.
"Oh . .uh . . .yeah, something like that."

There was an awkward moment of silence as Officer Ellis looked at her in the same way she had looked at him. Only his eyes were filled with noticeable hunger and lust. His tongue darted out to slowly lick his bottom lip again. That made her shift because her mind began to wonder about that tongue as his eyes traveled across her body, like finger tips across her skin. Sara was half uncomfortable, half aroused and her whole body felt like it was vibrating. She suddenly found her mind filled with thoughts of being handcuffed and violated-that only made her eyes unconsciously dart to his handcuff holder and then back to his face. Where were these thoughts

34

coming from? Sara was not acting like herself, it was as if the images were suggestions from another source. Almost like someone had reached into her mind and placed them there. Ellis caught her eye movement and a slow smile crept across his lips as that tongue flicked out to wet them and she could swear she felt it dart across the apex of her thighs. That made her shift and her eyes began to nervously dart every which way but him.

"Well . . .uh . . .see ya."

She nearly ran for the cash register. The urge to drop what she was carrying and run for the door, was over whelming. Sara fought to keep her body language and her every movement calm. In her twisted little mind, she saw him as a wolf and wolves smell fear. So she did not want to draw his attention any more than she already had done. As she moved cautiously toward the counter, Sara could feel his eyes roaming across her back and leaving a trail of heat where ever they lay. The officer who walked up beside Ellis, at first did not take notice of her presence. Sara however caught a brief glimpse of him out of her peripherals. He was nearly a head taller than his partner and his build reflected that of a man with far greater muscle mass. It was obvious he took great pride in his appearance. His uniform was pressed and the buttons of his shirt were perfectly lined up with his zipper. There was no hint of stubble along his strong jawline. Or faded scars decorating his features. There was a purposeful messiness about his hair but for the most part it too was neat. He had an obvious pretentiousness air about himself, as if he believed he was god. They seemed to be a mismatched pair but a second sideways glance gave her the inclination that they shared something. Beneath their authoritative exterior, she sensed a dark bond. It was during her second glimpse of the other officer that she noticed his stormy blue gray eyes. The way they looked at her, it was not right. Their position in society demanded more of them, higher standards. Therefore they should conduct themselves in a much different manner than they were at this very moment.

"I got the-"

Officer Ellis interrupted him with a back handed slap to the shoulder before pointing in Sara's direction. She did not see this action. The sudden quick response of his partner, as if to say 'shut up.' He was quick to silence himself and keep his attention on Sara. They both watched her for a few moments before getting in line right behind her. Now she was nearly shaking as she fought to keep her composure. She could feel him staring at the nape of her neck before his eyes trailed down to her backside. Those deep stormy pools burned through her as they disrespectfully roamed over her body. The line in which she found herself was moving far too slow. Sara struggled to maintain her seemingly placid exterior. Beneath her stony visage was chaos and senseless emotion. Her thoughts swam and swelled. While her over active imagination fueled the subconscious ramblings of her paranoia. It was only a matter of time before her composure cracked and the wolf smelled her fear. Sara knew better, she knew the rules of the game but she could not resist turning around to look at him.

"Hi." He whispered before flashing her what should be a charming smile.

She spun back around, fumbling with the locks as she attempted to set them on the counter. Her composure was starting to crack. As she stood at the counter to pay for her things, she glanced at Ellis's partner and at the name badge he wore - M. Harris. The clerk spoke to her and for a second she did not move.

"What?" She snapped out of her daze.

"Twenty dollars."

Sara pulled out a twenty dollar bill, shoved it at the man and then left as quick as she could. A sense of calm freedom passed over her when her feet touched the parking lot. She believed that she was in fact done with the eerie cops and the slow creepiness of this town. That was until she caught sight of someone walking through the parking lot wearing a big green coat and red trucker cap. 'No way. Not possible' This was all too weird and too close together to be a coincidence.

"Hey!"

She moved toward him at almost a run but as she started after him, he picked up his pace. If he followed her, then she was going to see his face. Sara needed to be sure. She wanted to memorize every aspect of him. A tougher person might have made him pay for stalking her but she was not a fighter.

"Hey wait!"

The bag full of locks was weighing her down, making it hard to run fast but she tried as best she could to catch up to him. He was unnaturally fast and for a second she could swear he was no longer running but somehow shifting around the parking lot in quick bursts. A blur in a field of endless cars.

"Stop!"

The figure blurred suddenly before he darted down a row of cars and she bolted down the same row.
Only to find that there was no one there, nothing but the cold autumn wind and a few pieces of trash blowing about. Sara looked around the parking lot, scanning every car window and the alleyway behind it. She glanced around a few more times before finally giving up the chase. 'Did that really just happen?' She wondered to herself. All the time failing to see the stranger hidden just by the corner of the hardware store. A slow smirk spreading across his face as the fear began to emanate from her body.

"What the hell was that? Am I hallucinating now?"

Sara continued to stand in the parking lot and look around at the small businesses lining main street. The electric glow of their neon signs seemed to suddenly peak to an unreasonable buzz as she took a moment to really look at the town. Something was very wrong about this place. Although she could see people moving about, she could not help but notice their almost robotic movements. As if they had been reprogrammed to move around town. They all seemed to be looking at her, not at the same time but at random intervals. There were no dogs barking and no children yelling. The wind rushed by her and for a moment she could swear it whispered her name. No one outside seemed even remotely stirred by its sudden movement. She backed away toward her car, keeping her eyes glued on her surroundings. As did, she bumped into a Collins Sherrif's car parked near hers. 'Was it there before?' Sara was officially done. So, she hurried to her car and climbed inside. When she pulled our her pack of cigarettes and flipped open the top, she realized that she was almost out. At this junction of her trip, the very last thing she wanted to do was visit a gas station. Sara did not wish to experience any more of the creepy vibe this town had to offer.

"Seriously?"

Starting the car she exited the lot and headed up town toward the tiny gas station. When she pulled into the gas station, they drove by, so she calmed down a little bit. Normally, (lately) she would have paid great attention to her environment. She was in such a mood right now that she did not bother to suffer the details. She headed inside keeping her face hidden in her hood. Sara felt the clerk working the counter staring at her the whole time. He was a young man in his thirties with noticeable dark skin and eyes. She assumed he was of some Latino descent but she could not be sure. From beneath her hood, Sara shot him a sideways glare to get him to stop staring at her, but he was not phased. That mildly annoyed her. After the eventful morning she had, she was in absolutely no mood for anything else.

She headed to the back to grab a pop and while she was looking, the bell on the top of the door chimed. A man entered and she ducked down slightly so she would not be seen. From this angle she could only see his slick back black hair, jean jacket, a zip up hooded sweatshirt beneath the jacket but nothing else. There was something odd the way he moved. It was as if he was out of sync with time. Or perhaps time had no meaning to him. The man said something in Spanish to the clerk at the counter and the man responded flawlessly. Sara wished she understood what they were saying. For all she knew they were talking about her. Then again, she not even be a thought in either of their heads. Had the man even seen her come inside? Her mind was rambling. She had to shatter the experience.

Sara closed the freezer door rather defiantly and the man half turned, looking at her from the corner of his eye and then said something else to the clerk before leaving. 'Damn' She wanted to see his face but he left too soon. So she payed for her pop, got a pack of cigarettes and headed home. It was during her drive that she noticed something else about this town-no matter what the weather, the town always had a tint of gray. As if it was really dead and the friendly outer appearance was only an illusion. That was odd and unnerving. It was about noon when she got home. She grabbed her bag on her way out of the car, stuffing everything in it before closing the door. The house too looked odd and for a minute she hesitated to open the door. As she grabbed the door handle, the wind rushed by and that time she did hear her name whispered. She jumped and spun around, dropping her keys.

"Who's there?!"

Sara scanned the front yard before moving away from the house and looking around the property. There was no one but her. She stepped back onto the porch, grabbed her keys and went inside, slamming the door shut behind her. The current lock on the door did not make her feel the least bit safe. Sara tossed the locks on the table before rummaging through a box by it to find her drill. It was not there, so she tore through the house to find that it was in fact, gone.

"Are you fucking kidding me?" She groaned in frustration.

That meant she would have to head back to the store or get someone to do it for her. It might be easier to just hire someone. Sara walked over and emptied the bag, grabbing her receipt (as it flew out) before it could hit the floor. As she threw it back onto the table, something caught her eye on the back of it. There was not a store number on it, but an advertisement for a local handy man. That seemed a little strange-her drill was gone but miraculously there was a number on the hardware store receipt for a handy man. 'Something about this isn't right Sara. Just get another drill, do it yourself.' Instead of listening to her instinct, she pulled her cell phone from her pocket and flipped it open. Picking up the receipt she hesitated when her thumb touched the keypad. "See, even you feel that something is not right.' She shook the thought from her head before dialing the number. The phone rang twice and then an oddly familiar voice answered the phone.

"Alex's Repair Service, this is Alex speaking."

"Uh . . . yeah . . . I got your number from the hardware store receipt and I need some locks installed."

"Locks huh? How many?"

His accent was familiar but she could not place the original source.

"About twenty. Three door locks and about eighteen window locks."

"What's the address?"

"Oh, 5102 Lillie Dr."

"I can be there at about three today."

"Today? Awesome, I'll see you at three."

There was no goodbye, he just hung up. She set her phone down on the table and looked around. If she was going to have someone here, she was going to need to clean up a little bit. Again that internal voice nagged 'Sara listen to me. Something is very wrong.' 'Shut up!' She mentally replied. Sara kept running the sound of his voice through her head, trying to figure out where she had heard it before. 'Where do I know you Alex?' The image of her faceless attacker flashed in her head. However, she refused to believe it was even remotely possible. Besides, it was not plausible. No one would drive nearly five hours to stalk and attack someone. With that conclusion firmly implanted, she set to picking the boxes up before the handy man came. Eventually, she knew she would figure out why his voice was so familiar.

Chapter 3

The events of the morning continued to play out in her mind as she sorted through her things. There were no curtains yet on the living room windows and its openness left her with a feeling of dread. She knew that he was miles away from her but the memories and emotions were not. A visible scar on her calf served as a reminder of that night. Try as she might, she could not get his silhouette out of her mind. Then there was Alex's voice, something about it was so familiar. Sara suddenly stood straight up from the box she was looking through. A slow silence had crept into the house and with it a coldness that made her flesh goose bump. She looked around the room. Everything was still but it all felt wrong. So, she stepped into the hallway and looked around. The unnatural stillness was here as well. She needed to shatter this quiet and fast.

"Time to for some music."

She looked around at the boxes, biting her bottom lip as she tried to focus her thoughts.

"But what box is it in?"

Sara scanned the room slowly until she noticed it half sticking out of a clearly over stuffed box, near her brown leather sofa. After kicking a few boxes out of her way, she finally pulled it out and sat it on the side table, before finding her booklet of CD's and flipping through them.

"Sara."

A disembodied voice whispered her name and her head jolted up right.

"Hello?"

She leaned back to look just down the hallway that ran along the left side of the stairs, a puzzled look etched into her features. She stared at the back door for a few moments before flipping on the hall light. Then she went meticulously through the house, turning on every light. There was no one but her in the large two story house. None of the windows were open for her to hear sounds from outside. Sara was standing in the dining room door when she heard it again

"Run Sara."

The voice sounded feminine. A hind of sadness, pain and desperation could be heard in its words. As if the bearer had suffered a fate worse than death and was now trying to spare her the same horrors.

"Is someone in here!? I'm not playing around!"

There was the sudden sound of crying and it ghosted by her before passing through the rest of room. Sara jumped away from the direction of the sound and dropped her CD case to the floor. Slowly she backed away, looking around and beginning to wonder if she had moved into a haunted house. Was someone trying to warn her of something? She paused in her movements and listened closely. When she did not hear anything, she picked up her booklet and began to slowly flip through it again. When she found what she wanted, she pressed the lid on the CD player and dropped the disc in to let it play. Once the music started she was a cleaning machine, she lifted and carried boxes from downstairs up to her room-trying not to think about what had just happened.

The house was simple in its layout. Her dining room sat at the front right corner of the structure and was seated just off the kitchen. Which was lined with all wooden cabinets and white marble counter tops. Across from the dining room was her living room and in the middle of the room was a white brick fireplace. All the bedrooms and bathroom were up on the second floor. Every room had oak hardwood floors that creaked as she stepped on them. Sara liked that because it let her know when someone was in the house. As she was cleaning she heard the hint of another Autumn storm rolling in and she grabbed a flash light from one of the boxes just in case the power decided went out. As she moved the boxes to their temporary resting places, she realized she was running out of places to put them and it was almost three. So she grabbed two of the boxes and headed towards the basement.

She attempted to balance them and get the door but it was not working out so well. So she set them down before grabbing the handle and giving it a hard turn. The door swung open so easily she almost fell down the stairs into the darkness below but she caught herself with her free hand and at the same time she found the light switch. Sara flipped it on and the basement became dimly lit by hanging yellow lights.

"I should have thought of this in the first place.."

She shook her head at her own stupidity and grabbed the boxes before descending the stairs to set them on the floor in front of an old work bench that she would probably never use. Then she turned and as she headed back upstairs, she noticed something about the basement door. Her brow furrowed and she ascended the stairs to get a better look at it. There were nails in the wood on the back side of the door as if someone had tried to nail it shut. The door frame was busted on one side where it had clearly been kicked open. Sara knelt down and ran her fingers over the remaining nails. On the wood, just barely visible to the naked eye, was a bloody hand print. There were scratched in the wood where someone attempted to buff it out. A sickening feeling crept through her stomach. Something horrible had happened in this house. 'Why would someone nail the door shut?'

"I don't know. But I don't like that. What happened in this house?"

She answered herself.

Sara knew now what she wanted that other bolt lock for, the basement would be her panic room if someone broke into her house.

"Sara."

The voice cried again and she found bolted out of the basement. She ran her nails through her hair nervously as the storm outside finally kicked up. Its orchestra only made her even more jumpy because she was not expecting a loud boom to rock the house. For a few moments all she could do was pace the floor and think about the events that might have lead up to the broken door frame Someone must have been truly desperate to nail a door shut. 'Who or what were they trying to keep out?' She wondered.

"What happened here?"

Although she had asked the question, she knew that part of her did not really want an answer. Even if she really wanted to know, there was no time to investigate.

It was now two thirty and she knew she had only a few minutes before the repair man came to install the locks. The last thing she wanted was to be unprepared for him. She needed a clear head and a calm demeanor. Even if it meant ignoring the feeling that she was not alone in the house. So she moved toward the dining room, grabbing the final box off the table and sprinted to the basement. The last box she set on the work bench and then turned to head back upstairs. Something caught her eye and it was not the sort of thing a person would notice unless they were looking for it. It was on one of the main support beams around the basement stairs. Sara moved toward it and what she found made her blood run cold.

On one of the wooden posts, someone had carved RUN rather crudely-almost as if they were in a hurry when they did it. She looked around as if she was being watched-or to see if she was being watched-she was not herself entirely sure what prompted her to turn around, but whatever it was, she obeyed the urge. Then with shaky fingers, she began to trace over the letters as if she would better understand their message if she just touched them. 'Could this be from the same person who attempted to nail the door shut?' Now she was beginning to think that she should just pack what she could into the car and go. Someone was clearly trying to chase her off or warn her of something.

"Don't let him in Sara."

There was the voice again.

"Don't let who in?"

Before the phantom voice could answer her, the doorbell rang upstairs and Sara cursed herself for not being completely ready for company. With the ghostly voices, cryptic messages, weird cops and mysterious strangers-her nerves were almost too rattled to deal with the repair man. She hesitated as she went up the stairs and closed the door behind her.

When her fingers touched the cold lever doorknob, she paused. The disembodied voice had gotten to her more than she cared to admit. It gave her reason to believe that she should not let him in her house. What could she do? He drove all the way out here, she could not just turn him away. That would appear suspicious and if he was bad, she did not want to let on that she knew. The black silhouette pounded on her door and made her jump. Outside the storm was blowing the trees about and had turned from a simple thunderstorm to a torrent of rain a matter of minutes.

"Hey, come on! Let me in, I'm getting soaked out here!"

Sara jumped at the sound of his voice and yanked open the door. The man standing in front of her was not overtly tall but he had broad muscular shoulders that strained against his brown leather jacket. His skin was the color of carmel and his eyes the color of dark chocolate. She could get lost in those dark pools. His gray shirt was so wet it clung tightly to his muscular chest. In one hand he carried a red metal tool chest and the other hand pushed back the dark wet locks that had fallen into his eyes. The jeans he wore were ripped in various places and they too were soaked. Sara glanced behind him to see his black work truck parked behind her car. The sign on the side of it read Alex's Repair Service in white decal letters. Alex's overall appearance did not seem sinister to her. An undeniable energy radiated from this man. Although he appeared placid, she could not ignore his over powering presence. His mere proximity to her was enough to make her lower belly tingle with arousal. Sara did not like that. Somehow he could evoke lust within her and all he did was show up. 'He needs to be gone and fast.'

She had a feeling she was getting closer to the reason that this town felt so dark. She needed the locks on the house installed, but perhaps she should have just bought a drill because she did not want to let this man in her house. The handy man flashed a friendly smile at her, but there was still something menacing in that-it was enough to make her back away from him slowly. For a brief moment she could swore she saw long white canines.

"Are you gonna let me come in? Or do I have to stay out here all day?"

Sara just barely caught the hint of an accent but it suddenly seemed to be gone with his next sentence.

"Oh god..sorry. Yes, come in."

"Thank You." He said, eyeing her as he stepped into the house.

"I'm Sara by the way."

"Nice ta meet ya."

The familiar tap, tap of water on wood, drifted up to her ears and she realized he really was soaking wet. That sound-so harmless- brought back a haunting memory that she had tried to forget. For a moment she was back in her old house and that man was with her again, his voice heavy in her ear. The sound of Alex's boots on her wooden floor made her swallow hard. Sara shook her head and flashed a forced smile before offering to take his coat.

"Can I hang that up for you?"

"Oh, yeah. Thanks."

He set his tool box down and shimmied off his coat, handing to her.

"Coffee?" She said as she hung it up by the door.

"Yeah if you have some."

"It'll take me a second to make some, if you don't mind. I'm still unpacking really." She chuckled nervously.

"You don't have to go to that trouble for me."

"It's really no trouble. I need some anyhow. Besides," She motioned to his damp tee shirt. "you need to warm up   before you catch cold."

He licked his lips before flashing her a rather charming smile, which made her stomach flutter with butterflies. Then he grabbed his tool box and moved closer to where she was fishing out the coffee maker. Those warm brown eyes, watched her as she moved and his tongue running along his bottom lip.

"I could always go without the shirt."

It was out there, the phrase just hung in the air and Sara almost dropped the coffee filters in her hand. She swallowed, trying to push the red out of her face.

"Uhh . . .Alex is it?"

She suddenly could barely look at him.

"I..uh..."

He laughed a little.

"I was not being serious,"

He moved closer to her still, his work boots thudding on the wood floor as he moved. Before he leaned on the counter next to her, his eyes scanning slowly over her delicate features.

"So you can relax. I'm just here to install the locks."

From this distance she could smell him, cigarettes, old spice and oil. This was a man who worked hard and liked to work hard. The more he watched her, the more she felt her body responding. 'Maybe he should work with his shirt off.' Sara finally managed to look into his eyes and smile nervously. If he had not come off so 'Kenneth Bianci' she might have paid for his services with an entirely different currency. Sara turned suddenly back to making coffee and found herself talking towards the coffee maker instead of addressing him. In a way, she was attempting to hide her reaction to him.

"I'm sorry...it's been a long day."

She poured half a cup of ground coffee into the filter before filling the coffee maker with water. This man was making her nervous and she had not been this flustered since her high school crush kissed her at her Junior prom. As she turned on the coffee maker she found her hands were shaking and she squeezed her fists to get them to stop.

"Maybe you've already had too much coffee." Alex had seen her hands shaking.

"What? Oh uh...no...this isn't from that."

"What's it from?"

Was he aware of what he was doing to her and trying to make things worse? There was something rather serious and seductive in his voice when he asked her. 'Avoid answering.' Her inner voice warned her-she needed to get him out of her house as soon as she could.

"So the locks are on the kitchen table," She pointed to the pile. "and if you could get started with the back door   actually, that would be wonderful."

"Whatever you want ma'am, you're the boss."

He winked at her.

Alex moved back to the dining room table to grab his tool box and then one of the bolt locks but paused when he started to head for the back door. Sara caught it, she had not told him where the back door was, so why was he headed in the right direction? Instinct? Or did he know more than he was letting on?

"Back door is?"

"Oh I'm sorry. This way."

Sara lead the way to the back door near the washer and dryer unit. As they headed down the hallway, the sound of his work boots on the wood floor made her skin crawl. Still, she could feel her lower back tighten and she was sure he was checking out every inch of her back side as they went. He had a friendly enough disposition, but there still seemed to be something darker underneath that visage. So long as he was here to install the locks, she would try to tolerate him and keep her imagination to a minimum.

She gestured toward the back door in a very mock Vanna White wave and without missing a beat Alex bowed with tool box in hand.

"Thank you M'lady."

It was a moment of friendly exchange which switched rather quickly back into a business discussion.

"Do you want me to leave the original lock on here because there's already one bold lock   here."

He was looking at the door as he spoke.

"Um..."

She peeked over his shoulder.

"How good is it?"

Alex fiddled with the bolt lock which appeared to have been broken once already. She scanned the door frame and found that it too was broken but someone had tried to mend it. Sara would say nothing to him about it.

"It's lose."

"No, just take it down then, I want strong locks."

"Expecting trouble?"

He looked up at her with a smirk that did not settle well with her. That was an interesting choice of words because it was exactly what Ellis had asked her.

She shifted a little.

"Um...not really. But I like to be prepared."

There was a moment of awkward silence and then Sara blurted out.

"So if you need anything, I'll be in the kitchen."

"I should be good. Thanks."

"I'll go check the coffee,"

She turned to leave, then turned back around.

"Sugar? Cream?"

Alex turned from the lock he had started taking off.

"No, black please."

"Okay then."

Sara headed back down the hallway and as she approached the living room, she realized the CD player was still running. So she headed into the room to turn it off and place it on the mantle above the fire place. The coffee maker was sputtering in the other room, which meant she would at least have hot coffee soon and could wake up a little more. When she set the radio down, she accidentally kicked one of the bricks that made up the ledge of the fireplace. If she had not had her boots on, that would have hurt. When she did kick the brick, she heard it shift and she knelt down to put it back. That was when she noticed something white tucked just beneath it. Sara picked it up to look at it, realizing that it was a folded up piece of paper. Someone did not intend it to be found very easily. She wondered who they were hiding it from and what did it say. The carving on the wood beam had been very vague. What was she supposed to run from? Who was leaving her cryptic messages and why were they leaving them?

"What the hell?"

"Hey, uh.."

Alex was suddenly in the doorway to the living room.

Sara jumped, spun around tucked the note behind her back. Only later would she come to understand her own actions in that moment and all of the answers to her questions as well. It was an instinctive action. She did not trust Alex and she somehow knew he would inquire about the paper. At the same time, she pushed the brick back with her boot and hoped he did not catch it.

"Yes?"

"Do you have a flashlight? The lighting by that door is impossible to see in and with the cloud cover I have no   light really."

The storm was still battering the house with wind and rain, although the thunder seemed to have stopped but she could have been wrong. With her attention focused on the mildly attractive man in front of her, there could have been a tornado outside and she probably would have missed it. For a second she just looked at him and then with an overly enthusiastic reply she headed towards the basement.

"I should have some in a box in the basement."

She was just stepping over the threshold of the living room when she tripped over Alex's boot-which she swore she had stepped over-and he ended up catching her before she hit the ground. His hands were strong and coarse but very cold.

"Whoa, careful there. That floor is unforgiving."

"Yeah . . ."

There was a pause in her movements, she was pressed almost right up against him and she could feel the muscles under his shirt.

"I guess it is..."

Sara was caught in those eyes, that smile, the intoxicating smell of him and the feel of his hands on her body. This man was charming alright and part of her did not want him to stop touching her-in fact part of her wanted to put his hands else where. She shook her head and pulled away from him, feeling her face flush with embarrassment and slight arousal.

"Right flashlights. Come on."

She waved a hand at him.

"I'm coming."

'If only.' She cleared her throat to shut her mind up-which had gone from afraid to aroused in the matter of a few seconds. The unknown fear was there still and perhaps it was the fear that was really causing the issues she was starting to have-whatever was making her flush with heat, she needed to make it stop. They descended the stars together and she began to shuffle through the boxes on the floor to find the large work light she had bought a some time ago. While she looked in the box, Alex wondered around the basement in such a way that he almost seemed to be looking for something. He would pause at random intervals and just stare at the small crevices that littered the entire basement.

"Ah...here it is."

Sara turned around, holding up a work light just in time to catch him kneeling at the post with the word carved into it and running a finger over the letters. That made her uneasy, something about the way he was looking at that made her nervous-as if someone just read her most intimate thoughts in her diary. Alex's body language changed slightly. His shoulders became more rigid and there was an air of disapproval around him. All at once the mood had shifted. 'He knows something.'

"I can buff this out for you." His tone was unnaturally serious.

"Alex?"

Even when he turned around and his tone softened, she felt uncomfortable. She knew she needed to keep him from noticing the blood by the basement door. There was something that glimmered in his eyes, a darkness that passed through momentarily. Sara took a step back toward the work bench and gripped the socket wrench with the hand behind her. Her other remained out stretched with the light.

"Oh good you found one."

He reached to take it from her and she let him. There was a moment of awkward silence between them before he gestured toward the stairs.

"Are you coming?"

Sara swallowed.

"After you." She replied.

" Oh, I *insist*. I'm a gentleman, ladies always come first."

Wanting to cut the conversation short and not appear suspicious, she let go of the wrench before heading up the stairs. She knew his intended meaning behind that last sentence. Alex followed close behind her and she hoped he did not see the door frame. After they exited the basement, she closed the door a little too hard. She was a little mad at Alex for offering to sand that carving out. This was her house and he had no right.

"Easy there Miss, that door is old. You have to be gentle with it."

"Sorry, it's a little lose on the hinges."

"You'll have that with an old house. I'm gonna get back to that lock, the coffee is done by the way."

Sara watched him walk away, half aroused, half mad and slightly confused about everything. The note in her back pocket would have to wait until he left. She did not trust him and she was beginning to not like his personality. One minute he was sweet and sexy and the next he was dark and cryptic. She sighed a frustrated sigh and walked into the kitchen to pour the coffee. A large red mug for him, a smaller blue mug for her with two scoops of sugar to kill the bitter taste. Alex was just putting on the new lock when she came to him with the cup of coffee.

"Hey I got hot coffee."

She tried to keep a friendly tone.

Sara set the mug down on the built in wooden chest by the back door and before he could say another word to her, she turned away from him. In the kitchen she popped a cigarette in her mouth and lit it, the cherry hissed as she pulled smoke into her lungs. The nicotine doing its assigned job of calming her down so she could think logically. Alex was just too weird, one minute he was sexy, and the next he was distant. She turned around to lean backwards on the counter and sip her coffee.

From down the hall she heard the sound of his work boots as he walked into the kitchen to grab another lock, and start on the front door. She watched him work, his strong hands making light work of an already easy job. The muscles of his shoulders and biceps flexed beneath his tight tee shirt. While she watched him, she bit her bottom lip, her eyes combing over the long black locks that fell about his face as he worked. Her mind drifted to thoughts of what that body was capable of doing to hers. This behavior and thought patter was uncharacteristic of her. All her behavior around him had been odd. Sara did not think about men in this way, at least not that easily.

"You know I can feel your eyes?" Alex said smirking.

Suddenly she flushed and found herself looking away in another direction to hide the red in her cheeks. Just a few seconds ago she was thinking about how creepy he was and then she was thinking about how she still wanted him. She was leaning on the counter when she heard his voice in her ear. Sara had not heard him approach.

"What do you want me to do with you?"

"What?" Sara turned around, even more flushed.

"I said what do you want me to do with this other bolt lock?" He asked, holding it up.

"Uh . . oh . . um . . . Basement door."

She shoved away from the counter, clearly flustered.

"Are you alright?"

He asked flashing one of those knee weakening smiles.

"Wha-yeah . . fine. Why?"

She sipped her coffee nervously, snuffing her cigarette out haphazardly.

"You seem a bit,"

He chose that moment to look her up and down before smirking. "shaken."

"Lemme show you where I want that."

She changed the subject, moving toward the basement. Behind her, she could hear his steady foot falls as he followed her to the basement. She stepped down just a little bit and waved for him to join her. Alex set his coffee and tools down outside the basement door and followed her down a couple steps. Sara closed the door just slightly and as she was telling him where to install the lock, she could feel his breath on her neck and ear. He was leaning too close to just be paying attention to what she had to say. That was not helping her to keep calm at all and she found herself clearing her throat frequently to keep calm. Then she heard the low rumble of his voice right in her ear.

"So you want it on this side of the basement door?"

She swallowed.

"Yeah."

"Ok then. I'll put it where ever you want it, how ever you want it."

"What?"

She half turned to find him a few inches from her.

"I'll put the locks where ever," He licked his bottom lip. "and however you want them."

She needed to get out of the basement and fast. This man was really starting to get to her and she was about to need a cold shower if she did not get away from him. Almost tripping over the steps, she ascended the stairs without saying another word and she closed the door behind her. When she got back to the kitchen-her sanctuary-she practically fell against the counter, leaning there to try and get herself to stop shaking. She nervously ran her fingers through her hair and exhaled a shaky breath-one thing was certain, it was getting much warmer in her house. Just when she had finally calmed her nerves, the power in the entire house kicked off. Now she was alone in a dark house with this man.

The darkness, ever present and thick, had rolled in like a shadowy fog. There was a presence in this darkness, Sara could feel it. The shadows felt alive and for a moment she swore they were moving, dancing even. Her eyes could have very well been playing tricks on her. A dim blue light from the well hidden sun was the only thing staving off the darkness that threatened to over take her house. Sara was more concerned with the stranger in here with her than she was the dark. Someone should have told her to be weary of both.

Chapter 4

It felt as if death had descended upon the house and all manner of evil with it. The house was heavy with a different presence than she had experienced before. For a few moments she only stood, staring into the black before her as if expecting something to happen. As if some demon might emerge from the shadows and reveal its awful face. A slow inaudible sigh passed through her lips. Her eyes scanned the room. What was she looking for? Even she did not know. Absent mind-idly she pulled the small led flashlight (she was still carrying) from her pocket and pressed the power button. Its brightness pierced the blackness in front of her, causing the shadows to recoil from the light. For a brief moment she could swear she head them hiss at her.

The silence echo in the house echoed as a high pitched hiss in her ears and the sound of her breathing as it came in slow shaky breaths. There was no sound from Alex at all and Sara had expected at least a protest from him when the lights cut out. But there was just the silence and the wind. She listened through the silence, through the storm and tried to hear the voices-she had decided-were trying to warn her of something.

"Sara."

She stopped moving and this time, tried to get more information from the whispering voices.

"I'm here."

"Watch the shadows. Beware of the shadows."

"What?"

"He's in the shadows."

"Who?"

"Not here, he's listening. Get out."

The room fell silent suddenly and the back of her neck prickled with nervous tension. Again, it all became very still. But then something moved just beyond her peripheral vision and she turned quickly to see it. A shadow seemed to actually move on its own from the doorway-it was darker than the rest, her eyes had adjusted enough for her to see it.

Without warning it seemed to disappear or meld into the other shadows around her. For a few seconds nothing happened and then she swore she felt hands on her. Sara batted the air around her but there was no one there to push away. The phantom hands moved down and worked their way into her most intimate depths. Her body betrayed her-as she attempted to fight whatever was happening-and she felt herself wet with ecstasy. She began to pant and put her hands out to try to steady herself as she lips with no visible owner began to kiss her neck. The flashlight fell from her hands and clamored to the wood beneath her before rolling into the dining room. Its glowing white beam painted the wooden legs of her chairs but left the rest of the room dark. She was not surrounded by perverse shadows.

"No, stop."

Sara was trying to fight it-the dream, shadow or psychotic delusion she was having but she slowly found herself growing weak to its touch. It was over whelming and she felt almost as if she was drowning in lust without a way to surface. But shadows could not touch, this was wrong, something was trying to get to her-trying to control her.

"No," She tried to push the feeling away. "Stop it!"

With another flash of lightning, the whole kitchen lit up and she suddenly saw Alex only two feet from her. When she jumped back away from him, she tripped over her own shaky legs and fell backwards. Sara was thankful that the feelings had stopped but at the same time, not happy to see Alex in her current state. She was panting, sweaty, extremely horny, parts of her were swollen and throbbing and she could feel the wetness her little shadow hallucination had caused.

As soon as she hit the floor she started scooting back away from him, there was something she did not like about the look on his face. By now of course her eyes had adjusted to the darkness and she could make out enough of his features to know what the expression was on his face. Alex followed her as she scooted backwards, he hovered over her with the most hungry, predatory look on his face and for a second she expected him to smile an flash a pair of fangs. In the shadows he almost seemed to emanate his own shadowy aura. Or was it a trick of her tired mind? Either way, she did not like it. Sara crawled for the flashlight, diving under the table and grabbing it in desperation. Then she turned its beam on him and the shadows that surrounded him. They slithered away, like serpents backing away from the flame of a torch. She laid on the floor looking up at him, ready to kick him if necessary.

"I didn't wanna have to do this,"

He continued toward her.

"But I'm afraid you leave me no choice."

"Alex please . . . whatever it is, please don't"

"If I don't get what I need, I'm afraid I'm gonna have to."

"Alex please."

She swallowed a lump of tears. Alex suddenly reached for her and she threw her arms up to protect herself. But he never touched her-he was only reaching to grab the flashlight from her.

"This ought to do the trick."

"What?"

"The other light is electric, it plugs in and I can't see in the dark."

Sara did not believe him because he had made it into the kitchen just fine in the dark. Why did he phrase things that way? The oddly cryptic way he had spoken, left her with a sickening feeling. It spread from her belly into her lower back before tingling through the rest of her. Alex reached down to help her up. She stared at his hand for a moment before she cautiously took it and he yanked her up so fast she fell against him. The feel of his hard body against hers made that hot wetness between her legs come to life again and she prayed at this range he could not feel the heat. The smirk on his face and the way he licked his bottom lip before letting her go, told her that he had noticed.

As he walked away, watched the steady shift of the muscles in his back, the way his arms flexed as he moved and the visible flex of the powerful muscles straining against his jeans. A brief image of him-slamming her against the wall and slicing through the straps of her thong with his pocket knife before shoving his hand down the front of her pants and shoving his fingers deep inside of her-came to her for just a second. It did not matter her little mini-fantasy made no sense, it still made her wetter and she dug her nails into her palms to calm herself before ducking to hide her pink cheeks.

Alex said nothing else before she watched him disappear into the darkness. The glow of white swallowed whole by the blackness surrounding them. She had no candles or extra lights. Which meant she was trapped in the dark with this man. The little sunlight outside was fading fast. Soon there would be no light at all. What would she do then?

It seemed rather odd that Alex would stay and work when there was no power. She figured he would leave and come back later. So what was the real reason he stayed? Did he have another reason? Sara would have time to think about all of this when he left. For now, she knew she had to get her wits about her and attempt to figure out what was really going on.

"What was that shadow thing? Did I imagine that?"

So shadows were moving on their own (or it was hallucinations of a tired mind) along with phantom voices and then there was Alex, who was somewhere between creepy and sexy. There was something about him that scared her. It felt like, without saying a word, he had claimed her and if someone else attempted to have her . . .he might hurt them. Where these feelings and thoughts were coming from, she did not know. The strange thing was, despite the fact his mere presence scared her, she still wanted him with every fiber of her being. It was an intoxicating combination of emotion, thought and sensation. At the same time it left her confused.

Those thoughts made her swallow nervously, her heart beginning to race even faster-its beat pounding in her ear and making her even more anxious. Sara stuck her head out of the kitchen doorway and looked for any sign of Alex. She heard his drill on the basement door. With Alex safely in the basement, she begin to listen for the voices again. This time she would speak first. So she whispered into the dark.

"Hello?"

Again, the shadows seemed to move on their own and then solidify right in front of her before fading again. But that time they seemed to form a masculine silhouette. Sara put her arms behind her-finding the wall-and backing into it, feeling much safer with something solid behind her. Without her light, she had nothing to keep the shadows at bay. No way to keep them from touching her again. How could he leave her in the dark like that? She looked around frantically, her throat began to dry, heart started to race and her breath came in shot quick gasps of air. When she tried to swallow, she almost choked on the lump of tears in her throat because it was so dry.

After what seemed like forever she heard a voice, not the same voice but a familiar male voice. The voice that haunted her memories and drove her nightmares.

"I will have you Sara." It whispered in her ear.

"No."

A single tear rolled down her cheek and she began to shake with fear, her breathing becoming low and shuddery. He was here, he had managed to find her in the dark. But how? Tears rolled down her cheeks as she braced herself for his attack. But it never came. She had heard his voice, she knew he she had. So far the shadows had not touched her. There were no invisible hands groping her and she did not hear his voice again. Nor did she feel his hard touch on her skin. She just stared in fear off into the distance and prayed silently to herself. 'Dear god, whatever this is, please make it stop.' Just when she though she was beginning to lose it, the power came back on. Again, Alex was suddenly in the kitchen with her. She had not heard him come in for the second time and somehow she did not see him enter. That bothered her even more than the voices. He was barely standing in the doorway, when he saw her, he moved slowly towards her.

"Miss?"

He ducked down a little to look at her.

"Are you alright?"

"I saw, it said..."

"Who said? Is someone else in here, did they hurt you?"

"What?" She shook her head. "No, nevermind."

She tried to shake it off, finally looking up at him. Alex saw the look on her face and that was what made him suddenly move closer to her.

"Hey," His voice was softer now.

The smooth raspy tone of his voice almost melted her entire tough girl act. Alex reached out and brushed her tear away with his thumb. The heat of his hands (which strangely had been ice cold hours ago) and the course texture of his fingers against her soft skin made her body begin to warm. Even with all that had happened, her lust was still stronger than her fear and the over powering lust that seemed to radiate from this man was suddenly more potent.

Now she was digging her nails into the wallpaper to keep from melting into the floor boards or from giving into this man. Although she had not realized she had considered letting him have her. She failed to realize her lust for him was that strong. In her mind though, he already had her arms pinned to the wall, his hard body pressed against her, his mouth was working down her neck-biting, licking, sucking. He had all the control and he would make her beg him to finish what he started.

"Hey? Hello?"

Sara shook her head to push the image away.

"What, huh?"

"Do you want me to put it in tonight?"

He had a slight smirk on his face, his head was tilted to one side and he licked his bottom lip when he asked the question.

"Excuse me?"

"The rest of the locks, do you want the rest put in tonight?"

Clearly he had changed the subject.

"I mean it is getting late an you seem,"

He scanned her body, licking his bottom lip again with a smirk.

"preoccupied."

As he said that last word he bit his bottom lip and gave her a once over. Those looks only served to make her problems worse.

"Wha-I-Um..."Sara was nervous. "just,uh,do my front-the front windows and we can call it a night."

Outside the storm was dying down and a few street lights were on now. There were visible branches down everywhere but as far as she could tell, no damage. Alex grabbed four window locks and headed toward the living room, when suddenly there was a knock on the door.

"I'll get it."

Sara said before she moved past him and opened the door. What she found made her blood chill as terror filled her veins and her head swim, she put her hand on the door frame to steady herself. It was Officer Ellis and Officer Harris, standing on her front porch. Alex had his forearm propped against the open door and was leaning rather close to her. She felt herself start to panic but she dug her nails into the door to keep her composure. After everything that had been going on, these were the last two people she wanted or needed to see. Alex's proximity to her, coupled with their presence, was making her stomach knot. Sara did everything she could to maintain her stony exterior.

"Evening . . . Officers," She choked out.

"What can I do for you?"

"We're sorry to bother you Miss but we need to speak with Mr. Reese." Officer Harris said with a smile.

Their smiles were friendly enough but she still was not buying into their good cop routine. That same hunger was still prevalent in their eyes when they looked at her. Sara zipped her hoodie up a little more, feeling incredibly naked all of a sudden. They needed to get off her porch and Alex needed to get the hell out of her house. She did not care how they left, just that they did and fast. In fact, she was perfectly all right with them leaving now.

"Something wrong?" She asked.

Those smiles faded and Harris glanced back at Ellis. Officer Ellis almost had a death glare now, his blue eyes twinkled with a coldness that made her step back from the doorway. When she did, she bumped into Alex who put an unnecessary hand on her waist to steady her.

"Whoa."

His voice was right in her ear. For a second she had to fight the shiver crawling up her spine. His voice was like honey in her ear, it tingled through her whole being. The two officers were not friendly now, instead they were smirking and they shot one another a knowing glance. It was obvious, they knew she was visibly shaken and now she was fighting to keep her cool. Sara looked at Alex one time and caught the same knowing glance. There was an invisible exchange of conversation going on between the three. They were up to something.

"It's a private matter."

Ellis responded, his tone alone almost commanded her to be silent.

Sara kept her mouth shut and she let Alex through the door. The three of them moved down to the end of the porch and huddled in a group. She could not hear what they were talking about but they were glancing in her direction. When she leaned out the door and attempted to figure out what they were doing, they suddenly went silent. Harris shot her a piercing glare. In the dark, she could have swore they were silver, like two mirrors looking back at her. Then the image was gone. Sara slammed the door before leaning her head against it. She was beginning to have issues distinguishing between hallucinations and reality.

After a while Alex shook Officer Harris's hand and came back towards the front door-she let him inside. Sara stood in the doorway and waited for them to leave. She wanted to be certain they were gone before she shut the door. Sara watched Officer Harris descend the stairs of her porch but Officer Ellis lingered, scanning every inch of her with his eyes before licking his bottom lip. When he grinned at her, she slammed the door. As soon as she did she found out that Alex had been standing behind it the entire time.

"Jesus!" She jumped.

"I didn't mean to scare you,"

He licked his bottom lip, those eyes roaming over her again.

"I just was waiting for you to close the door."

He moved to stand in front of her.

"So I can do what I need to."

Sara swallowed.

"So I can put it in for you." He continued.

Her knees weakened and Alex stepped forward, putting his hand on the door. There was no space between them now, she was pressed between him and the door. She was shaking and then without warning he broke the moment.

"The bolt lock."

"Huh?"

"Where do you want it?"

She swallowed hard before replying.

"The living room, first two in the living room."

"I'll do one at a time. I like to take my time...make sure I put it in right."

Sara gathered her senses and realized she had imagined being pressed against him and the door. She cleared her throat. Was he choosing that phrasing on purpose? He could have used any other wording because the phrases he chose suggested something else. Alex's whole body suggested some other meaning to their conversation.

"I'm going upstairs. If you need me, come get me."

"That's fine with me. It's your house."

As she moved past him and ascended the stairs, she did not see the smirk that spread across his features as if he knew what issues he was causing her. When she was out of sight, his entire demeanor changed. It was as if he was two different people, the friendly handyman and someone darker. Those deep browns scanned the room as if he had seen something above him. Or almost as if he was listening for something. The muscles in his jaw flexed and contracted with an unsatisfiable anger. Alex knew more than he was letting on. For a moment he listened to the sounds of Sara moving around upstairs and when he was sure she would not hear him, he spoke to no one in particular.

"Tell her anything else and you're done."

Then he headed into the living room and began the process of installing the locks. Not that any of her precautions would make a difference. For the creatures that would want into that house, could not be shut out by simple man made barricades. There was nothing she could do to contend with the evil that ruled this town and Alex knew it. An arrogant smirk crossed his features as he thought about her pathetic attempts to protect herself. He almost started to laugh. This little charade was entirely too amusing for him. Only a few more days and she would understand her place in this town.

Chapter 5

The storm had passed but the shadows remained and with them, the feeling of violation. Sara waited nervously in the dark, watching Alex. Without the flashlight in his hand, he was virtually invisible. Darkness seemed to encompass him, envelop him and radiate from him. It was unnatural the way the shadows moved around his form. In this brief moment, Sara discovered a new found fear of the dark. She could only compare it to being frightened as a child by something and then never wanting to sleep with the lights off. That was exactly how she felt, except in her case, something had touched her. Still she had doubts about that. Sara pushed her thoughts aside and crouched just out of Alex's view. She wanted to see what he would do without her around and he did not disappoint. He looked around as if he had heard the voices and then he said the oddest thing.

"Tell her anything else and you're done."

There was something going on here; now she was sure of that much and she was right to be suspicious of him. Alex knew more than he let on, he was not just a handy man. Before he turned around to start on the windows, his eyes shot up in her direction, but she was sure there was no way he could see her. At least she was hoping there was no way he could see her. Still, she leaned back out of his line of vision even more. With a slow smirk, he turned away to began his work. Sara nodded to herself, another inner monologue passing through her head. 'Get out of here Sara.' 'No, I need to figure out what is going on here. Alex knows something and I'm going to figure out what it is.' Before she turned into Sherlock Holmes, she needed to get herself back to a more logical state of mind.

Sara slid across the floor, feeling her way into her bedroom, not wanting Alex to know she had been spying on him. She took special precautions so the floor would not give away her presence. In her room were boxes of clothes and other items that she had just shoved in this room to get them out of sight. One of the boxes, if she could locate it, contained several large candles. She could easily light most of the house with them. So she picked a box at random and searched through its contents until she found her glass ashtray and the large candles. She pulled her lighter from her pocket and lit one of the candles. The small flame pushed the darkness back and cast the room in a flickering yellow glow. At least she could see where she was going now. By one of the windows, she had placed an old armchair and a table on which she set one of the candles and ashtray. She pulled out a cigarette and lit it. Then she strategically placed lit candles around the room in the areas she knew would not catch fire. When she was finished, the entire room was lit in a soft glow. It almost looked as if she was about to start some great ritual. At least the room was brighter now. With the room properly illuminated, she decided it was safe enough for her to sit down and relax, always she kept an ear open for the sounds of Alex. Sara stared out into the dark night on the other side of her window. The moon was hidden, so she saw only flames dancing on the glass and bouncing her silhouette around.

As the candles burned, the temperature in the room rose to and uncomfortable height. Sara needed to crack open the window before she began to bake in this room. She got up and moved over to it and tried to push the latch on top but it would not move. In frustration she hit the window frame with the butt of her hand and turned on her heels to go get Alex to open it for her. If she was paying him to put in new locks and had him for a few more minutes, she might as well get him to open the window.

"Don't."

There was the voice again but this time it was quieter, as if it was afraid of something. Sara paused in her movements and scanned the room with her eyes. When the voice said nothing more, she grabbed a candle and headed toward the stairs. Shadows crawled around the dim flame and the hairs on her neck prickled. That would not deter her. No matter what may or may not have happened, she would not let the dark win. It was an odd concept, the dark being thought of as a creature with conscious actions. She dismissed all of those notions for now.

"Hey Alex?"

"Yes'm."

The candle light flickered on the various items strewn about the house, casting odd shaped shadows that bounced around the room. As she approached the living room and watched the light cascade across his back, she begin to change her mind about asking him for help. There was nothing overtly sinister about the way he looked in candle light but she did not like him being in her house right now. So, she preferred him not come into her bedroom. By the time she finally reached him, she had decided to fix the window herself. He was still working on the lock with his back turned to her.

"Do you have a flat-head screwdriver that I could borrow?"

"Sure, check the top part of my toolbox."

She found the toolbox sitting open on the floor next to him, so she crouched down and pulled out a flat-head As she started for the stairs, Alex spoke to her.

"Something you need my help with?"

Sara paused. "Uh...no. I'm fine."

Before he could say another word, she headed upstairs and back to her room, shutting her door behind her. If her phantom whisperer wanted to speak to her again, she did not want to be interrupted. She headed over to the window and wedged the flat-head under the window latch, trying to pry it lose. The screw driver slipped and one of the corners, cut the side of the hand she had been using for balance. She cursed under her breath to keep from drawing attention and then she threw the screw driver angrily into the nearest box. In her anger she also punched the window with her good hand, sending shockwaves of pain through her bony knuckles. It helped her ignore the throbbing in the side of her other hand.

That was the breaking point, the emotional roller coaster she had been on the last couple days, finally broke free from its cage and she sank to the floor. The blood from her cut dripped rhythmically onto the wooden floor and she felt the memories come flooding back. The more this occurred, the flashbacks, the more insane she felt. This move was supposed to be her therapy and it seemed that it was driving her closer to madness. She had begun the obsess about the attack and turn every man into him. Any small thing could send her reeling into emotional turmoil. Sara fought the urge several times, to claw at her head as if she could rip the memories out.

In frustration, anger or just because she had become fed up, she kicked one of the boxes near her so hard that it hit the door. She leaned her head against the wall with knees pulled up and her left hand held in her right as tears began to roll down her cheeks. She just wanted it all to stop. The voices, the shadows, the strangers, and the chaotic stream of endless events. She just wanted normal.

"Please god, please make it go away."

Sara finally admitted to herself that she was terrified of whatever was happening and she did not know if she had the strength to continue going on. At that moment she heard the voice again.

"Sara get up! Sara he smells you, get up!"

A few seconds after that voice, she heard the floor boards shifting downstairs and knew that he was headed for the stairs. As much as she wanted to just tell the voice to go away and leave her alone, she could not help but listen to it. Even if what it was telling her did not make sense. Alex was not a shark who could smell blood in the water. Still, she stood from her place on the floor and headed into the bathroom. She turned the metal knobs of the sink, her blood covered hand leaving streaks of crimson on the dull metal and shoved her cut under the water.

Sara hissed in pain as the water hit her lacerated flesh but she knew she had to clean it and get it wrapped before he could see that her strong exterior shell, had cracked. Sara was quick to, wash her hand and wipe down the bloody knobs before bandaging up her cut.

The sound of stairs creaking told her she did not have much time left. A quick glance in the mirror reminded her to wipe the tear streaks from her face. As fast as she could, she rummaged through a box of clothes, found her finger-less gloves and shoved them on to cover her hand. Then she headed for the window which-for one reason or another-finally opened. She plopped down in the chair with just enough time to pop a cigarette in her mouth and light it before he knocked on the door. Sara attempted to appear calm and casual when she answered him.

"Uh...miss?"

"Come in."

Alex pushed the door open with unnatural ease, despite the heavy box in front of the it, and then stepped into the room.

"I'm all done with the front windows. But uh...I'll need my screwdriver back if you don't mind."

"Oh yeah," She pointed to the box. "It's in there."

He moved over, crouched down and picked it up. As he did, he looked up in the direction of her cut hand and she could swear his eyes were black in the dim light. 'Does he know?' He glanced in the direction of her bathroom and she could swear she heard a growl emit from somewhere deep in his throat. 'Why does he remind me of a predator smelling blood? Does he smell it?' When he stood up, she could swear he closed his eyes for a moment and sighed-as if to calm himself. For a few seconds he just stood there, back to her, screw driver in hand and that time she was certain she heard him growl. Sara swallowed nervously.

"Alex?"

He said nothing.

"Alex?"

"Ohh...Sara...I can smell you and now I want to taste you."

Was she really hearing this? The words "I want to taste you" made her mind run wild with the feel of his tongue across her swollen pink bud. She could feel his long dexterous fingers deep inside of her, stroking her into ecstasy. Sara dug her nails into the arm chair to ignore it. Who was this man? What right did he have to speak to her this way? How did they go from a casual exchange to this? The situation had evolved so rapidly.

"Alex!"

Sara stood from her chair and crossed the room to yell at his back.

"Alex! Look at me!"

When he turned to look at her, she had no idea what possessed her, but she slapped him across the face. It was hard enough to make his head reel and when he turned to look at her again, his eyes were full of rage. Why did she do that? That was the question in her mind as she backed away from him and he matched her every step. An inch of space was all that stood between her and his powerful body. They moved together in a dangerous tango. Sara quickly realized that slapping him was a grave miscalculation on her part. Without any warning he grabbed a hold of her and was pinning her against the wall-one hand on her throat. The screwdriver hit the floor and with his hand free, he found the tie on her cargo pants and slowly began untying them. Sara suddenly felt far away, as if she was on the outside looking in. She knew her physical body was in this situation but her mind had gone far away. Her every action now was merely out of instinct. The body knew hot to move on its own and therefore had switched to auto pilot.

"Alex please," Her anger gone. "P-please don't."

There was no fire or fight left in her.

"I just wanna know what you taste like."

Even though she was trying to fight him, even though his actions disgusted her, that little sentence made her body warm and wetness rush between her legs. She was split in two, body and mind. Where some part of her wanted this and in some twisted way enjoyed it, another part of her was disgusted. The unwanted hands touching her, made her cringe. If she had been of rational mind, she would have kicked him in the testicles. Instead she sat there like a dead fish and allowed him to do what he wanted. She felt the tie to her pants finally give and she gasp in shock, her body starting to shake with fear and arousal. Sara tried to beg him with her eyes to stop what he was doing.

"Some men," His voice was rougher. "can only take so much-"

Sara struggled. Alex squeezed tighter and slammed her against the wall again. Her head collided with the wood behind her and she bit her lip to keep quiet. The look on his face was a warning: the tight jaw as he pressed his teeth together hard and his once warm deep brown eyes, now a predatory black. She began to shake more as he ran his pointer finger across the waist band of her pants. Why was she not fighting him? Why was she allowing this to happen? This is not the way things were supposed to happen.

"And some men," He ran his finger just under the waistline of her pants. "have...certain...buttons...that a woman, like you...just...should not push."

"Alex-"

He put his finger to his lips. "Shh...I'm not done."

She bit her lip almost hard enough to make it bleed. As she was fighting every urge in her body, he began to run that finger along the top of her waistline again. When he moved it down and started running it just under the waistline of her panties, a gasp escaped her lips. Alex paused and looked up at her, his head cocked to the left, a slight smirk on his face.

"You like that?"

"Alex let go of me. Stop this."

"Make me Sara." He challenged.

Sara could only swallow. He then pulled his finger away and reached in his back pocket for something. She heard a click and caught the glimmer of metal out of the corner of her eye. A tendril of tears streaked down her face as she tried to pull back from him, afraid he was going to hurt her.

"I wouldn't move if I were you. I don't want to cut you."

So she froze, unable to speak, afraid to move and almost unable to breath. She watched in horror as he pushed the hip of one side of her pants down and exposed the strap of her bikinis. 'No Sara! Snap out of it! Fight!' But she did not, she could not. Her limbs refused to move. There was nothing she could do to stop him. Not recourse she might take to end his assault on her body. Alex looked up at her with a smirk, seeing her eyes widen in shock.

"Alex...no...Alex."

But it was too late; he had slipped that blade under the strap, the flat cold surface pressed against her flesh. He leaned into her ear.

"Ooh...I bet you would just about climax if I cut this."

He licked his bottom lip.

"Just one," He drew breath in between his teeth, hissing. "turn of my wrist and it would be gone."

She wanted to melt into a puddle on the floor right now, she could feel her knees weaken because of that statement.

"Alex-"

"Oops." He turned his wrist just slightly and the strap gave way.

Her breath hitched in her throat, she felt hot wetness rush down between her legs and her toes curled in her shoes. When she looked at him, he had his head lowered and cocked to the left, a half smirk on his face. But Alex was not finished yet. He stabbed the knife in the window sill behind her and then she felt his fingers rubbing through the fabric of her pants.

"Ohh...you are wet," He voice was slightly deeper as he whispered in her ear.

The tone in his voice made her breathing heavier and more shuddery. It seemed to almost travel through her whole body as if his very breath could give her pleasure. Suddenly, his fingers stopped and she felt that blade again, now it was against her neck and he was dragging the tip of it down her throat. Sara felt him lick the side of her neck ever so slowly, making her skin goose bump and her body shiver. Alex leaned into her ear to speak, the edge of that blade now rested against her throat. When he did speak, his voice was deep and gravely-almost a growl.

"You tell anyone . . .what happened here,"

He pressed the blade a little firmer against her throat.

"I'll come back for you. Understand?"

"Yes."

She whispered, scared he would hurt her.

"Good..."

78

Suddenly he let her go and she sank to the floor. For a few moments he just hovered over her and then he grabbed his screwdriver from the floor and turned, heading for the door. He paused a moment, turning to look at her.

"Hey."

She looked up.

"I'll see you again tomorrow."

He smirked and winked at her.

Sara waited until she heard him leave and then she broke into tears, sobbing heavily. Logically, she knew that should not have happened. How did things progress so quickly? The main point was that it did happen. To hell with the window locks. She could buy a drill and finish the job and he would not be getting one cent for his work. She would be calling the cops and telling them what happened, this was her house. She would be damned if he was going to get away this. Now Sara found her fire, after the fact and after he was gone. She was annoyed with herself for that. When she finally stopped crying and worked up the courage to go downstairs, she pushed herself from the floor and, grabbing a candle, headed to the dining room.

"Sara leave now. They won't help you."

"Why?"

She said grabbing her phone.

"They're all-"

"Hey wait!"

The voice was suddenly cut off as if someone was silencing her. Then she heard the crying again. It came breezing by her and she took a step back away from it. Behind that voice came another more masculine, angry voice and it made Sara jump back away from its path. The rush of air nearly blew out her candle.

'COME BACK HERE! YOU WERE TOLD TO STAY OUT OF THIS!'

Then they disappeared into the darkness beyond. When the voices had ceased, she looked around the house and felt a heavy presence in it. Slowly, as if afraid to piss someone off, she grabbed her jacket and headed out the door, almost running for the car. Sara blew out the candle and tossed it in the yard. From the driveway she could see the soft glow of candles in her room. For a moment she swore she saw the silhouette of a woman in the window. Then it was gone. Never mind the phantoms, she had something important to do right now. She would go to the police station personally and report the incident. If he thought he could scare her out of her house, it was not going to happen.

Jumping in her car, she started it and took off down Lillie and before taking a right onto Main St. That was where she had seen the small building that served as the police station for Collinstown. When she pulled up out front, she saw the two cars she had seen earlier in the day, at the hardware store and she swallowed nervously. For a second she paused, not really sure about going into the station with the two creepy officers inside. At this point though, any officer was better than no officer and they seemed to have a problem with him anyhow, considering they showed up at her house to talk to him. 'Rethink that Sara. Remember how they acted.'

Sara sighed, gathered her nerves and got out of the car. Just grabbing the handle of the door to the police station was like an electric shock of fear through her body. Her heart began to race and a mild vertigo passed through her head. 'Ok, you can do this.' When she opened the door and stepped into the police station, she nearly puked. The only two officers in the station were talking casually to Alex. The tears that she had managed to finally stifle after her attack, were resting just on her bottom lids now.

Alex, Ellis and Harris, all stopped talking and turned around when she walked into the station. Sara froze like a bird caught in the eye of a snake and began to slowly backing away.

"Something we can help you with Miss?" Ellis asked.

"Uh...no...never mind." Her voice was shaky.

Her gaze shifted once to Alex.

"You look like you could use some help ma'am." Harris replied a smirk playing at the corners of his mouth

"Nn-no." She was reaching for the door.

"She does look a little shaken." Alex said smiling like the Cheshire cat

"Why don't you come sit down?" Ellis said, standing from his place on the desk.

The three of them were watching her, like a wolf pack watching its prey. Before any of them could say another word, she shoved open the door, ran outside to her car and quickly climbed inside. She backed up and headed back down the street. Sara did not even bother to put her seat belt on.

When she pulled up in front of her house again and shut off the car, the tears she had been holding back, finally came spilling forward. She was terrified of everything going on. Of course she really did not understand what was going on. The things she had experienced were terrifying and mind boggling. Sara had no where to turn, she was stuck with the house and without real sanctuary. Some part of her was sure that the voice who had been warning her would not be speaking anymore and she wished she had listened to it the first time. 'The note, I still have the note to help me figure this out.' Sara fished in her back pocket for the note, she did not find it. So she checked the other pockets.

The note was gone. How did she lose the note? 'Think think think.' Then she thought back to when she first found it. When she tripped over Alex's boot and he caught her, he had 'accidentally' put his hand on her back side to support her. 'He took the note, he must have.' Even with tears in her eyes and her body full of fear, she still wanted to find out what was happening in this town. To make sense of things. She needed to know.

Sara suspected they all knew what was going on in her house and the town. Clearly, there was something wrong about the place. She could not be the only one to notice. There had to be someone else in the town that knew what its secret was. If she had to be stuck in this place, then she would find out what the townsfolk were hiding. After that, she would figure out who to call in order to get the creepy cops investigated. She refused to curl up in a corner and let them win. Even if she did break down several times, she would not give up

Chapter 6

The incessant beating of her heart had become the soundtrack for an endless series of unrealistic events. Her mind could not fathom or process what she had just experienced and therefore it removed her from the memory. She remembered it as a witness. Sara's body filled with a vibrating numbness, despite the adrenaline and arousal burning through her blood. The hot-cold sensation crawling across her flesh caused a mild vertigo and light headed feeling. Alex had touched, no, violated her and she knew that for a fact. Still, in order to save her sanity and keep her stable, it too was now a vague memory. It felt very dreamlike or in her case nightmarish. Why had she allowed him that touch? Why did she not fight harder? Her entire world, what she knew was reality, had been flipped and scrambled. There was no logic left, no bearings for her to grab onto and ground herself. They had looked at her, they knew what he had done and they mocked her discomfort. That alone should have sparked anger in her heart but it did not. Her body remained in a state of fear and confusion. The butterflies congregating in her diaphragm had morphed into spiders and now crawled up the inner wall of her stomach. All the tension binding her shoulders, now crept down her back and it throbbed with pain. She could breath fine but still felt short of breath. It might have had something to do with her never ending chain smoking as she sat in her car, staring at the house. The glow of her bedroom window gave her an urgency to get inside before it burned to the ground. It would be dark for a while and that was what she feared. Would the shadows attack again? Did they really attack before? If the answer was a doubtless 'yes', then she may have bigger issues.

Sara's mind continued to return to the facts she knew. Alex had touched her and she had been too terrified to react. The main point of that incident was it had gone wrong so quickly. He had been shameless in his assault. One minute he was repairing her home and then he was assaulting her. That scene, it made absolutely no sense to her. To add insult to injury, the police, they grinned at her pain and delighted in her suffering. She could only assume he went there to brag. Their words haunted her conscious mind, filling her with mild desperation. A small lump filled her throat and she fought to keep from crying. She knew she was already a broken woman and this was not helping. So, she had two choices, get tough or die. To anyone else, that might sound extreme but to a woman on the bring of insanity, it was motivation. She could not very well sit in her car for the rest of her life. There was no way she could just up and move again.

Sara lit another cigarette, inhaling the toxic smoke into her lungs as she sat and thought. One arm rested across her stomach and the other rested on top of it. She was afraid of what might happen if she did stay. At the same time, it there was something going on in Collins (and she suspected there was) then maybe she could stop it. Those cops needed to go any how. Sara had decided to get tough. Although the whole thing still felt like a bad nightmare.

When she finally emerged from the car, she forced herself to remain calm. The entire block was still dark and she could not remember if Alex left her flashlight. Sara reached under her passenger seat and grabbed the other one. Then she calmly proceeded toward the house. For whatever reason she was making a great effort to appear calm. 'Why does it matter?' She thought before answering herself.

"Because someone is watching." She whispered.

An unnatural stillness permeated the air. The storm had long sense passed and in its wake, left a cold breeze. Sara watched the shifting of the leaves on the treetops as the wind passed through them. Something about that made her nerves even more uneasy. There were no other sounds in the air, just the leaves moving in the breeze. She began to feel like she was living in a cemetery and that everyone else had died. All her neighbors were rotting corpses, sitting in their houses. The thought made her shutter.

As she surveyed the yard, she felt the temperature outside drop a few degrees more and she shivered. She had not dressed for this weather. Although her body was cold, the cold felt good on her tear streaked face. There was something grounding and cleansing about it as it filled her lungs. Slowly she moved toward the house looking and listening for what-she did not know. Perhaps she was looking for any sigh of life. Or waiting for the shadows to move. In any case, she needed to get into the house and look for other clues. Some part of had a feeling that there was more than one clue because there were several victims who lived in this house. Whatever was currently happening to her had been going on for a long time. 'Why did I think of them as victims? Why was that the first work to come to mind?' There would be no answer to her questions, not for a while. As Sara slowly pushed the key in the lock and listened to the tumblers turn, she glanced behind her. It was hard not to let her new found paranoia get the best of her. The door swung open into an empty darkness and it echoed as it collided with the wall behind it.

A heavy sigh escaped her lips before she bolted forward and bounded up the stairs. The beam of her flashlight bounced chaotically from one object to another. She could nearly feel the shadows closing in behind her. Sara sprinted for the safety of her glowing bedroom, leaping through the doorway and hitting the floor hard when she landed. Her movements greatly resembled that of a baseball player sliding into home. She lay there panting for a moment before rolling on her back and getting to her feet. Outside of her bedroom the hallway remained pitch black. The first thing she needed to do was get the rest of the house hit. Sara rummaged through another box and dug out a few more candles. At the very bottom of the same box she found an oil lamp. That was strange because she did not own an oil lamp. She stared at the foreign object for a bit and then looked around.

"All right, I am listening." She spoke to the voice.

There was no response at first but then the closet door swung open slowly.

"The closet, behind the wood." The voice whispered.

A loud crack came from the dark storage space and she nearly dropped the candles. Sara shined the flashlight into the closet and noticed the wood had been pushed forward. She set her bundled down and moved toward it. There was just enough space to fit her fingers in and pry off the large wood panel. In the dusty space behind it, she found a couple campfire lamps and a propane lamp with one extra tank. Whoever had hidden these must have known about the shadows. Sara left her candles for now and instead flipped on one of the campfire lights. Its white led glow lit the entire room, even with her candles blazing. There came another sound from the closet and she turned to find a pack of batteries at her knees. Looking up into the nothing above her, she whispered.

"Thank you."

Standing from her place on the floor, she carried the glowing torch into the hallway and set it down. In no time at all, it pushed the darkness away. Sara headed back into the bedroom, grabbed a couple more candles and the other lamp, hanging it from her arm. She held the large candles in one hand and her flashlight in the other.

When she reached the stairs, she turned the lamp on full blast and once again swore she heard the darkness hiss in pain. As she descended the stairs the entire kitchen was lit in a bright white glow. Sara set the lamp on the counter before finding her lighter and igniting the wick on the candles. Those she set in the living room on the mantle. With the house well illuminated she finally began to secure it. She locked every window and door, pulling the blinds shut as she went. Without the curtains open, the house became much brighter. There was no escape for the light now.

As she stood in the kitchen and looked around, she suddenly felt a cold chill coming from somewhere in the room it almost felt as if winter was blowing on her back. Slowly she turned and looked behind her for any sign of where that chill had come from. There was nothing in the house as far as she could tell. The more she analyzed the sensation, the more she began to understand it. She realized that she had felt the chill because someone was watching her. Normally, the feeling of eyes on her felt like a pressure or a head in the middle of her spine. For some reason this set of eyes gave her an all over chill. It made the room feel colder than the air outside. Whoever or whatever was watching her, was dangerous and for the first time ever, the scar on her leg began to burn. It not burn in the presence of Alex, which she found odd. Then again, would she have even noticed. Sara realized she needed to pay closer attention to what her body was telling her. She quickly switched back to her original thoughts about her secret stalker. All the blinds were closed, the house was locked tight. Had someone or something snuck inside? The door was open the whole time she was moving around lighting up the house.

Slowly, she turned around and looked behind her. Sara searched the entire first floor but found no one. Even if she did have power and the house was lit with normal lighting, she would not have seen him. There was a reason one of his girls had given him that nickname. Satisfied she was alone, she pulled out her cigarettes and lit one. The smoke curled up in spirals of white before hitting the ceiling. Against the ever present dark, its cherry looked like an angry red eye. As she exhaled the minty smoke from her lungs, she began to think out loud.

"So Alex took the note, the cops clearly know something and someone tried to silence the phantom voice. Why was it afraid of Alex? Who was the male voice? The angry voice?"

After much pacing she stopped by the kitchen counter and started drumming her nails on its surface like she always did before a tangible idea came to her. It was after her second round of tapping that she quickly turned around and started toward the basement but paused when she reached the dark hallway that lead to it. She turned and bolted for the stair, sliding into her room. Sara grabbed the propane lamp and the extra tank. Her flashlight dangled from her wrist as she slowly turned on the lamp. Its glow was brighten than any of the other lights she had. Her descent to the mail floor was not quick. The last thing she needed was to fall with that in her hands. She made her way into the basement, setting the lamp on the work bench and the extra tank on the floor. Then she moved over to the vandalized support beam and knelt down. Sara traced the letters with her fingertips and whispered to herself.

"What else did you leave behind?"

She looked around the basement for a moment, thinking out loud.

"You were smart enough to hide the note. But I have a feeling you weren't the only person here. So who else hid something?"

After standing there for about twenty minutes, she because frustrated and she started back up the stairs. That was when she finally saw it. How she had not noticed it before was beyond her. It was so small that unless you were looking for it, you would not see it. Just under the door frame there was one word carved, 'here.' Sara pushed on the wood paneling before trying to move it away from the bottom of the door frame with her nails. It was nailed to the bottom of the door frame, someone did not want whatever was behind there, found easily. She ran up the stairs, almost falling as she went and ran to the living room. There she rummaged through a box before finding what she was looking for a hammer. Then she ran back to the basement, sat down on the first step before she jammed the claw of the hammer between the wood panel and the bottom of the door frame.

Sara pulled the hammer backwards until she heard the wood panel crack and then she jammed the hammer down more. She pulled the handle back again. Finally the panel let loose and set the hammer down and pulled the panel off before squinting to see if she could see anything in the space behind the wood. It was too dark to see, even the flashlight still hanging from her wrist could not penetrate the small cavity. So she reached slowly into the darkness and felt for anything. At first she only felt cobwebs and then after patting her hand around for a bit, she found something. All she knew was that it was small and coarse to the touch. Sara grabbed the item and pulled it from the shadows.

At first it was hard to tell she was looking at but then she turned it over and, brushed the dust off before she looked at it in the light. It was a small leather bound journal and it had obviously been there a while because the pages were yellow. As if coveting some great prize she held the book to her chest and looked around. There were no windows here for prying eyes to see, so she shut the basement door and locked it. Here she would have complete privacy. She moved down to the work bench and under the light of her propane lamp, she began untying the leather straps holding shut.

The pages made a noise much like crinkling wrapping paper, as she turned them. At first she looked for a name and when she found no signature on any of the pages, she turned back to the first two pages. Written in what was clearly a woman's handwriting was a message for whoever found the journal:

If you find this I'm **Already** gone. But if you read what I have written here and you heed **My** w**A**rnings, it might **N**ot be too late for you. If you have alrea**D**y seen all of them or they h**A**ve seen   you then it **M**ight be too late. But maybe not if   you Ca**N** remember these few things. Do not trust the one with the d**A**rk **B**rown eyes, **B**ecause he is full of lies. Beware of the shadows, never let the house get dark. Do not trust the police, they are not real cops. Please get out before they get you. Use this book as a survival manual. Keep it close, hide **I**t, get out of the house, read this to survive, **N**ever let them find it.

A side from its cryptic contents there was something else strange about that first entry. Some of the letters were capitalized in the wrong places. Sara read the entry a few times before she began to understand the reason it was written that way. She pointed to each letter, saying it aloud as she did.

"A-M-A-N-D-A. Amanda. M-C-N-A-B-B. McNabb. Amanda McNabb, very clever."

Instead of signing her name in the stereotypical way, she had hidden it. The entire book was a vague compendium of research that its previous owner had done and little observations they had also noted. As she skimmed through the pages, she began to understand a few things. She understood the warning scrolled on its first two pages and that she was not the first woman. Whatever was going on here, had been happening for a while. There was one question that begged for an answer, how had no one noticed? Of course she realized that she may never have an answer.

Whoever Amanda had been or was, (there was no telling if she was still alive) she had guts. From what little evidence Sara had discovered, something horrible happened in this house. There was no denying the blood on the door frame. Or the fact that something lived in the shadows or possibly the shadows themselves were alive. It was an impossible idea but she had seen things herself and the journal confirmed it. Sara wanted to know more about Amanda and she needed to be sure that the journal was not another trick in their game. That Alex had not placed it there to drive her paranoia. If it was a trick, then how else could she explain the voices and what happened in her room. The person who hid the extra lights knew something about the dark. They seemed to know that someone else would need them and that inevitably the house would lose power.

Sara wondered if the local library still had power and a working computer. There was one problem, it was night now and dark everywhere. Her flashlight would be a glowing beacon in the dark. They could spot her from a mile away, it was a necessary risk. At least going on foot would make her harder to catch. There were endless alleyways for her to hid in. Of course they would all be dark too. It was either that or wait for them to make their next move. She was not going to let that happen. If Amanda was real and she was alive, Sara would not fail her.

The library was a few blocks from the house, she had spotted it on her way to the hardware store. She had another reason for wanting to walk instead of drive. If she traveled by foot she could get a closer look at the town, see the truth behind its visage. Maybe rip off its white porcelain mask and expose its disfigured face to the world. Now that she thought about it, it was no surprise that no one noticed the truth of this place. This was no destination spot. No one came here and stayed. They drove through it on their way to other places. As she thought more about it, she had a sudden urge to check her cell phone. Sara dug it out and flipped it open, no signal. That was rather strange, considering she had called Alex only about an hour ago. She nodded silently to herself before tucking it away and turning her attention back to the journal. 'Hide the book. Remember what you read but hide it.' Sara closed the journal before shoving it up into the rafters above her head. Then she flicked off the flashlight to save its battery and headed up the stairs. Before she headed out, she pulled her hood up about her face and zipped her sweater all the way up. She sighed slowly as her fingers gripped the door handle.

"You can do this."

That was all she said before leaping out into the night and dashing immediately behind the buildings. The temperature had dropped drastically and now her breath came out in white puffs. She would not be deterred. Even if the cops tried to stop her, she would not stop for them. They were not real cops, Amanda had said so herself. Slowly, she made her way across town, moving between buildings so she was never on the main sidewalk for very long. She expected to see at least one of them but there was no sign of them. Where were they?

As she moved down the sidewalk, listening to the sound of her own footsteps on the blocks of concrete, she began to realize that she missed having music when she walked. She had not used her Ipod since she moved here. It used to be whenever she went for a walk, she would put her headphones in and the world would fade away. 'Yes, but in all that time had he been watching you. The man who attacked you, he could have been right behind you and you never would have known.' At that thought, she turned around suddenly looking behind her. She scanned the whole walk and all the buildings behind her, looking for anyone. 'You've stayed in the open too long, get behind a building.' In no time at all, she made a dash behind one of the buildings nearby and for a few moments she hid behind it.

Slowly, she moved to the edge of the building and peeked around to look at the empty streets. It was not that late but there were no cars on the street and no one on the sidewalk. Had she not noticed this the day she came to look at her house? That question was for a later date. Sara moved down the back alleys until she came to another gap between the buildings and she paused. Across the street from this gap was the police station but what had caught her attention was the fact that there were no lights on inside. They had a back up generator for power, she knew they had to. Besides that, they had power about an hour ago when she stopped in there. It was a police station. There should be lights on all the time, even if they are not real cops they have to keep up appearances. Again, she decided just to make a mental note of it and move on for now. This part of town had to have power. The Victorian themed street lights were all on. Sara realized that could serve to be a good or bad thing. They kept the shadows away but also exposed her presence. She knew she had to move quickly if she wanted to keep from being seen.

When she finally reached the library, she paused to look over its exterior, it was a rather old building. The town had put no money into its up keep apparently because the entire front of it was cracked in different places. It almost looked like it was ready to fall down. But as long as it had power and a working computer inside, she would not care if the whole front of it fell off. The tricky part now was getting across the street without getting noticed. There was no one outside to see her, but there was the possibility of the boys seeing her. Just because she did not see them did not mean that they did not see her. Sara let out a slow calming sigh before she ran across the street, praying it was still open.

Sara was elated when she yanked the door open. It was thankfully still open. When she got inside, the old librarian behind the main desk gave her a nasty look. There was no time to be courteous, she needed to get in, out and back home before they realized she was gone. If they had not already. Sara kept her head down as she moved through the library and looked for a computer. After a bit of searching, she found one in the back corner and sprinted to it. She glanced around before pulling up the internet browser and typing in three words 'Amanda McNabb, missing. '

A list of different news sites popped up with those words scattered throughout the description in bold. Sara clicked the first link and a photo with an article popped up on the screen. The title was in big bold letters 'Michigan Woman Missing'. According to the article, her family had reported her missing only two weeks after she had moved to Collins. It went on to say that she had called and let them know she had arrived all right but then they stopped hearing from her. The article also said that with her demanding job it was not uncommon to not hear from her for up to a week. But when two weeks passed, they called and reported her missing. They spoke to the local authorities who claimed that they had no record of an Amanda McNabb ever living there.

On the bottom of the page was a link to a news video for Channel Five news. Sara clicked it and up on the screen popped Officer Harris, standing in front of a podium with five microphones mounted in front of him. Just off to his left was Officer Ellis. He did not seem the least bit concerned, he appeared rather proud of himself.

"People, people please. We are doing everything we can to help Miss McNabb's Family locate her. Unfortunately, we have found no evidence to suggest she was ever in Collins."

'Liar.' She thought.

"Officer Harris how can you be sure she was never here?"

"Because I know my town and everyone in it. I know who is in my town, what they're doing and where they are at all times."

Then the video stopped and Sara felt a tinge of nervousness climb up her spine. But she swallowed hard and sat back in the wooden library chair. 'So Amanda came here and went missing? Maybe I should take the journal, pack what I can into the car and run. Tell the authorities in the next town over what's going on in this town. But then again, I don't know what is going on here. What would I tell them? And . . . they would only see the uniform, they would not believe that Harris and Ellis are not real cops.' Sara sat there staring at the screen in front of her, contemplating her next few moves. What could she do? There were three of them and one of her. Exposing their crimes would be a dangerous task but it had to be done. Little did she know, this was going to cost her more than a few sleepless nights. It could very well cost her, her life. Then there were the shadows. How could she explain them? Her answers had to be in that journal.

Seemingly out of no where, she was suddenly snapped from her train of thought (almost like being shaken awake) and she jumped from her chair (nearly knocking it over) to look around. There were bookshelves behind her all lined up neatly and she could see down most of them. The air around her had become somehow thicker, colder, and the room, slightly darker. It was as if a dark cloud now hovered over her. How had she not noticed this transition? She slowly exhaled and tried to calm her racing heart. With careful observation she looked around for anything to banish the feeling of being watched. There were too many dark corners in this room. Sara scanned each shadow for a few moments before feeling sure nothing was hiding there. As her eyes started to move to the next dark spot, she saw a shadow shift, just slightly. It was enough to make her sprint for the exit, slamming her body weight against the library doors as she ran outside.

Sara was not sure how long she had been in there but it had clearly been too long. It was time to get back to her illuminated sanctuary and figure things out.

Their World

Chapter 7

It turned out they had been smarter then she had anticipated. Although she had managed to keep the information out of her mind so he could never reach it, they had found it anyhow. She knew she could not keep it from them forever. They were older, much older than they appeared and they were powerful. There was no way she could have expected to beat them or to even outwit them. They were forever and had been doing this a long time. At least the others had started leaving clues as well. But only one of them had the courage to take her own life before they could find her clue or before they could interrogate her. The normal predator of their species did not keep pets or prisoners like they did. But then again, what did she really know about them?

If only she had left more clues or had the courage the previous one had, maybe then she would not be here. Where was here? It was a cold brick building but it was not the same brick as the cell of her prison. This was newer, cleaner but still cold. She knew they had found it, when the shadows started moving in her cell, they were faster than normal-they were angry. The Shadow One, he was the strong one, the ring leader in charge of everything and the oldest one. She knew he probably could not die. If one believed the old legends, there were ways to kill them but she had a feeling that this did not apply to them.

So far, They had no name as a group or even a true name. She once read that to know a things true name was to have the power to weaken, kill or banish it. But they only spoke Their language when they were not in public. As far as she could tell it was not any known language. What they spoke was a something only known to their species-of course none of this was fact. Everything she believed she knew about them was from being here so long.

Now as she waited in this room, she started to pray silently because she knew that someone would 'leave' soon. Out with the rotten or used up and in with the new. She was surprised they had waited this long. What would her punishment be? What else could they possibly do to her? They would come up with something. Beings their age had many ideas. The last time she was bad, they let the

Chameleon play with her and he had delighted in knife play. There were still scars on her body and his name across her back to prove it. Unfortunately, it was not his true name, so it was of no use to her.

The restraints on her wrists were starting to dig and the bloody t-shirt (which was the only thing she wore) was providing no warmth. She just wanted them to get on with it so she could cry in her cell. If she was lucky they would kill her. Anything but leave her to the Shadow One. He could and would use the shadows to help him punish her. The Shadow One was in charge of the shadows and for that reason he did not even have to be there to torture her.

Her? That's all she knew about herself anymore, she was female and that was it. She could not remember her name, or any other defining characteristics about herself. What did she look like? Where was she from? What was her name? Name. That was something she had not heard in such a long time. They never called any of their keeps by name and they made sure not to let them see the outside. But still, why couldn't she remember her own name or anything else about herself? Did the Telepathic One erase her memories? She only knew what she could see with her own eyes. Every inch of her was covered in bruises and her thighs were still crusted with recently dried blood. The Chameleon had delighted in her pain only a few hours earlier. For a few moments she just stared at the edge of the table. It took her a bit to realize that the table was metallic enough to reflect the room around it. So, she slowly leaned forward until she could see her face a little bit on its surface. She could just barely make out her dark brown hair and the blur of her features. In that moment she started to remember.

They must have sensed it because the door opened suddenly and her head shot up. It was the Telepathic, dressed in a long sleeve black button down shirt, blue jeans and black dress boots. As he entered, she tried to look past him and see if she could tell where they were. But he closed the door, leaving her stuck with him in this small room. She felt herself start to shake and could feel the urge to cry quickly climb through her. He crossed his arms across his broad chest and just stood there staring at her for a moment. Those bright blue eyes of his were like daggers as he glared at her. They almost seemed to stare right through to her soul.

"You don't learn do you?" He snapped.

She squeaked out. "Please . . .I'm-"

He cut her off, holding up a finger and silencing her before she could say another word. When he started toward her, she ducked her head down and started shaking. Then she felt him grab her hair and pull just enough to hurt her before he whispered low in her ear.

"You better be afraid . . .he is furious. Who knows what he will do to you."

After that he let go of her and she began to cry. She knew that death would be too quick, that would be a gift and not a punishment. While she was slumped over crying, the door opened and when she glanced up to look through her tears to see who it was, she felt her heart quicken with fear. The Chameleon was still in his work clothes but he was no less intimidating and when she looked at him, she could remember the punishment he exacted on her like it was yesterday.

"No no no, please no!"

Before she could do anything else, he had his hand on her mouth and one of his knives pressed to the delicate flesh of her throat. She felt its sharp edge threatening to slice into her if she moved. So she stayed as still as her terrified body would allow.

"Ssh...if you make another sound."

A slow smirk crept across his lips. One that would make the devil shudder.

"We will play again and I will let him watch. Understand?"

She started to cry more as she nodded her head.

"Good girl." He let go of her.

Now she waited in fear, her whole body shaking from the adrenaline coursing through her veins. Her eyes bounced between them as she waited for him to get here, and as she did, she listened to them speak in their native tongue amongst themselves. They were talking about her, that much she knew from their gestures in her direction. She also had a feeling she knew what they were talking about, her punishment.

The air around them seemed to still suddenly. The two talking were unfazed by the change in air pressure because they were not the ones on trial here. She always felt him coming before she every saw him. It was the same stillness a hunter felt just before the kill, animals knew when death was coming, animals could always sense death. That was her nickname for him, Death. They all had nicknames because she refused to call them by the names they used. To her, they were Death (The Shadow One), The Chameleon and The Telepathic.

With a rush of cold air, the door opened and in he came, slamming it shut behind him. An angry sigh was all she heard from him at first. Through strands of hair she could see that his jaw was locked so tight the muscles were shifting just under his flesh and his once soft brown eyes were now jet black with rage. The room around them seemed to get darker just with his presence. She tried to curl up in the chair but couldn't with her hands restrained behind it. Now they all were talking about her and she glanced up to see them standing by the door before she dropped her eyes down to the floor. She could not bare to look at them.

When she heard them move, she looked up again to see what they were doing. The Telepathic was standing to the left of the table, the Chameleon to the right and Death was sitting in front of her on the table. She started to shake more, her whole body was trembling with fear and tears were streaming down her face.

"Shh . . .shh." Death tried to calm her.

She swallowed and became quiet. But she still flinched when he touched her face to brush her tears away.

"There now . . .that's better."

Death reached in his back pocket and pulled out a folded up piece of paper, laying it on the table. He had found it, he knew what it was and she knew he was enraged but he appeared extremely calm. That was not right, he was too calm. She knew she was in serious trouble.

"Oh," He was looking at her face closely, cocking his head to one side. "now tell me . . .did you leave this note for someone?"

His tone was soft, slightly mocking.

She could not bring herself to admit it. So she just jerked back away from his sight and tried to hide. But Death half turned and glanced at the Chameleon who moved to the table. The Shadow One (Death) moved away and the Chameleon leaned on the table, putting his hands flat on the top of it before he continued the interrogation.

"Sweetie did you?"

His tone was also too soft.

Still she refused to look at him or even answer him. In no time at all, his calm exterior disappeared.

"Did you?!" He yelled, slamming his fist on the table and leaving a noticeable dent.

She flinched, pulling away as much as she could in that chair. The Telepathic put his hand on the Chameleon's shoulder and pulled him back away from her. She could feel Death standing behind her now as the Telepathic moved to lean on the table and try to talk to her. Even without looking at him, she knew the evil being behind her was starting to lose his patience as well, she could feel his tension. She knew they already had the answer to their questions, the Telepathic had read her mind but they wanted to hear her say it.

"Hey." His voice was like honey. It was almost loving.

She could feel his eyes on her as he tried to get her to look at him. Now he moved closer to her.

"Come on . . ."

Slowly she lifted her head and found his eyes were now a soft blue. Her hair still hung in her face and he now pushed it from her eyes.

"There you are," He lowered his head to look at her more. "Sweetie you can tell me if you left the note. I won't yell."

After a few moments of looking at him to see if he was lying, she swallowed a lump of tears before speaking.

"Yes." She squeaked out.

Without warning he backhanded her across her face so hard that if Death had not been standing behind her and caught the chair, she would have been on the floor. The hit sent stars across her vision and she could taste blood in her mouth as more tears rolled down her cheeks.

"What should we do with her?" Chameleon asked.

After a moment of silence, she heard Death's boots hard on the concrete floor as he moved around to look at her. A slow smirk spread across his features and she knew what that meant. Before he even said a word, she began to shake her head 'No'.

"Shadow Cell."

Death would punish her. Although she knew that screaming and kicking would do her no good, she still fought against their iron grip. Her shrieks echoed off the unforgiving brick walls as she was dragged down the corridor and flung into another room. The metal door creaked on its hinges and slammed shut with echoing force. She was plunged into darkness, left alone with the shadows and their mocking, hissing voices. Maybe tonight would be the end of her and she could know peace.

"Sweetie did you?"

His tone was also too soft. Still she refused to look at him or even answer him. In no time at all, his calm exterior disappeared.

"Did you?!"

He yelled, slamming his fist on the table and leaving a noticeable dent.

She flinched, pulling away as much as she could in that chair. The Telepathic put his hand on the Chameleon's shoulder and pulled him back away from her. She could feel Death standing behind her now as the Telepathic moved to lean on the table and try to talk to her. Even without looking at him, she knew the evil being behind her was starting to lose his patience as well, she could feel his tension. She knew they already had the answer to their questions, the Telepathic had read her mind but they wanted to hear her say it.

"Hey."

His voice was like honey. It was almost loving. She could feel his eyes on her as he tried to get her to look at him. Now he moved closer to her.

"Come on . . ."

Slowly she lifted her head and found his eyes were now a soft blue. Her hair still hung in her face and he now pushed it from her eyes.

"There you are,"

He lowered his head to look at her more.

"Sweetie you can tell me if you left the note. I won't yell."

After a few moments of looking at him to see if he was lying, she swallowed a lump of tears before speaking.

"Yes." She squeaked out.

Without warning he backhanded her across her face so hard that if Death had not been standing behind her and caught the chair, she would have been on the floor. The hit sent stars across her vision and she could taste blood in her mouth as more tears rolled down her cheeks.

"What should we do with her?" Chameleon asked.

After a moment of silence, she heard Death's boots hard on the concrete floor as he moved around to look at her. A slow smirk spread across his features and she knew what that meant. Before he even said a word, she began to shake her head no.

"Shadow Cell."

Death would punish her. Although she knew that screaming and kicking would do her no good, she still fought against their iron grip. Her shrieks echoed off the unforgiving brick walls as she was dragged down the corridor and flung into another room. The metal door creaked on its hinges and slammed shut with echoing force. She was plunged into darkness, left alone with the shadows and their mocking, hissing voices. Maybe tonight would be the end of her and she could know peace.

The Journal

Chapter 8

The shadows crawled and crept where the light could not reach. Sara could see their skeletal fingers and tendrils dash between the lights before seeking the sanctuary of the darkness. She nodded silently to herself. They were not a figment of her tired mind or a hallucination created by her own growing paranoia. They were living creatures all their own. However, they no longer shook her foundations, she understood their weakness. So, like spoiled children pining for their mother's attention, she ignore them by turning her head to the overcast sky above her. There the moon highlighted an already eerie skyline with a crimson red glow. Would blood be spilled tonight? Is this when her confrontation with them would happen? Not unless it was on her terms. They may rule this place but she would be breaking all their rules and taking over their town. She decided that her responses to whatever happened would not be out of fear. Sara had lived in fear for too long and now refused to any longer.

It should have surprised her to find the streets desolate but it did not. She could no longer deny that a sickness plagued this town. No one had developed a cure for it yet but she was about to. A permanent vaccine for what ailed Collins. So, she was still not a fighter and she very much despised weapons. At this point, she understood that she needed to get something to protect herself from them. Besides, two of them were fake cops and although she knew that, nevertheless they were still armed. Sara had also become comfortable with the idea of hurting or at worst killing them. It might take a little more time but she would eventually feel the same way about murder as she did about breathing.

Sara shoved her hands in her pockets and slowly descended the stairs. It was strange (even to her), she ran through the library doors but not down the stairs. For some reason she had stopped herself. Even though she knew that the three of them might be roaming around, she stood her ground. It was a sign that despite all she had been through thus far, she was getting stronger. A necessary metamorphosis of her entire being was happening and instead of fighting it or denying it, she allowed the change to come.

As she made her way down the brightly lit sidewalk, a cold

breeze rushed by her, chilling her pale skin and whipping her raven locks around as if they were serpents. It had grown bitter cold since her adventure in the library and now her breath floated out as a white fog. The threat of snow tingled in her nostrils and she pulled her sweater tight around her. Perhaps that was the winds of change sweeping by, welcoming her into a new era of thought and action. Who's to say the winds of change are warm? Change often does not come quickly or without hardships. So the fact that the air was bitter cold and the wind made it feel even colder, seemed befitting. On her way home, Sara listened for any sound that would alert her to their presence. There was only the echo of her lonely foot falls on the pavement. Even if she did encounter them, she was not ready for any form of confrontation with them. So, if she did notice any sign of them, she would most likely jump behind a building or into an alleyway until they were gone.

In any case, this day had been far too long and eventful for her liking. All she wanted right now was to sleep, to pretend everything was fine. The survivor in her told her to keep going, to gather as much information as possible from that journal because now that it was out of its hiding spot it was also in danger of going missing. If it disappeared she would have nothing to help her. She was last man standing (or in her case, woman). Every woman who had lived in that house had (she assumed) disappeared and she knew they had something to do with it. How they had managed to sweep all of them under the proverbial rug was beyond her. The point was that they had done it and they probably had the same fate in mind for her. She would be damned if they thought they were going to get her too. Sara was determined to be the woman who ended it all, who shut their entire operation down and blew the whole thing to bits. The world would know what was happening in Collins and Sara King would be the poison on those boys lips by the time she was finished here.

One question remained, why had no one had stopped her from going to the library? She was tempted to sneak down to the police station and see if the lights were still off. It was too risky though, she could easily be spotted and she doubted that she could outrun them. Her best bet was to lay low and return home before anyone realized she had left. If they had not driven by the house or had seen her walk out the front door, that could explain why no one stopped her. Who was watching her then? Maybe the reason no one tried to stop her is because they had no idea what she was doing or why she was going to the library. Still it did seem that they used every opportunity to keep her on edge. So, why not rattle her nerves again? She was beginning to become a threat (little did they know). If they did not act soon and shake her foundations to the core, she would destroy their little game and ruin their kingdom. Suddenly she felt something brush across her back, breaking her train of thought and making her spin around to see what touched her. There was nothing, no one, not even a breeze.

"Sara . . . "

A male voice whispered behind her, spreading through the street like a wave. It echoed off the buildings.

Not a second after that voice, she heard a car engine. She did not even wait to see who it was. She dashed down an alleyway and crouched behind a dumpster. The car turned down the street she was on and seemed to slow down as it passed by the alley. Was she too late? Had they seen her already? With her nails pressed to her palms she waited to find out if she would need to run or if they would just leave. 'Maybe they're looking for you because they have no clue where you are.' She willed herself to breath slowly and keep her body ready but calm. If she allowed herself to panic, then she knew that her anxiety would take over and she would fail to react when necessary. Sara peered around the dumpster and could almost see who was in the car but the windows were tinted. Although she did not need to see the driver because she caught the reflective lettering on the side of the car and was now glad she had jumped behind the dumpster. Her quick reaction was a good sign, she no longer allowed her fear to dictate her actions. The woman she was before everything had happened, would have froze up and stood like a deer in headlights as the car made its way down main street. She would have been caught easily and would not have fought to keep her freedom or even went so far as to expose their crimes. That Sara definitely would have curled up in a corner and allowed them to take her. There was no fire in that woman or fight. She might have eventually ran from them but she never would have decided to stop them from doing whatever it was they were doing in this town. A small smile crept across her features as she felt courage fill her heart. She liked the person she was becoming and she understood why she had gone through hell.

When she heard the car turn onto another street, she slowly stood up and edged toward the edge of the alleyway. Sara slid her hand into her pocket and grabbed for the flashlight. If she had to face the darkness, she would not do it unarmed. The flashlight was not in her pocket. She frantically began patting her pockets for it. Her heart began to race and she felt her breath catch in her throat when she realized it was not in any of her pockets. Did she drop it? 'Oh god no! Please don't let me be alone in the dark with no defense from the shadows.' There was still one thing in this town she was afraid of because without light she was virtually defenseless from it.

"Sara"

A familiar male voice whispered above her.

She swallowed hard and slowly looked up. When she did, what she saw made her body begin to alight with fear. A pair of red eyes gleamed down at her from one of the rooftops and the shadow figure crouching there held the flashlight she had tucked in her pocket. Sara fell back away from the form as he jumped down from the building and melt into the shadows that encompassed her. It reminded her of watching water as it was poured into another body. The movement was so fluid that it made no ripple in the darkness around her. His solidity wavered momentarily before becoming once again the figure of a man. He was darker than all the shadows that surrounded him and as she watched in horrid fascination, she realized that the slithering tendrils she saw, moved around him. They reminded her of subordinates obeying their masters command and in that moment she realized they were. Sara could not stop the panicked breaths that escaped her. 'What in god's name is he?' Whatever this man, this thing was, she could not fight him. She had finally worked up to the idea of fighting the three ringleaders of the town. This however, she had no weapons or defense for. A sentient shadow with the anatomy of a man, who could take her light away from her and render her helpless to his shadowy servants. Sara hoped and prayed that Amanda had encountered this creature, only because if she had, then she may have figured out some way to defeat it. Or at best defend herself.

The shadow figured strolled casually toward her with her flashlight in its hand. As she backed away, her eyes caught in those glaring rubies staring down at her, she realized that his movements were very familiar (although at the time she was unable to place them). She knew she had to keep her mind from panicking. So she analyzed the demon before her, keeping the shadows around her in her peripherals. 'Who does he move like? Who does he sound like? Remember him and this moment. You will need to know this. Is he connected to someone here or to one of them?' Her thoughts and ideas seemed far fetched but so did the existence of a walking, talking shadow figure. If she had to deal with the realm of the metaphysical, then there was no idea or question right now that was too unrealistic. Sara backed toward the lit street behind her but the shadows were quick to stop her. She watched the light at the edge of the alleyway disappear as a wall of darkness went up behind her, blocking her exit. There was no escape for her at this point, except to charge through the creature in front of her and run for her house as quick as she could. She had a feeling though that it would not be so easy. They would not let her charge through them and besides that, she refused to back down. Demon or not, she was going to face whatever came from now on. The Sara King who used to jump at every little sound, was no longer here. She waited patiently to see what his next move might be. The apparition spoke to her.

"You should mind your own business Sara."

"How do-"He cut her off before she could ask the obvious question. The noticeable accent in his voice thickening with his impatience. "If you know what's good for you, you will go home before you make things worse for yourself."

"What? I don't understand. What are you?"

The shadow lost his patience. He threw her flashlight against the side of one of the buildings shattering the bulb and its glass covering, rendering it useless. Sara tried to run through him and from the alley but he was faster than she anticipated. The shadow grabbed her by her hair and pulled her back into the alleyway, pushing her face first up against the brick wall. She could hear remnants of her flashlight crunch beneath what sounded like cowboy boots as he moved closer behind her to kick her legs apart. Sara knew now that the shadows in her house had assaulted her and violated her. That she had heard them hiss and perhaps they were the voices whispering her name on the street. This one's touch was different, more solid than theirs and she could feel him as if he was flesh and bone. How was that possible? She wondered. Her mind questioning the event in an attempt to keep herself level headed (or at least as calm as she could be in such a situation). His shadowy hand left her tangle of hair and grabbed her wrists, slamming them against the wall above her head. Sara fought against his grip but no matter how hard she struggled, she could not wiggle free from his iron hands.

"I warned you. But didn't listen."

The husky sound of his voice as it traveled across her ear, caused her body to shiver, despite her disgust. Sara squeezed her eyes shut as she waited for him to decide what to do with her. It was all she could do at this point, wait for it to be over with and then deal with the aftermath.

"You were told to wait." There was the other male voice she had heard.

"Why?" He replied.

The next few sentences she heard were not English. That much she was certain. As far as she could tell it might not even have been a real language. There were two male voices (of that much she was sure), and they were arguing with each other about (she assumed) what to do with her. As they argued, she tried again to slip free but to no avail. After a bit she heard the other male voice speak to her.

"You should have stayed home."

They must have come to an agreement.

"If you scream . . .I'll slit your pretty throat. But if you're a good girl, I won't hurt you."

That was what her attacker had said to her. She fought to keep the phantom feelings from rising back up and over taking her. Sara refused to allow herself to be crippled by her past any longer. They would not break her new found constitution. Even if they were demons. Until she knew what to call them or what they really were, she would use that temporary label to describe them. The one holding her did have red eyes and as far as she knew, that fit every description of a demon she had read about. At the same time she was fighting, she tried to cry for help.

"Hel-"

Something was muffling her voice before the word could fully escape her lips. It felt like a gag but she could not see or feel anything wrapped around her face. She was fighting with everything she had to get away but she could not break the shadow's hold. Sara felt panic beginning to rise up from the depths of her stomach and she reprimanded her body for allowing such things. This was not where it would end. 'Be like stone, be like stone. Do not break, do not falter. Fight, fight, fight.'

"Sssh..." The shadow mocked.

"Don't fight or you will only make this worse for yourself."
The other warned.

No amounts of threats would make her stop. Sara fought harder against the grip on her wrists as she felt her pants unbutton and the zipper slowly pulled down before they were pulled down to her knees. Unlike before, this time she was completely helpless to stop what was happening. Again she could not see her attacker. This time there were two attackers and this time she did not know how they could hurt her. These attackers would not give up if hit with a lamp, if she could hit them at all.

"I'll bet she shaves." The shadow almost growled.

Those filthy disgusting creatures, how dare they discuss her most intimate parts as if she was a common whore. Although their words and their touch disgusted her, she still felt her body shudder. She felt dirty, the kind of dirty one gets from watching a rape scene in a movie. To be subjected to watching the act and to feel completely ejected from your comfort zone but at the same time you feel your body becoming oddly aroused. Then the disgust at your own reactions settles in and it becomes an endless cycle that nothing can stop. It was exactly how she felt and she hated herself for it. Sara fought harder as one of them pulled her panties aside and brushed their fingers over her bare flesh.

"Mmm...so soft.." The other one said.

"Wonder how sensitive," She felt the shadow push a finger between her outer folds and began to rub her sensitive pink bud. "she is"

This was wrong and every part of her mind told her it was wrong. Maybe that was the very reason she became aroused. None of this should have been happening or was remotely possible. Still it was happening and in her powerless state she felt a heat began to grow at the apex of her thighs because she could not stop it. The shadow who could touch was rubbing her swollen bud in all the right places. As much as her mind disagreed with the situation, her body still betrayed her, disobeying what her mind told it. She could not stop the noticeable shiver that traveled through her legs. Nor could she hide her arousal from her tormentors.

"You like that?" The shadow asked.

Sara did not answer. There was something in the way he said that, almost as if his words were a verbal aphrodisiac and they were meant to arouse her mind in the same way the dexterous digits aroused her aching core. Those few words fueled the growing ache between her shaking legs. It was, an innocent question (sort of) and at the same time a dominating statement as if he was telling her that she liked it. Letting her know he was aware of every dirty, dark, deep fantasy she had and he was going to explore them all. There was so much power in that one little sentence it was astounding or she was allowing there to be more power in it than there really was. They knew she was too far gone in the ecstasy of every element in her current situation to answer them.

Sara felt a long slender finger slide deep within her aching wet folds and rub tortuously over her g-spot. It was slow and deliberate as it rubbed in circles until she curled her toes hard enough for the knuckles to crack. She was shaking so hard she could barely stand without leaning on the wall.

"Mmm . . .she's so wet. Feel her."

The sound of his voice as he elongated the S in so and the W in wet, only made her shiver harder. What was it about them that made their words so potent? She did not know or care right now. This stranger was moaning at the feel of her and she was become more aroused (somehow) at the realization he was getting pleasure from pleasuring her. It took her a moment to realize what he had meant when he said 'Feel her' and then it hit her.

'No, they wouldn't.' She thought.

They would and they did. She felt the second figure slide a finger deep within her wet folds and began pumping in a different rhythm than the other digit. Sara would have sank down the wall if she was not being held up by her wrists. The two probing fingers in her both began to rub and stroke her g-spot, filling her body with pleasure she had never felt before. Of course, she had never had two different men finger her at the same time. Her nails were digging into and scratching against the brick as she moaned against whatever gag muffled her voice.

She had given up fighting them and just gave in completely to their torment The long fingers wiggling deep within her folds had subdued her a while time ago and now she was their willing victim. The thumb on her pink bud rubbed it in circles in rhythm with the two different fingers that pumped in and out of her. Without warning, two more fingers (one from each figure) slid inside of her, making her body jolt with more pleasure.

"Oh, she's close."

At this point Sara could no longer distinguish between voices, her brain was not functioning. With a hard shiver she felt the first wave of her orgasm hit her. The shadow whispered in her ear.

"That a girl."

It was the exact thing her previous attacker had said to her when she began to obey him. Only later would she realize just how much he sounded like the man who had attacked her in Layfayette.

"Be happy I forgave you for hitting me Sara."

That statement became a muffled sound against the background of her climax as it washed over her in waves and she let out a cry of pleasure against the gag. Her body shook violently, the stability of her legs weakening entirely as pleasure spread from her inner folds and flashed through the rest of her anatomy. Every inch of her flushed with a welcomed heat, quickening her heartbeat and coloring her flesh a rosy pink. The sensation of floating filled her and she desperately gripped the bricks in front of her for stability. For a few minutes after her orgasm, she just stood leaning against the wall panting as shivers continued to haunt her body and her mind attempted to come back down to reality. Sara knew she was asking a lot of a tortured, tired and now confused mind. Her previous train of thought had been abruptly derailed and she now fought to put it back on track. However, now was not the time or place to do so.

She had been so busy trying to gather her thoughts, that it took her a moment to realize that she was alone with her pants still down around her knees. Sara gathered what dignity she had left and pushed herself upright, praying that no one had seen what had just happened. Although she doubted anyone had, on account of the fact that the streets remained vacant. That did not mean one of the creepy men she was trying to avoid, were not still watching her and did not see everything that just happened. With shaky fingers she slowly pulled her pants up, fastening them and forcing herself to push her feelings down before heading back out on the sidewalk. Without her flashlight to protect her from the darkness, she had no other choice but to stick to the lit areas of Collins and risk being seen by the cops. Sara pulled her hood up and tried to fight the urge to cry even though every exhale was filled with shudders threatening at any second to send her tears flowing forward. Had that really just happened? Nothing made sense anymore but now was not the time to figure anything out. Nor was it the time to break down, she had to keep going. When she was safe behind locked doors, she could try to sort though her chaotic thoughts. At least then, if she became so over come with emotion that she finally broke down, she might be safer.

The walk home was slightly more difficult now because her legs were sore and she was fighting to keep her composure. Somehow on the last few blocks home, Sara had managed to push herself into a run. Why was she running? She knew she was not being chased and the shadows had not bothered her for a few blocks now. There were no signs of Alex, Ellis or Harris any where. So what had prompted her to start running? Maybe she thought if she ran hard enough that the memories, feelings or anything else she wanted to ignore, could not catch her. Maybe she thought she could outrun them. Logically she knew that no one can outrun a memory or try to hide from it because memories were not a living being. They could not be killed or caged. Once they are made, they cannot be unmade or if they are a bad memory they cannot be altered to become a good one. However, if running made her feel better than she was not going to analyze it. She would just push forward and run until her lungs burned from the cold air she was inhaling. Until her legs threatened to collapse or at least until she reached the safety of her front porch.

With every beat of her foot against the sidewalk, her body jolted forward, propelling her rapidly closer to home. She panted hard as she ran, her smokers lungs protesting the exertion. A steady pain began to throb in her lower diaphragm as her body begged her to stop this nonsense. Sara refused to listen to it. The house was slowly coming into view only a few yards ahead of her and she forced her legs to move faster. When she finally reached it, she jumped the steps to the porch and hurried inside, hoping that she could lock herself away from the evil that resided in this town, if only for a little while. That was really all she needed was a few hours of sleep, some food and a cup of coffee. She could figure things out in the morning. 'How do you know you have until morning?' She asked herself before realizing that was a morbid thought. As far as she knew they were not planning to kill her but there was a high risk in the journal going missing. Sara sighed realizing that she would have to go without sleep for a little while longer. At least until she gathered all she could from that leather bound survivors manual.

The front of the house remained lit by the camping lantern and the living room by the candles, whose wax was now covering most of the mantle. Before even thinking about heading back into the basement, Sara dashed up the stairs and into her bedroom to make sure that it was not about to catch on fire. She knew she would have to extinguish them for a while to avoid that. So, she headed back downstairs and grabbed one of the camping lanterns before running back upstairs and blowing out each candle, backing out of the room as she went. As each one went out, the darkness enveloped the area where their flame once stood. Sara grabbed the extra batteries before finally blowing out the last flame and stepping into the hallway. Her bedroom was a cave of solid black against the glow of the lamp in the hallway. She had never seen such a thing. The light she had coupled with the one she left sitting on the floor behind her, only served to keep them from reaching out for her but they did nothing to pierce the blackness of her bedroom. She backed away from the open doorway and headed back toward the main floor. A whispered hissing sound could be heard as her light permeated the darkness below and hurt the shadows waiting there. Sara smiled a little bit to herself. They could still be hurt, even if the shadow figure who attacked her could not be. She did have the power to harm his minions (she assumed they worked for him).

When she was finally safe within her lit fortress and all the doors were bolted shut, she let herself sink to the floor, leaning her back against the leg of her dining room table. She pulled her knees up to her chest, hugging them close as she tried to get rid of the violated feeling she felt again. The urge to break down and cry began to take hold but she fought hard to keep it at bay. Her lungs burned with every inhale and her right side still throbbed from the exertion she had put on her body. As she sat on the floor and examined her own behavior, a sudden anger flooded her body. They made her feel helpless again and made her remember him. How dare they do that to her. How dare they touch her like that and make her feel that way. Those demons forced arousal on her and although she may have enjoyed it at the time, it was nevertheless rape. They did not have to penetrate her folds with their throbbing members for it to be rape. She did not even know if they had such appendages but if they did, she wanted to kick both of them square in the balls. Whoever had been driving the cop car was as much to blame as they were. If they never turned down the street she was on, she never would have had to jump into that alleyway to avoid them. She wanted to scream now, to destroy something or even to hurt them if they could be hurt. One of them had been a shadow figure but she never saw the other one. Maybe he was made of flesh and bone and therefore could be kicked.

Sara suddenly grabbed her keys and tossed them in a direction, as rage filled her body and pushed all the other weak emotions away. She stood, screaming with tears in her eyes.

"What do you want?! Leave me the hell alone!"

They were not the tears of a woman on the verge of a complete and total breakdown but they were those of a woman who was ready to snap. She had been pushed far beyond her limit and now she wanted to make them pay. Although she was not even sure which them she wanted to hurt more, the ones she could not fight or the flesh and bone men who were her main issue. After screaming into the darkness and flinging her keys across the room, she sat on the floor panting. With a slow deep breath she began to calm herself. If she went at them swinging wildly without knowing what they were capable of and without being prepared to face them, she would lose. All her efforts would be in vein and she would end up another face on a missing poster. So she needed to calm herself, focus and regroup. First she had to come to grips with the fact that something had raped her in an alleyway and momentarily ripped her power away. That there were things in this town with the power to do that. Sara nodded to herself silently as she acknowledged this fact. Then she needed to get up off the floor and head back down into the basement where she could gather her thoughts. Again she nodded to herself before she, slowly pulled herself up off the floor and headed for the kitchen. From the drawer beside the sink she pulled the largest knife she could find.

Then she grabbed the lamp from the table and headed toward the basement, leaving the dining room to the shadows. The basement was still lit by the propane lantern from when she had found the journal. So she shut off the lamp and sat it on the workbench. Sara locked the basement door before reaching into the rafters and pulling the book from its hiding place. Sitting down on the stairs with the leather bound tome in her hands, she began to think. In the alleyway, when she was being attacked the shadow figure said something to her that she now remembered, 'Be happy I forgave you for hitting me'. Could it have been Alex? Or was it the man who attacked her? If it was the original assailant then the shadow form would explain why she never saw his face. Then again, he did not have red eyes. Alex clearly did not have red eyes either. That meant nothing. 'He is made of shadow. He could have seen you hit Alex and could have been playing off of what happened in order to mess with you.' This was not a far fetched idea. He was a demon or a shadow or a shadow demon, so in any one of those cases, he could have seen both assaults on her. So to cause confusion he could have said what he did, just to screw with her mind and make her even more confused. Still, she could not forget what the phantom voice said to her before Alex showed up and the fact that the shadow attack did not happen until he was here. Then again, when the power was still on, they would not have had the chance to attack her. Only when it was completely dark and the sun had set, did they finally make their move. There was a noticeable correlation between Alex and the weirdness. The voices started long before he showed up but they did seem to be trying to warn her about him. Or maybe the phantoms, (whoever they were) knew about the red eyed demon in the town and were warning her about him.

Sara had more questions than answers now. At least she was no longer frantic with emotion and running off on a panicked tangent. Her mind was working on a more logical (in a way) set of thoughts. She had begun to examine all the facts she knew, the things she had seen, heard and experienced. They all were related in some fashion but how, she did not yet know. She hoped that Amanda's journal might bring more light to the situation. So, she flipped it open past the first message and began to read its' first official entry.

You know that feeling of stillness, the one that feels too still? It's so still that you can hear it ringing in your ears and deafening you worse than any noise. In that moment of still, in the silence, I found the problem. It wasn't the stillness itself or the silence but the fact that somehow it had become that way without me noticing. That was not the moment however that I stood up to take notice. That moment happened a long time before the stillness.

This seems like an odd way to start a journal, if you could call it that. Think of this more as your survival guide. A way to keep from making my mistakes and maybe to get out before they can get their claws in you, so to speak. I was hoping to do the same thing myself, get out before they could figure out what I was up to. But they were smarter and faster than I anticipated. One thing I have figured out, is that They never go by the same name.

Always they keep the same occupation but never the same name. If you are careful and can find old newspapers in the archives at the library, you will see that the disappearances go back as far as the 1950's. Maybe even farther than that.

By now I'm sure they have taken the archives out of the library, so you may not find them. I would be surprised if the library still stands by the time you finally find this. If they haven't beaten you to it. But I'm getting ahead of myself and rather out of order. I am hoping that you have been lucky enough to avoid them and that you are confused by my ramblings. If not and if this makes sense to you, then you need to grab the essentials and be ready to move after you finish reading this. It is vital you read this because otherwise you have almost no chance of making it out of here.

For now, I'll start with the first few incidences that I feel are important and they started way before Collins . . .

Amanda McNabb

Chapter 9

The bitter caramel liquid scorched her tender throat, chasing away the tears that were filled with more than just emotional pain. On her face just above the cheekbone was a bruise that had darkened to a lovely magenta and was fading into a dark purple. She sat slumped in a leather recliner with half a glass of whiskey dangling loosely from her left hand. Her raven locks cascading across the back of the chair like a black velvet blanket. A pair of bright blue eyes stared into the flames, crackling the wood in the brick fireplace. She swore she would never deal with the likes of men ever again. The one who had managed to break down her wall, had hurt her the worst. Her once pouty rose lips were both split in various places. Amanda could still taste the blood seeping from the hole where a molar had been knocked out. At the hospital they said her jaw was fractured. She was a nurse, she already knew when his second hit came that it had given way. With another sip of whiskey she felt the numbness began. The noticeable warm tingle that spread through her limbs. On the floor next to her sat half a bottle of Jack Daniels, it had been full when she started. Her side table was littered with prescription bottles for anxiety and pain. Amanda knew better than to mix alcohol and Vicodin but after the month she had, had, she did not care.

It seemed that no matter how much she drank, she could never stop the pain. A single tear rolled down her cheek, burning over her tender swollen flesh. She swallowed her tears with a mouthful of whiskey. Telling herself, never again. James would barely receive a slap on the wrist for beating her, despite the fact that three of her ribs were broken. Every breath was a dagger in her lungs. The physical wounds would heal but her emotional ones would not.

Amanda knew what would happen when he got out. She knew he would be furious and that he would take every bit of his anger out on her. He would try anyway. Now, she had an equalizer, a . 12 gauge, double barreled, shotgun and both barrels were loaded. There was already a police report written about his assault. So claiming self defense would not be hard. Of course there were enough woods in Maine for her to bury his ass and they would not find him until spring. Amanda's mood fluctuated between fiery demonizes and heartbroken maiden. A haunting confusion remained, he swore he loved her and until now had never laid a hand on her. So what was it? Had he really been this brutal beast, masquerading as a sheep? The answer would never come. Sometimes things end in chaos without any logic behind them.

She already made up her mind though, if he came back, she would unload a two shells full of buckshot into his chest. Right where his heart should be. She would send him straight to hell where he belonged. Still some part of her wanted to believe it was all a horrible dream. The scars and fresh cuts that littered her wrists said otherwise. Like any battered woman, she loved him and some part of her still wanted him. So she ignored the other pain he had caused, which lead to her latest addiction. The way he would pick at every little thing about her. From her hair, to her laugh, her clothes and then there was his random apathetic moments. James would go cold on her for no reason. Or he might blow up at her for the most trivial thing. Often she would curl into a ball and lay next to him, crying. He never noticed her tears and he ignored the scars on her body. It was all about James, his pleasure, his happiness and what he wanted. She gave him everything he asked for, body, mind and soul. If she did not give him her body when he wanted, he would get mad. Most of the time he did not have to say anything. She could feel his anger radiate off of him in waves.

Now she waited, waited for him to come slamming up the driveway. He would not expect her to be sitting with a loaded shotgun. The addition of a gun safe was new in her small cabin. It had a few more weapons for her to choose from, although the shotgun should be enough. Amanda brought her glass to her lips, the caramel liquid burning as it passed through them and traveled down her throat. That was when she heard it, the hard sound of gravel sliding beneath heavy tires. Amanda stood slowly, pivoting toward the door before cocking the gun. James' footfalls could be heard thundering down the sidewalk. She raised the gun and waited. His tall silhouette shadowed the glass door and when he slit it open, she squeezed the trigger. The sound was concussive, the butt kicked into her shoulder as two shells of buckshot filled his large chest. James eyes widened with shock and he fell to the wooden porch. A spray of red decorated her sliding glass door and once oak colored walkway.

Amanda popped the gun open, kicking the empty shells from the barrel. They bounced to the floor, their vacant holes echoed a hollow plastic sound. She loaded two more shells into the gun and slammed it shut, aiming it at the twitching body on her porch. Slowly, she stepped forward, the gurgling sounds of blood as it filled his lungs was music to her hears. A karmatic symphony of pain and panic as he gasp for air. His dirty blonde hair and brownish red goatee glistened with fresh blood as he coughed more. It bubbled from his volatile mouth and poured down his face. A pair of dark blue eyes that she once found mesmerizing, now stared up at her in desperation. They would get no love or tenderness, not anymore. She used to see angelic comfort in those beautiful pools with their start burst of orange that surrounded his pupils. Amanda once told him they reminded her of a galaxy. Now that galaxy was fading, falling into a black hole. Would they give his bones a military funeral? Did he deserve one? Like any typical soldier, he had his unity patch tattooed on his right forearm just over a small scar where he had sliced his wrist after his first divorce. As she stood over his five foot, nine inch tall frame, she began to feel...better. Somehow filling him with buckshot had healed her broken heart.

"What's the matter James? Does it hurt?" She mocked.

A gargle was all she heard and then his body gave in and he fell into oblivion. At last it was over, the demon was dead. Amanda breathed a sigh of relief but her heart continued to race. She leaned against the side of the house, letting the gun dangle from her fingers. She now had to decide what to do with the body and fast. Someone may have heard the sound of the gun. As she pushed herself upright, the high pitched yowl of a wolf pierced the silence. In the woods behind her cabin, wolves were prevalent and they smelled the blood by now. They would not hesitate to attack. Amanda raised the gun and stepped off the porch, aiming for the woods. She stood combat ready, waiting for anything to move. The world around her became unreasonably silent against the sound of her heart in her ears. It seemed like an eternity before she heard anything. When she did, it was not a sound from the woods but a sound from behind her. The sound of something moving incredibly fast. Amanda spun around on her heels, shifting back toward her cabin only to find that James was gone. That was impossible, she had loaded him with buckshot. No one could have survived a blast like that. She knew he was not wearing a vest, her door was splattered with his blood. He was gone though and all that was left was a puddle of blood. Her breathing increased as the first waves of panic and fear crept over her. Another noise from the woods behind her and she spun around, ready to fire.

The world around her silenced as if death was passing through Wolf Creek and the woods had taken notice. There were no sounds of rustling leaves or snapping branches from the shadowy form that moved just beyond her vision. Amanda shifted uneasily, her eyes scanning the trees. If she had not mixed her alcohol with pain killers she would have clearer vision. It was hard enough seeing in the dark, let alone adding intoxication into the mix. She squeezed her eyes shut and tried to focus. Whatever it was, it stepped into her line of vision. Its silver gleaming eyes were all she could see. They seemed to glow with a luminescence all their own. Like two silver coins glimmering in the pale moonlight. Amanda lifted her head up so she could see over the shotgun and get a better look at it.

Her body suddenly filled with a coldness, the likes of which she had never felt before. As if it was looking right at her soul. She swallowed heard and then felt a semi-paralysis come over her. This thing was not human, she was not sure how she knew but she did. 'Shoot it.' Her mind told her but she did not move. Or could not move. It did not move either, it just stared at her, never once shifting. 'Shoot it! Shoot the god damn thing!' She fought to get her body to cooperate. Now she realized that during this supernatural standoff, her limbs had gone numb. The gun was still firmly secure in her fingers but she could not move them. 'Shoot! it! Now!' Something broke, she felt a sort of snap in her conscious mind and she squeezed the trigger. Another concussive blast was heard that night but this time the buckshot only peppered the trees. The thing in the woods had moved or disappeared. In its wake, it left a hollowness inside of her that she could not understand. How could it outrun bullets?

Amanda gasp for air, she had been holding her breath for some time now. The sudden inhale made her head swim and she stumbled backwards. She came to rest with her back against the railing of the porch, the gun having dropped from her hands into the dirt below. What in God's name was that? She wondered. There had to be a logical answer for everything or she would lose her grip on reality. She only delved in logic and reason. It was a large part of her profession. If you had a gash in your leg, a local for the pain and some stitches would fix the problem. Amanda fought to find reasoning, to make sense of a senseless situation. James sudden behavior change, coupled with the creature and the body. The body was gone. It could all be a mass hallucination brought on by a tired, drug altered mind. There was a large amount of alcohol in her and it had blended with the Vicodin. With a calming sigh, she pushed herself upright and grabbed her gun from its dirt bed. Then she headed toward the house.

As she ascended the stairs, she saw the crimson decorating her cabin. On the porch was a small puddle of blood and she stopped to stare into its glaring red surface. All of it could not be a hallucination. So what had she really shot? She knew she should spray the blood from the cabin before it dried but the sudden, very physical event had exhausted her. Besides she was miles from town and no one ever came to visit her. So she stepped inside, slamming the sliding glass door shut behind her before locking it and finally dragging herself to bed. She could deal with this mess tomorrow.

Amanda set the shotgun next to her bedside and flipped on the light sitting on her side table. She was not afraid of the dark or of anything that might be roaming in the darkness, normally. The encounter with that unnamed creature in the woods had left her shaken. It should not be able to enter the house but she did not trust that it would not try. Had she suddenly decided everything was real? Or was her thought process that of a tired mind? In her drug induced state had she become susceptible to suggestion and was she now letting the unrealistic thoughts come to her in one chaotic wave? Sleep, she needed to get some sleep and think about this in the morning. That had been her plan when she stepped over the threshold but something in the back of her mind would not let her drift off just yet. As she lay there, staring at the ceiling, she heard the floor creak with the sound of weight being pressed on it. He was back, he was here. Was it James come back from the dead for revenge? She shot straight out of bed, causing pain to lightning its way through her rib-cage and around her back. With her injuries, she could not move as quickly. Of course she would ignore the sensations of protest from the fractures in her body if it meant her survival was at stake.

Pulling her body from the bed, she grabbed the shotgun but in that moment she remembered the extra ammunition was still sitting in the living room.

"Shit." She cursed herself.

Still she was not without defense because sitting next to it, purposely placed there just in case, was a metal baseball bat. There was a risk of him getting a hold of it and beating her to death but if she caught him off guard, she could smash his skull in and ensure his death. Amanda slowly stood, raising the bat over her shoulder as if she was Sammy Sosa ready to hit a home run. She would hit one alright, the home run to end all. Her feet slid along the wooden floor, distributing her weight evenly ensured that she would not give her intruder cause for alarm. He did not have the layout of this house and he did not know its weaknesses, she did. She would use that to her advantage and take him by surprise. Amanda leaned her shoulder against the doorway and peeked down the hallway, looking up and down its dark corridor. There was no sign of the intruder anywhere. So she slid into the hallway and headed toward the living room. It too was empty and the sliding glass door was still locked. So had she really heard the floor creak? She let the bat lower and dangle between her fingers. A feeling of disappointment blanketed her adrenaline filled body. She had very much hoped to have the satisfaction of beating James's skull in and splattering his gray matter all over her floor. Her thoughts were very dark as of late, that was his fault. Most of the time she was a nonviolent person who occasionally threatened someone but never went through with the act. However, because of the hell he had put her through, she was non-tolerant, quick to temper and violent. A side from anger she knew no other emotions anymore. James was not the main cause for all of this hate but he was the man who broke the dam of emotion and sealed her fate. He was the reason she looked at men differently and the reason she never again wanted a man to touch her. The idea of sex made her sick to her stomach, she had no want for it anymore, that was his fault.

There was that sound again, the floor behind her creaked and when she turned on her ankles to swing the bat, she came face to face with the thing. It's silver eyes were even brighter at this distance, its male form was a black mass against the darkness in the house. Amanda wanted to move, she willed her legs to back away from it, she willed her hands to raise the bat and swing at it. Nothing moved, no part of her body would cooperate. A single tear slid down her cheek as she waited

for it to make its move. At first it did nothing and then it spoke.

"Amanda. That was not very nice. I just want to talk, why did you shoot me?"

"J-James?"

It sounded like him, it even moved like him but it could not be him. When she stuttered out his name, the thing began to laugh. It even laughed like him. All she could do was shake her head 'no' as her fingers went limp and the bat clattered to the floor with a hollow, metallic sound. A shadowy hand reached for her, grabbing her by her throat and slamming her up against the wall. Her toes barely touched the floor as it held her there. Somehow shadow could hold flesh and paralyze it. Its free hand slid just under her shirt and down the top of her sleep pants. Although he was shadow, his hands felt like flesh. She quickly realized what he was doing but she was powerless to stop what was happening. Those cold, silver eyes stared into her blue ones as she felt long digits sliding down over top of her shaven mound. Even his fingers felt like James fingers and she felt bile begin to burn its way up her throat. With one swift motion, it pulled its shadowy hand out of her panties and grabbed the top of them, yanking pants and all from her lower half, leaving her naked to its silver gaze. Amanda wanted to fight but she could not move, she could only watch as its fingers moved to the apex of her thighs and began to rub her tender flesh. 'Stop this! Fight it! Get it to let go!'

As if hearing her thoughts, it squeezed her throat a little tighter before its head dropped down and she felt a long tongue slide along the flesh where its fingers had once been. This was not James, he never would do that for her. He did not enjoy it, of course that was because he was a selfish lover. Her fight slowly began to melt from her as its tongue moved over her swollen bud, flicking expertly across the delicate flesh. She shivered and her head fell back against the wall behind her. A long digit slid inside of her delicate folds, stroking in and out of her in succession with its tongue. Amanda shivered again as its assault on her body continued. Her limbs went completely limp as her anatomy gave into the pleasure she was experiencing. For a moment she forgot where she was and who or what was touching her. Then something changed, the shadow yanked her from the wall and threw her onto the floor in front of him. Before she could even try to defend herself, she felt him thrust deep inside of her hard. That sent shooting pains through her entire body. His hands wrapped around her wrists and slammed them to the floor as he continued to thrust into her. With every movement of his manhood he caused pain to shoot through her lower body and his weight jammed into her rib-cage. The painkillers had long worn off and she fought now to keep from crying out in pain, she would not give this demon the satisfaction of knowing he was hurting her. He seemed to know that she was fighting to keep quiet because his thrusts became more aggressive and more painful.

"Scream for me. You will scream for me."

Its voice had changed, the voice it spoke with now was rougher and glazed with an accent. Still she refused to scream for him, she refused to let him hurt her and get any satisfaction from it. One man had already broken her ribs, she would not be letting another man thing, even a shadow one, have the pleasure of hearing her scream. Besides that, James had done this very thing once, when she did not want to give him sex. She had given into his demands only to save herself the pain of his anger. As usual it had not been pleasurable for her, it never was. Everything was about what he wanted, when he wanted and how he wanted.

Amanda knew she needed to find someway to get out of his grip and to get him off of her but her limbs still remained paralyzed. She would have to wait for him to finish and if he was anything like James, that would not take long.

The creature let go of her wrists, grabbed her by her hair and

126

yanked her up from the floor. She knew it was not finished with her yet. It tossed her toward the chair she had been sitting in and she knew what its intentions were. Thinking quickly, forced her body to move, grabbing a handful of ammunition from the box beside her chair before turning on her heels and dashing by the thing. She did not even know if that plan was going to work or not. Still she knew in that moment she had to try something, she was sure he would have grabbed her up. Then again, he did not count on her gaining her movement back and running past him into her room. She should have been still paralyzed by fear at least but the jolt of pain from being thrown against the chair had somehow canceled out the other. Amanda kicked the door shut behind her, flipping the lock on it before grabbing her gun and quickly loading it. She knew by now that it did not need to break down the door to get to her, it had gotten in the house without kicking in a single door. Of course she did not even know for sure if the shotgun would work against it, it was shadow. She had a theory though, if it could touch, then it could be touched and therefore it could be hurt.

The door rattled on its hinges as the creature knocked at it from the other side. Amanda sat with her naked rear on the floor next to the bed, aiming the gun at the doorway. Then she saw it, a shadowy hand slithered between the small gap in the door and unlocked it from the inside. Her bedroom door swung open and two red eyes gleamed at her from the other side. She realized that his eyes must change color when he is angry but she did not care and she did not hesitate. The moment she saw his shadowy form, she squeezed the trigger of both barrels and sent buckshot flying toward the shadow. It did roar in pain and curl up slightly where the shots made contact, so it could be hurt. The question remained, did it bleed? She grabbed two more shells, discarding the empty ones and reloaded. Then she pulled herself from the floor, cocked the gun and fired into it again. Another roar of pain echoed through the empty cabin and when it turned to glare at her with fiery red eyes, she could swear she saw two gleaming white canines. When she reloaded a third time and raised to fire again, it finally dashed toward the door, its shadowy form sliding through the glass, leaping over the railing of her porch before disappearing into the woods. She stood with the gun aimed at the sliding glass doorway, waiting for it to make another appearance.

After a few moments she realized that it was not going to be coming back, so she lowered her rifle and set it on the table beside her. Her legs were shaking, her body hurt more than it ever did before and she realized there was blood on her inner thighs. She needed a shower, another drink and some more pain medication. In the morning she would look for some place new. Wolf Creek was no longer safe for her. Whatever that thing was, she knew that it eventually would return and it would be more prepared. So would she because she would be so far away from this place that it would never find her. Between James and that creature, there was no reason left for her to stay here. She had been considering moving after he assaulted her and now she was sure she would be. James might or might not be dead and if he was not, she knew that she would see him again. He would come back and kill her. That was not something she wished to risk.

Amanda drug herself down the hallway toward the bathroom, flipping on lights as she went. It was in the dim hallway light that she noticed the blood on the floor by her doorway. She knelt down and touched it. It was the deepest red she had ever seen and when her fingers dipped into it, they began to tingle. As if the blood its self was alive. There would be no rest for her tonight, she had a mess to clean up before the morning light revealed what went on here. So she stumbled down the hallway and into the bathroom, by passing the mirror so she did not have to see the bruises decorating her face. The water burned her tender flesh as it washed the red from her body. She swore she would never shower enough to get the feeling of his hands off of her. A side from bathing in alcohol there was nothing that could get rid of that violation.

She quickly dispatched her towel and threw on clothes before heading back into the living room and taking another round of medication. A long swig of bitter whiskey washed away the raw feeling of holding back her screams. Amanda shuddered as it burned down through her system and met with the Vicodin in her belly. Then, before it all kicked in and she was too far gone to stand, she grabbed some cleaning supplies and began to scrub the blood from her floor. The visible pelts of buckshot were embedded in her walls as well as in the flesh they had connected with. That was fine, they were unnoticeable to the untrained eye. She slid back the glass door and stepped onto the porch, grabbing her garden hose from the side of the house before dousing everything in dish soap. Then she sprayed down the side of the cabin and every corner where blood might have landed. There was a permanent red stain on the wood where James body had been but she could throw a coat of wood stain on top of it and cover that up. She was surprisingly calm for a woman in her situation. That could have been very much because of the drugs now coursing through her veins. Give anyone enough whiskey and pain killers, they will forget about anything.

When the cabin was clear of blood, she tossed the hose into the yard and headed back in the house. The medication was beginning to kick in and she just wanted to go to bed. This time, she took the box of ammunition with her, leaving the useless baseball bat on the floor. Maybe if someone came back, they would slip on the darn thing and crack their head on her floor. That cartoonish thought made her chuckle. Amanda slammed her bedroom door shut with her foot and locked it behind her before climbing back into bed. Tomorrow was the start of a new day and a new woman. She had decided that she was not going to live in fear, no matter what happened to her. Every mythical monster could pour from the cracks in the walls and she would blast every one of them until her ammo ran out. No, James would not ruin her life. He would not cause her to live in fear. She was not changing her mind about men, that was for damn sure but she would not be afraid of them. That attitude would serve her well in the coming days.

She set the loaded gun beside the bed with the ammo on the nightstand and settled into bed. Maybe this time she could go to sleep without being disturbed.

Chapter 10

The days following the attack were filled with alcohol, pain killers and needless worrying. It seemed that no amount of whiskey or any other narcotic, could help to numb what she was feeling. She felt like a trapped rat in her own home. Usually she would go into town and find something to do, but she dreaded the looks she might get when people saw her busted up features. Then there would be the questions and she did not want to explain herself. Amanda felt weak, weakened by the physical ailments and even weaker still by the sexual assault. She could not tell anyone what happened to her after she went home. That was the worst part, she had to suffer on her own and find the strength all alone, to keep going. It was a chore to convince herself to get out of bed. Of course going to bed and sleeping was not much better. The nightmares and sudden manifestation of night terrors made it impossible to get a good nights sleep. She could find no comfort or rest, no matter where she went and she began to wonder when the normality would start again. At what point would her brain finally declare, enough and shove aside all the horrible thoughts in her head? She was used to horrible relationships ending in a chaotic explosion of final truths and unreasonable words. Then she might have her grieving period and eventually find her inner warrior so she could move on. This however, had gone on for far too long.

When nightfall finally came and she knew that most of the sympathetic faces were gone, she shoved on some clothes, her boots and shimmied into a coat that was big enough to hide her weapon. Amanda was out of booze and she refused to continue to deal with any of this under sober circumstances. There was one place she could go at this hour of the night and find whiskey. One place she could be left alone, for the most part. It was the only bar in town, just a hole in the wall and it sat at the very edge of town. On a Friday night, such as tonight, there would be nothing but drunk steel workers, loggers, and all the factory men. Although she did not want to ever look at another man again, it was the only place to get alcohol at this time of the night. The shops around Wolf Creek closed up early and this had to be the one town that did not have a twenty four hour store within ten miles of it.

Amanda's Jeep roared to life when she turned the key in the ignition. It had been a few days since she started it, the rumble of its engine brought her comfort. Her vehicle was a tank, last winter it had climbed through the snow drifts that had left even some of the one ton pick ups stranded. She had all terrain tires on it, four floodlights mounted on its roof and a suspension system that would make most men drool. There was almost nothing that could stop her when she climbed behind the wheel of her beast (as she called it). As she rumbled down the road, she began to think that maybe getting out of the house for a while was just what she needed. Although she knew that meant dealing with the rednecks and degenerates that frequented the local bar. When it came to Duff's, it was a hole in the wall. The building nearly resembled a shack, several boards were nailed to its exterior with different colors and type of siding thrown on top. It was one of those places that most people would look at and cast judgment on it without ever going inside. Of course she could not really blame their reaction, she would not step foot in this place without her .45 hidden safely under her jacket. Only the locals of Wolf Creek frequented the bar or even knew about it.

Just over the hill on the edge of town, that small wooden shack came into view and Amanda shifted slightly in her seat. What encounters would she have tonight? What sort of moron would attempt to bother her? Never mind their plans or intentions, she would handle them as they came. She was in no mood to deal with their drunken stupidity. The small parking lot that surrounded the bar was packed full of various trucks and other jeeps. Several of the vehicles in the lot were equipped with lift kits that elevated them more than four feet from the ground. As she drove into the lot, the bouncer was pouring the nights empty bottles into the dumpster out back, he was one of few she was acquainted with. She wondered if that was the first load of bottles or if he had been out there frequently. Amanda pulled into a parking spot and climbed out of the jeep. She trudged past the numerous beat up trucks and ignored the 'hey baby' from one red neck in a beat up red and chrome Silverado. She just barely glanced at the vehicle, noting its makeshift truck bed made of wooden boards. She snorted in disgust when she noticed his sweat and dirt covered flesh. That was all she needed to see, she averted her eyes, staring straight ahead at the bar and shoving her hand in her coat in case she might need to use it. The men in this area, were just about as bad as the wolves that roamed the surrounding woods.

From her place outside she could hear the noise pouring from the bar, laughs of drunk ecstasy, shouting and the loud music pouring from the disc jockeys speakers. The base of whatever he was playing, vibrated the sidewalk just slightly as she moved toward the door. There was a red and white sign posted on it that read "*No Weapons*", but no one ever obeyed and the bouncer never enforced it. She grabbed the door handle and braced herself for whatever was on the other side. As she pulled open the door to the bar, the cigarette smoke greeted her in a large rush of warm air. It was bearable once you got used to breathing in the second hand toxins. She pushed her way past the large men from the lumber yard and found herself a stool where she would not be bothered. A large, scruffy, balding man behind the bar, leaned on his knuckles before speaking to her.

"What'll it be?"

"Jack and Coke, no ice."

He nodded and while he was making her drink, she fished a five out of her pocket, tossing it on the counter. From the corner of her eye, she noticed two men entering the bar. They were evidently not from around here. The first one wore a black truckers cap and a heavy coat of army green, but from her spot at the bar she could not see much else. His companion she assumed was from the Silverado. He had spiky, jet black hair, inset deep brown eyes that seemed to undress her with every look. There were two metal hoops through his bottom lip and ink that decorated the back of his hands, trailing up his arms to the bottom of his short sleeve shirt. Amanda assumed they went further up and as she watched him make his way through the bar, she wondered what else might be pierced before shuddering at the thought. In her mind, freaks like that, not only stuck out in a crowd but were obvious trouble. They were almost comparable to a giant red warning label. It was weird to see someone without a coat in this weather. She eyed them out of her peripherals before coming to a simple and precise conclusion. '*They're gonna be trouble, I'm not gonna*

132

stay long.'

The bartender took the five and set her drink on the counter. Amanda kept a watchful eye on the men as they moved to a booth that was a little too close to her for comfort. She would rather they sit on the other side of the bar or play pool at one of the tables so she did not have to deal with them. She took a sip of her drink, letting the burning liquid calm her nerves. Then she instinctively clicked the safety off on the gun. That breed of men usually (like clockwork) were known to give her trouble. No sooner had the thought crossed her mind ,then she heard the voice from the truck behind her. *'Yep, he's the* **hey baby** *asshole from the truck. So much for a peaceful drink.'*

"You're brave coming in here all alone."

His voice was like that of some great rockstar, gravely and deep. It tingled the nerves in her flesh and she bit her lip to ignore it. The tone in his voice was mocking, laced with an air of over confidence that made her trigger finger itch. As she contemplated the situation, trying to keep it under her control, the smell of him drifted into her nostrils. He smelled like whiskey and cigarette smoke. There was the distinct possibility that he was already drunk. This also meant he already had a hard in his pants and was in here looking for something to help him solve it.

Amanda smirked, drink hanging between her thumb and fore finger.

"You're brave coming in here at all."

She could hear him scoff and shift his weight behind her. She rolled her eyes as she felt his hot drunken gaze drag down her body.

"Oh really? Hey! How bout you look at me when I'm talking to you!"

'My guess, drug addict, no surprise..And he's drunk too, here comes his mood swing.' That was the last calm thought she had before he grabbed her shoulder and she spun around, putting the gun to his forehead.

"I'm sorry, you're right, I'm being rude. How dare I come in here after a twelve hour shift,"She lied. " of doing nothing but taking care of other people, and not immediately jump your bones. How dare I expect to have a drink without you trying to fuck me. You're right, that is rude of me." She paused and waited for a response.

Everyone in the bar had stopped what they were doing. The punk in front of her backed away slowly with his hands up in mock surrender and a cocky smirk on his face. His friend in the booth, never said a word or even glanced up at them.

"That's a big gun for such a little girl. Lemme take that from you before you hurt yourself."

"Safeties off . . .I wouldn't try it."

"You remember to load it?" He said with an even cockier smirk.

"You wanna find out?"

He squinted a moment as if deciding whether to try taking the gun from her. Then he gestured to the scrubs she was still wearing.

"Didn't you take some sort of oath or some shit? You're a doctor right? So technically you're not allowed to hurt me."

"I'm a nurse and I'm off the clock. At this range you'd be dead, not hurt."

"But you're not a killer," He whispered, taunting her. "If I were you though, I would pull the trigger and made sure I was dead because if not," He leaned in a little bit, licking his lips before continuing. "when I got my hands on you finally, you'd beg to die."

Amanda pressed the gun to his temple and started squeezing the trigger. Then thought better of it. He would be gone by the morning, drifters always are, they only stop here to stir up some trouble. She would probably never see him again. So she flicked the safety on and pistol whipped him in the side of the head. It got the point across because he stumbled backwards. When he finally stood up right, she had the gun on him again and again he held his hands up, that cocky smirk still on his face, despite the fact that there was a small trail of blood slowly making its way down the side of his head. When he was upright again, she flicked the safety off.

"Sit. Down." She ordered.

Still smirking, he slid back into the booth and never said another word to her. Although the smell of him would drift her way ever now and again. She returned to her drink and holstered her weapon. It was surprising that they did not ask her to leave. She did not stay long anyhow. When her drink was gone, she tossed three ones into the tip jar and with her head down, she hurried out to her jeep. She would be happier when she was at home with her (now) usual creepy things.

Amanda pulled slowly into the driveway, flipping on her flood lights before hopping out of the jeep and pulling out her .45. She scanned the snow for footprints as she made her way around the side of the house. It had been only a week since the attack but with James, she knew better than to let her guard down. The body had never been found after she shot him and she did not trust that, or like it one bit. As far as she could see there were no footprints anywhere. After confirming that there was no sign of him, she walked back to the jeep and flipped off the lights. Then she grabbed her keys, headed to the door and unlocked it. She flicked on the kitchen light before shutting and locking the door behind her.

It was unfortunate that part of her evening had been ruined by the horny redneck. At least she could shower without the same issue. Amanda stretched and popped her back before finally heading to her room so she could undress in private. When she finally came out, she was wrapped in a pink bathrobe with her gun in hand. She shut the bathroom door, locking it before she finally disrobed and turned on the hot water. There was one thing she never could understand about creepy encounters with any sort of horny man, why did the image of them pop in your head only when you were naked? Was it just your mind tormenting you or what?

Now she could see that man and suddenly thought she could smell him again. It was a vivid enough episode to make her pause as she was going to get in the shower. The episode was over before she had time to really analyze it. So she shrugged it off and climbed in the shower. Maybe she could wash his undressing gaze from her flesh and feel a little less violated. When she was nearly done with her shower and just waiting for her conditioner to set in, she heard (or thought she heard) a noise. It sounded like boots. It was so brief and she only heard it once, so she shrugged it off. Tipping her head back into the hot water, she closed her eyes and let the water rinse her hair clean. With a sigh she opened her eyes.

Amanda felt her breath catch in her throat and her heart begin to race. Standing in her shower with her, was not the horny punk, him she could handle. Instead of the circus freak, she found James. The water was hitting his hard naked body and running down the length of things that she could not help but glance at. It made keeping her wits about her, almost completely impossible. 'How the hell did he? I didn't even hear him - nevermind that, get out of here.' His chest was unscathed, there was no sign of buckshot or even bruising from a bulletproof vest. Was she imagining all of this or had she imagined killing him? Her mind wanted her to just curl up and wish him away. However, her fight or flight instinct told her to get away from him. So she tried to get out of the shower.

James was too fast, he grabbed her by her hair and pulled her back to him so hard that her naked wet body slammed against his. Just the heat of his skin against hers was almost too much for her to handle. His hard, hot, naked wet body was pressing against her with the memorable force that he use to reserve just for bedroom play. Then she heard his deep gravely voice in her ear.

"We have unfinished business."

"You're not real, you're not here . . ." She kept repeating to herself, hoping to will him away.

"I'll show you just how Real I am."

James pushed her against the wall face first and kicked her legs open. Then she felt his mouth on her neck, hot and wet as he bit down into the tender flesh and pulled a yelp from her. His stubble scratched across her shoulder as he bit his way down her neck. With large powerful hands he pinned her wrists above her head and taking a free hand she felt his long rough fingers on her soft swelling bud. He rolled it between his thumb and forefinger, causing her legs to shake and her body to tremble. Amanda tried to keep her eyes from rolling closed but he still knew every one of her spots as if they were calling to him. She felt her whole body almost sink to the floor as he shoved a long dexterous finger in her deep and hard.

It was too hard to try to fight him, every time she tried to move her wrists, he would bite down hard on her shoulder and only excite her more. That finger deep within her folds found her G spot, teasing and stroking it until her body bucked under his assault. She felt an orgasm wash over her in a hard wave. Amanda attempted to control her reactions and keep from shaking but he seemed to know. In retaliation to her disobedience, he would find another one of her spots and incite another moan. When he momentarily took his hand from her wrists to drag his nails down her back, she almost lost any control she had left. James was an animal, that was what she had loved and hated about him. His aggressively dominate nature, the way he would rip all control away from her and return it only when he felt she deserved it.

He would growl, take what he wanted, bite, scratch and bruise her, she regrettably enjoyed every moment of it. When James was in control, he was in control. Amanda never had to give him control and she never could take the it back once he had her. This was why she had to quit him. If he told her what to do, she would listen or he would threaten to make her 'punishment' worse. Which usually, if she disobeyed, she could not walk for almost a week.

"Turn around." He growled.

She obeyed him, Amanda had already lost. The minute he

began to touch her, she became lost in the sensation of him. James crouched down and lifted her onto his shoulders. If she let him do what she knew was coming next, she would not gain control of herself for the next few hours. The thought had just entered her mind and then she felt his hot tongue caress her most sensitive flesh. Amanda reached up and grabbed the shelf mounted to the wall as James pushed his tongue between her folds to flick across her swollen bud. That was it, she was gone. Her eyes rolled back in her head and she was wracked with shivers and moans. His tongue flicked across her clitoris and dipped into her wet aching core, making her almost scream in ecstasy.

James was the caliber of man who would not cease pleasuring a woman until he was satisfied and he could go on for hours. Sometimes he went way past the point of climax, to the point that she could not stand to be touched anymore because she became so sensitive. Only then would he stop and allow her to recover. Today, he stopped when she could barely stand. He gently lowered her to his waist so she could wrap her legs around him. There was no point in fighting it now, he had her under his spell again and she would not be out of it until he wanted her to be. She obediently wrapped her legs around his waist and looked into his deep blue eyes.

Taking his hardened shaft in his hand, he began to tantalize her aching core by rubbing the head of it just around the outside. Every time it brushed across her, her legs would tense with anticipation and the ache deep within her would grow stronger. She knew how to make him stop this game. There was one sure way to make him bury himself deep inside of her and sedate her lust. Amanda took her nails and dug them deep in his back before dragging them down his flesh. He growled in response before slamming deep inside of her, making her cry out in a combination of pleasure and pain. Her eyes rolled back in her head as she felt him thrust in and out of her in long hard thrusts, making her toes curl so hard they hurt. The nails in Jame's back only dug harder as he held her up, filling her with every inch of his long hard shaft.

"Amanda . . ." He moaned.

She was not able to speak any audible words at this point, just winces and moans.

"Amanda," He growled. "Look at me."

There was something different about his voice when he told her to look at him, but with effort she opened her eyes to look at him. It was not James she was looking at now. It was the dark eyed punk from the bar. Amanda tried to scream but he put a hand on her mouth.

"Let go of me!" She screamed behind his hand.

"I told you to kill me. Now you'll beg to die."

He was inside of her, this man, this filthy creature was touching her. As she tried to figure out what exactly was going on, she started punching the man to get him to let go of her to get him off of her. Suddenly, he shifted back to James and Amanda could not stop herself. She felt the wave of vertigo wash over her. Before she knew it, darkness enveloped her and she fell unconscious. About few moments later, she woke up alone and freezing cold. The hot water had run out a long time ago. Although she wanted to scrub her skin off right now, the water was too cold and she could not afford to get sick right now. What she could afford to do, was to move out of this haunted hell house and transfer to another hospital. She would go somewhere remote but close to the city. Maybe a small town. It did not matter really, she just wanted to be out of this god forsaken place. Tomorrow she would check the newspaper or go to the library and use their internet. Either way, she needed to find a house before the end of the weekend.

Chapter 11

The feeling of being watched, the feeling of being followed or a feeling of being touched, these phantom feelings seemed to plague her for days after her attack. These emotional states would escalate to unreasonable heights and when she finally came down, Amanda was exhausted. It was as if the episodes drained her of her life force. What used to be an occasional feeling, she now found occurred more frequently. When she felt the eyes on her or the phantom touch, she would look for the source and subsequently begin to pay more attention to her surroundings. Call it survival instinct, call it paranoia, call it whatever you want, just do not call it crazy. Amanda was not crazy. She was not. Maybe she did not want to believe that her sanity was slipping away and that was the reason she never went to the hospital after passing out. The staff would call her delusional and say she was suffering hallucinations brought on by exhaustion, and they would probably attempt to commit her. What happened to her was no delusion nor was it a hallucination. One does not hallucinate sexual intercourse against a shower wall. She felt someone inside of her, she did not imagine that.

Nothing else happened after that incident, but the emotional turmoil, the mental anguish and the overall physical effect was enough to make her leave. She could no longer come home normal. The cabin she loved so much was now a cage full of nightmares. Every evening she would come home, flip on the floodlights and walk the parameter of the house before finally going inside. A week after the incident, she put her cabin up for sale, found another house in a small quiet town far away and put in a transfer to Creek County Hospital. She was lucky the hospital even had an opening for a nurse. It was also fortunate that her cabin sold quickly and the owner of her new home accepted her bid. Since the hospital was not expecting her for another week, she would have about two weeks to relax. She could unpack most of her things and have some time to settle in before having to go to work. A new town, a new house, a new life and no James.

The hospital and her father were the only ones who knew where she would be living. She was careful not to tell anyone else.

Amanda even considered changing her name or addressing letters home with a fake name that only her father would know. Then she thought that would seem a little too paranoid, so she scrapped the idea. She had hoped that her long drive to her new house would be relaxing but it was not. About halfway down Highway 33, she noticed a cop car behind her. How long had he been trailing her? Or did he just come up behind her? On a normal basis, cops did not bother her, but for some reason, this one did. She could not ignore the spider web sensation she felt when she glanced up in her rear-view mirror and saw the glaring lights of his cruiser. He did not pull her over but the car trailed her for a few miles before finally passing her. As he did, she glanced at the reflective lettering, on the side of the vehicle. It was a Collins Sheriff and he was way outside his jurisdiction. Amanda tried to get a good look at the driver, but he was hidden by dark tinted windows.

There was just something not right about him. Even though she never saw his face, she felt a cold chill wash over her. Unconsciously, she turned up the heat, even though she had a feeling the chill was not from the dropping temperature outside.

A side from the roar of the engine and the hiss of the heat, the jeep was silent after she saw the cop. The radio was out as well, so she had to tolerate the silence. Her stomach suddenly growled with the pangs of hunger. So she looked for any signs that might indicate the presence of a restaurant. About a mile from her stomach's first gurgle, she noticed a dilapidated sign advertising Maxine's Diner. It was barely visible behind the overgrown brush that surrounded the faded metal. For a moment she wondered if the diner was even open or operational. However, with it being on a major highway, there was a good chance the truckers were keeping them in business. Amanda traveled another couple of miles before noticing a small wooden building, the parking lot of which was packed with travelers of all types. She pulled off the highway and into its lot. As she was circling around trying to find a parking space, she spotted the cop car from earlier. The vehicle alone, caused her body to become hot and she began to sweat with anxiety. That sensation alone was enough to make her pull back out onto the highway and head in search of a fast food joint. At this point, she wanted to at least empty her bladder and grab something she could eat on the go. It was getting late and by the time she got home it would be dark. Amanda wanted to at least have the ability to stay awake long enough to shower. However, at the rate things were going, she would probably get home and just pass out. She shook her head, the mere thought of sleep being enough to make her slightly drowsy.

It was not until she drove into the town of Berne that she found a couple of fast food joints just off the main drag. She managed to find a Burger King that was still open, which was a great relief to her stomach and her bladder. When she climbed out of the Jeep, she stretched and cracked her joints. It had been about four hours of nothing but driving and her back was beginning to ache from the constant sitting.

Amanda headed inside, glancing at all the patrons leaving, the vehicles entering and exiting, before she darted into the building. As she stepped inside, she scanned the lobby. She was not even sure why or what she was looking for but she could not stop herself. It was a conditioned habit that she hoped to one day break. Subconsciously, she knew exactly why she did it and who she was looking for, although she doubted she would see him. Nevertheless, she did not trust him. He could have been watching her and could have followed her. James was no idiot, if he was still around (or alive), he had most likely been paying attention to her most recent actions. She felt it better to be safe instead of sorry. Amanda moved quickly toward the women's restroom, glancing once more behind her. With her bladder empty, she was quick to wash her hands, get some food and head back out. She ate while driving, hoping to make up for lost time.

The closer she got to Collins, the colder it seemed to get. Her want for stability made her deny what she was feeling and simply brush it off as a normality of winter weather. If only she knew how wrong she was, if only she knew what lay just beneath the surface of what she understood to be the truth. Of course she never would have believed it, mortals rarely wrap their minds around a truth so horrific. It's not in their nature to do so.

By the time she saw the 'Welcome to Collins' sign, the streetlights were on. As she slowly rode down the main street of town, she noticed something about this place. There was something off about this town, little did she know, she was not the first to notice. To her, it was like one of the horror movie, island towns. They looked so beautiful with their small town glamour but their reality was so much more grotesque. This town (like all towns) had secrets but something deep inside of Amanda, some knowing voice told her that this town's secrets were darker. The secrets here were even deadly.

That thought made her grab her .45 from its hiding place between the seats and tuck it where she could grab it quick. She was so worried about getting away from James that apparently she had barely looked at the town when she was here last. Now she was wishing she had looked around more. Still, it was too late to turn back now. So she turned off Main Street, onto Elsmoor Drive and made her way to Lillie Avenue. Before she finally pulled up in front of 5102 Lillie Avenue.

There is a feeling of isolation that people sometimes get. It makes them feel completely and utterly alone. Even if they are a strong, independent person it still has the power to make them feel helpless and indescribably small. When they're a strong person and they know it, they make the mistake of analyzing this feeling. The terror they are feeling eventually becomes so big that they cannot escape its hold. Now it takes every ounce of strength to keep from curling up inside of themselves. That was how she felt as she stared at the one bedroom, two story house with stucco siding.

For a few moments, she just sat there looking at the house, encompassed by darkness. Sure, Main Street was lit up nice and inviting. The other roads though were dark and sinister. There were no creepy neighbors or unusually odd things in the neighborhood. Still she could not shake the feeling she was utterly alone and isolated from the real world. Why now did the house itself seem to loom over her with its window eyes and porch grin? Was she really in such a hurry to leave that she bought this place without really looking at it? It was beginning to look that way.

Amanda wished the movers had at least left the porch light on when they left. Without any lights on the house looked dead and the barely managed yard reminded her of a cemetery. The house was a grinning stucco skeleton in a cemetery of melted snow and dead grass. Taking a deep breath she grabbed her gun from its hiding place and headed up to the house. She was quick to unlock the door and throw the lights on once she found the switch. A hot shower and sleep were her only plans for tonight.

This time her shower was blissfully normal. There was no James, no freaks and no phantom sounds. Just peace and hot water. She did not even mind her stiff limbs or her sore back. Those she considered the lesser of two evils. Things were returning to normal, despite the still eerie vibe the house seemed to emit. Again her strong want for normality, drove her to make excuses for that too. 'It was the emptiness of the house,' she would tell herself. She figured that once she got settled that the feeling would go away.

By the time she had finished her shower and locked the doors, she was more than exhausted. So when her head hit the pillow, she fell right to sleep.

Even settled into her bed, she felt as if she was trapped in this house maybe or trapped in a continuous nightmare. In reality she was trapped in her own skin, watching the scenarios unfold before her in a great chaotic opera. The sight before her was too horrific to behold but she could not look away, she could not escape. How could he be here? Had he followed her? Some part of her, some conscious, rational part of her mind, tried to tell her she was asleep that it was not real. She could not grasp that concept yet, she was too frozen with fear. So instead of running, she just stood there staring at him, whatever he was and in robotic fashion, raised her gun and fired. Even when the clip was empty, he still would not die.

Before she could turn to run, he was on her, holding her to her bed and trying to force her legs open. Amanda was sure it was James and despite the moonlight, she could not see his face. He was just shadow. They (who ever they were) were smearing blood on her as they ripped her panties from her body and man handled her tender flesh. She could feel their member pressing at her entrance, ready to thrust inside of her and fill her with pain. Before they could, she screamed. She screamed in the hope that someone would hear her.

She shot up our of bed screaming a blood curdling scream. When she finally stopped screaming, she gasp a lungful of air and let out a shuddery breath. For a few moments, she could only gasp heavily as she tried to come to grips with reality. There was a cold sweat glistening on her skin and her throat was raw from the violence of her screams. She was away from him and she was safe. There was no one in her room with her.

As she lay in bed, shaking and fighting tears, she fought to push the entire dream out of her head so she might get some more sleep. After a while of just staring blankly at her ceiling, she finally got up and opened the window a crack. The cold air prickled her wet flesh when it hit her, but it was a welcome relief to her. It helped to chase the image of the faceless shadow man and James from her mind. Amanda was not even sure it was him in the dream. Still her mind kept trying to turn the shadow into James.

Amanda leaned on the window, breathing slowly and trying to calm her racing heart. As she stood there, she could feel the wood cooling beneath her fed from the cold winter breeze. It's coolness further helping to sober her from her nightmare. She drummed on the sill a few moments with her finger nails before slapping it and heading downstairs.

It was just barely morning, the light outside was blue with pre-morning light. Amanda glanced at the clock on the stove as she headed into the kitchen, 5:00 am. Was there really any point in fighting to get back to sleep? At this point she was probably not going to get much sleep. Knowing her mind, she would go back to sleep and dream of James. 'No, thank you' So she turned on the pre-filled coffee maker (the only thing she unpacked and set up so far) and headed back upstairs to dress.

Turning on the light in her bedroom only revealed a days worth of boxes she would be unpacking. She threw her head back and sighed in aggravation.

"Guess I'll start work here. Why not?"

She managed to find a comfy black tank top and a baggy pair of blue jeans. The smell of hot coffee drifted up to her from the kitchen. So she headed back downstairs, leaving the light on in the bedroom. When she clicked on the kitchen light, she heard an electric snap and all the lights went out, leaving her in dim morning light.

"Shit! So much for unpacking."

The sun was coming up over the horizon, so she was able to at least find her shoes and jacket. Before even attempting to leave, she managed to find a travel mug and fill it with hot coffee. There was no way for her to locate her sugar tin, so she would have to choke down very bitter, black coffee. She had no idea who to call for this sort of thing, at least not in Collins. So she headed out the door. Nothing would be open at this hour in this small town but she would at least go look. She backed her jeep out of the driveway and headed out to the main drag. At least her coffee (although bitter) was helping to wake her up.

Slowly she rumbled down Main Street until she finally saw lights on inside a small brick building. When she took a closer look at the place, she noticed a police car parked in front. She paused. The last Collins police officer she had seen, freaked her out. Now she was more than apprehensive when it came to dealing with any cops. At this point though, she did not really have a choice. She sighed, gritted her teeth behind her pursed lips and pulled into the parking lot. If anyone would know who to call it would be them.

She hesitated as she approached the door. For some reason she could feel eyes on her back. They burned into her flesh causing her to bite her lip nervously as she slowly opened the door. The heat from a heater mounted above the door would have been a welcome relief if her temperature had not already spiked with anxiety.

The officer behind the desk was a man of average height with unkempt, dirty blonde hair and a prominent jaw line and a seemingly friendly face. He flashed a friendly enough smile at her as he looked up from his paperwork. When he spoke, his voice was not authoritative or dominating tone she was expecting to hear. In fact, he did not look like the uniform was made for him. It resembled a rather well made costume. The name engraved on his gold badge looked real enough. Her eyes scanned over his name several times, memorizing every letter. Sterling was the name that had been imprinted into the metal space just below the badge number. No matter how many times she read that name, it did not seem to fit. Everything about the man standing behind the front desk, was not right. He should not be here, in this building and he certainly should not be wearing that uniform. When he finally spoke to her, she jumped.

"How can I help you miss?"

"Um . . .yeah," She approached the front desk, "I have a dumb question."

Even if he was handsome and friendly looking, the knot in her belly warned her that he was dangerous. Something was not right about this man.

"Nothing of the kind."

He smiled a rather playboy smile.

"Heh . . ." She flashed a nervous grin.

"I'm new in town and I think I blew a fuse or something in my house. I have no idea who to call to fix it."

"Oh, well I can help you with that, you want James's Repair Service. I'll call him for you."

Amanda flinched at the name James.

"Wait," Sterling paused with the un-dialed phone in hand. "How long has he been living here?"

"Why?"

"Long story short, I had an ex by that name."

"I doubt it was him. He's lived in Collins for the past oh . . .ten years or so."

"Ok..."

She shifted uneasy. Sterling hung up the phone and leaned on the counter.

"I'll tell you what," He leaned close. "I don't normally do this but . . .I can pull up his photo and then if it's him, we can call another repair guy. Deal?"

He had such a friendly, handsome face and was so considerate that she almost had to say yes to him. So then why did she get the feeling he was trying really hard to appear friendly? It didn't matter what he said, Amanda couldn't (wasn't going to) ignore the feel of a wolf's teeth sinking deep into her scar. She nodded in an almost enthusiastic response. Without hesitation he tapped a few keys on the keyboard and pulled up James's drivers license. Then he spun around the monitor and she saw that the man in the photo was not her James. She was so relieved she felt her knees weaken slightly.

"You ok? Is it him?"

"No, thank god no."

"Are you sure?"

He smiled at her again.

"Yes, I'm sure."

"Good."

She squinted slightly at him in suspicion, he was far too happy and animated for an officer. They were usually far more militant. After spinning the screen back around, he picked up the phone and dialed a number.

"Yeah, James, it's Sheriff Sterling . . .I've got a young lady here, she's new in town and she says she thinks she blew a fuse in her house . . .yeah . . .uh huh . . .yeah . . .ok."

Sterling whispered to her "What's your address?"

"5102 Lillie Drive."

"5102 Lillie Drive," He repeated into the phone.

"Alright, I'll let her know . . .yeah . .oh yeah . . .you too. Thanks."

He hung up the phone.

"Well, what did he say?"

"Give him about an hour. He just woke up."

"I'm sorry for waking him so early."

"Don't worry about it. He'll do anything for a pretty girl."

That statement made her shift uneasily, in that same instance she noticed that he was licking his bottom lip and looking her over. While she was frozen in the uncomfortable moment, another officer entered the station, walking way to close to her. He stared hungrily at her as he went by. The look in his eyes was lustful, demanding and controlling. It caused the sick part of her mind to awaken and now she wanted to let him control her. Amanda realized she cold not break away from his gaze, her eyes were locked in his. When his tongue slowly ran along his bottom lip, she could swear she felt it on graze across her sensitive flesh.

Amanda unconsciously dug her thumbnail into the still healing cuts on her forearm. Without that sudden jolt of pain, she might not have broken from his gaze. What was it about his eyes that had her so enthralled? She looked at his golden shield, searching for the name engraved at the bottom, Miller. Although she had a feeling that his name was no more real than Sterling's. Something told her that things were not what they seemed in this town.

The pain in her arm had given her the ability to snap from the trance and head outside. She gritted her teeth against the pain and leaned against the jeep, hoping it would subside a little. Amanda could feel the warm sensation of blood trailing down her arm. She had dug her thumb nail into a fresh cut a little to hard and now it was staining the interior of her coat. After a few minutes the burning in her arm subsided just enough for her to feel a very familiar ominous sensation that was hovering around the place. It was the same eerie feeling she had when she saw the cop on he highway, trailing her. Was officer Miller, the Sheriff from the highway?

This of course was not the time to contemplate such things. She had a repair man coming over in a little while and she had stacks of boxes to unpack. So she pulled herself into the jeep, started it and left as quickly as she could without speeding. She did not want to give them a reason to pull her over or be near her at all. There was a good chance she could still salvage the day.

Chapter 12

The jeep slid when she hit the brakes and turned too sharp onto Lillie. Some part of her felt like a mouse who had just barely escaped the cat's claw. Another part of her felt, as if the so called cat was just behind her its hot breath caressing the back of her neck. Did she believe if she drove fast enough that she could escape the terrified, powerless feeling that gripped her heart? Amanda's knuckles were white from gripping her steering wheel so hard. She was nearly panting with fear. With every inhale, her breathing became more erratic and panicked. She was tempted to slam the accelerator to the floor and see if she could drive fast enough to escape that feeling. She kept glancing up in the rear view mirror to see if there were lights behind her. It was more unnerving to have that feeling of being followed and not see someone behind her, then it would have been to see the reflection of headlights in the mirror. She almost felt as if there were hands reaching for her, and the owner of those hands was just sitting in the back seat.

Amanda jerked the wheel, attempting to pull quickly into the driveway. The abrupt movement caused the jeep to slide on the freshly fallen powder and almost up into the yard. She hit the brakes so hard when she tried to stop, that she nearly collided into the wooden fence that fenced off the back yard. What was wrong with her? Had those cops rattled her nerves that bad? As she thought about it, she had a momentary flashback of the Officer Miller and the way he looked at her. The way they looked at her and the predatory, wolf-like glint in their eyes. Everything about their look and body language, defined them as predators. In Wolf Creek she could kill the predators that roamed her back yard with one squeeze of the trigger. But she could not shoot these men. They were not animals, they were officers of the law. Even they knew she could not shoot them. What would her excuse be? They attacked her? They made her uncomfortable?

Why was she considering killing them in the first place? Had they given her a reason to want to shoot them? A side from being emphatically creepy and completely inappropriate. They had given her no grounds to kill them. One question still remained: what if they did try something? They for one, out numbered her, and could (would) get away with it. No one would believe the new girl in town who just happened to tote a .45 everywhere she went. Everyone would side with the law. Was there any way to bring them down? Could she really take on the three of them and survive? They knew the town better than she did, so, they could be anywhere, at anytime and she would never know. So it was best to avoid the law and keep to herself. No matter what they looked like, some part of her knew that they were not cops.

It was half an hour before Amanda realized that she was still sitting in her jeep watching the snow fall outside. She did not want to be alone in the house, at least not while the power was out. So she waited outside for the repair guy, James to get there. It was another half an hour before she finally saw a beat up, black and white truck pull up in front of the house and park on the street. Amanda watched him for a moment as he got out of the truck. He was not exceptionally tall but still his mere presence was intimidating. There was a dark aura around him and it radiated from him as he stepped into the yard. It was cold outside but that was not what made the hairs on the back of her neck stand up and it did not make her shiver.

His movements were somehow strangely elegant. There was no shuffle in his walk, hunch in his back or swagger in his hips. Every step was sure and every move he made was as if watching water flow. Although his body language was all wrong for a man of his employment, he seemed to dress the part fairly well. James wore black work boots, faded blue jeans, a brown leather jacket and a black baseball cap that made seeing his face next to impossible. He was staring at the snow as he tried to navigate through the yard to the front door, so she would not see his face until he met her on the porch. She bit her lip nervously. In one hand he carried a red tool box. At least he seemed more normal, than the cops. However, Amanda could not ignore the fact that since he had stepped foot onto the property, the air around her had dropped in temperature. When he was half way up the yard, she stepped out of the jeep and headed toward the porch, pretending she did not see him. James spotted her as she started up the steps.

"Oh hey."

"Hi." She said nervously over her shoulder.

"I'm James, I'm here to fix your fuse box." He flashed a friendly smile at her.

Her intuition was not fooled. There was something dark in that smile, something dangerous in those eyes and power in the muscles hidden just beneath his clothes. She resisted the urge to shudder with discomfort.

"I'm Amanda." She said cooly, barely glancing behind her.

"What were you doing still sitting in your jeep?"

She wanted to tell him it was 'not his damn business.' Instead, she found an excuse for her peculiar behavior.

"No heat in the house right now."

She lied. There was a fire place in her living room but telling the repair guy 'I was spying on you' would probably not go over well.

"Well, if ya let me in and I'll fix that." He said with another little smile.

When she finally turned around to look at him, she found herself drawn in by his brown eyes and tempting smile. The hint of the accent she heard tingling in his voice the, seemed to be of Latino descent but she refused to make any assumptions. Even with the warning her body was giving her, she still felt herself wanting him in ways she should not. She found herself fantasizing about the feel of his lips on hers and the taste his kiss. For a working man (she noticed) he had rather delicate hands and long dexterous fingers, free of scars of calluses.

As she pushed her key in the lock, she could feel those imaginary digits push deep between her folds and his thumb begin to rub her pink nub in circles. Amanda bit her bottom lip in a attempt to calm herself. In her mind, his voice was like honey as syllables of Spanish left his lips. The words caressed her ears and although she understood none of it, she became even more aroused. She was so lost in her own mind that she did not realize how much time had passed.

"Miss?"

Amanda jumped when she heard the familiar voice behind her. When she turned around, James grazed his tongue across his bottom lip before a slow smirk spread across his features. The mere sight of his tongue flicking out to wet his bottom lip, made her body ignite with heat.

"Are we going to stand on the porch all day?"

"What . . .uh . . .no."

It took her a moment to realize that she had only put the key in the lock and never turned it. She flashed him a nervous smile before turning the key and opening the door. The house still smelled like coffee but now it smelled like old coffee. She felt a rush of cold air as James closed the door behind him. It was nearly pitch black in the house and it was getting colder. Amanda carefully moved toward the kitchen, pulling the blinds up to let in more light. By the time she turned around, he had a flash light in his hand and was using it to make his way over to her.

"Where's your fuse box?"

"Basement, I think."

"Hmm," He looked around, setting the box on the table.

He made his way to the living room.

"Do you have any firewood?"

"Huh-ouch!" She tripped over a box in the kitchen and

landed face first on the floor.

"Are you ok?"

He was suddenly beside her, helping her to her feet. She never even heard him approach.

"I'm alright-ow-just a little embarrassed is all."

"Are you sure?" He flashed a charming smile at her.

Amanda knew that smile was meant to pacify her but the spiders in her belly began to frenzy as she stood next to him. So they completely voided his smile. He was good, he even pretended to use the flashlight to look for injury. She had a nagging feeling that all of it was an act. After what happened in the sheriff's department, she refused to take away chances or trust anyone here.

"Yeah, I forgot that box was there."

James helped her to the living room and onto her couch.

"I'll tell ya what."

He moved over to the fireplace, shining his light up it to see if it was safe to use and not so clogged with soot that it would cause a fire.

"If you have any firewood, I can start a fire for you and while you keep warm, I'll fix the fuse box."

"I'm not sure, but there might be wood in the basement. I just got in yesterday so I'm not real sure if there is any at all."

"You stay here, I'll go look."

He picked up his flashlight and headed out of the living room. As he did, she spoke up.

"Uh . . .I didn't tell you where it is."

He paused, his body suddenly rigid.

"I've been in this house before."

James was quick to respond. The friendly tone having left his voice and been replaced by one of annoyance. It was not just the speed of his response that bothered her but his vocal change as well. He acted as if she was getting in his way or holding him back. There was something else too. One minute he did not know where the fuse box was (in the basement) but then he suddenly knew where the basement was located. Also, he claimed to have been in this house before, so he should have already known where the location of the fuse box His behavior gave her reason to be even more suspicious of him and to carry her .45 everywhere. While she was analyzing his behavior, her previous thoughts came drifting back into her subconscious.

It was almost as if her fantasy had a will of its own and it would not be ignored. This time the images were more erotic, more sensual. However, they begged the question, was she so attracted to him that she could not fathom the idea of him being a bad person? Was it just easier to day dream about him? Amanda felt torn, on the one hand, she was suspicious of him but on the other hand she felt incredibly attracted to him.

That second part of her wanted to feel that tongue flick across and lick her most sensitive flesh. To feel his fingers inside of her as they moved in perfect rhythm with his talented tongue. He tantalized and teased her, kissing her delicate folds. Her cries of pleasure were almost screams as his tongue moved back to her delicate bud. A shiver passed through her body from the mere thought of him touching her in that way.

"Found it."

"Oh god you did . . ." She whispered, her gaze far off.

"Huh? Amanda?" He waved his hand in front of her face.

Finally she snapped from her trance, looking up into his eyes and biting her lip to fight back the flush in her cheeks. She wondered if he could sense her arousal. Of if he had noticed the shiver that passed through her body.

"What were you thinking about so deeply?"

"Nothing . . .just tired." She dropped her eyes to the floor to avoid his gaze.

A smirk played across James's lips as if he knew she was lying. When he knelt down to load firewood into the fireplace, she shifted a little. Her eyes scanned over his back and she bit her lip. Amanda was glad he could not see her face because she realized that she was embarrassingly wet and for that reason she flushed red. Was that fantasy really that good? Or was he just that sexy? None of it mattered right now. She needed to regain her composure until he left. There was a particular box she would be unpacking when he was gone. She cleared her throat suddenly and finally spoke.

"You want some coffee? It's still warm."

"No, I'm all right,"

He half turned and licked his bottom lip before biting it. Another one of those almost seductive smiles played across his lips.

"Thank you though."

She managed a small smile that she hoped did not appear nervous. Did he know? The way he responded to her it was as if he knew how what she was fighting to keep out of her head and he was trying to make it harder. A few moments later, a small fire was flickering in the fire place. Its heat just barely reaching her.

"Come here," James waved her over. "give me your hand."

She obeyed. James's hands were definitely softer than a normal man in his line of work but at the same time they had the perfect texture for other things. Amanda was still fighting to keep her mind from drifting back to her previous train of thought. Normally, she was not like this, but today she was having thoughts, that just refused to go away.

As he gently held her hand near the fire, the smell of his cologne drifted up to her nostrils. It was slightly spicy but mild and certainly nothing like anything she had smelled before. There was something about his cologne that seemed to fuel the feelings she was already having. There was nothing at this point that could help keep her calm.

"You might have to sit here until the fire gets a little bigger. But at least you'll have some heat."

"Uh huh." She was suddenly stupefied by his touch.

"Good god your hands are freezing." He said, as he pulled her other hand toward the fire.

Before she realized what he was doing, he had already cupped her hands between his palms and began to breath hot air onto her fingers. That small, innocuous gesture made her body warm with an entirely different type of heat. It did not help that he was looking up at her with those deep chocolate browns as he attempted to warm her hands. The part of her fighting to keep control was praying he would stop before she lost it and mounted him on the hard wood floor in front of the fireplace. After about five minutes he stopped. When he finally did, she let out a shaky breath before biting her lip to stop it from quivering.

"Th-thanks," She cleared her throat. "Thank you."

"You ok?" He said with a smirk. His tongue darting across his lip.

"I'm fine." She lied.

If fine meant 'trying to contain her growing urges and arousal' then sure, she was fine. It was really beginning to look as if he knew what affect he had on her. When he reached for his flashlight that was lying just behind her, he leaned in so close that she fell back onto the floor to keep from making any physical contact with him. In doing so, she landed with him between her legs with one of his hands beside her to support his weight. This was not a good position to be in, considering her current state of mind. None of it seemed to bother James though because he casually spoke to her before standing up.

"Are you sure you're ok?" His breath smelled like cinnamon.

He smiled sweetly at her. Just what was it about this man that affected her so bad? She fought to ignore her racing heart and her throbbing flesh. It took her a moment to compose herself so she could answer him without a quiver in her voice.

"Yeah."

At this distance his lip lick and bite was a lethal blow to her willpower. Another section of her wall of restraint was knocked out from under her. When he finally headed toward the basement and she heard his boots on the wooden stairs. Amanda fell back on the wood floor and sighed in relief. She knew the wood beneath her would be cold. In fact, she was counting on it, she hoped it might rescue her from the fantasy filled day she was having. As soon as he was gone, some alone time would be in order. While he worked on her fuse box, her mind filled with erotic images but this time in greater detail..

James walked back into the living room but this time he was not wearing a shirt. He knelt down on the floor and taking her hand, he pulled her toward him. Amanda swallowed nervously. Although she knew what was about to happen, she could not wrap her mind around it. Slowly, he unzipped her coat, pulling it off and tossing it aside. While he was busy removing her clothing, she ran her fingers down his muscular arms, admiring his physique. She could feel the tension and strength of them and they only served to drive her arousal.

She glanced up at his face as she grazed her nails down his naked chest and hard stomach. He bit his lip in response. For a few minutes she admired his soft caramel skin and the way it lay perfectly over every inch of his hard anatomy. It would be nothing for a man with his muscle to hold her down. To pin her to the floor and take what he wanted from her. The thought provoked more moisture between her thighs and the realization that she wanted him to dominate her. That some part of her wanted him to break her and to own her. It was not a concept she had considered before but now she wanted it. Almost as if he heard her, he grabbed her by her hair as a look of predatory hunger crossed his features. As if he did not want to just own her but devour her. She was the last meal of a dying man and he intended to enjoy every last morsel. Those chocolate browns seemed to darken to an almost black; at the same time the fire from the fireplace reflected in his his pupils. Amanda shivered with arousal as he leaned in her ear and whispered in a deep husky voice.

"You're gonna be a good girl and do everything I tell you," His voice became more commanding."Or . . . you won't be able to stand tomorrow."

Her breath hitched in her throat when she tried to speak and for a second she had no voice. So she just nodded.

"Say it."

He said, biting off the words and pulling a little harder.

"Yes." She barely managed to say.

Then he let go of her hair and she pulled away so she could look into his eyes. Those eyes never changed in their darkness or intensity and the once sweet smile was completely gone. His expression was dominant and hungry. With a firm tone, he commanded her.

"Lay down."

'*Did he just growl? Never mind.*' Amanda laid flat on the wooden floor.

"Don't move or make a sound unless I tell you that you can."

She swallowed, feeling her arousal grow more as he took away all her power and gained complete control. Slowly he pulled her shirt up and began to run his fingers down her stomach, stopping just above her jeans. Amanda bit her lip to keep from gasping, he had warned her to keep silent. James leaned down and began planting hot wet kisses down her stomach to the top of her jeans, letting his tongue dip just below her belt line.

Amanda bit down harder on her lip, trying not to squirm. James glanced up, he could see her fighting not to move. If she had looked down at him in that moment, she would have noticed the smirk on his face.

With one quick motion, he unlatched and pulled her belt from her jeans. James made no move to suggest he would remove her clothes anytime soon. He wanted to tease her a little longer, that much was obvious. He began licking just barely under the top of her jeans, making her body wet with arousal. Amanda was struggling to keep quiet but she knew that if she bit her lip any harder, she would break skin.

She tried to pull her fist to her mouth so she could bite down on it. Before she could move, he was on top of her, slamming her wrists down to the floor, his almost black eyes glaring down at her. Amanda shivered, half with fear and half with arousal.

"I told you not to move."

His voice was deep with an almost angry tone. Amanda said nothing in order to avoid further punishment by speaking without permission. He leaned in her ear.

"Do that again . . .and you may never walk again."

That time she did hear a growl and she shivered beneath him. He moved back down her body, pulling the top of her jeans down a little more this time as he licked just barely across her delicate flesh.

How much more of this torture was he going to dish out? 'As much as he wants to give you' her mind said. She really had no choice but to endure.

Finally he undid her jeans and slid them off. Amanda glanced down at him in time to see him kneel between her thighs. For a moment she just watched the muscles in his upper body flex as he moved. James just barely grazed his digits across the fabric of her panties and she shivered.

A slight smirk played at the corner of his mouth when he realized just how sensitive his teasing had made her. Those long digits pulled the fabric of her panties aside, revealing her ever so sensitive flesh. She watched him lick his lips slowly before dragging his index finger just barely between her wet folds. She had to fight not to shift with frustration as he continued to tease her.

What he did next, nearly made her break all the rules of this game. She watched him put that finger in his mouth and suck her sweet nectar from it. That only made her body wet more with arousal. She fought to keep still, to keep from wincing in frustration and to keep from panting.

When he took that same finger and just barely began rubbing her swollen pink bud, she shivered and her eyes rolled closed. He pulled his hand away suddenly. Only to finally pull her panties from her body. James moved back up her body and whispered in her ear.

"Why are you so wet?" He almost seemed to purr.

"You . . .because of you." She answered obediently.

She could feel him hovering over her and she could not help but open her eyes to look at him. Amanda wanted to reach out and touch him, but she was afraid she might get in more trouble. It was too tempting to want to touch every inch of his well toned body. That caramel skin begged to be caressed.

Before she had a chance to 'break the rules' and touch him, he grabbed her wrists in one hand and pinned them above her head. With his other hand, he slid an index finger, painfully slow, deep inside of her aching wet folds. Ever so slowly, he began to move it in and out of her.

The rate at which he moved, only served to tease her even more. She wanted more, so much more. Somehow this man knew just how to make her ache more than she ever though was possible. His torture methods were exquisite and his ability to control her without trying was mind boggling. James was truly something else.

"What did I do, to make you so," He began to stroke her G-spot."wet?"

She shivered against his hand. It was almost impossible to answer him.

"You...oh..god," She was panting. "teased me."

She choked out.

"Did I now?" He growled.

With his mouth still at her ear, he began whispering in Spanish. She did not understand a word of it, but that did not matter and he seemed to know it did not matter. Just the sound of his native tongue coming out of his mouth was enough to make her shiver even harder and make her eyes roll back in her head. Without any warning, he suddenly stopped whispering and bit down on her neck so hard, she was sure that he drew blood. She yelped in pain. A second later, she heard his voice in her ear again.

"Don't. Make. Another. Sound." He growled, his voice deep.

She only shivered harder as he growled in her ear and commanded her silence. James suddenly pulled his fingers from her and moved back down between her thighs. His sudden pull from her body, left her hot and aching for his touch. Then he took her by her hand and pulled her to him, forcing her to sit in his lap just long enough to pull the last of her clothes off.

"Stand up."

She did. He laid down on the floor where she had once laid. Then he pulled her down so she was sitting on his face. At that angle, she had no power or way to get up if her body became too sensitive for his tongue. If he wrapped his arms around her small thighs, there was no getting up.

Just as the realization of this possible issue hit her, she felt that wicked tongue briefly flick across her swollen bud. The feel of his hot wet tongue, touching her so sensitive flesh so suddenly, made her jump. Then she felt him wrap his arms around her thighs and flick his tongue faster across her clitoris.

"Oh...shit...." She gasped and winced between breaths.

As his tongue plunged into her depths, she reached down and gripped his hair, pulling a little. That made him moan against her. She shivered harder and he licked harder in response. Now, he moaned on purpose, as he licked her until her body was racked by a torrent of hard shivers and orgasms.

His arms tightened their grip on her thighs as he locked his lips around her swollen bud and began to suck hard. Amanda's breath left her lungs in a gasp of pleasure and her toes curled as her climax washed over her in waves of ecstasy.

James licked her through her orgasm. Even when it had subsided, he did not stop. She was becoming too sensitive to even want to be touched anymore and so she fought to pull off of him. To gain some footing and give her body a small break. He was torturing her now. When she could not break free of his grip by force, she yelled in desperation.

"James please, stop!"

After about a minute or more of licking he finally stopped and let go of her. She pulled back with such force that she fell backwards on the hard wood floor. Amanda just lay there for a few moments, panting and trying to regain her strength.

While she lay on the floor, he got up and stretched a little bit. Then she heard his bare feet padding on the wooden floor and moving over to where she now lay. She could tell what he wanted by the look in his eye and by the fact that he was slowly pulling down the zipper on his jeans.

"Amanda?"

She heard his voice but his lips were not moving. Slowly, she watched the image of the shirtless James fade and become the clothed version of him. It took her a few minutes to realize that she had been day dreaming. She woke with a jolt.

Amanda looked down at herself to make sure she was in fact dressed, some silly part of her having been afraid that she had stripped in her dream state. She found that she was fully clothed and she was grateful for that but she was soaked. There was also a fully clothed repair man standing exactly where the previous, half naked version of him had been standing.

"What?!" She must have looked confused or startled because he suddenly seemed to be trying to calm her down.

"Easy, it's me,"

He knelt beside her.

"It's James, remember me?"

"What," She had a day dream flashback. "yeah."

Amanda tried to hide the flush in her cheeks and the arousal in her eyes by glancing everywhere but his face. As she tried to push her dream away and fully awaken, he started to tell her what was wrong with the fuse box. She was still trying to push away the feeling of his tongue and fingers. In the process of trying to do so, she found herself becoming more aroused than she had been while fantasizing.

" . . .so are you ok with that?"

"What?"

She snapped from her trance.

"Are you all right coming to stay with me?"

"Wait what? Why?"

"What's on your mind? You seem to be somewhere else today."

"Nothing." She looked away.

James smirked.

"It must have been something because you have not heard a word I said."

She glanced up at him. He had lowered his gaze, trying to get her attention and now he licked his bottom lip as he looked into her eyes as if trying to figure out what she might be thinking. Amanda shifted noticeably as she tried to ignore his tongue and what the mere sight of it was doing to her. She changed the subject, trying to avoid answering his previous question.

"Why do I need to come stay with you?"

He smirked. It was obvious in his face that he knew she was avoiding answering him.

"The fuse you need for that box has to be ordered and it won't be in for a week or so. You can't very well stay here in the middle of winter, you'll freeze."

"Why can't I just stay at a hotel?"

"There aren't any in Collins. I promise you'll be safe at my place."

'No hotels in Collins, how convenient. Heh safe . . .yeah sure.'

She knew it was a really stupid and foolish idea, but what choice did she have. James was right, she would freeze if she stayed in this house in the middle of winter. At least he was better than the creepy cops but not by much.

She really did not want to stay with him but some small part of her did. Amanda needed to spend that alone time she had been thinking about, since he came over. If she was staying with him, that might be a little more difficult. Could she really manage to stay with him and find some space for alone time? 'Wait till he goes to work' There was no other choice, she would have to stay with him. So she smiled nervously before she got up off the floor to pack.

Chapter 13

May 31, 2008

In the old days there was Jack the Ripper, and he was-
in some ways-easier to avoid. You knew not to go out at
night, or to venture the dark streets of White Chapel. Now the
predators are harder to identify. Now they run in packs and
they no longer hide in dark alleyways. They find you and
chase you into their neck of the woods. The modern day devils
do not come out of the darkness, they are the darkness. There
are no distinctive characteristics about them. No eye patches,
or horrific scars. The demons of the world now wear handsome
faces and tempting smiles. For these very reasons, you never
see them coming and that's why they win.

Thoughts....
      Amanda McNabb

Chapter 14

It stared back at her, reflecting her, reflecting nothing as she finished gathering things. 'What are you doing?' Her reflection asked her as she thought about the fact she would be staying with this stranger. 'Could this situation really be better than the one before?' Without the flickering flame of the candle sitting on the sink, her reflection would only be a shadow; a confused whisper of a phantom reflected in a pool of shiny glass. Still, her reflection did not reflect her properly. It failed to show the questions in her eyes, her discomfort and the fear overtaking her whole form. Fear of the unknown. A few hours ago he was a stranger to her. Who was she kidding James was still a stranger. For all she knew he meant to lock her in his basement and keep her prisoner. Her little shiny friends might have something to say about it.

Again the question arose 'what are you doing?' The answer to that question was more complicated than the equation 'what are you doing'. She understood the question but, to answer 'I don't know' seemed wrong. No one was forcing her to leave her new house and stay with him. So why was her only answer 'I don't know'? To answer that paradox was more simple, 'because I truly do not know'. So rather than continue to have round about question and answer sessions with her own decaying mentality, she went back to gathering things in her bathroom. She knelt down, opening the cabinet and grabbing her hair dryer from under the cabinet before standing and stuffing it in the overnight bag she had sitting on the sink. As she was double checking the items she had taken out of the medicine cabinet and making sure she had enough of everything to last her the week, something caught her eye. Something moved just out of the corner of her eye and she glanced up from her meticulous counting.

At first she thought it was just the flickering candle playing tricks on her tired eyes. Then she looked closer. It appeared as if her reflection in the mirror was moving on its own. Amanda leaned closer to the metallic glass to see if it was her own reflection moving. When she moved the image in the mirror did not. Suddenly, the silhouette in the mirror became clearer and she could now see it was the reflection of a young woman. She could not have been much older than twenty. The girl was bloody with jagged cuts across her bare breasts and blood running down the side of her face from a gash on her left temple. There was a violet fingermark bruise around her neck where she had been strangled and several bite marks along her shoulders. She was missing a great many of her teeth. The bruising that decorated her face suggested they had been knocked out over the course of several beatings. Blood dripped from her mouth in a disgusting mixture of saliva and crimson. This woman had been abused, tortured even and she could only assume raped. Why was she in her mirror?

Amanda stared in horror at the bloody and beaten apparition in her bathroom mirror. The woman staring back at her had once had bright vibrant beautiful blue eyes and long blonde hair. Now it was red with streaks of blood. The apparition held up her hands as if reaching out for help. Her lips moved in silent warning as but no sound came out. Amanda attempted to decipher what she was saying. The only words she could make out was 'help me'. How could she? Her hands were just as bloody as the rest of her, several nails were missing. They were ground down from possibly clawing on a surface. Suddenly the ghostly figure glanced over her shoulder and when she turned back, her eyes were filled with fear. Off in the distance Amanda could barely make out the shadow of a man. The woman let out a silent scream and punched the mirror from the other side, sending spider web cracks across its reflective surface. From the cracks in the mirror oozed tendrils of blood which dripped onto the bag she had sitting on the sink. Its crimson color stood out in contrast to the white porcelain. In some morbid aspect it could have been considered abstract art. True the conductors of this horrific scenery were masters of the arts. Just not any sort of work the world would ever want to see. Her heart was hammering in her chest as she fought the urge to slide down the wall and curl into the fetal position. She feared her mind could not handle much more of this debauchery. For a few moments she just stared at the mirror. As she did, her mind swam with questions. Who was that woman? What happened to her and who was the man behind her? The incident set her teeth on edge and she checked the gun in its hidden holster, for reassurance. 'One in the head, one in the heart.' That was her mantra for the day.

She raised the candle and used the flame to light the mirror. It was not cracked or bloody and there was no blood on her bag either. The reflection in the mirror was her own and not the other woman. Amanda absentmindedly ran her fingertips across the mirrors surface to see if she could find anything. There was nothing.

'How could there just be nothing? How could something be there one minute and then gone the next?' The mirror cracked, she saw the cracks on its surface and the blood that dripped from its jagged wounds. 'So how was it that one minute it was there and the next minute it was gone? What was that apparition? A hallucination? An omen?' As usual she had more questions then she did answers and again she felt more uncomfortable and nervous because she could answer none of them.

With the strange events of the day piling up, on top of one another, she began to feel as if she was somewhere between awake and asleep. Somehow trapped in a fun house that had turned on her. It no longer held the excitement of something new but now a more sinister feel hung over her new life. Why did she suddenly feel as if she had left her cabin only to live in the wolves den? In her tired state, her mind wandered into thoughts of delirious ramblings. 'Is it coincidence that the repairman's name is James? Maybe James is behind this.' She shook her head at that thought. Amanda knew she could not allow herself to begin thinking that way or it would never quit. She knew that she would spiral down into madness if she started that thought process.

In a matter of a few minutes she had gone from packing, to a hallucination, to paranoid delusions about James having a master plan to get her back and keep her. Or to perhaps drive her completely insane. Whatever she was thinking about or whatever idiotic thoughts were coming into her head right now, were not in any way sane or normal. She needed to get her things together and (when she got settled into James's) take a nap.

Ever since her mind started wondering off into that moronic train of endless thought, she had completely stopped moving. In fact, she was still standing staring, but not quite staring at the mirror. Her fingers were still pressed lightly to its cold surface and the heat from them had now made small ovals on its glass face. Even though she had become consciously aware that she was currently standing there, staring at the mirror, it still took her a few moments to snap from her stationary position.

Amanda cleared her throat before going back to checking to make sure she had enough of everything in her bag. When she was satisfied that had everything she would need for the week, she checked the holster one more time before pulling on her jacket to cover it up. She gave one last unsure glance at the mirror before she closed her bag and grabbed the candle off the ledge of the sink.

On her way out of the bathroom, she blew out the candle before sitting it on the window sill of her room. The breeze leaking in from outside would be enough to cool the wick and keep it from doing any harm. With her luck this week she was not stupid enough to tempt the fates. For some reason she had felt the need to close her bedroom door while she was packing. Because of the incident with the mirror, she found herself pausing as she reached for the handle to her room. She was not afraid that the mirror girl would pull a Jacob Marly and possess her door or anything of that nature. In fact it was not really the girl who made her uneasy … well, it was and it was not.

There was something in the girls face that told her to be cautious of the people around her. Or be cautious of James, perhaps even more than she already was. Did she think he was capable of doing something like that to her? No and Maybe. To be honest she did not really know the man. Ted Bundy was a really upstanding citizen and a very nice guy but he killed and tortured a lot of women. So she could not be sure if he was a bad guy or not. For all she knew, the man had a basement full of tortured and tied up women.

Amanda licked her lips nervously as she finally grasped the handle on the door and turned it. She expected to find James waiting on the other side of the door in one of his creepy ways, but she found the hallway blissfully empty and she could hear his boots pacing the floor downstairs. In the darkness of the hallway she paused and listened to his foot falls. The sound of hard soles on wooden floor never used to make her jump or cringe before. Since the attack, that sound was like nails on a chalkboard to her. She purposely closed her bedroom door a little hard in order to get his attention and at least make him stop pacing. Amanda did not want to hear the methodical, rhythmic, back and forth pattern of boots on wood. A brief flash-of his boots circling her as she fought to get her gun-came flittering into her vision. Then, as if it never existed, the vision was gone.

In the first few moments of meeting him, she had been somewhere between freaked out and extremely horny. Now as she descended the stairs and his image came into view more, she was hesitant. Was she nervous or just being cautious? There had been no outright sign that she should be extremely weary of this man, but she found herself now being more standoffish. Did the bloody girl have something to do with it? Why would that apparition appear to her if she was not somehow relevant to Amanda's current situation?

As she descended the stairs she glanced out the window just beside the door and noticed that it was snowing harder then it had been earlier this morning. There was only one other time that it had snowed that hard or that much. When he broke into the house. It seemed that everything around her was trying to force her to remember James and perhaps cause her to associate this James with the one she had tried to kill. Amanda felt a momentary deafness come over herself. For a moment a cold sensation over took her body and she could only hear her slow, steady breathing. The room swayed and she began to feel light headed. James's image blurred and for a brief second she was back on the floor in her house, struggling for her rifle. The pain in her jaw was excruciating and the copper taste in her mouth nauseating. She squeezed her eyes shut and shook her head. The hallucination drifted away, leaving her feeling out of touch with reality. Although the flashback was gone, the taste of blood remained. In that moment of thinking, she suddenly became more aware of the weight of her gun and she absentmindedly pulled her coat closed more.

Now that her mind had shifted to the grounding thought of weapons, she remembered why she had wanted her bedroom door closed when she was packing. In the bottom of her bag, she had placed her new sawed off shotgun and a box of shells. She did not know this man who she would be staying with and for that reason she wanted as much protection as she could get her hands on. For extra reassurance, she had tucked a large folding knife in the top of her boot.

Remembering that she had armed herself rather well, she felt her smile and confidence come back. The previous discomfort had faded. If he was a psychotic killer, then he would only get to attempt murder with her. It's a little difficult to kill someone when you have a quarter inch hole in your head. That thought made her smile. For the second time today she was considering the thought if she had to kill someone. She was beginning to get the feeling that her mind itself was trying to tell her what her body did not sense. Even though she had ignored his smile, James was unfazed. He flashed her another smile before speaking and pointing in the direction of the truck.

"You wanna just follow behind me?"

"Yeah, that'll work."

"Here lemme take that for you." He reached for her bag.

Amanda jerked it away from him.

"No, I got it."

James furrowed his brow but before he could say anything she spoke again.

"I'm stubbornly independent."

He just nodded, seeming to accept her lie. The wind nearly knocked her over as she stepped outside and turned around to lock her door behind her. Amanda paused as she slid the key in the lock. There was something on the other side of the door, she could not feel it but she could sense it. She glanced behind her at the growling truck parked on the street. Whatever was on the other side of that door, she could feel it beacon to her. It begged her to stay in the house. In the small rectangular window by the door, she could just barely make out a figure with blonde hair. 'Could it really be the girl from the mirror?' Amanda squinted trying to make out what exactly she was seeing. The figure lurched forward and stood in the window. Her broken, battered nudity was in full view. There were hand bruises on her inner and outer thighs, which were decorated by the crimson liquid that ran from the apex of her hips. All of it pointed to obvious signs of rape. Again, the woman screamed in silence before slamming her bloody palm against the window. This glass did not break but with the slam of her hand, she vanished in a spiral of black shadows. It was enough to make her stumble backwards. Amanda glanced behind her, wondering if James had witnessed any of that. She swallowed in a hopeless effort to calm her nerves. Then she reached forward and locked the door. The storm had picked up fury since five o'clock this morning and now the trees in her front yard could barely protect her from the ice nips of the snow flakes as they whipped by her. This wind was not quite a blizzard and if she was lucky it would not turn into that. Otherwise she might be stuck for a large portion of her week in the house with James. Things were awkward enough without her being literally trapped in the house with him. Especially if the bloody girl decided to follow her. She could only hope that she was bound to the house.

The sound of his rumbling truck was almost inaudible through the whistle of the wind. It was cold enough that -when it hit her face-took the breath right out of her lungs. She tucked her head down in her jacket and zipped it up tighter. Amanda ran at an awkward pace to her Jeep, throwing her bag on the passenger seat before fighting to pull the door shut. As she started it she could hear the wind whistling, as it passed between the mirror and the door.

At least the roar of her own vehicle would drowned out most of that noise and hopefully the radio could help sooth her fraying nerves. Even if they only had to drive a few blocks, she wanted to listen to the weather to see if this wind and snow would shift its way into a full blown storm. Before backing out of the driveway, she flipped on her radio and fumbled the buttons until she found a news station. Then she glanced up in the rear-view mirror and saw that James had pulled forward just enough so that she would end up behind him if she backed out of the driveway. Slowly, she maneuvered the Jeep onto the snowy streets and behind the rumbling truck. After her last vehicular skating escapade, she wanted to make sure she did not slide into his company vehicle.

James slowly started down Lillie and back towards main street. Every fiber of her being told her to find another way. To figure out something else but do not stay with that man. If the bloody apparition was not enough of a warning, then what else would be? This might be one of those time when her stubborn defiance would get her into more trouble than even a shotgun could fix. Amanda refused to let fear hold her back. As he applied his breaks to stop at the stop sign, Amanda heard them squeak loudly in protest to the cold wet environment around them. She had to put her index finger to her ear to block out some of the painful noise.

Something on the radio caught her attention and she turned the volume up to hear what was being said. A rather alarmed but pleasant male voice was saying something about a missing person.

"There is still no sign of Rachel Brown in the third week of the search for her. Police say they are not giving up hope. The family is praying for the safe return of her and have even offered a reward for any information leading to the location of her body. This is the fourth missing person from this area in the last four years. Law enforcement is warning all women to stay in at night, lock your doors and do not answer them at night.

Remember Rachel Brown is five feet tall with long blonde hair and bright blue eyes. She was last seen wearing white snow boots, blue jeans and a heavy brown, winter coat. If you have any information, you are asked to contact local authorities.

Such a sad story. We at WKJL are hoping that they find her soon, especially with the weather that is going to be blowing in. Now we go to Janet Coulter in the weather center for the latest on this building storm."

"Thanks John." Yes, this weather is set to turn ugly. The low tonight will be around 12 degrees but with a windchill of 1 it will feel much colder. We have a cold front moving in from the North which will bring more snow with it. Tonight we expect to see winds in the fifteen mile per hour range or even higher. There is the possibility for freezing rain as well, leading to severely icy conditions on the road ways. So if you have to venture out do be careful. That's all for me here in the weather center. Back to you John"

Although the weather was bad news, she was still focused on the fact that four people are missing from this area. It was a little unnerving. If the weather did turn south like they were predicting (and like the evidence around her suggested), then she might be completely up a creek without a paddle. That was not where she wanted to be. Between the possibility of disappearing and the possibility of being stuck in a house with a strange and mildly creepy man, her odds were not looking so good. The problem with James was that he was not outwardly creepy. He was not the type of man who fit the description of a sex offender, sadist or serial killer. Then again, they quite often look normal. They can be handsome and seductive, luring their victims with false promises. At least she knew the Jeep could handle the weather if she needed to get out of the house.

Her mind kept jumping from the weather to the report about the missing girl. 'Blonde hair and bright blue eyes . . .' Suddenly her mind flashed back to the mirror, the window and the bloody girl who tried to break it. Amanda was so entrenched in her thoughts on the news report about the missing woman, she did not realize that James had stopped. She nearly slammed into the back of his truck when she hit her breaks and slid on the fresh powder. Through his small rear-view window, she could see his truckers cap move as he glanced up in his mirror to see what the heck she was doing. She smiled sheepishly and waved and apology wave. When he looked back at the road in front of him; shaking his head and probably laughing, she went back to her thought.

'*Did that missing girl live in my house?*' The description was so common that it could have been a coincidence. Still, there was no denying what she had seen. That poor battered and beaten girl. The horrors she must have experienced. Her description fit that of the girl on the radio but how could she be sure? It had no voice, no real way to communicate with her and tell Amanda her name. Of course the creepy law enforcement probably would not tell her if she asked about her. It also would not be wise to suddenly go poking around for information. The police might have cause to start paying a little more attention to her. That was the last thing she needed right now. 'You're new in town and telling them you saw her in your bathroom mirror might come off a little crazy.' Right then and there, it was decided that she would not tell anyone about her ghostly visit. Or go poking around and drawing attention to herself. For now she pushed it out of her mind and concentrated on her surroundings. Which now looked completely foreign. How far from home was she? Where was she? It was almost impossible to tell through the wall of white. Her only guides were the red tail lights in front of her. She had no idea how she had gotten to this place. Somehow she had driven through the snow storm without issue but no matter how hard she tried, Amanda had no recollection of her journey. She barely remembered stepping off her front porch. It was uncharacteristic of her to forget though.

They were stopped at another light, its red glow pierced the wall of heavy falling snow. There was a police car sitting across from them at the intersection and when she finally noticed it, she felt herself unintentionally shudder. Amanda subconsciously touched the .45 on her back and flip the safety off. She had already decided that she could not legally shoot one of them because they did wear the uniform. Although she was certain neither one of them were really cops. The problem would be proving that in court, after she filled them with holes. As the car passed by them she felt the muscles in her entire back tense up. There was something wrong here, something completely wrong. Never once had she heard police sirens go off since she had been here. Aside from that, there were only two cops in the entire town and they only seemed to show up when she was out. It begged the question, were they following or watching her? She shifted uncomfortably as she stared at the tinted windshield of the cruiser. The light changed and they passed by one another. Amanda dropped her head slightly so she could hide her face.

James turned onto a street and pulled into a driveway by an older two story, ranch home. There was just enough room left in the driveway for her to park next to his truck. So she slowly pulled in before jamming down the parking break and shutting off the engine. The house they pulled up to was a little rough on the outside. There was white paint peeling off the woodwork, an array of random car parts, an overturned grill and random bits of junk scattered around the yard, all of it now covered by snow. On the side of the garage she could see at least one truck on blocks that had clearly been sitting there for a while. It was almost completely rusted through. Even the garage that they pulled up to was starting to fall apart. This was surprising because she expected someone who fixed things for a living to keep up on his own house. But she supposed that if you spend all your time fixing other peoples issues that you probably would not have time to fix your own.

As she climbed out of the Jeep with bag in hand, the wind ripped her breath away. The precipitation had turned from snow to sleet and was now slicing her forehead as it whipped by her face. Amanda hurried toward the direction James had gone, running up onto the porch and into the house behind him. Even though the wind was pushing heavily against the door, he shut it without issue.

'That was a bit strange.' She had known men twice his size that (against a good wind) would have still struggled to close a door that heavy. The front door was made of heavy cherry oak and she noticed that the back side of it had at least four bolt locks on it. Was he paranoid? Did she just agree to stay with a crazy man? This was one little quark she had to ask about.

"Uh . . . James..."

"Hmm?"

She was staring at and pointing at the locks.

"What? . . .Oh oh those? Those are um . . .well . . .a little old lady used to own this house. She was a bit of a shut in. I just never took them off."

Amanda was not buying it, his hesitant explanation gave her room for doubt. Besides that a little old lady could not move that thing. Even she was probably going to have trouble with that door. The bolt locks required a key to lock and unlock them from the inside. Unfortunately, she would have to investigate that strangeness later when he was at work. Right now, she was so tired that nothing else mattered. There could be dead bodies in his basement for all she cared at this point just so long as she got some sleep. For now she pretended to accept his explanation. She was not too worried, she had a cannon strapped to her back for protection.

"You wanna go ahead and get settled in?"

James interrupted her train of thought.

"What? Uh yeah."

"You all right? You've been drifting in and out all day."

"Yeah, just tired."

"Then I'll show you to the guest room."

James gestured toward the rear of the house, where she assumed she would be staying. They headed down a long hallway, dimly lit by the fading blue light of winter. The walls here were also dark cherry oak, which served to make the hallway even darker.

"Didn't sleep well last night?" James asked as they walked.

"No...not really."

"Bad dream?"

She could swear she heard a smirk in his voice. Then again, she wondered if she was just being paranoid because of the days' events. Still, it was slightly odd that he asked that specific question. Most people ask 'why?' They never straight out ask if it was a nightmare or bad dream. On top of that, he was way too nonchalant with his question, taunting, playful even, but in a slightly darker more sadistic sort of way.

"Excuse me?"

"Well this is your room."

He pushed open a door at the end of the hallway, cutting off her question.

Amanda tried to pretend she was not annoyed or unnerved by his casual, quick change of subject. She knew she heard him ask that question but she also knew better than to confront him. So she played along with this casual game.

"Oh, awesome."

James flicked on the light switch and a small lamp on the bedside table lit up.

"Bed." He pointed at it."That's a brand new mattress and sheets. So you enjoy those."

He winked at her. 'Pervert.'

"Bathroom is down the hall, third door on the left. Oh and if you open that door," He pointed at the dark oak door in her room. "it has more than enough closet space."

"Is there a lock on the bathroom door?"

"Of course. I like my privacy just as much as the next person. Oh, there's also one of those vibrating shower heads too if you like."

He winked at her and smirked. '*Pervert.*'

"Ok . . ."

She looked around. The curtains were dark, the furniture was dark and the lamp on the bedside table, barely illuminated the table.

"Um James?"

"Yeah?"

"Is there another light I can put in here? I mean I might need more light than this to read."

The friendly attitude and smile on his face quickly faded. There was a visible tension in his body which made her uneasy. James jerked his head quickly to one side, popping the bones in his neck before speaking. His tone was deeper than it had been previous, laced with anger.

"That is all the light you will need. If you need more light, take the damn shade off of it and you can read just **fine**. "

All she asked for was more light. It was a little strange that this request offended him.

"Ok . . ."

"If you need anything else, my room is down the hallway, the door is always open so you'll find it."

"So why don't you have your room upstairs?"

James's eyes seemed to darken now but maybe it was just the shadows around them getting bigger as the storm raged on outside. He looked more sinister, almost predatory in this light as he glared at her from beneath his dirty cap.

"You probably want to get settled in. I won't be going out to my other jobs right now on account of the storm. So I'll be in the living room if you need me."

From the sound of his boots as he left, she could tell that she had pissed him off. Although she failed to understand why, the fact still remained that her current host was mad. Somehow she had a feeling that she never would find out. That he was purposely trying to make sure that she knew nothing about him. What was he hiding? When she had some time alone, she would figure it out.

The town was eerie, the local law enforcement was slightly off and now the handyman was getting creepier by the hour. She knew that the apparition she had seen in her mirror was probably not helping her paranoia or mindset on the whole situation. Even if she had not seen that girl, she might have still come to feel this way. James was menacing but sexy, and other times he was down right frightening. His mood could jump from friendly to angry in the matter of seconds. So, either he was hiding something or he was severely bipolar.

Amanda breathed a slow steady sigh and then shut her door as quietly as possible. She wanted to pretend that he had not unnerved her and to keep him from hearing her door close as if that somehow would prove that she was not becoming mildly anxious around him. The gun on her hip was no longer grounding out her nervousness or her paranoia. Even the knowledge of its power was not helping to sooth her.

On a tired mind though, thoughts can race and become so chaotic that one can feel as if they are no longer the one in control of their brain. She was running on only a few hours of sleep and she had already had a long day. Although the darkness around her was mildly unsettling it was making her more tired. So she picked up her over night bag from the floor and moved it into the closet she could unpack it properly. Outside the wall of white blowing by the two small windows, was blocking enough light for her to leave the curtains open. Even though the walls of the room were white, every bit of furniture and fabric in the room was dark and that only helped to suck the rest of the light from the room.

There was no lock on her door, so she grabbed a heavy wooden chair that sat in the corner and jammed it under the handle of her door. She would be sleeping with no pants on and she did not trust him not to try to sneak in her room. God forbid she wake up tied to the four post bet with nothing covering her but a black sheet. Some part of her excited at the thought.

With the bedroom door secure, she tossed her heavy coat on the floor and let her boots thud on the wood beneath her as she pulled them off. Then she pulled her gun from her belt, tucking it and its holster beneath her pillow before finally shimming out of her pants. The man could at least pick good sheets. They were Egyptian cotton and the comforter was a down feather comforter. She scooted down under the blankets with her head facing the door. Amanda did not trust James and for that reason she kept ever watchful, even while she slept. When her head hit the pillow, an almost comatose sleep overtook her and she drifted quickly into pleasant but erotic dreams. Her dreams had been rather unusual as of late. They fluctuated between horrific and erotic. There would be time to analyze the cause of these dreams but right now she could care less.

Chapter 15

The massive structure loomed over her like some ancient evil castle. With its' tall smoke stacks and solid brick walls stained with the grim of abandonment, it seemed like the perfect place to hide something. Why had the thought occurred to her that something could be hidden there? Was her psyche trying to tell her something that her conscious mind was unaware of? After looking at the building for a while, she decided to investigate the mysterious factory. Although, she was suspicious of it and its motives, if a building could have motives. She was more suspicious of what it was and what was inside of it. There should have been nothing inside of it but for some reason her gut told her otherwise. What had brought her to the base of this structure? How did she get here? She could not remember. Even though she was in control of herself and she had not been brought here against her will, she could not remember how she arrived here.

The tall chain link fence that lined its parameter, had razor wire spiraled around top of it and its barrier was lined with no trespassing signs. Amanda knew there was no way she could have climbed over the fence without getting cut. There were no gashes on her legs or arms and with the clothing she had on (or did not have on) she would have gotten cut. Why had she left the house in barely anything? Somehow she had even left her gun. That in its self was unusual because she never left home without it, ever. Now she stood at the base of this large monument with barely any clothes on and no weapon to defend herself should something go wrong. The situation before her seemed to be slowly molding itself into a bad horror movie.

There was the possibility that she could get hurt or killed if she went into that place. Despite the fact that she knew this, there was still a stronger force, propelling her to go inside. She looked around the courtyard at the vast nothingness of loose gravel and dirt, before she proceeded toward the large concrete structure. She had seen the factory when she first came to Collins and she had been suspicious of what it was then. There was nothing particularly unusual about a large factory that had been shut down in a small town. It happened quite frequently. There was a mixture of feelings that came over her when she looked at this place, sadness, despair, hopelessness and fear. This place stank of fear, almost as if the very bricks it was built with were made from it and the mortar were made from the rest of the emotions.

As she made her way toward the factory, the sharp rocks dug into the bottom of her bare feet. She knew she should probably just turn around, find a way out and head back to the house for clothes before she went exploring. God only knows what they could have made in this factory before it closed. There could be hazardous chemicals for her to step in or sharp metal fragments for her to cut her feet on. For some reason she did not head back to the house and get dressed. Of course, even if she wanted to, she had no idea how to get back to James's house from here.

The only door that she could get to, to even get inside, was a heavy, pale brown, metal door with another 'No Trespassing' sign on it. Before even turning the handle, she pressed herself up against the brick of the building and moved slowly over to a broken window to look inside. All she could see was a large empty concrete room, dimly lit by the various shards of light from other broken windows. Why was she being so cautious? Did she really think that someone was in there? But then again, how could she not be cautious? She was a half naked woman, she was new in town, she had caught the eye of the local police and now she was going to explore an abandoned factory with no weapon to defend herself. She considered turning around and just leaving. If someone was in there, they could be a bigger danger than her trying to scale over the fence without getting cut. She would be better off cut than raped.

The brick wall scraped her skin slightly as she moved away from it. This building had obviously sat for a while unused because there were brick dust piles in various places along the ground. It had no security to keep people out, no cameras or any other means to keep squatters from sleeping in it or to keep teenagers from using it as a drug house. So the possibility of finding someone else lurking around the factory (other than herself) was moderately high.

When she was almost certain that she was alone, she grabbed the handle on the heavy door and turned it. To her surprise, the door was not locked but it was heavy enough for her to have to use two hands to open it. Amanda managed to slide inside before the it slammed shut so hard that it echoed throughout the empty building. She flinched and dove behind one of the heavy brick columns in the middle of the room, in case someone had heard that. For a few minutes she paused, not moving from her hiding place as she waited to see if she was alone.

After about five minutes she decided that she by herself. So she moved from her place behind the column. It was cold in this place and the concrete floor under her feet was even colder still. Amanda felt as if she was walking barefoot in the snow. Now she wished she had at least tried to go back to the house, she was nearly shivering. Even though she was almost certain she was alone, she tiptoed as she moved across the room. On the end where she had entered, there was what looked like a large furnace. It ran from the floor she was on up through the ceiling and after that she assumed it ran up through most of the building. On the other side of the room, off to her right there was a doorway where a door used to be. It was providing the most light for her to see.

She turned to her left and tiptoed through the other large doorway that led into more of the factory. In the next room she entered, she found various conveyor belts and machines that were still hooked up but not in operation anymore. This room had large windows all around the ceiling and in through them poured evening light. Only a few minutes ago it had been sometime in the afternoon and now it was nearly dusk. That seemed a little strange to her but she shrugged it off as perhaps a change in seasons. As she was making her way across the room, she swore she heard the sound of cowboy boots on concrete floor. For a second she froze and just listened.

The sound stopped and she realized that she had quit breathing. That was fine because she was trying to listen for that sound. Just when she thought it was gone, the sound started again. This time it was coming down the same hallway she had just been down and it was moving closer at a rapid rate. For a second she began to panic and then she dashed across the large room and turned quickly into the next available room. It was an office, lined with windows so someone could see both the rooms she had just left. So she crawled under the desk and pulled the chair in with her so that no one could see her if they were standing in the rooms.

The cowboy boots moved across the large room, their mere sound making her start to shake with fear. A fear that normally would have been dispelled by the handgun on her hip. However, her weapon was not with her and now she was left to face the fear. She could see the boots in her head, hear them 'clop' across the solid floor and watch them turn the corner in the same direction she had just run. They came closer and closer to the door of the office in which she was hiding. 'Oh god oh god please go away go away.' As if by some miracle, she heard the boots pass by the door and head away from her. Amanda knew better than to try and move right away. So she stayed under that desk until she was sure that he was gone.

By the time she crawled out from under the desk-dirt and grime coating her hands and knees-it was night time. There was barely any light to see in the darkness of the factory. The security lights that would normally come on had stopped working a long time ago. Now she was left to grope in the darkness of the office and try to find the door handle. She ran her palms along the brick wall until she felt the peeling paint on the warped, wooden door and the cold glass panels of its window. Being careful not to get a splinted, she lightly grazed her fingertips down the door until she found the cold metal handle before slowly turning it. Amanda was being as careful as possible not to make noise as she left the office.

It did not matter if she left the door open, she would be leaving anyhow. She did not want them to discover that someone was there now. Some part of her assumed she knew who it was because only one person she knew wore cowboy boots and only one person had that familiar long stride.

She tiptoed as fast as she could from the open office door to the large room with all the machinery. Then from there she made her way slowly along the wall toward the room she had come through. There was moonlight pouring in through some of the windows here and for that much she was grateful. Still, there were far too many shadows for her liking. She was almost out of this place and home safe. All she had to do was leave out the way she came and figure out how to get over the fence without getting cut on the razor wire.

As she tiptoed across the floor, she squinted to see if she could see anything in the dark. It was far too dark to see much of anything. A noise behind her caught her attention and she turned around. The darkness blinded her with its unwavering black wall. When she turned back around, her ears caught the hint of the sharp metallic click characteristic of a Zippo lighter being opened. Then in the dull flickering flame of the lighter she glimpsed his all too familiar features. It was James, her James. He lit a cigarette as he looked down at her. Now she wished she had gone back to the house. In nothing but a t-shirt and her underwear, she was fair game for whatever he had in mind.

James flicked the lighter shut and now all she could see was the glow of his cigarette as he inhaled its toxic smoke. The aroma of it filled her nostrils and triggered memories she had tried so hard to bury. Amanda slowly backed away from him, shaking her head in disbelief as she did. He was not dead, she knew she had loaded him with buck shot and he was standing before her, alive as ever.

"Miss me?"

"No, go away. Get-"

She tripped over her own feet as she backed away, cutting off her sentence as she fell back to the concrete with a hard 'thud'. Now she crawled backwards, trying to get away from him.

James licked his bottom lip before speaking.

"I think you did miss me. In fact, I think you've been aching to see me."

"Stay the hell away from me James! You're dead, I know you're dead."

"How do you know I'm dead? You never found a body."

"Touch me and I will give them a body to find!"

"How ya gonna do that? You hiding a gun in your panties?"

"Screw you James!"

"My intentions exactly."

He tossed his cigarette before moving toward her. His hand dashed out and grabbed her by her wrist . . .

Amanda shot up out of bed, she was panting, her heart was

pounding violently against her rib-cage, threatening to break free from it and her body was glistening with a cold sweat. For a few moments she just sat there in bed, panting and looking around to be sure that she was not in that god forsaken place anymore. As far as she could tell, she was alone in the dark guest bedroom with no James in sight. The heavy wooden chair was still lodged firmly under the handle of the door and her gun was still sitting just under her pillow. Outside the wind still whistled fiercely as the wall of white continued to rain down on Collins. It was night time now, according to the single clock on her dimly lit night stand. After waking up in a nasty cold sweat, she decided that she needed to take a shower and find something to eat.

The mattress groaned as she stood up from it and stretched, cracking her neck in the process. She put on the jeans she had been wearing only a few hours ago and headed to the closet to grab some clothes and her toiletries. There was no way she was going to use his shampoo or even his body wash and smell like him for the rest of the night. It was bad enough having to stay with him until her fuse box could be fixed. Amanda fished out what she needed from her bag before pulling the chair away from the door and heading into the hallway. She paused as she gripped the door handle. 'Should I hide my gun or take it with me to the shower? Where would I hide it in the shower?'

Before she headed for the bathroom, she grabbed her gun and hid it in her overnight bag. She did not want him to somehow find it while she was gone and then take it away from her. With that taken care of, she slowly started down the hallway toward the bathroom. As she did she noticed that there was a light on in James's room and the door was partially cracked. So she set her things down on the counter in the bathroom and moved quietly down the hallway.

The light from his room poured into the hall from the crack of the half closed door. It was evident that he was not shy or ashamed of his body because he was toweling off with the door barely closed. From what Amanda could see, he had no reason to be ashamed. Time seemed to slow as she watched him from her place in the hall. The water still clinging to his muscular form, ran down in several tendrils before dripping onto the floor. She bit her lip as she watched him move, every muscle in his body flexing just under his perfect caramel skin. Although she knew she should not be watching him, her curiosity and mild attraction to him made it hard to pull away.

Behind her, somewhere down the hallway, she heard the floor creak as if someone was walking toward her. She turned from the door to peer into the darkness and see if she could locate the source of the noise. Amanda did not see anything that could have made the floor creak. She shifted uneasily at the thought that something was there beyond her vision. To keep her imagination from running on some wild tangent, she turned back to James.

After a bit she decided it was time to go. So she slowly started backing away. The wooden floor threatened to alert him to her presence, creaking just under her right foot and giving her reason to pause. She prayed that he had not heard her. There were not enough shadows in the hallway to hide her. Without warning, he opened the door, sending tendrils of light pouring into the hallway. A hissing sound came from behind her as if the light had offended some great serpent but that sound paled in comparison to the sight before her. In the doorway he stood there looking at her with a slight smirk on his face as if he knew she had been there watching him. She could not stop the fever that flooded her cheeks.

The jeans he wore were resting low enough to show off his Adonis belt and the line of black curls that told her he was not wearing anything underneath. Whatever body wash he had used was now drifting off of him in fragrant waves, tantalizing her senses. His raven locks that were once tucked under his truckers cap, now hung about his head in a wet mess and bits of water dripped from several strands landing on his once dry chest. Amanda's eyes followed the path of one particular bead of water as it traveled the length of his abs and disappeared into the visible line of black curls. Her eyes fluttered up rather quickly when she realized what she was doing. All she could do was watch him lick his bottom lip before finally pulling a over his head. James said nothing with his mouth but everything with his dark eyes as he scanned over her nervous form. Those dark brown pools seemed to burn through her clothing and rake their way down her naked flesh as he looked her over.

It felt as if he was not just looking at her (drinking her in), but as if he was seeing every thought in her head. She felt naked in front of him. Which seemed ironic because only a few moments ago his taut muscular form had been bare for all the world to see. As she stood in the hallway, dumbfounded as to how she might explain herself, he adjusted his shirt, smirking slightly. There was no denying it. He knew she had been watching him, he even knew the effect it had on her and he reveled in the power he had over her. She would be incapable of explaining her way out of this situation, James already knew the truth.

It was obvious that he knew what effect her had on her. James stepped over the threshold and out into the hallway. So she moved aside to let him by, pressing her back against the wall to put as much space between them as possible. He moved in front of her so she had no where else to go. His chest was only a few inches from hers. Amanda tried to slide across the wall to her right in an attempt to get away, he slammed the palm of his hand on the wall near her head, blocking her path. She tried to slide to the left but he slammed his palm on the other side of her before moving closer pinning her to the wall. Now, there was no way to hide from him (which was all she wanted to do right now).

She swallowed nervously before she felt his knee start to press between her slightly spread thighs and move upward to brush against her through her jeans. Amanda was in too much shock to move, try to fight him or even verbally protest. Her toes curled against the wooden floor as she tried to keep her reaction from going to her face. James moved his hands from beside her, only so he could grasp her wrists and hold them above her head. The feel of his knee rubbing against her was only helping to sexually frustrate her even more. She knew she had to try and ignore it.

It was not enough to pin her with his body, James grabbed both her wrists pinning them above her head in one of his large powerful hands. Although they looked delicate, they were strong. She tried to pull free but could not break the hold he had on her. James took his free hand and used his forefinger to lift her chin and force her to look at him. Slowly he leaned in and just barely kissed her, flicking his tongue out enough to tease her. When he pulled away from her, her lips were tingling slightly with the whisper of his kiss. That only made her want more. He moved his free hand away from her face and brushed his fingertips down her neck, making her skin goose bump. She was barely breathing now as she felt him run his fingers across the skin exposed between the gap of her shirt and belt line.

His fingers brushed just briefly under the top of her jeans and for a second she stopped breathing. With a sly smirk James let go of her. He left her leaning against the wall of the hallway in the dark, slightly aroused, moist and confused. 'What was that? What had just happened? Why did I let him do that?" All this time she had been trying to keep him from touching her and now he had not only touched her, but he had kissed her and violated her. What was she supposed to do? Hit him? Then she would have to brave the storm to find another place to stay. Why did she freeze up completely when he touched her? Actually, she realized that she had frozen up when he caught her watching him and then she realized, that he had allowed her to watch him. It was obvious that he had known she had been watching him because he opened the door with a smirk. None of that mattered. What mattered, was that she had allowed him to over take her without protesting.

She was half shocked, half angry at herself for not saying anything. After waking up from the dream she had, having James touch her was the last thing she needed. Now she desperately needed a cold shower or even a longer shower than she had anticipated. At the moment she could not understand what had just happened. Perhaps, tomorrow he would not be home and she could spend a little time alone. With the way the storm was raging on, she doubted that she would. All of that would have to wait.

Amanda knew that now was not the time to think about the incident. She headed back down the hallway and into the bathroom, shutting the door behind her. Thankfully the bathroom had more lights than her room. There was a long halogen light mounted above the bathroom mirror. At least she would not have to shower in the dark and there was a lock on the bathroom door so she would not have to jam a chair under the handle for privacy. For now she might have to settle for a little shower play to keep her sanity. It was better than nothing.

She pulled the knob on the shower and turned the handle until she found the temperature of hot that she could stand. Before stripping down she locked the bathroom door and double checked that it had locked tight. Then she stripped off her t-shirt and now sticky pants and climbed into the shower under the stream of hot water. Its warm touch felt good after waking up in a cold sweat.

That place she dreamt about had seemed so real that for a second she wondered if she had been there once before. She had never seen inside a factory, and to dream of one in that much detail was a little more than unnerving. The fact that there really was a factory like that in Collins was a little disturbing. Why had her mind drummed up that dream? 'That dream.' Those words echoed in her head until the flashback of dream James came rushing into her vision. Would that demon from her past haunt her forever? Then again, she knew that everything in dreams had a symbolism to it. So the dream James could mean nothing at all. However, Amanda also knew that he represented nothing good and that she should take his presence in the dream as a bad omen. She would feel a slight uneasiness for the rest of the day, a feeling that she was not quite centered or fully rooted to the earth. As if somehow she had been split between two worlds and that somewhere another part of her was still trapped beyond her reach, in hellish nightmares that were doomed to repeat themselves. She shook the thoughts from her mind, wishing to dwell on them no more. Amanda had more important things to take care of at present.

She leaned against the tile of the shower wall and found it pleasantly warm. Then she placed a foot on the ledge of the bath tub so she might have some extra support for her upcoming activities. She would need some sort of fantasy material to get the job done. After a few moments of wracking her brain, she gave up and decided that her handyman would have to do. Slowly she moved her hand down the length of her body and to the apex of her thighs. There were no curls to get in the way of the task at hand and so she traced her fingers across the bare flesh there, teasing herself as she fantasized about what she might have let him do to her in the hallway.

She ran her index finger just barely between her folds and rubbed her swollen pink bud around in little circles before pulling her hand away. Although he had already teased her, she was teasing herself more this would prevent him from having any effect on her later. Or so she hoped. Again she reached down between her legs and rubbed in slow circles, her toes curling against the ledge they were resting on as she braced herself for the shiver that would run through her body.

Amanda bit her lip to keep herself from making any noise and drawing his attention. She slid her fingers from her swollen nub and pushed two fingers deep into her wanting hole, pumping them in and out of herself. Her free hand grabbed onto one of the shelves mounted in the shower as another shiver hit her and she felt the first wave of her orgasm hit her. 'Oh god James. Yes! James.' She was moaning in her head to keep from moaning out loud. But the closer she came to climax, the more difficult it was becoming to keep from making noise.

Now she was panting as she pumped her fingers in and out, faster and faster, her toes curling against the ledge even more as she struggled to keep from sinking down the wet, tile wall. A squeak escaped her lips as she felt her climax start washing over her and when it finally did hit her, she had to put her free hand over her mouth to keep from yelling James's name out loud. It washed over her in heavy waves of ecstatic bliss. By the time her climax had finished washing over her, she was panting heavily and the water was starting to get cold.

Under the stream of lukewarm water she washed her hands and her sensitive flesh to remove the sticky mess and smell. Just in case this James also had an abnormal sense of smell, she did not want him to know that she had been pleasuring herself in his shower. The moment she was clean again, she quickly turned off the shower before it became ice cold and dried off. By now he was probably wondering if she had drowned in the shower. At least she hoped that was all he was wondering. There were no shadows beneath the doorway of the bathroom to indicate that someone was spying on her. So, there was a good chance he was in the living room, waiting on her to come out of the bathroom. She knew from this moment on that her stay in his house would be more than a little interesting. In the very moment that thought crossed her mind, she heard a familiar knock on the bathroom door.

"Hey, you all right in there?"

Amanda, licked her bottom lip before momentarily biting it. She was still attempting to calm herself back down from her recent exploits. So, she waited for the second knock before she said anything, pretending she had not him the first time. Also, she needed some time to come up with an excuse for her rather lengthy shower.

"Am I going to have to come in there?"

"No, no. I'm fine."

Before he could say anything else, she spoke up.

"A girl's gotta shave doesn't she?"

He chuckled on the other side of the door. Then she heard nothing else, not the sound of his feet moving or even a sigh. James just seemed to disappear from the other side of the door. That made her even more uneasy. She knew that floor should creak with the weight of his steps but he just seemed to vanish from beyond that door. 'All right so he can move about the house without being detected. Good to know.' She thought to herself. Now she wished she had figured out a place she could hide her gun and bring it with her to the bathroom. It was fine, she would holster it when she finally dressed. She made sure to do so rather quickly, pulling her hair back into a wet ponytail so it was out of her way. Then she reached slowly for the handle of the bathroom door, as if it was a serpent that might strike her hand if she moved too fast. Perhaps she had put herself in more danger than she could have anticipated. After today, she would know for sure.

Chapter 16

Amanda opened the door slowly and poked her head out into the hallway before fully deciding that James was not hovering near by. She tiptoed down the hallway and to the guest bedroom where she promptly tossed her clothes on the floor of the closet. Outside the wind had not changed in its ferocity but there was something in the wind that had changed. A sort of foul energy now seemed to hang within the storm as the snow poured down around the slightly damaged but solid structure of a house. Slowly she moved over to the far window that faced the front yard and she looked out into the darkness to see if she could pin point the eerie feeling crawling up her spine.

It was far to dark outside to see anything and with the snow visibility was impossible. She knew if she attempted to open a window and try to poke her head out, the snow and wind would be too harsh for her to handle, so she was better off trying to peer through the glass. After a few moments of useless squinting and staring off into the abyss, she gave up turning her attention back to the feeling hanging in the air. Maybe it was the atmosphere in the house that had changed.

The air around her felt thicker, heavier even. The shadows around her appeared much darker and denser in some areas. 'Can shadows change consistency?' Something about that thought made her even more nervous and she quickly shuffled over to the lamp on her bedside and removed the shade. It illuminated the room about as much as a bright night light but it was still better than nothing at all. Somehow she would have to learn to deal with this place for the next few days. Within that time she hoped that the snowstorm outside would stop.

A gurgling sound in her stomach made her realize that she had not eaten in a few hours and she needed to before her stomach began to hurt. Before she did, made sure to arm herself before venturing into the rest of the house. Amanda grabbed her .45, she slipped it into the rear of her jeans and pulled her shirt down over top of it. Of course she knew that she could not really just shoot him in his own house but then again, the snow storm would be the perfect cover for the noise if she had to do it.

The extra light in the room did not serve to relax her any, so she decided to head out to the living room. As she started to leave, she could swear she heard someone breathing just within a few feet of her. Amanda paused and listened for the sound again. Being a rational woman, she would have to hear a sound like that again before she begin to believe she had heard it at all. Even then she would most likely try to justify that it was her own breathing she heard. She listened, her eyes scanning the room for any signs of anything that would come close to that sound. There was nothing.So she slowly closed the door behind her, leaving the lamp shade off in case she did decide to retire for the night. She much preferred to not have to fumble for the light switch. Amanda silently slipped through the threshold of her room and out into the dark hallway. The wooden floor felt exceptionally cool under her bare feet as she made her way toward the kitchen.

There was almost no light in the room as she tiptoed toward the counter to see if he had made any coffee. To her disappointment, there was not even a coffee maker. Amanda scratched her head as she stared at the blank space where she thought the coffee maker would be. If she had known that he did not have one, she would have brought hers. At any rate, she still needed to get something to eat but she felt rude rummaging through his fridge to for food.

She made her way toward the living room (where the TV provided the only light) and leaned on the back of the couch to ask him if he was hungry. He was not on the couch where she expected him to be. There was some hunting show on and they were just getting ready to skin a deer (or so she read) based on the subtitles at the bottom of the screen. She was quick to find the remote on the side table and change to anything but that. Although she was a nurse and she had seen many horrific things, seeing someone skin a deer was a whole other thing. Besides that, she knew she it would only make her sick because she could feel the nausea of hunger just starting to show its ugly face.

After what had happened in the hallway, Amanda was attempting to avoid James as much as she could. Although she was still uncertain as to what exactly had happened. Did he really pin her against the wall and do that? As she tried to think back to what had happened, the memories of that brief event became mildly fuzzy. It was as if she was watching them play through someone else's eyes. All of it was too much for her to process in her current state. She was still so exhausted that she almost wondered if it had been a hallucination.

In all actuality, it might just be better for her not to think about it and to pretend that nothing happened. If she had to be in this house for more than a couple days, then she needed to keep her wits about her. By letting the memory of what had happened get to her and by not erasing it from her mind, she risked him having power over her. She knew all too well these mind games and this power struggle. Her James had played the very same mind games when he was stalking her. All of it was just a matter of willpower. By pushing the memory, and all thoughts associated with it, from her mind she would gain back the power that he was trying to take from her. Amanda knew she needed to figure out where he was and find something to eat.

"James!" She yelled into the house.

No answer.

"James?!"

Still no answer.

She was not going exploring to see if she could find him, considering how touchy he was about things in his house. Amanda feared she would anger him and make her stay much more unpleasant. She plopped down on the couch and flipped through the hundreds of channels there were to choose from. At least he had cable and the wind had not knocked out the power, but the night was still young and the storm was probably not even close to being done. She crossed her fingers momentarily and knocked on the wooden table beside her. It was best not to jinx herself. As she sat there watching some cooking show with the volume barely up and the subtitles turned on. The shadows reflected off the television and bounced every which way around the room. It always puzzled her, how people moving on television can cast a shadow across a wall. In the night it's hard sometimes to tell if the shadow-that just passed across the blue lit wall-was really a person, some phantom shadow or just a shadow from the movement on a lit screen.

So she ignored the shadows bouncing around her in the dark living room, writing it off as just television light tricks. Amanda neglected (in her ignorance) to realize that some of the shadows were free moving and not bouncing with the changes of light being cast around her. Maybe if she had noticed this, she might have gotten smart and tried to leave his house. Even if she had noticed, the storm outside would prevent her from going anywhere. The show on the screen in front of her was hypnotic and now she was just staring at the screen. Part of it was because she needed more sleep but another part of it was because the monotone voice on the screen was lulling her into a sleep like state.

There was a thud above her and she shook her head, realizing that she had just been staring at the screen and not really watching what was on. Her head shot up to look at the ceiling and it took her another moment to realize that the sound had come from upstairs. She got up slowly, setting the remote on the couch and heading toward the stairs. As she moved, she looked around cautiously for any sign of James. Amanda wanted to call out and see if maybe he had been working up stairs and had been hurt, but some instinctual part of her told her to keep as quiet as she could and to head for the stairs.

Slowly, she started ascending the stairs to investigate the source of the noise. She was just lucky that the stairs made no sound as she moved up toward the landing at the top. The first thing to come into her vision was the sight of a door with several locks on the outside.

Amanda furrowed her brow. It seemed a bit strange to have locks on the outside of a door. That was unless you were trying to keep something in that room. For a few moments she just stood there on the fourth step and stared at the door with the gleaming locks on it. 'I should probably leave. Something isn't right here. What or who is he keeping in that room? Is he even keeping anything in that room or is he just trying to keep people out of that room?'

It was not even the right room for it to be the source of the noise. Somehow she had missed the sound of the door opening behind her and the rush of cold air from outside because the next thing she knew, she heard firewood being purposely dropped into the wrought iron container by the fireplace.

"What the hell are you doing?"

Amanda jumped and turned. Looming by the fireplace was James. How long had he been standing there? She wondered. None of that mattered at the moment because the more she looked at him in the dim light of the fire, the more she realized, he was furious with her. But why?

"I uh-"

"Stay the hell away from the upstairs. I do not even want you on that fucking staircase. Do I make myself clear?"

She only nodded and quickly moved off the stairs. There was something about him in that moment, that she feared. What it was she probably would never figure out. Amanda sensed a warning in his voice as he spoke. The warning in his voice coupled with the cold, black stare in his eyes when he looked at her, made her body jolt with fear. It did not matter that she was armed or that her right hand had instinctively reached back to grip the gun tucked away in her back, she was still afraid of him. When he moved past her to hang up his coat, she found herself pulling away from him more as he walked by. James glared at her as he hung his coat up to dry. His once soft brown eyes seemed almost black now in the dim light and when he looked at her, they seemed to stare right through her. Something about the look in his eyes told her that he would not be brought down so easily. An icy chill crept up her spine and she knew it had nothing to do with the cold wind outside.

The sound his boots made when he walked back into the living room, made her flinch. Even the breeze his body made as he moved past her was charged with his current emotion. Amanda reached back to click the safety off her gun. If something was going to happen, then she needed to be ready to defend herself. As her thumb touched the button, he looked at her-almost as if he knew what she was about to do- and she froze. Why was she suddenly so afraid of this man? She felt tears forming just above her bottom lids and she could feel her body wanting to shake with fear. It was becoming hard to fight off the terror that he had instilled in her.

There was something cold, distant and almost inhuman about the look in his eyes. The light that caught in his eyes made them appear almost silver. Amanda considered just going back to her room, jamming the chair under the door and spending the rest of the night in there. It might be safer for her to do that, rather than face him right now. What had she really done? Why was he so upset? Maybe she should try to talk to him or wait until he was calm and then attempt to talk to him. While she quietly weighed her options, he began to put wood into the fire place.

What really baffled her were his manic mood changes. When she met him, he had been so sweet, so helpful and slightly flirtatious. She had been so lustful when she looked at him the first time. What had happened? In the matter of a few hours he had gone from being one sweet person to a completely different man all together. Where there was once lust, she now had fear and it was slowly molding back into some sick twisted sort of lust. Amanda was undoubtedly turned on by the fact that he scared he so much. However, if he could turn so quickly, then she should be weary of his temper because if she was not, she might end up dead before the week was out. 'So what now? How do we handle this one? Tread carefully, stay away from upstairs and as soon as the weather clears, get OUT.'

"You know . . ." James started.

Amanda jumped when he spoke.

"I don't ask much..." He placed another log in the fireplace. "respect my house . . .obey my rules . . .and . . ." He turned around to look at her. "keep your nose out of my business..."

She had not realized she had begun backing away from him, until she felt her back hit the wall. Right now she could not look him in the face. Only later would she understand why.

"Am I asking too much?" His eyes seemed to glimmer as he looked up at her, two metallic black pools of onyx lit by the glow of the fire.

"N-no James...and I'm sorry. It will not happen again."

"It better not," He growled.

"There will be consequences *if* it happens again."

His tone seemed slightly distorted, with an almost demonic quality to it and for a moment she could swear she saw two gleaming canines in the dim light of the fire. Amanda swallowed nervously as she tightened her grip around her pistol. She would unload the entire magazine into his body if she found it necessary.

"Understand?"

She nodded slowly at first. Then she realized that he wanted a verbal answer.

"Yes James."

When he finally turned back around, she realized that she had not moved since he had looked at her. 'You need to be cautious.' There was clearly something wrong here and she wanted to figure out what it was, but she feared James too much to go poking around in his house. What had he meant by consequences? She really did not want to find out what he meant.

The soft glow of a fire was starting to emanate from the fireplace and when James turned around to look at her. It was now in the low glow of the television and the fire, that she noticed there was something at the corner of his mouth. '*Is that? It can't be. Is that blood? I think it is. Why is he bleeding? Maybe he was chewing his nails. Or biting his tongue to keep his patience. It doesn't really matter how it got there does it? I suppose not. It just matters that it's there.*'

Amanda thought better of mentioning the drop to James because he might take it as a criticism. So she bit her tongue and kept her eyes glued to the dark wooden floor of the living room. It was no surprise that her appetite was gone. The best thing she could do was to wait until he had gone to bed and at least get herself a glass of water. There was a part of her that thought about trying to brave the storm and head back to her place. Even with no electricity she could use her fireplace to keep warm and the stove was gas so she could heat water if she had to. Every part of her wanted to escape from this house and to do so unnoticed. 'Escape...why am I thinking about it as if I'm a prisoner? I'm not a prisoner. I'm free to go anytime I want to!' She told herself that in her head but some part of her did not believe it.

If she was going to get through this ordeal, then she was going to have to do everything in her power to keep James from knowing he scared her. So she gathered herself and tried to pretend that she was not afraid of him and that he did not make her nervous. Of course in all reality, he terrified her beyond rational thought. It was the first time in a long time that she had froze completely. In fact her thumb was still on the button as she stood there looking at him like a deer in headlights.

"You hungry?" His tone still was not very friendly.

Although her appetite was gone, she nodded to keep him from getting more angry. He looked at her, his head slightly cocked and his eyes squinting as if he was trying to read her thoughts. When she glanced up, he was licking his lips and looking at her. Then as if nothing had happened, he headed toward the kitchen. Those now jet black pools never leaving her as he passed. There was something about his eyes that not only pinned her to the wall but made her lower half ignite with arousal. '*Stop it! Do Not let him get to you!*' James headed for the fridge and started looking through the freezer. Just over his shoulder she could see that there was not much to eat at all. There was maybe all of one frozen pizza. '*Why is he pretending to look so hard?*'

James pulled the pizza out of the freezer and dropped it on the counter. Was he annoyed with her still? His body language told her that he was annoyed and a little angry. He almost acted as if she had actually broken something in his house, something he would have to fix. All she did was go halfway up the stairs. 'What is he hiding? What is upstairs that he doesn't want me to see?' A sudden chill passed through the room as if someone had walked by her. It was enough of a breeze for Amanda to start rubbing her arms and trying to will it away. That little breeze had made her lose focus on what she had been thinking about.

"Did you feel that?" She asked James.

"What?"

His back was still turned to her.

"That gust of cold air."

"Stand by the fireplace. This house gets very cold in the winter and with the wind blowing, you're going to feel a lot of random breezes."

She did not believe his explanation of the phantom breeze. Even though she was a rational woman, she knew that there was something strange going on here. The fact that she hesitated when her thumb was on the safety, was strange to her. She never hesitated when she decided to even pull her weapon. Now one look from him had caused her whole body tense up. What sort of power did this man have over her? Maybe it was not the man at all but the situation that had the power over her. She was after all trapped in a house with a man she barely knew and in a town that she had just moved into. So maybe it was all of those elements that were influencing her mindset.

'Maybe if I wake up and actually look at things with a more stable mind, they might not seem so off. But still, his odd behavior over the light and the upstairs...that was not created by tricks of my mind. And what was that noise I heard?' Almost as if hearing her thoughts about the upstairs and the noise, James suddenly spoke up from the kitchen.

"I thought I'd let you know that if you hear any strange

sounds, it's probably the pipes. They have a tendency to bang and clank. It's an old house and I've not gotten around to fixing that."

"Oh..." Amanda paused.

"So I guess no running to you in the middle of the night if I hear a strange sound?"

She was trying to lighten the mood.

"No."

His answer was cold.

"Hey James?"

"What?" His back was still to her.

"Do you have any coffee?"

There was a moment of awkward silence between them. For a second she wondered if he had heard her at all.

"Jame-"

"No, I ran out earlier in the week and was going to pick some up on my way home from work today but the storm prevented that."

His answer was laced with annoyance. It seemed at any moment now he was going to snap. Amanda swallowed before speaking again, her voice cracking a bit with nervousness.

"A-anything hot to drink at least?"

Again there was a moment of silence between them and within that silence, she knew she heard him say something but not to her.

"...do not get shitty with me...I'm working on her...you should have done more when you had her..." He whispered.

"James?"

"What?" There was anger seeping into his words now.

Amanda jumped when he spoke and she had to bite her lip to stop it from trembling. It was one of the things that would give her away the easiest.

"Never mind." She mumbled.

She would rather do without than to provoke his temper. Besides, she wanted to eavesdrop in on his conversation with the invisible person. Maybe she would figure out that he was entirely insane and that she was just dealing with the average schizophrenic person. That she could deal with. That she knew exactly how to deal with. But in order to figure out if that was the case, she was going to have to get her hands on a notebook or something and start documenting his behavior. Better yet, she had better start keeping track of all the strange events that were going on around her. Even if she did figure out that he was mildly psychotic, she knew that would not explain everything else. Being of sound mind, she knew she had to figure things out before she too lost her sanity. For now she sat quietly on the couch, listening to him talk.

" . . .do it . . .touch her . . .taste her . . .no man. . . it's cool, it's cool . . ."

Suddenly, he stopped talking and she saw him lift his head slightly as if someone just told him she was listening. Amanda was quick to turn around and stare at the television. She grabbed the remote and started flipping through channels as if she had been doing it the whole time. Something in her very gut told her that things were going to start getting even more strange. She needed to be more cautious and maybe it was for that reason that she finally took the safety off her gun. Even if she never had to use it, she wanted to have it ready just in case. It was going to be a long night. James was not going to make her stay here easier. In fact it was probably going to get harder and if the storm continued to rage she would have to keep from breaking before the week was out. Under extreme pressure Amanda knew the mind had a tendency to cave and the aftermath was a series of documentable mental disorders.

'*Why do I get the feeling that he was talking about me? But who the hell was he talking to? Himself?*' She had been locked so deeply in her train of thought, that without realizing it she move to the living room and settled on the couch. When she finally heard James begin moving from the kitchen to the living room, she pulled all the way to the corner of the couch. She did not want to be closer to him than a couch length, especially in his current state of mind. As she had predicted, he was not going to make things easy. James sat down right next to her and put his arm across the back of the couch. The exotic smell of him drifted across the void between them and the heat of his body caressed her bare skin. Amanda casually tried to look at him without him noticing. What was it about him that drove her mad? How could he terrify her one minute and then seduce her the next?

From the corner of her eye, she admired his caramel skin and dark mass ravel locks. She watched the calm rise and fall of his muscular chest as he was hypnotized by the droning television. Amanda could just make out the definition of his legs beneath his ratty old jeans. They were the same powerful legs that had made her body shake when they were grinding against her. James shifted slightly and Amanda tried to pretend she had been zoned into the television the whole time. When she believed that it was safe again, she let her eyes drift over to look at his best feature, his hands. She admired the smooth skin of his palms and his long dexterous, artists fingers.

Again, she pretended to be watching TV as thoughts of his hands tried to drift into her conscious mind. She didn't need those thoughts in her head right now. Not with him sitting this close and not with the urge to let him have her, growing stronger. Amanda's behavior as of late, had been very uncharacteristic. She did not think this way about a complete stranger. To lust after someone she barely knew, was nothing like her.

Amanda could hear James tapping his finger on the fabric of his jeans in a rhythmic, yet impatient beat. 'Tap, tap, tap.' Was he counting down for something? Was he nervous? 'Tap...tap' Had she done something? First his finger started tapping and now she could hear him bouncing his boot heel off the floor as his leg bounced up and down in a clearly nervous gesture. What was he so nervous about? 'Tap.....tap' On the last tap, he suddenly grabbed her thigh and in one swift movement, he yanked her toward him. Before she could stop him, he was on top of her, pinning her arms above her head. One hand was still holding that thigh and the rest of him was between her legs.

The whole event had happened so fast that she had no time to react. Now she was speechless with shock and so she just stared into this black pools. James said nothing.

'What now?'

Chapter 17

What now?

It was the question that begged to be answered and it hovered in the air above them. Although it was a logical inquiry for an illogical situation. There had to be a course of action she could take in order to get free from his grasp. His body pressed down firmly her soft frame, sinking her deeper into the couch, making escape almost impossible. Amanda was only barely maintaining her calm exterior. The last James had already broken her, beaten her bloody and managed to turn her into a shell of a woman. This one would not be allowed to have that power over her. She knew she had to do something soon or this might turn deadly.

At this distance his allure was lethal. She was bombarded by his intoxicating aroma and hypnotized by the predatory look in his dark pools. James gazed into her eyes as if he was attempting see her very soul. He tightened his grip on her, even though she had not struggled to get free. She was smart enough not to fight him until she had better footing and had put some distance between them. Amanda was well aware of his mental psychosis and that short temper. It was in her best interest to avoid having any physical relationship with the man. The only thought in her mind right now was 'get away from him'. Which she was already planning on doing, but she knew there was only one way to accomplish that. She was going to have to hurt him.

As long as he did not come after her when she escaped his grasp, she might have time to figure out her next course of action. She would sneak out into the storm if she had to and knowing her father as she did, he would fight to get to her. Then again, Amanda did not want to drag anyone else into this mess. If she could she wanted to avoid endangering anyone else. There would be no collateral damage in this fight. Keep the causalities of war to a minimum.

As she lay there, processing her thoughts and trying to maneuver her leg between his, a thought occurred to her. It was more a strong urge that she could not shake. She wanted to go home. The problem was, this crazy nightmare happening all around her was home. Somehow she had managed to willingly walk straight into this horror show without even bothering to look for the monsters and without paying attention to the obvious signs. She had ignored every omen and was not suffering for it. Would things get worse before it was over? Those words only taunted fate, they dared the demons to emerge from their hiding places and show her what true evil looks like. Now she had to suffer the consequences of being careless enough to allow herself to step from one bad situation into another. Without giving it any thought. Everyone she encountered in this town was more insane than the last. Did she willingly put herself in an asylum too? Or was that just a side effect of the other terrible situations that she kept finding herself.

The cops were certainly abnormal and James' moral compass was completely broke. She had no sense of balance in this place. Amanda had to get out of this house, away from James and possibly even out of Collins. Otherwise she might find herself in an irrevocable situation.

For a moment she glanced past James to look out the window behind him in an attempt to distract herself. She was beginning to feel the last of her nerves slipping away. In order to keep her composure and get away from him, she mentally talked herself through the situation. '*Step one: Knee him in the groin.*' When she raised her eyes again to look into his, she felt a bolt of fear strike her heart. So she inhaled slowly to keep herself calm. A sly smirk crawled across his lips and now his tongue played with his bottom lip. Those deep browns had gone from an animalistic glare to a lustful stare. '*Oh yeah, this situation is about to get worse. He's gonna be pissed when you run, so be ready to jump out the window.*'

As Amanda started to move her leg between his, she felt his grip on her wrists tighten again. They would be bruised in the morning if he held them any tighter. She managed to get her leg between his but to keep from raising any suspicion, for a few moments played his willing victim allowing him to lean down and kiss her. While he was distracted, she brought her knee up hard and fast. It slammed against his growing erection and at the same time, she bit his bottom lip hard enough to make it bleed. James let out a grunt and she managed to roll him off of her before she vaulted over the couch. As she ran for her room, he trailed behind her.. Apparently she had not kicked him hard enough. A few feet from her room, she heard him picking up pace.

Amanda managed to get into her room before he could grab her. She quickly jammed the chair under the door and pulled her colt, aiming it at the door. The sound of the door shaking against its frame, told her that he was ramming it with his shoulder, trying to break it down.

James found it a bit comical that he was keeping up this charade, he could easily kick this door down without much effort. However he knew it was best he not let her know about him too soon. So, he would pretend to have the strength of a normal mortal and fight against the chair she had shoved under the handle. Thanks to his blood brother, he knew her next move even before she executed it. It was too easy for him to be one step ahead of her. This was all part of the hunt, trickery and games. Let her believe she is in control and let her believe that the cannon in her back pocket with stop him or even slow him down.

James gave up ramming the door and instead he kicked it open. There was a loud crack as the wood of the door frame splintered and the chair slid across the floor hitting the night stand, nearly knocking over the only light she had.

"James stay the fuck back!"

He peered into the darkness in the most unnatural way. In the little light there was, she could just barely make out his silhouette and for a second the color of his eyes. They appeared jet black and the edges looked as if they were lined with blood. James tilted his head as he looked at her. Those unnatural eyes squinting as he looked at her.

"You gonna shoot me Amanda? In my own house? How are you going to explain that to the cops?"

"Explain what? If I leave town, they'll never know something happened to you."

"I knew there was something I liked about you," he swayed as he spoke. "you got some fight in you . . .I like that."

211

As he said that, he ran his index finger along his bottom lip and then sucked on it. She knew now that she had drawn blood. Maybe she had given him a message that he would not soon forget. Even if the lip bite had not gotten the message across, the gun pointed at him, just might. They both stood there a few moments and as they did, she swore she heard a low growl come from him. It was not from hunger either.

"You know I could take that gun from you...trust me. . .you don't want me to come in there and have to take that away. Now . . .be a good girl . . .put the fucking gun down and come here."

Somehow, in the last few words she heard his voice change. It did not get deeper or louder. In fact it did not sound human anymore. Was it her imagination? 'Stay focused!' Amanda could not allow him to get away with speaking to her that way.

"Fuck you James . . .I'll fill you full of lead before you can even touch me."

"Mmm . . .," He did growl that time. "I thought you might say that."

Amanda suddenly noticed the shadows in the room seemed to shift around him. What the hell was happening? Something was not right. Now she was thinking she should have listened to the apparition in her bathroom mirror. It was trying to warn her. There was something seriously weird going on here. She broke from her train of thought to look at James.

"Come," He grabbed the night lamp from the table and threw it into the wall. "here!"

"NO!"

The lamp hit the wall with such force, she heard the dry wall crack and heard the lamp shatter into a thousand pieces. Now she was stuck in complete darkness with a gun in hand that was useless if she could not see. All the terror she had been trying to fight was staring to over take her and win. The room was pitch black and its shadows were as thick as fog. Somewhere in the dark she heard a piece of broken glass crush under James's boot. Then everything went silent. Was he just toying with her? It was possible.

"Can you see in the dark Amanda?"

She heard his voice suddenly in her ear and she swung around to pistol whip him. But she caught nothing but air. Then she heard him chuckle.

"You can't hit what you can't see."

He was right in front of her

"No but if I fire in your general direction, I am sure to hit something."

Suddenly the room fell dead silent and Amanda paused in her movements to see if she could tell where James was. There were no sounds. Slowly she reached down with her free hand and slipped on her boots. She could not see them but she knew approximately where they were. Amanda slid from the bed and felt her way across the floor, heading for the closet. The room remained silent as she helplessly groped for her bag. Upon finding it, she jammed her hand in the bottom of it but found her shotgun gone. Her flashlight was also missing. She refused to play his game any longer. 'Ok, ready . . . one . . . two . . .three!' Amanda bolted from the closet, running for the window she knew was on the other side of the room. As she crossed the threshold from the closet to the bedroom, she tripped over something solid and fell hard on the wooden floor. A sharp pain shot through her free hand as it landed on a lamp shard and the gun in her hand fell, sliding across the room to the wall. 'Shit!' She was still on the floor when she felt cold steel pressed just under her chin and a sharp pain at the back of her head. James had grabbed her by her hair and was using it to help her off the floor. He had her own shotgun under her chin.

"Get up!"

Amanda said nothing. As he lead her down the hallway, she could feel the blood starting to trickle from the palm of her hand and down her fingertips. James let go of her hair momentarily and then she heard the sound of a door opening in front of her. Then she heard a click as a light was turned on to reveal wooden basement stairs. He gave her a slight push with the barrel of the gun.

"Walk!"

"James-"

Then he did something she had not expected, he stepped back away from her and kicked her in the small of her back. Amanda lost her balance and went tumbling down the stairs. It did not kill her but it did knock the wind out of her and she was in enough pain for her vision to blur momentarily. From her place on the floor, she watched him casually descend the stairs with her shot gun in hand.

"You know Amanda . . .I tried to be nice . . .I tried to be reasonable . . .but you," He paused to crack his neck on one side. "well you just can't play nice."

James was standing over her now as he spoke. In the light she could see the blood on his bottom lip. That animalistic look had returned to his eyes and the tension had returned to his muscles. What bothered her the most was the way he was so casual about the whole situation. It almost qualified him for sociopathy. Although he had the upper hand, she was still trying to figure out how to get her gun back from him or at least how to get away from him.

"James please . . ." A tear rolled down her cheek now.

"Please . . .let me go home . . .you'll never see me again. I promise."

"Shut up. I'm not letting you go anywhere so you can just knock that shit off right now."

With that he grabbed her by her hair again and drug her over across the concrete floor to an old mattress sitting in the corner of the cold, dingy basement. There were shackles permanently attached to the floor. Amanda wondered to herself, if he had done this before or if he had been planning this. Everything was happening so fast that she barely had time to decipher her new surroundings. She was looking for tools that might help her escape. That was when she noticed the two metal shelves full of boxes, filled with random items. There was a chance she could find something useful in them. James shoved her down onto the mattress and held the barrel of the shotgun at the middle of her chest. She instinctively put her arms up by her head signaling her surrender and when she did that, she felt him lock cold metal around each wrist before shackling her ankles. Now she was shackled to the basement floor, on a dingy old mattress where he had possibly raped women before.

"What are you gonna do? Rape me?! Go ahead!"

"I'm not gonna rape you. I'm gonna wait for the storm to calm down and then the cops can deal with you."

As he said that, an unnerving smirk played at the corner of his mouth. He knew something about those cops. Somehow she had a feeling that they would not just arrest her. They would probably be the ones who made her disappear. All the anger she had just spewed at him, faded as she realized that she was in bigger trouble than she realized.

"James no . . .wait James . . .I'll do whatever you want . . .just please don't call them."

For a moment he paused, relaxing his grip on the shotgun and letting it hang loosely in one hand. This posture made all the muscles in his arm even more prominent than they were before. His tongue played slowly across his wounded bottom lip before a slow toothy smirk crossed his features. Amanda stared as hard as she could at him in the dim light and as she watched that smirk cross his features, she swore that his canines were longer. When her eyes met his, she could swear that his iris's were lined with blood. That was impossible and completely illogical. He slowly crossed the concrete floor.

"You'll do . . .whatever I want?"

He set the shotgun on one of the higher shelves and stripped his shirt off. For a few seconds she she could only stare at his incredibly toned and tempting physique. James knelt down on the end of the mattress and slowly worked his way up her body. The powerful muscles in his back and shoulders flex just beneath his perfect caramel skin. Amanda could see the tension in every move of his body. She dropped back against the mattress as he made his way up her small frame. James leaned down, his lips inches from hers as he spoke.

"James please . . .I'll-"

He pressed his finger to her lips.

"Shhh ..."

Then she felt his fingers gliding across the flesh of her stomach where her t-shirt had come up because of the position her arms were in.

"The price of your freedom is higher than you're willing to pay."

"Please . . .I'd rather deal with you...please."

"Oh, would you now?"

She felt that hand slip from her stomach, past her jeans and into her panties. His fingers came to rest on her soft, shaven flesh. Amanda gasp in shock as she felt his fingers spreading her folds and one finger begin rubbing across her sensitive pink bud. It was so sudden that she could not stop her legs from shaking or her body from quivering.

"Are you really willing to pay the price? You kicked me . . .remember . . .why should I not call them and tell them you threatened me?"

He was biting off his words now which was only making her more aroused and the exotic smell of him was filling her senses. Something in the cologne he was wearing or something in his scent tantalized her. When he voiced the question, she tried to come up with an answer for him, as she opened her mouth to speak, he shoved a long finger deep into her wet depths. It flicked and rubbed against her sensitive pink flesh, sending her into a torrent of shivers as she attempted to form an answer.

"I don't know!"

"Not good enough."

With that, he yanked his hand from her panties so quick that he left her throbbing and aching even worse than she had been before. When he stood up, stepping away from her, he forced her to watch him suck her juices from his fingers. Then he grabbed his shirt from the floor and the shotgun from the shelf and without saying another word, he headed upstairs.

"James please! James!"

Her cries for sympathy fell on deaf ears. James said nothing as he flicked the basement light off and slammed the door behind him, leaving her in total darkness. Everything had gone from bad to worse in a matter of a few hours. How had she managed to screw things up this quickly? She should have just pulled the trigger the first time and splattered his brain all over the wall. There was no use dwelling on what she did not do. Now she needed to devote all her energy into getting free.

For a few moments she lay there in the dark, hoping her eyes might adjust enough for her to see but this darkness was too thick. So she closed her eyes and let her other senses take over. Above her she could not hear any sound to inform her of James movements. The wooden floor did not creak, she did not hear the sound of the heat kicking on or the wind outside. It was silent, nothing but darkness and silence. Amanda moved her wrist, trying to see if she could wiggle her arm free. But the shackles were tight and they prevented her from even sliding her wrist around inside of them. In the solitude of the basement, her mind filled with thoughts.

'*We should have never come here. We should not have stayed with him or even remotely considered it. We're gonna disappear and-WAIT! The hospital is expecting us, someone will come looking for us!*' There was a glimmer of hope than began to grow in the back of her mind. It was possible that someone might come looking for her. It was just enough hope, to give her the power to fight for her life. As far as she was concerned, her life was in danger at the moment and she certainly would not go down easily. She had to try. Amanda moved her feet a little bit to see how loose the shackles on her ankles were. They were even tighter than the ones on her wrists. So she went back to fighting with her wrists again.

The shackles on her wrist would move more if she had something to loosen them or they would pull her skin off. She leaned over as far as she could and started licking the bottom of her hand. When she thought she had enough saliva on the bottom of her hand to slide her wrist more, she started to pull her arm downward. At first it was slow going and her hand almost got stuck on its slide down. After a few moments she managed to get her right hand free. With one hand free, she began the process of freeing the other hand. Again, she drooled on her own hand in order to get herself free from her restraints. Amanda managed to pull her other hand lose and then she began the process of trying to free her ankles.

There was no way she could free her ankles as easily as she did her hands. Amanda knew she would need something to help her get the shackles off her legs. She crawled through the darkness on her hands and knees, until she reached the shelves. The chains scraped across the floor as she groped her way through the darkness.

It amused him to watch her pathetic attempts to get herself free. He would allow her to succeed and run about the town for a while. There was no where for her to run or hide. His brothers would assure that she would never make it out of this place. For now, he watched her through the eyes of the shadows as she desperately crawled through the darkness. He gave the command for the shadows to keep their distance. Let her move about freely. In a matter of a few days she would be writhing desperately beneath him as he tasted her blood and felt her flesh. A smirk crossed his features before he made his way back through the shadow realm and headed upstairs.

She started padding down the shelves to see if she could find any tools or even a flash light. During her search, she accidentally hit a box and sent it crashing to the hard concrete floor. It landed with a loud crash and she heard several items skid across the floor. 'Shit' For a few minutes she did not move, just sat there staring in the direction of the basement door and listening for foot steps. When she was sure James had not heard her, she began to search through the items that had fallen.

She felt an old metal pipe, some wiring, a couple bolts and then she managed to find a small mag light. A small cry of joy almost escaped her lips when she turned the end of it and it lit up. Now she searched the boxes for a screw driver to help her pry the shackles open. Amazingly she found one at the bottom of one of the boxes. Amanda held the flash light in her mouth as she sat on the mattress and tried to pry the shackles open. At first she could not even manage to get the screw driver head between the two pieces of metal that the made up the shackle. After a little working, she managed to get the head just barely between the thick metal.

It was about ten minutes of struggling before she could get the shackle to let her ankle loose and she had to crank the screw driver so hard that she made her ankle sore. In total, it took her twenty minutes to get free from her restraints. She did not even bother to put the tools up, he would know she was gone when he woke up in the morning. As she made her way slowly toward the stairs, pointing the light to the ground in order to not give away her movement. Amanda had more than enough of this place. Screw the job, screw the house and screw this town.

Slowly, she ascended the stairs, careful not to make them creak. Amanda gripped the door handle with a sweaty palm and slowly turned it. The door groaned as she opened it and she paused for a moment to make sure that she had not drawn attention to herself. When she heard nothing after what seemed like forever, she slowly made her way out of the basement and toward her room. The plan was to grab her things and leave...

Chapter 18

For the first few minutes of freedom, Amanda crouched on the stairs. It was dead silent in the basement and in that silence an eeriness crept over her, starting at the base of her spine and moving up to the back of her neck. The feeling was no where and everywhere at the same time. It enveloped her, suffocating her, drowning her in panic. Somehow, she was alone in that basement but she felt an invisible presence. Was this house haunted too? She wondered. A chill now worked its way through her and made the flesh on her arms goose bump. She shuddered trying to shake the feeling away but it clung to her like a bad after taste in the back of her mouth. What was wrong with this place? Well, she knew what she thought was wrong but she had a feeling there was something just underneath that wrong, something darker and more sinister. Whatever was making her uneasy, gave her cause to turn around and look behind her. There was nothing but darkness. The darkness seemed to move and shift. It was impossible, shadows and darkness were not sentient beings. They could not move on their own. Before her very eyes she watched them weave and snake around on the very stairs she was sitting on. The darkness was starting to wrap around her legs, like vines of some large plant or deadly black serpents. There was no where for her to go to, she could not move from that place just yet. She had no idea where James was and she dared not risk running out of the basement and right into him. She had nearly forgotten about the flashlight in her hand. A feminine voice that was not her own, whispered to her, advising her. '*Point it at the shadows.*' They hissed as if they heard the voice as well. Amanda followed the phantoms advice, aiming it at the shadows that were wrapping around her ankles.

That time she unmistakably heard their hisses of protest. The flashlight was helping to keep them at bay just enough to calm her. What would she do when the light ran out? When she had no way to keep the shadows from touching her? There was no way she could stay in this basement all day. She also could not keep the darkness at bay and keep an eye on him until he left. James needed to leave, she needed him out of the house. When she turned back to look out through the crack in the door, she saw James standing in the kitchen.

A few seconds ago he was not there and now he was washing his hands. When he turned around, there was a tendril of thick, dark red liquid running from the corner of his mouth. She could no longer deny that it was blood. It was the second time she had seen it and she had a small notion that it was not his blood. '*But why would he be drinking blood?*'

Time seemed to pass in slow motion as she watched James pick up the kitchen rag and dry off his still blood spotted hands. Amanda shifted nervously as his tongue licked the last of it from the corner of his mouth. This James was more dangerous than she thought. He was not afraid to kill or possibly even torture. For all she knew, he could be sexual predator, a serial rapist. The thought was enough to make her shudder and her blood run cold. Some part of her wanted to cry, she was choking on terror but if she let it over come her, she would be a dead woman. Other than anger (if she could muster it) emotions would do her no good.

Amanda shook the fear from her mind as James wiped his mouth with the hand towel he had just dried his hands on. Was her mind making up ridiculous fantasies to make him out to be worse than he was? Or was her subconscious picking up on something that she was unaware of? 'You're just going by what you see.' There was still room for doubt. As it was highly possible the blood she had seen was not from another human. Although she could push out the unfounded thought that he was drinking blood. What she could not ignore was the red tendril that had been at the corner of his mouth. She knew what blood looked like in its many forms. So she knew that there was no way she could sit and deny what she saw. There were many reasons for that to be there. It was possible that he got hit in the mouth. 'When? By who? The storm has been going on for the past few hours now and no one can get through that mess. Not even you in the jeep.' A bar room brawl might explain the blood but he had no way to leave the house and in her drive around town, she had not seen a bar. There was no other reason for it.

As she crouched somewhere within the doorway of the basement, she wished that he had shown his true colors earlier and saved her from becoming trapped in his house. Men like him (psychotics, maniacs, sociopaths) never let the monster out of his cage until they have you where they want you. Until the storm died down and he left the house, she was stuck in that dark cellar. The advantage of all of this was that she would have time to come up with a proper plan to leave this place and disappear off their radar. Their, they, why was she thinking in multiples? Was she actually considering the cops as an issue? Then again, could she really ignore their unusual behavior? At this point it was best not to throw anyone out as a suspect.

James paused in his movements, he could feel her eyes as she peered at him through the crack in the door. He knew she was slowly starting to catch onto what was really happening. Eventually they all did but they were always too late. Even if they knew in the beginning there was nothing they could do about it. Still she was smarter than the last one, he would have to move up the timeline.

Now Amanda watching him casually pace back and forth from the kitchen to living room. It was as if he was waiting for someone or something. Was he killing time until the storm died? What was it that had him so agitated? Even in his pacing movements, he walked with the confidence of a man who was very pleased with himself. There was something else in his movements as well, he moved quicker, smoother almost. It was almost as if he was in the world but not at the same time. Somehow he seemed to move out of time, his movements were too fluid and quick. None of it was natural. He some how seemed inhuman at this very moment.

James turned on his heels and headed in her direction. If she had paid closer attention, she might have seen the blood on his shirt. Amanda gasped and moved back from the edge of the door, afraid he might have seen her. Her heart thumped against her rib-cage She whispered to herself, to the darkness, to god himself.

"Please go away. Please, please, please."

She swore she heard a giggle in the dark. Was it laughing at her misery? He paused when he turned toward the bedroom. The smell of her fear was intoxicating, it tempted his inner beast and he fought to keep it down. All in due time, she would be his. James felt a growl forming in his chest.

Amanda leaned forward and peered through the crack in the door. Why was he just standing there? He lifted his head and awkwardly adjusted his posture, cracking his neck. James rolled his shoulders and sighed before pulling his shirt over his head. She swallowed hard as an unwanted heat began to grow between her thighs. The affect this man had on her was unfounded. Fear and arousal had become common emotions for her. Now they were almost indistinguishable to her. She watched him step out of his room with a shirt thrown over one bare shoulder. The muscles of his powerful chest flexed with every step. James turned, headed through the kitchen, throwing the shirt on the counter and headed upstairs. For a little while she heard nothing and then she swore she heard a growl, like some animal readying for attack. After that the sound of a woman whimpering, then crying and finally a thud as something hit the floor. When he came back down, there were tendrils of blood running down his stomach. Amanda clasped a hand over her mouth to stifle her gasp. He nonchalantly grabbed a hand towel and wiped his chest off before zipping his fly. 'What did he just do?' She had a feeling she did not want to know.

James grabbed the comb he had tucked in his back pocket, using it to slick his hair back with a little water from the kitchen sink. Then he slipped on the black long sleeve shirt he had thrown on the counter. He buttoned and tucked it into his jeans. Oddly enough he reminded her of a backwoods preacher, the fire and brimstone type. Amanda knew better. Like all great evil men, he was charismatic, eloquent and convincingly innocent.

He disappeared from her field of vision and when he returned he was carrying something. It was a pack of cigarettes. She did not think he smoked but apparently she was wrong. Turning around, he leaned backwards against the counter and pulled a cigarette from the pack with his lips. Then he flicked open a silver Zippo with one flick of his wrist, tilted his head and as he did, he looked up in her direction. Amanda stopped breathing the second he looked her way and she felt her heart start pounding in her chest. Had he seen her or heard her? Was he looking right at her? She swore that he winked at her before lighting the cigarette and flicking the Zippo shut. The whole process took a matter of seconds but it reminded her of the James she left behind. She shuddered at the thought before swallowing tears.

All memories of him only brought her pain. With her free

hand, she ran her fingertips across the spot on her cheekbone where he had split her skin with a hard fist. Amanda slid her fingers to her lips, grazing them across their chopped surface. She swallowed a lump of tears before raising her eyes to look at James. That would not happen again.

From her place on the stairs, Amanda watched him smoking the cigarette and pacing. All the while wondering if he knew she was no longer chained down and if that was the case, she wondered how he knew. James ashed his cigarette in the sink before she heard the sound of his boots crossing the floor back toward the living room and listened to the firewood hiss as he shoves another wet log into the flames. She carefully cracked the door a little more and listened. Amanda listened past the fire, past her own breathing and she searched for the sound of the storm. There was nothing. The wind had all but died down to a manageable breeze. As far as the snow, she could not see outside to tell if it was still snowing or not.

Before she could try to peak her head out and look out a window, a shrill ring pierced the silence of the house and echoed off the wooden structure. Somewhere in one of the rooms beyond her vision, there was a phone. She heard James's boots cross the wooden floor and then heard him answer the call. As she crouched and listened, the smell of cigarette smoke drifted into her nostrils and she had to fight the urge to gag. Even as many times as she had been around her ex when he was smoking, she never could stand the smell of it. In order to hear better, Amanda decided to take a stupid risk. She slowly opened the basement door and then carefully closed it as to not make any sound. Then she slid across the floor on her knees and crouched at the end of the hallway, with the flashlight turned off and tucked in one hand. If she had to, she could possibly injure him with the light.

"Yeah . . .No . . .I've got the bitch chained up . . .yeah. I'll be there soon . . .I figured he'd give you shit . . .no no . . .she has no idea it was not him . . .don't worry, I'm gonna keep it that way. He'll be dead soon anyhow . . .yeah . . ."

She heard his boots pounding harshly against the oak floorboards as he moved towards the door.

"I'm leaving now . . .yeah . . .bye."

He pulled on his leather coat and a black beanie, then headed out the door. 'Who was he talking about? Who's gonna be dead? James? MY James? Can't be. Who was he talking to?' It did not matter. She needed to get out of there as soon as humanly possible. Even though every part of her wanted to just leave, another part of her wanted to follow him and for some reason she had a distinct idea of where he was going. When she was sure he was gone, she hurried from the basement, ran into her room with the flashlight blazing and threw on some more clothes. Then she grabbed all her things and dashed towards the door. Amanda was almost to the front door when she heard the key sliding into the lock. James was coming back into the house. Had he had forgotten something?

Almost slipping on the wet wooden floor, she hurried for the hallway and just barely made it into the closet in her room before James opened the door. Amanda hugged her bag to her chest as she heard his hard footsteps moving her way. Amanda flicked on the flashlight, aiming it toward the rear of the closet to keep the majority of shadows at bay. She carefully set the back on the floor and slid it in front of the crack under the door. It would be just enough to keep him from seeing any light that might leak out. She heard him move down the hallway to his room and so she slowly let out a sigh. Suddenly, she heard his boots stop and turn. He was headed her way but then he stopped short and she heard him fiddle with the handle of the door. Finally she heard the sound of a key sliding into a lock and the click of the lock as it secured the basement door. He gave it a couple hard tugs to be sure it was locked tight. A small smile of victory crossed her features as she realized that he still thought she was tied up. Or he was playing that he did?

Of course he would play along. This was all part of his intricate plan. He did it with all of them.

The sound of his foot falls seemed to march in rhythm with her heart beat as she heard him head into his room and then for a bit she heard nothing. After a while she heard him head for the front door and she grabbed her bag, ready to move at any moment. Timing her movements with the sound of the door closing and locking, she moved stealthily toward the guest room door. Only when she heard the low rumble of his truck did she sneak quickly down the hallway and crawl on her stomach toward the front door, the beam from her flashlight bounced awkwardly as she moved. With the light from the dying fire in the living room, James could have seen her if she stood up.

At this point Amanda wanted so badly to be brave and to just charge out of the house and right to the jeep. She wanted to ignore the terror that she had been fighting and just pretend she was not afraid. But she was terrified. This was not something she had faced before and she had nothing to defend herself. How had things gone so badly so quickly? As she sat with her back to the front door waiting to hear his truck pull away she felt a single tear slide down her cheek. At the realization of this tear and the acknowledgment that it was in fact a tear and not water. She began to cry. It had finally caught up with her. All the feelings she had been fighting off were now taking over her and she was sitting on the floor with her knees pulled to her chest, tears streamed down her face, her whole body shook and she could not get herself to stop. Amanda wanted to give up, she wanted to just stop fighting and let James do whatever it was he wanted to her. It was not because she really had a desire to sleep with him, it was purely for the fact that she was afraid and exhausted.

The fighter in her screamed for her to get off the floor, to stop crying and to fight. She was so tired, afraid and alone. Amanda was up against impossible odds, she knew it, they knew it and she had no idea how she would get out of it. Even with what she had seen so far, she wondered if things really would not be that bad. Somewhere a voice said 'don't be so stupid.' She wanted to just let the darkness pass over her and to give in. Maybe it would not be so bad if she just gave up and let him have her. To just let everything take its course and not to fight anymore. As she sat there contemplating throwing herself into the fire and letting it consume her, a curious thought hit her. Before she knew what she was doing, she was heading back toward the hallway and into his room. Amanda reached for the light switch, flipped it and found that there was now a bulb in the overhead light. So she grabbed the flashlight that she had found in the basement and stuffed it into her bag. Then she began to poke around his room. What was she looking for? That was a question she had no way to answer. When she picked up the gray t-shirt he had worn earlier, she found it covered in blood. It looked as if he had murdered someone. Amanda started frantically picking up clothes that were strewn across the floor and on every other article she picked up she found blood.

The room started to spin and she felt light headed. It was not the sight of the blood that was bothering her, it was the thought that she might just have caught the attention of a serial murderer and now had no way to hide. She took slow deep breaths for a few seconds and eventually managed to calm herself down. Then she started for one of the drawers in the nightstand. Amanda was not even sure what drew her attention to it, all she knew is that she needed to get it open. To her surprise it was not locked and it was fairly easy to pull open. Inside of a small drawer at the bottom of the night stand, Amanda found drivers licenses of different women. All of them were around the same age at the time the license was valid but some of the licenses dated back to the 60's. 'Wait a minute! He could not be that old, could he?' The more she looked through the drawer, the more she found. There were wedding bands, earrings, car keys and various other items. All of them appeared to be from female victims.

Amanda felt her stomach turning as the room threatened to spin again as she felt terror clamp its icy hand around her heart. This could not be happening. When she slammed the drawer shut and started to stand up, her whole body was shaking. The tears were streaming down her face again. She had not even realized that she was crying until a single tear dripped onto the wooden floor. With flashlight still in hand she backed slowly out of the room as if the drawer was going to pop open and all the various items would come flying out at her. The bulb above her began to flicker on and off. In the space between the light she heard a hiss and a cackle. They were laughing and waiting, the shadows. As she yanked the light from her bag and flicked it on, the overhead went out. She was plundered into darkness again. In the beam of light that just barely pierced the darkness of the room, she saw something dash through it. For a second she thought it was a bat or maybe even her imagination. Then she saw it again. It looked like a sentient shadow was flying about the room on its own. Amanda watched for a few minutes more and that was when she realized the shadows around her were moving again.

Something in her told her to 'run' and at the sound of her

internal voice yelling, she turned on her heals and ran out of his room and toward the door. She really needed to get out of that house, to figure out where he went at this hour of the night and who was on the phone. Although some part of her told her to leave, she knew she had to find answers to her questions. There were more now that she had been through his room and found the things she found. As she unlocked the door and grabbed the handle to leave, she swore she heard someone say something behind her. So she turned around and peered into the darkness of the hallway. Some how the dark of the hall had gotten darker and thicker. The shadows now seemed to breath. Amanda knew she heard the low sound of someone or something breathing. It was the second time in this house that she had heard breathing that was not her own and had no source. The first time she heard it, she was not entirely sure she had heard anything. Now she was certain she had heard breathing. For a second she glanced at the stairs and considered trying to get into one of the bolted rooms up there. Then thought better of it, considering the fact that the shadows in the stairs seemed themselves to move in the dying light of the fire.

If she stayed any longer, she would be left in complete darkness in the house. So she ran out into the bitter cold of late night. The snow was piled in drifts all across the porch and around the driveway. She would have to engage the four wheel drive to get out of the driveway. As it blew, the wind seemed to cut through every layer of clothing she had piled on and into her very core. At least the Jeep would provide shelter from the cold and in a little while she could turn on the heat. She tucked her head down as much as she could within her jacket and headed for the Jeep. To her surprise, her keys were still in her jacket where she left them and the lock on the door was not frozen shut. Amanda tossed her bag in the back before climbing in and starting the engine. Then she put it in reverse and managed to back out of the drive way.

As she shifted into four wheel drive, she thought about the turn of events in the last few minutes. She still felt the urge to curl up in a ball and cry. Or just let him take her. At the same time she was hoping to blow the lid off what ever messed up thing was going on in his house and this town. It would be easy just to give up and let him win. All her problems might just disappear or they might multiply.

She knew what she really should do. Ignore all the nagging questions and just get out of that town. Forget even calling the hospital. Amanda needed to go back to her parents for a bit and disappear from the rest of the world entirely. It was easier to deal with blood thirsty wolves everyday than to deal with this mess. Following the fain tracks in the snow, she turned right at the end of the street. She followed a narrow pot hole filled street for about two miles before she found herself in front of a colossal structure.

The dream she had about this place came rushing back to her and suddenly she knew a back entrance where she would not be seen. Slowly, she drove by the thick gate that had a large sign on it which read *"No Trespassing. Violators will be arrested."* Sitting almost right in front of the gate was a Collins Sheriff's car. There appeared to be no one in it but parked just beside it was James's truck. Sometimes she was so right that she even scared herself. Amanda headed just past the factory and turned down an alleyway where she parked before making her way around the back side of the building. On this side she managed to find a small hole within the brick wall that surrounded the place and she slipped inside. To her surprise there was less snow piled up around the factory than there was anywhere else in the town. The snow crunched softly under her feet as she cautiously made her way toward the doorway with no door attached to it. Before even ascending the three stairs that would take her inside, Amanda knew exactly what room she would find herself in when she put her foot through the door. So how did she dream about a building she had never before seen? That question would probably never be answered.

Somehow the factory inside was colder than it was outside and as she moved through the room she felt her whole body goose bump. Amanda had a feeling she was close to James and at least one of the creepy officers whom she had run into. She made her way across the room with all the equipment and followed the wet footprints toward the other room she had not seen in the dream. When she got to the doorway, she paused because she heard the sound of voices. Someone was cursing, someone was threatening and then she heard a loud thud. From her place by the doorway she could see someone tied up to a chair and someone else had kicked the chair backwards. There were two silhouettes moving around the seated figure. It was too dim to figure out who was who but when the more shadowed of the two spoke, she knew who it was. So what was James doing here and who was in the chair?

The other figure moved and lifted the chair back on its legs with one hand before landing a hard fist to the side of the victim's head. When he moved away from the figure in the chair, Amanda had to slap her hand over her mouth to keep the whimper in her throat. Her James was tied up in a metal chair with blood pouring from his mouth, a gash just above his eye and several cuts across his face. She could not piece together what she was seeing. Is that who they were gonna kill? But why? He had not done anything to them as far as she knew. She sat there listening and trying to figure out what was going on.

"Just kill the fuck already."

The other figure spoke.

"I'm not done fucking with him yet. I want him to know that Amanda is ours now. Even if he could move, he can't do shit about it."

"F-fuck you . . ." James said through bloody spittle.

The two figures turned toward him and then the other one she did not know, kicked the side of his chair so hard that he flew across the room and hit the wall hard enough for it to crack. The amount of force that he kicked that chair with was impossible for even the strongest man to exhibit. There was no way she had seen that. This had to be a dream or even a nightmare, but it was not. Other James walked over and picked up the chair with one hand before walking over and setting it back down in the same spot. Somehow her James was still mildly conscious but probably would fade quickly if he did not receive medical help. She knew his ribs were probably shattered and a concussion was possible. He hit the concrete wall hard enough for his head to collide with it. Amanda decided she had to get a better look at what was going on so she slowly started to move further into the room. As she was quietly sliding along the wall, the other unidentified figure was moving toward her James.

Then she heard what sounded like an animal growling and the guttural sound of blood pouring into someone's throat. When she looked up, she saw her James twitching and the unidentifiable figure appear to be biting his neck. The faceless figure jerked back violently, tearing the entire front of his throat before spitting it onto the floor. There was blood pouring from the hole where his throat had been.

Strands of flesh, muscle and what was left of his trachea, hung pathetically from the gash in his neck. An endless stream of blood poured down his esophagus and chest. Amanda listened to the sounds of him drowning in his own fluids. He gasped desperately for air as the thick red liquid slowly filled his lungs. She heard him cough twice before his body finally went limp. Amanda had wanted him dead, she had prayed for it, but not like that. She knew it took about five minutes for a person to choke to death on their own blood.

Amanda gasped before she could stop herself. The other James leaned his head up as if he might have heard her and when he turned around and looked right at her, she knew he had. Before he could say anything, she scurried up from her crouching position and nearly slipped on the steps on her way out the door. Suddenly she heard a noise behind her and she turned to look for source. She ran into a solid figure. It felt like she had hit a brick wall. She bounced off of it and fell into the snow. Looking up from her position on the ground she found James hovering over her.

"Shit!"

Amanda tried to get up and head back for the factory so she might hide but she ran into another figure. This one did not knock her down but she did back away. Still dressed in a bloody uniform, was Officer Miller. There was blood both corners of his mouth and something was different about the color of his eyes. The irises were luminescent blue and appeared to be outlined in blood. She backed away from him, glancing over her shoulder every now and again to see where James was.

"Come on Amanda...make this easy on yourself." Miller said.

"It will feel so good if you don't fight."

Suddenly James was whispering in her ear.

'How did he sneak up on me so fast?'

"Fuck you both!"

She tried to dash out from between them and toward the small gap in the gate but Officer Miller was fast. Before she could get more than two feet, he was on top of her and she could feel his knee pressing into her back as he tightened handcuffs around her wrists.

"Get off me! Let go of me!"

Amanda was yanked, not so gently, to her feet. James was standing no more than a few inches from her. When he reached for her, she fought against her captor but Miller held her firm. No amount of movement from her could sway his grip. His hands felt like iron claws as they dug into the soft flesh of her biceps, holding her still for whatever James intended to do. Those long fingers that she had stared at and fantasized about so vividly now ran slowly down her cheek and across her neck. Then James wrapped his hand around her throat and squeezed it just enough to let her know how easily he could crush her windpipe.

"I promise you . . .you'll come around. All the other girls did . . .or you'll beg to die before we're done with you."

She wanted to utter an insult, to give him some attitude and show him she would not be swayed by threats. The hand on her throat made her think otherwise. James released her as if nothing had happened and he nodded his head to Miller who drug her kicking and screaming toward the cop car out front. As they headed around the building she noticed the red and blue lights that were bouncing off the brick wall and the factory. How did he call for back up that quickly? She never heard him radio for anyone. Standing just outside his car with a cocky smirk on his face, was Officer Sterling.

"Let go of me! Help! Someone help me! "

"You can scream all you want darling, there's no one around to hear you." Sterling said.

When Miller opened the door to push Amanda into the car, she kicked it shut. Without warning he threw her against the car and slammed her head into the trunk. She did not see stars but she could taste blood in her mouth. What in the hell was going on around this place? Corrupt cops? Blood letting? Murder? This was not going to go unnoticed, she was sure of that. Amanda spat blood into the snow.

"Police brutality you stupid pig! I'll have your badge for that!"

"I did not see any police brutality. I just saw a bitch resisting arrest." Sterling replied.

"Fuck you too pig!"

Suddenly, Sterling pushed her up against the car, she could feel his erection brushing against the back of her thighs. Then he pulled a switch blade from his back pocket and flipped it open. It was now pressing dangerously into her neck.

"Come again?"

Amanda momentarily stopped breathing, as she felt that blade drag down the tender flesh of her neck. How was he getting away with this? They could not be the only cops around here. She needed to get a hold of county officers or even state troopers. Someone needed to know what these boys were up to.

Amanda said nothing.

"I can't wait to see if you come around . . . I'll enjoy playing with you..."

"You're not gonna touch me." Amanda just barely managed to say.

"Oh?"

Sterling said glancing at Miller. Then she felt him press the edge of that blade into her throat.

"I wouldn't move if I were you." Sterling said.

Miller move closer and he kicked her legs apart with one of his boots. She felt cold air rush up her shirt as Sterling pushed a leather gloved hand up her shirt and then slowly down into her jeans.

"Stop-"

Sterling pressed the blade a little firmer into her neck as she started to protest. Then she felt his leather gloved fingers sliding over her shaved flesh before finally she felt them rubbing her pink bud in slow circles. Amanda winced in disgust as she felt him push a finger into her wetting depths. Even though she did not want him to touch her, she could not deny what the leather did to her and she could not keep her body from reacting. After torturing her for a few minutes, Sterling stopped and before pulling the knife away from her neck, he whispered in her ear.

"You will give in . . .I can feel it."

With those last words he wiggled the hand that just violated her. Amanda tried to leap at him, she would find a way to hurt him even with handcuffs on. Miller grabbed her by her hair and shoved her hard into the cop car.

"Get in the fucking car!"

She kicked the back of the seat for a couple minutes before settling down. Just outside the window she watched the three men (if they were that) stand together talking. Every now and then they would glance her way. At some point she grew bored with watching them and then she heard the drivers side door open and Miller climb inside. As they pulled out of the factory lot, she glanced at James who winked at her with a smirk on his face that made her shudder. '*What the fuck did you just get yourself into?*' She knew she screwed up. Amanda had to figure out how she would get herself out of jail, figure out what really happened at the factory and get out of this town. Was it really worth risking her freedom to find out what was happening in Collins?

Chapter 19

Amanda knew there was no way she could break the handcuffs and manage to get out of this moving car. Besides that the doors in the back did not open from the inside. So unless she got them to open them somehow (and that was a risk in its self) without some help she would be escaping the confines of this car. Even if she did get the handcuffs off or maneuver them in front of her, she knew that the glass on the back windows would not break so easily. Also, assuming that Miller is paying attention (and she assumed he was) the first kick to the window would alert him and he would hit the breaks before she could execute the next kick. The thought had no more than passed through her brain when Officer Miller hit the breaks.

The sudden stop jolted her forward so hard she hit her head on the metal fencing and sent a jolt of pain through her already sore face. Amanda was quick to move away from the door that Miller was opening. She knew she had to be quick on her feet, she had to think fast and move fast. If she wanted to survive this ordeal. She should have grabbed her pistol from the bedroom floor. James probably already had it. He seemed to have inhuman night vision. The way he moved through the darkness, it was wrong. She shook her head, she needed to stay focused. Amanda could not let Miller get his hands on her again. There was no time to think, she knew if she did not act quickly, it would be too late. So, she decided to fight back. Although she knew there was a chance she would fail and they would beat the hell our of her or kill her. At least she would have the satisfaction of knowing she fought for her life.

In the few moments before she saw Miller's face, the memory of James came flooding back to her: all of the beatings, the words he said, his empty promises and finally what they did to him. It gave her the fire she needed. If she could not take her revenge on him, then she would take it out on them. They could taste the lead she had intended for him. 'Kick his teeth in!' Screamed a feminine phantom voice. The second he opened the door, she kicked both feet toward his face (intending to do just that) and she heard something crack. It sounded like she had broken a few teeth or even his nose. Not that it mattered any. The dirty prick deserved much worse than that. She wanted him to feel the pain he had inflicted on her. He reeled back away from her, blood dripping from his lips and ran from his nostrils before hitting the seat beneath her and coloring the fresh powder. Amanda heard the sound of the door behind her opening before she was yanked out of the car by the back of her coat. She fell hard into a snow mound on the side of the road. The cold rushed up the back of her shirt. It was just the shock her system needed to keep her motivated. From her place on the ground, she looked up to see, Officer Sterling hovering over her with the blade of a knife glinting in his fist.

"Shit!"

Amanda tried to somersault backwards and kick him in the groin or even the knee. The snow did not provide the footing she needed so she failed to execute the move properly. It made it too easy for Sterling to catch her foot and yank her onto her stomach. Then grab a hold of her hair and pull her to her feet before he grabbed her by her arms an tried to slam her against the trunk of the cop car. She jumped and kicked the side of the car, sending Sterling backward into the same snow mound he had dropped her into. While they were seemingly distracted, she struggled to her feet and started to run for an alleyway. There was a roar as James stepped on the gas and breezed past her. His truck skidded sideways, stopping just in front of her, blocking her path and giving Sterling and Miller just enough time to grab her again. Even with pain shooting through her arms from the grip they had on them and through her skull from Sterling holding her hair, Amanda fought. If they were going to take her in, they were going to have to fight to take her in. She had laid down once for a man and it did not gain her any sympathy. This time she would give them reason to hurt her.

Without warning she pulled her foot up and smashed it hard against Miller's kneecap. That made him grunt in pain but he did not move. Sterling slammed her head into the glass of the truck window, splitting her forehead and sending a tendril of blood running down the top of her nose. Amanda watched black and white stars bounce around in her vision. Through the blur of disorientation she watched James slid out of the truck. The two officers let go of her and she knew (from the tension in the air) that something far worse was about to happen. He grabbed her by the side of her face (gently at first) and stared into her eyes. There was a rage in his dark pools, unlink any anger she had seen before. This was different, deadly. She knew that look on his face, she had seen it before, it meant that pain was coming her way.

"When you don't cooperate Amanda,"

His voice was a growl.

"I have to hurt you."

"You don't have to do shit! You want to hurt me. It delights you, hell it gives you pleasure,"

She glanced behind him, instinct told her to   avoid direct eye contact with him and she listened.

"Fuck you James and your pigs."

There was a hint of amusement on her face now. Perhaps she surprised him a little. It did not last long though. James cocked his head to the side before leaning in and whispering.

"The question is sweetheart, how much pain will it take for you to learn your place?"

With that he threw her away from the truck. She landed about ten feet away, just barely managing not to knock her head on the ground as she slid another ten feet down the icy road. The handcuffs on her wrists sent a mild jolt of pain through them as they dug deeper into her flesh, creating shallow cuts. How had he managed to throw her that far without any effort? James had tossed her like a rag doll and his fellow companions never batted an eye. Was it adrenaline that game him the power to perform that feat? Not even the strongest human could have accomplished something like that. As if hearing her thoughts Miller spoke up.

"If you think that is impressive, just wait. You ain't seen nothing yet."

Amanda refused to allow herself to wonder what he meant. That was a dangerous road. Now, as she crawled backwards trying to find a way to get to her feet, the three of them moved toward her. James was suddenly standing over her, where a moment ago he had still been walking toward her. In just a matter of seconds he was hovering over her and then he pulled her to her feet and shoved her face first to the cop car, pressing her face down hard. The pressure on her jaw sent shockwaves of pain through her skull. She grit her teeth to keep the pain from her face. Then she felt the blade of Sterling's knife on her throat pressing dangerously into her flesh. Amanda stopped trying to fight them momentarily and pretended to be complacent. If she moved now, she might end up dead. Sterling's blade was pressing so hard into her flesh that any small twitch would cause her harm. She could still give them hell but not right now. For now, it would have to come in small bursts.

"Stupid little bitch,"

Sterling had her hair in his hand suddenly and a knife to her throat.

"You wanna kick me! Big mistake!"

Officer Sterling shifted the blade in his hand and now she could feel it pressing against the meat of her shoulder. Before he could start slicing into her James grabbed Sterling's arm and twisted his wrist backwards. She heard the bones snap and he grunted in pain. Then he pulled the knife from his limp fingers and she watched him stab it into the hood of the cop car inches from her face. The sound of metal scraping metal was deafening. The displays of strength this man was exhibiting, were not normal. They were borderline human and logically she knew they were impossible. 'What are they?' She could not see what was going on but she could hear them talking.

They were no longer exchanging words in English but some other language she could not distinguish. Slowly something inside of her stirred. Despite her theory that these three were something other than human and despite her feeling that they could easily destroy her. All these facts were pushed aside and what she was left with was raw emotion. Amanda did not try to rationalize her feelings this time. There were no logical or poetic thoughts this time. The emotion over took her, filling her veins with a white hot fire. She was not just angry, she was vengeful and bloodthirsty.

It was at this point she wished she had her gun on her. Amanda no longer cared about going to jail for killing the fake police officers. It did not matter if the rest of the world believed her. Nor did she care if she emptied a whole clip into James and left him to bleed on the fresh fallen snow. The vengeance in her would enjoy that. Something inside of her had awoken or had just completely snapped. Whatever was going on in her mind, it had killed the unmanageable lust she had previously felt for any of them. Even though she felt no want for them, she could feel a whisper of the lust lingering in the back of her mind. If she did not at least try to fight them off and she just let them take her, she would hate herself forever. The moment she felt the two officers pin her arms down to the cop car and she felt James starting to unbutton her pants, she kicked at his knee trying anything to get him away from her.

Unfortunately her little kick only served to annoy him. The result was her being yanked away from the cop car by her head and tossed into the side of the truck, leaving a dent in the door and a smear of blood. She felt her head slam against the metal door and her body shudder in protest. Amanda could feel her body trying to shut down on her. James's image was starting to blur as he moved toward her and she sank down the side of the truck. If she did not find a way to keep herself to stay awake she would lose consciousness soon. She had to get away from them. Amanda was certain something was fractured, she heard something in her face crack when she hit the truck the second time. That was good, she was grounding herself with medical facts. Analyzing her injuries would give her something to focus on and help her to stay awake. It was one of the first few things she learned in medical school. If the patient is suffering head injury, keep them focused on something to keep them coherent.

With her hands cuffed behind her back it made trying to stand more than difficult. When she shifted her eyes up to look at them, she felt her head swim and the cars around her started to blur. It was clear that she had some cranial damage and possibly internal bleeding. Her eyes rolled as she tried to stand up and her body teetered before she fell to one side. The three of them watched her struggling to stand up. Like a pack of wolves toying with their prey.

"It doesn't have to be this way Amanda..." James said.

"If you just cooperate all the pain will go away..." Miller continued.

They were like circuits switching off and on. When one sparked the other one already knew what to say.

"Do you really think I am that stupid? I have heard these same empty promises before. I obeyed. And the pain..." She spat blood in the snow. "it was never-ending."

Despite their offer and the throbbing pain in her head, Amanda was no where close to giving in. She would rather die in the middle of the street with a large gash in the side of her head then to subject herself to their torture. Upon trying to stand again her already shaky legs found a patch of ice and she slipped, nearly knocking her head on the truck again. 'Stay conscious Amanda. Get up! Keep your eyes on something! Focus! God damn it focus!' While she tried to will herself back into a more coherent mind, James and the other two began talking amongst themselves. The possible, mild concussion had left her unsure as to what language they were even speaking. She managed to catch bits and pieces of their conversation.

"We should just bend her over the squad car right now and take her here."

"What do you wanna do with her?"

"I've got a better idea . . .but first . . ."

James let his sentence trail off before looking up and smirking.

"We will have to teach her. She needs to learn her place here," He looked back at them. "twist her mind and Sterling get out your tools. This little bitch is not as tough as she thinks she is. By the end of the day, she'll be begging for it."

Amanda dreaded to find out what it was. In that moment she made a promise to herself, no matter how much pain they inflicted on her or what every else they did to her, she would not give up. She knew from experience that begging would not get her mercy. So she refused to waste her breath.

As she struggled to stand up (ignoring most of their conversation) her mind wandered back to her previous home and to the wolves that used to stalk across her back yard. Why in this moment was she thinking about them? On occasion when the wolves were dealing with a bigger prey, they had a tendency to just injure it a little bit and wait for the injury or blood loss to weaken it. Then when the timing was right, they would go for the kill and finally bring the creature down. So how was this thought supposed to help her? 'Do Not let them go for the final kill.' Amanda managed to get her vision to stop blurring and she finally looked around. The truck behind her was still running but her hands were still cuffed behind her back. If she could get inside of it though, lock the door and then work her hands in front of her, she could drive with her hands cuffed.

Amanda tried to run around to the other side of the truck but before she could even move more than a foot from her original position, James was on her. All she saw was a blur and then felt his hand on the side of her head and the bed of the truck hitting her fact. Her head bounced off the truck. It felt as if someone was trying to compress her skull but her brain throbbed on the inside, threatening to explode. Dull pain shot through her upper half and she grit her teeth to ignore it. She wanted to fight off the black sheet that was starting to take her. In her semi-consciousness she heard one of them speak.

"She's a tough one. This one might be even more fun to break than the last one."

Amanda wanted to say something but when she opened her mouth, only blood came out. Through her fading vision, she saw the red patches in the snow. She felt blood running down the side of her face, its bitter, copper taste lingered in her mouth. Slowly she slid down into the fresh snow beneath her and she knew her head hit the snow covered pavement but after that everything went black. When she finally started to regain consciousness, she barely wanted to open her eyes. A piercing light beamed down on top of her and every flutter of her eyelids sent white hot pain through her head. The first attempt to open her eyes failed miserably. She felt as if she had been hit in the face several times by an aluminum baseball bat. Amanda shifted a little, trying to will her body to move. Her limbs felt heavier than usual and the surface beneath her felt hard. She remembered the mattress being oddly firm but not hard and cold like the one she was laying on. Something was wrong. The last thing she could remember was being in bed. Everything after that was a blur. Amanda fought to keep herself from panicking. She concentrated on trying to get her body to move.

She tried to pull her arms under her so she could push herself up from the cold, hard surface. When she tried to pull her arms toward her, they would not move. That was a little worrisome. She knew she had to open her eyes. Despite the excruciating pain the light brought her, she slowly lifted her head. She had to figure out why she could not move. When she did open her eyes, she felt panic at first and then rage. Amanda was naked, bent over a steel table in a windowless room and her arms were each handcuffed to a different table leg. The light above her was blindly bright but at this point she was just happy there was a light so she could avoid the shadows she had see in James's house.

It's amazing what you start thinking about when you find yourself in an inescapable situation. At that moment all Amanda could think about was James tied in that chair in the factory with blood pouring from his throat. To see someone so strong be reduced to a broken and bloody man terrified her. If they could so easily bring him down, then she knew for a fact that even if she had managed to maybe hit Miller in the face and break his nose or injured Sterling, there was no way she could actually beat them. At least not without her gun. She had no idea where it was and she probably was not going to get free from them long enough to trek back to the house to look for it. Right now she wanted to kick James in the groin until she heard his pelvic bone snap. That would at least make her smile a little bit and maybe if he was seriously injured he would not slam her head into something again. No, he would send the other two after her. They would delight in causing pain for him. It would be worse than any pain she had felt before. There was no hurting one without retaliation from the other. What had brought the fire back to her veins? What part of her had lost its patience and made her want to rip him in half suddenly? She could figure that out later. For now she needed to at least try to get away from them, even if she only ended up hurting and regretting it.

The cuffs around her wrists were too tight for her to slip out of them so she tried to see if she could get her feet under her and maybe push herself to the other side of the table so she was at least standing on her own two feet again. When she tried to pull her feet up she found that they too were bound, they were shackled to the floor. This was not going to end well. In the very moment that thought popped into her head, she heard the only door to the room open with a large metallic squeak. To her injured skull that noise was a million jackhammers pounding into every part of her brain. Amanda braced herself for what might come next. Three sets of footfalls entered the room, one stopped just in front of her and the other two stopped behind her. She felt completely exposed, helpless and mildly disgusted. Some small part of her missed James at the moment because psychotic or not he would have still gotten her out of this situation. She heard the large metal door close with a bang and then the room fell silent. 'Whatever you do, do not scream. Do NOT give them any satisfact-' Her train of thought was derailed by an all too familiar hand running up her inner thigh.

Amanda shivered as she felt those long musician's fingers graze the apex of her thighs and send her body into arousal. It was not a wanted arousal, it was merely a bodily response and that was fine with her. They could have her body but they would not have her mind or her spirit. Those were hers. No matter how much they thought she belonged to them, she would never fully belong to them. Even if she died trying to get away or ended up so bloody her own mother would not recognize her, she would endure the pain because she would not give them the pleasure. If given the chance she would kill all of them and then leave town without talking to anyone. 'So fine you perverts, touch me, rape me, but you won't break me.'

'*Yes we will.*'

There was another voice in her head, it was not her own, it was a male voice and mildly familiar. This version of the voice sounded older with more wisdom than the voice but she was sure it was Miller. It sounded like him but with her concussion, she could not be certain. If she could have see his face she would have know sure she heard his voice in her head. That was impossible. People do not just hear your thoughts and then project a response into your mind. That doesn't happen. As she was trying to build up the fire she would need to survive this ordeal, those long fingers were starting to rub her delicate flesh. Amanda made sure to bite her lip to counter act the pleasure he was trying to stir in her nether regions.

'*Do Not fight it Amanda, you're only going to make this   worse. We can give you so much pleasure.*'

'*All these things I will give thee if thou will fall down and worship me. Is that right Satan?*'

'*Do Not make me force you again.*' His tone was threatening.

'*Again?*'

Before she even realized what was happening, she was no longer biting her lip and her legs were shivering from the long dexterous fingers now probing her depths. Every time she tried to cause herself pain to ignore what he was doing to her, she found that she had no control over her own body. Some how, someone or something was controlling her. 'It could not be, it's impossible!' That time she heard no response from the voice she could not truly identify. What was happening to her? The feeling of being out of control, of being completely unable to fight was too much for her and she felt tears running down her nose before dripping onto the table.

Her tears did not stop any of them from touching her. Amanda felt a second set of fingers rubbing against her swollen pink bud as the same familiar fingers continued to probe her inner depths. They were working in teams.

There was no getting free, no shutting it out, she could do nothing to save her sanity or try to stop them. Someone was in her head and two others were touching her. Even with the intruder in her head, she tried to concentrate on anything that would help her to ignore their touch. Suddenly the image of her James all bloody and broken on the cold concrete floor of that factory, came rushing back to her. It was not much but it was enough to help her keep from being sexually aroused by the perverted wolf pack now circling her. So she held his image in her mind as much as she could, even with the one still keeping control of her. 'Remember James, remember what they did to him.'

'Shut up!'

'Fuck you no! Remember how they beat him.'

'Stop it!'

'Fuck you I do not belong to you!'

'We will break you...just concentrate on the feel of their fingers in your tight wet pussy.'

'Ignore him Amanda! Ignore his vulgar words. Remember the blood pouring from James's throat-'

She suddenly felt as if her mind was splitting in two and the image of James's bloody body faded. Someone else was taking control of her mind and now she was back to being jello in their hands. Amanda was merely a piece of flesh for them to play with and to do whatever else they wished to do with her. For a few moments the hands violating her stopped and then she heard footsteps moving around her. They seemed to be changing places and then she felt different hands gripping her thighs. Amanda heard footsteps stop near the side of her head and she turned to look at them. Standing a few inches from her, dressed in a black shirt and jeans was Sterling. In his hand he kept playing with a switchblade, flicking it in and out. The small click of the knife was enough to make her flinch. But why? Would her really cut her? It seemed silly to ask that question.

Without warning she felt thumbs spreading her open and a hot, wet, tongue licked slowly around her inner folds. Amanda jerked violently against her restraints, which only incited a small chuckle from the other two.

"Yeah, get her." James said.

Then that probing tongue began to flick against her swollen pink bud. 'Mmm you taste so sweet.' The voice was in her head again. Amanda fought to ignore it and the tongue between her folds. At the same time she glared at Sterling with a 'fuck you' glimmer in her eyes. She let herself fantasize about breaking that blade off in his skull. Then she began to wonder if he would like a new hole to breath through. 'You like it when I touch you? '

"Shut up!"

The voice in her head was pissing her off and yelling at the voice with her own internal voice just would not be satisfying enough. So she screamed and her scream earned her more pain. Sterling grabbed a hold of her hair again, making her head pound as the knife was pressed to her throat. His interference was unnecessary because as soon as she protested, she felt a pressure on her mind. It forced the conscious thoughts (about Sterling's demise) from her mind and forced her to feel the tongue violating her. She could not escape it or ignore it. She was trapped in this torture until they had their fill of her. Amanda felt tears of desperation spill slowly down her cheeks. She knew the desperation was only temporary but it was still heartbreaking to feel this way. She was developing a plan to remedy this situation, now it was only a matter of time. For now she would stomach their torture and allow her pain to fuel her cause.

Chapter 20

The pain in her head was starting to overpower the forced pleasure. No matter what way she turned over the situation, it was still rape. In every aspect, they were raping her; of her freedom, her control, her body and her mind. Still there were portions of her they could never touch. They might succeed in breaking her spirit but that did not give them any right to touch her soul. The other part of her they would never touch. No matter what they did to her. It was a fairly new addition to her arsenal but it was very powerful. This thing was responsible for war, murder, vengeance and all the ugly parts of humanity. Like all great things it could be used for good, evil or in her case survival.

Some where back at that factory when they grabbed her it was born. That was the moment she first felt it and somehow she thought they knew it. They were unafraid, unshaken and out of disrespect (or some other reasoning) they chose to mock her. It was as if they were daring her to react. This thing inside of her had started small at first, but very rapidly it grew. As it developed it devoured her lust and swallowed her fear. This thing was not something she needed her mind or her body for, and this thing fed on pain. That was the fuel that kept it going. The thing growing in the pit of her chest that spread like a virus was something, none of them could kill. Not unless they killed her. If they did, she would welcome the freedom from this level of hell and in turn, would haunt these demons.

Amanda wanted to be the one woman they regretted kidnapping and torturing. Or the phantom from their worst nightmare. If they thought the ghost she encountered was bad, she would make her look like a saint. Of course these were only rage fueled theories based on her own observations. As she felt the pressure increase in her mind, she looked up at the creature (she was sure at this point was not human) and felt that dark, growing thing twitch inside of her. It wanted a piece of him. Hell, it wanted him in pieces so it could devour every last bit of him. Amanda could feel the control on her mind press harder and she pressed back now.

The dark little thing in her heart helped her ignore the pain. She had been pushed far enough, and now a fire had begin to build. It morphed into a hatred that quickly became vengeance. Everything else but that blood lust seemed meaningless. Only one thought remained, 'kill them all and anyone else who stands in your way.' Between the thoughts of anger, she still felt the tongue flicking and swirling around her swollen bud. His fingers continued to pump in and out of her depths. It was only a physical sensation but it brought her no pleasure. These sick twisted perverts would never coax a moan from her or an orgasm.

Again she felt that pressure on her and she used her hate to press back even harder. She was trying to hurt whoever and whatever was hurting her. Amanda did not just want to make them stop, if she could, she wanted to kill them with her mind. For a moment she felt control come back and it was so brief that it shocked her. She was quick to regain concentration. The throbbing in her head made thought almost unbearable. Still she pulled strength and ignored the pain long enough to project a thought to the mind controller.

> '*Take my body, rape my mind, keep my freedom. I am not like the other   girls you took, I will not cower or cry. I won't beg for my life. You still don't scare me. You'll never have all of me. You. Can't. Have. Me. Cut me, beat me, kill me. I'll never let you have me. You can go to hell!*

The mind controlling abuser, must have heard her because she felt everything stop, all at once. It could not have been because she was now planning to kill them and they knew it. That was not something she was thinking, it was something she felt. So maybe, after everything, she shocked them. Maybe they never expected that out of her.

Whatever it was, she suddenly felt them (the one with his tongue in her) stop touching her. As she lifted her head up and looked around, she heard the sound of something liquid, hitting the metal table. Amanda looked down and saw blood where her face had been. She realized her nose was bleeding. Amanda could only assumed that her little mental fight had something to do with it. At this point she did not care. After what seemed like an eternity of silence, Miller spoke.

"Let's try this a different way."

Without another word, she felt her legs being unshackled and then she watched Sterling unshackle her arms. Amanda had plans for him. When they pulled her to her feet, she used her hatred to keep herself standing, it gave her the power to overcome her current weakness. Although her arms felt numb, she still knew that they would work for what she was about to do. So when Sterling was in range, she balled up a fist and slammed it into the left side of his face. It felt as if she had just punched one of the concrete walls around her. She heard her knuckles crack and felt a sharp pain shoot from the bones in her hand, down her wrist. The equivalent of smashing her palm with a sledgehammer. Amanda shook her hand, trying to will away the pain and braced herself for the punishment to come. It was a hard enough blow to make him reel back. The assault only managed to piss him off. When he looked at her. It was not the same 'handsome' face she had known.

The look in his eyes was enough to halt her anger for a brief moment. There was something cold, distant and inhumane in them. They were like looking into the eyes of the corpse. It was as if her hit had knocked whatever soul he had, out of his body. A chill crept through her now, Amanda knew he was not dead, he was up and moving around, still she could not ignore the cold steel that was hidden in his gaze. 'How could his eyes look so old and so dead but his body be so young and strong?' She thought to herself. 'How did I not notice this before? Because you weren't paying attention.' She answered her own question as she continued to stare into that death like glare.

Before she could even try to move, he had her by the throat and she was flying through the air into the nearest brick wall. The sound of her back hitting the wall echoed with a resounding slap. Her back scraped against the course brick as she sank down the wall, leaving small scraped on her skin. She bit her tongue to keep from hissing in pain. Without the rage still coursing through her veins, she might have passed out from the pain. 'How the hell is he so quick? He is definitely not human.' She was holding her own mental conversations again, she had full control on her mind again. But as she slowly stood up-none of the three offering her help-there was a mocking response to her thought that was not her own.

'I promise, you will learn just how not human we are, unless you behave.'

Amanda looked up in time to see Miller smirk. She made a quick mental note of that before she turned back to Sterling. Again he came at her, his movements too quick for her to see. He grabbed her by her throat and this time she hit the metal door. Amanda heard her shoulder crack when she collided with the unforgiving solid steel. Again she grit her teeth, refusing to give him the satisfaction of hearing her cry out in pain. She may not have been able to stop them from hurting her but she could keep him from enjoying it. It took every bit of hatred she felt for them, but she managed to push past the pain and stand up once more. Even though every inch of her body hurt, she still had enough left in her to glare at them. Miller was the first one to say anything. He broke the silence with a mocking statement.

"Oh Sterling she is mad at you," He chuckled. "look at the fire in her eyes. She wants a piece of you."

Sterling flicked out a switchblade and started toward her.

"I guess she hasn't had enough yet. You want some more bitch? I'll give you more, more than you can handle."

James grabbed him by his shoulder and pulled him back. With one look, he made Sterling put the switchblade away.

"Not yet. No no no, we got plans for you sweetheart. Don't you worry about that. Depending on how you act, will determine how our plans play out."

She continued to glare at them, never backing down or flinching. Without warning, James grabbed her by the back of her fractured skull and pulled her face inched from his. Still she refused to blink or stumble. They would not make her flinch, even standing in front of them naked would not shake her.

"Think you're tough bitch? Think we won't break you?" He growled.

James let go of her, tossing her back as he did. Sterling smirked.

"We can show you more pain that you could ever imagine," He was fiddling with the switchblade again. "or we can show you more pleasure than you could ever dream of."

Amanda was not hearing a word they had to say.

"I'm gonna have fun with this one." Miller said.

"Look at that boys, I think she wants to hurt us. Can you see the hate in her eyes?" James said with a smirk

Let them mock her for now. She new she was not on even ground, three against one was not fair odds. For now she could spit insults and threats. Later, she would fill them full of lead and watch the light leave their eyes.

"I don't know what you are, I don't really give a damn. When this is over, one way or another, you three will be dead. I can promise you that. "

Sterling smirked and looked at James.

"What's the matter Sterling, you need permission?" Amanda mocked.

He turned on her and in the blink of an eye he had that blade pressed against her cheek.

"You wanna hurt me Amanda?" He drug the blade down her

face. "Really think you can kill me?"

"I will kill you Sterling. I promise I will kill all of you."

He leaned in her ear, his free hand squeezing her windpipe.

"Good luck with that."

Then he let go of her.

When she looked up, noticed Miller's eyes had changed. She was positive that they had become a blood red color. Before when she thought they changed, they still held their blue coloring. Now his whole iris was blood red. James turned from the group and headed for the door.

"Take care of this. You know what to do."

He padded Miller on the shoulder when he said it. Both officers looked at her as the steel door slammed shut. Its sound echoed in the empty space. A blur suddenly came flying across the room and something that felt like titanium struck the side of her face. The assault did not immediately knock her out. At first her vision only wavered and she watched their blurry forms approach. Then the black sheet of unconsciousness drifted over her and everything went black.

The first thing that she felt was cold. But it was not the type of cold you could measure on the thermometer, it was the sort of cold that touched the soul and shakes the nerves.

At first the hairs on the back of her neck stood up and then her body flushed hot-cold. This was a sensation that she knew all too well. It started in in the middle of her chest and spread to the rest of her in rapid waves. Terror was nothing new to her. Neither was panic. However this time, when she felt these emotions, she chose to ignore them. She was sure she was still unconscious. If she was, how was she aware of this feeling? Amanda reached up and started to rub her eyes in an attempt to wake up from her coma-like nap. Only after poking her eyes did she realize she was already awake and her eyes were open.

How long had she been out? How long had she been awake? 'Where am I?' She posed the thought cautiously to herself, fearful that someone else might be listening. After her last mental battle, she did not wish for another headache. The pain in her head was already excruciating and she was sure her skull was trying to split in two. It did not help that her head had also met the side of James's truck, shortly before her telepathic battle with what she suspected to be Miller. The throbbing pain in her head was bad enough to make her stomach turn. Amanda tried to fight it but there was no controlling her bodies natural reaction. All she could make out was the taste of bile in her mouth and throat as she vomited in the dark. It slapped against the floor with a moist mushy sound. Like wet dog food being dropped into a bowl. After a bit she could only dry heave.

For a few moments she just sat breathing in the dark, trying to calm herself. At least the wood floor beneath her was cold, it soothed her nerves and nausea. Now that her stomach had quit turning, she could try and figure out where she was and how to get out. Amanda slowly crawled back away from the pool of vomit on the floor and started crawling toward what she hoped would be a wall.

There was not one shred of light in the room. When she finally found a wall, she leaned against it and tried to calm her head. She knew her skull was fractured and she may have a few other injuries that she needed to address. Her first priority was to get free from these sex crazed, sadistic, murdering psychopaths. As she leaned there trying to get her head to stop throbbing, she stared into the thick dark of the room and tried to make out the area around her. It was too dark to see anything. There was no way she would be able to make out the room around her. Within the impenetrable darkness, something caught her eye. Amanda saw something move. She squinted her eyes, trying to see better. Whatever she was seeing, it slithered and coiled like a serpent in the dark. Then she started noticing other things moving in the darkness in a similar fashion. The shadows that tried to grab her in the basement, they had returned to torture her again. She was in no shape to handle them or anything else for that matter.

"Amanda . . ."

A deep, familiar voice whispered in the dark.

"Stay away from me!" She shouted into the dark.

"Wanna play . . ."

"Wanna play . . .wanna play . . ."

The voice whispered it once and several voices around her hissed the same phrase in a sick echo.

"No! You're not gonna touch me!"

"So much fun . . .when you scream . . ."

Only the shadows whispered   now.

"Shut up!" She screamed.

"You're so soft inside . . ." They chimed.

"No no no!"

She covered her ears to block out the voices.

"Let us touch you inside . . .deep inside . . ." The shadows hissed.

"Shut up!"

Amanda curled into a ball and held her hands over her ears for a while, rocking back and forth. 'I am losing it.' It was a full ten minutes before she realized that the room had fallen silent again. Slowly, cautiously, she pulled her hands away and lifted her head. Then she struggled to her feet and started sliding quietly along the wall in an attempt to find a door. She was sliding along when she realized that she could hear the sound of hard boots on wood stairs.

'*No!*' Even though her whole being protested the thought, she quickly realized that she could not stop what was happening.

There was the deafening sound of locks being unlatched on the door. When she heard the locks coming undone, she started backing away from its location. The sound of laughter pervaded the room and she almost screamed in horror. Before the door even opened, she knew who was on the other side. Amanda knew that somehow the shadows around her were alive. For whatever reason she also knew that they were related to him. The door creaked on its hinges as it was slowly opened and James's silhouette became visible.

The light from outside poured into the room, blinding her momentarily. It was a few moments before he said or did anything. Amanda stood there staring in horror at the man before her. She was afraid of him but not because of his physical body. It was the unexplainable things going on around her (that she knew had to do with him) that had set her nerves on edge. James seemed to be capable of impossible things. Still she knew that fear was not an option. No matter what happened, she could not allow herself to feel that. When he finally moved, she realized that the telepathic intruder, she had battled, must have told him of her thoughts because he responded to her threat now.

"We don't care if you are afraid of us. But you should be. You have no idea what we could do to you."

He paused and licked his lips, smirking.

"Do you really believe you can fight us and win? Oh, how I would love for you to try. It will make the game so much more interesting. Besides, you taste so much better when you're afraid. At least that's what Miller told me."

She wanted so back to hit him, or tell him to go to hell. Something made her decide better of it. Again, he paused and before she could flinch, he had her up against the wall by her throat. She could feel his bare muscular chest up against hers. That, however, was the least of her concern. James had her throat in his palm and was holding on enough to let her know just how easily he could snap her windpipe.

His voice was deeper this time. It was almost not human and she could swear his eyes were blood red, just like she swore Sterling's eyes had turned.

> "We really don't give a damn about having you. Not in the way you think. We just want pieces of you, certain arts . . .the parts that are useful to us. Keep your fucking soul. We stopped caring about souls years ago . . ."

When he spoke again, his tone was slightly softer.

> "And as far as 'you not giving in' . . .I can promise you, when we're done with you, you'll be begging for us to touch you," His voice became a whisper. "or you'll beg for death."

Then James tossed her toward the darkness and she felt things wrap around her arms and legs, pulling them apart as far as they could go. The door behind James slammed shut with an ear shattering bang. If she was not afraid before, she was now. There were shadows holding her legs open for him, in some perverted bondage scenario. How was she supposed to fight shadows? This whole event sickened her. It was the same sickness she felt for a rapist or a child molester, complete and utter disgust.

> "Mmm . . .there's the fear I was looking for."

> "Don't fucking touch me!"

> "Oh, Amanda I am going to do more than just touch you. I am gonna make you scream."

When the light was no more, and the darkness enveloped her, the shadows came alive. They hissed their twisted words as he began to touch her. At first it was just her thighs. James gently ran his strong hands up them and then when he reached the corner apex of them, he dug his thumbs in hard. The jolt of electric pleasure and pain tingled up through her body from her womb. Amanda's whole body shuddered and pulled against the tendrils of shadows that held her. She tried to gather her thoughts (to gain some footing) about her situation, James pressed harder on those pressure points. Another jolt of electric pleasure and pain mixture shot through her even harder now. Amanda bit her lip to keep from giving him any knowledge of her enjoyment. Again he pressed his thumbs harder into the pressure points that were causing her to shake so hard.

Somewhere in the back of her mind, she fought against the pleasure controlling her body. Amanda was trying to find the hate she had before but something was blocking it. When he finally stopped she let our a shuddery breath. Suddenly, from no where and everywhere she heard his voice around her.

"Don't fight this Amanda . . .you know you're enjoying it."

It was true, her body was responding but she was determined not to give in. Now she could feel him standing behind her, she could feel his warm muscular chest on her back and his breath in her ear.

"Be mine . . .let me in."

There was something in his voice, something about the way he said those words in her ear. They caressed every inch of her, melted her control and tantalized her senses. The lust she had felt for him, came rushing back ten fold. Her body was suddenly hot with desire and her core was now aching for his touch. Amanda squirmed against her shadowy restraints, but now it was for a whole different reason. She no longer wanted to get free. Amanda wanted to feel those long fingers deep inside of her. She wanted him all over her.

James was still behind her when she heard him laugh. It was deep, malicious and seductive. She felt it rumble through her whole body and vibrate her core. 'What did he just do to me?' He laughed again.

"Darling, it's not what I did to you. It's what I am about to do to you that really matters."

With every move of his body and every sentence he spoke,

Amanda found her pleasure centers overloading. Every nerve in her body vibrated for his touch and every movement he made sent her shivering with thoughts of what he could do to her. She winced in frustration for him to touch her but he only teased her. James ran his fingers lightly between her breasts, and down her torso toward the apex of her thighs, before moving around between her legs and pressing hard into those pressure points. Amanda bucked against the restraints still holding her and moaned an intelligible moan. Then he suddenly stopped and she could hear him moving away from her. She could hear the sound of boots on the hardwood floor, as he circled her. Amanda yanked at her restraints, wanting relief from the ache in her lower regions. Suddenly, his footfalls stopped and the room fell silent. Not even the shadows spoke. Fearful he had left her in this state, she begged the darkness for a response.

"James?"

There was nothing.

"James?"

Silence.

"James? James please answer me."

There was desperation in her voice.

"James . . .please don't leave me like this . . ."

"Oh?"

"Please."

"Please what Amanda?"

She shivered at the very sound of her name falling from his lips.

"Touch me."

When he spoke again, she could hear his voice low in her ear. It only made her ache more.

"Touch you? You told me not to."

"I take it back, please James."

"Not until . . .you apologize."

"I'm sorry . . .James please I'm sorry."

James made no sound as he crossed the floor and then she could feel him standing between her thighs. She felt his long fingers brush against her outer folds sending waves of shivers through her body. Ever so slowly, he pushed a finger between them and ran it down over her swollen pink bud, making her whole body buck upward. She wanted him to touch her more.

"Tsk tsk tsk...we work at my pace."

"James . . ."

She winced in frustrated desperation. She felt him lean against her, his hot firm body pressing into her soft flesh. Then she heard his voice in her ear.

"Do you ache for me Amanda?"

She could only wince in response. James laughed a deep throaty laugh, he was enjoying this too much. Those long fingers ran slowly over her swollen pink bud again before he grabbed it firmly between two fingers. Amanda shivered hard as he pinched her throbbing clitoris between those strong fingers and rolled it in circles. She shivered hard, panting and moaning as waves of orgasms hit her body hard. By the time he stopped, her legs were already sore and her core was dripping with wet juices. Still she wanted more. James took his fingers from her swollen bud and slid them down to her hot core.

He slowly circled a single finger around the outer edge of her aching heat. Amanda pulled at her restraints, wanting to just shove those digits deep inside and stop the ache. But the shadows held strong.

"Tsk tsk tsk . . .do you want me to stop?"

"No . . .please . . ."

"Then don't move . . .be a good girl and be patient."

Even in the dark she knew he was grinning and she hated him for it. James slid a long dexterous finger deep inside of her wanting depths, sending a shiver through her and making her moan. Then he began to pump that finger in and out of her tortuously slow. Before she felt his tongue began to flick slowly against her swollen bud. Amanda sighed a moan.

"James . . .oh . . ."

For a second her breath left her lungs and she struggled to breath as even harder orgasms racked her body repeatedly. She tossed her head side to side as he flicked his tongue against her faster and faster. Sometime between his tongue speed increase and the climax that took her breath away, they had moved to a bed. Instead of air beneath her, there were now black satin sheets caressing her hot flesh. The shadows here were thicker and without her vision, she was forced to rely on her physical senses alone. Now she could feel James on top of her, his naked flesh melding with her softness. His hot mouth came up to meet hers and she moaned as his tongue wrestled with hers.

Amanda could taste herself on his tongue but she did not care. Two fingers found one of her sensitive nipples and twisted it. Again she moaned. Then she felt that hand move further down and she felt the head of his steel hard member, rubbing against her still swollen bud. Before she felt it start rubbing against her wet core.

"James . . ." She begged.

This time he answered her by slowly pushing inside of her inner folds. She felt her body stretch to accommodate him. Where there should have been pain, there was only pleasure. But not for long. The shadows latched onto her wrists again, holding her arms down. James pulled all the way out before thrusting all the way back in, hard enough to send pain jolting through her lower belly. It was painful and at the same time, she loved it. Although she would probably never understand why. He continued to thrust in and out of her harder and faster with every stroke. Despite the pain, she shivered as waves of orgasms ripped through her body. James never let up.

When she was close to climax, he suddenly bit down on her shoulder and she knew he broke skin. Amanda could feel blood running down her neck and dripping onto the bed. Her orgasm hit her and she screamed his name.

"James!"

The orgasm that hit her was sobering. When it finally passed, she could feel the pain in her shoulder and in her lower body. In pain, anger, vengeance or just an attempt to get him off of her, she bit down on his shoulder hard. Amanda felt her own teeth break his skin and she could taste his warm blood in her mouth. It was hot and sweet. In the same moment that she tasted his blood, she felt her body fill with a lust and a power that she had never in her life felt before. For a few moments, all the pain in her body subsided and she could feel her body get stronger.

James was quick to pull away and back hand her hard. It was hard enough to knock her out but this time it didn't. Was she building up a tolerance to their abuse? Or was something else happening? Whatever it was, it pissed James off enough to grab her by her hair and toss her out of bed. The wooden floor was like concrete when she hit it, but it did not hurt as much as it had before. Amanda slowly pushed herself up off the floor. Before she could get to her feet, she felt a cowboy boot press into the middle of her back and shove her back down to the floor. Somehow, James had dressed in only a few seconds.

"Where the hell do you think you're going?"

James pressed his boot into her back even harder. It was enough to keep her pressed to the floor and hold her there, long enough for him to call for back up. In mere seconds, she heard the door open and someone else come in.

"What happened?" Sterling asked.

"Change of plans."

Amanda felt James move his boot and then someone grabbed her by her hair and yanked her to her feet. They drug her out of the shadows and into the light. From what she could tell, they were in James's house still. In that moment something deep inside of her finally let go and she jammed her heel into the leg of the person holding her. There was the sound of bone snapping and they dropped her on the floor.

It took her no time to get up and turn to face the person. Stirling was hunched over, the bone of his knee was sticking out the back of his leg. When he managed to push the bone back in and stand up, she could finally see the real thing that he was. She could see it but she did not in that moment believe it. His iris's were blood red and his canines were long than they should have been. Amanda began to understand why James got so mad when she bit him. Some part of her knew she should be afraid of this creature, of all of them, but she was not. Not anymore.

Amanda knew she needed something to defend herself. She dashed into the kitchen and grabbed a kitchen knife, ready to defend herself. Before she could do anything, a voice slammed into her head and commanded her to sleep. She felt her body go limp and she tried to hold herself up by grabbing the edge of the counter top. There was no fighting off the effects that voice had on her. Everything slowly began to fade and then it all went black.

Chapter 21

All the sounds around her were amplified and to her they were nails on a chalkboard. She could hear the harsh electric buzz of the lights above her. Every sense in her body was heightened to an unbearable level. The smell of sulfur and copper assaulted her nostrils. It made her stomach ache as if she had not eaten in weeks. Amanda felt a hunger, the likes of which she had never experienced. When she tried to open her eyes, the light hurt them. As if a thousand suns were beaming down upon her. She could see the most delicate cracks in the aging concrete around her. The throbbing pain in her body was now gone. She did not understand what was happening to her. Even with the sensory issues she was having, it took her half the time it had before, to wake up. Either she was becoming immune to their games, or they just were not trying as hard.

While she pulled herself back to consciousness, Amanda began to process the last few memories she had before the blackout. It took her a bit to find her memory, but she eventually recalled everything that had happened. Amanda could still taste James's blood in her mouth and feel his flesh in her teeth. She could remember Sterling's face, his true face. Now, she had an idea of what she was dealing with. It was weird to even think the word, but she knew that it was the ugly truth. They were vampires, killers, fiends. These creatures had no love for anything but the blood that flowed through her veins and they were sadist. 'Really Amanda, Vampires?' She was beginning to form a theory as to what was happening to her. James was one of them and she had tasted his blood. So was she changing into one of them?

Amanda made another attempt to open her eyes and look around. Through the blinding glare she scanned the room, it was solid concrete like the last room she had found herself in and there was a solid metal table pushed up against one of the walls. A steel chain was bolted to the middle of the floor and one end of it was locked around her right ankle. She picked up some of the links and turned them over in her hand. It would not be easy to get free from this situation. Unless she could break the chain or rip the bolt from the floor. With a groan and the support of one of the walls, she pushed herself to her feet. From this angle, she could see the array of knives laid out on the table in neat little rows. There were scalpels, hunting knives, boning knives and a various mixture of saws. Some of them still had microscopic traces of blood. The sight of which made her mouth water.

From behind her she heard a noise, the inaudible sound of metal creaking and clicking. To her ears it was a knife scraping across glass and she pulled her hands up to cover them. Her head snapped up in the direction she heard the noise. Through the four inches of solid steel she could smell a copper, sulfuric smell and the over powering scent of cologne. Were they trying to cover up that disgusting smell radiating off of them? There was a rhythmic thumping sound and the rushing of liquid through a hollow space. Was she hearing the plumbing? She heard them exhale slowly before an ear shattering creak overcast the other sounds. The lock on the door clicked open. This was her one opportunity to defend herself and get out of this place before they could stop her from leaving Collins.

All sound, thought and reason became muffled as he walked into the room. Amanda began to crawl backwards. She knew there was no escaping him as he slammed the door shut behind him. It would be impossible to keep him away from her, to keep him from touching her. There was nothing she could do to stop him. Amanda shook her head no and she was saying it aloud.

"No no no no."

As if she believed verbally rejecting the image of him (his presence) would be enough to make him disappear. The sight of him filled he with terror, she began panting and tears rolled down her cheeks. She was crippled with fear, outside of the monster before her, it was the only thing she was aware of. Amanda was shaking, her bottom lip quivered and she stared with tearful eyes at him as he strode toward her. She just sat on the floor trying to comprehend what was happening. Her mind reeled as it attempted to understand, she felt light headed and sick to her stomach.

The pungent smell of Marlboros wafting off of him, the sound of his boots on the floor, and his look were just as she remembered. She should not be seeing him at all. He was dead, he was supposed to be dead. There was a smile on his face as if he was proud of something he had done. James stood six foot four but at this angle he looked eight feet tall. His hair was buzzed short in the same militant style he always wore. This man, her James wore a black t-shirt, blue jeans and his infamous black work boots. He was square shouldered with long muscular legs. It would take nothing for him to break a grown man, let alone her. Amanda knew the power in those large hands and the excruciating pain he was capable of inflicting. Her body had not forgotten, there was a fading scar on her cheek to remind her.

"There you are, I've been looking all over for you."

"James please . . ." She choked out.

"Please what?"

He cocked his head, seemingly puzzled.

"Didn't you miss me? Do you miss," He moved slowly toward her with every sentence. "the feel of me inside of you? Because I did. I miss it very much."

"Shut up please. Go away, please go away. Leave me along, I just wanna be left alone."

James crouched down in front of her, staring at her with his piercing blue eyes. Amanda started to pull her knees to her chest but he grabbed her ankles and yanked her toward him. She waved her hands in the air, desperately trying to slap him. James grabbed her wrists and effortlessly pinned them to the floor above her head, holding them in one large hand. The other one began to brush up her inner thigh.

"James please don't . . .please stop."

"None of that now. I know you missed me too. Why are you fighting this?"

His thumb brushed against her shaven folds and she turned her head away so she did not have to look at him.

"Oh, I miss that sweet pussy. Don't you miss me Amanda? The feel of me thrusting deep inside of you."

"James stop it," She began to cry more. "God please stop this."

She was so terrified of this man, of this monster with angry fists that it did not register he was dead. The demon she was looking at, that she was so afraid of, was still lying on the cold factory floor. His body discarded as if he were only roadkill.

"We're gonna have some fun."

"No, no more please."

Although she knew begging would do no good, she could not stop her natural reaction. James leaned down and ran his tongue over her delicate folds. She got no pleasure from his touch. When he put a saliva soaked finger inside of her, the only warm liquid her enticed was her bodies reaction from the stimulation. James pumped a long thick finger in and out of her until he felt she was ready for him.

"James, don't do this, please don't"

"I love you Amanda. Don't you understand that. I've missed you so much. I have to feel your warmth again."

She heard the sound of his zipper and then she felt him thrust inside of her. He was bigger than she remembered and with every assault on her lower regions, a pain jolted up through her womb. It felt as if someone was continuously hitting her in her lower belly, hard enough to make it collide with her pelvic bone. An endless stream of desperate tears flowed down her cheeks and through her sobs she begged him to quit.

"James please, you're hurting me! Get off me."

His hot breath beat in pants against her ear as he whispered.

"I love you Amanda. Oh god I love you. I missed your sweet pussy."

Every word out of his mouth disgusted her, she fought against his iron grip. There was nothing she could do to get free. She prayed he might finish soon. In hell though, the devil is the only entity who can answer her prayers and she knew he would not. The pain between her legs was excruciating but she could do nothing about it. James was too strong. He began to slam into her even harder, moving ever faster as his grip tightened on her wrists. Amanda heard a crack and felt one of her wrists pop under the strain. He had fractured one of them and did not care or notice. After a few minutes he shuddered, pulling out of her to spill his hot seed on her stomach. It was thick, sticky and warm on her chilled flesh.

James finally let go of her and stood. Amanda pulled her shaky hands down to her face, her whole body shaking as she sobbed into them. A sharp pain shot through the side of her wrist as if a gutter nail was being driven into it. With her good hand she reached down and cupped her abused flesh. When she lifted that hand, she saw crimson running down her fingers. She used her elbows to help pull herself into a corner so she could assess the damage her had down. While she examined her bloody womanhood and broken wrist, James began to browse the knives. She should have never taken her eyes off of him.

There was blood smeared on her thighs, dripping from her aching core and leaving a small puddle where ever she went. Amanda swallowed her tears now, she knew she had to fight this demon or he would kill her. He might kill her anyhow but she at least had to try. The smell of blood pervaded the air, she knew the smell of it but only in large doses. Now it seemed she could detect the most minuscule amount. None of those sensations were relevant to her or important at that time. She had to stay focused on surviving. The sound of James's voice pulled her from her thoughts.

"These look like fun. Wanna see?"

He selected a scalpel from the array of knives.

"No!"

She tried to get up and run across the room but the muscles in her legs had atrophied from the assault. So they collapsed under her weight and she slammed into the floor, skinning her palms an cracking her teeth as her chin hit the cement. She tasted a sweet liquid in her mouth, unlike anything she had experienced before. The pain in her body was less than it should have been but she dared not question it.

"Come on, don't be like that. These could be so much fun."

"Stay away from me!"

Before she could move, he was on her, holding her to the floor and she felt the sharp bite of the blade. He began to lay little cuts up and down her body. She cried out in pain as he decorated nearly every inch of her flesh with gashes from various knives. Every slice was hot, searing pain and she could feel the warm crimson as it ran from her wounds. It was unclear how he managed to get to them but the details no longer mattered. When James was satisfied with his work, he pulled her up by her hair and slammed her into the table, bending her over it. Amanda had no energy or strength to fight him. This time there was no warm up, he thrust into her tender flesh hard. The sensitive skin resisted his motion as skin rubbed roughly against skin. Everything in her lower region burned and she cried out in pain. James must not have liked that because he slammed her face into the metal table hard enough to break her nose and knock out a tooth. The room around her swayed as blood from her face dripped onto the the table. As he continued to tear her inner folds with his hard, dry thrusts, he dug his strong fingers into the wounds on her thighs. It felt like fish hooks were jammed into the tender inner flesh. She grit her teeth against the pain to keep from making any sound and invoking his wrath again. Through her locked jaw, she sobbed, tears dripping onto the table below her and mixing with the blood pool.

Again when he was finished using her, he shot his load on her mutilated flesh. Its salty liquid burned in the cuts on her thighs. His previous ejaculate was already drying on her stomach. James yanked her away from the table and tossed her to the floor. Amanda no longer fought the landing, she allowed the pain to come. Her woman hood hurt so bad that she could barely close her legs without feeling sharp tendrils of pain. What did it really matter anymore? As she lay on the floor, staring off into nothingness, he moved around the room. She heard cloth rustle, then the sound of something heavy being lifted off the floor and finally there was a hissing sound. Amanda glanced up in time to see him coming toward her with a red hot brand.

She tried to push herself up off the ground but he put his boot in her back and before she knew it there was a burning pain in her left butt cheek. The smell of scorching flesh wafted into her nostrils and she had to swallow bile because of it. Amanda screamed, she screamed until her lungs hurt, and she was gasping for air. Amanda lay there shuddering in pain, her body going into a mild shock from the third degree burn. As he branded her, he whooped in excitement.

"Yee haw, I got me a live one."

She heard him throw the branding iron to the ground before hopping up on the table to sit down. Amanda was still gasping for air as she pushed herself onto her side. It took all her strength to do that. Her body twitched violently from the assault, she fought to ignore the aching wounds on her body. She slowly lifted her eyes to look at the figure sitting on the table. It was not James she saw but Sterling, he was sitting playing with one of the bloody knives.

"Shit!"

The mere sight of him gave her enough of an adrenaline rush to get up off the floor and back into the wall. Sterling's anatomy shifted for a brief moment into James and then back into himself. His blue eyes sparkled menacingly, contrasting the almost charming smile on his face. She did not understand just what had happened or what he was but one thing was certain. He was not human. Somehow, seeing him in his normal form, helped her to remember that James was dead. None of what had transpired in the last few hours could be his doing. Amanda pointed a bloody finger at him as she spoke, her hands still shaking.

"You . . you . . .son of a bitch!"

His smile widened.

"Oh sweetie, what's the matter? Aren't you having fun? Didn't you enjoy that?"

"Fun? Fun? Enjoy that? Are you out of your mind?! No, no I didn't! You're sick, you're fucking sick. What the hell is wrong with you?"

Sterling's smile widened even more, his lips curved up in an unnatural way, almost contorting his seemingly charming features. He jumped off the table, the movement causing Amanda to twitch. Her body expected more pain. They had warned her she would either obey or wish for death. Even in her broken state, she refused to collapse under the torment. After the torture he had put her through she began to understand a few things. The apparition in her house was Rachel, the missing girl and that James, he was not the person she had shot on her porch that night. This thing, whatever it was, this chameleon was the thing she had shot. Amanda slowly looked up at him.

"You bastard! You hurt her, you tortured her! It was you I shot, not James, its been you this whole time. What the hell are you?"

272

A toothy grin replaced his clown like smile, it was almost as if he had hoped she might figure it out.

"Hurt? No Amanda, you have it all wrong. I never hurt any of my girls. What I did to you, that was foreplay."

She was beginning to understand what level of psychotic sadist she was dealing with. He took pleasure in what he did to her and he believed it was arousing for them. Amanda realized he had avoided answering her on a few things, so she reiterated.

"Rachel! You tortured her and raped her! You're a monster, a demon!"

Sterling laughed, amused by her disgust toward him.

"Tell me what you are. Tell me it was you on my porch that night." She growled.

He stopped laughing, turning back to the table and dropping his head before he finally spoke.

"We watched you for weeks on end. Watched you go to work, saw James punish you for your insubordinate behavior. James did come back that night but he never made it to the door. That buck shot was rude by the way," Sterling cracked his neck before continuing. "And Rachel, oh she was so much fun. Her screams were tantalizing, music to my ears. I loved the hours we spent together. But don't let her fool you, she loved every second with us. She was just so disobedient. She just . . .she just couldn't get it right, ya know? We tried so hard to teach her but she never could understand her place, she had trouble following orders. So disappointing too. Her sweet twat was...well... to be honest it was better than yours. She was virgin when we found her, Miller was the first to break her in. Unfortunately, we had to let her go. Like any bad pet, sometimes you just have to put them down. I will say, she was much more entertaining after that."

Amanda could not believe what she was hearing. Did he really just elude to the fact that he was also a necrophiliac?

"You're all sick. Rachel did not enjoy that, your perverted ass did. I don't let you do the same thing to me. I'll kill myself before I let that happen."

"Heh, you don't have a choice. We told you, learn to obey or you will beg to die."

"Go to hell. Whatever you are, go straight to hell and tell the devil I sent you."

"The devil," He laughed. "that's only a myth parents tell their children so they'll behave. No no, I am much worse than he because I'm real. And hell, heh, you're in hell sweetheart. You wanna know what I   am . . ."

Sterling was a blur to her as he lifted her from the floor and she just caught a glimpse of red eyes before a stabbing pain shot through her shoulder. He held her up off the ground with with one arm, his had gripped the back of her neck. The pungent smell of fresh blood tingled her nostrils and with her heightened hearing, she listed to the sound of him swallowing her blood. Amanda tried to pull him off of her, screaming for him to let go of her. As she clawed at his flesh and beat at his back, she felt her anger grow. How dare he drink her blood. He thought he had the right to torture her, feed from her and rape her without consequence. No matter the fact she found her anger, the blood loss was making her weaken. She resurrected her fire a little too late. Her arms became limp, her legs could no longer hold her weight and her head began to droop to one side.

When she was subdued and he was satisfied, Sterling pulled his mouth from her. He dropped her as if she were only a piece of meat. Through her fuzzy vision, Amanda watched him clinch his fists and arch his body as he threw his head back and growled. It was as if her blood had filled him with new power and he was adjusting his body to accommodate for it. When he lowered his head, she could see his crimson eyes and hear the liquid as it dripped from his sharp canines.

Amanda wanted to get up and hurt him but she had no strength to move. There were worse monsters than James and now she was trapped in their carnival of pain. If she did not get out of here, she too would end up a corpse. A discarded toy they had grown bored with and thrown away. She tried to grab for his leg so she might pull herself up but he stepped back from her. Her hand fell to the floor with a slap. There was no strength left in her limbs and without rest, she would not regain any of it. She winced weakly, her hand just barely lifting in the air. Amanda begged with her eyes, begging for mercy and praying that god would help her.

Sterling crouched down to look at her, blood still glistening on his lips. He continued his previous explanation.

"What am I you ask? I'm the monster your people tell stories about. The demon watching you from the darkness. I'm your nightmare. Only, I'm real. All the myths are false. We are capable of so much more than you humans realize."

"God, please help me." She whispered to herself.

He cocked his head, tipping his ear to the ceiling.

"God?" He began to look up and around, mockingly.
"Oh god! Hey god! Where are you god?! Amanda needs your help!"

He dropped his head, pursing his lips and shrugging, his eyes still tilted upward.

"I guess he's not coming. Maybe he doesn't love you. I mean he let James beat you didn't he?"

Amanda squeezed her eyes shut, her body began to shake as she started to cry.

"God, there's no god here. We're god. We can be merciful gods when you obey our rules."

"You don't know the meaning of the word." She mumbled.

Sterling grabbed the back of her head, lifted her up and slammed his fist into her jaw. A resounding crack echoed through the room and she spit two molars on the floor. Her jaw felt as if someone had hit her with an aluminum bat or she was hit by a truck. She lay there letting the blood slowly drip from her mouth.

"You will learn your place or you will end up like Rachel. You only speak when spoken to. I didn't ask you a question so you keep your fucking mouth shut!"

"No." She mouthed.

Her eyes were growing heavy but she dared not close them around him. With every passing second, her breathing became more labored and he r body became even weaker. The wound on her shoulder was still bleeding, as were her gashes and her womb. Everything around her began to blur even more. Amanda was aware of the sound of the door opening behind her and the two distinct sets of footfalls that entered the room. She flinched unconsciously as they passed by her.

"No no no, god please stop them. Don't let them touch me."

She whispered to herself.

Bits of their conversation drifted to her ears.

"Wow, you did a number on her. I think she's worse than the last one."

"But she's so much more fun that the last one. She actually tried to pray to god. Hell, she even thought she could fight back."

There was an eruption of laughter among them. They mocked her pain and suffering, they enjoyed it. Amanda recognized one of the voices out of the group.

"Is she ready for me?"

"Yeah, take her. I'm done with the little whore."

She could feel their eyes on her naked, battered frame. They stared down at her like she was their last meal. Amanda pulled her arms under her and managed to push to her feet, half stumbling, half running for the door. Although how she managed this, was unclear. Outside of that room was a long metal walkway, she just barely caught a glimpse of it before Miller blocked her escape. He too was wearing the same clothes as he had before. He bit his bottom lip as he strode slowly toward her, his body swaying slightly with every step. There was no emotion on his face but there was a hungry lust in his eyes that made her diaphragm tighten briefly with nervous tension. Amanda glanced behind her, hoping there was another exit available. James was standing there, blocking her from heading in that direction. Of all these men (if she could really call them that), she feared him the most. So she dared not even try to get by him. Sterling leaned in the doorway, watching them with a look of amusement on his face. He seemed to be enjoying her futile attempts at freedom. As if he knew full well, she had no chance.

"Where ya going Amanda?"

"Please no more."

Tears rolled down her cheeks.

She struggled to stay on her feet, her knees threatening to collapse on her at any moment. Miller cocked his head to one side.

"Oh baby, we're just getting started. We have so much more to show you."

He held his hand out as if he expected her to willingly take it.

"Come here, come on. Make it easy on yourself."

"No," She shook her head.

"I wanna go home. Please let me go home. I won't tell anyone. You can go about your business in peace."

"Home?" He smirked.

"You are home." James whispered in her ear.

He had snuck up behind her when she was distracted.

"No."

Her whole body began to shake and she froze where she was standing. As James wrapped his arms around her, her knees gave out but he did not let her fall. They moved down the long walkway to a large concrete structure and she realized they were in the factory. She had been right to fear this place. She should have left well enough alone. Amanda could hear female voices within the cement walls, there were steel doors on the structure. They were rooms, cells, four in a row on each side of the factory. She understand what was locked in James's house upstairs. The sounds of fists pounding on the steel, begging for freedom and mercy, were deafening. Some of them just sobbed in the darkness. Amanda began to cry more, the sounds of their hopeless pleading and helpless suffering, broke her heart. How did no one notice what was going on in this town? How could they ignore that? Were they completely heartless? Someone had to stop them. It would not be her, she did not have enough power, strength or ammunition.

They stopped in front of a door and Miller opened it before he turned to look at her.

"What's the matter Amanda? Where's your fight? Aren't I

supposed to be dead by now? Or are you all tired out? Is your anger all gone?"

He looked at James and they laughed. Those heartless, evil beings were mocking her pain. They were taking enjoyment in the breaking of her spirit.

"Man, she couldn't kill a mood right now, let alone one of us. Not that she could before." James laughed.

"I'm in a mood right now." Miller said, grabbing his groin.

"Come on man, let's get this bitch in her cell."

James moved toward the doorway and she pushed back into him when she saw the darkness. For within the corners of her cell, she could see tendrils of shadow moving, waiting for her.

"No, James please. Please don't"

He leaned in her ear, his voice dropping an octave, so it was gravel to her sensitive ears.

"What's the matter? You don't like my friends? They love you. The sound of your moans as I touch you and the feel of your sweet twat. Oh they like that very much. My boys like your sweet pussy as much as I do. Why no let them play with you a little bit. They can be so much fun."

With that he shoved her in the cell and Miller slammed the door shut. She tried to run for the entrance but she was too late. Her palms slammed into the hard steel and she began to beg for them to stop this.

"Please! Let me out! Don't do this!"

Her hands slapped desperately against the door. Amanda's cries for sympathy fell on deaf ears and she sank, defeated, to the floor. Still, she prayed for release from this level of hell, promising whatever she had to, to convince God to help her. Again, he did not answer her. She was beginning to believe he could not hear her or he was ignoring her. Within the dark of her cell, she heard James's voice.

"No one's gonna save you Amanda. You belong to us now. Even he knows that."

She lay on the floor, curling herself into a ball as heavy sobs wracked her body. She cried until she had not tears and her lungs hurt from her ragged breathing. The shadows left her alone for now but there was something else. Through the cement wall, she heard grunts of pain as clear as day. They were female in nature and the growling that accompanied them, she knew was from one of the boys. Amanda crawled over to the wall, pounding on it and screaming.

"Leave her alone you bastard! You hear me! Let her go! I'll kill you, you son of a bitch!"

It was not out of anger she did that, she no longer felt that emotion, only coldness. She no longer cared if she lived or died. Although she knew her death would not come quickly. At least resigning herself to this state of mind would ensure some form of survival. Embracing the void of emotion might help her to bring them down or keep them from getting pleasure from her pain. Amanda did get a reply to her threatening screams as a voice slammed into her head with such force that she fell over.

"Try it!"

"Ahh!"

She gripped her skull as her mind began to throb from the psychic pressure being put on it. Amanda writhed in pain. He increased the pressure in her head.

"Ahh! Stop! Stop!"

The last word came out of her mouth coupled with a forceful thought and she felt the pain in her head suddenly cease. She gasp in relief. Before she could begin to gain her bearings, that voice slipped back inside. It commanded her to *sleep* and although she tried to stop her bodies reaction, she was no match for him. Her limbs went limp and then her eyes slowly fell. Amanda was plummeted into darkness and horrific nightmares of which there was no escape.

Chapter 22

Amanda had forced herself from the coma, hours ago, and in turn was greeted by a blinding, white hot pain. It jabbed at the side of her temples, stabbed at the tip of her skull and dug deep into her eye sockets. The apex of her thighs throbbed and burned as if her womanhood had been set on fire. She could still feel blood trickle slowly between her thighs. A majority of her body had atrophied from blood loss, lack of movement and muscular trauma. Although it was nothing in comparison to what James had done to her. The final beating he had given her, the final straw of their relationship, may well have been a gift. It prepared her for what she was to endure in the undetermined amount of time she would spend with these men...these monsters.

Some part of her subconscious mind knew what they were but her logic refused to accept it. All her mind refused to declare it true, to acknowledge their existence, for many reasons. It would mean that everything was not as she once knew it. It would mean that the world she thought she knew was only a surface, an airbrushed beauty, meant to hide the ugliness of the world. To keep people from knowing the truth and maybe it was all for the best. How many could handle the fact they were real? Chaos and discord would ensue if the rest of the world became aware of what she knew. Or would they be better off knowing? Would it be better for them to learn about these things and therefore allow them to mount a defense against the real evil of the world? If they were real though, what else existed? What other creatures had the mortal world been convinced were myths so they could sleep better at night? Was the Devil real? Did he exist with the red horns and forked tail of the mythology? Her mind swelled with questions. She was not prepared for this, any of it. But she knew that she was not being given a choice. Her fate had been sealed, the wheel of fortune had been spun, and now she could only hang on for the ride.

The voices, the screams, their prayers for mercy and salvation. They came on suddenly and without warning. It did not start with a small trickle but a waterfall of thoughts-heard through dense concrete dividers, but as a landslide. Then there were the voices, all of them speaking at one time. Some of them raspy and faint, others even weaker. Amanda fell to her side, curling herself into the fetal position and holding her hands over her ears to try and will the voices away. She writhed on the bloodstained floor of her cell, barely able to hold back a scream as her psyche teetered on the brink of insanity. What was happening to her? She pressed her teeth together hard, sending sobering bolts of pain through her lower jaw.

'*Stop it! STOP IT!*'

She was screaming inside her own head, hoping she could make it stop as she had the Telepaths control over her mind. Amanda rolled onto her other side, scooting herself back into one of the dark corners, paying no mind to the shadows that continued to slither there. She knew that her thoughts would have easily reached the Telepath's mind, and he would undoubtedly respond.

Suddenly, everything stopped all at once. Amanda squeezed her eyes shut tight, waiting, bracing herself for whatever else was to come. There was nothing. No sounds through the walls, no other voices in her head but her own. A slow sigh left her lips and she pulled her hands down from her ears. She looked around in the darkness of her cell, listening for the slightest sound. Again, there was nothing. Her head fell back in relief, its light collision with the wall reminding her that she had sustained injuries to it only a few hours ago. She let out a wince but nothing more. The cold of the room around her was helping to sooth the pounding in her skull.

The large puncture wound on her thigh had continued to bleed, she could feel the warm sticky fluid running down toward the crack in her buttocks. Every movement sent pain shooting through her extremities. She could smell the Chameleon's juices that had dried to a white crust over the bloody flesh. Amanda shuddered at the thought of him ever touching her again. The bastard had posed as her James and worst of all, he had raped her as her James. On her back side, where the branding iron had been pressed, she felt the familiar burning of blisters forming. Without the cold floor beneath her, she might have been in more pain. Her back was still sticky with the blood that oozed from her cuts.

As she sat there, leaning her head on the wall, she felt her bottom lip began to shake. Her body was threatening to betray her, tears beginning to form on her lower lids. Now, was not the time to break down. When she was home again, safe from the clutches of them, she could cry but not now. No matter how much pain they inflicted on her, she refused to give them the power to bring her to tears anymore. Only one man could do that and he was dead. For all she knew, the James she loved had been kidnapped months before she was attacked. If it was true, that meant she owed them for more than her suffering. She would repay them for taking away the man who had promised to love her forever. Amanda wondered, did he fight for her in the end? Is that the reason for his defiance, even in the face of absolute death? He could have told her the truth and they demonized him for their own selfish desires.

Another sigh passed through her, nausea chasing closely behind it as she pushed to find her strength. She knew she needed to get to her feet before they came back. But she would have to do it in such a way as to not give her plans away to the Telepath. She would have to be irrational. Do the things they would never suspect she might do. If the Chameleon had been playing the part of James for an extended period of time, it meant that he had been watching her every move. Therefore they believed they could predict her. A slow smirk spread across her lips.

Amanda placed her hand on the wall beside her, pulling her feet under her and gritting her teeth against the agony of moving. She squeezed her eyes shut as she forced her legs to bare her weight. They wobbled under the pressure, threatening to collapse at any moment. With a throaty growl, she summoned all her strength and pushed to her feet, using the wall for support. Through grit teeth, she huffed out pained breaths. For a moment she only leaned there, panting.

There was a resounding creak and then she heard her door groan on its hinges. She squinted as she looked up in the direction the noise had come from. In the doorway, illuminated by the bright factory lights, was the silhouette of the Telepath. Amanda could only assume he had heard her thoughts or perhaps her grunts of pain.

The small light of hope that she had gained when she managed to push to her feet, was gone in an instant, replaced by anxiety. Amanda swallowed hard, pushing herself back into the farthest corner of the room. She did not want to see him again. Somehow she knew he was the one who had forced her body to submit to their sexual deviance.

Amanda felt a growl crawling up her throat, it was weak but it was there none the less. The Telepath seemed to hear it because he cocked his head to one side as if attempting to listen better. Then he spoke.

"Oh Amanda…if only you knew the things I'm about to do to that pussy. Maybe then…you wouldn't be so brave."

There was a threatening undertone to his every word, and his voice was a soft whisper. A far cry from the anger she had heard dripping from his lips only hours ago. Something was very wrong, she could sense it with every fiber of her being.

As he stood in the doorway, staring at her, he shifted his weight from one foot to another, his arms swaying senselessly. She could hear his teeth scrap along his bottom lip and the audible sucking sound as he pulled it into his mouth. He seemed to be either contemplating his next move, or waiting for something. Was he waiting for them? Even in the dim light she could make out the narrowing of his eyes as he stared into her soul. After minutes of silence, she heard his voice in her head.

'Amanda…come with me. I can give you so much pleasure.' His voice was honey in her *mind.*

She felt the tension in her body began to relax and the fire in her belly start to fade. Maybe if she cooperated, things could be wonderful.

'That's my girl. If you come with me…I promise there will be no more hurting. No more pain. You can be with us…let us love you.'

Amanda licked her bottom lip, cocking her head to the side and looking at him. The fury and pain in her eyes softened. She became less aware of the pain in her limbs and the pounding in her head. Her eyes felt heavier than they had been before and she felt this unquenchable urge to be near him. She had to have him, to be close to him. If she could not consume him, she might surly fade into the darkness and disappear. Going with him was the right thing to do.

The Telepath extended a hand into her cell as if to lead her in a dance. Amanda leaned against the wall and attempted one of many steps in his direction.

'Come to me Amanda. Poor thing, I'll get you cleaned up. If you be good, I will get you food and dress your wounds. You'll know only love.'

With every step, she moved slowly closer to him, reaching out desperately for his hand. Her fingers barely brushed his and she stumbled. To her surprise, he caught her, lifting her up and helping her to walk the rest of the way. Not another word was spoken as they made their way across the narrow bridge that spanned the two upper floors. For a moment she feared she might never hear his sweet voice again or that she had done something to anger him. Amanda looked at him with longing in her eyes and finally she heard him again but not in her head.

"Ssh…quiet your racing mind. I'm not mad at you. Do I look mad? It's all right Amanda. Everything is going to be okay."

She was taken into another room, it too was solid concrete but in the middle was a claw foot bathtub. Steam rose from the middle of it, disappearing into the cold. With a gentleness she was unaware he was capable of, he lifted her into the tub. A thousand hornets stung her open wounds as the hot water seeped into them. She winced in pain but then she felt something come over her, as if blanketed by morphine and it was gone.

He washed her carefully without a word. Amanda never noticed the smirk on his face or the glint in his eyes. She only knew she had to be near him, she wanted him to touch her. He had to make love to her, to feel every inch of her, or she would surely die.

The Telepath lifted her from the tub and carried her down the hallway into another room. This one was white tile from ceiling to floor and a long double sided mirror spanned one wall. On another was a metal table, which she took no notice of because her eyes were glued to him. He was her everything. How had she lived without him? Could she ever live without him? She knew the answer was No. There was nothing before him or after him. There was only him.

In the middle of the room, was another white table and above it, hung a chain. He laid her out, pulling the damp towel away from her, and stepping behind her, he placed his hands on her thighs. Amanda felt panic but it too was gone.

> '*You trust me. You have always trusted me. I want to play with your sweet pussy and watch my fingers roam over your delicate clit. To see them as I spread you and push my fingers deep inside. You like that, don't you Amanda?*'

"Yes." She sighed with excitement.

> '*Yes what baby girl? Tell me in detail what you like.*'

"I like when you spread my labia and rub my clit. I like when you push your fingers deep inside of me."Her answer was almost robotic, mindless.

"Oh...ooo." He moaned as he slowly opened her legs toward the two way mirror.

Then his hands ran down the length of her body and he spread her labia open.

"Oh, look at that sweet pussy. That delicious little clit. I can't wait to wrap my lips around it. Flick my tongue all over it."

She purred in response, unaware of her audience on the other side of the mirror and unable to break free from his spell. Amanda had no comprehension of what was going on. No idea that she was being influenced by his telepathic powers, so he could do what he wanted to her without a fight. She was a puppet in his hands, caught in his thrall.

The Telepath began to rub her pink bud in slow circles, watching himself in the mirror as he did. She moaned, her hands gripping the side of the table.

"Oh look at that. Look at that sweet clit. You like when I play with it, don't you Amanda?" He asked, grinning wide as he watched her obey.

"Yess...yes...play with my clit. Rub it. I love when you rub it." She replied.

The Telepath pulled his finger away and she winced, feeling the absence of his touch on her delicate flesh.

"It's okay...it's okay. I'm gonna make it all better. You want me to make it better?" He asked, bringing that finger toward his lips.

"Yes. I to make it feel good. Make it better." She said.

"That's my good girl." He replied before shoving that finger in his mouth and wetting it.

Then he brought it back down and began to circle it around her tight hole, dipping inside only briefly. She winced in frustration. With a grin, he glanced up at the mirror and then slowly slid that finger inside of her. Amanda moaned, her head dropping back slightly on the table.

"Oohh...you're so wet. Why are you so wet? Are you wet for daddy? Ooo...look at that...ooo...your pussy feels so good around my finger."

His sick twisted words, the way he was talking and touching her, it should have disgusted her. She should have grabbed him by his hair and slammed his head into the table. But her mind was mush. The

Telepath had complete control over every sensation she felt, and every thought she had.

"I'm wet for you. Finger my pussy. Play with it,   I like when you play with it." She said.

If she could have woken from her trance for a moment, only a moment and heard what she was saying to him. She would have hated herself. Their fantasy world would have come crashing down because their puppet would burn it down.

"Are you my good little girl? My little girl?"

"Yes."

"You wanna make me happy?" He said, his finger still working inside of her.

"Yes. I wanna make you happy." She said.

"I will keep playing with your pussy and make you cum but you have to do something for me."

"What? Anything."

He unzipped his fly and she felt something press gently against her lips and waited. Amanda obediently opened up and allowed him to push into her mouth. She began to roll her tongue around the tip, moving her head up and down in sync. The Telepath let his eyes flutter for a moment but managed to keep them open and continue violating her.

Behind the mirror, greedy eyes watched with accompanying hungry smirks. He had turned Amanda into a living doll, obedient because she had no control over her own mind. If only they knew, she was not entirely gone.

In the back of her mind, she watched herself helplessly obey his every sickening whim. He undressed as she worked her mouth around him. She had to do something to break out of this trance before she was raped again. Amanda kept him distracted with her talented tongue, while the part of her that was fully aware of her situation. Began to push him slowly out of her head. Without his full concentration, he was susceptible to losing control. She was certain this had not been the case with the other women. However, she was stronger willed, more intelligent and had already dealt with men like them.

Amanda's eyes flew upon and she glared up at the Telepath. There was the sound of rattling glass as the window in front of her began to shake on its foundations. They were trying to get his attention but it was too late. When he finally looked down at her, she clinched her jaw hard, sinking her teeth into the tender flesh of his manhood.

The Telepath roared and she felt the painful effects of it in her mind. Her brain threatened to explode at the sound of his screams, both internally and externally. A drop of blood fell from each of her ears, hitting the table below her. She could taste his blood as it filled her mouth and she tightened her jaw, cutting deeper into his flesh.

A fist slammed into her right temple and then another collided with her jaw, cracking her teeth. Amanda let go, and when he was free, he grabbed her by her hair, throwing her to the floor.

"You bitch! You little skank!" He shrieked, looking down at his battered manhood.

She said nothing as she lay there on the floor, grinning. Blood dripped from her bottom lip and her smile widened. She did not care what names he called her, she had injured him where it would hurt the most. It was her victory. Let him call her whatever names he felt were appropriate, whatever would make him feel like a man again.

The Telepath snatched her by her hair, dragging her face up to look at his injured groin.

"Look what the hell you did!" He slapped her hard. "Fucking bitch!"

With every chaotic movement, his cock flailed about helplessly, blood flinging in every direction. His pants had dropped around his ankles and his balls had shrunk up to his body in the cold air of the room. It was a pathetic sight to see him this way. She almost felt sorry for him. Almost.

Grabbing her hard by her jaw, he dug his fingers into her broken teeth as he lifted her face to his.

"You wanna bite me bitch?!" He yelled.

Amanda only smirked, knowing that nothing she said ever mattered to them.

"I'm gonna wipe that smirk off your face." His words dripped with malice.

He tossed her to the floor, under the chain she had seen dangling in the middle of the room. Then she was lifted by her wrists and secured with the silver chain she had seen. She could hear the hiss of her flesh as it burned into them. It was pure silver, or at least silver plated. So, she was not the first of the women to accidentally become a vampire. But she was the first to make it this far.

Amanda ignored the pain in her arms. She began to focus her attention elsewhere. She knew that she was about to experience more pain than she had in her entire life. That what James had done to her would pale in comparison. A slow sigh left her lips as she attempted to prepare herself for the next few moments.

The Telepath moved over to the table she had seen shoved against one wall and she heard something metal slide across its surface. Closing her eyes, she listened to his foot falls, the muffled sound of his voice as he continued to berate her and the soft metallic clink of whatever was dangling from his hands. It was a chain, most likely some sort of silver chain, meant to welt and burn her flesh.

White hot fire burned across her back as the first of many lashes connected with her skin. She grit her teeth against the pain, refusing to allow him to hear her scream. Every strike of the chain was harder than the last. It was long enough that it wound around to the front of her, welting and cutting her breasts. He hit the back of her thighs with such force that she heard her calf muscles fracture, and her ankles break.

Amanda panted through her teeth and glared at the two way mirror. She knew now that they were watching. It was all a part of their sick game. They got off on the depravity and the carnivals of horror that each one enacted on the girls. She began to understand that submission did not matter. At some point in her, or any woman's captivity, they would find an excuse to cause them pain.

Her body rattled against the chains as he hit her one more time with all the strength he could muster. With her keen sense of smell, she could detect trace amounts of blood still dripping into his boxers. Biting him had been worth it. She had done that for her, and all the other women locked away in their concrete cells, losing hope of ever being rescued.

She turned to look as she heard him toss the chain onto the table. For a moment, his hand hesitated between a pair of bloody pliers and a cat of nine tails with metal embedded in the leather. He snatched up the whip and moved over to her side, so he would not block the window.

"Think you're pretty funny huh?" He asked.

She swallowed a mouthful of blood before nodding toward the glass.

"Your boys enjoying the show?" She asked, flashing a bloody smirk.

The Telepath growled before drawing his arm back and bringing the whip across her torso. Its jagged blades dug deep, embedding fire into every wound, and leaving even deeper cuts in her tender skin. The blades sank their silvery teeth into her, and then she felt the pull of the whip as they were drug through her skin. It might have been tolerable save for the feeling of her skin being pierced, tugged and then sliced open. He had used sterling silver shards for his whip and they left behind an unbearable burning sensation with every cut, as if he had poured gas in her wounds and lit them with a match. Blood ran down the front of her in long deep red tendrils. Amanda felt her stomach churn, threatening to give up at any moment. She had to breath heavy to make the pain bearable.

Again, he hit the front of her, barely missing her womanhood as it cut into her legs, exposing muscle and tendons to the stinging air. Bile began to crawl up her throat as lightning bolts of pain coursed into her from every direction. The whip connected with her backside and her body jerked forward in unconscious movement to get away from the pain. Her muscles tensed as the whip connected with the back of her legs, and she felt it slice through her Achilles heel. She could not live through this. It was not humanly possible for her to survive the blood loss he was inflicting.

A small ruby puddle had began to form beneath her feet, and her body was beginning to shake. She was starting to exhibit signs of shock. Amanda had to do anything to help stable her mind, to distract it from the situation at hand. There was no telling what he would do to her if her body shut down and she blacked out. *'James... focus on James. You didn't let him kill you. Do not let this asshole get away with it.'* She sighed, slowly working herself back to a more level point.

On the glass in front of her, she could make out the deep cuts that littered her body. The white of tendons, the red of muscle and the yellow of what little body fat she had left. She wondered if the silver would cause her wounds to scar. Would she be marked for life? Even if she survived and gained her freedom, would the rest of the world know who did this to her? In the end, it was all meat, food for the scavengers, and blood, for the monsters that held her in captivity. Her mind was beginning to fracture, attempting to spare her the pain of reality by mulling over useless information.

Through the fuzzy incoherent noise, the buzz of the lights above her, the sound of his footsteps and the ringing in her ears from the pints of blood now pouring out of her, she could just barely make out the clinking of pliers being drug across the table. Her eyes shifted unsteadily, and the world around her spun. The human body was not made to endure this much torment. Even if she was no longer fully human, she was not full vampire either. He could not expect her to hold out for much longer.

The Telepath stood in front of her, a pair of pliers dangling from one hand as his weight shifted and swayed from one leg to another. His arms swayed loosely at his sides, his head cocked awkwardly to the right as stared at her fading strength. It was almost as if he was contemplating what he would use them for, or he knew and was having second thoughts about using them. Perhaps he enjoyed watching his victims squirm and suffer. Delighted in watching them slowly fade, only so he could bring them back from the edge of death, and start all over.

Her glassy gaze drifted down to the tool in his hand and then back up to his face. Every minuscule movement made the world around her spin and bile climb further up her throat. Amanda swallowed hard, attempting to prepare herself for what he was going to do.

"I'm gonna teach you not to bite people."

He was seething with rage, his jaw tightened and the muscles in his arms flexed with unreleased anger. Then, he grabbed her chin, he wrenched her mouth open with his hand. She tried to jerk her head out of his grip but he was digging his fingers deep into the broken bones of her face. The Telepath clamped the teeth of the pliers around one tooth and with no effort at all, he pulled out one of her canines.

Electric jolts of pain shot down through her mouth, and around the sides of her head. The roots of the tooth he had pulled, slapped loosely against her gums. Amanda spit blood onto the floor beneath her, tasting it as it pooled on her tongue. She closed her eyes a moment to steady herself, but before she could, he ripped another tooth from her bottom gum. Blood ran over her bottom lip as pain traveled down her face and into her ears.

"This is what happens to biters." He said, waving the bloody pliers at her.

Their session continued on in that manner until her body refused to content with the agony anymore and she succumbed to unconsciousness. She was suddenly greeted by an icy shock as cold water was thrown onto her naked, battered frame. Amanda woke with a start, shaking from the sudden onslaught.

"No no, I want you awake for this next part baby." He whispered in her ear.

She wanted to retort with something smart. To say anything that would make him mad. To provoke him into ending her life and sending her from this hellish place. Her mouth was numb, filled with blood. There were no teeth left in any of her gums. After she passed out, he had continued to rip them out. Rachel must have bit him too, or perhaps he did it for his own amusement.

The Telepath stepped behind her, and she heard his filthy mouth as he sucked his fingers, wetting them. Then he brushed his fingers across her delicate flesh, enticing her body to become wet for him.

Amanda tossed her head from side to side, fighting off disgust. She felt his middle finger, force its way into her inner folds, thrusting with no hint of intimacy. His digits violated her until she was moist enough for his intrusion and her body had physically readied itself. Although it should have been pleasurable, her anatomy only understood pain. She was numb, dirty, sticky, and a constant torrent of nerve grinding sensations, waved down through her body. Her head lolled to one side, and bloody spittle dribbled from the corner of her toothless mouth.

He lowered the chain slightly, and then she felt the head of his shaft position at her entrance. Amanda closed her eyes, preparing for what he was about to do. But how does one prepare for such a thing? The Telepath thrust into her, hard and fast. She was not wet enough for his violation, and the skin of his cock rubbed hard against her delicate inner folds. Amanda could feel the flesh began to tear against his hard onslaught and she squeezed her eyes shut harder. Having no teeth to grit against the pain, she groaned and winced as he shoved into her hard. She tossed her head from side to side, praying he would finish soon.

What seemed like hours, had only been a few meager minutes. Then he pulled from her, stepping in front of her and grabbed her bottom jaw hard in his hand.

"Open your eyes!" He demanded.

She disobeyed. He dug his dirty fingers into her face and then commanded her again.

295

"Open your eyes! Look at me!" He growled.

Amanda weakly obeyed, her eyes opening only slightly. Her lids drooped with the threat of unconsciousness. She could not endure much more of this torment.

"Oh...stay with me baby. I'm not finished with you yet. You bit me, now, you're going to swallow my cum."

Despite her pain, her weakness, she managed to gather bloody saliva onto her tongue, and spit it in his face. She already knew the punishment for her transgression but she was beyond the point of caring. It did not matter if she obeyed him or not, he would find an excuse to hurt her. So, she was going to give him enough of a reason that she could fall into unconsciousness. It was not fun to torture a woman who could not scream, or cry, or fight back.

The Telepath drew his top lip up in disgust, wiping her spit from his face before backhanding her hard enough to make her sway against her restraints. Much to her disappointment, it did not knock her out. The changes taking place in her anatomy ensured a larger pain threshold. It would take more than a backhand to send her into the darkness. '*Damn.*' She thought.

"Puuckk y-you." She managed.

"Fuck me!" He screeched. "Fuck you bitch!"

Reaching above her, he unwrapped the chain from her wrists and she heard the hiss of the metal as it touched his flesh. The smell of silver reaction with the undead hands that continued to violate her, reminded her of burning pork. It caused empty stomach to turn and bile to creep onto the back of her tongue. With a grimace, she swallowed it.

Amanda fell to her knees on the bloody concrete floor and heard the bones in them crack on impact. Her hair was wound around an angry fist, and her head yanked into position. She was staring at his bloody member, the smell of her own sexual fluids drifting into her nostrils. Amanda glanced weakly up at him, thinking to herself '*he does not seriously expect me to do this.*'

"You wanna know why Rachel lost her teeth? She tried to bite too. When you bite, you get your teeth taken out." He said, positioning the head of his member at her bloody lips.

Why was he bothering to explain any of this to her? Why did it even matter anymore? But it did matter. It would matter when she regained her bearings. When the pain had long subsided and her strength renewed. Then, she would remember what he said and it would give her more power to push through.

"Open your mouth..." He commanded before leaning down into her ear. "Suck it good for daddy."

Her upper lip twitched with disgust at his filthy words being whispered in her ear. Did he have an incest fetish she was unaware of? Not that she really cared but her curiosity had gotten the best of her. To avoid further pain, she allowed him to slide his cock into her battered mouth. It grazed across her gums and tears ran down her cheeks.

"Oh yeah...that's my little girl." He said, letting his head fall back slightly.

Amanda sucked and allowed him to control his rhythm and how far he slid into her mouth. Saliva, blood and precum intermingled in her mouth. With every swallow, she felt her stomach protest but she fought to keep the vomit down. Thankfully the Telepath did not last very long and his salty, bitter load shot across her tongue. It burned as it touched the holes where her teeth had been.

She prepared herself to spit it onto the floor beside her but he pulled from her, grabbing her chin.

"You're gonna swallow it." He demanded.

Amanda shook her head as best she could. He leaned closer, and his grip on her hair tightened.

"**Swallow!**" He commanded, his voice booming in her mind.

With a wince, she did as she was told, and was finally let free from his grip. Amanda gagged, squinting and trying to crawl away from him. She would lick the blood from the floor if that was what it took to get the taste of him out of her mouth. Blood continued to drip from her wounds and slowly dribble from her bottom lip. The friction of his member against her swollen gums had caused some of the holes to open more. She could feel the roots of her teeth, slapping around in her mouth as she moved.

Amanda managed to make it to the table on the other side of the room, and as her fingers hooked over the edge of it, she felt pain course through her ribs. She heard the impact of his boot as he kicked her in the side. Her body gave into the assault, collapsing on the floor as the world around her began to fade. She looked weakly up at the Telepath, and heard the door to the room open. That was the last thing she remembered before her body shut down, and she fell into unconsciousness.

Chapter 23

The hours seemed to merge as the days bled from one to another. There was no distinguishing between pain and pleasure, they seemed to enjoy both. It should have come as no surprise to her that creatures such as them were sadists. Amanda could barely remember being drug into her cell and dropped onto the concrete. She could still feel the shards of metal in her thighs as her flesh healed and pushed them out. Her healing process was still more accelerated than normal but slower than it should have been. The blood drain had dulled her enhanced senses to nearly human. Where pain used to be manageable, without blood, her pain was even worse. A small cut felt like a gash. So she lay on the floor, curled in a ball, writhing in agony. The feel of her bones resetting was as if someone was pulverizing her bones with a sickening, sucking sound and hear the grinding as they rubbed together. Amanda twitched and bucked like a fish out of water. She gasped for air as more of her body shifted back into place.

When the process finally ceased, she let her eyes slowly fall closed. There would be no sleep for her tonight though. The sharp sensation of cold hit her and when she bolted upright, she realized a bucket of water had been thrown on her. Two figures came at her, one held her and the other shoved something in her mouth. Then she tasted warm, sweetness and greedily drank it down. Whatever it was, it curbed her pain and gave her strength. They yanked the thing away and she was roughly pulled to her feet before someone tossed her down the metal stairs. Amanda tumbled head over heels, breaking more bones until she collided with the solid concrete. She winced for a few moments before she tried to will her body to get up.

Although she had more strength than a mortal, she was still too weak to move. She heart the metallic clink of chain links and then the sound of them singing through the air before they slammed into her back. All the air left her lungs, her back arched and she gasped in pain. Her eyes began to water and she clawed the floor, trying to drag herself away. The muscles in her arms bulged and her nails scraped the concrete, breaking off at crude angles, some of them pulling completely from the flesh. Her fingers left weak bloody marks as she clawed the floor. Amanda cried out in pain, no longer able to hold her tongue. They hit her again and again, until her entire body was decorated with wounds. She could smell blood running from the gashes on her flesh and her legs were not paralyzed from one of the hits to her spine. She panted as she tried to desperately drag herself away. The burning sensation on her skin, told her they were using silver chains. There would be more scars on her body. As she lay gasping and trying to stay conscious, she heard James.

"Get her chained up."

A pair of gloved hands grabbed her wrists and another pair (also gloved) wrapped the length of chain around her forearms, the metal burned her flesh like fire. Then they carried her naked and battered form out into the cold. They wrapped the chain around a pipe in the middle of the yard before stepping back and admiring their work. Miller and Sterling glanced at one another before nodding and stepping away. Standing in front of her with a sledge hammer in hand and a lit cigar in his mouth was the Shadowed One. Amanda slowly lifted her head to look at him, shaking it 'no'. He lifted the hammer and looked at the head.

"Too much? Yeah, maybe a little over kill."

He tossed it into the snow before stepping closer, blowing smoke in her face.

"The question is," He gestured to her with the cigar. "have you learned yet? Hmm? You gonna cooperate now?"

Amanda breathed slowly for a few minutes, closed her eyes and looked up at him. Even with the continuous burning in her arms, she refused to give into them. She had made a promise to herself and to the silent victims haunting her dreams. The pain she had endured would get worse if she did not give in but there would be more bodies, more women if she did. She knew the needs of the many, outweighed the needs of the few. So she would endure, survive and find a way to kill them. Amanda braced herself for what was about to come.

"Got to hell." She replied, spitting in his direction.

His upper lip flinched, the muscles in his jaw tightened and he pressed the hot cherry into her scarred flesh. There was a hiss and the smell of burning skin in the air. Amanda grit her teeth, breathing heavily through her nose as he twisted the cigar. Although she had caved once, she was determined not to let them hear her cry out in pain. James licked his bottom lip as he pulled the cigar away and jerked his head to the left, gesturing to someone. When he stepped aside, another bucket of ice cold water was thrown on her. The cold outside was already turning her porcelain flesh, blue and the water on her froze into small droplets. Snow continued to trickle down, covering her bloody form in white fluff. Her shivers rattled the chains above her, their metallic sound echoing off the building beside them. How much more did they plan to do to her?

Behind James she could see the glow of a fire and several iron handles sticking out of the fire pit. Somehow she had missed them building the fire. How long had it been going? Long enough apparently to turn the end of the fire pokers red hot. He walked over and pulled one of them from the pit, its cherry glow the only light in the dark courtyard. She heard his boot steps behind her and then she felt searing pain coupled with the smell of burning flesh as he drew the hot metal across her back. A mixture of blood and bile crawled up her throat and she vomited into the snow beneath her. The pain being too much on her weakened anatomy. James repeated the process several times until her body was shaking from the shock that had set in. If she had still been mortal, she might have gone into shock sooner. She coughed, gagging at the smell of her flesh and panted slowly in an attempt to calm her stomach. Overhead she could hear a crow screaming somewhere in the distance. Was it a sign that her suffering would end soon? Amanda knew it was only wishful thinking. The Shadowed One tossed his last iron poker in the snow and stepped away from her.

In her peripherals she caught the sight of him jerking his head in her direction again and her body was hit with another bucket of cold water. Then a cup was shoved to her lips and (this time she knew what it was) blood was forced into her mouth. Amanda swallowed it hungrily (some of it dripping from her lips into the snow beneath) understanding now that it would heal her wounds. She could feel her flesh began to repair its self, much like when a scab is pulled off. It was almost as painful as their creation.

The cup was ripped from her lips and James came back to stand behind her. She heard the moist, sloppy sound of his tongue on his fingers before they were shoved between her thighs and used to stimulate her. That was the furthest thing from her mind, sex. They did not care and she knew it. When he was satisfied with her wetness, James rammed into her, rocking her body. He grabbed her hips and thrust even harder inside of her, finally finishing on the back of her thighs. At least she had learned to block that much out. If they were torturing her, then they were leaving the other women along, for now. Amanda saw herself as sort of a sacrificial lamb. Even distracting them for a few hours was worth all the pain and suffering she would have to endure.

She grit her teeth and managed a laugh, causing the three of them to look at her puzzled.

"What's the matter boys? You running out of ideas as to how to punish me? Or break me? Your attempts, although painful are pathetic. You've tried all the tricks you have on me, we both know it. You might as well give up now. Admit your defeat."

There was a collective growl before Miller stepped forward and grabbed her by her jaw.

"You think so? Maybe I should rip those pretty little teeth from your mouth and skull fuck you. Just like I did to Rachel."

Amanda glared up at him as he said her name. That poor innocent girl, how they must have tortured her. How dare he even speak her name. She jerked at the chains holding her in place, wanting so badly to tear into him. Her actions only invoking a laugh from him.

"I have an idea. Bring her inside, to my room and then meet

me in the hallway. I know one thing that will change her tune." Sterling said.

There was an air of seriousness in his voice that was unnerving. In all the time she had dealt with him, she had not heard him say anything with that tone. Something was very wrong.

The chains above her were unlocked and she was drug back into the factory. Her legs scraped against the metal stairs, slicing them up as they carried her upstairs and back to the Chameleons room. Amanda had become numb to the horror that surrounded her and the monsters that mutilated her flesh. She could almost say she had grown bored with them. Which was an odd concept, to become displeased with her torture and suffering. To be disappointed because it lacked creativity. Still, she could not deny what Sterling had said and the way he had said it. There was a fear in her heart she did not understand, her body knew something worse was about to happen.

The door creaked open and James stepped into the room. There was no emotion on his face, the visage he had kept up, long gone. No more pretending to be something else, she had already seen the demon and the evil that it was capable of inflicting. The two minions under his command walked into the room, carrying a small woman with short raven hair. She was covered in bite marks, bruises, scars, cigar burns and deep lacerations.

"Over there, on the table."

They bent her over the metal table, tying each her wrists to a different leg of it.

"What are you doing? Let her go! Leave her alone!"

Sterling walked over to Amanda with a knife in hand, dragging the blade lightly down her flesh as he spoke.

"Since pain doesn't seem to affect you anymore, we're gonna have some fun with her . . .and you get to watch."

"No, leave her be. Hurt me, not her. She hasn't done

anything!" Amanda screamed in desperation.

A slow smirk spread across his features before he moved over to the girl and drug that blade down her back. She screamed in pain, her cries echoing harshly off the brick walls around them. The sound of the strange woman's agony caused Amanda's inner animal to come out. Her canines grew to long sharp points and she roared at them, pulling hard at the restraints. Wanting nothing more than to break every bone in their body and slowly peel their flesh away. No more women should suffer or die because of them.

"Take your hands off her!"

With a toothy grin, he licked the girls blood from his fingers before using those same wet digits to finger her. Amanda growled, pulling harder at her restraints, every cell in her body wanting to tear into his flesh. James and Miller stood there, watching in amusement. Sterling glanced over his shoulder at her as he unzipped his fly and she watched in horror as thrust forcefully into her. The woman began to cry and beg him to stop but that only seemed to arouse him more.

"Get off of her!"

Hours must have passed as they forced to watch the rape, beat, whip and cut this poor defenseless woman. No matter how hard she pulled, she could not break free from her restraints. Still, she swore she would not give up, she would get free and when she was fully healed, she would kill them. When they grew bored with their toy, they cut her restraints and drug her limp form over to Amanda. They held her up so Amanda was forced to look into her eyes.

"Look at her Amanda. You did this to her. This is your fault." Miller said.

"No, let her go! "

"You want us to let her go?" He nodded to himself. "What do you think boys? Should we let her go?"

"She's served her purpose." James replied.

The tone in his voice told Amanda that they were not going to let her go in the way she intended.

"All right," Miller nodded. "Sterling."

He grabbed the woman by the back of her head and drew a knife quickly across her throat, spraying arterial blood on Amanda's face.

"No!" Her scream came too late.

As Amanda listened to her gurgle (as blood filled her lungs) and watched the light fade from her once green eyes, she cursed the laughing demons around her.

"You bastards! I'll kill you for that! I swear I will!"

"Why? You did this to her." James replied.

A blood red tear of rage and sadness ran down her cheek. That woman would be another discarded corpse or another unmarked grave. All because she had failed to save her, so they were half right, it was partially her fault. She could not reverse her death but she could avenge her and make sure she did not die in vein. The blood on her face was beginning to drip onto her scarred chest and dry to a dark crust. She replayed the last few moments in her mind until she was consumed by rage and adrenaline filled her bloodstream. Until everything around her appeared to slow down and she could see every trivial movement they made. A growl left her lips and she pulled at the chains with all the strength but still they did not budge. However, the lights around her began to flicker as the rage in her chest grew.
It was short lived, a fist slammed into the side of her jaw causing her body to wave. Amanda shook her head and the world around her resumed normal speed. Sterling had punched her in the jaw, but why? Was she close to breaking free or was it something else?

She knew she had done something to rattle his nerves, the look on his face told her that much. They all seemed a little shaken as they surrounded her like wolves with a large prey. James stood in front of her, a stack of faded, torn papers in one hand. He stepped closer to her, speaking low.

"How does it feel to kill an innocent? Her blood will always be on your hands, all because you couldn't play by the rules."

"No, her death was not my fault. You knew after I bit back that I would never submit. Don't act like it surprises you."

"You're right, it doesn't. But how many more women must die for you? Hmm?"

He stepped back and began throwing one sheet after another on the floor beneath her. Amanda looked down and realized they were missing posters he was tossing at her feet.

"Her? How about her? Or even her?"

He hung one of them up so the boys could see.

"She is so much fun."

"Oh yeah, lemme see that," Miller said grabbing the poster. "Sterling remember her?" He turned the picture toward the Chameleon.

"Ohh she screamed so loud." Sterling said laughing.

They were having a laugh about what they had done and would do to those women if she did not submit. So either she gave in to protect them and the boys continued to torture them. Or she kept fighting and they killed them faster, which in her eyes was a blessing for those girls. Amanda thought about something, it had not occurred to her before now. There were not enough women in their factory for them to keep killing them off at an accelerated rate. For the boys to resupply their stock, they would have to get sloppy and risk getting caught. They had to know this and were just hoping that she did not figure it out. Amanda began to laugh and James threw the rest of the posters at her.

"What's so funny bitch?"

"You're a fucking moron." She laughed.

"So, you think I'm playing games with you?"

"You won't kill more women. You can't afford to. There is no way for you to replenish your supply as fast as you knock them off. Not unless you want to draw the unwanted attention you have spent so many years avoiding."

James jaw tightened, his tongue rolling around in his mouth as he decided what to do with her. He turned his back on her before spinning on his heels and slamming his fist into her rib-cage until she was spitting blood. Her diaphragm seized momentarily and she gasped for unnecessary air. She no longer needed air to live but breathing was a hard habit to break. A laughed escaped her ruby lips between coughs. Was insanity setting in? She was mocking their anger, they knew she was right.

"Oh, James are you mad? I guess I'm the one woman you'll come to regret taking." She continued to laugh.

"Miller." James snapped his fingers, holding out his hand.

The telepath handed him the cat of nine tails and he began spinning through the air, rotating his wrist to build up speed. Then he brought the whip across her torso hard, he hit her until her blood dripped from all nine tails. Her breasts and stomach were covered with deep lacerations. Blood poured down her midsection, trailed down the length of her legs before dripping off her toes. As her body swayed and the tails hanging loosely from his hand swung with the movement of his body, blood began to fall in droplets onto the faded faces below. The many innocent eyes looking up at her, begging for help, became soaked in the crimson that fell to the floor. It almost felt symbolic. She had planned to save them from this hell and was willing to bleed for them. Dare she sound blasphemous but it was very Christ-like, except she was dying to save their lives, not absolve them of their sins. Amanda licked her lips before spitting blood from her mouth in a gesture that told James she still would not give up. That her resolve was absolute. He sighed heavily in anger before flinging the whip behind him and knocking all the knives from the metal table. His fists creating large dents in its metallic surface and then he turned to her, his face mere inches from hers.

"You will break Amanda, eventually they all do. I know you've got it in your head that you're gonna get free and be some big hero. That you can take us down. But you never will. You'll die before that happens."

"If you're so confident, then why even worry about me? You've been getting more nervous with every passing hour. So, who are you really trying to convince? Me? Or your boys? The situation got our of your control a long time ago. You know it, you've just been trying to convince them of that."

James pursed his lips, licking his bottom one and nodding. His dark pools stared angrily into her own eyes as he spoke, never turning his head away.

"Sterling, your turn. We'll see how confident your sweet ass is when he's done with you." He said, his voice dropping an octave lower.

Amanda knew she had rattled them, their body language was not so confident. Sterling moved over to his favorite table, grabbing his butcher knife off the floor.

"Come on Sterling, get creative. We've already done this song and dance. Is that the best you've got? The knives?"

The Chameleon smirked as he walked over toward her and

drove the knife deep into her thigh, slicing through the bone. Amanda grit her teeth breathing heavily as a new brand of pain shot through her leg. The muscles in her appendage twitched and just when she was beginning to come to grips with what was happening, he drove another knife into the opposite thigh.

"Creative enough for ya?" He whispered in her ear. "What I'm about to show you is an entirely new brand of pain. Baby girl when I'm done with you, you'll be begging for forgiveness."

As blood poured from her wounds, her eyes began to grow heavy. The blood loss was not enough to cause her to pass out, only make her feel a little drowsy. She knew she needed to get away from them and back to her cell to rest, so she could execute her plan of escape. It would be painful, what she would have to do to get free but not nearly as bad as what they had already done. So she pretended to pass out and she waited for them to carry her into her cell. One of the times they had drug her across the factory floor, a large sliver of metal became lodged in her thigh and when they were not looking, she pushed it in deeper. She let the wound heal over, holding the metal in place by tightening the muscles around it.

When they dropped her on the floor, she shoved her fingers into the gashed on her legs and pulled the shard from her flesh. As they started to close the door, she slid on her own blood trail and shoved the metal in front of the latch. The door never fully closed and she knew they were so worked up by what she had done, they never noticed. Even the Telepath could not focus properly. All she had to do now was wait for nightfall and then make her move.

Chapter 24

As she lingered in the confines of her cell and stared into the darkness around her, something inside her began to change. It was not the way she wanted things to happen but she had come to a realization. If she was going to survive then she would have to accept the demon she had unintentionally become. A ruthless, cold hearted, killer with a craving for human blood. Now she understood the premise of their hunting strategy or at least when it came to her. The chameleon had posed as James, beat her within an inch of her life and had done it all to drive her to Collins. How was he so sure she would move here? Unless the Telepath suggested it to her. Then why bother with the charade? Perhaps to shake her nerves, throw her mindset off kilter and make influencing her that much easier. Their plans were not as air tight as they believed. Her mind went back to that night, back to the feelings she had when she pulled the trigger. If she was angry then (angry enough to kill) how did she feel now? After being treated like an object and watching them hurt that girl.

Every strike of Sterling's boot, every cut from his blades, the lashes from Miller's whips, the beatings that James had dished out and then the rape, all flooded into her minds eye. The memories flooded her senses as she stared blankly into the distance, a small flicker of rage (like a candle flame) ghosted through her eyes. Her body flinched and twitched at the feel of the whip. The pain did not break her as they had hoped.

When she was finished with them, there would be only pieces. Their deaths would be slow and more agonizing than any pain she felt. She was vengeance incarnate but not just for herself. There were others here, suffering along with her and for some unexplainable reason she wanted to avenge them. The women before and after her, whose families mourned their loss every night, staring hopelessly out the window, wishing they would come home.

The more the change took hold, the more Amanda could see the cracks in the illusion. She began to notice days ago but never let them know it. What she saw were decaying buildings, cracked streets and falling signs. She knew the Telepath was responsible for everything looking the way it did. The more he was in her head, the more she learned to block out his influence and the more she learned about him.

In the cell next to her, she could hear Miller's voice yelling at the woman as he man handled her. Amanda listened to her cries of pain, the yells as he hit her repeatedly and she began to tap her hand on her kneecap. With every cry from the next cell, she flinched but not out of fear, it was a combination of muscle memory and rapid deterioration of her patience. She was not a battered woman beaten into submission. No, she instead was a pissed off vampire whose patience seem to thin with every passing minute. Tap, went her hand with the next whelp, tap again and then one last tap. Amanda clinched her fists, digging her nails into her palms until they bled. With every tap she told him to leave her alone. Tap, 'leave her alone', tap, 'leave her alone' and then her thoughts ceased. He was ignoring her and she did not take too kindly to being ignored. Her patience had come to an end.

"Leave her alone!"

It was not a threat she was issuing, it was a promise. If he chose to ignore it (and he seemed to be doing that very thing), then she would help him to understand new definitions of pain.

Amanda continued to growl, her thoughts loud enough for him to hear them. She had meant her exclamation to be a threat. Now her thoughts were an attempt to provoke a reaction from him. If she was insulting and disobedient enough, he may feel it necessary to come deal with her. Despite the excruciating pain she was in, she would rather be the sacrificial lamb. For some unknown reason she felt and urge to protect the other women. Call it motherly instinct, call it a hero complex, call it whatever, she so desperately wanted to sage them. At some point in her own torture, something inside her stood up and declared No. They were not going to hurt innocents who could not protect themselves. She on the other hand, could and she was prepared to take whatever they dished out. 'To hell with nightfall.' She thought.

Amanda pressed her palm to the cold concrete wall, pulled her legs under her and dug her nails into the side of her cell as she attempted to pull herself to her feet. She tightened her jaw and grunted quietly, breathing irrationally as sharp daggers pressed deep into her legs. The still open wounds on her body posed red and ran down, gathering in a puddle on the floor. Her nails left jagged indents as she dug them deeper into the wall beside her and with a growl, pulled herself to her feet. Even with adrenaline flowing through her veins, her vision blurred momentarily and her body swayed.

Through the thick factory wall she could hear the continued yelps of pain as the Telepath struck the woman repeatedly. On quivering, bloody stems, she moved to the back of the cell and pressed her ankle into the wall. Amanda tucked her head down, turned her body so her shoulder was more prominent and then forced herself into a run. There was a loud bang followed by a screech of metal as she slammed her full weight against the door, fracturing her shoulder and pushing the door open.

As she stumbled to the next cell (leaving a blood trail with every labored step) the demon inside began to take hold. There was a sharp pain as her canines grew to their full length and then the world around her grew brighter. The weakness in her body subsided, her head stopped swimming and she felt stronger than she had before. She exhaled and her breath was a guttural growl. Amanda clinched her fists until every knuckle cracked. Within the darkness of the cell, she could see (as if by day) the Telepath raising his arm to stick the small woman again. The bloody form in the corner gasped at the sight of Amanda and began pointing irrationally. That was fine, she wanted to see the look of desperation or (more enticing) pain, on Miller's face as she served him some of his own torture.

"What did I say? Did I not tell you, no, work you to take your hands off her? What did you not understand about that?"

"Get back in your cage before you really get hurt. Or have you forgotten what I am capable of?" He warned.

"Oh, I'm fully aware. See that's the beauty of it all. I know what you can do. Do you want to learn what I can do?" She grinned.

Whatever humanity she had, was dying with every passing second. She was beginning to like the darkness inside. It had not only become part of her, it was taking over.

"Amand-"

Before he could say her name with that acidic mouth of his, she closed the gap between them and silenced him. The sharp white daggers in her mouth pierced the soft tissue of his neck. She wrapped her legs tight around his waist as warm, red liquid poured down her throat. It tasted sweet beyond comprehension and her body buzzed as it filled with age old power. She could only equivocate it to being fueled by large quantities of caffeine. Her body swayed slightly as if comfortably buzzed and her wounds (some of them) began to close. There was a sickening wet sound as the flesh healed, followed by a shift and grind when her broken bones healed.

Miller tried hard to pull her off of him but she had her legs locked around his torso. The nails on her fingers had grown to sharp talons during her feed and in return she buried them in the meat of his shoulder. He had no chance of pulling her away from him now.

When she heard the beat of his heart slow to a near stop, she let lose her grip and he fell to the floor. Amanda slowly stepped back away from him, blood coating her lips and dripping onto the floor.

A purr rolled through her chest as his life force revived her strength. By now, she knew the others were no longer in town or they would have come running. They were hunting for another girl to replenish their supply. That meant she had plenty of time to do what she needed to do. She glanced at the girl who was now hovering in the corner, staring at her with wide eyes, the bitter smell of fear radiating off of her. Amanda licked her lips and allowed her body to relax. The color of her eyes faded to normal and her canines retracted to their human length. She made no attempt to pacify the young woman, knowing it would do no good.

"I'm not going to hurt you. I'm not one of them. I can't take you with me right now, not yet. I will come back for you."

That was all she said before she grabbed Miller's body and

hoisted it over her shoulder. It was a nightmarish sight, a woman covered in wounds, nude and bloody. Her hair was soaked with it as if she was Elizabeth Bathory reborn. However, she did not bathe in the blood of virgins but instead in that of her captors.

Her feet made a wet slapping sound as she padded back to her former living quarters. Amanda dropped his body carelessly on the floor and slammed the door, locking it. Then she headed back to the other cell and regrettably closed that door too. The sound of that lock felt like a death sentence. She paused before heading for her exit, her fingers smearing the door with blood. Now, was not the time for sorrow, it would only make her sloppy. Her mind quickly traveled back to the task at hand.

That cell would only hold Miller until the rest of the cavalry returned. However, that was not its purpose. When the others returned to find their brother was missing, they would have to search to find him. He would be out for a few hours so there would be no way for him to telepathically tell them his location. It bought her more time to do what she planned. She very well could have killed him but she had other plans for him.

Amanda headed down the walkway, leaving small blood droplets as she went. In the dim light of day, she looked almost amazonian with dirt and blood covering every inch of her.

The sunlight finally began to fade as she searched the factory for some clothes. She went from one room to another, finally finding a single box with some ratty jeans and shirts. Every article of clothing she found was torn or cut. They were remnants of previous victims. Although, why they keep any of them was beyond her. Among the clothes, she managed to find a pair of black jeans, boots and a holy tee shirt. Then she headed down the hallway and slipped into Sterling's playroom. There was fresh blood still drying on his floor and the nauseating smell of non-consensual sex. Amanda shook her head and shoved her emotions down as far as she could. There were more pertinent tasks at hand. She searched his collection of knives until she found the one blade that burned her flesh and she tucked it in her belt.

Silver would not kill them but it would slow them down. Amanda's sudden vampirism did not make her immune to them. Nor had it given her the power to defeat them. She knew enough to know that they were far older, wiser and stronger. Now, was not the time to be arrogant and take them on. However, there was nothing wrong with enjoying her victories thus far. Amanda also knew there was a chance she would not make it out of Collins alive. She had to make sure the if she died, it would not be for nothing.

A sigh passed through her as she boldly, daringly walked out the front door of the factory. The illusion that was Collins had begun to fade. She no longer wore the rose colored glasses of Miller's creation. The wall surrounding the factory, was not solid brick as she once knew, it was only an illusion. There was nothing keeping anyone in or out. On to one side of the snow covered property was a barrage of cars. If she planned to escape this prison or inflict some damage before she died, it was a necessary part of her plans. It was the perfect time to test her boundaries and discover her full capabilities. So she crouched down and pushed with every muscle in her body, leaping into the air and landing on a rusted out vehicle with most of its parts missing.

She moved from one hood to another until she located hers. Amanda yanked open the drivers side door, jumping down off the hood and began searching for the keys. They had been shoved in the visor, falling into her lap when she pulled it down. Pushing the key in the ignition, she started it and smiled when she heard the engine roar to life. Amanda flipped on the lights and bounced out of the abandoned lot, fish tailing onto the street as she headed, not for the house but instead for the police station. She had a feeling she would find her Mossberg there. It would not kill them, she knew that but she had a plan for it, something that would slow them down. Everything else she needed, she could find at James's house and the hardware store. At least she hoped she would find what she needed.

The snow had drifted heavily across the street since it fell, so she had to switch the Jeep to four wheel drive to get it through the large mounds piled around the town. She slid to a stop in front of the building, turning on her floodlights before climbing out of the car. There was no power in the entire town, she knew it, they knew it and she refused to deal with the shadows. To her surprise the door was locked, which she thought was ridiculous. Who was around to try and break in? Besides, few people would dare to break into a police station.

Amanda stepped back and slammed her foot into the lock, bending the door frame enough so when she yanked on the handle the lock snapped under the strain. She was not worried if they came back and saw the damage. What else could they do to her? Kill off their entire supply trying to break her? Or kill her? That would be a blessing, they knew it too. So, she knew they would not do that.

What shadows were lingering hissed at her and she growled in response. The shadows slithered and whipped about, hissing at her as the light from the Jeep's floodlights poured inside. Amanda rolled her eyes upward and glad at them with annoyance. A low growl of warning rumbled through her chest. She scanned the small building until she located the metal gun case behind the long counter. Aside from breaking through another door to get to the back of the station, her only other option was to jump or climb over the counter. She placed her hand on the counter top and pushed herself up over the ledge with one arm, throwing her legs on the other side. She landed silently and made her way over to the safe. It towered over her small frame, its massive turn style nearly the size of her head. Amanda stared at it in an attempt to discover its weakest point. There was no easy way to break the three titanium bars keeping it locked. She looked down at her right hand, clinching it into a fist and thinking only, 'this is gonna hurt like hell.' There was an echoing thud followed by the cracking of bones as her fist slammed into the edge of the door. She could feel the snap in her hand as her bones broke and the metal gave way under her first hit. Amanda hit the door until the titanium bars weakened enough for her to pull the door open. By that point her knuckles were smearing blood on the face of the safe and was limp from the crushed bones in her hand.

With time, they would reset themselves and heal. The other hand was still in tact and she grabbed one of the large tumblers, yanking with all the strength she had. There was a metallic groan, as if an old ship coming to port and then a deafening snap. The three bars holding the door closed had snapped under strain and the safe opened wide. In the corner of the iron box she found her Mossberg 500 and on the top shelf extra ammunition.

Above the safe she spotted a black bag, (the type one might use for tactical missions) she grabbed it awkwardly with her broken hand. Then she shoved all the ammo she could into the bag and tucked her shotgun on top. She grunted as she moved, switching the bag to her good hand.

Amanda turned around (leaving the save open) and headed for the Jeep, sitting the bag on the passenger seat before backing out and heading for the hardware store. She knew it was the only other building in town that might still be in tact. It was where Sterling could get his knives sharpened and Miller could get his chains. They needed that place. How else could James pretend to be a handyman? She scoffed at the thought of him. He most likely knew nothing about tools, let alone how to fix a fuse box She was willing to bet it was already broken to begin with, and Telepath let the truth show through when the moment was right. Amanda half smirked and shook her head. '*Idiots.*' She thought. It was a pacifying statement. She had to admit their plan, up till now, was airtight and well through out. Find a way to lure women into your territory, isolate them, trap them and then have your way with them.

The hardware store was darker than the police station. Although none of that came as a shock to her. She had left the floodlights on for that very reason. The door on the hardware store remained unlocked which defined its level of importance. They were hiding nothing within these walls but its lack of security seemed strange. She knew its purpose in their games, so why not protect it? Using her partially broken hand, she pulled the heavy door open with a grunt of pain. The smell of stale death wafted out to greet her, assaulting senses with its sour stench. She pushed the back of her hand against her nose to dull the aroma. That fragrance made her stomach roll and at the same time it fascinated her. She was amazed by how things smelled, felt and looked different with her enhanced senses. The aroma was one of old death, over powered by the sulfuric smell of old blood, long sense desiccated. It coated the floor of the center isle, turning dark brown when it finally dried. Without Miller they could never have pulled this off. Only he could make an entire town disappear and anyone's memory along with it.

In the back of the store, she found the tools she could use to load her shells with something more useful than buckshot. As she was loading her supplies into a heavy toolbar, something caught her eye. In the far corner of the building, disagreed like trash, were two shriveled husks. They were still wearing their blue work vests (stained with blood) the store name remained embroidered but faded. Those people deserved to die with more dignity than that. Amanda did not have the time to give them proper burial. So, she turned from them and headed down another isle, grabbing emergency candles, propane lanterns with canisters, flashlights and the batteries that had not expired. Then she carried it all out to the car, loading it all in the back seat.

At the realization that her journey was not complete, she placed her hands on the seat in front of her and sighed. The thought of going back into that house, willing stepping through the door, sent her into a panic attack. She clinched her fists to steady herself, jerking her broken hand back when she felt the sharp pain of its still broken bones. There was no tie for an emotional break down. So she slammed the door and climbed in the drivers seat.

The Jeep slid around the corner as she turned sharply, heading for James's house, suddenly remembering how to get there As if an invisible force was guiding her. On James's street the snow was much higher and large snow drifts were piled across his driveway, making parking impossible. There was only one place left for her to park. She pulled up into the front yard, and parked so her lights lit up the entire front of the house. Again, she left the engine running as she hurried into the house and made her way into his room. The shadows were thicker here and they hissed at her as they tried to keep her from the room.

"Back off! I'm in no mood!" She growled.

With hesitant movements they obeyed, slithering back into the corners of the room. She fearlessly stepped over the threshold. The Dark (she pretended) meant nothing to her anymore, she could see in the dark better than she could the light. So locating the drawer was nothing for her and picking out the silver was easy. Whatever burned her flesh, she knew was the metal she needed. Why did James bother to keep any of it? She wondered. Was he keeping trophies of his past victims so he could relish in their deaths? It was not enough that they kept the girls for days, weeks or even months. He wanted to revel in the horrors they introduced them to and remember their even more painful deaths. 'Bastards' She thought. Gathering the silver into one of his clean socks, she finally headed back to her house. With the boys gone and her strength renewed, she was feeling a bit cocky but she knew better than to let that attitude get the best of her. It would make her sloppy and she might be caught before finishing the task at hand. The dilapidated buildings around town looked like giant skeletons frozen in hell. If only she could have shown the other girls, enlightened and empowered them, maybe they would try to fight back.

There were a lot of possibilities but it was up to her to give them the tools they needed. Amanda slid up into the driveway, hitting the garage door in the process. She climbed out of the Jeep (disregarding the broken door) with tools in hand and headed in the house. The door to the house shook as it hit the wall beside it. She wasted no time closing it. Instead she ran for the basement, leaping the last few stairs on her way down.

The workbench would finally come in handy. She shoved everything off the wooden table, and dropped her bag of tools in their place. Then she began the process of melting the silver and pouring it into a mold. When the molten metal cooled, she tapped the mold on the table and gathered the ball bearings. Amanda replaced the buckshot with silver and sealed the shells back up. The entire process took nearly three hours to complete, but when she had finished, there was enough for a box and a half of ammunition. The rest of them she left filled with regular buckshot, loading one of each into the shotgun and cocking it. That metallic crack was deadly music to her ears, even though she knew it would only stun them, having at least that much, was empowering. The sadistic side of her wanted to test it out now. She missed the buck of the recoil as she squeezed the trigger. However, she had other plans for her modified weapon.

Time was running out, she had to move fast or miss her window of opportunity. Amanda grabbed the box of lights and her weapons before heading back upstairs. When she reached the bottom stair on the first floor, she dropped the black gun bag and headed up to her bedroom. Once there, she pulled off the back panels of the closet wall and hid the majority of lights, all save for one, a propane lamp.

Her actions reflected that of a woman who could sense her own demise. Amanda was preparing for the chance she might fail and they might lure another woman into this house. From one of the boxes in the living room, she grabbed the leather bound journal she had brought before everything happened with James. Then she stashed the shotgun with ammunition, beneath the last stair by prying up the board. Maybe the next girl would get out before it was too late. She set up the propane lantern and cranked it up until the light was bright enough to light her whole front room. Snow continued to drift in through the front door and the wind had chilled the room around her to an almost unbearable cold. She walked over and slammed the door, huddling near the light for warmth.

Amanda set to documenting everything she had gone through, writing down everything she knew about the boys. So if their next victim was smart enough to follow the clues, she might have a chance to get free. Or maybe end this thing. When she was nearly finished documenting the series of events that lead up to this point, she heard the tap tap of someone knocking on the door. She jerked her head up in the direction of the noise. Even through the glass she could tell who was on the other side. Of course it was him, it would always be him. Amanda slit silently across the floor and flipped the lock. It would not keep them out but it might buy her more time.

Before they could catch her and she knew they would, she pulled the silver knife from her belt. She knew she could not fight them all and if they caught her, they other girls would pay for her crimes. That was the only way for them to punish her because hurting her, no longer did any good.

There was moment where everything stopped and she sat staring at the silver knife in her hand. Amanda had only one option available and she knew it would be the end of her. She stood from her place in the floor and ran to the basement. There she sat down on the top stair, pried the board from under the stairs before driving the blade in her heart. An indescribable pain shot through her chest, spider webbing out from the wound and paralyzing her lungs. Her next actions seemed irrational but she knew what she was doing. If she was going to die, she wanted it to be on her terms and she wanted to document it.

As she waited for death or them (whichever came first) she wrote her last few thoughts, drops of blood dripping onto the pages.

I'm not sure who left the claw marks on the floor. Who they might have drug out of here. I just know that blade brought me peace. Sure it hurt like hell but as the blood left my body, I felt a sense of accomplishment.

They could no longer have me. I can hear them roaring in anger right now. Its amazing how little pain you feel when the blood starts to flow.

Everything around you becomes so quiet and time seems to slow. I knew my death would be slow but they would suffer more because I had won.

This is my last entry. I pray you get our alive . . .

Then she closed the journal with shaky hands and shoved it under the stairs, carving another message with her nails before slamming the basement door. Amanda flipped the lock on it as the front door busted off its hinges, her hands leaving bloody smears on the wood. Amanda moved down the stairs to carve one last message on one of the support posts before collapsing on the floor. She stared up at the wood beams above as her vision began to fade.

Present Day

Chapter 25

There was a stillness in the air like a storm was brewing. In a way it was, Sara knew what she had to do, what was being asked of her. Although she dreaded every second of it, she understood that she was going to have no choice. Amanda needed some help from the outside. Sara was the only girl to discover the journal and therefore she had to help her. Together they had a chance for revenge and not just for themselves. Shedding their blood and sating the girls lust for vengeance, would be the first time that fury did some good. Through their united hatred and pain, they could kill the demons responsible. Neither one of them knew how to kill a vampire but maybe after being turned, Amanda learned how. Sara knew if she was going to achieve this goal, she needed to get blood to her partner in crime. But how? There were no blood banks readily available. She surely would not sacrifice one of the girls. If she could cripple one of the boys and drag them to the cell, that would work. If she had the strength to move their unconscious body. Unless she could get some blood from them while they were incapacitated.   Sara would have to risk getting caught and sneak into the factory so she could physically talk to Amanda. She knew she would have to give her some of her blood to start the healing process. Although how she got past them without being detected would be another story. Her time was running out, they only kept Amanda for a few weeks before capturing her. She set the journal on the floor before jumping to her feet and moving frantically around the basement. There was a shotgun hidden upstairs but she knew she would need a hammer to get it. Sara tossed boxes around on the floor until she found a claw hammer and headed upstairs, taking the lamp with her. Her movements resembled those of a schizophrenic as she ran to the upper staircase and dropped to her knees. Setting the lamp on the floor, she jammed the claw under the top board of the bottom stair. The wood creaked and groaned as she cranked the hammer. There was a pop as the wood gave way under the strain and she tossed it aside, plunging her hand into the cold, dusty space. She groped desperately for the black canvas bag. It was, to her, her holy cross and defense against evil. She felt as if having it in her possession would somehow save her from them.

Shatter the unbelievable nightmare she found herself trapped in. Her fingers brushed the coarse fabric and she grabbed the bag, yanking it from its coffin. Sara unzipped it, pulled the Mossberg out and stuffed her pockets with ammunition. She did not want to be caught without any or get low and not be able to defend herself. As she was rummaging around, her hand brushed against something cold and metal. It was a small thermos and on the side was a note. She recognized the writing as Amanda's.

'Drink before going out. It will hide you.'

When Sara unscrewed the cap, the over whelming smell of blood wafted into her nostrils. She turned her head away a moment exhaling hard to get the rancid smell out of her body. With her stomach turning in protest she put the neck of the bottle to her lips and poured a swallow of the liquid into her mouth. Then begrudgingly swallowed it down before putting the cap back on. It was like trying to swallow honey but without the sweet taste. The world around her swam, her hearing sensitized and her vision became unbearably sharp. She could see the shadows moving in the dark corners of her house. Amanda's blood not only would hide her but it also gave her enhanced abilities. She shoved the blood back in the bag, zipped it shut and headed out with Mossberg in hand.

As Amanda's blood flowed through her system, the illusion that was Collins, began to crumble. The once beautiful architecture of the buildings was now skeletal with fallen roofs and busted windows. None of the streetlights worked, the sidewalks and roads were littered with weeks that poked through their cracked pavement. There was only one source of light in the distance, its windows glittering like stars in the darkness. Which seemed ironic considering the horrors its walls contained. That was the one place she did not want to be and it was exactly where she was going.

Sara pulled herself into a run, moving between houses to keep from being seen by one of the boys. She dashed across side streets decorated with the bare frames of vehicles, long since forgotten by their owners. Or not forgotten at all and their owners were dead. It should matter to her that they may be dead but it did not. Death, blood and bodies had become normal to her. Not just normal, familiar. That was and uneasy realization.

She heard the rumble of an engine on the next street and she ducked behind a house, gripping the shotgun in both hands. The vehicle sat for a while, not moving as the beam of a spotlight ran across the houses. Slowly, it began to make its way down the street. They were looking for her. Sara hurried around the other side of the house and waited for it to pass. Her heart hammered in her chest, she was not ready for this confrontation. However, she realized she may have no choice. There was a chance that nothing could go according to plan but it would still be better than the alternative. The breaks of the vehicle squealed in protest and then the light lit the back of the house where she had just been. For a moment she felt as if she had been spotted. If they wanted her, they would have to come to her. The vehicle passed her location and turned down another street. Sara waited for it to go a little further before forcing herself to move and continue her run. They knew she was not at home anymore but they could not detect her. She smiled to herself, thinking about how mad they probably were. If she was caught, she knew she had better be ready to pull the trigger. The consequences of her actions up to this point, would be severe. Sara pushed her body harder as she hit the last block and ran around the back side of the factory. Slipping in through the hole in the fence, she ducked behind the cluster of abandoned vehicles, moving between them to find the Jeep. Amanda's car was more sturdy and would make a better escape vehicle. It could go off road if necessary. There was only one problem, they could not fit the other girls inside. They would have to figure out another plan for them. Right now, she had to take them down. That was plan 'A'.

In the far corner, closest to the side gate, she found the Jeep. It was a little dirty and beginning to rust but she had a feeling the engine was fine. At least she hoped it was all right. Sara glanced toward the factory before opening the door and searching for the keys. She found them tucked in the glove compartment, she shoved them in her pocket before quietly closing the door. Sara moved between the cars to crouch down beside them and watch the factory. Minutes moved into hours and for the longest time nothing happened. She considered trying to move toward the factory but something told her not to. They were baiting her, trying to trick her into coming out of hiding. She would not fall for that again.

Her eyes began to slowly drift closed as exhaustion started to take hold. That was when she noticed it, a dark silhouette in the courtyard, watching her. The sound of water dripping off him was only noticeable because of her enhanced hearing. Her blood flushed cold as her body flushed hot. Sara's mind revolted at the thought. She white knuckle gripped the gun to her chest and fought back the panic. A voice pierced through the silence.

"Be a good girl and I won't slit your pretty little throat."

His boots crunched the gravel under his feet as he moved toward her. She slowly slid between the cars, moving back away from him, the monster from her nightmares. As she was fighting to keep from running or firing the shotgun and drawing unwanted attention. Someone else was manifesting in the shadows. She stood behind him, her image flickering as she used all her strength to save Sara.

"Leave her alone."

The sound of her voice made Sara pause and stand to see who was speaking. Even without ever seeing her human form, Sara knew in her gut that it was Amanda. Sara's demon, the unnamed man, paused and his body language told her he was pissed. Slowly, he turned to look at Amanda. Even though she was there to protect Sara, she knew she could not keep that form for long.

'Can you feed in that form?' Sara thought.

Knowing Amanda would hear her.

'Not for long.'

Sara bit her bottom lip, sucking it in her mouth before she nodded to herself and yelled to get his attention.

"Hey! Over here!"

The shotgun was hidden behind her back, she just needed him to get close enough. All predators are the same in a fir of hunger, they zone out everything but their target. So when he was within range, Sara slammed the but of the gun into his head. It collided with his forehead and he collapsed on the ground unconscious. That was a risky move because there was no way of knowing if he was only a shadow. His body hit the ground hard and it was then that Sara learned who her attacker had been. The cause of her moving here. It was Alex. A growl escaped her chest and she pointed the shotgun at his face, her hands tightening around the barrel. Her fingers flexed and loosened as she shifted her weight to and fro.

"No Sara don't. Not yet."

Sara's upper lip twitched in anger and she huffed out a heavy exhale before lowering the gun. Then she spun on her heels and paced the area around his body, running her fingers through her hair. He was the reason she was here and he was right there for the taking. She could shoot him and go home, she wanted to so badly kill him. A rage filled her once fearful heart, reminding her of why she was doing this.

Amanda was already feeding on him, her shadow form darkening as she regained strength. The sound of a car was the only thing that made her quit. Sara dashed behind a car and Amanda disappeared into thin air. This plan was not going to work. Desperate times called for desperate measures. They would not be able to rescue all the girls if Sara did not take a chance. She needed to get Amanda more blood than that. Sara would have to either leave town or give the weaker girls to Amanda.

"No Sara. Not the girls."

That meant going to the next town, without being detected. She would have to steal one of their vehicles to do that. The cop cars were out of the question but Alex would be laid up for a few hours. Ellis was helping him to the factory, any moment the Chameleon would be showing up. It was now or never. When the boys were out of sight, Sara made her move. She dashed across the parking lot and headed for his truck, parked just behind the building. To her relief, he had left it unlocked with the keys in the ignition. They would not notice it gone for hours. Their over confident sense of control, ensured they would never look for it. Sitting the gun on the seat beside her, she flipped on the lights, started the truck and headed out. She was gone before Harris ever arrived.

Crossing the border of Collins was both sad and surreal because she knew she would have to come back. Also, she never thought she would leave again, it may be the last time she left. As she drove off, going where, she did not know. Amanda spoke to her one more time.

'There's a hospital in the next town over. Get into their blood storage unit.'

Sara knew that access to that floor would be restricted. She would have to steal a badge to get in. Time was of the essence, so she pressed the accelerator to the floor. The truck engine roared to life and she held a steady speed of ninety until she saw the next city lights. Their hospital was on the edge of town, lit like some great monument. Its endless windows glittered like a thousand diamonds in the night. She slowed the truck to a mere thirty before pulling into the lot and parking near their emergency entrance. The hospital was smaller than most which would make this task a little easier but not much. She exhaled slowly, trying to calm her nerves. Then she zipped her hoodie, pulled the hood up to hide her face, grabbed her bag and slipped out of the truck.

Sara moved around the parking lot until she saw a doctor leaving for home. Moving up behind him, she jammed the butt of the gun into the back of his head before grabbing his badge. There was no time for niceties. She rolled him over and shook him until he snapped out of his daze. He held his hand up to shield himself from the barrel of her rifle.

"Please..."

"Shut up. Look I'm not going to kill you. I'm real sorry about this doc but I need blood. Where do you keep it?"

"I-I-"

"Tell me!" She growled.

"B-basement. It's a large freezer."

"Thanks."

She flipped the shotgun around, cold cocked him and moved his body so it was not visible. Then she put the weapon in her bag and ran for the hospital.

Sara located the staff entrance and slipped inside, keeping her head down to avoid being seen by cameras. She sprinted for the stairs and descended into the basement. Between avoiding other staff who were down there and getting lost several times, it took her nearly an hour to find the storage unit of blood. She swiped the doctor's badge and slipped inside. The room was a steady six degrees Celsius Its walls were lined with several metal shelving units. On each shelf were bags of blood, piled one on top of another. All of them were labeled as to what type they were, but she doubted it mattered. She filled the bag with as much blood as she could carry (about ten bags). Then she snuck back out of the hospital, heading for the truck as fast as she could with the bag weighing her down.

It would not be long before the hospital staff realized what happened. Sara hopped in the truck and peeled out of the parking lot. She kept the peddle pressed to the floor until she reached her destination. There were mere minutes left for her to park the vehicle and hide before they realized she had stolen Alex's truck. The factory was still lip up, so she knew they were still there. Hurrying out of the cab she slid behind a row of cars, leaving a blank trail of dust under her body. She scraped the skin off her arm and hand in the process but she was out of sight. Sara frantically dug to the bottom of the bag for her thermos, choking down another mouthful.

A crowd of angry voices erupted in the courtyard as Alex, Harris and Miller gathered. She peered around the side of the car she was behind, crouching with one leg out stretched, ready to move at a moments notice. They were yelling amongst themselves, the sound of their shouts echoing off the building.

"That bitch! How could you two let this happen?"

"Us? You're the one who let yourself get knocked out! By a human no less!"

"Fuck you!"

"Miller, got anything?"

"No, I can't find her."

"Don't just stand there! Get out and find the bitch! Go!"

The two cops climbed in their cruisers and headed out.

"Morons." Death whispered under his breath.

'Why is he still bothering to use their given names?' He must know by now that I am not fooled by the costumes they wear.'

Then he too headed for his truck and she prayed he would not notice the heat coming off the hood. He climbed in and took off himself. In his blind fury, he had failed to even notice the gas gauge was lower. Sara waited a few minutes after he left before she printed for the factory. Following Amanda's description of the place, she had a good idea where to find her. The first cell on the left hand side of the walkway was where she hoped Amanda was locked up. She braced herself for what she might find when she opened the door. There was nothing she could have done to prepare herself for the sight before her.

In the far corner of the dark cell was a bloody pale form, her body decorated with bite marks. Sara set the bag on the floor before slowly entering the cell.

"Amanda . . ."

No answer.

"Sweetie, it's Sara."

She heard the sound of chains moving and then Amanda came out of the shadows. Her hair was falling out, her body withered and her face was bruised from her jaw being broken repeatedly broken. She resembled that of a woman far older.

"Oh my god."

Grabbing the bag, Sara dropped to her knees and began to shove the bags of blood at Amanda.

"Hurry, we don't have much time."

One after another, Amanda bit into and sucked the bags dry. Sara dropped the empty ones in her bag, hiding the evidence. She saved one bag for emergency purposes. After Amanda finished, her skin was flawless porcelain, her hair more lustrous than it had been before and her face was beautiful beyond reason.

"I've gotta go. But I'll be back."

"Wait."

Her voice was soft and sweet, like the clinking of wind chimes. Its melody enticed Sara to turn back around.

"Come here Sara. You'll need more strength."

The mortal moved toward the pale frame and knelt down beside her. It was then that Amanda wrapped her in her arms and pulled her close.

"This will only hurt for a moment."

Sara felt soft lips on the tender flesh of her neck and then a sharp pain as canines pierced her flesh. For a few moments the world around her fell away and she was floating in a sea of black. While she hovered between life and death, she heard Amanda's voice in her head.

'When you have drank from my body and the change begins to take hold, you will need blood. Consume what is left in the thermos and then head for the house. You will need to distract them for a bit.'

The world rushed back to her and the next thing she felt was the flesh of a wrist pressed to her face.

"Drink Sara."

Pulling the appendage to her lips, she sucked the blood from the gash there and swallowed a few mouthfuls. It was like coming up for air when she finally pulled away. They had no time for lessons or explanations.

"Go Sara. Run now."

Amanda shoved her to her shaky legs and tossed her things behind her. Still in a daze she slammed the cell door and locked it before stumbling down the stairs.

She barely managed to make it out of the factory lot before the boys returned. Sara dropped to the ground and fished out the thermos, downing the rest of the blood before finally heading toward the house.

The new blood over taking her body, coupled with the vampiric change was disorienting. As she ran, the world around her sharpened and blurred. Her muscles tightened with new found power, giving her more speed and strength. Every sound and smell became unbearable as her sensitivity rapidly increased. By the time she reached the house, the change was complete. Sara stumbled onto the steps falling on the porch and beginning to desperately dig for the bag of blood in the bottom of her bag. She grabbed it with the ferocity of a starving man and bit into the plastic, sucking the contents down. What once tasted bitter, now tasted like a sweet shake. It was filling in a way that food never had been. Her body absorbed the crimson substance, enticing her animal side. Sara purred as she tossed the bag and wiped her mouth with the back of her hand. The game was changing. No longer did the boys have full advantage over them. There were two female vampires (that although they knew the men were stronger) who were willing to stand against them. They were still afraid and would much rather run but they knew they would be pursued. Things would not stop unless the girls stopped them.

Amanda needed a few hours for the blood to take full effect. After running from the factory, she realized there was no time to watch each of them individually. The boys were on to them. So they did not have hours. Sara needed to do something brash, even if all those girls escaped, there was no guarantee that they would stop. If they could not kill them, then they needed insurance that the biggest part of their predatory games was destroyed. Sara was trying to reason with herself but in reality she just wanted to destroy the place responsible for so much pain.

When she stepped into the house, she proceeded to set lit candles and propane lanterns all around the up and downstairs. This time she was not intending to chase the shadows away. Sara grabbed a length of clear hose and two buckets from the basement. Then she siphoned gas from her neon and poured it all around the house. Finally, she did something she had not done since she arrived, she lit a cigarette with Alex's lighter (which she had stolen from his truck). The lighter spun as she tossed it and watched it fall into the puddles of gasoline. A vengeful mix of orange and red, raged across the sea of noxious liquid. Sara watched its quick precision with a satisfied smirk. How mad would they be when the house exploded? She wondered.

Her night was just starting though. Before leaving the blazing structure, she grabbed a set of clothes from her car, moving quickly to the other side of the street and hiding behind the decaying skeletons. Once they were all in front of the house, she could head for the factory.

There was a large pop and then the windows blew outward before the house its self exploded with an ear shattering bang. She felt the vibrations where she sat. It was mere seconds before the boys pulled up out front and began to pile out of their cars. They cursed and roared, one of them shattered the window of their car with their fist.

For a few moments she just stood watching their fits of anger. Sara took another drag from her cigarette, a tendril of blood still drying at the corner of her mouth. Her eyes glimmered silver in the dark as she watched them in amusement. Then she exhaled, flicked her cigarette to the side and turned from them. Time, she knew, was no longer a luxury. If they had been looking for her, then they knew something was up. The girls would have to ready themselves and take the boys out now. Otherwise there was no way to get the girls out of there safely. Sara never heard the footsteps following her or notice the outline of a man against the trees around her.

Chapter 26

The house fire had served its purpose, drawing them away from the factory. It would buy her enough time to get Amanda clothes before they descended on the brick structure again. They would not touch any of those girls, not without a fight. Amanda and Sara were more than happy to oblige them. That thought made Sara purred as she ran through the front gate of the property and up to Amanda's cell. She opened the door with such ferocity that it slammed into the concrete beside it, cracking it. Her newly gained strength was something she would have to get used to and fast. There was no time for the usual vampiric mentoring or the discovery of her full abilities. That was a luxury provided to a luck few. Those who were not trapped within the hell of Collins, fighting to escape its prison. As it was, no one had ever heard of anyone performing suck a feat successfully. They would soon. At best, she had her shotgun and the rage burning deep in her heart. Besides that, she was not alone in this war. Sara threw the clothes into the darkness and waited for her companion to emerge. A familiar voice behind her, shattered the ever present stillness and startled her.

"What the hell do you think you're doing?" The voice demanded.

She turned to find Harris (or Sterling as Amanda knew him) standing there and she attempted to raise her gun to fire. He shoved the gun up with one hand and punched her in the jaw with the other. Sara reeled backwards and fell, crawling away from him. Sterling looked over the gun, then at her, as if he was deciding whether he wanted to use it or not. Sara felt nearly relieved when he tossed the shotgun aside and it skidded across the floor. He moved toward her matching her every movement as she fought to get away. Even though she had become one of them, she still struggled to ignore the fear he could ignite. The fight she originally had was gone melting away the moment she laid eyes on him. She felt trapped, helpless and in her short time of desperation, she began to cry. It was an unconscious reaction that she was unaware was happening. Sara so wanted to believe she could handle the situation but the truth was obvious.

"Where ya going Sara? I just wanna talk to you." Harris whispered softly.

"No. Get away from me! You're not going to touch me!" Sara shrieked.

"Oh ho ho, I'm going to touch you, I'm gonna do a lot of things to you. You're gonna scream and protest but in the end, you'll give in. They all do."

It was more a suggestion than a statement.

"No! Stay the hell away from me!" Sara continued to scream.

She reached for the rifle but he put his boot on it and scooted it out of her reach. Sara looked up at him in desperation. Was this really about to happen?

"Come here, make this easy on yourself." He said calmly in an attempt to pacify her.

As he reached for her, she heard someone behind him.

"Sterling." A female voice warned.

Slowly, he turned to look behind him and from her place on the floor, Sara saw Amanda in her true form. There were black pools where her beautiful eyes had once been and her top row of canines were four sharp daggers. She had become something more predatory, darker than they could ever hope to be. Somehow, she had surpassed them in power.

"Get. Away. From. Her." Amanda growled.

"Ha ha….or what? You're gonna kill me? You don't have it in you bitch."

Amanda cracked her neck, dropped her head and raised her black eyes. Then her fist collided with his chin, sending him flying a few feet away. His teeth broke as they were forced together, she heard his jaw snap and the back of his head hit the wall behind him. Amanda watched his body jolt violently when it collided with the brick. As he slowly got to his feet, she spoke.

"I don't? Oh, Chameleon I can promise you I do. I've watched you boys work and listened to the cries of pain and desperation from these women for long enough. It helped me to build up a tolerance to you,"

Amanda's voice was steady as she spoke.

She walked toward him as she continued.

"You know what else it did? It gave me the unwavering resolve I need to deal with you. Kill you? No, I'm not going to kill you exactly, not yet anyway. I'm going to make you beg for Death. Repay the favor you gave me so many times. I promise you Chameleon, I do have it in me now, thanks to you,"

She stopped only a few feet from him, staring him down as if he was no longer a threat.

"So, here's what's going to happen . . .you're going to deal with me. Not her," She pointed at Sara. "And she is going to fill your boyfriends with silver. Then, we're going to take all these women home, while you all burn in hell. Sound good?"

Amanda grinned.

"Little girl, you're asking for it. What I did to you before, that was just being playful. Now, you're going to see the devil." Sterling warned.

"Oh, I love it when you talk dirty to me. Come on, give me some." Amanda beckoned, glancing over her shoulder at Sara.

"Head downstairs and watch the door. Shoot whoever tries to come through it."

Sara glanced between them before rolling over and grabbing the shotgun. As she stood to descend the stairs, the Chameleon lunged for her but Amanda was too fast for him. Her hand wrapped quickly around his throat and she was throwing him against the side of her cell before he could come within inches of Sara.

"What did I just tell you? I said you're not to touch her."

Chameleon groaned in pain as he stood from his place on the floor, cracking bones back into place and spitting blood.

"What's that? No witty retort? No threat? You're losing your touch." She said sarcastically.

"Shut your fucking mouth bitch!" Chameleon's voice boomed.

His arrogant composure was beginning to break. The Chameleon pushed himself to his feet. There was blood dripping from his mouth onto his shirt. He wiped it off with the back of his hand before stripping the bloody garment from his torso.

"You're going to pay for that." He warned.

"Am I now?" She asked rather matter-of-factly.

She beckoned mockingly with one hand. The Chameleon pulled a knife from a sheath on his back, flipping the blade under his fist and bringing his hands up near his ribs.

"You think I'm that stupid? That I'm going to make the first move?" She said snidely.

"All right bitch, have it your way." He warned.

Then he stepped forward and began furiously, slicing through the air at supersonic speeds as he tried to connect the blade with her flesh. Things were different this time, she was too fast for him to touch her. She dodged and ducked his senseless efforts. Before she dropped down and swept her leg at his ankles. There was the resounding echo of his ankles breaking and he collided with the floor.

"Come on. Are you even trying?" Amanda asked, mockingly genuine.

He growled as he jumped to his feet, increasing his speed to match her own. There were a few moments of missed hits and her avoiding his every advance. She made the mistake of getting overly confident and the knife cut through the flesh on her upper arm. A hiss of pain emanated from between clinched teeth. That gave him the opportunity to slam his free fist into the side of her jaw and send her stumbling backwards. Amanda shook her head to regain her bearings and glared at him. Her eyes flickering between the open laceration on her arm and the blood dripping from his blade. Those red eyes followed her line of sight to the slow rhythmic drip of blood falling from the knife. Chameleon lifted it to his mouth and licked her blood off the blade. He was daring to taunt her. That was fine, she had no more time to toy with him.

There was a long stillness in the air followed by a chill. Even he felt the shift in energy. Amanda glided around the room, her every move becoming a blur. Her fist collided with his sternum hard enough to crack it. Then his throat and she watched him stumble. However, she did not let up. Her right knee made contact with his rib-cage before she leapt in the air and kicked him in the side of the head. Chameleon's skull whipped to the side from the onslaught and he came to a rest with his back pressed to her cell wall for support. One arm wrapped around his mid-section comforting his ribs as he leaned there panting. He licked his bloody mouth and spit on the floor.

He found his reserve of strength and stood, spinning the knife in his hand once more before executing another attack. He must have been holding back because he was too fast for her to avoid. His hard boot kicked the front of her right knee, breaking it and his knife simultaneously sliced through the flesh just beneath her ribs. Amanda stepped backwards, the bones of her kneecap grinding together as she did. The nails on her fingers extended to sharp points and she braced her body for the trauma she was about to put it through. Chameleon looked down at her hand and she watched his eyes widen with shock.

"You looked surprised. You've never dealt with a woman like me before? No, I bet not."

There was a long moment of silence as they circled one another, each one trying to decide their next move. Chameleon looked at the knife in his hand and then glanced at the metal upper railing. He sheathed his knife and grabbed one of the bars, ripping it from the concrete and swinging it at her head. His movements were faster than she had expected and the chunk of concrete at the end of it caught her in the temple. Amanda stumbled backwards and had barely recovered before he hit the other side of her face. There was the sickening sound of teeth cracking and her jaw breaking. Then he hooked the pole behind her knees and pulled, sending her to the floor. Chameleon proceeded to hit her torso until she spit blood. Before slamming the pole into her face.

When he was finished, he tossed his weapon aside. Amanda had broken ribs, most of the bones in her head were shattered and she was coughing up mouthfuls of blood. She rolled on her stomach to protect herself from further injury but he used that opportunity to kick her in the back several times. So, she lay there trying to fight through the pain. As she drug herself desperately across the floor, Chameleon began to circle her. He opened his mouth to spew insults, while she forced her body to cooperate and stand.

"All your power and your talk. Where are you again? On the floor like the whore you are. You just don't get it do you Amanda?"

He grabbed her by her throat and hauled her to her feet, dangling her a few feet off the ground.

"You are ours now, you belong to us. That means you leave when we say you get to leave. You're going to spend the next few years paying for what you have done today and Sara . . .oh lemme tell you . . .we got plans for her."

He disgustingly licked his fingers. The thought of Sara screaming in pain and going though the agony she had experienced. Just the idea of them hurting her and raping her repeatedly, coupled with the sound of his laugh as he said it, it awoke something in her. A growl crawled from deep within and slowly up her throat, despite her lack of air. From her place on the floor she managed to look down at him. Something was happening that even they could not explain. Amanda rolled on her back, ignoring the agony it caused her.

"You will never touch her!" Every word dripping with malice.

She brought her leg up and kicked him in the groin before rolling backwards away from him, landing in a crouched position. She was panting from the pain in her body. However, she focused on her anger and her eyes faded to black, her claws extending in turn. This time she planned to use them, he would not get the upper hand again.

"Oh, little girl has some power." He mocked before insulting her.

"Give it up Amanda. You've already lost."

That was all she said before she began to move around him in a blur, her claws slicing the tendons in the back of his legs and severing his lower spine. When he realized that he could not move his limbs, he dug his fingers into the cement floor beneath him and began trying to claw his way to the stairs, using only his digits.

"Tsk tsk tsk . . ." Amanda slammed her ankle into his spine.

"Aagh." He cried out in pain.

"Where ya think you're going? I'm not finished with you yet."
She said sweetly.

Walking up his body she grabbed him by his hair and slammed his
face into the floor, breaking his nose.

"Remember that Chameleon? Or should I call you James!?"
She screamed.

He said nothing.

Stepping away from him she moved to his ankles and put one
of her bare feet on his right one.

"You should stop this before you really get hurt," He groaned.

"They're going to come back and you're-"

"I'm gonna what? Pay? You're boyfriends aren't going to rescue
you, not this time. It's just you and me baby. We get to play
all by ourselves. Aren't you having fun yet?" Sarcasm dripping
from her words.

"I'm gonna kill you slow bitch." He threatened.

"Hey Chameleon, remember all the times you kicked me?"
She asked.

Applying pressure to his ankle, she snapped first one and then
the other. He screamed through his teeth, still trying to pull himself
away from her.

"Oh no sweetness, you're not going anywhere." Her voice was
eerily calm.

With that she progressively snapped every the bone in his legs with her bare feet.

"Agghh . . .fuck you. You're nothing but a fucking whore!" He growled.

"Oh, I'm so hurt. You cut me deep." She said cattily.

She sliced through the flesh on the back of both legs, cutting all the way to the bone.

"Aaahh . . .you-fuck-bitch."

"We're just getting started . . .I'm being gentle right now."

"You're," He panted for a few moments. "dead!"

Amanda grabbed him by his hair again, lifting his face to hers.

"I died a long time ago. You three killed me." She whispered, a hint of melancholy in her voice.

As she was holding his face up, he spit a mouthful of blood into her eyes and she pulled her head away quickly, wiping the blood off. She had enough of his antics and as far as she was concerned, their conversation was over. Through the red warpaint coating her face, she glared down at him. Amanda slowly moved toward him, having decided his fate. She stared down at him, her eyes falling on the knife still strapped to his lower back. It was time for him to feel the bite of his own blade.

"All the times you raped me," She kicked his pelvic bone so hard it snapped.

"The times you broke my ribs," She stomped on his ribs until the bones protruded through his flesh. "and you cut me . . ." She began to slice into his torso with his own knife.

The red tissue of his muscles gaped open, revealing the white bone beneath. Amanda cut him deeper than he ever did her and she reveled in his pain as he squirmed under the torment. A laugh escaped her lips as she watched shock take over his body and he began to shake from the blood loss. Although he was a vampire, his body in some ways continued to function like a human. Which also meant he could still go into shock. With one foot she flipped him onto his back, sending tendrils of pain coursing through him from the wounds there. By the time Amanda had finished, she had nearly stripped the flesh from his body. When she finally stopped, she sat down on his torso. He no longer had the strength to groan in agony, only twitch in pain. Grabbing him by the back of his skull, she lifted his face to hers. As her tongue ran up one of her bloody claws, she moaned.

"You don't taste too bad yourself," She held the claw in front of his face. "Wanna try?"

His top teeth scraped his bottom lip as he tried to tell her 'fuck you' but he did not have the strength. Amanda laughed before hitting him in the face so many times his cheekbones and eye sockets both shattered.

Then she leaned in his ear and whispered.

"Your days of horror are over. There's a new monster in town." She grinned.

Then she grabbed both sides of his head and twisted it sharply snapping his neck. It echoed off the factory walls. To see his body lying beneath her, a broken battered mess, was some how therapeutic. He could not hurt anyone ever again. A moment of relief came over her and she had to fight the urge to cry. Now was not the time to break down and this was not the place to do it. She had given enough blood and tears to this hell. It would not get anymore, not ever again. Right now, she had two more demons to deal with and when they were dead, she could rest. All the women could go home and break down.

There was this over whelming desire to save them and continue protecting other innocents. Even if they never knew that she was hiding in the shadows to keep them safe. Amanda still had to do it. She had to accepted the fact that she had, had to become a demon (like them) to defeat them. It was a burden she was willing to bare. Although she knew that this transformation was irreversible and she would never be able to see her family again, she knew it was better for everyone. Now, she had to help Sara face the other two.

A wicked thought occurred to her and she decided it would be too much fun, to ignore. She picked up the mutilated corpse of the Chameleon, his hanging flesh slapping about with a sickening wet sound as she moved and tossed it through one of the upper factory windows. The glass shattered and the metal bent upon impact. His lifeless body hit the ground with a sloppy thud, sending the cut flesh peeling from the bone in chunks. Amanda's laugh echoed through the factory as she cackled with amusement. They were going to be enraged when they saw what she did to their brother. She could not stop smirking.

While Amanda was upstairs breaking the overly arrogant Chameleon into nothing, Sara was preparing for the arrival of his back up. She got down on one knee, shoving the butt of the rifle in her shoulder and leaning her head down so she had a better aim. Then she just had to wait for them to arrive. A few moments later, it was not the sound of their vehicles she heard but the soft thud of a body hitting the pavement outside. Its sound and sudden appearance making her jump. Looking up she saw what was left of the Chameleon, a bloody battered mess. There was no time for her to enjoy it because the glow of red and blue lights came tearing down the street toward the factory. She whispered to herself.

"Here we go." She lined her eye up with the sights on the rifle.

Their tires slid on the broken pavement as both vehicles sped up into the lot, stopping abruptly. They jumped out of the cars, heading quickly for the front entrance. Sara exhaled slowly, reducing her breathing to nearly nothing as she waited for them to come within range. The sound of their boots sounded like gun fire to her sensitive ears. In her head she was counting, '1...2...3...4...5...' Then she squeezed the trigger of the rifle, sending a spray of gun powder and silver buck shot at both men. They jumped out of the way but she still managed to clip the telepath's leg with silver. He limped to his cruiser. So she stood and aimed at Death, emptying the barrel into the hood of his truck before reloading and firing one more time. His engine hissed in retaliation and as he tried to back out of the lot, it died.

Sara exited the factory and continued to unload one round after another as she pursued him. Somehow he managed to dodge every round she fired in his direction. Instead he looked over his shoulder at her once, a smirk forming at the corner of his mouth before he disappeared into the shadows of town.

"Shit!" Sara yelled.

She tried to run out after him but he was gone before she could even try anything.

"Shit shit shit!! Amanda!!" She continued, slightly panicked.

There was a response from behind her and Sara jumped, not expecting the woman to be there so quick.

"Go after the cruiser. I'll get him." Amanda said, her voice low.

She growled the last word before Sara watched her body fade into the shadows of the factory. When Amanda disappeared she ran for the Jeep, jumping in it with shotgun in tow. There was no time to waste, that cop car could easily hit one eighty before her jeep even got up to fifty. Sara started the Jeep (flipping on the flood lights), backed over the curb and took off in the direction she thought he had gone. Those cowards, when confronted with a real fight, ran scared. They only seemed to like to hurt innocents they knew could not fight back. As the thought occurred to her, Sara pressed the peddle to the floor. Knowing him like she thought she did, if he was injured, he would con some poor woman into pulling over so he could have his way with her before feeding off of her. She was not going to have that, not as long as she was still standing. No matter what she had to do, she would do it to protect those who could not fight for themselves.

The highway was bare when she pulled onto its long stretch of pavement. Still she knew that he would be out there somewhere. Minutes stretched into hours as she continued to search for any sign of red and blue flashing lights. Sara was beginning to lose hope that she would ever find him, that he would get away and start this horror all over again. It was in that very moment she saw the sign she had been looking for. As she approached the cop car, she slowed way down, she needed to be sure it was him.

On the side of the cruiser, she saw the familiar lettering and the silhouette of him sitting in the drivers seat, pretending to be something he was not. Sara flipped the Jeep into four wheel drive and drove over the grass median so she could turn around. The telepath must have seen her because as she was pulling back onto the opposite side of the highway, he drove around the vehicle, abandoning his victim. He was attempting to run from her and if she did not do something to stop him, he would manage to get away. She pressed the accelerator to the floorboards and the vehicle jolted forward. Unfortunately for him, he had not been fast enough. Sara's bumper was right near his now, she needed a little more speed to do what she wanted to do. There had to be a way to slow him down.

Grabbing the loaded shotgun from the seat beside her, she set it in her lap and rolled down the window. Then she aimed the shotgun out the window at the rear tires of his cruiser and pulled the trigger, hoping that he was not smart enough to get police issued tires. The first shot missed, as did the second but finally she managed to hit his right tire. His car swerved as he tried to keep it from flipping off the road. Now she could do what she planned. Sara lined the front of her Jeep with the rear of his cruiser and watched the look of anger come over his shadowed face as she caught up with him. She jerked the wheel to the right, clipping the rear of his car and sending him down into the embankment. The car flipped roof over wheels before coming to rest upside down. To stop, she had to yank the emergency, screeching the tires on the asphalt as she slid to a halt.

Sara needed to be sure that he could never come back. The task was up to her. Without Amanda to protect her, she was on her own. So she pulled the Jeep up to the place where his car had flipped and climbed out, loading the shotgun as she headed down the steep embankment. She no longer needed a flashlight to see in the dark, so when she got to the bottom of the hill and saw his drivers side window busted out, she knew he was gone.

"Son of a bitch." She growled.

On the other side of the over turned vehicle, she heard laughter emanating from the woods that lined the highway. With a nervous sigh, she racked a round into the chamber of the shotgun and headed into the darkness of the trees. Her vampiric eyes scanned every bush and tree top for any sign of him. Although with him, she knew better than to trust her vision. Unlike Amanda, she had not had the time to build up a resistance to his telepathic illusions.

"Come out here and face me asshole!" She howled.

"What's the matter Sara? Don't you like hide and seek?" Telepath mocked.

Sara slowly moved around the forest, careful not to step on branches as she went and making sure to never keep her back turned in any one direction for too long.

"You're a coward! You can beat on helpless mortal women but you can't handle your own kind! What's the matter limp dick? Don't we do it for you?" She asked.

There was silence for a long time and she worried that he had in fact ran from her. She did not hear the sound of him landing in the mud behind her.

"Oh no Sara, you, you do it just fine for me." He purred.

She spun around and fired a shot at his silhouette but it disappeared into thin air. Just an illusion. His voice was behind her again, whispering in her ear.

347

"I remember the taste of you on my tongue. I don't think I'll ever let you go, you're too much fun." Telepath teased.

Again she spun in his direction and fired another shot at another illusion.

"Ellis stop this shit right now! I'm in no mood."

She felt his lips on her neck.

"No but I bet I could get you there."

Although she wanted to shoot the image she saw before her, she knew it was another illusion. So, she turned the other direction and fired instead into thin air. When the Mossberg was empty, she felt a hand grab her by her hair and toss her body into the nearest tree, causing her to drop the gun. Her forehead hit the base of the tree and she slid to the ground. Telepath walked over and grabbed the rifle.

"We don't need this anymore do we?" He tossed the gun.

Sara felt an all too familiar fear begin to fill her body. She might be one of them now but she was newly turned, not sired and much younger. What was she supposed to do now?

"And you certainly don't need these." He said holding up his fist.

He dropped handfuls of shells into the dirt. How did he manage to do that? She wondered. Now Sara had no way to defend herself. She scooted herself backwards into the tree as much as she could.

"What's the matter," He began walking toward her unbuttoning his shirt. "not so tough without Amanda around?"

"Stay the hell away from me!" She shrieked.

He laughed. "Oh no, you and I are going to get well acquainted." He said, stripping off his shirt and beginning to undo his belt.

"You're not gonna touch me!" Sara yelled louder.

"Touch, lick, fuck...heh we're gonna have a lot of fun, you and I." His voice was laced with sex.

'*Amanda if you can hear me, help me!*' She thought.

"Oh no, don't call to her. She can't help you right now anyhow. Alex has her and I'm sure he's having his own fun." Telepath said grinning.

"Stay out of my head!" Her voice cracked.

He paused in his movements, cocking his head to one side and looking at her.

"I'm sorry. Where are my manners? Would you prefer I look like this?" His voice changed with his appearance.

The Telepath's boyish image faded and before her was the silhouette of the man who had attacked her. She knew who that man was now, so the fear associated with him was gone. As she pushed herself to her feet, she heard Amanda's voice in her head or thought she did.

'*Get up! Fight! Do not go out this way, you have come too far. Concentrate, will him out of your head. He's right in front of you, I know it doesn't look like it but he is.*'

Sara trusted the female voice in her head and in that voice she found the strength to stand. She swung her fist with all the strength in her body. She heard a grunt of pain and the telepath stumbled backward, the image he had conjured up, wavering. The voice in her head spoke again.

'Force him out of your head. Push him.'

"Get. Out. Of. My. Head!" She growled.

The telepath suddenly put his hand to the side of his head as his other hand held his clearly broken jaw.

'That a girl. Get mad. Embrace the demon. Become the darkness. Remember what they did to me, remember all the missing women. Think about all the discarded bodies. Because of them you'll never see your family again.'

A growl hummed deep in the bowels of her chest and she felt her canines extend to sharp points. She glared at one of the vampires responsible for the suffering of so many innocents and for destroying her own life.

"And stay out!" She demanded.

"Gah!" He groaned in pain.

She watched a tendril of blood began to trickle slowly from his ear as she continued to push her way into his mind now. It was time he experienced all the torment he had issued to the women they kept locked up in the factory.

"Yeah, you and I are gonna play all right. But we're playing by my rules." Sara grinned a toothy grin.

"Fine," He said, shaking off the effects of her attack. "Have it your way."

Sara bared her fangs, balling her hands into fists and raising them.

"Come get me." She replied.

The telepath stepped forward, swinging his fist at her jaw and she blocked it with one arm before kicking his knee hard enough to snap it. He stumbled sideways as he fought to keep his balance. Sara did not let up, she did not waver or give him the chance to recover. A Valkyrie scream echoed through the woods and months of anger came pouring forward. She leapt into the air and kneed him in the jaw. Then she slammed her fist into his temple, sending him to the ground. At this point she did not care about a fair fight or giving him equal opportunity to defend himself. Grabbing him by his broken jaw, she squeezed it between her fingers as she tossed him across the forest floor and into the nearest tree. His body hit the oak with a resounding snap as his ribs cracked. For a few moments she stood, watching him struggle to get to his feet.

"Get up! Fight me you coward! Or is that all you have, just head games and tricks?" She asked, her voice dropping as she spoke.

He chuckled, looking up in her direction.

"No Sara, I've got something for you."

The Telepath pulled himself to his feet, realigning his knee before she felt him forcing his way into her head again. An over whelming arousal filled her body and she fell to her knees. Sara dug her fingers into the cool earth beneath her, trying to force the feeling away. While she struggled to get him out of her head, he slowly moved toward her. Although she knew the feeling was false, she was having trouble ignoring it. It was so over powering that it crippled her, any small gesture that signaled she might get to her feet, was dismissed by another wave of arousal. Telepath cocked his head to the side as he moved toward her, watching her twitch.

"What do we have here? Are you giving up Sara?" He dared to mock her.

"F-fuck you!" She shouted.

He smirked before he put up two fingers and made a thrusting motion. Sara could feel them inside of her, violating her, touching her. She did not want to but she moaned and dig her nails harder into the dirt.

"St-stop it!" She demanded.

"Ooo ho ho, you are fun." His every word a perversion.

She grit her teeth and closed her eyes, trying to concentrate on anything but what was happening to her. Sara willed her mind to think about all the things they had done, all the lives they had stolen and the families they had broken. In her mind's eye, she could see what Amanda looked like when she found her, the apparition that she had described and hear the agonizing screams of the women. She could hear them calling out to her in desperation, reaching to her with blood covered hands and begging her to save them.

The Telepath was standing right in front of her, she could feel his aura touching hers. His boots were almost against her knees. Sara stifled the growl that wanted to come. She wanted him to gain the same false sense of security that he had given the girls time and time again. Right before he raped them and hit them with that whip. The image of them screaming as he laughed at their pain, came flying at her. A barrage of sights and sounds filled her mind. It was the fuel she needed to over come him.

"I'm gonna enjoy this. If you're good, you might get to enjoy it too." He said as he unbuttoned his pants.

"Oh, I will get to enjoy it more than you will." She mumbled.

With that, Sara stood, her image becoming a blur as she punched him in the throat so hard she put her fist through it. His eyes filled with shock and he stumbled backwards, dropping his pants in the process. He put his hands to his neck, trying to stop the bleeding but his attempts were futile. The Telepath looked grossly pathetic with his pants around his ankles and his phallic shaft flopping about. Sara cocked her head to one side, watching him for a moment.

"This won't hurt if you cooperate. Wait, no, that's a lie. This *IS* going to hurt...a lot." Her voice now a demonic whisper.

A blur was all he could see as she proceeded to break his ribs, shatter his jaw, crush his pelvic bone, and snap all the bones in his legs. She was not done with him yet. As he lay on the ground, twitching in pain, blood pouring from the wound in his throat, she began to break each one of his fingers and wrists.

"You like to hit women asshole! Try even touching one with a broken hand!"

She snapped another bone as she said that. Sara looked into his face and could see the light beginning to fade from his eyes.

"Oh no, stay with me. I'm not quite finished with you yet. Remember the girl who's teeth you ripped from her mouth? This is, my dear, for her." Sara was almost growling.

She kicked him in the mouth until every tooth was a tiny busted pearl and he could only spit blood.

"You're a strong one. I like that. What other fun can we have? Oh, I know. Since Sterling is dead, how about..."

Sara kicked him in the side of his face with suck force, she shattered his right eye socket, causing his eye to droop sickeningly to one side of his head. He reminder her of a Salvador Dali painting she had seen once, only more gruesome. She walked around his broken form, surveying the damage she had done. This was not how she had expected it to end, she thought she might lose. Whatever strength she had summoned, gave her the power to destroy him. Now it was time to finish the job. Amanda was still in Collins, searching for the Shadowed One. They still needed to get those women out of that hell and back home to their families. There were more important things she needed to be doing at this point.

"Wow are you fragile. Now I understand why you're not a fighter. In any case, it's been fun but I've got somewhere else I have to be right now." Sara said rather matter-of-fact.

"S-a-hara" He uttered.

"Ssh . . .It's all over now. You lost, nothing you can say will change the situation. Have fun in hell."

Crouching over him, she grabbed his head in both hands and twisted his neck quickly, snapping it. A gurgled sigh escaped his lips and then silence.

Sara stood, looking around at the large pine trees that surrounded them. It had been a long time since she was able to enjoy the outdoors without fear. There was nothing she was afraid of anymore, or there would not be soon. Once the last one was taken care of, she would be able to live again. Not in the way she had before but in a new sort of life. She sighed, glancing down at his corpse. Then she nodded to herself, grabbing her shotgun and made her way out of the woods back onto the highway.

It was strange, her Jeep and the cruiser were still sitting on the side of the road undisturbed. Now, she understood why the boys had chosen this stretch of pavement for their stalking games. The place was so deserted that would have seen anything, if the boys did do something. Sara climbed in the Jeep and started it, heading back toward town. She had no clue as to where to start searching for Amanda or what's his name. The names of the boys were irrelevant to her at this point because they had so many of them and none of them was real.

Sara roared down the highway at a steady ninety, until she reached the edge of Collins, passing by the rotting welcome sign as she entered town. Where in the world were they? For a second she considered starting his house on fire and seeing if that would entice him to come out. She realized it was a trivial act. The Shadowed One was not concerned with material things, he had been around for years. There were only a few things he cared about, other than himself. Still she could not leave Amanda to fight him on her own, she had to do something. But what?

Chapter 27

A culmination of dark storm clouds now rolled across a gray sky as Sara made her way back though town. It seemed a befitting background to the finality of their battle in Collins. The rotting skeletons (now abundant and visible) were cast in erratic shadows that creeped and crawled across the cracked pavement. Patches of dying grass and weeds poked up through, where mother nature had begun to take hold again. How could she sit by and watch this go on? Was the creator, so blind to the trespasses of these demons? Or had she no angels to fight them? No one brave enough in the heavens to come down and dispatch them back to hell? The thought occurred to Sara, perhaps she and Amanda were the angels placed here to penetrate their strong hold and dissemble their town. Perhaps it was true, sometimes in order to destroy evil, you have to become evil yourself. This was not what she had planned for her life. However, now was not the time to be selfish and self pitying. Did she believe the other women who were still trapped here, had planned for their lives to end this way? Most certainly not. She knew in her still beating heart that they had families somewhere and that they were praying for the safe return of their girls. That those poor souls were tricked into believing the false authority of Collins, believing that they would find their women and return them home safely. How they must have laughed at their pain.

Slowly, she made her way through town, heading toward the still engulfed house as she attempted to find Amanda. Without access to the shadow realm (that they both held) she was of no help. The only thing she could do, was to head back to the factory and sit in the parking lot, guarding the girls from further attack. Even if it meant her death (she had settled with the idea) she would not let another one of them be hurt. They were going home, one way or another. So, she turned the Jeep around and headed back the other way. It was eerie to hear the sound of her engine as it echoed off the abandoned buildings. Large monoliths of a time long forgotten. The structures that once stood as a representation of safety and security, were now reduced to their most basic form. They were brick and mortar, wood and drywall. These were facts, undebatable facts but beneath the fallen snow they had transformed into skeletons. The reality that she and the rest of the world knew, was now gone. What was left of the houses served as a warning, that there were monsters in the world who were capable of devastating destruction. That they walked among us and that there was no where safe anymore. These ideas, this knowledge would haunt her, even if she did leave. She was certain Collins wound not leave her. In a way, there was no leaving Collins, it stuck with a person for eternity.

She dared to wonder how they managed to make a whole town disappear in a night. When did they arrive? Were there other towns like this? Did they slaughter everyone who lived here, just so they could have a point from which to operate? The thought made her shudder, some part of her was still human, still emotional. It was better if she stopped thinking and kept her eyes open for any glimmer of shadows.

The incorporeal world that was the shadow realm, enveloped her in its icy chill. It was oppressive darkness with no aroma or taste. Within its confines she could hear the hiss and slither of his companion shadows but there were other things. They growled and roared, slashing through the air with unseen claws. Amanda roared back and bared her own claws, daring them to try. The dark was a wall, always pushing her back. She fought through the black, moving ever deeper into him territory.

Death knew this place better than she, he was of this world and therefore could lose her quite easily. That was something she was determined to prevent but he had jumped in first and continued to out run her. Even with her novice experience, she managed to get her hands on him a few times. In this realm, he was not solid matter, nothing was. So causing injury to him was nearly impossible, unless she had some form of light (that was only a theory). However, she had not thought to grab and bring a light with her. If she could contact Sara and get her help, there was a possibility of success. In the back seat of her Jeep, she knew there were two bottles of bourbon she had brought with her when she moved to Collins. They had become her therapy, a way to help her deal with the abuse that James had enacted upon her. By now they would be more potent, but she had no idea if they would light in this realm. She had to try. So, from the confines of her shadowy prison, she reached out with her mind, praying that Sara could hear her.

'Sara!'

Her thoughts projected through the thick black and into the Earthly realm. The solid physical world that Sara found herself trapped in. As she was sitting in the factory lot, waiting for a sign of either one of them, she began to hear Amanda's voice shouting in her head.

'Amanda? Is that you?' She responded cautiously.

A sigh of relief came over Amanda when she heard Sara respond.

'Yes, it's me. I need your help.' Desperation and panic evident in her voice.

'How? I cannot enter that place.'

'In the back seat of the Jeep, you will find work rags and two bottles of bourbon. I need you to take the caps off the bottles and stuff a rag in each one. Then I will need a lighter.'

Sara understood all too well what Amanda was asking of her, she was about to try and throw a Molotov cocktail into the shadow realm. Without hesitation, Sara reached behind her, grabbing desperately for the bottles and rags.. Then she tore one of the rags into two long strips and (using a Phillips head screwdriver) she jammed a rag down into each bottle until it was dangling in the liquid. She had used the Shadowed One's lighter to blow the house up, so she searched the Jeep for a lighter. Under one of the seats, she found one with barely any fluid left and she prayed that what Amanda was trying to do would work.

'Ok, how do I get them to you?' Sara's thoughts radiated with fear.

'Hurry, I need you to get out of the Jeep and find the darkest

shadows you can. Then wait.' Amanda replied.

Sara climbed out of the car and ran for a corner of the yard, the caramel liquid inside the bottles sloshing about as she moved. She found what Amanda had instructed her to find and then she waited. A second ticked by and the silhouette of her companion was standing in front of her. This would have startled her at one time but she had grown used to shadows appearing out of no where. Especially ones that had saved her life on more than one occasion. Sara handed the items to her shadow sister and watched her disappear back into the shadow realm. All she could do was wait. She needed a cigarette so bad right now but without a lighter, there was nothing she could do. Instead she paced the parking lot, walking a few times around the building to ensure that no one had breached the parameter.

Without prior experience or knowledge of the occult underworld she had been thrust into, the shadow realm was the equivalent of navigating through a thick black fog. There was no way of knowing how far he was from her or how close the other things were that she hear, slithering and screaming around the realm. No concept of time or space was evident.

Amanda moved further into the realm with her newly acquired weapons in hand. She knew there was a chance that the light would hurt her as well, but it was a chance she was willing to take. If it meant stopping him from ever hurting another woman again, she would handle the pain. Besides, she had experienced agony far worse than a burn. When she was in position, where she believed him to be hiding, she clicked the lighter. It did not light and she feared for a moment that no light was allowed to penetrate this realm. Amanda refused to give up though, she flicked the wheel across the flint one more time and the flame came to life. A smirk came over her face as she touched it to one of the rags and tossed the flaming bottle into the darkness. It pierced through the shadows and exploded in a fire ball as it came in contact with a solid presence. In that moment, she saw the image of him.

"You son of a bitch!"

Just as quickly as she saw him, he was gone again. His

laughter filled the endless silence and seemed to echo mockingly all around her. It only served to enrage her even more. Amanda lit the other bottle and tossed it in the direction she had seen him go. It exploded in bright flames of red before burning out. This time there was no sign of him, not anywhere. She cursed herself continuously. Had she lost him already? Had they really come all this way, only for her to lose him in here?

"Shadowed One!!" She shouted, her voice disappearing into the void.

Again he laughed.

"What's the matter, you afraid to fight me? Worried that you'll lose? You've already lost, your brothers are dead!"

Silence.

"You wanna know what else? They begged for their lives before they died."

There was nothing and then she felt something hit her with enough force to send her flying from her place in the shadows and she landed hard. So, this world did have solid matter in it. She assumed it was him, attempting to get back at her for killing his vampiric family.

"I have no more time to waste with you child." His voice was husky, deeper than she remembered.

Amanda laughed.

"Excuses . . .always excuses with you."

"You're a powerful little bitch . . .I'll give you that. But I'm older and wiser, you'll never defeat me. Maybe some day, you will have your chance . . .today is not that day."

Somehow she knew he was about to disappear forever and if

she did not stop him now, then all their efforts would be futile. They would have expended all that energy for nothing.

"Come back here!" Amanda demanded.

"Goodbye Amanda." His voice faded as her name slipped from his lips.

"Noo!!"

Her cries were greeted with silence. He was gone. After all their fighting, their hard work and their planning, they had failed to catch the one thing that had started all this. Their ring leader and sire. For a moment, Amanda could only stand there, staring helplessly into the dark. She had not felt this way since they put her in that cell and began torturing her three times a day. A sigh passed through her and she felt tears began to well up in her eyes. The sensation of cold started slowly at the pit of her stomach and spread through her like fire. How could this happen? How could she let this happen? Her anti-climatic revenge. It was as if someone had ripped out the pages of the book. Shock and dismay was all she understood. There would be no satisfaction for them. Both girls would have to look over their shoulder for the rest of their eternal days. She felt slightly lost, what would she tell Sara? That she failed to kill Death? Closing her eyes, she sighed again. At least the girls were safe for now. However, she knew that it would be up to them to continue to protect them until the last member of this vampiric cult was dead. Not just dead, dismembered and the pieces scattered to the edge of the earth. With his shadowy power, there was no telling if he could reassemble his own body. If destroying his physical body would be enough to stop him.

The momentary melancholy passed and her body became filled with a slightly different emotion. Amanda balled her fists so hard that her nails cut into her palms and her muscles tensed with fury. A Valkyrie scream pierced the never ending shadows, causing the entire realm to shake and tremble. She screamed until her lungs burned and her voice ceased to exist. The creatures of that shadowy place, slithered and scattered away. Even if it took centuries she would find and kill him.

Hours had already passed since Sara last had any sign of Amanda. Her pacing had growing increasingly worse and she worried that the Shadowed One, had killed her best friend. It was a weird concept to call the woman that, but what else do you call someone who had saved your life more than once? Who had no apparent ulterior motive. Some part of her felt much closer, that was her blood sister. Both bound together by vampiric bond and circumstance. They were the stalkers in the night who chose to protect innocents. Their actions were more human than they realized.

Slowly, the sad silhouette of a woman formed in front of her and Sara felt her heart skip a beat. She was alive and unharmed but her body language said something had went wrong. There was not the satisfied posture of a woman who had overcome her kidnapper. Instead, her head hung and her shoulders slumped with disappointment. What was wrong?

"Amanda?"

The shape solidified into her human form and she stared at the ground as she spoke, sorrow evident in her voice.

"I...I...lost him." Her voice cracked as she spoke.

"Come again?"

"Sara I tried...the bastard disappeared further in the shadow realm. Then he was gone."

Sara sighed. She could not be mad at the woman, she tried with everything she had. It was not her fault, they had an advantage on both girls. All they could do now was plan for their future and figure out how to handle things from here.

"All right, what now?"

Amanda lifted her head, mildly surprised she was not being yelled at for her failure.

"You're not mad?"

"There's nothing you could have done. We just have to take care of the girls now and make sure they leave them alone. Even if it means visiting each one and checking on them frequently during the night. At least until we track his ass down."

Amanda nodded.

"All right, let's head inside and see if we can get them out of here. Even if we have to go to the next town and call for help. We cannot move all of them on our own."

As they were figuring out what to do, in the shadows at the corner of the property, a set of glowing red eyes watched them with a deadly pearl smile. He would be damned if they took anyone out of here. Slowly, he faded back into the shadows and disappeared from sight.

Amanda and Sara headed into the factory, being cautious that the Shadowed One could show up at any moment. They headed up the long metal stairs together and as they did, the pungent smell of fresh death greeted them. A fearful look passed between them and they ran up to the top of the stairs. When they got their, the sight before them was more horrible than they ever could have imagined. The cell doors were flung open and the nude girls were hanging across their thresholds. There they lay with their throats ripped open, blood pooling slowly around their mangled bodies. Their once bright eyes, now glazed and wide with shock. They had died staring up at their killer. The Shadowed One had come back and was so determined to not let them return home, he would rather kill them.

Time seemed to slow as they ran to the separate walkways and each took a girl up into their arms. Some of the women were not even women yet, mere teenagers, most likely snatched from rest stops. Or lead foolishly from the diner by Death's haunting good looks. These young ones never had the chance to learn about life before theirs was snatched from them. Sara looked up at Amanda with bloody tears in her eyes.

"Why?! Had they not done enough to these girls?!"

Amanda appeared beside her, looking down at the small corpse.

"Because they could, because it delighted them, because no one else gets to play with their toys. Because they are monsters, they have no feeling for anyone. They do not care about life. They're emotionless, spineless cowards who prey on the weak. No Sara, they had not done enough. This was Death's doing. He was determined to not let us leave with them."

Amanda had spent enough time as a vampire that she could shut off human emotion and become heartless. She understood why her charge could not. The girl was only newly turned and she was still very much human. After a few months or days, she would learn how to shut off that part of herself. For now, Amanda reached down and pulled Sara away from the mangled body of the young brunette.

"Come on sweetie. We need to give them a proper burial. We need to make a funeral pyre for them. A mass grave as it were. I know you're not going to like this and you're going to have a hard time dealing with this, but in time you will come to understand it."

Sara sniffled and wiped the bloody tears from her cheeks. She knew her sire was right. This was a deadly game they were playing, as long as Death still lived. There was no time for emotion or tears. No time for sentimental burials. If she wanted to survive, she needed to become as cold and calculated as they were and fast. She nodded to Amanda and they began to gather up the girls, one body at a time, laying them down on the asphalt behind the factory. They stacked them one on top of another in a triangular formation. Amanda siphoned gas out of the truck still sitting on the front of the lot, pouring it into the gas can she pulled out of the bed before dumping it on the bodies and setting them on fire with the lighter Sara had given her.

The flames crawled quickly up the pile and the smell of burning flesh permeated the air. Both girls pressed the back of their hand to their noses until they became used to the smell. Sara held her free hand to her heart and began to say a silent prayer for their souls. Not that she really believed in God at this point, it seemed like the appropriate thing to do. They watched the fire as it consumed the bodies, its glow lighting up the side of the factory. It seemed befitting that the burning bodies of the women it once housed, not illuminated the structure in a red-orange light.

Amanda glanced at Sara, seeing the ever present sorrow in her face and feeling a tinge of humanity touch her heart. It was time for them to leave, that poor girl did not need to see any more of this place. No more horrors for her to behold, not until she was ready.

"Come on. I'll drive." Amanda said, touching her shoulder.

They headed to the Jeep, Sara curling into a ball as she climbed in the passenger seat. Amanda started it and headed out of the factory lot, putting Collins far behind them. Although she had no idea where to go and what to do. There was no way either of them could go home and they did not want to live anywhere close to this place. So Amanda drove until she could smell the heat of the sun beginning to come up over the horizon. Still she had no reason to stop, she knew that sunlight was not something that affected her. They passed through one town after another, wondering if they would be next. The girls had no destination in mind. They had no where to go anyhow. So, Amanda continued to drive.

As she drove, she contemplated how she would do it. She realized a long time ago that Sara would be safer without her. The thought crossed her mind and it was at that point, she spotted a rest stop up ahead. Amanda pulled the Jeep into the lot, glancing at the sleeping form in the passenger seat. The best thing she could do for Sara was to leave her alone. Death would not come after her, if Amanda took herself out of the picture. It was her who had challenged him to a fight and had decided to break up his happy home. There was no reason for him to come after Sara. She whispered a silent good bye before slipping out of the vehicle and disappearing into the night.

When Sara finally woke up, she found the drivers seat empty and as much as she searched, there was no sign of her sire. What was she supposed to do now? She was on her own, without any guidance. Why did Amanda leave? Did the Shadowed One come back for her? There were so many questions and no answers to be had. She absentmindedly touched the seat next to her before climbing behind the wheel and leaving the parking lot. She would have to figure things out on her own...

Sara's Story

Chapter 28

The nightmares, the broken bottles and jagged scars could not curb her pain. She had lost everything because of them and the ghost town in front of her. Worse than the nightmares were the thoughts. They were her destruction, her obsession her sickness. Although she hated them, she wanted them in ways she could not fathom. The telepath had nearly raped her and she wanted him in sickening ways. Those fantasies would come on strong, almost forcefully and she would scream until they passed. She was not as strong as Amanda, she could not resist them because she had none of the hate her Sire did. Sara was unsure if she could handle this fight.

What if Death came for her? Would she give in? To end this hell for sure, she had to set fire to this prison, burn their world to the ground. She wanted so bad to curl up inside herself and just give up. Her days were filled with restless sleep and her nights brutal agony, followed by one bottle of whiskey after another. Although the alcohol had no effect on her and she would smash the bottles (in frustration), screaming at a deaf god. No one heard her cries or knew her lonely suffering. Sara knew she had two options; lay down and die (if she could) or get mad and fight. There was still one a live and many more like him.

Things improved when she let the monster take over and began to take her hatred out on the evil men of the mortal world. If she could not have Death's head, she would have all aspects of him, including his kind. They were her kind too now but she chose not to identify with them. Besides, vampires had been responsible for destroying her life, so she took theirs as payment. She would paint Chicago with their blood. With immortality on her side, she had time to learn their weaknesses. Decapitation seemed to be the most efficient way to dispatch them. It also gave her room to worry. The Chameleon and the Telepath were never beheaded, there was a chance they were alive. How they managed to heal was another question.

Sara had found another use for the empty bottles she had, with a few gallons of gas, she planned to have her own Devil's Night. The Jeep roared as she drove into the middle of town with twenty Molotov cocktails in a wooden box in her back seat. She parked and grabbed a couple of bottles, beginning to ignite the rotting skeletons around her. With every burst of glass and flicker of hot orange, she felt her life coming back in small pieces. It was as if she was waking from a nightmare and the last bits of it were starting to fade away slowly. She stood watching the town burn, the light and shadows bouncing off her features, her eyes glowing, giving her a more demonic appearance. Sara remembered the night she burned the damned house on Lillie. That too, she believed would end things. No, burning the town would not make her human again or undo the damage done but it would help her sleep better or so she hoped. As long as she knew they had no way to lure women and start their game again, it might help her forgive herself. Her failure to protect the prisoners of Collins, was enough to make her loathe herself. Though now with the vampirism infecting her, she could not end her suffering.

"You took my home from me!"

She screamed at no one, wanting Death to hear her as she threw another bottle. Sara made her way down the streets, throwing bottles and screaming with tears in her eyes, somewhere between rage and sorrow.

"You destroyed my life!"

The hardware was next.

"You hurt my best friend!"

Another bottle shattered as she chucked it into the library.

"You raped them! Tortured them and ran like damn cowards! You killed them!"

The remaining bottles hit separate buildings in rapid succession. When the town was burning around her, Sara screamed into the heavens, her vampiric features emerging as she did. Her fists balled tight and her nails cut her palms, causing droplets of blood to drip onto the concrete beneath her.

"Come out and face me Death! You spineless bastard!"

There was no response from Death. He may have been laughing from the shadows. It angered her that he was ignoring her and disregarding her as a threat. She wanted to be though, she wanted to be the thing that he feared. Instead she knew that he was mocking her from the darkness. It only gave her reason to keep killing his kind, she would kill them all and burn everything to the ground, leave him no place to hide. The fire would burn across the world until there were no shadows left.

"Fine then," She said, staring at the heavens. "their deaths are on you."

Sara jumped back into her vehicle, headed to the edge of town and poured a line of gas before lighting it. Then she drove out to the other side and repeated the process, surrounding the town in flames. She sat in the Jeep a few yards outside of town and watched it burn. Sara thought the destruction of Collins might bring her relief but she felt only emptiness. She dug deep within to try and find some sense of satisfaction but it was like grabbing at clouds. She could feel it but never catch it.

With a sigh she backed away and left, not before setting the Collins sign on fire. The town burned so fiercely that its blaze could still be seen in her rear-view mirror as she drove away.

The lights of the city glimmered in the distance, their glow hanging over the horizon. This was home now, hiding among the humans and feeding on their scum. Sara was nonviolent as a mortal but the more she found (the rapists, psychos and sadists) the more enraged she became. In all of them, she could see the wolf pack's mocking faces. Although she had no fighting skills, she made up for it with intelligence and anger. Nearly all of the vampires she had killed were animals, driven by lust and hunger. She was driven by something entirely different, her humanity having died off months ago. Every now and then she would lose control of her inner beast and get a little sadistic. Watching a rapist beg for his life as he tries to drag his half paralytic body across the pavement. For them, she had no mercy. None of their deaths brought closure or satisfaction but they helped to quell the ever present anger inside. Sara walked between worlds, choosing to belong to neither one. Both sides were full of an evil, a sickness she did not with to contract As far as she was concerned she was a plague. The rider on the pale horse with the free will to choose her participation in the apocalypse. She did not need to catch the sinful nature of mankind. However, she had been given power and she chose to counter their actions.

Neither world could comprehend the horrors she relived every night and one side would not care. They might even be entertained by it. Without Amanda, this was a burden she was destined to bare alone.

The streets were barren this time of night, when the predators came out from their hiding places. A mixture of cops, pimps and drug dealers filled the night. That was fine with her, she had worked up an appetite burning Collins down. There would be plenty of time to hunt, she needed to change and gather supplies first. Her clothes reeked of gasoline and hard liquor. Sara headed toward the south end of town, where even police preferred to avoid. She had obtained a room at a rather seedy motel and paid for it with the money she stole from her kills. As one of the undead, she found she did not need much; a pack of cigarettes, shower supplies and gas for the Jeep were all she bought. It allowed her the luxury of buying any weapons she might need. She had purchased a single katana at an army surplus store, for her hunts and a sharpening tool.

The motel should have been condemned a long time ago, its parking lot was barely concrete anymore. She imagined (before the stained surfaces and worn mattress) that the motel had once been a decent place. It's location and current state did prove to be an advantage for her. She was right in the heart of one of the worst neighborhoods.

Sara closed the door to her room with her foot and dropped her hooded sweater on the floor before beginning to strip off the rest of her clothing. She headed into the bathroom and filled the sink with ice cold water, its temperature making no difference to her. The mirror just above the sink was cracking in the corners but there was enough of it left to reflect the unrecognizable woman staring into it.

She had used the blade to chop her hair down nearly nothing. It was cut so close to her head now that she was often mistaken for a boy but that was fine. In her research of the missing women she suspected the wolf pack (as she had come to call them) took, she noticed a pattern. They preferred women with long hair, because it made grabbing them easier It was symbolic for her, it meant, they would never touch her again. Although she knew that if Death wanted to get his hands on her, there would be virtually nothing she could do to stop him.

Sara scooped some water from the sink and splashed it across her face and head. Grimy black dripped from her pale skin into the sink as she washed the ash from her face and hair. She would rather not go out smelling like gasoline and give her presence away.

To think that the predator's of the night were now beginning to fear something else, something far worse than they, was albeit satisfying. Still, there were those who refused to obey and stop their criminal ways. That was fine, it made feeding easier. There was no guilt if she killed someone who spent the majority of their day harming others. Drying her head and face, she headed back into the main room and pulled her clothes for the night from the closet. On the bed she tossed a black shirt, a pair of black B.D.U.'s and her leather jacket. She shimmied into her work clothes and grabbed her katana from the wall, holding it sheathed in her right hand. Its smooth black handle and sheath gleamed in the dim light as she moved toward the door.

Sara stepped outside and headed toward the main part of downtown. She slipped like a shadow around and among the criminals that roamed the streets, waiting for one of them to get out of line. Sara had somewhat a code of honor, she would not kill them unless they hurt someone. The drugs that dealers sold to their willing participants, were harming them already but they allowed that to happen. She was looking for the rapists and the vampires who did more than just feed.

The moon hung high above the city and on this night she was not the only predator hunting their own. A silhouette watched her from the alleyways as she moved about. She had sensed him when she first left the motel and had kept an eye out for him but never could seem to catch him. Unsure of his intentions or if he was an extension of the one's she had killed in Collins, she was ever ready.

Her vampiric eyes shifted about, looking for any signs of her own kind. It was what she heard, not what she saw that set her on edge. Through the sounds of cars, voices and the buzz of dozens of streetlights, she heard a woman's voice begging for mercy. Sara cocked her head, shifting her eyes upward as she attempted to pinpoint the source of the sound. The smell of fear drifted into her nostrils and she took off down the street, scaling up fire escapes and leaping from one building to another. She stopped atop a bakery on the southeast side of town, crouching on it's rooftop and watching the scene in the alley below.

There were two vampires who were cornering a scantly clad woman. The smell of sex and uncleanliness drifted into her nostrils from the naked flesh between her thighs. She had several customers already and never bothered to wash between them. She most often rescued prostitutes from the bloodsuckers she hunted. They were easy prey and the scum she killed, liked it that way. These were the type of vampire that made her race look weak and pathetic, just like the wolf pack. Why hunt anything challenging? No, they chose to hunt the helpless who already had nothing. Those weak and broken, who had been beaten down by circumstance and society. Sara shook her head as she watched her soon to be kills, analyzing them for any signs of weakness.

There was one who looked like a bad eighties villain. He was shaved bald and covered in a variety of piercings, with a mishmash of tattoos from his face to his fingertips. The other one was twig skinny with an electric blue mohawk and large gauges in his earlobes. They were both wearing leather, old band shirts and plaid of some color, as if they were trying hard to fit the ideal profile of a punk. Their auras exuded arrogance as they began to corner the woman. Sara lifted her head slightly, the dim lights flickering across her pupils as she decided her next move. She knew she wanted to kill them, but how? Slowly perhaps. The over confidence they displayed, aggravated her to no end. No one told them, there was a new monster in the city and alpha predator. How many years had they killed without consequence? Tonight would be their last.

The prostitute they had chosen looked no older than sixteen, dressed in a red mesh dress with nearly nothing beneath it. She had already been stripped of the fake fur jacket she had been wearing. There were tears streaming down her cheeks and in that moment Sara saw every woman she had failed. Telepath's laugh echoed through her mind as she remembered her own moment of desperation and the cruelty she had seen. Their voices echoed up to her ears from the alley below.

"Come on baby, we just wanna have a good time."

The mohawk grabbed her by her hair and pulled her close, running his pierced tongue up her cheek. She grimaced in disgust and tried to pull away.

"Ah . . .where ya going? We're just getting started. Ain't that right Sam."

"Oh yeah, you ever been bent over by a vampire? I promise it's one experience you won't forget."

His human features faded as his eyes turned a bright iridescent blue and two large canines extended from his mouth.

"No! Please don't . . ..Help! Someone please help me!"

"Yeah, scream. I love it when they scream."

Sara stood and stepped off the roof, dropping gracefully two stores down into the alleyway landing silently a few feet from the two thugs.

"So do I. . . I love it when you boys beg for your life." She replied mockingly, her voice a deep growl.

They momentarily turned away from the woman in front of them to look angrily at Sara. Good, she had their attention. If she could get them to let go of the prostitute, it would allow her to escape.

"Who da fuck are you? Are ya suicidal? Interrupting us like ya are."

"This is my territory and you're hunting in it."

"Is it now? Well, I don't see your fucking name anywhere. We can settle this right here, right now."

Sara cocked her head at the sound of that word, it grated her nerves and made her muscles tense.

"That word . . .I don't like that word. You would do well not to use that word when addressing me. And my name is everywhere, you just didn't look. Have you not heard the rumors of a vampire killing her own kind?"

"What word don't you like bitch?" The mohawk ignored anything else she had said.

"Ah see, there you did it again. I'm trying to be civil here but you're testing my patience."

It would appear that these two goons, did not belong to a coven or socialized with any of the community or they would have heard about her. She slipped into one of their hangouts every now and again to listen to their conversations. Sara knew that she was an enemy to the entire vampiric race, save for one and she was fine with that. They could all try to kill her, she had no fear of death in fact she welcomed it.

"What ya gonna do, kill us? Do you have any idea who you're talking to? We're the Sampson brothers, killers of vampire hunters and hell raisers of the night."

They took this moment to whoop and dollar in some poorly synchronized display of macho bravado and unity. Sara rolled her eyes, they were growing steadily worse.

"So you're self entitled now? Did you boys have a vote on what your name would be? So I guess you're dumb" She pointed at the bald man. "and dumbass, right?"

"Keep talking bit-"

Sara was tired of hearing that word come out of their mouth. Her form became a blur and she slammed her fist into the Mohawk's jaw. She was back in her original place before he realized what had happened. The mohawk reeled backwards as blood dribbled from his lip.

"I said . . .I don't like that word. Perhaps we understand one another now. It seems you only seem to know pain, I figured a broken jaw would help you learn."

"Ya broke my fucking jaw! I'm gonna kill you for that!" Mohawk said, spitting blood as he spoke.

"You can try." Sara responded calmly.

His threats were hollow, they probably worked most of the time on mortals. She was not them, she was something entirely different. The blood flowing through her veins, although diluted by Amanda's, was from an older line. That much she had come to understand from interrogating the elders she killed.

"I'm going to tell you boys one more time. Let the girl go. Or things will get very . . .unpleasant."

The bald vampire holding onto the girl, tossed her to the ground and pointed at her.

"Don't you go anywhere. When I'm done with her, we'll play."

"No you won't." Sara said.

"You won't be alive to do so."

"You're cocky aren't you? Girly you have no idea who you're messing with."

Sara beckoned to them with her right hand, the left one still holding her sheathed katana. The mohawk tried to swing at her but she slammed the metal sheath into his arm, hard enough to break it before cracking him under the jaw with it. He stumbled backwards and the bald one moved forward, his movements hesitant. The bald one attempted to kick her but, she caught his leg wrapping her right arm under it and pulled down on his kneecap breaking it. Then she tossed him backwards away from her so she could deal with the mohawk now swinging a board at her head. She danced around his desperate movements, blocking the wood several times with her sheath. He took a swipe at her knees and in an effort to knock her down but she blocked the board again and broke his nose with her other fist. With the sheath tucked under her elbow, she drew the sword and decapitated him in one flawless move. His head bounced when it hit the ground and rolled a few feet, stopping somewhere further down the alley.

Sara let the sheath drop to the ground and turned to face the other vampire. He was pathetically attempting to stand. She cocked her head to the side as she sliced through the flesh of his thighs, just above his knee. He screamed in agony as he stared down at his bloody stumps. These were the moments of pain and suffering she enjoyed.

"You crazy bitch! My family will find you, they'll kill you for this."

"That WORD . . .I told you, I don't like that word. Why must I repeat myself?"

She followed him as he desperately tried to pull himself down the alleyway and get away from her.

"Shit…shit…shit…" He said, grunting in pain with every word.

"You really think anyone in the vampire community, let alone your family, really gives a shit about scum like you? I'm doing them a favor. I've killed dozens of you and to date no one has raised a hand against me."

Sara pushed the sword slowly into his lower back, watching his body squirm in response as she paralyzed his lower half entirely.

"If you knew anything, you'd know I come from an older line. Your kind, save for a few, will not dare touch me."

"Fuck you! Fuck your bloodline."

She sighed.

"As it is, I've already wasted too much time with you. So, if you'll excuse me…"

Sara brought the sword down and cut his head from his withering body. Using his shirt, she wiped the blade clean before finally placing it back in its sheath and whispering a silent prayer. That was a ritual she started weeks ago as a way to not lose sight of why she was hunting. She asked God everyday to forgive her for what she was and what she must do. In some aspect, she felt as if killing her fellow demons would some how cleanse her soul and save her. That maybe when she did die, he might absolve her of her sins and allow her into the kingdom of heaven. Maybe he would understand she was a victim of circumstance and that if he had rescued her before, she never would have become the monster she is today.

Looking down at the bodies before her, she realized she had allowed her anger to take control of the situation and now she would have to look elsewhere for food. She refused to feed on the prostitute still shaking by the dumpster. The girl needed a hot bath and some help to get herself out of this situation. Sara closed her eyes and willed her inner animal to go back into its cage. The last thing she needed to do was traumatize the girl any more than she had already. Sara sighed slowly as she felt her beast fade. Then she turned her attention to the girl, who immediately began to beg for her life.

"Shh..." Sara whispered, crouching down to her level.

"Please-"

"I know, you're scared. I would be too. I'm not like them, I'm not here to hurt you."

"You . . .you killed them. Oh god you killed them. Troy is going to be so pissed at me."

"If I didn't kill them, you'd be dead."

"No no . . .you don't understand. I'm dead either way. Troy is gonna kill me if I don't bring him his money."

Sara fought to hide the smirk on her face. She delighted in killing pimps almost as much as vampires. Those pieces of garbage deserved to die nearly as much as the rapists. They treated women like objects, using their bodies to help them make money because they were too stupid or lazy to get a job.

"No, he won't."

She handed the woman back her jacket. "What's your name?"

"A-Ashley."

"Okay Ashley, let's get out of this dirty alley and somewhere a little safer. There's a battered women's shelter close by and trust me, he won't be able to get to you there."

Only because he would be dead before the night was over. There were a lot of women she had lead to the shelter and none of their pimps ever came after them. None of them could when Sara was finished with them. She was helping Ashley to her feet when from behind her, came the sound of a deep voice. It echoed through the small space, causing the hairs on the back of Sara's neck to stand on end.

"Ashley! What the hell you think you're doing?" The voice demanded.

"Oh god." Ashley's voice crackled as she spoke.

Sara could feel her began to shake and she let go of the girl's hands, whispering to her.

"It's all right. I'm not gonna let him touch you."

"He-hey Troy. I-I just." Ashley stuttered.

"You just what bitch?! You better have my money." Troy was threatening with every word.

"Don't use that word!" Sara growled in response.

The figure finally stepped into one of the dim lights of the alley. He was a dark complected man with spiky black hair, dark eyes and the build of a line backer. None of his muscle would help him now.

"What the hell did you say to me? Who the hell do you think you are bitch?!"

As he moved toward Sara, yelling and pointing, he seemed completely oblivious of the dead bodies all around him. Sara cracked her neck to one side, resting her sword against one of the dumpsters nearby.

"Shut your eyes Ash." Sara said over her shoulder.

"Ashley get over here!" Troy turned his attention back to the prostitute.

A slow growl worked its way up her chest as the animal began to emerge. Troy reached past her and grabbed Ashley's wrist.

"You're coming with me!"

"Hey..." Sara whispered.

"Oh it speaks! What the fuck you want?"

"You wanna know who I am? I'm the nightmare you never imagined. I'm your death . . .I'm everything you should fear but are too stupid to realize it."

"Oh really? You're gonna be my death?"

Troy pulled a chrome plated .45 caliber from the front of his baggy jeans and pressed its cold metal at her forehead.

"Kill this!"

Then he squeezed the trigger and she felt the bullet tear through the flesh of her head and out the back of her skull. It was only a minute before she was standing again and watching him as he yanked Ashley around, slapping her several times. Sara took a good hard look at him this time, his body language and dress reminding her vaguely of the Chameleon. She was far too hungry to deal play with him. She moved like lightening, appearing by Ashley long enough to tell her to close her eyes. Before shifting back to her original place and calling for Troy's attention.

"Let her go!"

He paused in his movements and turned to face her, a look of shock filling his features.

"What the hell?! All right, you want some more?"

He was either too stupid or too high to realize what just transpired. Troy pulled the pistol again and began to march toward her aggressively with his arm outstretched. Sara shook her head before letting him see what real evil looks like. Her iris's became a deep crimson and her upper canines extended to their full length. By the time he finally realized what was happening, he was too close to get away from her.

"Oh God, what the hell are you?"

Grabbing him by his muscular throat, she pulled him forward and sinking her teeth deep into his neck. The sweet taste of blood filled her mouth, its warmth caressing her throat as she drained him. Sara dropped his body in a dumpster. That was one of the benefits of feeding on this side of town, no questioned the bodies that piled up here. Most of the cops attributed it to gang violence.

She wiped her mouth with the back of her hand, she looked up to see that Ashley had run from the alleyway sometime during her kill. She would probably return with cops. That was not something Sara wanted to deal with, so she grabbed her sword and ducked into another alley. She was beginning to cross an intersection of alleyways when a voice interrupted her movements.

"Not bad lass. But if ya thinking those same techniques will help ya against the Wolf Pack . . .I hate to tell ya, but that kind of sloppy shite is only gonna get ya killed."

Sara pulled her katana from its sheath, the metal covering clattered to the ground as she stood ready for a fight. She spotted him leaning casually against a brick building his face, cast in shadow and his body cloaked in a black trench coat. He was approximately six feet tall with broad shoulders, salt and pepper hair slicked back behind his head. With the shaded covering, she could distinguish nothing else about him, other than he was Scottish. He seemed to wholeheartedly disregard her as a threat, that angered her to no end.

"I've got a lot more where that came from. Wanna find out?"

She had no way of knowing if he was involved with them or if he had some other agenda in mind. Still, she was not the woman she used to be, she would not take any chances. Sara slid her feet across the ground as she advanced on him. He leaned his head up slightly.

"I wouldn't do that lass."

"Fuck you!" Sara yelled defiantly.

"Hm...Yer asking' for a beaten' ya don't want...I can promise ya dat." He said, lifting his head slightly

Sara refused to drop her blade. The Scotsman was in front of her and then he was not. He moved so fast that she had no time to react, she had never seen one of her kind move at that speed. As her sword began to cut through the air, he caught her wrist, bending her arm over her shoulder so fast that he snapped every bone in it. Then he kicked the back of her ankles, sweeping her off her feet and sending her falling to the ground. When he finally let go of her, she was staring up at him and her katana was in his hand. He promptly tossed it on the ground, moving around her as he spoke.

"What good is a weapon if you don't have any fighting skills?" He asked, his Scottish brogue even thicker.

"You bastard. You broke my arm!" Sara screamed, anger dripping from her words.

"Aye. But we both know that they'll do much worse if you don't learn to fight better," He crouched down over one of her sprawled out legs. His endless hazel pools stared fiercely into hers. "Or do ya wanna end up as one of their pets again? Being fecked daily, beaten and tortured until you are nothing but a dried up . . .used . . .cunt."

Even though he was leaning over her, the few lights in the alleyway, provided her no hint of his features. She needed to get a look at his face, to know who she was speaking with.

"What do you mean they? There's only one of them left alive." Sara said, doubt in her voice.

"Is that so? Are ye entirely sure of that lass?" He responded.

"We left two of them dead in Collins. Amanda practically skinned the Chameleon alive."

"The Chameleon . . .you must be meanin` Shane Finley. That's what he be callin' himself these days."

"Sean Finley?"

"Ye mean to tell me ya don't know? Oh yeah, he's got himself a nice Hollywood life now. And there's Nathan Reilly, he's doing some telly show these days."

"The Telepath and The Chameleon are alive?" Sara sat up slightly, still holding her wrist.

"It takes a lot more than a few broken bones to kill these lads."

His tone deepened as he spoke, there was something he knew that he was not telling her.

"So then just who the hell are you and why do you even care?" She asked defensively.

The Scotsman smirked and leaned a little closer, even at this distance she could barely see his face.

"Why don't cha come with me and find out?" He said, smirking.

"I'm not that stupid." She replied.

"Really now?" His brogue was like gravel, it made her shift uncomfortably.

Sara was still nursing her arm, which was healing as they spoke. She looked at him mildly puzzled, he had still failed to answer her question. For all she knew it was a trick and he was an extension of the Wolf Pack, sent to retrieve her. However, she had no other choice. Take a chance and risk being tossed back into their world or find a worthy alley in this battle. Amanda had certainly not shown up to help her figure everything out, so this was what she was left with. After a moment, she spoke.

"Let me see your face." She demanded.

There was a pause and then, she was being lifted to her feet by the shoulders of her coat. The brick wall of the building behind her pressed sharply into her back as she stared into his eyes. Seeing his face had not done anything to pacify her. Her heart was pounding against her chest as she looked him over. His once black hair, slick back behind his head, faded into salt and pepper, complementing his goatee. Sara barely noticed the scars that traveled up both sides of his face, disappearing somewhere beyond his cheek bones. He towered over her small form, more intimidating than any member of the Wolf Pack had ever been. His breath smelled of fresh blood and even fresher cigarettes.

Sara swallowed nervously. The proximity between them was discomforting, she needed to put some space between them but she could not budge him. He (unlike the Wolf Pack) was an unmovable force, which unnerved her even more. Should she ask him to please step back? To give her some space? Or would that give away her anxiety.

The stranger leaned forward, his hot breath brushing her hair as he whispered in her ear.

"Not gonna happen lass. And I already know what yer feeling right about now."

His deep brogue and the gruffness in his voice made her breath hitch in her throat. As he pulled away to look at her face, she could see the start of a smirk, playing at the corners of his mouth. He was enjoying this too much.

"Better?" He asked.

"What?" Sara was so distracted, she forgot where she was for a moment.

"Ya seen me face, does it help ya?" He asked.

Sara ignored his question, choosing instead to change the subject.

"What's your name?" She asked.

"Finn. Now we're all acquainted an shite, can we go already? " He replied, rolling his eyes in annoyance.

"Who the hell do you think you are?! You show up, break my whole damn arm and   demand that I go with you. What the hell you gonna do if I don't?! You gonna kill me?" She yelled, having had enough of him.

Finn had her katana in hand before she could even blink, the tip of it was pressing gingerly against the bottom of her chin. She swallowed nervously.

"Listen good woman," He growled, his voice like gravel, his accent so thick she almost could not understand him."If I wanted ya dead, you'd be dead. I wouldn't be wasting my freckin time out here in some bloody alley, arguing with ya about why your ass needs to come with me. It makes no feckin difference to me, I'll take you willing or not. One way isn't so pleasant, of that I can assure ya. The other, is a nice trip to another part of town, with no restraints,"

From his left pocket he pulled out a set of silver handcuffs, slapping them on the wall next to her head, his face mere inches from hers.

"Decide, how ya want it lass?"

His body was solid iron, pressing her into the brick wall, threatening to crush her under its power. He had already pulled her sword from her possession with barely any effort. Sara was not stupid enough to test him and find out how much more he could do.

"I'll go, I'll go." She squeaked out.

With another growl, he pushed away from her, offering the handle of her katana to her and waving the cuffs at her before shoving them in his pocket.

"They're still an option, remember that lass." He threatened.

Sara gingerly took her katana from him. He watched her every move, his gaze firm, the tension of his muscles a passive threat. She knew if she dared take another swing at him, it would not end well for her. So, she sheathed her sword, never taking her eyes off him as she did.

Glancing around the alleyway, he seemed to be listening for something. The muscles of his jaw flexed as he pressed his teeth together hard, his hands closing into fists in anticipation of something. Sara followed his movements and sensed what he must have been picking up on for a while now. They were not alone, someone or something was watching him and it did not have good intentions. She now understood the urgency in his wanting to leave but his refusal to leave without her was confusing.

"Come on." He commanded.

They headed further down the alley, their figures disappearing into gaussian blurs as they shifted into a run. Two strange shadows in the night, moving among the sights and the sounds of the city, headed in an undetermined direction. Sara could not understand what exactly she thought she was doing but at this moment, she had no other option. He could be worse than Death or he could be the very thing that Death feared. Somehow she hoped that he was the one nightmare these three bloodsuckers had.

Chapter 29

The building, was three stories of dark brick and blacked out windows. A row of houses flanked it on either side, mirror the building before her. All of them had exposed tresses, gothic windows and intricate statues lining their rooftop. Sara estimated they were built somewhere around the 1800's when Chicago was first being established and over time they had been forgotten as the city grew. Only one house however, had snarling stone gargoyles glaring down at them. They sat perched on the corners of the stone columns that made up the doorway, like vultures in the desert. Their peering stone eyes seemed to stare through to her tainted soul. However, that was not the reason for the cold shill that had begun to slowly creep up her spine. Another set of eyes were watching her, they had been since she stopped moving. Pressing her thumb to the metal hilt of her sword, she pushed the blade out a few inches and gripped its handle in preparation of an attack. Sara's crimson eyes scanned the silhouettes around her, searching for the source of her discomfort. Her body knew more than her conscious mind and in her short time as a vampire she had come to trust her instincts. They had saved her life more times than she could remember.

If they had stayed in her territory, it would have been would have been easier for her to spot a stalker. In this portion of Chicago, there were more bodies, human and vampire alike. Their energies mingled with one another and the mortals casually spoke to their predators as if they were friends. It made distinguishing from one to the other more difficult. Vampires passed among humans and the humans, unaware of what they were talking to and interacting with, went about their business as if nothing was amiss. Sara shook her head at the blatant display of idiocy. Of course she could not blame the humans for having no idea of the creatures that roamed the streets at night. For being unaware of the truth. At one time she too probably spoke to one and had no idea, until Collins.

He was stationary, that was the only reason she was able to spot him because he was the only one not moving about. This one, vampire or not, was brash. To be standing across the street, staring her down as if he had no sense in his head. Or perhaps there was something she did not know about him. Still, when she saw him, she knew immediately what he was and who he was or thought she did. The question was, did she really see him? It seemed improbable, no impossible. She should have known better though. Only months ago, she had learned there was no such thing as impossible or improbable. There was a world in which these terms, these actions did not exist.

Sara turned to face him. The fear she once associated with the silhouette in front of her, gone for now. She knew what he was capable of, the sick twisted things he delighted doing to innocent women. He was wearing the exact same thing he had been wearing, the night he attacked her. At this distance she could smell the leather jacket and the rain dripping from his fingertips. It had not rained in over a month but in her emotional state, this fact had slipped her mind. All she thought was that she must kill him before he disappeared into the shadows again. Sara was filled with rage at the very sight of him and in her quest for vengeance, she did not stop to think. As her foot touched the cracking asphalt of the street that separated them, she felt a heavy hand on her shoulder.

"Easy lass. Don't let them distract you. It's an illusion." Finn whispered in her ear.

"How can you be sure? Death is familiar with the shadows, he can appear any way he wants to."

Sara's voice was low as she spoke. She never took her eyes off the figure.

"Trust me lass. It's only meant to stir you up, to make you impulsive."

Finn pulled on her shoulder, trying to move her back toward the house Even with Finn's words ringing in her ears, she refused to turn away. So he leaned closer and whispered to her.

"Think of it as an omen. A warning maybe even a threat. They know you're here, they've always known and they've been watching."

Sara moved her thumb and pushed the blade back into its resting place before giving the illusion the middle finger. In a gust of wind, it disappeared and faded as if it had never existed. She turned her attention back to Finn.

"How did you know it wasn't real?" She asked.

Finn smirked before heading up the stairs and opening the door, waving her inside. She cautiously looked around, catching a few glares from a handful of her own kind. Let them hate her for killing them, she did not care. Sara took one last look around before she was satisfied that they were no longer being followed. So, she headed into the darkness of the house, her nerves climbing again. The door creaked as it was shut behind her and then she heard a loud click as the main power to the house was turned on. It lit up with a variety of lights, the likes of which she had not seen. There were flood lights in all the corners, white Christmas lights hanging along the walls, desk lamps, side table lamps, tall lamps and even a couple theater lights. Every inch of the house was lit in bright white light. Sara squeezed her eyes shut to stop them from watering, the sudden onslaught of light causing them to burn. When she opened them, she looked around one more time and noticed that there were iron bars on every window. On every surface of wall that could be spared, there were mirrors, tall, short, decorative and hand mirrors. Sara turned to look at Finn puzzled.

"What's with all the mirrors and iron and lights and crap?"

"The lights the little Shadow feck, the iron that nosey little Telepathic shite and the mirrors for that little weasely shapeshifting feck. The Chameleon as you call him, mirrors reveal his true face."

"What if I put a piece of iron in my pocket?" Sara inquired.

"It'd keep that 'lil feck outta yer head. It'll give em' a nice 'lil headache as well." He responded, pointing in her direction.

"Keep a shard of mirror in yer other pocket, if ya wanna keep that lizard from pullin any of his shiftin' shite." He said before turning toward the staircase by the front door.

"What about the shadows?" Sara asked.

"Floodlights." He responded cooly as he headed upstairs.

Sara looked about the interior at the peeling red wallpaper and faded Persian rugs, left behind by the previous occupants. There was dark oak, everywhere else in the house and a single set of stairs that lead to upper bedrooms. Finn seemed to use only a small portion of the building, the rest looked empty. He waved her upstairs and they ascended into a large upper floor, not filled with bedrooms as she had assumed but rather one room. It had swords and knives hanging on the wall. A large map of the United States (decorated with several multicolored dots) hung on an opposite wall, a desk sat below it with several newspapers stacked on top, so many of them that they had at one point fallen over. They now formed a small moat at the base of the desk. He had pushed an old military cot into the furthest corner of the room and from the looks of it, he rarely used it. In the center of the floor, he had placed several mats. She was not the only one who rarely slept, his pile of gas station coffee cups on the floor under by his bed, told her that he spent most nights working late. On what, she wondered. Finn tossed a blood bag on the small bed in the corner.

"I'm headin' out for a bit. In the meantime, ya eat something and get some sleep. Ya look like a junky whore. Take a shower too, ya smell like one."

"Excuse me!" She exclaimed, slowly pulling her sword from her sheath.

It was unclear if he sensed her intention, read her mind or hear the hiss of the blade sliding from its sheath. Finn was on her before she could move it another inch, his fist wrapping around her throat as he held her at eye level. The katana slipped from her fingertips, clamoring on the floor beneath her. His blade was silver and as it pressed into her flesh, she could feel it burn.

"Don' test me lass."

His body felt like titanium as he pressed her up against the wall. Sara began to choke for air, realizing in this moment that she had miscalculated his abilities and made a poor choice. Ignoring the pressure on her windpipe, she began to try and wiggle her way away from him. The pain in her throat she could handle, but him pressed up against her was too much. Finn let up the pressure on her throat, leaning forward he whispered in her ear.

"What's the matter lass?"

He was smirking when he said it. Sara could hear it in his voice. He damn well knew what was the matter. She felt the pressure on her throat let up entirely and instead, he had a large paw on her stomach, holding her up by her torso. However, he did not back away from her, he continued to push her into the wall.

"Put. Me. Down." She demanded.

"Put ya down? Are ya sure about that lass?" His eyes twinkled as he asked the question.

"Yes." She replied nervously.

"All right then." He said.

Finn sheathed his knife, grabbed her by her hips with his large hands and slammed her on the bed behind him. For a moment he hesitated, hovering over her, his eyes glimmering in the light. Sara knew he was thinking about something and she had a feeling that she did not want to find out. He stepped back, dropping the blood bag he had given her, back into her lap before turning from her.

"Eat." Finn said as he was walking away.

Then he was gone, locking the door behind him. Sara sat there staring at the red liquid resting in her lap. Sleep, he expected her to sleep. That was something she had given up a long time ago. She moved over to the hardback wooden chair by the window, staring out at the clouding sky as she sat there waiting for him to come back.

Silence, was not good for her. In the nothing, she could hear their cries, see their faces, remember their bodies lying there in the doorways of their cells.

'*Sara . . .Sara . . .Sara . . .*' She heard them whisper in her head.

"Shut up!" She screamed into the silence.

'*Sara . . .*' A faceless voice cried.

"Leave me alone!" She screamed, throwing the chair across the room.

She had to do something, silence the voices in her head. Sara could not take it anymore. Every night it was the same thing. Glancing up at the window one last time, she stormed into the small bathroom upstairs and turned on the bathtub, filling it with scalding hot water. Sara began to search the room, she was looking for one of his silver knives.

"I'm sorry, I'm sorry, I'm sorry. I can't . . .I can't . . .I can't do it." She whispered.

If she was going to do anything though, she had better do it before Finn came back. The next few hours were a blur, she remembered stumbling into the bathroom with a silver blade in her hand. There was the feel of hot water and then everything went blank. She could not remember anything else. He should have never left her alone.

"Nooo!"

Finn roared, stumbling into the bathroom and dropping to his knees. She was laying in a pool of red, blood continuing to trickle from the deep gashes on her wrists, one of his silver knives dangling from her fingers.

"Gahh!"

He growled in shock and frustration before slamming his fist through the wall in front of him. Finn stripped off his coat and scooped her out of the bathtub (water and blood soaking his long sleeve shirt). He lay her out on the floor.

"Why lass? Why? Come on lass. Breath for me. It's not your time love, not yet." He whispered.

Then he leaned down and laying his hand on her stomach, exhaled into her mouth. There was a whispered hiss and then a minute later Sara gasped. She coughed at first, the sudden rush of air into her lungs causing them to cease momentarily. Her eyes opened and then closed. Then her head dropped back onto the floor.

"That a girl. Come on Sara."

Finn coaxed her back to consciousness as he ripped a towel into shreds and began tying it around her wrists. There was a small whimper that passed from her lips but that was all.

"Aah . . .wake up lass. Stay awake. It's ol' Finn, come back to me."

He slid his arms under her and lifted her off the floor, laying her unconscious body on the bed. She needed to feed, he had to find some way to get blood into her. Grabbing the blood bag off the floor, he bit off one corner and shoved it into her mouth, squeezing it slightly.

"Drink Sara. I need ya to drink love." He was almost begging.

The sweet liquid touched her tongue and she weakly swallowed some of it. Ever slowly she drank the contents of the bag he had been trying so hard to get her to feed on.

"That's me girl. Keep going love. A little more."

He said, sliding his free hand behind her head and lifting it slightly. Finn continued to glance down at the gashes in her wrist that were slowly beginning to heal. Sara finished the contents of the bag and then lay back down on the bed. She was weak but she was alive. Finn pulled back away from her, sitting with his back to the wall as he watched her recover.

"Why tha' fuck did ya do that for?! Huh! Answer me Sara!" He yelled.

"I didn't kill them. The voices I didn't kill them." She mumbled.

"What voices?" He asked leaning forward.

"The girls, the ones they killed. The ones we had to burn at the factory. They won't leave me alone." She groaned.

Finn ran his pointer finger across his mustache, looking down at her. He had not realized her turmoil was this bad. Although he could read her every thought, he still could never have prepared himself for this. He had pulled her through the worst of it, back through the veil. She was gone the moment he arrived, he knew that. The next few hours would determine if she was going to stay with him or if all his work had been for nothing.

He stayed by her side, watching her toss and turn in her sleep, sweat glistening on her skin as she fought through another nightmare. Every few hours he would wake her enough to help her feed from another bag of blood. The wounds on her wrists would scar from the silver inlayed in his blades. Why did she do it? Why?

Sara suddenly gasp in her sleep, wincing and waving her arms around. If he did not calm her, she would rip the gashes open again and he would have to start the process over.

Finn knelt by the bed, gently stroking her hair, his other hand holding her arms down to her chest to protect her wrists.

"Sssh . . .love. It's all right. . .Finnie is here. Come on love . . .pull through, ya hafta pull through. She's gonna need ya." He whispered softly.

His heart felt like stone as he watched the turmoil pass across her face. The Wolf Pack had done a number on her and he worried she might not be strong enough to pull through. She had been fighting, she had kept going but only out of necessity.

"No!" Sara jerked, yelling in her sleep.

She shot straight up out of bed, pulling herself back against the wall and looking around frantically. For a moment she forgot where she was, she forgot who he was and she panicked.

"Sara . . .Sara . . .its me Finn. Sara look at me." His voice was soft, it soothed her frayed nerves.

Sara was panting, her eyes fluttered and tears spilled down her cheeks.

"I didn't kill them. I didn't kill them Finn." She repeated.

"Who didn't you kill? Who?" He asked, looking into her reddening eyes.

"The girls Finn. I didn't kill them. He keeps telling me I did it. It's my fault. I didn't stop him. I couldn't stop him." She was rambling.

"Who keeps tellin' ya love?" He asked, gently placing his hands on her knees.

"James . . .Alex . . .the Shadowed One . . .he slit their throats. He left them naked, hanging out of the doorways of their cells. He treated them like cattle. I have to see it, I dream it everyday." Sara began to cry.

Finn stood, sitting next to her on the bed and pulling her head into his chest.

"No lass. You didn't kill them. That's what these bastards do, that's on them. I'm sorry Sara . . .I shoulda' never left ya alone." He whispered, stroking her hair.

She gripped onto him, holding his shirt in fistfuls as her bloody tears soaked the fabric. Why did she trust him? How could she trust him? It did not make any sense but she did and right now he was the most solid thing she had to hang onto.

After a few minutes, he gently lifted her head and looking into her eyes he spoke. It was as if his words held some sway over the nightmares and the memories she carried everyday.

"Look at me Sara...you didn't kill them. That dodgy coward woulda' killed them even if you were there. Don' let em get in yer head." His thumb brushed away another tear.

"I don't have the power to fight them Finn. Amanda was the strong one. Look, I just tried to kill myself." She said gesturing at the still bloody bathroom.

"No, you've got power love. I'm here to help you learn what you can do. Ye' were put in a hell of a situation and ya survived. A fledgling against an elder. That takes bullocks." He said with a wink and a nod.

Sara sat there in silence thinking about what he had just said to her, gingerly moving the gauze away from her wrists to look at the gashes. She should be dead right now. Somehow she knew she should be dead right now but she was not. She looked up at him with a curious look but thought better than to ask.

Finn was right though, even as a human she managed to out run them and survive their little game. She even outsmarted them a time or two. He looked down at her as she stared out the window, knowing she was thinking about what he just said to her.

"Think about it Sara. Mind games is all they have left to hurt ya with. They won't dare come near ya. Not now."

He said before climbing off the bed. Sara sat there staring off out the grimy window on the opposite wall until exhaustion finally took hold. It had been weeks, maybe months since she had a decent nights sleep. This time, there were no nightmares. Nothing but peaceful darkness.

Chapter 30

The bed was suddenly lifted from the floor and slammed down hard, jarring her out of a deep sleep. Sara bounced on the mattress and nearly fell off. She awoke ready to kill someone.

"Oh good, yer awake." Finn said, moving away from the bed.

"You son of a bitch! I'm gonna-"She started.

His hand squeezed her throat just enough to cut off her air.

"Do what?"

When she did not move, he let go of her, shoving her backwards.

"That's what I thought. Now sit yer arse down." He demanded, pointing at the wooden chair.

Sara begrudgingly followed orders, settling into the hard backed chair with a groan.

"That little stunt ya pulled yesterday was not funny and it cost us time." He said as he looked down at her. "I'm here ta teach ya what ya need to know to fight them. I can't do that if yer killing yerself every feckin' day. No more of that shite! Understand?! Or next time I'll do the job myself,"

He paused, then gestured at a blank spot on his wall of weapons.

"Hang yer sword up."

"What? No. Fuck you." She said, letting her irritation slip.

"Cop that feckin' attitude again with me girlie, and ye'll be pullin' it out of yer ass. Hang it up." He growled.

Sara hesitated, son of a bitch thought he was in charge and had the right to give her orders. Was she really going to do this? Leave her only source of protection behind and trust that he was not one of them. They were known to play a great role of disillusion when they wanted to con someone into their world. If he had wanted her dead though, he could have left her floating in that bathtub or finished the job. Finn must have noticed her nervousness.

"Knock it off. If I'd wanted ya dead, ya would still be in that bathtub. I'm gonna teach ya how to blend into a crowd. Ya hafta' be able to get close to them without being detected."

His voice seemed to vibrate through her as he spoke and she shifted in her chair. Sara hated crowds, she always had. Now he was expecting her to go into a crowd where they were and stay calm.

She began to unconsciously tap her leg on the floor in rapid succession. Their faces flooded her mind. Her skin flushed hot and she began to shake her hands slightly (perspiration forming on her forehead) to calm herself. Sara panted slightly, her breaths rapid and frantic now at the thought of seeing them again. Suddenly, her stomach lurched and she darted to one corner of the room, leaning against the wall as blood spewed from her mouth. Through crimson soaked lips, she mumbled one word.

" Hell, no I'm not going anywhere near them. You'll have to kill me before I do that."

She did not consider the gravity of her words before they left her mouth. Finn was quick to respond, hauling her up off the floor, the blade of his knife pressing dangerously into the soft flesh of her throat. Sara dangled there helplessly, looking down at him as the silver of his blade scorched her flesh.

"That can be arranged, real easily love. Just say the word."

His tone was cold, it sent a shiver through her body that she could not control.

"Let go of me!" She managed to choke out.

"What'll ya do if I don't?" He challenged.

Sara was stunned, she did not know what to say or do. He had the upper hand and she had no training to get herself out of this situation. She coughed as the world around her began to blur. That was when he finally let go of her, dropping her harshly to the floor and stepping over her.

"Ya've got a lot to learn lass," He said moving toward the opposite side of the room.

"Your first lesson starts," The click of the main power switch could be heard and she was plundered into darkness. "Now."

When the lights went out, she panicked. The darkness had never bothered her before Collins, before the Shadowed One. This was where he thrived and where he was most powerful. Although she could see in the dark, she could not find Finn. His voice was a phantom to her, moving about the room as if he too was made of shadow. She had made a mistake trusting this man.

"Control your fear . . .he feeds on it. That is what gives him the most power." His voice drifted through the air.

"Finn? Turn the lights on!" She screamed in desperation.

The fighter in her had disappeared and there were now tears flowing down her cheeks. Her breathing became frantic and she pushed her back against the wall she had been leaning against. She could not do this, the dark was where things happened she wished to forget. It touched her, molested her and violated her very senses. Even if she could now see in the dark and know the difference between shadows and the absence of light, it made no never mind. How did he expect her to control her fear? It was then, she heard his voice in her ear.

"Concentrate, breath, know that you are in control. He cannot hurt you unless you allow him. Do not fear him." His brogue brushed across hear ear. She could only guess he was inches from her.

Following his advice, she inhaled slowly and exhaled even slower. Concentrating on the beat of her heart, she forced it to slow to normal rhythm. Then she began to look around, Finn's voice echoed in her head. 'Do not fear him . . .you are in control.'

"I am in control. I am not afraid." Sara whispered to herself.

"Good lass. Now, grab the shadows." He whispered.

"What?" She asked slightly puzzled.

"Grab em' Sara!" He commanded.

"How? His shadows aren't here Finn."

"But he is . . .he has been watching you always. He just found a better way to hide them from you. See the darkness as a fog, know that when you reach out, you can grab the tendrils he controls."

Sara furrowed her brow but she followed his instruction, she jabbed her hand into the dark before her and felt something touch her hand. It slithered by her. To her it felt like ice water, passing across her skin. She nodded to herself. If the darkness was a fog, then perhaps she could part it. Lifting both hands, palms up, she spread her arms as if pushing aside curtains. That was when she saw what he meant. The darkness before her, slid slowly aside like mist on the water. Beyond the blackness, she saw thousands of slithering shadows, moving all about her. She squinted her eyes and reached out again, grabbing one of the ice cold creatures, yanking it forward.

"Good! You got it lass. Now, kill it!" Finn shouted.

"How?" Sara asked.

"Let your instincts guide you." He replied.

Taking the creature in two hands, she bent its serpent body downward and felt it writhe in pain before going completely limp. Something metallic brushed her fingers and she felt Finn push the sheath of her sword into her right hand.

"You understand now. Your sword is an extension of your power. So use it. Clear the space of his pets, let him know you're not afraid of him." He whispered.

Passing the sword to her left hand, she pushed the blade from its casing with her thumb and pulled it out. With a spin of her sword, she began to slice through the withering creatures and watch their shadowy bodies fall to the floor. They dissolved as they hit the wood beneath her. These things had caused more harm and pain than the Wolf Pack, ever could. To have the power to destroy them was exhilarating. It felt as if some part of normal was returning to her world and that she now had the chance to rebuild her life. Tears of a different kind ran down her pale cheeks, relief filled her body and a new found confidence replaced her fear. She laughed slightly and at the same time cried. Her body was filled with over whelming emotion. The Shadowed One could not hurt her anymore and he could never hide any aspect of himself again.

When there were no more shadows to kill, she collapsed on the floor, sitting on her feet with her katana lying in front of her. She smiled and lifted her head to the ceiling. They would not dare return to this place now. She had discovered her ability and in doing so had also regained some of her personal power. There was still much more she had to learn. Finn flipped all the lights back on helped Sara off the floor.

"Ya've had the power all along but yer fear was holding you back."

Sara sat for a moment, staring at the sword in her hand. She had accomplished the impossible, what she believed could not be done. Slowly, she looked up to see him watching her reaction, studying her every move.

"What else do you know?" She asked, here eyes wide with shock.

A satisfied smirk spread across his face, she was beginning to understand. Finn wasted no time. She was told to hang her sword up again and they ventured out into the night. They visited a nightclub where her kind frequented and he taught her how to move through the crowd only inches from her intended victim, without them sensing her. Night after night they practiced this skill until one day, something changed. Finn did not take her back to the same place or even a similar place. He gave her no warning as to where they were going. The Jeep stopped outside a club somewhere in New York, and she was handed a sliver of iron to put in her pocket.

"What are we doing here Finn?"

"He's here." Finn said, nodding toward the entrance of the club.

"He . . .which HE?" Her voice heavy with worry.

"The one you call the Telepath." He replied, coming his loosened gray locks back behind his head.

"No no . . .Finn I can't do this. Not him. I can't do this with him."

"Then why the feck are you wasting my time?" He replied irritation in his voice.

"Excuse me?!" Sara said, furrowing her brow.

"All the days we've spent training. Suddenly now, you wanna

lose your shite. Then take me home and don't bother me   again."
He growled, his brogue thick with anger.

"Fuck you Finn! You've never been one of their pets, you don't
under stand a damn thing about them. You don't know what
they are capable of!"She roared, part of her wanting to break
his teeth for daring to say that to her.

"Yes I do." He said solemnly, staring off into the distance.

"The hell-" Sara started.

"I do!"

He growled at her, grabbing her by the neck of her shirt and
then quickly letting go. Sara dared not to say anything, at this point
she knew what he could do in the blink of an eye. Still she wondered,
how could he know anything about them?

"I used to be one of them lass."

"What?! What do you mean you used to be one of them?"

Finn sighed.

"When they started kidnapping women, I went along with it.
They didn't always hurt them like they do now. Before, we
would feed on them a little, maybe play with them but never
torture them. Believe it or not, they would enjoy it. But their
Sire, that sick heartless bastard, he twisted them into what
they are now. If I had been smarter, I could have kill him . . ."

"So you have the same Sire?"

"No. My Sire...she tried to stop their Sire and he killed her.
Not just killed her, he tortured her ...he did things to her
that ..."

His words drifted off and he stared out the window. Sara dared to think about the things they might have done to her.

"Finn?"

"Get in there if you're going. Otherwise take me home." He said waving his hand toward the club.

It was apparent that he did not want to talk about what happened to his wife. Not only had their Sire killed his, he had tortured the woman Finn loved. Now she understood his reasoning for caring what happened to her and for wanting to help her get her revenge. Sara had a new respect for him.

She slid from the Jeep and made her way inside. When her feet crossed the threshold of the clubs entryway, she felt his energy. In this small enclosed space, above the noise and the gyrating bodies, she could sense him. The music thudded against her ears but she heard none of it, she saw nothing going on around her. Her only focus and concern was for him. Sara wanted so bad to kill him but knew that it was not the right time. There would be time to get her hands on him. So, she followed his scent, and found him sitting at a table with several women. If only they knew the truth about him, would they still find him as desirable? She scoffed at their ignorance, even she knew something was not right about him from day one.

Sara slithered through the crowd, watching him from a few feet away and waiting to see if he spotted her. Finn had told her that in order to be successful she needed to be able to get inches from him and disappear back into the crowd. It was tempting to let him spot her one time but she still had more work to do. She did not need him warning anyone of her presence. So she circled him a few times before moving quietly up behind him and brushing the back of his head with her nails. Again, she faded back into the mass of bodies, watching him as he scratched the back of his head and looked around. He never saw her. With a sly smirk, she pulled the hood of her long trench coat, up about her face and moved in again. This time she whispered his name in his ear, the one he had used with her.

"Ellis."

This time he jumped up from his seat and turned around. She was already on the other side of the room. Sara ducked down and slipped out a back exit, heading quickly toward her vehicle. Her excitement was evident as she neared the car.

"I take it you were successful." Finn said with a smirk.

"I got close enough to whisper in his ear. He never saw me."

"What did you say to him lass?" There was concern in his voice.

"Ellis . . .the name he used when I was in Collins."

"That may not have been a good idea love. You've alerted them to your presence."

"No, I haven't. They already knew I was here. I just did not want them to know what I do now."

"Mmm..." He shrugged.

Sara traveled from New York to California, practicing on each one of them before Finn was sure she was ready for the next stage. In his eyes, training her on how to fight, would do her no good if she could not get close to them. He knew they would run if she attempted to confront them again. That was, if the Shadowed One (Death) was not there to back them up. They were nothing without him running the show.

Finn spent the next few weeks training Sara on hand to hand combat, knife fighting and improving her sword techniques. She worked and fought until her body was nearly too weak from lack of food and sleep to continue. He would push her beyond those limits and teach her how to ignore her bodies demands for sustenance.

"Stop I need to rest." Sara said, holding up an arm for protection.

"No. Do you think they will stop? Or maybe you have forgotten just how cruel they are. What do you think they will do if you get to this point and do not have the skills to push through?"

"Finn, I'm exhausted."

"Uh..huh . . ." He nodded.

Then he wrapped an arm around her waist, yanking her from the floor and bent her over the desk in the corner.

"Maybe you forgot what they do to women."

She heard the click of a pocket knife and felt the blade slide beneath her belt. 'He would not dare.' She thought. Then she felt him beginning to pull at the back of her pants.

"No!"

Sara would not let that happen again. She slammed her foot into his knee, hard enough to hear the bone snap and then head butted him in the nose. Finn stepped back but not for long. He grabbed her and tossed her down on the floor, reaching for the top of her cargo pants again.

"Keep away from me!"

She kicked him in the nose and crawled back away from him. Still, he came at her, managing to get on top of her and pin her arms to the floor. His hand began to slide down the front of her pants and she stopped breathing.

"Finn stop it!"

His fingers were resting at the top of her shaven pubic line where he finally did stop. Sara could feel a heat beginning to grow between her legs and she pushed the thought from her mind.

"Just remember, they won't stop if you show weakness for one second. And if they get you in this position, you'll have to concentrate hard on keeping your wits about you."

Sara was panting as she tried to ignore the slow ache coming on. She needed to get away from him and fast.

"Finn-"

Her voice caught in her throat as she felt that hand push a little further down, resting atop her outer folds. Sara bit her lip hard, puncturing flesh as she attempted to hide her arousal.

"Even if they," He pushed a finger between her folds. "Do this, you will have to use everything you have to keep from becoming aroused. Do you understand?"

Then she thought about them and what they did to those women. Her mind narrowed in on the girls and the description Amanda gave of Rachel, the apparition in her house. She held on to that image, the broken battered blonde, covered in blood. Sara found her strength to ignore what Finn was attempting to arouse within her, she slammed her knee into his groin and he rolled off of her.

"They don't arouse me! Using yourself as an example is unfair!"

Finn scooted back to a wall, still gripping his groin. The dynamic of their relationship had taken a sudden change. She used to view him in an entirely different light and now she was not sure what way she should look at him. He was no longer just a mentor. Or was the change in their relationship all in her head. She had to let this go, there was no time to get attached to anyone. Sara had made the same mistake with Amanda, now she was gone. So, she knew that she had to be willing to lose anyone and not care, that was the only way she would survive. At least until they were dead.

"Why is it unfair?!" He asked with a grin.

"Fuck you!"

Sara stood and headed for the door but Finn blocked her way.

"Move Finn!"

"I'm sorry Sara. I did not mean to upset you."

Her eyes were beginning to change as her anger got the best of her. Finn was being honest, she could see truth in his eyes.

"Why the hell did you do that?"

"I don't know."

Their conversation fell into silence. From that moment on, they pretended nothing had happened. The idea of ever being in a consenting relationship was something Sara never considered. She quickly pushed the thought out of her head. This would only complicate things and slow her reaction time. Sara knew that if he was going to fight along side her (she had no way of knowing if he would) she would need her head clear. No emotion, no attachments. To beat the devil, she had to be cold hearted, give them nothing they could use to hurt her. They had already used Amanda once against her, she would give them nothing else.

"So how do we kill these bastards?" She was quick to change the subject.

"Right."

Finn pushed himself up off the floor and moved over to the desk, pointing at the map above it.

"First, we need to locate their living quarters. Now, I've grabbed every newspaper and missing person's ad. I will tell you love, they're not just kidnapping women anymore. They're going after the men who keep them safe. In the last few months, they have killed dozens of men to get to their women. They'll stop at nothing. The disappearances are spread out, so it makes it harder to determine where they are. Although the police are investigating the disappearances, they have yet to find any evidence."

Sara stood from her place on the floor, straightening out her pants and moving cautiously toward the map. She stared at the multicolored dots on its surface, Finn's voice fading into the background. Her focus blurred a moment and then clarified. Grabbing a black sharpie from the desk in front of her, she pushed the desk away, sending missing ads and newspapers falling to the floor. Something was drawing her, guiding her to where she needed to look. The marker in her hand moved as if it was being lead by an unseen hand and she circled New York and Los Angeles, California.

"Two of them live in California, one of them in New York down in China Town."

The fact that they are getting more aggressive with their hunts and killing the men that stand in their way, did not bother her. It proved one thing, they were getting desperate. So, her and Amanda had succeeded in a portion of their quest. Without Collins serving as their home base, they were struggling to find a new way to gather their victims. Which also meant they were getting sloppy, it gave her an advantage. She had gotten more calculated, more organized and with the help of Finn, she had become even more a threat to them. Although they would never dare admit, one of their former captives now had them on the run. That they had turned on them and become something of a threat to their existence. A slow smirk spread across her features, their blood would taste even sweeter now. Sara was still staring at the map when his voice interrupted her thoughts.

"Sara?!" He growled in her ear, breaking her trance.

"Huh?" She turned to him.

"That's it girlie. You've got em' I knew ya could." He said.

"Really?" She turned to look at him, leaning on the desk.

"And just how did you know Finn?" She crossed her arms across her chest.

"Ya've had the second sight since ya were turned. I've sensed it in ya from day one." He replied, leaning in as he spoke.

"So, then you know if I can kill them or not." She implied.

"Nay," Finn shook his head. "That's up ta you lass." He said pointing at her.

"But I can give ya the things ya need ta stick it to the bastards." He finished, clinching and waving his fist.

He moved over to a black cabinet in the corner of the room, there was a large lock on its doors bolting it shut. Finn opened it and pulling out a small box.

"Ya' have the rest of the weapons yawl to kill the other two. This however is hard to get. It takes a good   smith to make one of these for you."

There was excitement in his voice, he only rolled his R's when he was worked up about something. That much Sara had come to learn about him in the few days they had spent together. He set the small metal box on the desk next to her.

"Open it." He said softly.

Finn leaned against the wall next to her, crossing his arms

across his broad chest as he watched her reaction. Sara opened the box and inside she found an iron spike with silver inlayed on all sides.

"This will kill the Chameleon but cha' haft' to get it in his heart. Some of the myths about vampires are true. But they vary from one bloodsucker to the next."

"What about the Telepath and the Shadowed One?"

"Ah . . ."

He turned from her, walking over to her banana and pulled it from the wall, handing it to her.

"Take it out." He said, nodding in her direction.

Sara slowly pulled the blade from its sheath as he had asked. It looked slightly different than it had a few months back.

"What did you do to the blade?" She asked.

"Your katana works on younger vampires. You can decapitate them and that's it, they die. But you're dealing with elders now. As a vampire ages, it builds up a severe allergy to silver. Only if you take their head off with a blade that has been inlayed with silver, will you kill them for good. Otherwise their Sire, like the prat helping these bastards, can regenerate the body. This is the only way to kill the Telepath. Take his head off and burn it. If you don't burn his head, he can transfer his consciousness to another body." Finn's Scottish brogue thickened as he talked about killing the members of the Wolf Pack.

"Sounds more like a demon than a vampire." Sara commented.

"These twits are only a fraction away from being demons. More the shite under my boots. Even our own kind looks down upon them. The younger vampires, those anemic fanboys, they revere them. Like they're some sorta gods," His words dripped with disgust." One more thing lass..."

Finn moved over to the cot in the corner and from under the bed, he pulled a box of Molotov cocktails.

"That shadow fleck'... he can die...but only by fire. Ya have to make sure his body burns to ash," He said, gesturing at her with the bottle.

"Scatter his remains in a large body of water. Do not let him turn into shadow," His voice deepened as he cautioned her. "If he's shadow, fire won't work on him."

Sara ran her fingers through her hair, feeling slightly over whelmed by the task before her. If he was not going to fight with her and if Amanda never showed up again, there was no possible way for her to complete this task on her own. She could not take on all three of them by herself. No matter what weapons or training she had at her fingertips. She reached in her coat pocket and pulled out her last cigarette, lighting it. The nicotine had no effect on her anymore but it had become such a habit in life that she could not bring herself to give it up. For her, it was the last piece of her life she had to ground herself to this world, to remind herself that she had once been human. She looked at Finn with worry in her eyes.

"Are you coming with me?" Sara tapped the ash into an empty cup.

"No lass. That is not my fight." He said softly.

"I cannot do this alone." She was desperate.

He smiled a soft smile as he looked at her.

"You won't be alone." He replied.

The words only left his mouth and then there was a hard knock on the door. Sara turned her head sharply in the direction of the noise, setting her cigarette on the edge of the window sill and grabbing her katana. She descended the stairs with a prowess that would unnerve even them. With her hand wrapped around the handle of her sword, the other one reached for the doorknob, slowly turning it. With a nervous exhale (her heart hammering in her chest) she yanked the door open. At first she could only blink as she stared in shock at the sight before her. The woman had shoulder length dark hair, her eyes reflected pain and exhaustion. There were numerous scars decorating her face. A long coat hung about her, hiding the ripped up t-shirt and black leather pants she was wearing. Sara never thought she would see this face again.

"Amanda?" Sara asked, unsure if she was really seeing her.

"You ready to go?"

Amanda asked, glancing over her shoulder at the towering figure behind her. A low growl crawled up her throat. Who the hell was that? She wanted to know. Who dared to come near her friend? She did not care if it was the Master himself, no one should be so stupid. She could not see his features in the dim light, but she caught the glimmer of a blade, the soft wave of a long coat and the movement of his hand as he pushed his hair back behind his head.

"Who the hell is that?" She demanded.

Sara barely glanced in his direction before quickly replying.

"No one."

She knew her Sire would not hesitate to attack him and she knew that it would not be a good idea. Finn had more power than both of them combined. Although she had never seen him use it, she could sense it rolling off of him in waves, especially now. The growl she heard Amanda utter had caused him to become defensive and she was standing between them trying to keep the peace. Sara's answer was almost enough to pacify her, still she saw Amanda hesitate before slowly turning for the black Chevelle rumbling outside.

"Wait-" Sara started.

"Grab what you need, I'll wait in the car." She said, glancing over her shoulder once more at the man in the shadows.

Sara sheathed her sword and rushed upstairs to grab her things. She stepped into the bedroom, and wanted to tell Finn goodbye before she left but he was gone. She wished she had more time to look for him, her heart ached at the prospect of never seeing him again. But why? She shook the thought from her head before gathering the tools he had given her. Sara took one last look around the room with a longing in her that she never thought she would feel again. Amanda was the only person she had become attached to, that she had missed and now, she found herself missing him too. She hoped when all this was over that she might see him again.

Turning from the room, she thundered down the stairs, slamming the door behind her as she left. She never noticed him step from the shadows to watch her leave.

"Got everything?"

"Yeah, uh, wouldn't the Jeep be better?"

"No."

All conversation after that was covered by the sound of squealing tires and the growl of the engine. They were headed out of the city and fast. Sara hoped Amanda knew where to look for the Wolf Pack's members. Their reunion was awkward enough without attempting to fill it with small talk. So, Sara said nothing as they sped through the night.

Amanda's Story

Chapter 31

The remnants of police tape, whipped violently about as the wind drifted between the tall skyscrapers and down into the ghettos of New York. In the dead of night, among the homeless figures, the drug addicts and the scarlet women, a small shadow moved about. It flickered between the yellow, buzzing street lights and around the graffiti covered buildings, an unnoticed phantom. They would pay her no never mind, even if she remained solid and walked boldly down the middle of the street. Who would dare look at a hooded figure covered in blood? Her features disfigured by the jagged scars covering most of her body. A large puffy violet scar spread from her forehead to her right cheek. The one that lay across her left eye, made closing it nearly impossible. None any of the withering figures that littered the street corners and alleyways.

There was a darkness here she could not understand. Nothing made sense to her anymore. The dark feeling that hovered over her, that clung to her, she knew had nothing to do with New York. What was left of her clothing whipped about her as she headed deeper into the ghetto, pulling her arms around her torso and tucking her head down. The smell of factory smog, old blood and sewage, assaulted her senses. Garbage and old furniture littered the empty chain link lot across from the row of boarded up house fronts. Bullet holes decorated their siding and the casings remained scattered in the street. The sound of dogs barking, shouting voices and screeching tires echoed through the night. Off in the distance, over the piercing scream of an Amtrak, she heard gun shots rattle in rapid succession. Another body would be headed to the morgue, she could smell the fresh scent of blood from here.

A rat scurried across her boot, heading for one of the turned over trash cans, with a one eyed cat not far behind. She considered feeding on the cat and putting it out of its misery. But she could not bring herself to kill an animal.

Amanda passed shivering bodies curled against foul smelling dumpsters in an attempt to stay warm as fall's harsh wind whipped their tattered clothing about them. Her humanity (what little there was) begged her to stop and help them, put them out of their hopeless misery.

It was not the weak and helpless she wanted to kill but the evil men that roamed the streets. There were plenty of them to provide her with adequate food, without her feeding on crack addicts and prostitutes. Those scarlet women, some but not all of them had never been given a choice as to their lot in life. They were forced into their profession, out of survival and sometimes, out of fear. There was no reason to punish them.

Amanda understood all too well, what it was like to be used for your body alone and receive nothing for all your suffering. Although she herself was still dealing with her own agony, she felt obligated to help them. They did not have the power to fight for themselves. Besides, what was one more scratch on her karmic record? Who would bat an eye at another dead gangster? When her death came, she knew that Hell was inevitable, so why not make her suffering worth it? If she had the power to kill James (back when he had turned her face into his own personal punching bag) she might have done it. Or at least beat him within an inch of his life and ensure, he never touched another woman in anger. There was no point in dwelling on the past.

She was a single woman, with no weapons to defend herself, aside from the demon dwelling within. The clothing she wore was not helping to block the cold and although she would not die from frostbite, she was uncomfortable. It would only get colder as winter approached. Amanda was so deep in thought, she startled when a police car screamed by her. The sight of it sending her into a mild panic. Her heart hammered against her rib cage as she watched its lights disappear down a side street. Amanda exhaled slowly (her claws retracting back to normal length) and looked around to see if anyone had noticed. If they had, no one was daring to look in her direction. As far as she could tell, she was alone. She closed her eyes, squeezed them tight and licked her lips. It seemed, no matter how far away she went, Collins would always be with her.

Evidently tired feet moved forth toward an undecided location, her body was in need of rest and recuperation. Though she had no idea where she might locate a hotel and the resources to pay for a room. As her wavering eyes stared down at the broken blocks of concrete beneath her, they scanned over the miles of garbage, discarded needles, condom wrappers and commercialized food packaging. Even if she had not been covered in filth of her own, just walking through the area would have made her feel disgusting enough to bathe. She would not find all that she needed here. A meal at best but not the finances she was desperately needed. Unless, she found a drug dealer or a pimp. Sure, dealers were not directly guilty of the death of their patrons but they did pollute the city every year and their money helped to contribute to the sex trade. Besides, the body of a drug dealer in an alleyway would go mostly unnoticed and the police would brush their death under a rug. In the matter of a few days, they would be forgotten about.

Realizing her limited options, Amanda headed for a more populated area, the red light district would be her best bet. So, she summoned what energy she had to shift between the shadowy doorways the few shadows provided and headed into a more lively part of New York. Within the confines of the shadow realm, she peered through the fog, searching for frequent headlights. Somewhere between 48th street and 59th, she spotted the small curvy, scantly clad figures shifting about on the sidewalks. Their skin pink from the cool night air. Amanda slowly stepped from the shadows, her body lacking the proper energy to maintain her shadow form. So, she was careful to stand back within the safety of the alley. Hours passed by before she finally heard the angry shouts of a pimp, scolding his property for not bringing in enough money. Still, she waited. He grabbed the woman and yanked her in the vehicle, squealing his tires as he drove off. Amanda followed him, speed meaning nothing to her.

The vehicle pulled to a stop behind an abandoned building, where he drug her out of the car and proceeded to beat her for her indiscretions. Amanda recognized the sickening sound of his fist as it collided with her diaphragm, the sound of the stomach fluids swishing around internally as her body rejected the assault. She heard the woman gasp for air before his hard hands insulted the delicate features of her face. The vampiress pressed her teeth together hard, his actions remnant of her own abuse. Her muscles tensed in response as her canines extended, she would enjoy his death. She would have to proceed with caution. There were at least three other men in the car with him.

"What the hell have you been doing?! Where is my fucking money!?"

He was screaming questions at her which he knew she had no way to answer and that no answer would sate his anger. His fury was driven by the alcohol wafting off of him and the cocaine she could see, lining the bottom of his nostril. Amanda was going to take great enjoyment in killing him. Slowly, she melted between buildings until she was a few feet behind the black, musclebound, angry pimp. Cocking her head, she stared at the barely visible tattoos on the back of his bald head. Did he really think those baggy pants and black tank top looked good together? Who was he attempting to impress? Could he not afford a belt? She never could understand their ways, their dress and who in the world told them that showing their boxers off, was a style.

"I'm talking to you bitch! Answer me!"

He raised a fist to hit her one more time, the prostitute by this point having curled up in a heap on the ground to protect her already bloody face. Amanda caught the wrist of his upraised arm, just as it was coming down. The black man turned to look at her and with a very calm tone, she spoke.

"Don't do that."

Her demeanor was calm, as if nothing out of the ordinary was happening. She knew with his hot blooded temper and his alcohol infused rage, her relaxed attitude would entice him to be stupid. He angrily yanked his wrist from her grip and then turned on her, his putrid breath assaulting her senses. She blinked annoyed as a torrent of curses and droplets of spit sprayed her face.

"Who the fuck are you and why the fuck is it any of your business?! Dis' bitch is my property, an I'll do what da fuck I wan' do with her! An ain't no body, not even you gon' do nothin bout it!"

Aside from the fact he was still spitting on her (which she wiped off her face), his evident lack of intelligence was an insult to her ears. Did he not understand proper English? Most likely not. She assumed his upbringing was rather lacking in the educational apartment. Again she sighed before letting him continue on his tirade.

"Now ya better get da fuck up outta here," He pressed the barrel of a 9 mm to the side of her hooded head. "for I splatter yo' brains on dis here street."

"Mmmm." She growled.

Her head remained slightly down as her eyes filled with blood and her canines extended to their full length. His threat, his stupidity was what she needed. She was playing with her meal, invoking his anger and enticing his minions to get out of the car.

"No you won't."

As she spoke, she slowly raised her head so he could see the red of her iris's and the deadly smirk revealing her long sharp canines.

"What the fuck!?" He shouted, jumping back.

His men piled out of the car.

"Shoot that bitch! She's possessed or somein' man!"

A rapid flash of lights and the concussive sound of gunfire filled the alleyway. Amanda weaved between them, dodging bullets, her claws slicing through the delicate flesh of one man's throat. The echoing crack of breaking bones echoed through the alley as she grabbed another men, shattering his ribs and his legs. She left him to drowned in the blood that was now filling his punctured lungs. The last, aside from the pimp, attempted to crawl back into the car and drive away but she broke the window, snatching him out by his throat.

"Hi." She whispered as she stared into his fearful gaze.

Then she opened her mouth wide and sank her teeth into his neck, draining him. His body dropped loosely from her arms, landing on the concrete with a soft thud. The pimp attempted to run, screaming desperately for help. No one would hear his cries tonight and even if they did, in this part of New York, they knew better than to get involved. By now, blood was running off her fingertips and dripping from the end of the sharp daggers at the end of her hands. It soaked her clothing and ran from her lips. She was an intimidating sight to behold, a different woman than the one she had been a year ago.

She turned to kill the man she had originally set her sights on but he was running away from her. Amanda frowned mockingly and pursued him with the excitement of a child. His futile attempt to escape only increased her animalistic hunger and she quickly closed the gap between them. She was not subtle about it either, she dashed past him in a blur of speed and as she did, she swept her foot at his ankles. There was a resounding snap as his calf bones broke violently, their jagged white ends poking grotesquely through the skin. He screamed and fell to the ground, pulling himself desperately along by his fingertips. The pressure on his nails, slowly began to pull them from his flesh as he clawed desperately to get away. Amanda moved slowly toward him, watching his pathetic attempts to get away with curious amusement. Crouching down beside him, she tapped him on the shoulder.

"Where do you think you're going?" She asked, cocking her head to the side.

He grunted in response as he continued to try to crawl away from her and he felt another fingernail rip from the bed. The broken bones sticking out, snagged on the concrete, causing the flesh to gape wide as it tore. Amanda glanced up in the direction he was attempting to go.

"No one is going to help you." She said, her tone grim.

Shaking her head, she rolled him on his back.

"Do you know how pathetic you look right now?" Her voice remained soft.

"What the hell do you want from me man?"

He had stopped crawling long enough to ask her the question.

"Your life."

In one fluid motion, she moved over him like the angel of death passing over the city to kill their first born. He had no chance to escape. As she sank her fangs deep into the tender flesh of his neck draining him of his crimson essence, she tasted his anger, fear, and the variable narcotics he had been injecting. Her mind swam with his memories and her body buzzed from the heavy drugs streaming through his system. Although they did not effect her in the same manner as a mortal, she did get a lovely floating feeling. She purred as she dropped his body to the ground, his blood providing her with the healing she so desperately needed. Though she now had more energy to continue on her journey, sleep was a necessity if she was ever going to hunt down the Shadowed One.

Shoving her hands in his pockets, she set to robbing him and his minions, taking the wads of cash they carried. Feeling no guilt for the death of any of them, she decided to take their car as well. She have considered taking keys and heading to the listed address on his drivers license but she already had drawn more attention than she wanted. So, she chose to head in a different direction, using his GPS to help her get there. The vehicle bounced with a rhythmic thump as it rolled over one of the bodies. There was no need to dispose of them. Even if the police noticed the bite marks and the autopsy revealed a lack of blood, no one would believe what they found. It was the only reason the Wolf Pack had been able to go this long without being detected.

It felt strange driving again but at least the vehicle would blend into the neighborhood. The prostitute she saved was long gone, most likely ran off to tell the tale of the monster who killed her pimp. That was fine, perhaps the rest of them would think twice about their chosen profession.

New York on the other hand, continued on about its nightly business, paying no mind to the death of four miscreants. At the corner of 12th Avenue and Amtrak, she found a two story brick building with the letters Motel painted on its front in faded yellow lettering. Amanda pulled the black cutlass to a stop on near the buildings door, leaving it there for the police to tow. She would not be keeping it, it was more evidence of her involvement in their deaths. There was a large glowing vacancy sign in the window of the Motel's door. If they had rooms at this hour of the night, she was sure she would be able to check-in when she returned. First she needed to obtain some different clothes. Using the GPS she punched in a search for an army surplus store and a clothing store. They would not have women's undergarments at the surplus but she could find some more durable clothes.

A few miles from her location, she found both. She shifted into the clothing store and snatched a pack of underwear. Amanda was careful when moving through the surplus store, staying in her shadow form so she did not set off their security system. She filled a green duffle bag with two pairs of black combat boots, a few pairs of black B.D.U's, long and short sleeve black shirts and lastly a black trench coat with a hood. Amanda set a few dollars on the counter to cover most of what she had taken, feeling slightly guilty about stealing from veterans. Although she knew that if they had been in her situation, they would understand.

With her supplies acquired, she slipped back onto the vacant streets and headed back for the Motel. It would have been faster to move between the shadows draped across the sidewalks and occupying the overpasses around her but she wanted to walk. For just a little while she wanted to feel some sense of normality, to feel something solid beneath her feet and to know she was still on the Earth, even though she knew things would never be normal again.

As she walked, she contemplated all the questions she had acquired over the course of a year as their prisoner. There was freedom now to think for herself without looking over her shoulder every few seconds. If the Chameleon had been James, then at what point did he take over and become her James? Or better yet, how did he find her? Why did he choose her and how were they choosing the women before her?

For a moment, her thoughts drifted back to Sara and how she had left her. Amanda did not want to remember such things but her mind would not allow her to forget. After all the hell they had been through, how it had bonded them for life, she did not want to imagine the hurt Sara felt or the confusion. Only a few hours into her vampiric birth, she had been left without direction, without a home and without a Sire to guide her. She probably believed that Amanda no longer cared about her or that she had used her. That being far from the truth. It was because she loved and cared about the girl so much that she knew, she was safer if she distanced herself. However, now there was no one to protect her from her own kind, those who would pray on the weaker. Amanda's heart skipped a beat as fear trickled into her bloodstream. Was leaving Sara really the best thing she could have done for the girl? She was no longer sure. Either way, Sara was still safer without Amanda around.

She knew that the moment she watched them rip James's throat out and leave him bleeding on the concrete. They killed him because he came looking for her. Or maybe they did it for their own amusement. She would never know. Did it really even matter? Some part of her regretted not burning him or burying him properly. Although he had beat her within an inch of her life, at least, that was what she had been lead to believe. The sudden change in character would make more sense if the Chameleon had taken James's place sooner. James could have been innocent of the crimes she had accused him of, his doppelgänger may well have been the guilty party.

In any case, the Shadowed One would be looking for one of them, the one person who ruined his little kingdom of atrocities. He would hunt her for all eternity and when he found her, her death would not come quickly. What if she was wrong and the Shadowed One decided to kill Sara just to get to her? It was not that

unreasonable to consider, he had done it before in Collins. Amanda
needed to stop thinking that way. It would make her act irrational
and she knew that was a quick way to end up a corpse. She needed
sleep, she needed to get her head on straight before she did something
stupid.

A small bell above the Motel door, rang as she pushed it open
and stepped into the yellowing lobby. It's wallpaper was peeling,
floors were stained with rusty water that had leaked down from the
ceiling tiles and the air stank with the pungent smell of cigarette
smoke. This may have well been a decent place when it was first built
but years of neglect had taken their toll. From behind two coke bottle
glasses, an older Indian man stared at her judging her disheveled
appearance but doing so cautiously. His white hair crowned around
his upper skull in a horseshoe, there was a few days of white stubble
on his chin, and a mustard stain on the belly of his white shirt. A
heavy accent made him nearly incomprehensible, but she managed to
understand enough.

"What you want?" He asked, curling his lip up in disgust.

"I need a room. Not sure how long. A couple days at most."

"No no, we don't do that type of business here." He said,
waving his hand at her.

"Excuse me?" Amanda growled, insulted.

"You sell sex else where." He said, pointing at the door.

Amanda had to bite her tongue to keep from being completely rude.

"Look, I'm not a damn prostitute. And," She pulled three
hundred dollar bills from her pocket and put them on the
counter. "I pay cash."

He looked at her over the top of his glasses before handing
her a pen and pointing to the next line in his ledger. Amanda found it
strange, he never asked for an identification card or drivers license.

She could only assume that he did not care enough to bother. So she signed Jane Doe on the line and he handed her a room key before pointing to the only other door in the office. It was the only way in or out of the Motel besides the emergency exits.

The yellow lights above cast a sickly green color on the stained and faded red carpeting. It stank of old cigarettes and long forgotten memories of family road trips. There was a sadness to the appearance of the Motel that sickened her. It was like a forgotten relic in an overgrown, over developed city. Or a used woman, cast aside when they no longer enjoyed her company, befitting really. Amanda trudged past rooms with screaming orgasms, rooms with snoring sleepers and the rooms with the television too loud for any one person. At the end of the hallway, she located her room number 20 and unlocked the door, slamming it behind her. Her room was riddled with burn marks and if she had not been so tired, she might have turned around to demand a new room. It was most certainly infested with bedbugs and it held the pungent aroma of a moldy blanket.

A small desk was pushed up against one wall, with its mediocre supplies resting on one corner, they even provided a comment card. She would not bother to fill that out. The pad of paper had nothing written on the top of it, except for the motel's address. It was almost as if they did not want anyone to recognize their stationary. Her nightstand held the ever so common King James bible, with gold lettering pressed on black leather. There was barely any light in the room, one weak lamp with a stained lampshade sat on the right side of the bed, nearest the window and its paisley brown curtains. She felt more like she was in a mental institution than she was a motel room. It's drab depressing state only adding to her already depressed mood.

Amanda sighed and dropped her bags on the bed. Pulling the curtains shut, she set to the task of peeling off her soiled clothes and stuffing them into a garbage bag. They were soaked with a combination of old blood, fresh blood and sexual fluids from the endless rapes she endured. Not to mention the stains from her own wounds, although they had long healed. In her nudity, she could now see the evident scars that spread across her midsection and down her legs. As she headed into the bathroom, she dared to stop and look at herself in the full length mirror, to see the damage they had inflicted on her. Delicate scars lay across the bridge of her nose and beneath her eyes, where the whip had caught her face. They would never heal. The rest of the scars on her breasts, stomach, legs and back were large and puffy. Their off white color a glare on her once flawless porcelain flesh. Even her eyes, although they bared no visible blemishes, had a lifelessness to them as if all happiness and joy had been drained from her. They used to be bright and beautiful, even that was now gone. Amanda knew it was best not to dwell on the past and to keep the mirrors out of her sight. She contemplated breaking them, all of them but decided better of it.

The bathroom was worse than the rest of the room, cracking tiles, iron stains on the tub and sink, a self standing toilet paper holder was shoved to one side of the toilet. Amanda turned the knob for the hot water and the shower groaned to life, brown at first and then clear. She wondered if bathing in the cities sewers would be just as sanitary. Grabbing the motel's toiletries on the narrow top of the tub, she climbed under the scalding stream of water. A foul mixture of blood, dirt and chunks of flesh swirled around the drain as she washed the filth of Collins from her body. She could wash Collins from her flesh but never from her mind. Amanda was beyond exhausted, so she washed quickly. The towels the motel provided felt somewhere between actual sand and fine grain sandpaper. After the discomfort she experienced for nearly a year, these were a blessing. Having no other clothes to speak of, she shuffled to the main room and climbed beneath the covers. Their cheap fabric scraped against the still open wounds that were slowly healing from the silver blades on the Telepath's whip.

Amanda's attempt at sleep was useless. A thin sheen of cold sweat glistened on her ivory skin as she thrashed violently, crying out for salvation. They were hurting her, they had her and they were hurting her. She was in a cell, not in Collins but somewhere deep in a wooded area. It was a cage, small and cramped. She was bloody, most of her body broken from the incessant beatings they laid upon her night and day. A pair of pale blue eyes looked up at her as if to ask her why. He found her, Death found her and made her pay for Amanda's crimes.

"No! I didn't do this! No!"

Then she was back in Death's bed, restrained by thick silver chains, lying between the black silk sheets. His hands were on her most private flesh, touching her, violating her. Amanda tossed in her sleep, throwing her body about violently as she fought against nonexistent chains.

"Get off me! Don't touch me!"

A shadow muffled her screams, she was human again, she had no power. That was the moment she knew it was a dream and she screamed at herself to wake up. Still she was trapped in the nightmare. So she roared at herself until she felt something snap and she was jolted awake. Amanda sat quickly upright, her heart hammering against her rib cage, her breathing shuddery. Her eyelids fluttered at first and then she swallowed hard before bloody tears began to flow down her cheeks. Grabbing her knees, she hugged them to her chest as she sobbed heavily. 'She was there, they were there and Sara . . .they found her. Oh, god he had me, he had me.' She thought, the words repeating in her mind several times. It took her a few minutes to pull herself out of the anxiety attack she was experiencing. When did she become this woman? When did this happen? She was allowing herself to feel emotion and that would serve no purpose.

Throwing back the covers, she grabbed a washcloth and wiped the bloody tear marks from her naked form. Then she put on the stolen clothing from last night and plopped down at the small wooden desk, pulling the glass ashtray toward her. Her mind swam with an uncomfortable vertigo and her body swayed. Amanda put a cigarette between her teeth, lighting it and tossing the lighter haphazardly on the counter where it bounced a few times before sliding to a stop. She was disoriented and felt as if nothing around her was real anymore, the nicotine was not helping to center her. Was she losing her mind? Was it all part of a psychotic breakdown? She swallowed the lump in her throat. Staying here, sitting in this room was not doing her any good. Amanda grabbed her room key and headed out.

It was nighttime again, the perfect time to search for her kind. First, she would visit a gun shop if she could find one and get something to maker her hunt easier. Perhaps killing would help get rid of her memory of the dream. The pimp's car from last night was already gone, as she suspected it would be. So, she headed out on foot. Some part of her wanted to track down Sara and make sure she was all right. Then again, Death could be wanting her to find Sara for him. Without the Telepath, he would have to track her on foot or through the shadows and he would have to come through Amanda to get to her. She dared him to try.

In the bowels of the city, past the prostitutes and the ghetto clothing stores, she found the gun shop she was looking for. It was not guns she was after but something a little quieter and a little more personal, because it was personal. To her all of the bloodsuckers that roamed this great city were guilty of the crimes in Collins. Every pimp, sadist, rapist and murderer were a part of what happened to her. They were the reason she suffered and why she wore the scars on her body.

Amanda headed inside, keeping her head down as she went. The man behind the counter eyed her with unease. She paid him no mind, he was not a threat to her. He was a portly gentleman with a closely shaven head. His face was clean except for the jowl hanging down beneath his chin, there was a hint of white stubble. A Smith and Wesson was strapped to his right hip and she watched him briefly touch the grip when she entered the shop. At least until she suggested he not do that, her eyes glimmering momentarily as a warning. From body language alone, she could tell he had been prior military. She would give him as much respect as she showed her, despite his service.

"Can I help ya find something miss?" There was a slight twang in his voice.

"A sword. Something functional."

He scanned her once before deciding she was not one of the general population who frequented his store. As he turned toward the wall behind him, she glanced down at his .45 and felt a nostalgia for her own. It used to be her main protection and the one thing she knew would kill anything, until she learned that some things did not die by bullet, no matter what caliber it might be. From the wall behind him, he pulled a black handled katana with a black sheath. The finish on its sheath glimmered in the dim light of the store. She slowly pulled the blade from its case and held it up to the light, examining it for any nicks or bends in the metal. There were none, it was perfection at its finest. Amanda grazed her thumb across its surface and felt its bite. The shop owner would never notice. Her cut healed as soon as it appeared.

"Do you mind?" She asked raising the blade.

She wanted to hear how it sounded when it cut through the air. He cocked his head to the side and looked at her for a moment before nodding in response. Amanda brought it down hard and listened to its harmonious tone. Her skin goose bumped and she felt the power within its folded metal. It would taste much blood before the night was over, it would drip with rubies and together they would paint the city red.

"How much?"

She asked while gently sheathing the blade, her eyes remaining glued to the blade.

"Maybe more than you can afford." He replied shifting his weight and looking down at her.

Amanda sighed, why did this have to turn nasty? She had not been rude to him, she had allotted him control of the situation and treated him with respect. So, what was the problem? When she turned to speak to him, looking him in the eye with a cold glare of irritation, her tone and demeanor had changed.

"I'll ask you again. How much?" The threat in her words was evident.

Even if she did not have it in cash, she still had the pimp's credit card and she knew it was not shut off. The carrier was dead.

"Three thousand." He said with a scoff.

"I need a wet stone as well."

She said as she, pulled the handful of cash from her pocket, she counted it and found she had more than enough to pay for the weapon. Amanda snidely set it on the table. As she waited for him to take the money, she raised her eyebrows and waited to see if he would say something else. He dropped his eyes, taking the cash off the table and putting it in the cash register before handing her the sharpening stone. They now had an understanding. At that notion, she was gone. The sound of the door closing was the only thing he noticed when he turned around to hand her a receipt.

New York had been awake in one respect for a while now but now she was really beginning to liven up. Amanda headed into the downtown area with the katana hidden off to her right side. The last thing she needed was a police officer stopping her for carrying a weapon illegally. She was not the thing they needed to worry about, she had no qualms with them.

For a while she moved around the downtown area, looking for any sign of her kind. Being newly acquainted to their world herself, she had no idea where they normally amassed. In her search for the heathens, she found something else, someone else who dared to show their face.

On a street corner, diagonal from the alley she was lounging in, she saw three vampires who should not be there. Was she seeing things? Beneath the dim streetlight they were standing under, she just barely caught their faces. What or who rather, she believed she saw, was Death, the Chameleon and the Telepath. They were smiling at her, mocking her. There was no way that those two were still alive. They had nearly dismembered them back in Collins. A voice in her head, told her that she was seeing them.

'Did you miss me Amanda?'

"No! You're dead!"

She recognized that laugh, it echoed through her mind and sent chills down her back. They were alive, all of them alive and standing in front of her. How was that remotely possible? She had only nearly recovered from what they had done to her and although she had faced them, she was not over her fear. It came on strong as ever. The emotions she worked so hard to bury, now crippled her and she sank down the side of the brick building she was leaning on. Before she could pull herself out of it, she was curling up against the dumpster behind her in an attempt to make herself as small as possible. She was trying to hide from them. All she could think was 'Not again. Not again.'

The laugh in her mind grew louder as she pulled back into herself and became the frightened woman she had been when they first tossed her into that cell. The memories she thought she had killed, were very much alive. She only managed to be strong because Sara needed her. Without that need, that want to protect her, her strength was gone.

"Sara." She was all Amanda could think about.

Amanda looked up, realizing she had left the girl alone and unguarded with no way to defend herself. If she had to burn them to ashes, these boys would die a thousand times but they would never lay their hands on Sara. Not as long as her black heart still beat in her chest.

When she found the strength to stand she turned to grab her sword and when she looked up they were gone. Had she really seen them she wondered? Or was she experiencing a hallucination? She needed to kill, to get her mind right.

The smell of fresh blood drifted through the night and she followed it. There she found what she had been searching for in the downtown area. In an abandoned church, not far from her, was a woman lying near the base of the altar. She was still alive because the leech feeding on her, had been taking his dear sweet time. A vampire who looked no older than nineteen by human standards, sat perched atop the marble top altar. He was using the wooden cross as a sword, having a mock sword fight with himself. A patch work of poorly constructed tattoos and piercings littered his body. The tight leather pants he wore on his skeletal legs, squeaked as he moved, his black shirt was gauze thin and to add to the mismatch he dawned a pair of laceless combat boots. Amanda rolled her eyes at him and shook her head.

Although she could have easily wiped him out, she was cautious as she entered the church. Her footfalls were light and precise. The mirage out in the street had left her visibly shaken. Where once she had certainty, now she felt a tingle of fear. As if she was still in Collins, they were still in charge and her escape was only a dream. At any moment they could come out of hiding and toss her back in the cell. Amanda approached everything now as if the Wolf Pack was involved and it was all a trick. She nervously tightened her fist and forced herself to move. Every action, even her arrogance, was an effort. But she did everything she could to make it believable.

"Isn't it past your bed time?" She asked, sarcasm dripping from her words.

He looked up at her, annoyed. Amanda smiled to herself, that was what she wanted. If he allowed his emotions to get the better of him, he would make the first move and he would get himself killed.

"So what if it is? What the hell you gonna do about it?" He replied jumping off the altar.

Amanda smirked.

"Oh, I hoped you might say that."

The sheath clattered to the floor as she pulled the katana in one swift motion.

"Why's that? You think you can take me? Do you know what I am?"

"An eighties throwback?"

"All right, you want a piece of me? Then you'll have to take me and my friends."

He wolf whistled and a series of footfalls could be heard all around her as ten like him dropped from rafters, jumped in through broken windows or stepped out of the shadows.

"You can't take us all."

"You are gravely mistaken. Believe me, I have dealt with worse."

Dropping her hood back, she revealed the scars that covered most of her face, they would know who had done it to her. She was intelligent enough to know that they would recognize the Telepath's handy work. The kid stepped back a bit and then laughed, pointing at her.

"Oh ho ho . . .sister lemme tell you, if you won, its because they let you. The Blood Kings do not give up that easily. Did you remember to kill their Sire?"

Amanda said nothing, letting him talk would be the best way for her to find Death.

"No? Oh ho," He clapped his hands excitedly, jumping around in amusement.

"Oh baby doll, then you're fucked. You didn't kill shit."

"Hmm . . .maybe I did . . .maybe I didn't . . .but you . . .you're dead already. You're just too stupid to know it."

While he spoke, she had been shifting the shadows under her control into place around his companions.

"See . . .what you don't realize," Her iris's filled with blood.

"Is that my bloodline is derived from them. What do you think that means?"

His mouth dropped open as she looked up at him and he now realized that the shadows were gathering in a thick fog. Their first priority was to protect the girl at all costs.

"Kill her! Get that bitch! She's King blood!"

She heard the air shift and she flipped the katana, driving it all the way to the hilt into the vampire standing behind her. With fluid motion, she spun on the balls of her feet and sliced his head from his shoulders. Amanda drifted through the room, like a phantom in the wind, her blade singing through the air as she sliced repeatedly through flesh and bone. The blood coating her katana, dripped on the forgotten pews and spattered across the relics the church left behind. Her shadows dispatched the others with a quick twist and pull of their head. Their spines still clinging to the base of their skulls as they were dropped to the ground. Amanda felt nothing when she killed her own kind. So, she felt nothing now.

Amanda cocked her head to the side as the leader of the group attempted to run for the door. With a slight jerk of her chin, the shadows rose up above the windows, encircling both of them in darkness. She knew he could see through the dark but there was no way he could fight off what she had conjured up. He turned to look at her, slack jaw and wide eyed.

"Your . . .your bloodline . . .it's . . .Prince of Darkness."

"Stop giving them noble titles! There is nothing noble about what they do!"

His comment had angered her. Grabbing his bald head in one hand, she looked him in the eye and spoke.

"This territory and all the mortals in it belong to me."

He opened his mouth to speak but she silenced his words, drawing her blade one last time through his neck, finishing her tirade of murder. Then she set his severed head atop the altar, driving the wooden cross into his skull before turning to the bloody woman on the floor. She was trying to crawl away from the horror above her. Amanda knew she would not get very far in her condition. So, she walked over and sheathed her blade before wrapping an arm around the young girls waist. The woman (as expected) began to panic and beg for her to let go. Amanda dropped her sword and lifted the girl to face her.

> "Hey, hey . . .it's okay . . .it's all right. I'm not going to hurt you! Okay? I'm here to help you. You need to get to a hospital. I'm going to take you there, okay?"

At first she only nodded, her blood soaked blonde locks and vibrant blue eyes reminded Amanda so much of Sara. She felt her heart began to ache for the woman but she quickly brushed it off.

> "Those guys," She pushed her hair behind her ears as she spoke, looking around nervously. "they . . .they kidnapped me. I don't even know where I am."

Amanda cupped the woman's face in her hands.

> "It's okay. You're in New York City. Where are you from?"

> "Wolf Creek."

A cold recognition fell over the vampiress as she heard a name she never thought she would hear again.

> "I was in a bar-"

> "I'm gonna get you home." Amanda could not bare to hear anymore.

She hugged the girl close. "Close your eyes and hold onto me."

Amanda grabbed her sword and wrapped her arms around the woman. With the help of the shadows, she made it to Wolf Creek within a matter of a few minutes. It was best if she took the woman to a hospital back home, where they could not touch her again. She wondered if the 'Blood Kings' (she rolled her eyes at the thought of the name) were involved in that kidnapping. Did they do that on purpose, to mess with her? To try and throw her off? Had they planned for her to find this woman? No, she would not do this to herself or allow them to succeed. If they had something to do with this kidnapping, her best coarse of action was to shut down. No emotion. She could not let them get to her, not again. Somehow this felt like a set up. She gently let go of the girl and pulling her hood up, stepped just inside the hospital.

"I've got an injured woman! She's bleeding bad! I need a doctor!"

Amanda shouted for some help before quickly moving away. She watch from a safe distance as nurses ran out to the sidewalk with a wheelchair. It saddened her to watch someone else do what she loved so much. That used to be her running outside to assist the sick or injured. Amanda turned away (assured that the woman was now safe), and she headed back to the church in New York. Something was amiss, there was something not right that she just could not put her finger on. Her intuition was trying to tell her something. Amanda cautiously headed further into the more populated area of the city. She watched for any sign of the Wolf Pack. There were too many factors pointing to their involvement and their resurrection. She would remain cautious, until she was certain they were back.

Chapter 32

Amanda felt disoriented, out of touch with the physical world that surrounded her. But why? She was here, she was touching the ground, smelling the air and tasting the blood she drank nightly. What was it that made her feel so disconnected to this place? New York was not a dream or some vacation, it was most certainly was not her ideal city. It was a nightmare she could not escape. She wanted to forget the things that had happened to push them from her mind. This was supposed to be her escape from Collins. Instead, everything reminded her of that ghost town. Around every corner and beneath every scrap of trash, was something that reminded her of that place.

Although her hunt was successful, it was not as satisfying as she had hoped. It did not ground her to the earthly plain and the leech she dispatched, gave her some disturbing information. They were known among the vampire community and yet, they still lived. Did none of them realize that eventually the 'Blood Kings' would be caught and then the entire world of vampires would be revealed. Or were they so arrogant, all of them, that they did not care? And where were the hunters in all this? Were there no hunters left in this highly technological age? Had the idea of the vampire become such an out dated concept that hunters, no longer existed? It was a disturbing thought. Then again, Satan's greatest trick was convincing man he did not exist.

As she was passing one of the numerous abandoned buildings in this section of New York, she paused. Something caused her to stop, almost as if she had collided with a brick wall. It crippled her, gripped her in her most uncomfortable flesh. She had no explanation for the sensation that came over her or why. After her nightmare in the hotel and her forced memory of driving to Collins, she recognized what was happening, its symbolism. Just not the reason it was happening.

"No," She began to pant. "Stop."

Amanda put her free hand on the side of the burnt structure and slowly began to sink to the ground. The still healing muscles in her thighs, tightened uncomfortably as she knelt down hard. She was back in Collins, chained to that table, feeling the blades slicing through her flesh. Before she was raped, passed around among them like a prison prostitute. She could feel their touch, smell the familiar smells of blood and sex. Again, she willed it, whatever was happening, to stop. There was nothing she could do to break out of this flashback. Her only option was to wait for it to cease.

Amanda clinched her fists, digging her nails into her palms until blood oozed between her fingers. Her flesh lightened to a sickly pale-blue as the ever present sapphire veins in her body became more visible. She was panting heavily, pressing her knuckles into the concrete beneath her. At the height of her episode, she did not feel pain, in the sense of the physical. So, splitting her knuckles on the tender flesh of her fists was nothing, especially in comparison to the remembrance of silver shards digging into her back.

When the memories stopped, she was soaked in sweat, panting heavily and staring off into oblivion. The wale of a siren was the first Earthly sound she heard. Then the whole of New York flooded into her senses, breaking whatever invisible wall had been holding it all at bay.

Amanda moved slow at first, leaning forward beads of sweat dripped onto the concrete below, splashing in their own segregated puddles. A ruby tear fell from her cheek and she realized, she had been crying. For how long, she did not know. Somewhere between the time it hit her and her struggle to regain control, the tears had started. The remembrance of pain or the inability to fight it, must have been the cause. Now, she could began to recover.

She lifted her hands, unclenching her fists, she looked at her blood soaked palms and knuckles. Her hands were shaking. Amanda dared not ask why. There were too many answers, too many reasons. She did not want to think about them. They all lead to a dark place. The kind of places that would cripple her, render her useless. Perhaps that was what they intended. She had to stop. They were dead, that was the only healthy way to think of them.

Her body trembled as she pushed slowly to her feet, looking around as she did. If anyone had seen her breakdown, they had already seen too much. She would not give them anymore. Her mind continued to ask questions she told it not to ask. Would these flashbacks ever stop? Was she going crazy? Would she ever be normal? She swallowed hard and willed herself to stand again. 'Come on, you have to get up. You have to keep going. This is not the place to break down. You don't have time to break down. You'll be fine, you're okay, you'll be fine…you'll be fine…you're okay.' That became her mantra and at some point as she was making her way down the sidewalk, she began to whisper to herself.

"You're okay…you'll be fine…you're okay…"

She was not okay, she was not fine. They had succeeded in breaking her, just not in the way they expected. The physical damage they had done to her, had driven her to this point. Sara might have helped her keep from slipping into this dark pit but she was not there.

Facing James, being willing and able to kill him after he had broken her, reestablished her power. The Wolf Pack was not as easy to kill, so there would be no regaining her power this time.

The tangible, low rumble of thunder drifted through the vacant city streets as the piercing sound of a car alarm echoed through the street. Something in the air had changed, it had turned foul. She sensed an eeriness that she could only associate with one person. It started as a cold chill that tantalized the flesh and caused it to goose bump. Then the hairs on the back of her neck slowly began to raise in alarm. Amanda turned around sharply, her hand white knuckle gripping the sword that stood faithfully by her side her blood soaking the cloth wrap on its handle. It had already tasted blood once tonight but it would feed again if necessary. She could smell moisture, alerting her to the oncoming rain. Squinting, her animal began to emerge from its fleshly cage and show its predatory face. Although her body stank of fear (radiated with it), begging her to turn on her heals and run. Do not face that demon alone, it said. She ignored it. As far as she was concerned, her emotions, her feelings and her pain was unimportant. The mission was to kill him and anyone else who got in the way.

If she did not stand up and fight him, destroy him, he would be free to cause more pain and damage. That blood would be on her hands. Everything happened for a reason, she knew this and for that reason, she understood that there was a reason she had been put in Collins. Sure the boys had lured her there but whatever supernatural power ruled the universe, it knew she would not lay down and die. That despite all odds, she would be the one to break the pattern and destroy the beast.

A breeze brushed her raven locks around and she swore for a moment she felt a hand touch her face. Again, she wondered if they were really under that streetlight. Death knew he could not hide in the shadows, not from her. So why bother trying? Why play these games with her? Did he know she was not fully healed? That she suffered some type of post traumatic stress disorder, which crippled her when it struck. A voice whispered at her from the darkness and she turned to face the host.

"Amanda? Do you wanna play?"

When she turned to look at him, she recognized the outline of the Telepath. With fear radiating off her body, she lowered her head and growled, willing it away. Amanda forced her emotions to mutate into anger, hatred and rage. They were the only thing she could use to survive this ordeal, real or otherwise. She was not going to be leveled by another episode.

"Sure…come out of the darkness and we can play." She said as she began pulling the blade from its sheath.

As she felt the flat part of the cold, blood crusted metal pass across her index finger, another voice whispered behind her.

"Oh baby doll, I don't think you wanna play our new game."

Quickly she turned to face the other voice, recognizing his dirty blonde hair, even in the dim light around her. In his hands, he was holding a large hunting knife, its metal glimmering in the streetlight he was standing beneath. How did they sneak up on her? This was not good. One she could handle but not two at once. As she finished drawing her weapon, deciding that attempting to fight them was better than backing down, she heard another whisper on her other side.

"Are you so sure, you want to do that?"

There he was, the bastard that had run from her like the coward he was. Her red eyes shifted from one silhouette to the other, readying herself for anything. The streetlights around her began to flicker as she called her shadows to the party. If they wanted to fight her, they would have to do it on her terms. This was not Collins, they were not in charge and she was not their property. The Telepath was still as strong as ever, her responded with a sly smirk to the thoughts swimming around in her mind.

"You are ours Amanda."

Almost as if they were a collective mind, the Chameleon responded without missing a beat.

"You belong to us."

She may be a broken woman, she may have mental and physical ailments that they caused, but she was not the same Amanda they had known. With a toothy grin she glanced between them and responded.

"Then come get me."

A growl drifted across her lips and she spun her sword, antagonizing them.

"All in due time."

The silhouette of Death began to fade and she screamed in alarm.

"No!"

With her sword raised in the air, ready to strike, she ran at him and sliced through the air where he had been. When she turned to get the other two, they were also gone. She shook her head 'no'. The katana clattered to the ground as it slipped from her grasp. She was losing her mind. Was it a hallucination? Amanda stared at the blood crusted metallic blade before her, her breathing heavy. Her arms hanging loosely at her sides and her head whipped about. Where were they? What was that? Again she thought about Sara. If they were all alive, then she was in imminent danger. She needed to find her but not before confirming she did see them. There was no point in running off half cocked and leading Death straight to her. Although by now she was sure he was not hunting either of them or he would have attacked by now. Then what were they up to? They could have easily grabbed Sara or killed her already. So, what were they planning?

Her thoughts were quickly interrupted by the downpour of rain that suddenly came. It should have been calming, cleansing, grounding but it did none of those things. She stared vacantly down at the sword lying at her feet, listening to rain bounce off the metal. Picking it up, she placed it back in its sheath and she started for the Motel.

The thunder rumbled and the lightning flashed across the New York sky as a storm raged far above the skyscrapers. Its torrent winds rushed by her, chilling her flesh and driving the rain deeper into the fabric of her clothing. Amanda pulled her trench coat tightly around herself, feeling more isolated than she had before.

On her way back to the place she called home, she saw the horrors this city had to offer. A mixture of abandoned animals, whimpering in the rain and young runaways beneath the railway overpass (mostly women), hugging themselves and trying to keep warm. It was a depressing sight. She shook her head, these ladies were ripe for their picking. Tomorrow she may not see them. Tonight however, she was finished with her hunt. She was only one person against an entire city of vampires and monsters, she was doing the best she could.

By the time she reached the door of the Motel lobby, her clothes were dripping wet, her black hair clung to her face in tendrils. Still that feeling of something being wrong had not left her. Her body continued to fluctuate between hot and cold, not deciding on what it wanted to do. Amanda shuddered as she entered the lobby, even the Motel felt wrong. She glanced at the man behind the counter, he had his head down, she assumed he was asleep. The door to her hallway creaked on its worn hinges when she pulled it open. For a moment she back stepped away from the hall. That energy she had felt on the street was strong here. Had they followed her? Were they here?

This was not them, this was stronger than any of their energy. She sniffed the air before stepping over the threshold. What engulfed her was an old energy, it was strong and thick. Sleep was no longer an option at this point, she knew that something was here. Whatever it was, it was not vampire and certainly not human. She drew her sword once more and slowly headed toward her room. This location had been compromised, she needed to leave tonight. Amanda cautiously unlocked her door, pushing it open with her back and searching her room. There was no physical sign of anyone in the room and no shadows, save for her own. She did not like this.

Grabbing her green military duffle bag, she hoisted it onto her shoulder before stepping back out into the hallway. She needed to get to the bottom of what was going on. Everything had been calm, she had, had time to deal with her mental and emotional anguish. Something in the city did not want her to heal from what they had done. Perhaps now was not the appropriate time. It seemed she would have to shove all her issues down and deal with the task at hand. When they were long gone, dead, with no way of returning, then she could break down. That was her mistake, she had let her guard down and they took advantage of it.

Amanda managed to get out of the motel without being stopped but the feeling followed her. She looked all around her for the source of the energy but was never able to place it. Her diaphragm tightened with unease and nervous tension. There were no other hotels on this end of town, she would have to find somewhere else to bed for the night. Even if it was a dirty mattress in an abandoned apartment.

She walked a few blocks before she found a decently suitable place to sleep for the night. Scaling the old fire escape, she climbed inside a window and settled down in one of the dark corners. No power, meant that she would have to rely on her shadows to watch out for the Wolf Pack. Still, without rest, she would not be no good to anyone. So, she lay her bag out for a pillow and used her trench coat as a blanket, despite the fact it was soaked.

Sleeping tonight would be something she would regret for the rest of her life. They were waiting for her to lay down and close her eyes. A dark blanket enveloped her as she drifted off. Amanda fought as she slept, kicking her legs and tossing her head violently. She screamed in pain, roared in anger and begged for salvation.

The Chameleon and an unseen face held her down to a mattress in an undisclosed location. No matter how she fought, they held her tight. The Telepath and the Shadowed One took turns violating her. Each of them thrusting into her womb so hard that she felt tendrils of pain travel up through her lower belly. Even in the dreamworld, tears ran down her cheeks as she fought to get them off of her, telling her dream self that it was not real. Trying to will her body to realize it and her mind to take over, to kill them. There was no hope. For what seemed like hours, she was forced to endure their continued assaults. They laughed at her, mocking her pain and taking amusement in her struggles to get free. When they had their fill, she was able to wake up.

She sat up straight, pulling herself back against the wall as she looked around frantically. The pain she experienced in the dream, she now felt in her nether regions. It throbbed as if someone had done that to her and the rest of her body hurt as if she had been restrained. Amanda pulled her hand up and looked at her wrists, there were no bruises. However, she knew if anything was going to show up, it would take a couple days. She bit her bottom lip hard as she fought to push the emotions down into their cage. There was no time to deal with this now. Although she had no proof that they were back, (only vivid hallucinations), she knew for her safety, she needed to treat the situation as if they were.

With a strong inhale, she pushed herself to her feet. They needed to see that their efforts were futile, that she was unbreakable (she had to be). So, she held her head high and with an arrogance that rivaled the Chameleon, she spoke to the empty air.

"Is that the best you can do? Did you think that would still work on me? You wanna attack me! Quit being cowards and come face me!"

She was screaming at the end of her tirade, throwing her bag across the room in her fury.

"You hear me!? I'm coming for you boys!"

The sun was only barely beginning to graze the horizon, its few rays trickling in through the busted windows around her. Her vampiric bloodline did not have a solar allergy. With sleep out of the question, decided to grab her things and head out. Amanda ducked through the window and dropped from the fire escape. A majority of the energy she felt earlier, seemed to have dissipated for now. Although she had seen nothing during her search of the hotel, where the energy was most prevalent, she scanned the alley for signs of a tail. Someone or something was following her. She thought living in a big city would help her to hide, now she felt more nervous. Every window, car or alley provided a million places for someone to hide. Amanda continued to search for signs, using all her senses to detect the slightest hint of anything.

She pulled her hood up to hide her scars as she made her way down the sidewalk. In this vapid society, she knew that her imperfect features would frighten the general public of the daylight hours. So, she chose to keep her head down and hide in shame. They did this to her, making her a social pariah. She dreamt of the day when she could get her hands on some silver and scar up Death's face beyond recognition. Her morning was filled with anger, that was good, she would need it.

Amanda turned down Houston Street and headed east, stopping off at the Remedy Diner. She settled into the corner and waited for a waitress to approach her table. Coffee did nothing for her fatigue but she ordered a cup anyway, perching a cigarette between her lips as she waited.

The diner felt a little safer than being on the street right now. Between the nightmare and the episode from last evening, she was visibly shaken. She would not admit it to herself. They were back, she was nearly certain. The Wolf Pack had brought something with them, she could only speculate what it might be.

Slowly, she sipped her coffee and smoked her cigarette. She was stalling and she knew it. The daylight would not protect her from them and she knew she could not hide forever. A flicker of light

447

through the large window beside her, caught her attention. She squinted as she peered out into the bright light of day, (thinking briefly to herself that she really needed sunglasses). Across the street from where she sat was the figure of a man with aviator glasses and a brown leather coat. Against the glare of the sun she could barely see his dark hair, slick back behind his head but she did not have to, she knew him.

His boldness and arrogance should have angered her, instead she began to worry. Pulling her attention from the man outside, she began to look around the diner. Where there was one, the others were not far behind. There he was, sitting at a table only a few feet away, the Telepath, sipping a cup of coffee and watching her. His baby blue eyes twinkling with arousal, highlighting the blue button down he was wearing. He looked indescribably human.

Glancing up at the clock then back down at him, she pushed the hilt of the katana, sliding the blade an inch from its sheath. This was not where she wanted to do things. The ask of her cigarette, resting on the edge of the ashtray, fell silently onto the glass. Everything slowed and she knew they were doing it. How they were doing it and how she knew, was an entirely different story.

The scarlet second hand ticked with her movements. Another tick coupled with the sound of a car horn. She allowed herself to become distracted by the noise and when she looked back they were both gone.

A quick glance around and she pushed the blade back in the sheath with her thumb. No one seemed to notice what happened. On the table where she spotted the Telepath, sat a steaming cup of coffee. It was not her imagination, she knew that now.

Slapping a twenty on the table, she shuffled out of the booth, making sure to hide her weapon in her coat. Throwing her bag on her back, she left the diner and headed out into the city. She continued to look over her shoulder, something she had not done since Wolf Creek, since James.

As she rounded a building, heading for a more prestigious side of town, something made her pause, muscles twitching. She lifted her head, looking from beneath her hood. Her intuition was trying to tell her something. Amanda nodded, she was listening. When she was passing the newspaper stand only then did she understand the reason behind her bodies reaction. Her diaphragm tightened with a familiar uncomfortable anxiety. Slowly, she turned to look at the variety of images displayed on the front of the stand and that was when she noticed it. On the cover of three different magazines were announcements about the next series of entertainment to come. There they were, the Telepath featured in a television show, the Chameleon starring in a movie and Death in a movie of his own. She had to be sure she was not seeing things, so she grabbed up each one and stared intently at their covers.

From beneath the dark hood, her red eyes glared down at their smiling faces. They mocked her from the cover of People, GQ and Entertainment Weekly. Amanda fought to keep her composure, they were watching her. If she allowed herself to fear, they would smell it and know that she lied about their inability to affect her. A growl crawled up from the bowels of her belly. They were dead, they were supposed to be dead. Not only were they alive and healed of all the damage she had helped to inflict, they now had infinite power at their fingertips. Being actors would allow them to have access to as many women as they wanted, they could hide themselves (keep their addresses private) and their influence would be more extensive. They would also be surrounded by people on a nearly constant basis. She would have to be more methodical in how she went about killing them. If someone found their body, it would be all over the news. She did not want to make a public spectacle of their deaths. Either way, killing them or not, their fans would not change their mind.

Their fame also posed another problem, conventions and public appearances. The ability for them to sweep women under the rug on a constant basis and wipe their memory out, multiplied. What had been a major issue, had now developed into a disaster. Even if she warned their fans, they would not believe her. 'Shit.' She thought to herself.

As she stared at the covers of the three magazines in her hand, she thought to herself. Sometimes it becomes entirely necessary to be seen as the bad guy. It is essential, in order to do the right thing, that you must be willing to sacrifice your life. If she wanted to protect the rest of the women they would now have access to, she needed to be the enemy. Let them see her as crazy, evil or a murderer. They would be safe from a worse fate than hating her forever. She was willing to accept the burden of her task. It was now time to find Sara. The girls were connected by blood, all she had to do was close her eyes and feel for her energy.

Amanda flung the magazines down, barely hearing the vendor shout at her for damaging his product and drifted into the shadows of the abandoned building behind the stand. Traveling by shadow was convenient but not economical, especially if she was taking Sara with her. Still, if she was going to steal another vehicle, then she needed something with more horsepower.

She had a vague idea of where to find something that might fit her needs. So, she walked a few more blocks until she located a vehicle repair shop. There was a black Chevelle she had seen sitting outside every morning until the shop closed. It belonged to one of the young mechanics she had seen coming out of the shop. Although she regretted having to take it off his hands, she needed it for something more important that picking up tail.

Amanda slipped inside, tossing her duffle bag in the back seat before searching for an extra set of keys. She hoped he was trusting enough to leave a set in the glove box. The back lot where the mechanics parked was fenced in and had surveillance cameras mounted around its chain link fence. Shaking her head, she pushed the key in the ignition and turned it. The engine, roared to life and she shifted the car into gear, just in time to see the owner come running out of the garage.

When she was out of the city before anyone could stop her. Amanda was shifting through gears, pushing the car to its maximum speed. She did not have time to waste. Chicago was nearly ten hours from her location and the longer it took her to get there, the greater the risk of them getting Sara. The engine growled as she shifted one more time and pressed the pedal to the floor. Sara was in danger, she never should have left her alone. Amanda would do anything to get to her. Even risk them following her because together they could take the Wolf Pack. They were not going to get her, not this time. Amanda was her Sire, she was in charge of her in every sense of the word. They would have to kill her to get to Sara. Although she was sure, they would not mind the challenge.

The speedometer climbed quickly to 140 miles per hour and she was not slowing down anytime soon. Sara needed her, that was all that mattered.

Reunion

Chapter 33

There was a long awkward silence between them as the Chevelle roared down the deserted stretch of highway, a black blur against an ever darkening horizon. The gas gauge steadily dropped as they sped along at a steady ninety miles per hour. Sara lit another cigarette, chain smoking and staring at the moonlit sky through the gap in the window. She stared out the window, watching the silhouettes of trees and fields fly past them. Although she knew they were safer in numbers and that her sword was resting by her side, she felt anxious. There was nothing to stop Death from watching from the shadows, interfering with their plan. She turned to look at Amanda, watching her as she drove, in an attempt to ignore her emotions.

Aside from telling her to get in the car, her Sire had not said a word to her. Her body was rigid, one hand gripping the steering wheel and the other resting on the stick shift. Sara wanted to say something, she wanted to ask why she left, did she dare? Would Amanda even answer her? There was also the question of where they should head to first. Were they driving endlessly with no destination in mind? Did Amanda know where the Wolf Pack was?

Sara sucked her bottom lip into her mouth, chewed on it for a while and then spoke, her eyes drifting to the windshield.

"So…while you were away, I discovered the location of the Chameleon and the Shadowed One."

Amanda glanced up at her.

"They're living in Los Angeles. And they're movie stars," She said with sarcastic excitement. "It might make things difficult for us."

"I know. And things are already difficult, it makes no difference to me. I'll kill them in front of the cameras if I have to."

Their conversation was very minimalist, almost militant. As if keeping their turmoil of emotions at bay would somehow make them go away; or it would help heal them the damage the Wolf Pack had inflicted. Amanda continued, sharing what she knew with Sara.

"While in New York, on a hunt, I learned the vampire community refers to them as the Blood Kings."

She glanced at Sara as if waiting for a response. Both women rolled their eyes, knowing all too well they were the furthest thing from kings. That the title they allowed to adhere to their reputation was more of an insult to the girls than anything else they had done.

"They refer to Death as the Dark Prince."

"Dark Prince my ass." Sara replied, scoffing at the notion before continuing.

"We should stay for a couple days in LA and see what we can find out about them,"

She lit another cigarette.

"There's another thing…and you're not gonna like it…they're nearly impossible to kill."

"If their Master, is hanging around, nothing we do will mean shit. We could dismember them and he can still put them back together. He did it once already." Amanda added.

"Actually…I have weapons that will kill the Wolf Pack and there is nothing he can do about it."

Amanda glanced doubtfully at Sara.

"I hope you're right. I'm tired of hunting these bastards."

They drove until the sun came up and the sun went down

453

again, several times, stopping only a few times to fill up for gas and feed. Being careful to only take the scum that frequented the truck stops. They continued to travel in silence, neither one of them wanting to discuss the obvious. The sun was coming up over the Los Angeles skyline when they finally made it to their destination. It should have been a glittering horizon filled with hope, brimming with inspiration. However, for them, it was their war zone, ground zero for the execution of the Blood Kings.

When they got into the lower class area of LA, they procured a cheap hotel room and made their best attempt at sleep. That was not a privilege allowed to those touched by darkness. Collins was a part of them, it and all its horrors was burned into their mind, under their skin and in their blood. There was no way for them to close their eyes without seeing it, it and all the tortures it contained.

They tossed and turned until first mornings light. Rays of sunlight crawled slowly across their sleeping forms, releasing them from their unrestful sleep. Amanda was the first to stand from the floor and look around. She seemed to be searching for something that was not there, her shoulders were square and her movements quick. Her nightmares, were becoming more realistic and with the Wolf Pack alive, she knew things would only get worse. The lines between dream and reality were easily blurred with them. Amanda was slowly beginning to recover from the dream she had, stealing one of Sara's cigarettes and lighting it.

Sara on the other hand, sat staring at the wall, she was hugging her knees to herself. A visible tremor of shivers coursed through her body and she rocked slightly. Amanda looked down at her, dropping to her knees so she could take the woman's head in her hands, being careful not to burn her with the cigarette.

"Hey, look at me. Hey! Sara, its okay. I'm here."

"They're here...I was there...I was back in Collins...they raped me...they raped me...they raped me..."

She continued to repeat in absent thought as she stared blankly at the wall. Amanda hugged her close, anger surging through her body as she watched the trauma Sara was going through. The

Wolf Pack may never have tossed her in a cell but to look at her, one would not know any different. 'How dare they do this to her!' Amanda thought, angry at the fact they were tormenting the woman who had little involvement in their downfall. They were attacking the weaker of the two and they knew it. That only proved how pathetic they were. None of them wanted anything to do with someone who could fight back. They did not want or believe in a fair fight. Last time they ran from her.

Amanda knew she needed to get her level headed again and fast. For all she knew, the Chameleon could be standing nearby watching in amusement as Sara slowly broke. This was what they wanted to happen. They were wanting the girls to become so hopeless that they give up so the horrors would stop. She shook her head, knowing full well that things would only get worse. As much as she did not want to hurt her, she knew there was only one way to snap Sara out of her trance. So, she leaned back and slapped her across the face, knowing that would trigger a violent response.

"What the hell did you do that for!?" Sara roared, eyes reddening and canines becoming more prominent.

"Snap the hell out of it! You're no good to me a quivering, blabbering mess. Do not let this break you."

A low growl left Sara's lips before she finally settled back down. She sighed, dropping her head and fumbling for her pack of cigarettes. Her hands were still shaking, although she was no longer afraid of the attack, she was edgy. She had gone from afraid, incomprehensibly so, to enraged and ready to kill anything that came within reach. Sara managed to put a cigarette in her mouth and light it, the nicotine helping to center her. She raised her eyes to Amanda.

"I'm sorry. I'm still not as strong as you are."

Amanda was leaning against the opposite wall from her, the bottom of one boot pressed against the same wall. She tapped the ash of her cigarette into the glass tray next to her, looking up at her before calmly replying.

"Yes you are,"

She moved across the room, sitting down in the chair by the small desk, taking one more drag before snuffing the cigarette out.

"You took on the Telepath. You fought him, hell you nearly dismembered him as bad as I did the Chameleon. Even if he was only dead for a few days, you, afraid as you were, you fought him. And you were only a few hours into your change, that's saying something. Only if you believe that you are not strong, then it will be true."

Sara stared at the floor for a bit, glanced at the window and then back at her Sire.

"Should we get out of here? We have a lot of work to do."

"Yeah, come on."

They grabbed their bags and headed out, setting their keys on the desk of the hotel lobby. When they rented the room, they payed cash so no one would ask questions and each signed in as Jane Doe. It gave them the freedom to come and go as they please.

Los Angeles was awake and alive at this hour of the day, cars flew by, drivers honking angrily at one another, shouting and sirens. It was an average day for the humans that moved past them in hoards. However, for these women, it was the start of an apocalypse of sorts. The means to an end that was long overdue.

They were feeling a little more confident this morning, despite their restless evening and continued exhaustion. So, they headed into a small coffee shop on Wilshire Boulevard to discuss what to do next, settling into a corner booth where they would be left alone. The middle aged waitress behind the counter, came over to ask for their order. Amanda ordered them a pot of coffee. Although it would have no effect on them, it had been one of their normal morning rituals when they were still human. It was the only familiar thing they had left to cling onto, the only thing normal left for them.

The bitter taste and the heat would help them to ground themselves and shake the rest of their nightmares off. For now their bodies recognized the substance and responded accordingly, it was a false caffeination. Sara slid the glass ashtray away from the wall and lit another cigarette, looking around at the human patrons that surrounded them before leaning in and her voice low. She was careful not to let others hear their conversation. As she spoke, the smoke from her cigarette curled up, dissipating when it hit the light mounted just above.

"Alright…while I was in Chicago, I had a little help to learn more about these bastards."

Reaching into her bag, she pulled out the iron, the small mirror and a bottle of cheap whiskey, laying each of them on the table in front of her.

"According to Finn-"

"Who?"

Amanda was quick to cut her off, hearing an unfamiliar name unnerved her. She looked up from the objects on the table, her eyes losing all sense of warmth. For a moment, Sara felt like she was looking into the eyes of the Shadowed One. It seemed Amanda had a little more of him in her than she knew.

"The reason I'm still alive." She replied firmly.

Amanda looked doubtfully at her partner before nodding for her to continue.

"So anyhow, according to him," She pointed at the bottle. "The Shadowed One can die only by fire," Then she pointed at the mirror. "The Chameleon's true face is revealed by a mirror and if you keep one in your pocket, you will be free of his deception."

Sara held up the small box with the iron spike inside.

> "In this box is a spike made from iron and inlaid with silver. It's the only way to kill the Chameleon. You have to drive it into his heart. I've got the sword which will kill the Telepath if I cut his head off, but the bodies all have to be burned to ash. They can die."

Sara paused long enough to hand her a small iron nail and a piece of mirror.

> "Keep these in your pocket. The iron will keep the Telepath out of your head. Although you can handle him, it's easier if he stays out. The mirror, you already know how it works."

Their waitress came over and set their pot of coffee on the table, pouring each of them a cup before walking back behind the counter. Sara lit another cigarette before continuing.

> "So, we know the general location of two of the members here in California. The Chameleon lives in Rancho Carne California and the Shadowed One lives in Studio City California."

Amanda nodded, a smile of satisfaction crossing her features. Her fledgling vampire had blossomed into an intelligent, methodical killer. She beamed with pride.

> "Then perhaps we should check property records for the areas you named and check for appearances. It might even be a good idea to visit one of their scheduled appearances. We can see them in action. I want to track them a bit longer, find out where they feed and live. We need to learn as much about them as we can. No mistakes this time." Amanda replied, taking a sip of coffee.

> "I agree." Sara said, adding another pack of sugar to her cup.

The space between them fell silent and they exchanged a knowing glance Now, came the hard conversation, the one Sara had thought she could ignore until they were finished. She realized if her head was not clear and she was still focusing on the matter, that she would be no good to Amanda.

"Amanda…" Sara said.

"Hm?"

When she looked at the blonde across from her, she sighed. She knew what Sara was about to ask her and she braced herself.

"Why did you leave me?"

Closing her eyes, she licked her lips and then spoke.

> "I thought you would be safer without me. Death was after me for attacking him. He had no reason to come after you. I thought it was best if I was as far from you as I could possibly get-"

> "Well you thought wrong! I couldn't sleep, I had nightmares and hallucinations. They tormented me night after night. They reminded me of how I failed. Told me you left because you didn't need me anymore."

> "No," She shook her head. "I worried about you every day. I realized after I left that I had put you in more danger that way. I know what you are dealing with. I have them too."

> "I dreamt of Collins so much…I finally had to go back and burn it down. I burnt the entire town to the ground. Still…still the shit didn't stop. They'll never stop."

> "Sara I'm sorry…"

Sara swallowed hard, her eyes filling with blood tears.

"I dream of them…those girls…I see all their dead little eyes. They ask why I failed them…but we failed them. We did…"

"I know. I know that. I dream about them too. I fucked up. Okay? I fucked up that time but I won't this time."

"You started this Amanda and you drug me into this shit."

"Would you rather have been one of their toys? Should I have let you get raped over and over? I was not gonna let that happen. I may have started this, but do you think if you walk away, that they will really stop? I hate to tell you. That's not how they work. Unless you submit, admit you belong to them and let them do whatever they want to you, they will never stop."

With a shaky fist, Sara tapped her cigarette on the side of the ashtray and watched the gray fluff drop into the glass container.

"Shit."

"Yeah…I'm sorry they drug you into this. But we're gonna end this. We're gonna get our lives back. Maybe not the same ones we had, but we're gonna build a new life. Each of us. Don't you want that?"

"Heh…I can't have that, ever. I'm a god damn vampire Amanda. How normal a life could I really have? I can't go back to my family."

"Maybe not. But you have someone sitting here, who is willing to go through this hell with you, all over again. You're one hell of a friend Sara. I would not go through this with anyone else. You forget, it was you, who pulled my ass out of that cell. That takes balls."

Sara snuffed her cigarette out in the ashtray and looked up at her Sire. Somehow telling Amanda exactly what she thought, made her feel a bit more together. With a nod, she looked up and spoke.

"Then we better get going. We have work to do."

As they headed out of the diner, Amanda replied.

"We need to find a computer."

"I know. I spotted a library a few blocks down the way."

The sun burned down upon them as it rose high in the California sky. They were an intimidating sight among all the colors of LA. Two black silhouettes with pale skin and piercing eyes, a katana in their opposite hands. It was as if they were twins, clones, two souls on the same wavelength. A single mind operating between two flesh bodies.

As they made their way to their destination, people scurried out of their path, shooting them disgusted glances. The girls exchanged amused smiles between one another. There was something satisfying about seeing people scurry like mice, perhaps it was the animal in them. Even the police cars that passed by them, did not dare to stop.

A tall white building with white stone columns out front and a long staircase, stood as the only library on this side of town. Normally, the librarian might have stopped them from going any further than the front door and security would have been there to escort them out. It only took a glimmer of those red irises to make them change their minds and of course a little influence from Amanda. They did not have time for any of their drama. Sara hurried behind an abandoned desk and went to work. Her hands moved in a perfect symphony of digits and button presses.

Amanda stood just behind her, watching as the screens flickered by in rapid succession. Sara searched and backtracked until she found the information she was looking for.

"Alright, they're using their celebrity names on all their documents. So their houses are listed under those names. The Telepath is at 132 Baxter Avenue. Apt C New York, New York. Death is at 12933 Bloomfield. Studio City, California. The Chameleon is at 35 Amantes Rancho Santa Margarita California."

"Hang on. I wanna see something. Move a minute."

Sara slid out of the office chair and Amanda began to pound her fingers on the keys, using the available search engine to find out when they would be making appearances. She ripped a piece of paper from the notepad by the computer and jotted down a few dates. Then she typed each one of their names into the same search and began to look through the forums, message boards, chat rooms and blogs. Their enthrallment of fans had grown to a sickening proportion. Women willing to fight over them, hurt people over a simple disagreement, dissolved relationships and friendships. It was no longer admiration but obsession, with women dedicating their entire lives to following, writing about and creating art of them. Even begging them to marry them. Not the innocent declarations of the nineties boy band fans, these ladies were serious. Some of them spending nearly all of their income to make every convention that the Wolf Pack or separate members of the pack would be showing up.

The two hunter's eyes scanned over their messages in disgusted horror. How could they find them so attractive? How did they not see that something was wrong? No matter that two of the pack had taken wives. It was a visage, just a game to them. So the public would believe they were normal, upstanding, human citizens. Amanda scoffed and sat back in the chair.

"You see this? They think these boys are god."

"Should we tell them? Would they even believe us?"

"I've got an idea. It might not work. I sure as hell have to try. At least one of them has to see the truth. They cannot all be so blind."

Cracking her knuckles, Amanda began to type a message and posted it in every possible place she could, hoping and praying that one of them might read it and see what they really were. Then she sat back and waited for a reply, knowing that these brainwashed humans (mainly women) spent a majority of their time hanging around in the blogs as if the pack was their god and their websites, the church. When the barrage of replies began to pour through, she closed her eyes and shook her head.

"They think I'm crazy. The boys have such a hold on them, they cannot see the truth."

"Damn it!"

"Our only option is to kill them and accept the position of social outcast. It's a necessity of the mission we decided to take," Amanda spun around in the chair and faced her.

"Are you ready for this?"

"What other option do I have? They already took my life from me. At least this way I will be able to live with myself."

Grabbing their things, they headed out of the library and back on to the harsh LA streets.

"So, what now?" Sara asked.

"We head to the Chameleon's house. Just observe, do not attack yet. If we get impatient and sloppy, they will have us. They've got years on us, they're stronger than us and for the most part, smarter. But they're getting sloppy. So, we have to outsmart them. When the time is right, we will take them out one at a time."

"We'll have to wait til dark. Or he'll spot us."

"No," She shook her head. "He won't."

They nodded and climbed into the Chevelle, each feeling a tightness in their chest. Wanting so bad to have their revenge, to have his blood on their swords and see his body fall for the last time, that it would take everything they had, not to kill him when they saw him. Each of them felt as much fear as they did hatred, favoring one over the other. It was time to work, they had a job to do.

The Chameleon

Chapter 34

A flash of lightening electrified the air as ever darkening clouds reached down to brush the tips of the glittering buildings that made up the Los Angeles skyline. The rumble of thunder that followed it, signaled the threat of rain. Amanda stared for a moment at the power of mother nature, wondering, if there was something up there. An omnipresence watching them carry out their work. Her hand rested on the skull head of the shifter, her foot moving fluidly between brake and clutch as she weaved her way through the morning traffic. She could sense Sara's unease but knew there was nothing she could do to pacify it. Had she been attacked during a thunderstorm? Amanda wondered quietly to herself but knew better than to ask. Memories can hurt, sometimes worse than any knife. They dig in places that cannot be healed.

On the corner of one street, she saw the shriveled shell of a woman (the kind of woman she had once been) and she knew that she was ripe for the taking. If the Wolf Pack saw her, they could snatch her up and tear her to pieces. Sara white knuckle gripped the hilt of her sword, wringing her hands around it. The image of that frail figure served as a reminder of what she was fighting for. Her time was running out, she knew it. So she planned to use what little of it she had left to do some good in the world.

The steady, rhythmic beat of rain against the windshield became their soundtrack for the next few miles. Amanda flipped on the wipers and listened to the obnoxious while of them as they scraped across the glass. When was the last time they had been replaced? She wondered.

Sara cranked her window down an inch, droplets of lukewarm rain, hitting her coat and face as she did. She pressed a cigarette between her pale pink lips and lit it with shaky fingers. Her nerves were climbing with every passing mile. Would it be the Chameleon, the Shadowed One or the Telepath who would get their revenge? How would her life end? She thought as she exhaled the smoke from her lungs, enjoying the taste more than ever before. Her Sire had no idea that she was cherishing these last few minutes, no matter how hellish they might be. The rain smelled a little stronger, the seat she was lounged in felt more comfortable and the menthol of her Marlboro was smoother than she remembered. Sara was at peace, if only for the moment.

Amanda glanced at her passenger, she had been acting rather strange, calmer than she should have been. What was going on with her? Why did she give up the weapons? Was she planning to leave? There was something going on with her but she could not put her finger on it.

The torrent of rain had turned the highway into a black sheet of ice, but she refused to slow the Chevelle. It was not as if an accident would kill either one of them, it would hinder them momentarily. She gave a hard pull on the wheel as she merged left onto US 101 South, which would take them toward Rancho Santa Margarita. They were an hour from their final destination and as long as nothing came between them, they would make good time. Amanda pressed the clutch and shifted again, the speedometer climbed quickly to ninety. She knew the speed on this stretch was only seventy and she dared anyone to be ignorant enough to pull her over. As far as she was concerned, human laws no longer applied to her.

If the Wolf Pack could torture women, change their names, take celebrity status and do it all without persecution, she too could break the law. In the rear-view mirror of the Chevelle, Amanda caught red and blue lights, coming up on her and fast. She smirked, accelerating again before weaving between the other cars in front of her. The police were no match for her, if she so desired, she could tell them that they saw nothing. Why drive a car with this much horsepower if she was not planning at some point, to open it up?

Sara seemed too perplexed with the scenery passing them by, to notice or care about what was happening. She dropped her cigarette out the window and lit another one. How many had she smoked already? Then again, did it really matter? She would never die of cancer. Something was obviously bothering her, she had become more agitated when the storm started.

"Hey, what's going on with you?" Amanda asked, passing another car.

"Huh...hm...nothing. Why?" She replied.

"You've been puffing down those cigarettes since we left the diner."

"Yeah..."

"Sara?"

She turned back to the passenger window, not able to look Amanda in the face at this moment. Her mind flooded with memories of that night, of the reason she was even in this situation. It was how she ended up in Collins and why she feared Death most.

"It was thunder storming that night, the way it is now. The sky was darker than I ever remember it being and the rain had done nothing to stifle the heat. The humidity was god awful At the time, that was my only worry. Trying to sleep comfortably in a house with no power and the humidity climbing steadily. I had no idea that there were things that hid in the shadows and attacked you mercilessly," She paused, licking her lips before continuing.

"The cops said that the Shadowed One, the assailant as they called him, had used a flat-head screwdriver to punch the lock on my back door. Now that I know what he really is, I wonder why. Why bother to use a door at all?"

"Sara?"

"I can remember three things from that night. The sound of the rain dripping off his coat, the smell of his cigarettes and what he said to me. He said . . .he said . ..If you scream . . .I'll slit your pretty throat. But if you behave I won't hurt you... I remember that Amanda . . .every time I shut my eyes I can hear his voice."

In that moment, she squeezed her eyes shut and clinched her left hand into a fist as she tried to level herself. She could sense Amanda's want to comfort her, so she held up the palm of that same hand in a gesture meant to reassure her. Or at least push her away and make her pause in her actions. They were not in therapy and there was no time to deal with their emotions and Sara had no plan to deal with them anyway. She preferred to shove them down and pretend they were not there.

"I'm fine. Let's get this over with, kill these bastards and move on with life."

Life. The word almost made her laugh. In a twisted way, the word was humorous to her because she knew that hers was quickly coming to its completion. Perhaps her only purpose was to rescue Amanda from Collins and then make sure that she went on to kill the Wolf Pack. The only reason her death would make sense, is that it would fuel her to go on. It almost seemed unfair that she had gone through all of this to end up dead a few months later. Then there was the question on Finn, she wondered how it would affect him. Here she was, thinking about her death when she had swore she would not. When she told herself that she was going to accept it and not let Amanda know about it.

The long line of ash, barely hanging onto the end of her cigarette now fell into her lap. It was the distraction she needed and a strong sign from the Fates, that she needed a new idea.

"Shit."

Sara cursed, brushing her pants off and tossing the butt out the window. Opening her pack, she looked disgustingly at the two measly cigarettes staring her in the face. She desperately needed to stop and get more before they ventured into the Chameleon's house. There was no logical reason for her to need them but as far as she was concerned her reasons were her own. She wanted them, that was it, she wanted to fill her undead lungs with as much tar as she possibly could. After all, she was going straight to Hell when she died, the black muck coating her interior might help her withstand the fires.

Sara smiled a little bit. She gracefully accepted her demise, with dignity and felt peace wash over her. It was a feeling that she had never achieved, even in her human life.

"Hey." Sara said, lighting another cigarette.

"Yeah."

Amanda replied, having forgotten their previous conversation entirely.

"Mind if we stop for cigarettes? I'm almost out."

"If you quit smoking like a chimney, you wouldn't be."

Sara looked up at her with annoyance.

"Spare me the lecture. I'm not gonna die from it, so why does it matter?"

"It doesn't really. I was just pointing out the facts."

"Thank you captain obvious, I'll put that in my little book of I don't give a shit."

"No need to bite my head off. I'll find a gas station."

The Chevelle rolled into a newly built truck stop, parking on the edge of the lot to avoid being bothered. Sara stepped out of the car, throwing her cigarette somewhere into oblivion, paying no mind where it landed. Why should she care? She was (not only) a vampire but she knew her death would come soon and her attitude reflected that.

Amanda sat in the car, waiting for Sara to join her again and as she did, she watched the coming and going of the customers in the truck stop. Her thoughts drifting off to the diner where she first (unknowingly) encountered the Shadowed One. If only someone told her, if she knew somehow, she could have avoided Collins and the tortures that took place there. Was there any point in thinking about the past? About the what ifs?

During her observation of the people around her, she spotted a man, about five feet, eight inches tall. He was wearing a brown leather jacket and his raven colored hair had been expertly slicked back behind his head. There was not a hair out of place. Amanda narrowed her eyes, watching as he moved toward the front of the building beside her. Would Death dare to show up here? Did he really believe scare tactics had an affect on them anymore? Her hand fell to the handle on her door, and she began to pull. That was until, someone shouted his name and he turned around to answer them. It was not the Shadowed One, not even close. The resemblance was uncanny, however.

When she was sure it was not him and that it was not some trick, she let go of the door and settled back down. What was taking Sara so long? Was the man she saw meant to be a distraction? That was it, Amanda opened the door and headed toward the door. She should never have let Sara go inside alone.

There she was, standing at the counter, paying for her next pack and talking with the clerk. Amanda shook her head and went inside. She needed to be sure. The Wolf Pack was clever and although the girls had a bit more footing than they did before, now was not the time to get sloppy or comfortable.

Upon first entering the store, Sara felt an inexplainable paranoia wash over her and she frantically looked around. She remembered the gas station in Collins and the way they looked at her while she was inside. Amanda must have seen something or sensed her discomfort because a few minutes later, she spotted her walking toward her. There was no reason for Sara to be afraid, it would all be over soon but it was out of habit that she felt this way. Or perhaps her subconscious had picked up on something her conscious had not. That was becoming a frequent occurrence and she learned in Collins that she should listen to that part of her. The last time she did not, things went wrong very quickly.

"You ready to go." Amanda said, glancing behind her at the clerk.

"Yeah, everything all right?" Sara asked, shoving her money in her pocket.

"We'll talk in the car." She replied, looking once behind her.

"Okay." Sara nodded.

It was obvious something had given her a start, enough to send her flying into the store. They headed out, climbing back into the car and squealing out of the parking lot. The truck stop quickly disappeared behind them, fading into the darkness as they headed down the highway. It was not until they were miles down the road that Amanda finally told her what it was that had given her such a start.

"Back at the truck stop," Amanda glanced in her rear-view "I thought I saw the Shadowed One. It wasn't him . . .but you understand I'm sure."

"Yeah, I do."

Sara began packing her cigarettes, they were getting ever closer to the Chameleon's house and her anxiety (despite her knowledge) was growing worse. She would need another pack before they were through with him.

The car decelerated as Amanda slowly turned onto Antonio Parkway, they passed several uniform housing additions before making a right onto Las Banderas. Sara tossed another cigarette out the window. She could almost feel his energy suffocating the area. Was this where it ended for her, in the suburbs? It did not seem even plausible that he would take up residence here.

Amanda turned onto Amantes, passing one stucco house after another. The entire neighborhood was built in the Spanish style that had become so popular in Southern California. Every house had a white stucco exterior, and angled roofs with faux red clay shingles. Amanda hated housing additions, they were not quite factory built homes but they were close enough. Each building a reproduction of the other.

Why? Why in hell did the Chameleon chose to live here? In of all places a sweet, white picketed fence subdivision. Sara could only figure he was trying hard to convince his human fans and the humans around him, that he was a completely normal human man. She felt outraged and disgusted. How dare he do this! How dare he masquerade among the mortals and continue to commit his crimes behind closed doors. He had no right!

The Chevelle drove past 35 Amantes and parked three houses down, in the driveway of a house with a for sale sign in the front yard. Parking in front of a home would create less suspicion than parking on the street. Even if their car was a black blemish against the pale white buildings surrounding them. She knew it did not fit the neighborhood and that people would be watching them. That was, if she allowed them to do so. With a simple thought, she could blind all of them.

As they exited the car, both tucking their perspective weapons within their long coats, they looked around. Although they each had a piece of iron and a piece of mirror in their pocket, there was one more they knew could be watching them even now. Not Death though, he would not dare to come near them, now that they were together again. Their Sire, the girls had heard about him but still had not seen him. It was unnerving. From what they understood, he was protecting the Wolf Pack. There was no telling how powerful he was or even his capabilities. So, they proceeded with caution, moving toward the house in slow unison.

"Doesn't it seem strange to you?" Sara whispered.

"What?"

"That, after what we did to them in Collins, we found them so easily. You would think they would have hid better. And it seems a little odd that there were no roadblocks, so to speak. Nothing trying to stop us from getting to the Chameleon's house."

Amanda said nothing at this point, she only looked at her

with concern. She hoped Sara was wrong, that they were not walking straight into a trap. Her eyes faded to their true crimson color, giving her enhanced vision, lifting the veil and allowing her to see the truth. If there was any truth to see. She sniffed the air, felt the energy with her own and listened beyond the sounds of the neighborhood. There was nothing unusual, at least nothing she could detect.

Sara sensed the change in her Sire and she followed suit. She too, saw, felt and heard nothing out of the ordinary. Although she knew not to let her guard down, not to trust that something might be going on. There was the small issue of their Sire. For all she knew, this could be a trick, conjured up by what she imagined was a hooded figure.

In the brief moment they had taken to investigate their surroundings, the rain and wind had almost turned into a miniature hurricane. It was bending the tops of the palm trees and the rain felt more like hale. They would be soaked and leave wet indents in the carpet if they did not get inside soon. The point of their visit was to gather information and in the meantime, not alert him to their presence. Leaving muddy, watery footprints would certainly create an issue.

The image of Amanda slowly faded into a black fog as she blended with the shadows, using their endless doorways to make her way into the house. Sara on the other hand, moved toward the garage door, not meaning to enter through it because she knew it was locked. However, there was a balcony just above and a sliding glass door through which she could enter. She had spotted it on their way past the house.

The wind kicked up again, whipping her dampened hair about, cutting through her soaking wet clothes and chilling her flesh. It was not the sudden gust that caused her to look around but a newly fallen silence. Sometime between their exiting the car and walking across the front lawn of Amantes 35, it had crept up on them. Was it slow, methodical in its movements and that's why she did not notice it until now? Sneaking behind the sounds of the storm that raged around them. Or was it because it had come on so quickly? Moving in violently with the gusts of wind, flashes of lightening and quaking booms of thunder.

It was reminiscent of Collins, this silence. Sara did not like it and she was quick to let Amanda know about it. 'Something is here.' She thought, pushing her thoughts into her Sire's mind. 'I know.' Amanda responded.

One last glance and Sara pushed herself gracefully up into the air, landing silently on the stucco balcony above. There she waited for Amanda to come and let her inside. After a few minutes, the door before her slid back and there she was, a black silhouette against a bright white room.

"You have to see this."

Those were the first words out of her mouth. Sara furrowed her brow as she stepped into the room. It was only then that she learned what Amanda was talking about.

The room she was standing in, was (as she already expected) a bedroom. However, everything about it was wrong. Its walls were checkered ivory, as was the bedspread, and the carpet. Sara became annoyed, determined, she was not sure at that point but she felt electrified. She marched toward the closet, throwing back the door, she looked on the shelf above and rattled the empty hangers. Then she moved to the dresser, pulling open one empty drawer after another before finally searching the nightstands beside the bed. There was nothing, no clothes, no shoes, absolutely nothing to suggest that anyone used the room. Or that anyone even lived there.

They moved downstairs, not bothering to look at the whitewash bathroom, knowing they would only find more empty cabinets. However, as they passed by, they failed to notice the blonde apparition watching them from the mirror. It was an omen they should have seen and one they should have payed attention to but they never bothered looking.

So, what else were they expecting to find? Well, with his carefree attitude, his lack of concern for the two hunters who meant to kill him, they hoped he might be sloppy. That he might slip up and leave something, a clue of any kind. They separated when they reached the first floor.

As Amanda moved into the large living room, she was confronted by a sandy colored dog in a kennel. It barked and growled, spittle flying off its jowls with every snap of its jaw. She narrowed her eyes, growling deep and letting it know she was the superior predator. First it lowered its, eyes and dropped its head. The aggressive stance melted away and it turned to curl up in the corner if its cage. Amanda shook her head at the notion, he had even gotten a dog.

She wondered how no one had become even remotely suspicious about his behavior. When would they realize that anyone who acts that pure, is full of it? They allowed themselves to be fooled by what he wanted them to see. That coupled with his adolescent humor, his charming demeanor and his holier than though, arrogant attitude. It created the perfect setting, the perfect image for him to appear human and carry out his monstrous atrocities in the evening hours. No one would suspect and therefore no one would oppose him. Hell, the fans who worshiped him only confounded the issue by drinking up this ridiculous behavior. Those masses of simpletons, looking for a way themselves to be famous, none of them would judge him based on morality, they would not dare. They were so enthralled, he could beat his wife in an inch of her life, in front of them, with news cameras surrounding him and they would applaud. Most likely they would think it was staged.

"Amanda, come see this." Sara whispered from the other room.

Amanda looked round the living room once, deciding there was nothing of interest here, she turned and headed in Sara's direction. She found her staring at the row of photos on a wall nearest the dining room. Her face was flush with anger, irritation and a bit of disgust.

"Look at this." Sara said.

Her sire said nothing but her eyes scanned from one small framed photo to another. There he was, the Chameleon, posing with his wife, him on a bicycle with his dog and then, the last one made her pause.

"Sara." Amanda nudged her with her elbow.

"Yeah." She said, leaning closer.

They stared at it with awe. What was the point of it? They wondered. Why would he bother? On the wall, at the end of the line of photos was the Chameleon, in a blue Karate Gi uniform. The patch on the left side read Aikido Center, the rest of the print underneath was too hard to read. Again they wondered, what would an elder vampire with his skills and powers, need with an Aikido class?

"Why . . ." Sara started, then stopped, her mouth dropping open.

Amanda was silent for a few minutes, her mind coursing with possibilities. She was thinking about all the things she knew about him, what she had learned first hand, his thought patterns, techniques, his every movement and what he was doing now. The Chameleon never did anything without reason, well not never, he did let his anger get the best of him. She glanced around and then it hit her.

"The very same reason he became a celebrity." She said, her tone serious.

"Protection, security, influence? I'm not quite following you." Sara replied.

"He's not taking the class," She turned to Sara. "he's teaching it. Spreading their influence . . .the disease that is the Wolf Pack. He's almost the equivalent to a sexually transmitted disease. No one knows he is there, they don't see him coming until its too late and like the plague he spreads fast. Consider there are three of them doing the same thing in their own way."

The sound of a car engine pulling into the driveway, interrupted their conversation. They exchanged a knowing glance and for a moment Sara felt a sense of panic. Was this it? She wondered silently to herself.

"Go. I'll stay. Get in the car and wait for me." Amanda said passing her the keys. "If I'm not there in twenty minutes, get the hell out."

Sara wasted no time, running back up the stairs and waiting in the bedroom for the sound of the front door. Her heart was racing in her chest as she crouched by the balcony, looking around the bedroom, some part of her expecting a guillotine to come crashing down on her. Or to see the Shadowed One stepping out of the darkness of the closet. There had to be something, some trick, some occurrence, she knew the Wolf Pack, she would not get out unscathed. She had no protection from the shadows but they had not bothered her since she left Finn's. Was he watching over her?

There it was, the front door slammed shut and she heard his cowboy boots resonating on the tile floor downstairs. With an inhale and a sudden exhale she carefully slid the glass door open, being cautious to make no sounds. She quickly closed it behind her, praying he did not sense the change in temperature from the gusts of wind. Or hear the sound of the storm growing louder and realize someone else was in his house.

From her place in the shadows, Amanda watched the Chameleon's head jerk up toward the upstairs bedroom. He had sensed something, she had to do something to distract him. Anything to keep him from going into that room. So, she moved within inches of him and brushed her translucent, shadowy fingers across the back of his neck. He shuddered at the feeling of cold air touching his flesh. It was enough to take his mind off the bedroom for a moment.

Chameleon moved quickly toward the stairs, leaping them two at a time and headed quickly into the bedroom. He walked to the very spot Sara was hiding only minutes ago. The door was locked and there was no sign of anyone having ever been there. His eyes scanned the room, the closet and then he unlocked the door, stepping out onto the balcony.

Sara pressed her back against the side of the garage, out of his sight, her nails digging deep into her palms in an effort to calm herself. The wind whipped her coat about her and the rain continued to soak her clothes. She did not move, she knew better.

The Chameleon looked over every edge of the balcony, scanning the neighborhood until he was sure certain that he was alone in his kingdom. He turned back to the house and headed inside, descending the stairs as quickly as he came.

When she was sure he had left, she ran for the Chevelle, her feet barely touching the ground as she moved. It was not until she climbed in the car, shutting and locking the door, that she finally realized she had not taken a breath for some minutes now. Her sharp inhale burned her lungs, making her cough and her exhales were shaky. He could still rattle her nerves and catch her off guard. However, she was still alive. Perhaps the Chameleon would not have a hand in her death.

Sara pulled herself up out of her huddle and looked around the neighborhood. Something in the rear-view mirror caught her eye and she slowly looked to see what it was. There, in the silvery surface was the woman from their house in Collins. She was sitting in the back seat, staring at her. Sara turned quickly to look in the seat behind her and saw nothing. When she turned back to the mirror, the bloody apparition was writing something in blood on its surface.

'N-U-R.'

It was backwards but she recognized the word, even backwards. The entity was telling her to RUN. Then, with a silent screen and a slap of her bloody hand, she fractured the mirror and disappeared. Sara's heart was pounding in her chest and she gripped her katana. When she looked back in the mirror, the bloody writing was gone.

Amanda sat in the shadows on the stairs and watched him for a bit. She wanted to know why he was even here. There were no signs that he lived in the house, so what was he using it for?

The Chameleon walked through the dining room, into the kitchen and from her place on the stairs she heard a heavy lock. Then there was the sound of a door opening and she recognized the quiet whimper of a woman. When he walked back toward the dining room, he was dragging a busty blonde figure, his fist wound in her hair. She was dressed in a black satin negligee, which exposed the new scars, old jagged scars that puffed up away from her skin and new lacerations only now beginning to scab over.

Amanda recognized her as his wife and knowing what he would do to her, she shifted uncomfortably. She did not want to sit and watch him torture this woman but in a way she had too. Not because she needed to know if he was up to his same old games but for his wife's sake. Hell, for her sake even.

"Please don't, not today." The woman begged.

"Shut up!" He said as he tossed her onto the tile floor.

There was a moment where he stood over his wife and watched her trying to crawl backwards away from him. It amused him to see her fighting for her life, begging for mercy and knowing all the while that he had none. He grabbed her left ankle and drug her back toward him, the bottom of her gown rolling up around her hips, exposing her womanhood to his greedy eyes. She fought to pull her gown down and received a hard backhand across her face for her insolence.

The Chameleon reached down and grabbed the front of her gown, ripping it to shreds, leaving her scarred nudity exposed. Amanda turned her head slightly, not wanting to watch him do this, fighting back the urge to kill him. Her thumb had unconsciously began pushing the katana from its sheath as she watched him hurt this woman. It was taking more strength to keep from attacking him, than it was to sit and watch him.

He yanked her up off the floor by her throat and roughly cupped the apex of her thighs, his fingers working around the tender flesh there.

"This belongs to me. Got it! I'll touch it, look at it. I'll do whatever I want to it. Including letting my brothers play with it."

Then he turned her around and pushed her face first onto the dining room table, his mouth spewing forth phrases, disgusting enough to make Amanda plug her ears. He brought the hand he had used to violate his wife, sucked his finger and shoved it inside of her until he was satisfied she was ready for him.

Amanda faded further back into the shadow realm, using its foggy clouds to obscure her vision as he thrust into the battered blonde and began the process of sodomizing her. With every buck of his hips, she yelped, tears beginning to run down the side of her nose and drip onto the wood beneath her. He kept his hand wound in her hair as he pressed her face into the table hard. The tile floor glittered with a mixture of sexual fluids and droplets of blood as he pushed into her with enough force to break her pelvic bone. There was the sickening slap of flesh against flesh and the moist sucking sound of fluids as he continued to force into her with ever increasing force.

The Chameleon paused only to strip his shirt off and toss it across the room. His wife's thighs were beginning to look like a bad Jackson Pollock painting, with the mixture of red, white and the barely visible flesh color. He increased his speed, pressing her face harder into the table, his fingers digging deep into the tender flesh of her hips. She would have new bruises to go along with the internal injuries she was obtaining. An echoing grunt was heard from the Chameleon and pulling from her, he ejaculated his load onto the back of her legs. Then, with his fingers still in her hair, he pulled her from the table and tossed her on the floor.

Amanda heard a crack, recognizing it as a bone breaking and she flinched at the sound. She remembered how many times they broke her own bones and cut her own flesh. Without thinking about it, she stood.

He was hovering over his wife, looking down at her and Amanda recognized that look in his eyes. The Chameleon was contemplating killing her.

Amanda's nails extended to sharp daggers and the muscles in her body tightened. She did not want to break from the plan but she would not allow him to kill another innocent and in front of her no less. 'Don't even think about it asshole.' She thought, knowing he would have no way of hearing her. Still, she stepped back a step or two when his head jerked in her direction. There was no way he could see her in the confines of the shadows but she would take no chances. Her eyes, red as rubies, snapped from him to the battered woman beneath him. Amanda's upper lip twitched and her breathing became heavier as her fingers flexed. She was fighting with everything she had to keep from killing him right now.

The Chameleon turned his attention back to his wife, yanking her off the floor by her throat and kissing her hard. Then, as he was carrying her back to her prison, he whispered in her ear.

"I love you, you know that?"

"I know."

Amanda glanced between them, she was confused. How could that woman believe he loved her? Unless it was a conditioned response, a way to survive and keep him from causing her any more harm. Amanda knew if she did nothing to intervene, that there would be no way to rescue this woman. So, she said something only the woman would hear.

> '*Fight. He's going to hurt you if you fight or not, so you better fight like hell. If you want to survive, if you want to live, you better dig deep and find some strength. He won't ever stop. Trust me. You're not the first woman he has done this too. I had to bury the rest of them.*'

There was a sudden eruption of noise, anger and it was coming from the cracked, pale lips of the blonde.

"No, you don't love me! Take your damn hands off me!" She shouted.

"What the hell do you think you're doing? You're gonna tell me no?" He responded.

Chameleon clinched his fist and hit her hard, knocking the fight out of her. She crumpled to the floor but even through her fading consciousness, she spit out two words.

"Fuck you."

Then her eyes rolled back in her head and she fell unconscious. It was not exactly what Amanda had in mind but maybe she would survive long enough for them to kill the Chameleon and get her out of there. This time however, she would not dwell on the woman's death. She had to be more cold and calculated. Keep the mission as her number one thought and push everything else out of her mind. The most important thing was to kill them. If other innocents died because the Wolf Pack killed them, she would not take that onto herself, not this time. She knew they would use that against her if they could, so she shut off that part of her. The human part of her.

Again, Chameleon looked up toward the stairs where she was hiding, he was panting, blood smeared around his hips and chest.

"Where the hell did that come from?"

He quickly tossed the naked woman back into her cell and locked the door. Then he moved over to the white phone hanging on the wall and began to dial a number.

Amanda knew he was calling one of his brothers. She had stayed too long and been too bold, he was suspicious. It was time to go. So, she moved back through the shadow realm and came out in the garage at the house the Chevelle was parked. She walked out the side door and climbed in the drivers seat.

Sara had hunched down in the passenger seat, gripping her sword between two pale hands. She sighed when she saw the familiar face climb behind the wheel.

"What the hell took you so long?" Sara asked.

"Why didn't you leave like I told you to do?" Amanda replied, glancing at the clock.

"I don't know." Sara replied.

She was being honest, she really did not know. It was a pointless discussion, Amanda knew the answer. She never left her in Collins, the girl would not leave her now.

"We have to get out of here and quick. Chameleon is already on the phone with one of the others." Amanda said, starting the car.

"What the hell did you do?" Sara asked with alarm.

"I'm not sure. He was suspicious before I told his wife to fight or he would kill her."

"Shit."

"Yeah."

Amanda backed out of the driveway and pressed the accelerator hard. The vehicle bucked and they sped down the street, making a hard turn out of the addition. Its engine growled, whined and roared as she shifted gears as fast as the car could handle. If the other members were going to show up, they needed to be far away from the Chameleon's location as possible. They needed to stop and regroup before paying a visit to the next member. Although she felt fine, she could tell by the look on Sara's face and the body language she was displaying, that she needed minute. Amanda needed her stable and level headed. Or there was a strong chance one of them would do something stupid and get themselves killed.

The Shadowed One
(Death)

Chapter 35

Amanda did not want to admit it, she did not want to believe he could still make her feel that way. But he did. She felt her body flush hot and her skin flush cold. A slow sigh left her lips as she pushed the car faster because fast was not fast enough. Far was not far enough away from that house. Although she failed to realize she was also moving closer to the worst one of them all. He was the one that kept them apart, he had attacked them both and the first one to rape her. It was his every word that lead to the tortures she endured. Perhaps Collins, was all his idea. Amanda could feel the accelerator nearly touching the floor but it still did nothing to quench her anxiety. Oh, hell, she should call it what it was, fear. She was undoubtedly still afraid of all of them. Despite having escaped their grasp and nearly killing one of them. All her power, her immortality and the weapons (that now felt heavy in her interior pockets) she felt small. It was as if in one swoop he had stripped it all away.

Sara herself was dealing with her own battles, she was on the verge of tears. Her mind repeating 'I can't do this. I can't do this.' The Chameleon had come inches away from her. Although she managed to out fox him and make it to the car without being caught, she still could not shake the feeling off. Being that close to him, was too much. She did not have the strength Amanda did, or the resilience. How was she supposed to pull herself together? They were headed to the Shadowed One's house, gaining on his trail at too fast a pace. She was in no hurry to see him. Neither one of them were. Then there was the little matter of the apparition who refused to leave Sara alone. It had warned her to run for her life but she would not listen. She would not allow Amanda to face these wolves alone. Even if she knew that her death would be long before they had the chance to kill them. The ghost, still staring at her from the side mirror, could not understand that. Unless, dying at the hands of one of the Blood Kings, did not mean true death. Did they hold that much power? The ability to keep a spirit trapped on this plain. Sara glanced at the speedometer and then at Amanda's face. They needed to slow down.

"Amanda! Amanda stop!"

Sara's voice was a muffled sound as the voice of the Chameleon filled her ears. She remembered everything he said and did to her. The silver chains that dug deep into her flesh and the rapes. That was the worst part. Amanda was panting and gripping the wheel as if it would save her from this nightmare.

"Damn it Amanda Stop!" Sara demanded.

The needle on the speedometer continued to climb as the roar of the engine became deafeningly loud. They were going to crash if she continued to drive this way. Her eyes flickered between the rear-view mirror and the windshield in front of her.

Sara turned around to look behind them and it was then she understood why Amanda was driving so erratic. An old Ford pickup, with a spray paint black exterior and no make or model marks on it, was trailing them. Where did he come from? How did she not hear him approach? Sara planted her hand unconsciously on the dashboard as she continued to stare at the vehicle behind them. She could not see the driver through his nearly black tinted windows. But did she really need to? Was it, could it be? She wondered. There was no possible way that the Shadowed One could know they were there. Unless Amanda lost her temper and killed the Chameleon already. 'Never mind that', she thought. They needed to lose the truck and fast.

"Amanda go go go! Lose this fuck!" Sara screamed.

"Hang on!" Amanda replied.

Finally, she could hear Sara and with one more glance in her side mirror, she made a hard left onto I-5, heading North. The Chevelle fishtailed on the wet pavement and for a moment Sara thought Amanda was going to lose control. She held the wheel tight and shifted through one gear after another.

Sara thought they had lost him but she looked behind them to see him gaining on them. No matter how many cars Amanda passed or how fast she drove, he never seemed to falter.

"Who the hell is this guy?!" Sara yelled over the roar of the engine.

Amanda's eyes shifted once in her direction, as if to ask don't you know? It was not possible, it was in no way possible. How could they know? In that split second, Sara made a decision. She stripped her long coat off and fished the bottle of whiskey from the interior pocket, tossing her coat in the back seat.

"What are you doing?" Amanda asked, glancing from her to the mirror to the road.

"Getting rid of our friend." Sara said with a sly smirk.

She then cranked her window all the way down, ripping a piece of fabric from the bottom of her shirt and using her finger to stuff it down into the bottle. Then, she unfastened her belt and climbed halfway out the window. Amanda's maneuvering made it a little hard to aim, but she would manage. It was a good thing her Zippo was wind resistant because at this speed, she knew lighting that rag would be nearly impossible if it was not.
Sara flicked open her lighter and touched the flame to the bottom of the rag. It flared up the strip of fabric, stopping at the top of the bottle.

"Hey asshole!" Sara yelled at the truck. "I got something for ya."

She waited until he was in direct alignment with the rear of their Chevelle and then she threw the flaming torch at the hood. It shattered and the flames spread all across the front of the truck. There was the hard screech as his tires locked up and he slid sideways. Sara watched as he lost control and the truck flipped roof over tires. A crowd of cars piled up behind him, bringing traffic to a halt.

"Yeah!" Sara shouted.

She pulled herself back into the car and rolled the window up behind her.

"Nice." Amanda commented.

"Thanks. We'll have to stop for another bottle."

"That's fine," She replied glancing in the rear-view again. "We've got time."

Sara had to resist the urge to smile at the word time. Hers was quickly running out. So, if she planned to help, to make a bit of a difference, then she needed to take risks that Amanda would never take.

They turned off the highway at some point and headed down Sunshine Terrace. Sara shifted nervously in her seat, she could feel the distinct chill of his energy. She knew they were close and in that she knew, her life was ending. It only made sense, the Shadowed One was the wolf Amanda had left to protect her from. So, why not have him be the means to her end? However, she hoped that he might kill her with some dignity in tact. She glanced once at her partner in crime and thought I love you for the last time. Amanda had, in a way, become her mother and her sister. They were bonded by blood and circumstance. After seeing her reaction to the Chameleon, Sara knew her death was necessary to numb Amanda from the power the Wolf Pack still had over her. She only prayed that her death would have the opposite effect (of what it was intended) and break Amanda.

"We're here." Amanda announced.

Amanda said, breaking Sara's train of thought. Before them stood an apartment building, the corner of which faced the street. It was lined with balconies, their glass railing and gold painted posts glimmering in the dim light.

This was where the worst of the worst, the ringleader, the sadist, their leader, lived. It did not fit. To think that he would enjoy sun lit balconies or bright colors, seemed a bit off. Then again, the Chameleon was playing house, so why not? Sara rolled her eyes, forgetting for a moment why they were here and what it meant for her. Her annoyance at his arrogance overpowered her fear for him. She calmly reached in the back seat and pulled her coat back on, the wind having turned bitter cold by this point. It was colder than California should have been. At least she thought so.

Sara closed the door and looked up at the building, her eyes settling on the one balcony where she felt his presence strongest. She no longer needed the address to know where she was headed. It was as if something was calling to her, drawing her there. With a sigh, she accepted that whatever happened was meant to happen and with a glance in Amanda's direction, realized it was up to her to forgive Sara for allowing this to happen. Sara swallowed, having accepted her fate did nothing to curb her nervousness. She could hear her heart beat, slow and rhythmic. When she closed the car door, she hesitated to move. She knew what he was capable of (to a point) but she had no idea, how her death would go. 'Please do not let me leave this world without my dignity intact.' She thought.

"Come on. He's on the third floor.

Amanda headed for the front of the building, intending to take the stairs and avoid drawing any more unwanted attention. Sara's little stunt on the highway (although effective and necessary) had already done that. She wanted to avoid getting anymore. Sara looked around, then she began to back away from the building.

"Sara what are you doing?" Amanda asked.

With a smirk and a wink, she ran toward the building and leapt into the air, grabbing the top of the glass railing on the fourth balcony up. She only briefly touched the glass before she landed on the cement holding it up. Sara did not bother to wipe her fingerprints off the glass, she was not going to be on this Earth much longer.

Amanda cursed under her breath before ducking into a shadow and stepping into the white on white living room of his apartment. Why did she do that? What the hell was she thinking? She would deal with Sara after they were through, right now, she knew she had to be ever vigilant because his shadows were clever.

Sara slid open the glass door of the balcony, the wind brushing back the white gossamer curtains as she stepped inside. She turned and shut the door, being careful not to catch the fabric in the railing. When she turned back around, she had to press her hand to her mouth to keep from making a sound.

There he lay, a silk black sheet draped low over the apex of his hips, curls of black poked out just over the edge of his silken cover. His hair was longer than she remembered it being and it lay across his pillow, a river of feathery charcoal. Sara had never seen him like this, she was not prepared to see him this way, her mind reeled back, trying to center itself. Every inch of him was flawless caramel, the tight muscles of his stomach and chest flexed with every breath he took. She could not move or speak, only stare at him in awe. Everything she knew about him was forgotten in that moment. It would be that moment, that would cost her.

A slow smile played across his thin pale lips as he lay, half covered in the black satin sheets he had shared with Amanda. The memory of her terror, her screams and the way she felt as he thrust into her, it played in his subconscious. Sure, he would play along, pretending to be asleep as they searched his house for clues they would never find. Nothing had changed. Finn had not done Sara any favors by giving her the stake and altering her sword. He had been keeping an eye on both of them since they escaped Collins. He could feel Sara's eyes scanning over him, he had almost forgotten that she never saw him this way. It was the upper hand he needed. The Shadowed one moved his right leg, letting it hang over the edge of the bed and he shifted his body just slightly to one side. What little cover he had, pulled aside, revealing the parts of him Sara had not the privilege of knowing.

With her hand over he mouth, she backed away slowly, her hand reaching for the handle behind her. She meant to keep her eyes fixated on him, not because she was now being overtaken by lust but because she knew better than to take her eye off him even for a second. There was a noise behind her, just a small one and she turned to see what it was, that was her mistake. When Sara turned back to look at him, he was gone.

"Shit." She whispered.

She turned to head back out the way she had come but she ran into something, or rather someone solid. Sara backed away quickly and reached for the katana still hidden within her coat. But he was faster and before she had the chance to react, he grabbed that hand, pinning it and her to the wall. His nudity pressing into her hard, his deep brown pools stared down at her, weakening her resolve. She tried not to look at him, she fought to pretend it was not happening so she might gain control. Amanda, she needed to get her attention.

"Amanda! He's awake!"

"Shh sh sh." He whispered, his voice soft and low.

It tingled the hairs just below her earlobe, causing her to shift her hips slightly to ignore what he was doing to her. That only made things worse, her movement had given him access to the apex of her thighs, which he was now taking advantage of, pressing his member between them.

"It won't hurt if you don't fight." His voice was warm velvet.

"Amanda!" Sara shrieked.

There was the sound of footsteps and then she saw her face, but only for a moment. The Shadowed One turned to look at the door.

"No no, you wait your turn."

As he said that, the door slammed shut, locking Amanda out. Sara could hear her shouting and ramming it, trying to break it open.

"Fight him Sara! God damn it fight him!"

Sara knew she would never get out of here alive if she did not do something stupid and irrational. Summoning all the strength she had, she called to the demon inside and allowed it to take over. Her canines extended to their full length and her iris's became red with blood. Before Death could say a word, she bit deep into his shoulder, not meaning to feed but so she could rip flesh. He hollered in pain and pulled away from her. Sara spit the flesh from her mouth onto the floor. For a moment she thought he was going to attack but he steadied himself and lowered his gaze to meet hers.

"Sara..."

He said, cocking his head to the right, his eyes softening. The sound of his voice made her stumble slightly as her knees began to weaken. Her eyes fluttered and she fought to keep them from closing. What was he doing to her? She felt her body began to warm.

"What are you doing Sara?" His voice was lower this time, softer even.

Sara's head wavered and her body became slack.

"Come here." He beckoned.

From the other side of the door, she could hear Amanda screaming in desperation.

"Sara don't! Don't listen to him!!" Her voice boomed.

Sara slowly made her way toward him, her feet felt like lead weights. She drifted side to side as she walked, almost as if in a trance.

"That's my girl." He cooed.

The Shadowed One reached into the interior of her coat and pulled out the katana, dropping it onto the floor.

"We don't need that anymore do we?" He asked, cupping her

face in his hands.

"No." Sara mumbled, unaware of what was happening.

"Sara snap out of it! Sara!" Amanda screamed.

She would have walked through the shadow realm to get her but he was blocking her somehow. Amanda had no way to get in. Every time she attempted to become one with the shadows, she was snapped back to her solid state. She never believed it possible. Amanda backed up and using all her strength, she rammed the door one more time. It would not budge, bend or break, no matter how much force she put behind it. There was no time to go back downstairs and come up through the balcony. However, she would not leave Sara in the clutches of him. So, she continued to look for a way to get the door down.

The Shadowed One, slowly stripped off Sara's coat, pulled her shirt over her head and dropped her pants around her ankles. He guided her to the end of the bed, where he bent her over and removed the last bit of clothes from her lower half. Sara was defenseless, she could not even understand what was happening. He had full control over her body.

He lifted his hand to his mouth, wetting his fingers with his tongue before spreading her legs wide and beginning to rub the pink bud hidden by her outer labia. She made no sound, having no feeling in any part of her body at this point. When he felt she was moist enough for him he thrust into her hard. It was not pleasure he was after but humiliation. He knew that hurting Sara would hurt Amanda in the process.

It went on that way (with Amanda continuing to ram the door) for nearly half an hour. He figured she would have stopped by now but she refused to give up. That was his favorite thing about her in Collins, she could handle what ever they threw her way. It meant they could have as much fun with her as they pleased and know that she would live out the night for them to do it again.

His body began to shudder and he pull out of Sara, shooting his load onto the small of her back before shoving her down on the mattress. He was going to enjoy this even more than he did her tight hole. Grabbing her by her hair, he yanked her to her feed, holding her nude body in front of him for protection before picking her sword up off the floor. With the flick of one wrist, the sheath fell off and he allowed the door to finally open.

Amanda came limping into the room, one of her legs and shoulders clearly broken from her attempts to break in. Her eyes widened with horror and shock when she looked at Sara. He had drugged her and raped her, or somehow hypnotized her. There was nothing in her eyes, as if her soul had died.

"No," Amanda held up her hands. "no, Sara? Sara can you hear me?! Sara look at me?"

"She can't hear ya honey. I'm the only voice she hears right now." Death said with a smirk.

"Look at her Sara." He whispered in her ear.

Sara's vapid eyes looked up at Amanda, her movements were robotic. He had done something to her, she had no control over herself.

"God damn it let go of her! Or I swear I'm going to-"

Death pressed the point of the katana to Sara's back, pressing just enough to break the skin.

"You're gonna do what?" He challenged.

"Stop! Stop it! Let go of her." Amanda was on her knees, begging.

"You're begging now. I like when you beg. It gets me all," His hand traveled down to the apex of Sara's thighs and he cupped her womanhood. "excited."

"You arrogant piece of shit!"

"Come on honey, wake up." He whispered in Sara's ear and she jerked her head backwards as if breaking from a trance.

Her eyes fell to Amanda and she could now feel the air on her naked flesh. There were tears in her voice when she spoke.

"Amanda help me please. Don't let me die this way." Sara begged.

"I won't. I swear I won't." Amanda replied.

"Aww isn't that sweet. You two love each other." Death said before turning his attention to Amanda.

"But you shouldn't lie to the girl, you shouldn't make promises you can't keep. Didn't you swear to rescue the other girls?" He asked, cocking his head. "Hm? And how did that work out?"

"Fuck you!" Amanda screamed, hatred dripping from her every word.

"I already have and I gotta tell ya, not that great. Really, you could stand to learn a thing or two from Sara here. Now Sara…" He paused to lick the side of her face and sniff her hair. "Oh, she's got just the sweetest, tightest-"

"Shut up!"

Amanda demanded, cutting him off so she did not have to hear the filth that was about to come out of his mouth.

"Ya know it's rude to interrupt other people when they're talking." He acted genuinely disgusted.

"What do you want Death? What? What will it take for you to let her go?" Amanda was bargaining now.

"Oh, you want to make a deal. What happened to that whole, I'll kill you bravado? No? You wanna know what I want Amanda? I want you to stop hunting me and my brothers. To apologize for what you did to them and me. And, oh yeah, come be our good little pet again. But this time, you have to be willing." He was gesturing at her with the tip of the sword.

"I thought the only way you could get it up, was by raping women. Isn't that your thing?" She replied.

"I didn't rape Sara. She loved every minute of it." He said.

"Bullshit. Hypnotism, drugs, alcohol . . .its still rape if she didn't say Yes."

"I gave you a chance. A chance to right your wrongs and you didn't wanna play along. That's fine. Just remember that you got Sara involved. So, everything that has happened to her today, is on you."

The Shadowed One shoved Sara away from him and before Amanda could grab her, he sliced through the delicate flesh of her neck, decapitating her.

"NO! Sara!" Her voice rattled the walls around her.

Amanda was quick to turn her attention to Death, forgetting the reason she came here in the first place. He was gone before she had the chance to pull her sword from its sheath. Instead she fell to her knees, scooping up Sara's headless body and rocking with it in her lap. She needed time to grieve but the Shadowed One was not going to give her that right.
There was a shout and the sound of footsteps coming up the stairs that lead to the apartment. She glanced over her shoulder and listened for a moment. The bastard had called the police on her, claiming she had broken in and killed his girlfriend. According the the radio chatter and the voices in the hallway, that's what he had told the cops. He was going to masquerade himself as the victim. The

press would eat it up and her chances of getting close enough to kill him would be cut in half.

"Damn it!" She mumbled.

Amanda stood quickly and ran for the door that lead to the balcony. The glass pane shattered from the impact and with one push of her foot, she leapt over the glass railing. She could feel shards poking out of her flesh and other areas where she had been scratched by the jagged pieces wedged in the door frame. She could hear the footsteps behind her as the officers outside began to pursue her on foot. Although the last thing she wanted to do was kill a lawman, she decided that if it was necessary, then one would have to die. Just not today. There had been too many innocents murdered today.

Amanda made it to the Chevelle and was already on the highway, headed out of California before they managed to get a patrol car out. She drove through the night, not stopping unless she needed gas. What happened back there she knew, was not entirely her fault. She also know if she did not get out of California, she could forget ever taking them down. Amanda had to get somewhere, where she could pull herself together. But where?

Finn

Chapter 36

Sara was dead, that fact was inarguable. No matter how many times Amanda repeated it, her mind still could not accept it. Before she had time to mourn she was being chased out of the apartment by brainwashed human cops. She could well have killed them and in turn went after the Shadowed One but the amount of damage she would have sustained from the bullets, would have left her too weak for a fight with him. Besides, there were other forces at work in that place. How else could she explain the door and her inability to get back into the Shadow Realm. Was his Master hanging around in the safety of the shadows?

The car gunned forward as she pressed the clutch and tapped the shifter into the next gear, forcing the speedometer to climb higher. Everything around her passed by in a blur as she sped down the highway at a hundred and ninety miles per hour. One hand white knuckle gripped the wheel and she glared forward at the hot asphalt strip before her. Her eyes slowly faded to their crimson color as bloody tears flowed down her cheeks. She was numb, she did not feel them. Or the shards of glass still protruding from her flesh or the blood that continued to ooze from her open wounds. What was the point of everything else? The pain in her chest was worse than any torture the Wolf Pack had put her through. It was enough to make her want to die. In one simple act, they had managed to destroy her, level her. Even though a voice whispered to her from somewhere far off, '*You're not dead.*'

Amanda could not hear anything over the continuous roar of the engine and the ringing in her ears. Her fingernails were crusted with Sara's blood, her hands nearly covered and her clothing was beginning to stiffen as it dried. Part of her wanted to make them pay for that but the other half of her, the one that was mourning, wanted to give up. She needed to make a decision but it seemed they were going to do it for her.

A few miles down the way, Amanda spotted something that made her undead body run hot. She was warmer than she had ever been, even as a human being. How dare they! She thought to herself. Are they serious right now?! Her fist tightened her grip on the wheel and she reached down grabbing the shifter to her right. Did she dare push the car into last gear and hit him? As she contemplated her next move, she opened and closed her hand around the metal skull mounted on top. Deciding it was better not to wreck the car just yet, her hand quickly moved to the emergency break and she yanked it up. The tires squealed and the car lurched forward. There was the smell of hot rubber as friction and speed caused the tires paint the sun bleached concrete with two thick stripes of black. White smoke wafted around the rear of the car and breezed past her open drivers side window.

Amanda continued to open and close her hand angrily around the top of the steering wheel, her other hand following suit on the lever of the emergency break. The urge to run him through, continued to scratch at the back of her mind. He was the unknown element she knew nothing about. As angry as she was though, she did not care but the logical part of her brain or some unknown force cautioned her 'don't'. For now, she stared hard at the hooded figure before her, continuing to rev the engine in warning.

"What are you doing Amanda? There is no where for you to go, no where to run and hide this time."

His voice was booming gravel and she knew it was not coming from his lips. She was hearing his voice in her head. The sound of his voice, the fact that he dared to speak to her was an insult.

"I'm not running and I'm sure as hell not hiding. One of your bastard children killed my best friend, my fledgling. I don't take too kindly to that. One way or another, they're going to pay for that and you're going to pay for letting it happen."

Their conversation was over as far as she was concerned. He and his coven had no right to speak to her. In one fluid motion, her steering hand tightened, she slammed down the emergency break and shoved the shifter into gear. Her foot pressed down on the accelerator so hard and fast that for a moment the rear tires only spun, kicking up smoke and the rear of the car fishtailed. The sudden exerted force on the car, pushed her back into the seat as she sped forward, meaning to run him through. Damn the car, damn her because she was on a suicide mission. If she injured him and died in the process, so be it.

There was no crunching of metal, no thud of a body hitting the Chevelle's hood. He was already gone, disappearing into the nothingness around her as if he had never been. She slammed her palm on the steering wheel in frustration and cursed the air.

"Damn it!"

He had been able to find her, without ever seeing her face or the vehicle. His appearance in the road had told her one thing, he was partially responsible for Sara's death. That he was the reason she could not get the door open, no matter how hard she rammed into it. Her shoulder was still throbbing from the impact and blood continued to ooze from her wounds (none of which had begun to heal) around the large jagged shards of glass protruding from her flesh. Without grief numbing her entire body, she might have noticed the pain. Amanda needed to take care of them, it was hard enough to stay hidden without the scent of fresh blood giving her location away.

She could feel the steering wheel beginning to give way beneath her iron grip as she squeezed harder to keep her hands from trembling. The rest of her body was shading from the encounter with their Master. Although she had maintained her composure, it had left her with a fear she could not seem to shake. The longer she drove, the more Sara's death began to sink in, her mind filling with memories of their time together. She knew she needed to push the grief aside, long enough to think.

Amanda headed a few more miles down the road until she found a truck stop. It was busy enough that her presence there would most likely go unnoticed and right now she did not have the energy or the mindset to manipulate the masses of bodies occupying its parking lot. She pulled into a parking space near its exterior bathroom and grabbing her bag of clothes from the back seat, headed in, locking the door behind her.

The room smelled pungent with the odor of stale urine, crack cocaine long since inhaled, meth and alcohol. Its walls were covered with graffiti scrawled in permanent marker and spray paint. In one corner was a used condom, dried and stuck to the bottom of the trashcan it had been tossed toward. This was one of those moments she regretted having a superior sense of smell because the discarded needles in the trashcan were odorous with dried blood. She looked around with disgust before setting her bag on the floor next to the leaky sink. The yellow light mounted above the mirror cast everything in a sickening flaxen glow.

Amanda peeled off her bloodstained shirt and tossed it into the overflowing can next to her. She glanced down at the bloody black pants she was wearing, knowing that she could not slip them off over the glass daggers in her legs. Pulling her boot knife from its sheath, she sliced down the left side of the pants, pulling them off around the shards in her legs. Then she set the blade on the side of the sink, she would be needing it again. Her body resembled that of a voodoo doll with various sizes of glass poking out from her torso and legs. It had to be done though, she knew it would hurt but it was necessary.

Slowly, she began to pull them out and drop them into the sink, they clanked emptily one after another as they piled up before her. It was a long arduous task, and several times she had to stop because the pain was too much. They gone through bone in certain areas, and she screamed as she pulled them out. Her hands smeared blood on the filthy sink and the corresponding walls behind it. Amanda was holding on to anything she could to stable herself as her body wavered with blood loss. She was breathing unsteadily, huffing out her exhales in an attempt to keep the bile in her throat from spilling forth into her mouth. Another huff of air and she turned her head, puking onto the floor beside her. Amanda's body lurched and another stream sputtered forth, landing on the tile with a sickeningly wet, slapping sound. She gripped the side of her sink as her body shuddered, working slowly back down to a more balanced state.

Amanda looked down, staring for a moment at the large piece of glass that was embedded in her left femur. She was anticipating the pain but nothing could prepare her for what she would experience. The metal she had to pull out of her body in Collins, did not hurt nearly as bad. With an unsteady hand she reached down and wrapped her fist around it. The sharp edges pierced her palm as she began to pull. The blood pouring forth from the wound and her lacerated hand making the glass slick. She grit her teeth hard as she pulled her free hand from the sink and wrapped it over the other. Amanda tightened her grip, digging the glass further into her left hand as she finally yanked the shard from her leg, it pulled free with a sickening pop. She dropped it onto the floor before she herself collapsed from the effort.

Her hands continued to shake and her body protested movement but she forced herself to stand. She washed and wrapped her wounds the best she could (binding them with gauze and electrical tape) before gingerly slipping on a clean pair of clothes. The bathroom resembled a crime scene with the blood smears across the wall and the puddles on the floor beneath her. Her boots squeaked and slid as she made her way toward the sink.

Placing her hands on either side of its faux porcelain bowl, she stared at the bloody glass piled inside. Her mind swam with their faces, laughing as they tortured her, laughing at her pain and mocking Sara's death. The look on Sara's face before she died, the helpless confusion forever etched in Amanda's mind. What the Master said to her, the Master, standing there staring at her in the middle of the freeway.

These thoughts played through her mind in rapid succession. The things they dared to say to her, the way they disregarded her as a threat. Their blatant disrespect. Amanda began to rock, the muscles of her jaw flexing just beneath the skin. Her muscles tensed and she rolled her shoulders forward, sighing heavily. There was something new happening to her, she sensed her inner demon coming forward but behind it, stirred a darkness she never felt before.

The hairs on the back of her neck prickled, causing her to pause in her movements. It was a familiar sensation, one she only experienced while living in the house on Lillie. Someone was in here with her and they had only just arrived. Amanda slowly raised her head, looking up into the face of a bloody apparition. It stared back at her from the confines of its reflective surface. She knew this face, she had seen it before. Her name was Rachel and to Amanda's surprise, she, was still with her. Despite the fact the house had burned to the ground.

Neither one of them said a word to the other one. There was a moment, an unspoken thought that they both understood. Rachel did not appear to be in as much pain as she had been. Instead, she looked rather defiant, even in her battered state. She nodded a ghostly nod to Amanda, sparking something in the her that she had desperately needed. In response, Amanda slammed her palms on the side of the sink hard enough to crack the base.

She grabbed up her bag and coat, hurrying out to the car. There was the sound of quick rubber on broken pavement and then a growl as she sped back out onto the highway. Although she had no idea where she was going or what her next move might be. The sun was passing down over the horizon as she headed into the next county.

"Raadiiooo."

A phantom voice passed by her, causing the hairs on her arm to stand at attention. Amanda glanced in the rear-view mirror, then she looked around. Cautiously, she reached forward (obeying the ghostly request) and turned the knob for the radio, scanning through channels until something told her to stop. Turning it up, she began to understand why something or someone had told her to turn it on:

> *"Today funeral services for Ashley King, the girlfriend of actor Colin Caine were held today. If you remember, she was killed when sources close to the actor say that Colin's stalker broke into his apartment and cut her head off. Some of the people in attendance were Colin's close friends actor Shane Finley and Nathan Reilly."*

Really! Amanda thought as she heard the news report. They not only dared to frame her for a murder she did not commit but they were daring to publicize and claim that she was the Shadowed One's girlfriend. The Wolf Pack had buried her under a false name. Did they really think changing the first name was not going to change a thing? Who were they trying to fool?

Amanda cranked the wheel to the left, driving over the grass median and into the opposite lane, gunning the engine as she headed back toward Los Angeles. She had an idea, something to prove to them that they had not yet defeated her. It was something she knew that would have made Sara proud.

The police would still be looking for the car, let them find her. Right and wrong were blurred lines to her in this moment. If she made a public display of the vampire and exposed them in the process, it would at least put a slight wrench in their plan. Her soul was already damned, so why should she care who else she killed?

She reached down and switched stations to something more appropriate for the drive ahead. Before she got to the cemetery, she needed to get a sheet, some boards, a can of gas and a thick chain. A smirk crossed her lips as she thought about what she was planning on doing. Sara needed to understand that Amanda would pay her respects but after that she would be moving on and doing what needed to be done.

It was dark when she finally made her way into the cemetery, she needed the cover of darkness for what she was about to do. Sara's grave was not hard to find, she was only buried this morning. Digging her up would be a breeze, they most likely paid for the cheapest coffin they could get their hands on. She would not need a crowbar to pry it open. Amanda paused to stare at the name carved on the generic floral headstone they had chosen for her. Sara would have hated it if she could see it. Maybe she could, who knew.

Amanda popped the trunk of the car and set to her work, stacking the long boards so their ends crisscrossed. Then she laid a few on the very top, creating a small platform, just long enough to hold a body. She built it in the middle of the roadway of the cemetery. It was a definite message and she knew that when the groundskeeper came to attend the site in the morning, he would report it to the authorities. With the celebrity names involved in this case, it would take no time at all for them to call the Wolf Pack and inform them of what had just happened. That was fine with her, she was going to deliver one message personally. She would give it straight to the person responsible for her death.

With the funeral pyre set, Amanda began to claw her way down into the hole, ripping the flimsy coffin door from its hinges and tossing it aside. They never even bothered to have her head sewn back on. Amanda's blood began to boil but what she did not notice was the darkness around her thickened with her anger.

Heading back to the car, she grabbed out the sheet she had purchased and laid it out on the ground next to the open coffin. Amanda gently lifted the stiff, lifeless body out and laid her carefully on the sheet, setting her head just above her. She then wrapped her entire body with the sheet and then set her atop the pyre. With a soft sigh, she doused Sara in gasoline and then lit a matchbook, tossing it on top her. Fire spread across her and down the pyre, quickly consuming the wooden platform and Sara's lifeless body.

Amanda could feel it now, the grief, it hit her suddenly, crippling her as she stood watching her best friend burn. Crimson coated her cheeks in long red streaks. It was inarguably her fault, she had allowed this to happen. The Shadowed One was right. The guilt of her death was nearly as overpowering as grief. What was she supposed to do after this was all over? She was alone, Sara was the last bit of humanity she had left in this world. As she stared into the flames, she began to speak, telling Sara (if she could hear her) what it was like without her.

"I watched the sunrise without you today. It was nothing, it felt cold to me. Depressing even. I don't sleep anymore, knowing that I failed you. Death was right, I drug you into this. I wish we could have met in a different life. Not here. Not in Collins. I'm not sure how I am supposed to do this without you. What's the point in continuing? I am just going to fail again."

"I don't blame you for my death…" A voice said from beside the flickering flames.

Amanda stepped back, ready to defend herself, almost certain that this was a trick of the Wolf Pack. A figure slowly moved toward her, coming into view. It was Sara. She was dressed in a white gown, her hair lay down her back in long waves and a thin line of blood ran the circumference of her neck.

"Sara?"

The apparition nodded.

"Amanda I chose to go with you. I chose to rescue you too. It's not your fault, do not let those bastards convince you otherwise," Sara paused, dropping her eyes, her body language becoming increasingly nervous.

"Amanda listen, I only have a few moments before he realizes I am here. I'm trapped here until he is dead. We all are. It's not enough to torture us in life. He holds sway over the world of the dead. You have to kill them. They are hurting more people now. You have to end this."

No sooner had the last word left her lips before Amanda recognized another figure behind her. It was the Shadowed One, Death himself come to claim her.

"What the hell are you doing here?" His voice boomed.

He wrapped his arm around her waist and proceeded to drag her back through whatever doorway he had come.

"Let go of me!"

"I told you to stay put! Come here!"

Even in the afterlife, Sara continued to fight him every step of the way. They were beginning to fade.

"Let the hell go of her!"

Amanda moved toward them as if she could rescue Sara for one last time. The shadows around her moved with her and for a moment she could swear that Death paused.

"Sara!" She screamed as she attempted to grab her ghostly hand.

There was nothing but cold and then they were both gone. Amanda stood there staring into the nothingness in front of her. No, no, she did not have time to be standing around crying over Sara's death. Besides, the woman had come back in spirit form, risked her own hell to tell Amanda that even after death there was no peace. She now understood that the Shadowed One was more powerful that originally anticipated.

With anger and determination, she headed back to the open trunk of the car and pulled out the length of chain she procured from the hardware store. Amanda wrapped it around the headstone with the name Ashley King scrawled on its surface. If they wanted to dare bury her friend and dare to put a fake name on the headstone, then she was determined to make it cost them a little more than money. Heading back to the rear of the Chevelle, she hooked the other end of the chain to the bumper and climbed inside. Amanda smirked slightly as she started the car, glancing in the rear-view mirror at the stone one last time before she hit the clutch and tapped the stick shift into second gear. Her foot pressed the pedal down hard and the car jerked forward, yanking the headstone out of the ground.

She stopped the car, climbed out and loaded it into the trunk before taking off out of the cemetery, squealing her tires as she pulled onto the main road. Amanda was almost laughing hysterically as she headed toward her destination. She disregarded caution, speeding through the downtown area, passing police officers and fire stations. They had no photo of her, no identification even on file. None of the Wolf Pack knew her real name, nor did they care to know. This would be the one time that would work against them.

Amanda stopped in front of the very same place that was responsible for the death of her best friend. Getting out, she popped the trunk of the car and grabbed the headstone. She already knew he would be out, cruising the town for new property. That meant, she had all the time she needed. There was enough gas left in the can, that if she wanted to, she could burn his place to the ground. Using the shadows to her advantage, she made her way into the Shadowed One's apartment, where she promptly dropped the stone in the middle of his living room. The floor cracked from the impact and the weight. It set awkwardly in the wooden hold it had created. She could not wait for him to come home and find that.

Again, she considered taking advantage of the fact they were all out for the night and would be for a while. She could fill some bottles and have her own Devil's Night, head to each one of their houses. They needed to know she was not done with them and that their little stunt, would not be enough to bring her down. For now, she would settle with the headstone in the living room. They would come to learn how not done she was with them.

Amanda headed upstairs, back to the scene of the crime and began to look around. There, on the floor, in the spot where Sara's head once lay, there was a bleach spot. It glared at her, mocked her. She knelt down and touched the spot, running her fingertips over the shaggy surface, now stiffened from the chemicals they had used to clean up the blood.

She was so enamored with the spot on the carpet that she did not feel the shift in the air around her or hear the creak of the floorboards behind her.

"She's nae here. You're nae gonnae fin' 'er" A thick, solemn Scottish brogue broke the silence.

In one flawless movement, Amanda stood, turned and pressed the tip of her katana to the throat of the man now standing in front of her. Her eyes were crimson with anger and grief. He had interrupted her moment of peaceful melancholy and for that he would pay.

"Who the hell are you and what are you doing here?"

A tendril of blood began to run down the flesh of his neck, Amanda did not let up on the pressure of her blade.

"Ah could ask ye th' same thing. 'En again, Ah kno' who ye are. Ah kno' a lot about ye Amanda." He said, his hands raised in the air now in surrender.

"I'll ask again and this time, if you don't answer me, I'm going to leave you here . . .in pieces." She growled, she had no patience for this.

"Easy lass. Ah ain't here tae hurt ye. Besides, if Ah was you'd already be dead.

Sara had never described the man to her, but Amanda felt something as she looked over his appearance, something she had not experienced in a long while. She was so busy being disgusted with the Wolf Pack and their perverted, masochistic ways that she forgot what it was to feel this way. He was taller than she anticipated, she would guess around six feet with powerful broad shoulders. They stretched the long leather coat he was wearing, threatening to bust the seems with the wrong movement of his arm. His salt and pepper hair (once a solid black) was slicked flawlessly behind his head, perfectly complimenting the similarly colored goatee he wore. The eyes she could feel staring at her were hidden behind a pair of dark sunglasses and his upraised hands cloaked in tight black leather gloves. Amanda gave him a once over as she continued to press the blade in to his throat, black, hard soled boots tucked under even darker leather pants. A black t-shirt hung loosely about his torso, giving no indication of what amount of physical power he might hold. The longer Amanda continued to stand here and look at him, the more she noticed a heat rising in her that she thought had died a long time ago.

Her crimson pools came back to rest on his smirking face. What was he smiling about? She did not like it, it was making her uncomfortable and more nervous.

"What are you smiling about?" She asked.

"Ye see somethin' ye like Darlin'?" He asked, licking the corner of his mouth.

His brogue was thicker this time and it made a warmth spread through her chest. Amanda knew what that feeling was, all too well. She needed to stifle it and fast.

"Shut up," She blurted out, her confidence shaken. "Take off your sunglasses. Let me see your eyes."

The smirk on his lips widened as he reached with his right hand and using two fingers pulled his glasses off by the end piece. Telling him to remove them was worse than having him keep them on. There was a twinkle in his eyes and a heat in his gaze that made her shift slightly. She felt butterflies flutter in her stomach, something she never expected to happen. His eyes were hazel with prominent lines of green that twinkled mischievously in the dim light.

"Better lass?" He asked sheepishly.

He knew exactly what he was doing. Amanda cleared her throat and pressed the sword a little firmer against his neck, attempting to remain calm. Moreover she was trying her best to keep control of the situation. Even he could feel the slack in the pressure of the blade.

"What's your name?"

Her voice cracked slightly. She barely caught it before the question was asked and she knew he heard it as well.

"Mah names finn. Now we're acquainted, would ye put doon th' god damn sword already?"

Amanda hesitated but eventually lowered the katana, placing it in its sheath. She sighed. What was she supposed to do with him? Sara had mentioned a man by the name of Finn. The man before her was not what she had expected.

"All right Finn," She stressed his name, coating it in irritation. "What do you want? Sara's dead and I have no use for you."

He stepped forward, moving quickly into her personal space and leaning down to talk to her.

"Oh Ah hink ye do. Ye cannae tak' them on alone, nae yit. I'm nae gonna interfere wi' yer wee plans. Ah have me ain reasons fur wantin' them dead. I'll just make sure ye don't get killed."

Amanda could feel heat coming off his body, a warmth she knew should not be there but it was and it tingled across her skin. She needed to break this moment.

"How dare you! Where the hell were you for Sara! She died right here," She screamed, pointing at the bleach stain in the carpet. "she was raped and killed here! Where the hell were you then?!"

Before she had the chance to move, she was pinned against a wall with a leather gloved hand wrapped around her throat.

"Ye listen tae me ye wee tart.," Finn said, his breath wafting her hair with every word, he was growling as he spoke.

The weight and strength of his body pressing against her hard as his eyes seemed to stare right through her.

"I expected ye, 'er charge, tae dae yer damn job an' protect 'er. That's wa Ah did nae come. It was up tae ye. Ye turned 'er, it's yer job nae min' tae ensure 'er safety. But ye couldn't dae 'at! So, what in heel makes ye hink ye can kill them aw by yer lonesome?!"

Then he let go of her and she dropped two feet to the floor, her legs collapsing under her. He was right, she knew he was right and it crushed her to admit it. Amanda sat there, staring off at nothing as tears began to fill her eyes.

"I . . .I didn't want this. I didn't want any of this. You're right, it was my job to take care of her and I failed her. I should have never found her again. I should have left her with you. I should have done more to protect her. The Shadowed One was right, I killed her-"

Finn growled, hauling her up by her shoulders.

"Get tae yer feet! Ah cannae hae ye loch thes, yoo're nae good tae me broken an' blamin' yerself fur 'er death. Ye waur a bampot an' glaikit walkin' intae his apartment loch 'at. Ye hear me?" He said, shaking her.

"I killed her. Sara's dead and it's my fault."

That was the final straw, the dam broke open and tears flowed forward. Amanda felt every bit of sadness she had been holding back, coming surging through.

"I killed her-"

"Stop it! Shut it! she is dead, ye need tae deal wi' 'at. Ah need ye tae accept it."

Then he did something that Amanda never expected, he wrapped his arms around her and pulled her into his chest. Without thinking, she clung to him, holding on in desperation as she sobbed heavily. Her fingers dug into the fabric of his coat as if she would sink into the floor and be lost forever if she did not hold on tight.

"Aam sorry lass. 'at arsehole, he wasn't right. He's ne'er right. Ye understand? Ah needed ye tae deal wi' 'er death an' tae stop thinkin' you're in control ay everythin' that's happened tae 'er. 'At ye could hae done anythin' different. It's nae yer fault! Dae ye hear me? It's nae yer fault."

As she cried and listened to the softer sound of his voice, she realized he was right and she understood what he had been trying to do. She could not rightly take them on with the thought of Sara's death still dominating her mind. If she was going to succeed in this endeavor, they both needed her to have a clear head. Perhaps he was as good a man as Sara had said.

"I failed her Finn." She said before another torrent of sobs racked her body.

"Come 'en lass," He replied, holding and rocking her. "let's get ay haur. Thes is nae where ye need tae be right now. Ye need tae feed an' get yer strength back. We'll take care ay them. Ah promise ye, they will nae get away wi' what they've done." His voice had softened.

How far had she fallen without realizing it? She wondered to herself. Here she was, standing in the room of the Shadowed One, on the very spot where he had decapitated her best friend, sobbing into the arms of a man she did not know. A man, who she would not admit to herself, could stir in her emotions and sensations she had thought were dead. The idea of . . .a relationship . . .a connection to anyone other than her charge . . .it had never crossed her mind.

Amanda was careful to keep these thoughts locked away in the deepest parts of her mind. The last thing she needed was to get attached to someone, it would give them another way to hurt her. She needed to keep a steel wall up around her heart and not allow him inside. If the Wolf Pack had any inclination of her caring about someone, they would kill him. She could not have that, she could not do that again. Besides, the last man she let in, he nearly killed her and he was not one of the undead.

Although she pushed the thoughts away, her body language, her energy and her aura gave her away. He could see the signs and unbeknownst to her, he planned to act on them, when the time was right. She did not have to worry about his safety, he had more strength than she knew. Having a connection with another being would not make her weaker, it would give her more than she could possibly understand. Then again, he knew more about her than she did about herself.

With Amanda still encompassed in the safety of his arms, he moved them outside, laying her in the back seat and taking the drivers seat. She curled up, leaning her head on one of the narrow windowsills. Finn, headed out of Los Angeles, taking her somewhere more secluded where he knew they could never reach her and with him around, they would not dare.

Chapter 37

It was darker than Amanda had ever remember the night being. Every minute ticked by as an hour. Finn sat across from the bed, in a hard back chair. He sat watching her, sorrow in his eyes. Silver strands of hair hung down in his face, the ashtray on the floor next to him was over flowing with cigarette butts. There was nothing he could do to take away her pain. He understood what she was feeling more than she knew.

Amanda sat with her back to the wall, tears flowing down her cheeks as she stared out the window. The red flashing of the vacancy light outside, casting her face in a translucent pink. She saw nothing, her mind was locked somewhere else, dealing with the memories that continued to haunt her. Finn had tried several times to get her to eat, all of them a failed attempt. She brushed away every cup and blood bag he handed to her. They surrounded her, a deathly confetti of forgotten sustenance.

As gruff as he had been with her, she sensed a gentleness in him that she never knew in life. Why did he care what happened to her? Why was he bothering to waste his time on her? What did he want? The questions coming forward told her two things, one, she was beginning to find her strength and two, she was pulling herself out of her grief induced coma. Amanda glanced his way, her iris's beginning to fade back to their more human color. She watched the muscles in his shoulder shift just under his black t-shirt. He had noticed and she saw something in his eyes that made her stomach tighten, hope. The concept, the word, made her uncomfortable. For her, it only came with death and disappointment.

"Come 'en lass," His voice gently caressed her ears. "ye have tae eat somethin'. Yer wounds will ne'er heal if ye dinnae feed."

Amanda's shoulders began to shake as she spoke through tears.

"What's the point Finn? Why should I bother? I cannot beat them anyhow. I'm not strong enough. You should just leave me. Why do you care what happens to me?"

Finn only sighed.

"Don't you get it! I don't have the strength to keep doing this anymore!"

"Aye ye dae.. Ye need tae deal wi' it lass…Sara is gone." He said firmly.

"And then what? Everything magically gets better!? No, it doesn't change a damn thing! She's dead. If I stop to deal with it, if I break down here, I will never pick myself back up!"

She was shrieking at him and in her fury, she grabbed the lamp on the table beside her, flinging it at his head. It was as if he already knew she was going to do that because he only slightly moved his head out of the way. The lamp shattered against the wall behind him. When she picked up a bag of blood and tossed it at him, she missed and it exploded on the wall beside him. Droplets of blood sprayed onto the side of his face. Finn stood up so quick, he knocked the chair backward and grabbing her by her shoulders, he lifted her off the bed. Amanda was unsure if he was pissed about her throwing things or if he was tired of hearing her yell, whatever it was, his hands were iron and his dug into her flesh.

"Aye ye will! That's why aam here! Do ye nae get it?! Aam nae gonnae let ye stay here!" He growled, before dropping her back on the mattress.

"Even if I don't end up breaking down permanently…I couldn't protect Sara, what makes you think I can take down these demons?" She mumbled.

By this point, he had stood the chair on its legs and was sitting by the window again. Finn dropped his head, his shoulders slumped and he sighed. Then he raised his eyes to meet hers and stood from the chair. His weight made the bed (she was sitting on) shift slightly. He was close, closer than he had been when pinning her against the wall. With every word, his soft brogue caressed her ears, tingling her nerves.

"Ye have more strength than ye kno'. Ye can beat them, trust me when Ah tell ye, ye have power ye haven't begin tae use."

"You didn't answer my question, why do you care?" She demanded.

He turned from her, licked his lips and when he turned back, he pressed his lips to hers, pushing her back on the bed. Amanda gasped at the sudden intrusion and he slid his tongue into her mouth, running it softly across hers. She could barely catch her breath before he wrapped his arms around her waist, pulling her closer to him.

She lost all sense of time and space. Everything she had known in the last few months was suddenly gone. All pain, the tears, her screams and Sara, they had disappeared in a moments notice. What was he doing to her?

When he finally pulled away from her (maintaining the closeness he had before) she gasped, licking her lips. His kiss tasted like cigarettes, blood and whiskey. She rolled her tongue along the interior of her mouth, wanting to never stop tasting him. Amanda felt disoriented, confused, there was no way this was happening. She was damaged goods.

"What-"

"Ah needed tae shut ye up somehow." His response almost seemed cold.

"Son of a bitch." She replied..

Then without thinking, she brought her hand up to slap him but he was much faster than she, he caught her wrist in one hand and pinned her to the bed with the other. They were both panting as he pressed her into the mattress. She did not like this, she was feeling something for him. He was laying on top of her, between her legs, his face mere inches from her and she could feel her body responding.

"Get off me!" She growled.

"Try tae slap me again," His iris's were black now. He glared into her crimson pools. "Ah daur ye Amanda." He growled.

She could not stop the hitch in her breath from the look in his eyes and the feel of his body against hers. Amanda knew he felt it too because slowly a smirk formed at the corners of his mouth.

"Get! Off! Me!" She demanded, her nails extending.

"Nae!" He responded.

"Finn, you're going to get yourself hurt. I don't want to hurt you."

She was trying to reason with him now, while at the same time, trying to wiggle out from under him.

"Hurt me 'en." He pressed her body to the mattress a little harder.

Amanda's control was beginning to waver, her breathing was increasing as a warmth began to spread down between her thighs. She needed to do anything to get him off of her, to keep him from feeling it.

"Stop it! Finn stop it!" She yelled, her voice cracking.

There was something in her words, perhaps her desperation that caused him to let go of her wrists and pull away from her. An awkward moment passed between them and then she asked again (trying her best to ignore the sensations he invoked in her).

"Why do you care what happens to me Finn? You barely know me." Her voice was soft, she wanted to know.

Finn raked his hand through his hair, pushing his sunglasses back on his face. With a sigh, he finally answered her.

"Ye remin' me of mah wife."

That was all he said before shoving a lukewarm blood bag at her and telling her to eat. She could hear his hard soled boots on wooden floor as he left the room, heading, where, she did not know. Amanda continued to stare at the bag in her hand, her stomach throbbing with hunger pains. She knew he was right, she had to get up and keep going or Sara died for nothing.

After nearly two days of staring off into oblivion, she allowed her hunger to come and she fed as if she had never eaten before. Amanda drained one bag of blood after another, blood dribbled down her chin, dripping onto her filthy clothes.

She tossed the last empty plastic container on the floor in front of her and pushed herself off the bed. At first her legs protested and she swayed against the sudden kinetic movement. Looking around, she noticed her bag sitting propped in one corner of the room. There would still be some clean underwear and other clothing inside. Amanda grabbed it and headed to the small bathroom, dropping her bloody clothes onto the white tile below. The towels would be stained red when she was finished.

Something inside her, a thing she believed she had killed, prompted her to turn her naked form toward the mirror and look at the scars covering her body. The new and the old. She was deformed by them, the memory of the Wolf Pack and Collins forever embedded in her skin.. Even if she killed them, there would be no moving on. She had only one option when this was all said an done.

"Nae ye don't lass." Finn's voice startled her and she scrambled to cover her naked flesh.

"What the hell do you think you're doing?" She yelled, angry.

"Stop thinkin' loch 'at. Ye are nae scarred fur life. At least nae in th' way ye hink. Don't lit them control yer decisions." His brogue was soft.

"What the hell would you know Finn? You seem to think you know everything!" She yelled, suddenly forgetting her nudity.

She seemed to forget his lightning reflexes, he grabbed her by her wrist and yanked her forward, pulling her face close to his as he ran his pointed finger down one of his deep scars.

"Thes is whit happens when ye challenge th' master an' lose. When you're arrogant an' irrational. When ye dinnae watch yer are. He takes a silver chib an' carves deep intae yer flesh, so deep 'at ye have tae tak' a needle an' sew th' flesh yerself. that's after he has had his turn at rapin' yer wife!"

Amanda tried to pull back away from him, to get free from his grip. For the first time in a long time, she was afraid. The anger she had been using as fuel all this time was gone in a matter of minutes. She swallowed hard, suddenly feeling as if she was back in the Wolf's den and he was James.

"Please don't." She squeaked, a single tear rolling down her face.

"These," He said, brushing his coarse fingers gingerly across the scars on her stomach. "dinnae exist. Ah dinnae see them," He was looking down at her bare skin as he touched her. His eyes shot back up quickly to meet hers. "Dae ye understand?"

He let go of her and without thinking, she brought her right hand up, her claws slicing through the flesh on his already scarred face. How dare he look at her nudity so boldly! How dare he touch her without invite!

"Don't touch me!"

Amanda turned from him but he was not having any of that. He had his arm wrapped around her waist before she could move an inch away from him. She had enough, he was not going to treat her this way. She slammed her elbow into his rib-cage, stomped on his right foot before wrapping her left hand behind his head and yanking him over her shoulder. He landed on the floor below her with a thud but pulled her down with him.

There she was, naked on top of him with no way to protect herself. He did not let up this time when he pulled her into a deep kiss. She could no longer resist, she ripped through the fabric of his shirt, digging her fingers into the hard flesh of his chest as she deepened the kiss. What was she doing, she barely knew this man? But it felt as if she had known him forever.

Finn stood with her in his arms and she wrapped her legs around his waist. They stumbled into the bedroom, kicking empty blood bags out of their way as they went. Amanda fumbled for his belt, shoving his pants down over his hips to expose his erect, throbbing, manhood. It seemed as if an eternity had passed since she wanted this, since it meant something other than carnal pleasure.

She did not know him any more than she knew the Wolf Pack and yet she wanted him, she wanted him to devour her. His kiss was intoxicating and breath taking, she never wanted to come up for air.

A sigh left his lips as he laid her down on the bed and stripped off the rest of his clothes, his hand coming up to gently cup a scarred mound. Those hazel pools, scanned over her broken flesh and he leaned down, planting wet, hot kisses over every inch of her nudity. It was true, he did not seem to see the scars or the wounds she carried.

Amanda could not understand how this man had given her peace, joy and dare she think it, love again. She thought after James and after them, she could never see a man this way, she could never feel this way again. To want a man at all, to even let him touch her or make love to her. She winced as she felt his hot tongue on the more tender parts of her body. Her eyes rolled back in her head and her hands combed through his hair as he licked her into ecstasy. Amanda felt as if she had melted into him, her flesh became his and there was nothing but pleasure. What was he doing to her?

Finn slowly made his way back up her body and then she felt him, resting at her heated core. He seemed to be waiting for her to tell him it was all right. As if he knew where she carried her real scars.

A fear tingled in the back of her mind, was she healed from the endless assaults? Or would this bring back all pain and memory? Timidly, as if still a virgin, she nodded her head.

He was slow and gentle as he parted her folds. Her head fell back against the pillow and she felt him pause, so she wrapped her arms around his broad back to reassure him that she was not in any pain. With every move, he made her body tingle, her hands gripped the comforter and she arched her back wanting more of him. When he was certain he was not causing her any pain, he increased his speed, his breaths coming out in pants.

Amanda tossed her head back and forth, panting, her nails digging into one of his shoulders. She wrapped her legs around him, pulling him in deeper as she felt her orgasm coming ever closer. All breath seemed to leave her lungs, she was gasping for air, her whole body tightening and shuddering hard. For a moment she thought her head was going to explode. No man, should be so good.

Finn pulled her close, in a tight embrace as he too began to shudder. He leaned down and kissed her deep, pulling a wince and a moan from her lips. Amanda felt a growl pass through his chest and she shivered in response. Everything about him was driving her over the edge.

"Finn…oh god…Finn."

She just barely managed to say his name before her entire body tightened, she pulled him close and her climax washed over her in waves. Her eyes rolled closed and she gasped for air. Never in her life had something felt so good. Finn's fist tightened around one of the bed posts and he shivered hard. Amanda felt his heat spill into her core and he continued to thrust into her as he slowly came down from his own climax. Then he collapsed on top of her, laying his head in the crook of her neck. One arm wrapped around her torso as if he would lose her if he did not hold onto her.

They lay there curled in each others arms, their breath synchronized in heavy, satisfied pants. Neither one of them moved, holding each other tight as if the slightest movement and the other one might disappear.

Rays of sunlight slowly crawled across the worn motel carpet, making its way up the chaos of covers and then up their naked sleeping forms. When the bright yellow light of day hit Finn's eyes, he brought his hand up to shield them from the harshness. He too was immune to the burn that daylight caused but his eyes were human. Sometime in the night, Amanda had ended up on top of him, her head lay on his chest, her breathing slow and steady. He had not seen her sleep since they checked in and he knew sure she needed it.

Slowly, carefully, he lifted her small form off of him and lay her back down on the bed, pulling a sheet over her. For a moment, he stood and watched her sleep, she made no movement or sound. She was dead to the world. That meant he needed to get dressed and ensure no one dared to bother her. He knew the Wolf Pack (as she called them) would never come near her with him around. They were not that stupid. Even the Master had reason to fear him now, a reason that, in time, Amanda would come to understand. She would also learn why they were so bent on destroying her. It had nothing to do with her hunting them but it had everything to do with what happened last night. He hoped she might remember her true self and soon.

Amanda continued to pretend to sleep, she had awoken the moment he moved. The bed was emptier than it had been and the one thing helping her to sleep soundly was now standing behind her watching her. It was sweet that he tried so hard to keep from waking her up. Without the safety of his arms (which was an odd concept), her rest was disturbed. For whatever reason, Finn grounded her, he had steadied her and made the confusion come to order. Things suddenly made sense. He made sense.

She felt those warm, soft lips making their way down her neck and the shift of the bed as he put his hands on either side of her for support. Amanda purred in response, pulling her hands down beside her in preparation to get herself out of bed.

"Ah hink ye need tae get up." A gruff, Scottish brogue whispered low in her ear.

If he continued whispering in her ear, they would be going back to bed for several more hours. He needed to stop doing that. She stretched her arms above her head and slowly began to roll over. Her hair was a tangled mass, her body still covered in smears of dried blood and now other body fluids were drying between her thighs. For once, in all these horrific months of hunting, hiding and nightmares, she felt happy. She was happier now than she ever had been before. Amanda knew she had to prepare for the upcoming battle but now things were different. Now she had something to lose. Something she never thought she would find and it terrified her.

"What did Ah tell ye abit thinkin' 'at way lass?"

Finn said, as he was headed toward the bathroom. It was almost as if he was replying to her thoughts. Was he telepathic? She wondered.

"Yes Lass!" He said from the bathroom.

'*Asshole.*' She thought.

"Ah heard 'at." He said, opening the bathroom door and closing it again.

Amanda heard the sputter of the shower turning on, glancing down she looked at her nudity. She needed to get clean, when was the last time she had a real shower? When was the last time she was not covered in blood from the night before? As she looked at the scars, the patches of dried blood and the smears of dirt covering the majority of her body, she realized something. It was strange, impossible but she was looking right at it. The scars that decorated her legs, the thick jagged cuts and the gash in her thigh from the glass shard, they seemed to be less visible. Or perhaps they did not bother her so much. She knew they no longer bothered her. Was it only because they did not seem to bother Finn?

"Get yer arse in thes shower woman! Ye stink'!"

'*You son of bitch! How dare you-*'

'Dinnae make me come it there love.' Finn interrupted her thoughts, inserting one of his own into her mind.

"Get out of my damn head Finn!" She yelled at the door.

"'En stop thinkin' out loud.!" He replied, slightly sarcastic.

She tossed her legs over the edge of the bed and pranced (in all her nudity) across the room, heading into the steaming bathroom. Amanda paused at the shower curtain, she could just barely make out the blur of his silhouette as he rinsed shampoo from his hair. Making love to him the night before was one thing but seeing him in his full nudity was entirely different. It had been dark the night before so she never saw anything.

"Eep." Amanda yelped as she was yanked into the steaming shower.

"Ah said get yer arse in here." He growled.

What is he going to do? She wondered. With her wrist still in his hand, he turned her sideways and gave her a playful slap on her backside.

"Clean yerself up." He replied.

Then, he moved toward the rear of the shower and stepped out, wrapping a towel around his waist. Amanda was more than a little surprised that their shower encounter had not turned into something else.

"Ah thought about it love. I did." He said.

"Damn it Finn, knock that off!" She said.

Amanda was frustrated with his continued invasion of her thoughts. That iron nail she still had in her coat would stop that right now. With wet messy bangs, he poked his head back around the curtain, as she was soaping up.

"Won't work on me love." He said smirking.

"Grr. How did Sara put up with you?" She asked herself.
"Shut up!" She yelled before he could respond.

Through the bathroom door, she heard him chuckle. He was
one of the most maddening, irritating men she had ever dealt with
and she was madly attracted to him. For a few hours she felt (dare she
say it) normal, almost human.

The water rinsing off her body and swirling down the drain,
ran red. She washed weeks of blood, dirt, smoke and sex from her
flesh. Her hair was more vibrant now than it ever had been, she
combed chunks of flesh from her now shoulder length strands,
washing it too down the drain. Amanda was a new woman, she felt
that way anyhow. Whether it was, last nights activity, or this
mornings shower, something had revitalized her.

As she stepped out of the shower and wrapped her towel
around herself, she glanced in the corner of the room. Where were
her clothes? Her under garments were there but the rest of her clothes
were gone. What the hell did he do with her clothes? She quickly
dressed before storming out of the bathroom.

"What the hell did you do with my clothes?" She demanded.

He was sitting in the hardback chair, tying his boots when she
came bursting into the room. Glancing up, he continued what he was
doing as if he had not heard her. Strands of silver hung about his eyes.

"Finn! Answer me!" She said, putting her hands on her hips.

She used to be able to maintain an angry outer shell, to
maintain a sense of authority and fear. Finn had taken all that away
from her. He was neither impressed nor intimidated, the look on his
face reflected his passive emotions. Which only infuriated her even
more.

With a smirk, he sat up straight and with one hand grabbed her bag, flinging it out the open window beside him.

"What the hell!" Amanda started toward him.

Finn stood, towering over her and she slowly backed away from him. He pointed at the black canvas bag sitting on the bed next to her katana before pulling on his leather jacket. This time, he wore a shorter one, with the same black clothes she had originally met him in. How many pairs of black did he own?

She turned from him and slowly headed for the bed. Nothing he was doing right now made any sense. The sudden switch in body language made her nervous. Amanda pulled the zipper back on the bag and inside she found an entirely new set of clothes. Behind her, she could feel him, leering over her shoulder, his breath hot on her bare neck.

"Your clothes, they stank ay blood. Any well trained vampire could smell you from a mile awa'. I found ye somethin' better suited."

His Scottish brogue was thicker this time, she was beginning to understand that meant he was serious. They were about to embark on a journey in which she did not wish to travel.

Amanda pulled out a pair of black mid-calf leather combat boots with buckles on the back of them. There was a pair of black leather pants, a black long sleeve heavy shirt with a hood and even heavier lining on its interior. Finally she found a black leather bustier in the bottom of the bag, it buckled all the way up the front. Why in gods name did he pick this out for her?

"Th' shirt has a built in scarf..."

Finn grabbed the remote and flipped on the television, flipping through news stations. "in case ye did nae notice, yer 'lil arse is aw over th' news," He walked over and picked up the bustier and pants.

"This will be a lot easier tae clean aff than th' cotton shite ye have bin wearin'"

She had no idea why but she listened to him, everything he was telling her made sense. So, she squeezed into the tight leather pants, slipped on the snug black shirt, tightened the buckles on the bustier and laced up her boots tight. On the side of her outfit, she slid her katana into the heavy leather holder that had been sewn onto the bustier. She then pulled up her hood and tied the scarf across her face, draping it across the bridge of her nose. Amanda knew there was a reason, he had picked these clothes out. Now, she had a right to know why.

"Where are we going Finn?" Her tone was serious.

"Th' Telepath-" He started to say.

"No, hell no! I'm not going back there. Did you not hear me, I cannot do that. I cannot, I cannot. I already got Sara-"

She was babbling, her eyes wide with borderline madness. Her decision, iron clad, set in stone, she wound not go.

"Stop it! Amanda knock it aff! Ye dinnae have a choice! Ye..." He trailed off.

Finn was across the room before Amanda could even sense his next movement. He grabbed her by her bicep but she was not going to allow him to over power her again. Leaping into the air, she flipped her body backwards, catching the back of his head with her boot. He stumbled forward, giving her a few feet of room to move.

"You're not dragging me back through that realm!" She growled.

"Do you not get that the Shadowed One, Sara's murderer holds sway over the afterlife? He has her soul trapped. How am I supposed to contend with that kind of power?!" She said as they circled one another, her nails slowly extending.

"Nae, he doesn't hold sway. He is usin' stolen power 'at disnae belong tae him. He is meddlin' where he disnae belong. They have nae real power, it's aw parlur tricks an' min' games." His brogue was so thick, it was nearly impossible to understand him.

"You're not taking me anywhere near them!" She shrieked before leaping in his direction, her nails leaving deep lacerations in the side of his face.

"Th' hell aam not."

He growled back, resisting the urge to pin her to the bed again and exhaust some of her aggression. Finn grunted in pain as he felt her slice through his flesh. That was fine, if she wanted to fight, if she thought she could take him on, he would give her what she wanted. As her feet just barely touched the floor from her leap at him, he caught her by her throat and (knowing it would not kill her) tossed her out one of the windows.

There was the sound of shattering glass and a yelp from her lips as she fell through the small pane. Finn moved over, looking out the window, hands resting on either side of its frame. She caught him off guard, her boots slammed into the bridge of his nose as she came leaping back into the room.

"You son of a bitch! Did you just throw me out a window?" She looked at him shocked.

"An' what did ye dae tae me?" He asked pointing at the healing gash on his face.

"You're gonna pay for that Finn." She said as she balled up her fists.

He responded, planting his feet firm, and turning his body sideways, one arm in front for defense. With his defending arm, he beckoned to her.

"Come get me then lass." He was unnervingly calm.

Amanda charged across the room, her right hand meant to collide with his face but he was faster than she and more trained. He brought her arm down and around behind her back, wrapping his left leg around hers and bringing her to the ground hard. Her face slammed into the dirty carpet they were standing on and he pressed all his body weight against her.

"Get off me!"

She growled, fighting as hard as she could to get out from under him.

"Get me aff ay ye 'en. Come 'en now. Ah thought ye were gonnae kick mah arse."

"I'm not going there! I'm not fighting them anymore! Do you get it!" She was no longer screaming but demanding.

She could feel him nodding as he lay on top of her.

"That's why Ah need ye tae see somethin'. It might change yer perspective."

He said solemnly before yanking her up off the floor and shoving her hard through the silvery door that had formed sometime during their fight. Finn was not giving her a choice in the matter, for some reason he thought she was strong enough to handle them. She did not want to disappoint him but she was in no way as strong as he believed.

In his words, the last thing he said before shoving her into the Shadow realm, she could sense hesitation, even he did not want to go where they were headed. That gave her more reason to worry about stepping through that silvery doorway. Not much seemed to startle, surprise or rattle him. If he was unnerved, then she definitely did not want to go.

Blood Kings

Chapter 38

The feel and smell of wet mud was the first solid matter she noticed. Then the sounds of nature filled her ears and she looked around, having not been this close to woods in a while. Where were they? Where had he brought her? Amanda hesitated, feeling as if she had been lead straight into a trap. Had she made the mistake of trusting the wrong man?

Finn had already begun moving toward the edge of the woods, as if he knew the land. He never once looked around. Amanda gripped the handle of her sword. Although she knew he was faster and stronger than she could hope to be. She refused to go down without a fight. Suddenly, he paused and turned to look at her, his aviator glasses resting on the bridge of his nose, his head cocked to one side and one shoulder leaning in sync with the movement of his head.

"After all this time, ya still don't trust me lass?" He asked annoyed.

"I don't put anything past anyone Finn. I learned that lesson in the past and I paid for it." She replied, pointing to an old scar on her cheek.

He stepped closer, looking down at her over the rim of his glasses.

"I'm not James."

That was all he said before turning back around and heading toward a weedy clearing that was now coming into view. They had to hack at the overgrowth of thorny vines that lined the edge of the forest. Just over his shoulder Amanda could make out the roof of a cabin, it looked abandoned. After her stay in Collins, she knew better. The Wolf Pack preferred discarded buildings, no one bother to check in on them. How did he know about this?

"Ah found it when Ah was followin' Mark," He glanced over

his shoulder. "That's yer wee Telepath's real name love. It sits exactly five miles from where they are filmin' his tele show."

As they moved closer to the building, the smell of blood, decay, death and feces drifted out to greet her. Amanda feared what she might find locked inside.

"Ah will warn ye lass, what is inside is appallin' tae say th' least."

"What are we doing here Finn?" She finally asked.

"Ah, still speakin' to me are ya?" He replied, slightly irritated.

"Finn? What the hell are we doing here?" Amanda replied, pushing her sword from its sheath.

"Ah have tae shaw ye somethin' lass. Ye need to know why ye cannot give up." His tone was serious now.

The door of the cabin was secured with heavy bolt locks. Finn gave it a hard tug, ripping them from the thick logs that made up the outer wall. When the door opened, the smell that had been mild from the outside, overpowered their senses. They gagged, covering their noses with the back of their hands. Amanda did not want to go inside, she knew what that smell meant. She had come to know it in the factory back in Collins.

"I can't go in there." She said, shaking her head.

"Ye have tae lass." Finn replied, holding out his hand. "Come en'."

With a deep inhale, she grabbed his hand and stepped inside. The wood floor of the cabin was stained brown and red, with fresh and old blood. There were heavy animal cages sitting in a semi circle around the edge of the cabin and in each one, was a nude woman covered in the same filth. Some of their wounds were only a few hours old and others were a few weeks, the boys obviously had their favorites. Amanda could tell by the wounds on their bodies, which Wolf played with which woman. The floor around the cages was covered in fecal matter and the bottom of them were worse. In one of the cages, a small framed woman had curled herself in a ball and died some time ago. How could they leave the body there? Let her rot away? Could they not smell the stench? Or did they just not care? Somehow, she had forgotten what sort of cruelty they were capable of exhibiting.

In the center of the room, hanging from a hook in the ceiling was the Telepath's cat of nine tails and lining the walls were the Chameleon's knives. They had made themselves at home here. The sight of their torture implements was more than enough to cause Amanda's hands to shake. There was a metal fire pit with iron pokers on the far side of the room. A metal table with chains around each one of its legs sat pushed up against a bare wall. There was evidence of its use, blood smeared on the top and legs, also barely visible sexual fluids drying in various areas.

"Ya see," Finn said gesturing at the room. "this is what they have bin daein' since ye have bin moornin' Sara's death. They know it has crippled ye. They will keep daein' thes if ye dinnae fight them lass."

Amanda could only stand there and stare at the whimpering figures in the cages before her. There was no way to get them out of here. She knew that half of them, even if they did survive, would never be able to function in normal society. The most humane thing she could do, would be to put a bullet in their heads and burn the cabin to the ground. She turned and looked at Finn.

"Get me a gun." Was her only response.

He knew what she was about to do, what she had to do. His image faded into the ever present shadows around him and he reappeared in a matter of minutes. In his right hand, he was holding a Sig .357. There were enough bullets in it, for each one of the women.

Amanda moved over to the first one and pointing the barrel at the woman's skull, pulled the trigger. The concussive blast made her ears ring, the others still alive began to scream but she could not hear anything over the sound of the gun. Blood, skull fragments and brain matter now coated the feces covered floor. One after another, she went and put them out of their misery.

When she was finished, she tossed the empty gun aside and looked at Finn. Her eyes were red with the start of tears, which she had no time to deal with. He handed her a one gallon container of gas and she began dousing the interior of the cabin. Its toxic fumes making her undead lungs burn and her already teary eyes, water even more. With the cabin prepared, they stepped just outside the door.

Amanda fished her Zippo from her pocket and lit it, tossing it into a puddle of gas on the floor. Flames quickly crawled across the floor and up the walls. She held up her hand to shield herself from the intense heat, stepping back away from the building to watch the fire consume it.

She had to do some dark deeds in her time fighting the Wolf Pack but this she was sure, was the worst. At the same time, it was the most humane thing she had done in all the while. Perhaps, if she had done the same thing for Sara, she could have saved her the hell she endured.

"Nae lass." Finn said, replying to her thoughts.

"I could have saved her from a worse fate." Amanda said softly.

"Aye...but ye needed er'." He said.

Amanda looked at him puzzled.

"Ye will understand in time." He replied.

Amanda pulled down her scarf, squinting as she stared into the flames, remembering the cries and screams of the other women she could not save. Listening to their unanswered prayers through the thick concrete and them not realizing that someone heard them. She did not mean for any of this to happen and at that thought, the tears began to flow down her cheeks. A mixture of blood and ash coated her pale skin. Amanda closed her eyes and turned her head as the wind shifted the smoke in her direction. Her mind filled with the images of them clawing at the walls, screaming in pain, and begging for mercy that would never come. All the time wondering why no one was coming for them. Being convinced that no one cared what happened and their families had forgotten them. The lies the Wolf Pack must have told them. Finn wrapped his arm around her shoulders, trying to turn her from the scene.

"Come en' lass. This isn't gonna do ye any good." His voice was soft.

Amanda jerked away from him with fury in her eyes. How dare he tell her what will be good for her. He brought her here.

"Are you kidding me!? Won't do me any good! I killed innocent women, I am burning another pile of bodies! Won't do me any good?! The Wolf Pack is not doing me good! That's the only thing hurting me! How dare you tell me it won't do me any good! How fucking dare you perceive to tell me anything!" She screamed.

Finn stepped closer, bringing his face two inches from her. Every word he spoke was a guttural growl, so thick was his Scottish brogue that she could barely understand him.

"Aye Ah brought ye haur! Aye Ah am tellin' ye 'at standin' haur cryin' about it ain't daein' ye any good! Ah have been fightin' fur ye lassies fur months. Ah brought Sara back after she killed herself! Ah have fought ye tae save ye from yerself. Ah am daein' aw thes fur ye! Ye wanna spend the rest ay yer life crayon' ower Sara's death! 'En fine lass! Ah wulnae waste anymair time on yer arse," He then pointed at the flaming cabin. "Just kno, 'At, wulnae be th' last time they do 'at 'en. Soe ye decide. Thinkin like ye ur, will get ye killed."

Amanda stood there, stunned, fury slowly fading from her eyes. He had defused her rampage in a matter of a few words. She was mainly awestruck at the fact Sara tried to kill herself. Why? She thought. Finn combed his fingers through his hair, scratching his head and turning to look at her again.

"She couldn't deal wi' ye leavin' 'er. She couldn't deal wi' Collins. She said she was still hearin' th' voices of th' dead ones. 'At shadowy snake was whisperin' tae 'er in th' dark. In 'er dreams, he woulds tell 'er it was 'er fault." He replied with a sigh.

She had grown quite used to him responding to her thoughts.

"No...no," Amanda shook her head. "She never told me. It was lies, he was telling her lies. She...oh god. He never did leave her alone. I thought I was protecting her by leaving. Finn she was my best friend. I loved her like a sister."

"Ah kno lass. Did ye tell 'er 'at?" He asked, resting his hands on his hips.

"I never had the chance to...he killed her." She closed her eyes, more tears flowing forward

Finn sighed, wrapping his arms around her and pulling her close.

"Come en lass. Ah need ye angry. Ye have got tae fin' yer strength." He said, brushing a tear from her cheek.

She sniffled and wiped her face, pulling her scarf back over her nose. Swallowing down her sadness, she nodded for him to go on. They stepped into the woods again and then through one of the shimmering doorways. In a matter of minutes, they were outside a Marriott hotel where hundreds of costumed patrons were coming and going. There were people wearing orange shirts at every entrance, ensuring that only ticket holders came in the door.

"What are we doing here Finn?" Amanda asked, confused.

"Follow me lass." He said, heading for one of the doors.

The pair walked by security without once being questioned. Amanda could only assume he had done exactly what she would have, influencing the man at the door so he never even saw them. Finn turned down a hallway, heading to one of the large ballrooms, stepping into the last one on the left.

"Look there lass." He said, pointing at one of the tables.

Her eyes moved to where he was pointing, and there she saw what he wanted her to see. The vinyl sign with his face, various movies and his current name, Nathan Reilly were the first things she noticed. Then, just below it, she caught him moving about, taking photos and signing autographs with fans. He was smiling and laughing. The fans around him saw things differently than she did. For her, the world slowed down and she watched his smile form and disappear, listened the the sound of his laughter over the roar of the crowd.

Her eyes slowly started to change. She was having trouble controlling her beast. Amanda's right hand slid onto the handle of her katana and she felt Finn's hand on her forearm.

"Don't lass." He cautioned, looking at her sideways. "We are nae haur fur 'at. Ah want ye tae watch th' fans" He said, looking around.

She let go of the sword and began to scan over the crowd of women, seated in front of his table, waiting for their turn. The line that went all the way out the door and around the side of the building. Their obsessive nature, the sickness that was the Telepath, spreading like wildfire and all the while, none of them realizing anything was wrong.

"This will get worse, unless ye dae somethin' about it. He's amassed himself a nice 'lil followin'. Aw while ye have been sittin' on yer arse." Finn said.

"Sitting on my ass? I'm sorry, did you miss something. My best friend is dead." She replied with disgust.

"Ya' Ah know. An one ay th' wankers responsible fur it, is sittin' reit thaur. Instead ay ye gettin' it there an' killin' th' slimy bastards. you're sittin' in mah hotel room cryin' yer eyes out. Doubtin yerself. So, sittin' on yer arse is appropriate." He replied, cooly.

Was he trying to make her mad? He was doing a good job if that was his intended goal.

"Fuck you Finn." She said.

"We already done that lass." He whispered to her with a smirk.

Amanda shot him a sideways glance before shaking her head.

"Come 'en. Ah got one more fur ye." He said, tapping her shoulder.

They turned away from the Telepath (Amanda fighting the urge to kill him now) and headed through the Shadow realm. This time he gave her no warning as to what she was about to see. Perhaps, he did that on purpose. She knew he had a point to everything, but what?

The Shadow realm enveloped them in its cold touch, it felt cooler than she ever remembered it being. She glanced at Finn to see if he was feeling it as well. His body language told her nothing. As they neared their exit, he turned to her, pulling his sunglasses off his face.

"Remember lass, we are haur tae observe only…." He started, pointing his finger at her.

"Why-" Amanda started to ask why.

"Observe only." He stressed the words.

They were in California now, on Sunset Blvd. Finn had brought them to a club called Bootsy Bellows. It's neon red sign glared against the darker complexion of the building to which it was attached. A line of hopefuls ran more than halfway down the block, although they knew they were not getting inside. Amanda spotted a large black bouncer at the door, he was in charge of admittance.

"What are we doing here?" She asked.

"Watch." He growled, silencing her.

Amanda recognized him, the moment she saw him climb out of a black Cadillac Escalade. He was dressed in a pair of blue jeans with an American flag bandanna hanging out of his back pocket, a black button down shirt and a gray scarf around his neck. His hair was longer than she remembered it being and it hung down around his shoulders.

A low growl crawled its way up from her chest and she instinctively reached for her sword, her left thumb pushing the hilt.

"Observe." Finn growled again.

The Shadowed One disappeared inside the club and they moved through the shadows, following him. Amanda was surprised that he had not detected the movement. Being so acquainted with the realm and the movement of the shadows around him. She thought he might sense a shift but he did not.

Somewhere above them the clubs speakers thumped with some pop stars latest song, its vibrations traveling through the crowd, hypnotizing them with the beat. Bodies gyrated, grinding against one another as their sexual energy climbed. Amanda could smell their arousal floating in the air just above their heads. Between the bodies, behind the social props, she watched the Shadowed One at work.

He flashed that handsome, tempting smile at the woman he was talking to and then whispered something in her ear. No one else would hear it or notice what he was doing. The music could not stop Amanda from hearing him. He was trying to convince her to go back to his hotel with him or at least leave with him. She shifted uncomfortably, she wanted to either go back to her hotel or kill him. The urge was stronger to kill him but their were too many witnesses.

His filthy hands brushed up the woman's thigh, slipping slightly beneath the short dress she was wearing. Those dark pools of his flickering intensely with hunger, which the poor unsuspecting woman mistook for sexual arousal. Amanda shook her head, watching him work his lies, the pretentious ass was charming and humorous. If everyone knew the truth about him, things would be different. When he finally stood and began to leave, Finn and Amanda glided just behind him.

"Go to the roof lass. Trust me." Finn ordered her.

Amanda did as she was told, leaping from the alley on the side of the nightclub and landing silently on its rooftop. Moving from one building to another as she followed them, a phantom gliding above them unseen.

The Shadowed One and the woman walked a little ways down the sidewalk from the club, guiding her into the nearest alley. He spoke softly, his fingers brushing through her hair gently as he lead her to her death. Amanda swallowed as she watched him work his game on the next innocent destined to die because of this monster. She clinched her fists as she fought her animal, the part of her that wanted so much to peel his flesh from his bones. How did Finn expect her to do this? She could not just sit back and watch this happen.

'Ye' have to love.'

Far above the Shadowed One and out of his sight, she began to pace the rooftop. In the last few days since Sara's death, she had not been able to overcome her grief of fear of them. Now, all of that seemed to suddenly be forgotten. What she did not see, was Finn glance up at her and a small smirk began to form.

The Shadowed One licked his lips, and grinned about something his meal had said to him. Then he turned from her momentarily and when he turned back, Amanda finally saw his full demon. There was no white left in his eyes, they had become dark pools of black and he had two sets of sharp canines, top and bottom. The blonde he had lead into the alley started to run, but he had her by her hair before she could move and was throwing her into the nearest dumpster.

"Where are you going sweetie? I'm just getting started. We're about to have lots of fun." He said to to the blonde.

She was clenching and unclenching her grip on the handle of her sword. The words he was using, the sound of his voice, his every movement was bringing back memories she had buried deep. He grabbed the woman throwing her to the ground and he began to rip at the skimpy clothing she was wearing. Most likely picked out with the intention of drawing attention but she had grabbed the worst sort. It was something Amanda's father had warned her about for years, little did he know, there were worse monsters in the world, than men. The woman began to scream for help but he was silenced her with a hit to the face.

From the alley below, she heard him chuckle.

"I'm going to enjoy this."

"Please don't..." The woman began to cry.

Amanda clenched her fist so tight, blood began to ooze between her fingertips. Was this what he had been up to every night since Sara's death? Is this what was happening because she was too busy mourning? He was hunting boldly and fearlessly because he had no one left to fear. She shook her head. He was going to beg her for death and she was not going to give it to him that easily.

"Please god help me." The woman begged.

"God…baby doll," He pulled her up by her throat. "I am god."

He squeezed the woman's throat enough to make her choke for air, then he shoved her against a dumpster so hard that it moved slightly, she cried out in pain. The charming movie star had faded away and the truth was revealed. Death did not even give her the courtesy of getting moist, unzipping his pants, he then shoved himself into her hard and thrust with all the strength in his powerful hips. His growls echoed through the alleyway but no one came to the woman's rescue.

'*Finn. I cannot sit by and watch this.*' Amanda thought.

'*Trust me lass. Just watch.*' He responded.

Amanda begrudgingly obeyed his orders, pacing all the while. Why was he forcing her to watch this? Why would he not let her attack? Was this what he got off on? What was the matter with him?

'*No, I get no enjoyment outta this.*' Finn's voice boomed in her head.

When the Shadowed One was close to climax and they both recognized the signs, he tossed his head back and sank his fangs deep into the front of her throat. There was the guttural sound of blood pouring into her lungs as he drank down her life force. He almost laughed as he was feeding on her and ripping away her last bit of innocence. As he tossed her lifeless body into the dumpster, he chuckled to himself and zipped his pants. He headed out of the alley to the vehicle waiting out front to pick him up.

Finn moved to the other side of the club, leaning against one of the walls in the alley as he waited for her to come down off the roof. Amanda leapt down beside him and he could tell she was angry, not just with the Shadowed One.

"What the hell Finn? You force me to watch that shit! What is that what does it for ya? He was right there. I could have-" Amanda said.

Finn had enough, he grabbed her by her throat and slammed her back against the wall he had just been leaning on. He pressed his body weight against her, pinning her, his free hand resting on the handle of her sword so she could not pull it on him.

"Listen!" He growled. ""Listen! Nae 'at doesn't dae it fur me lass! I get nae stauner from watching him rape some slapper! Ye should kno 'at by now! Ye needed tae see 'at! Are ye wi' me lass? Ah need ye bloodthirsty, ragin' pitied!'"

At first she said nothing, she wanted to break something on him, preferably his groin. However, she understood. He was right. If she killed the Shadowed One before he killed the woman, before she watched him hurt her like he hurt Sara, she would have gone right back to being depressed. To see him do it again, reminded her of Sara's death. She had been so focused on her actual passing that she forgot about the way she died. As the memories came back to her, she began to tremble with fury, her eyes fading to a deeper red than Finn had ever seen them be. Her upper lip twitched slightly and all the bones in her fists cracked as she clenched them.

"Atta girl! Ya' ready-" He started to ask.

"I'm going to kill them all. I want them to suffer more than any woman they tortured ever suffered." Amanda growled.

When she finally looked up into his eyes, he stepped back, letting go of her. How did she allow herself to doubt his intentions? By now, she should have known that he was not one of them. He had never belonged with them. A Wolf would not have brought Sara back from the dead and sat up with her. He would not have fought this hard to help Amanda find her spirit. To find her hate and her anger.

She straightened her back and sighed a heavy sigh. The huntress was back and she had her sights on the Wolf Pack. If they were smart, they should sense her presence and run. It was time to come out of hiding, to make herself known again. It was time to end their rule, a new vampire was in town. Even the idea of their Master did not phase her anymore. Amanda turned to look at Finn.

"When do we start?" Her voice was laced with power.

"Tonight…" He said with a smirk.

They headed down the alleyway, walking into another shadowy doorway. Amanda could still feel the darkness she had felt back at the cabin when she executed the women. It was now growing, taking over slowly and she was willing to let it. She no longer cared who or what she was after tomorrow, as long as they were dead. Then she would know she went through hell for a good reason and she had served her purpose.

Chapter 39

A thousand glimmering lights in a never ending sea of darkness. The sound of stone on metal rang through the night. Her blade reflected their dancing flames as she sharpened it into a deadly edge. The fragrant, pungent smell of some herb burning on charcoal, permeated the room as she sat in silent meditation. She had become comfortable here in the shadows. Slowly, she rose from her kneeling position, the blade resting flat across one palm, the handle across the other.

Amanda's movements were silent and her blade swift. Her fingers curled around the handle and the sword passed silently through the air. It cut the wicks from the candles. They hovered in the air around her, dancing before falling to the floor, casting the room in shadows.

In the night, in the stillness, she began to hear Finn's voice. Amanda stood in the center of the room, back straight, shoulders back, ready. Her posture was calm, defensive.

"I need ya, focused," A hand shoved her shoulder, she did not respond. "not vengeful."

His voice deepened as he stressed the word.

She closed her eyes, listening to the sound of his boots on the wooden floor around her. It was one of her triggers, it caused her stomach to tighten, and her body freeze up. That was the exact reason Finn was wearing black cowboy boots, to reprogram her mind and her response to them. Their dull rhythm against the floor, used to make her body flinch but over the last few hours, she began to see them as only boots.

"Anger, hate, darkness...it's where they can hurt ya. It's how they can corrupt ya. Anger makes ya impulsive, sloppy."

Amanda opened her eyes in time to see the room around her fade and become Collins (before Sara burned it to the ground). Finn's voice continued to ring in her ears.

"Feel that fear," He whispered, his breath hot on her neck.

She slowly began to walk down the transparent street, turning onto Lillie she headed for the house. The door creaked on its hinges as it swung open, revealing the dark interior of the house. Amanda headed upstairs, looking around at everything, the place she was meant to start over and call home. Turning left, she headed into the bedroom and walked over to the large bed, brushing her fingers across the soft sheets. She could see herself, a translucent figure, sleeping on her stomach, tossing and turning as the Wolf Pack stood around her.

A series of events (in the form of translucent figures) passed all around her in no particular order; the first time he violated her, her hiding in the closet while the Shadowed One stood there in the dark, watching her struggle to find her way. The memory of the Shadowed One looked up in her direction, actually looked at the real version of herself. Was this real or a memory? She wondered. Did they travel back in time? Could Finn control the flow of time? How was he looking at her if she was not really here? She would normally feel fear or at this point, anger. However, she felt nothing, she was empty. Amanda stepped forward, warning him it would be a poor choice to challenge her and he stepped back.

She turned away, moving down to the living room, watching their uncomfortable exchange there. The Shadowed One and herself, passed by as if fog. Amanda was sure if she reached out to touch them, her hand would pass right through their gaussian forms. Then to the basement, where she watched herself attempt to commit suicide, only for her half conscious body to be drug out of the house. Amanda now knew, she was the one who left the claw marks in the floor.

Heading out of the house, she moved toward the monolith of a factory. It was there she watched the tortures inflicted on her. She saw herself, locked away in the cell, bleeding and fighting to survive. The whip of the Telepath, splattered the walls with her blood as he brought it back and struck her flesh again. That would have made her flinch before but now, she felt nothing.

"Acknowledge it happened...see it...then let it go."

Finn had given her the go ahead to turn away but she was not finished. She wanted to see it to the end.

"There's more Finn." She said before heading outside.

Events began to overlap as time melded together. She watched herself and Sara fight them in the factory, the bodies being piled and burned. Her body was a blur against whatever this was, memories, time travel. It was Finn's work and she was along for the ride.

There, in the street, that was the thing she needed to see. The first time she fought back against what they were attempting to do. Shadowed One throwing her head first into the side of his truck. All before she became a vampire and began to hunt them the way they were hunting women. Amanda nodded silently to herself.

"Forget Collins. It's the one way they can scare ya. It doesn't exist." His brogue thickened.

The scene around her, the houses, the streets, the town of Collins faded away as if it was a reflection in a pond. Her body felt weightless, her motions fluid. What was Finn doing to her? She trusted his reasoning and his decisions but did not understand them.

There was suddenly the unmistakable feel of carpet beneath her boots, chalk white walls began to fade into view. She moved slowly down the hallway, her limbs felt as if she was moving through molasses. Her body was heavier here and Finn's voice sounded far away.

"Lass . . .yer bout to go through somethin' I cannot help ya with . . .I need ya to do this."

Amanda knew where she was and what she was about to see. The other version of herself stood staring in horror as Sara as the blade of her own sword sliced through her neck. She watched Sara's head fall to the ground, blood beginning to pour from her neck, coloring the white carpet crimson. She felt grief and sadness blanket her.

"Why are you showing me this Finn?" Amanda asked her voice cracking.

"Focus on the bastard that killed er'."

Finn appeared behind the nude Shadowed One, pacing behind him with his hands behind his back. The Shadowed One stood there, smirking, his body splattered with blood. Amanda clinched her fists, attempting to maintain her calm, trying to keep them from touching her inner peace.

"Be focused . . .determined . . .strong . . .but peaceful. They cannot touch ye there."

Amanda continued to stare at Sara's body with Finn whispering in her ear.

"Yer powerful Amanda," He whispered. "more powerful than the Master. Yer a Goddess love."

That last statement rang in her ears on repeat. She thought he was being figurative, attempting to build her back up, turn her into a better warrior. The more it repeated, the more she began to wonder if he was being literal. Finn stood in silence, letting her think over what he had just said.

After a few moments, he finally spoke, his voice no longer a whisper.

"How do ye feel lass?"

"Calm . . .Sara's death was not my fault. It happened . . .but I've made peace with it." She replied.

"That's me girlie." He said, placing his hand on her shoulder.

The apartment faded out the same way it had appeared.

Although this time, Amanda continued to glare into the face of Sara's killer. It was not a look of anger, but one of focus. She was determined now, nothing would stand in her way, nothing would stop her from achieving her goal.

White flakes drifted all around her, falling atop the cold blanket decorating the forest floor. Her steps made the slightest sound as they compacted the snow around her. Finn did not have to say a word, she knew where she was. She recognized the chill of winter, the smell of the pines, the silence, it was Wolf Creek.

Amanda turned to look behind her, seeing the cabin she once called home and wishing she never left.

"Ya must not regret what ya left behind . . .ya must learn to let go and move forward."

Finn's voice echoed through the trees, as if he had become the wind. She knew part of the reason, he had brought her here. Why she was forced to remember James and the things he had done.

She ascended the stairs, walking into the living room in time to see his fist slam into her jaw, breaking it. The former of Amanda drug herself across the floor, blood dribbling from her lips. He screamed before dragging her back to him, his boots hammering against her rib-cage as he continued to berate her. In the opposite corner of the room, she heard his words of hate, calling her derogatory names.

Amanda turned away from that brief memory to look at herself curled on the floor, her shaky hands dialing the phone. She watched him fighting against the cops as he was hauled from the house and placed in handcuffs. A paramedic helped her to her feet, laying her out on a gurney.

Her feet turned and she headed down the hallway toward her bathroom, to see herself sitting by the tub. A puddle of blood glared at her from the white porcelain tile. The woman she stood staring at, was not her anymore. That person was slicing deep into her wrists, wanting to make the pain go away. She remembered how she felt in that moment but she had changed, was changing, she could turn away with no sorrow in her heart now.

A sound from the living room, drew her attention and she

headed down the hall. There she was, the start of who she had become, sitting in her recliner loading a shotgun. Then she was standing, firing at James through the sliding glass door.

Amanda followed his body, moving quickly outside ahead of her phantom human counterpart. There, she saw what she had suspected and she understood. As he limped down the stairs, his form began to change. She did not have to see his full metamorphosis to know he was the Chameleon. The real James, might have been in Collins already or in jail. Where ever he was, the man she had known, the few weeks leading up to her shooting him, that had been the Chameleon. It explained his cruelty. The Wolf Pack, must have know she was stronger than the other women they had kidnapped. So, they worked early to weaken her and break her down.

She turned to look at the wall of towering trees behind the house. Something was drawing her into the woods. Amanda descended the wooden stairs, slowly heading deep into the pines she had never dared to explore in her mortal life. They were full of Wolves, the real ones. Hence where the town had gotten its name.

Its large paws were silent against the softly fallen powder. He moved closer to her without her ever realizing he was within inches of where she stood. From the cover of a brush, two ice blue pools watched her, studying every move. His breath fogged as he exhaled slowly, his panting having decreased to a crawl. Around him the remainder of the pack formed an invisible parameter.

Amanda could sense them as she entered the woods, despite their impressive camouflage. She was unafraid of this pack. They (although animals) had more sense, more reason and more kindness than the monsters she was now hunting. Uncorrupted by ego, greed and lust, they did not kill without reason.

She came to a small clearing and there she could feel several sets of eyes watching her every movement. Amanda dropped to her knees, sitting on her feet in the snow and placing her palms down on her thighs. There, she waited for them to come to her.

The woods fell silent, as if the trees knew what was coming. Finn's voice was the only sound she heard, it echoed through the woods as if he had become a corporeal, ominous presence.

"Tae kill a wolf . . .ye must learn tae understand them . . ."

Why? She wondered. Why was he suddenly being cryptic. The brash man she had come to know would not sugar coat anything. Until now, she was certain he had no tact. Now, he was acting as if he was her Sensei. Amanda knew he would never answer her. The wolves on the other hand, were more forward.

At first he only stood at the border of the clearing, staring at her intently. His coat a thick mane of gray and white, glistening with flakes of snow. He lowered his head, huffing into the snow. Then he glanced over his shoulder and moved closer to her. His face coming inches from hers.

Amanda slowly turned her hands over, allowing him to see the tender flesh of her palms. The large male sniffed her upturned hands, acknowledging her sign of submission. She cautiously reached up and stroked his fur. He responded, lowering his head and pressing his forehead against hers. They remained that way for a few moments and then simultaneously pulled away from one another.

She waited for him to move back to the edge of the clearing, before she finally stood. The wolf glanced over his shoulder once before disappearing into the brush. Amanda turned and as she was heading for the edge of the woods, she heard Finn's voice.

"Ye mist lea this behin' ," He said, stepping from behind a tree.

"Yer auld life . . .Yoo're deid tae them."

Amanda looked around, her eyes scanning the tops of the trees.

"Are we really here?" She asked, her voice echoing all around her.

"Nae lass, it's aw in yer mind." He responded dismissively, glancing away.

"But ye have tae lit go . . .It'll dae ye nae good."

She reached up, brushing her fingers across his face before

turning back toward her cabin. Amanda took a few steps toward it, looking one last time at the place she would always call home. Finn's footsteps fell behind her, she could feel his breath on her neck as he whispered in her ear.

"Troost me lass...it is better if ye lit go." Then he wrapped one arm around her waist.

"Close yer eyes."

With a sigh, she let her eyelids fall and the image of the cabin disappear from sight. Amanda felt light, as if she was floating, butterflies whirled around her belly and fluttered up through her chest. She felt the world around her shift and they were gone from the cold snow.

The ground beneath her was hard, the smell of extinguished candles still permeated the room and the air felt warmer. She rolled her eyes and then slowly opened them. Amanda blinked a few times to clear her vision. She was back in the house, standing in the exact spot where she had been before. Her mind swam, her head spun and her knees suddenly gave out.

"Amanda!"

Finn said, jumping up from the chair he was sitting in to catch her. She felt his strong forearm on the small of her back and then she was being lifted into the air.

"Ah got ye lass." He whispered, lowering her to the floor.

"Wha . . .what happened?" She mumbled.

"Memory recall can be exhaustin'. Yoo're just overwhelmed. Aam sorry lass. Ah shoold nae have done 'at." He said, placing his hand on her stomach.

"What are you doing Finn?" She asked.

"Ssh love. Ah got ye."

That was all he said before she felt electricity coursing through her body. Amanda gasped, sitting upright. Finn took his hand off her stomach, his other one resting on her back as she recovered from whatever he had done to her. She could only sit and stare at him.

"Easy lass, go slow." He coaxed.

"Who or what in the hell are you? What the hell did you do to me?" She asked, defensively.

"When yoo're ready I'll teel ye. Until 'en, just know, Aam nae here tae hurt ye. Aam here tae help ye." He said, lowering his gaze to hers.

She squinted as she looked into his eyes, staring for any sign of deceit. He was not lying to her, she was almost certain he had never lied to her. Still, she felt she had a right to know who or what he was if she was to fight next to him. In all their time together, he had never fed. She had not seen his eyes change, or his canines grow in length. Even the smell of him was different. It was not the sulfuric ting of her kind.

"Fine then. I need a break though." Amanda replied, standing up.

"Slow, go slow," He advised, standing with her, his arms nearby for support.

She felt suddenly claustrophobic, she needed some air and she desperately needed a cigarette. Finn seemed to understand because he was now holding her pack in his right hand, closest to the window.

"There's a fire escape 'at side." He said pointing to the window.

Amanda grabbed her pack of cigarettes out of his hand and

opening the unbroken window, climbed outside. She headed up to the roof, having to leap the last few feet because the fire escape did not go all the way to the top of the building. Once there, she found the highest point of the roof and sat down, lighting her cigarette.

The gray cloud cover above left the city with a dreary aura. It had rained nearly every day since she came to this town. She was beginning to grow sick of the rain. Amanda knew the day was not over with yet, they still had to plan their attack and find out where the Blood Kings would be tomorrow. Since her encounter with the wolf, real or not, she refused to call them the Wolf Pack, it was a name above them.

She never even heard his approach, she jumped when he finally spoke, causing her to nearly fall off the roof.

"Ye ready fur thes love." He asked, looking at her.

"Shit!" She said, grabbing the edge of the roof to keep from falling.

"Stop doing that to me."

"Sorry lass.

"Sae ye ready tae dae thes?" He asked again, running his fingers through his hair.

Amanda paused, taking a drag of her cigarette and exhaling the smoke. She dropped her head, rubbing her hands together and glancing up at him.

"Is the soldier ready to face the enemy? The victim, ready to face her attacker? The family ready to face their loved ones murderer?" She paused.

"No, Finn, I'm not ready to face the Blood Kings. They're all three of those things to me. No matter how you train, you can never be ready. But it doesn't matter . . .does it? My feelings aside, what I'm about to do is necessary. The needs of the many . . ."

She flicked her cigarette over the side of the building before standing and looking at him.

"So, how are we going to do this?"

She asked, changing the subject back to the task at hand.

"Come on." He said, jumping down onto the fire escape.

They headed inside, sitting down at the desk where he had a blueprint laid out. On the top of it, was the name Club Bootsy.

"You're kidding me? The same club we were at last night?" She asked as she stared at the paper in front of her.

"Aye, a soorce tells me they will be thaur at nine." He replied.

Finn began the process of laying out their plan of attack, his sharpie circling certain points on the blueprint. He scribbled notes, gesturing madly. Amanda did not hear any of it, he was not going. She already decided that he, unlike Sara, was not going to end up a corpse.

The weapons cabinet was big enough to fit a grown man inside and the lock he used to keep it shut, would keep him from getting out.

"Weapons?" Amanda asked, after a moment.

"Aye, thes way." He replied, standing up and heading to the large cabinet.

Finn handed her the same items he had given Sara before she was killed and Amanda set them on the table. She waited til he handed her a Molotov cocktail for the Shadowed One and the iron railroad spike for the Chameleon. Then she acted. Amanda stepped back, setting the items on the table beside her before picking up the small stone gargoyle statue to her right.

"Finn?" She asked, getting his attention.

He turned toward her.

"Aye, lass."

Amanda pulled him close, kissing him deep, kissing him goodbye. She had no way of knowing if she would ever see him again but it was a sacrifice she was willing to make for someone she loved. He would never know how she felt. She pulled away from him, stepping back to look into his eyes one last time.

"I'm sorry."

"Huh?" He replied.

That was all she said before she cracked him in the head, hard with the butt of the statue. He grunted, sliding down the side of the cabinet and sinking to the floor. Amanda dropped the gargoyle and proceeded to stuff his unconscious body into the cabinet before locking it. She even pushed the bed vertically up against the doors to ensure that he would not follow her.

"Sorry my love, I've already lost my best friend. I won't watch you die." She whispered.

Then, she turned from him and leapt from the broken window, landing in the alleyway below and heading for the club. The Wolf Pack would be there soon.

Chapter 40

As night fell on Los Angeles for the last time, a full moon rose red in the sky above. Amanda stepped through the shimmery doorway of the shadow realm and onto the roof of a building across from the club. She was silent in her movements, undetected by the Shadowed One himself. Pulling down the scarf she used to cover her face, her ruby eyes scanned over the club. A line of humans spread from the entrance down the sidewalk that ran beside the building. She spotted four other vampires, surrounding the exterior of the club, each of them armed with semi-autos. One paced the rooftop in front of her, seemingly oblivious to her presence. She would take him first if necessary.

Pulling her scarf up across her face, she stepped back into the shadow realm, emerging behind him. The razor sharp blade, sliced through meat and bone. His head bounced onto the pavement below her. Amanda flipped her sword and slid it back into the sheath on her left side. Then she dropped down into the alleyway below and moved quietly toward the next vampiric guard.

"Hey bitch, we knew you would show up. I got a little something for you." He said, holding up the gun.

"Hmm." Amanda smirked.

The guard squeezed the trigger, but even his gun was not fast enough to contend with her. She spun on her toes as if performing a ballet, her right hand grabbing the lower receiver of the gun and slamming it upward, breaking his nose. He had ruined the element of surprise, which was more than a bit irritating. Amanda twisted the gun from his hands, slamming the butt of it into his jaw before finally pulling it away from him. Then she pulled the silver blade she had grabbed from Finn's cabinet and drove it through his heart. He gasped before crumpling to the ground.

Her footsteps echoed off the walls as she headed toward the rear of the club, surprising the young vampire nervously pacing around. She did not give him the chance to get a shot off. Amanda drew her sword, shifting past him and decapitating him before his finger touched the trigger. Blood dripped off the end of her katana, decorating the dark wet pavement below.

She heard a sound behind her and she turned to find the last guard had moved to see what was going on. Amanda cocked her head slightly to one side, the sword held away to her right as she made her way bracingly toward him. He began to shake.

"Fuck this." He said, throwing down the gun.

"No no. We're not finished yet." Amanda replied.

She could not afford to let him escape and alert the others. The club music was loud enough to deafen even the humans to the sound of gunfire. She glanced down at her sword, then raising it, she threw it at the running man. It impaled him, sticking out the front of his chest but she missed his heart. Although, she already knew he was too weak to fight the silver poisoning his system. Amanda was on him before he had the chance to even attempt to stand up. She pulled her katana from his back and with the slightest movement, she cut his head from his body, leaving the bloody mess in the alley.

Then she slid her sword back into its sheath and glancing toward the top of the building, leapt onto its roof to await the arrival of the Blood Kings. She crouched unseen on the corner of the club, watching the mortals move about, unaware of the war going on around them. Amanda could not fault them for it, she herself was oblivious at one time as to what was going on for years.

Nearly an hour passed before each of the Kings began to arrive in their separate vehicles. The Shadowed one was the last to arrive in a black Cadillac Escalade. Amanda raised her head slightly before finally standing up.

"Here we go." She said to herself.

It all came down to this, she had been training for this particular moment. The finale, the end of an era. Although she should have felt some excitement, she felt nothing. Not anger, not hate but peace. She had made peace with what she had to do and made peace with the enemy. Amanda accepted what they did to her but she would not allow them to continue. Finn taught her that to fight with anger, would make her sloppy, it would only get her killed. So, she emptied herself, became a hollow shell and there she found a light in the darkness. It was not something she thought that she, a vampire, could ever find again. That was her new power.

As she started to leap from the roof, there was a familiar voice behind her.

"Amanda." It whispered.

Slowly, she turned and standing behind her, spreading from the club roof to the buildings around her were transparent figures. There were women from every era and at the forefront was Sara.

"Give em hell." Sara said.

Amanda nodded, looking at the faces of the women around her. There was defiance in them now, strength and the damage that had been inflicted was gone. Had someone released them from the Shadowed One's grasp? None of that mattered now. Again, she nodded before turning and dripping off the roof, near the back of the line.

She made her way toward the entrance of the club. Her eyes flashed red once at the bodyguard admitting people and he promptly unhooked the red rope blocking her entry. Amanda slide inside without her weapons being noticed, it also helped that she was influencing the humans to see another scantily clad club goer. These were the moments she enjoyed being a vampire, telepathy made some things almost too easy.

The clubs vibrating music thumped through the wooden floor beneath them, bodies gyrated around her completely unaware of her intentions. In the center of the room, amidst the flashing lights, the Blood Kings were seated at a table. The three sat drinking with their unsuspecting, would-be victims, laughing and carrying on. Their arrogance and the sight of them nauseated her to no end. It was time for her to turn the tables on them. She would not fight all three of them at the same time though, that would be a careless move that would only get her killed.

So into Death's mind she wend and there she concocted the image of a woman, she knew his type. Then, she glided past him, lingering long enough to catch his eye. When she had his full attention, she beckoned to him and then slipped into the crowd, heading toward the rear of the club. She already knew there was a storage room back there from the blueprints Finn showed her.

It took every ounce of strength she had to pull this charade off. Everything about him disgusted and enraged her. His smile made her skin crawl, his touch stirred bile in her throat and his voice evoked the animal inside. Her eyes flickered red as she slowly turned to him and revealed her true face. His response was not as she had suspected, his smugness remained.

"Didn't get enough the first time?"

"Ah yes, because you're such a delight to be around." Amanda replied sarcastically.

The Shadowed One grinned wide. Amanda's jaw flexed with rage and a sigh passed through her in an attempt to keep from becoming irrational. He was trying to make her lose her temper and do something stupid. She was smart enough to know better.

"Well, much as I've enjoyed our little reunion, if you'll excuse me, I've other things to do, something a little younger and less, used up." He said gesturing toward her.

"Oh, another teenager?" She asked. "Tell me James or whatever you call yourself these days. Is that what does it for you? Children? I knew you were sick but a pedophile, that's new. Are you getting so old that they're the only ones who will have you?"

Amanda may have become a peaceful warrior but that fiery attitude inside would never die. She could not resist the urge to insult him. If he became angry, then he would be the irrational one.

The Shadowed One had started to head back towards the main area of the club but her little comments gave him cause to turn back around. A deep growl rumbled in his chest. She could not resist the urge to continue

"By now I'll bet that you can barely get it up. What are you now? Two hundred? Three hundred? It's amazing it hasn't shriveled up and fallen off at your age." Amanda said, smirking.

"What do you think you're gonna accomplish here?" He asked, attempting to avoid her questions entirely.

"No no no…you can't just change the subject. I wanna talk about is, why children?" Amanda replied.

"You would know I can get it up just fine bitch! I fucked your sweet pussy many times and could do it again if I wanted to." He said, anger coating his every word.

"I'm not here to argue," She said, pulling the Molotov out. "I've brought you a gift."

"You are dumber than I thought. You realize that one thought from me will bring the other two." He replied.

"Go ahead. Call your boyfriends to rescue you. Prove to them that you're not the big boss you think you are." She said, pulling out her lighter.

He sucked his bottom lip into his mouth before giving her a once over.

"I've got something for you if-"

A streak of silver passed by his face, whipping his hair as it did, a thin line of blood began to appear on his cheekbone. Amanda said nothing, her eyes flickering deep crimson. Something was not right, his demeanor had suddenly changed.

His smile widened as he dabbed the blood from his cheek, licked it from his fingertip and turned once to look at the throwing knife in the wall behind him.

"Now, that wasn't very nice." He slowly licked his bottom lip before continuing.

"Come now Amanda, you know you missed my touch. I have missed the taste of you." He said as his eyes faded to coal black.

She was tired of listening to him talk, so she lit the rag and tossed the bottle at him. It shattered into pieces at his heels and the fire consumed the liquor but never touched him. The flames licked the air around him, as if there was a barrier keeping the fire at bay.

"Not what you were expecting?" He asked with a smirk.

"What the hell?" Amanda asked, shocked.

At first she only noticed a sensation as if all the air had been sucked from the room and then the ringing in her ears started. Someone had come to join them. Amanda stepped to the side in an attempt to avoid putting her back to the Shadowed One, and turned to see who was behind her.

A tall dominating figure, in a long black cloak, stood blocking her exit. The Shadowed One began to grin when he finally noticed the other man in the room. Amanda knew who it was and although she had no idea what he was capable of, she dared to fight him.

"Go, rejoin the others. I'll take care of her." The Master said to the Shadowed One.

He started to head for the exit but Amanda was not letting him get away so easily. She attempted to stop him, kicking the back of his knee to break it but his Master intervened. She felt the blunt part of his knuckles collide with the side of her face. Everything blurred and she fell to the floor. A millennia of power and strength had hit her full force. However, she refused to give up that easily. Pushing herself to her feet with blood dribbling off her bottom lip, she stepped back, pulling her katana from its sheath.

"Hmm...you're stronger than I thought." He said.

"Didn't they tell you? I'm the woman who helped burn Collins to the ground. But I'm not done yet." She replied.

Amanda spun her sword once and brought it down across his torso. She might have been fast but he was faster. The Master side stepped every swing of her sword, no matter how she moved, he out maneuvered her every time. She jumped back to give them some space and instead of attempting to cut his limbs from his body, she pointed her sword at him and charged in an attempt to run him through.

The Master swung his big arm, pushing her sword out of the way and grabbing her by her throat with his free hand. His grip was that of an iron vice, squeezing hard without mercy. Her larynx began to crack under the weight of his hand.

Her hand holding the sword loosened as the world around her began to blur and she fought to maintain consciousness. There was a sudden sharp pain as she felt something slide through her torso and out through her back. She looked down to see the handle of her own sword sticking out the front of her.

The Master yanked it sharply from her body and tossed it one direction before tossing her into the nearest wall. She collided with the concrete, leaving a large dent and chunks of it fell to the floor around her. He was not finished with her yet. Amanda used to think that what the Blood Kings had done to her was bad. Now, she understood that they were kind, compared to the man they followed.

His kick shattered her rib-cage, puncturing one of her lungs and causing her to spit more blood. Then he kicked her in the face, breaking her jaw, nose and she spit teeth. Amanda knew she had to hang on, she could not let him be the one to kill her. This could not be it, after all the work she had done.

"Is this all?" His voice boomed. "Is this what they were so afraid of?"

Even in as much pain as she was, she managed a growl. He had better kill her because if he did not, she would make him pay for every crime his children had committed. Amanda extended the claws on her hands, and digging them into the floor beneath her, she used them to began pulling herself toward the exit.

"Where are you going? I'm not finished with you yet."

He said, his right foot coming down on one of her ankles, snapping it. She grit her teeth hard, refusing to give him the satisfaction of hearing her cry out in pain. The Master knelt down beside her broken form, the sound of his voice caused her head to throb.

"I could have killed you already. You know that don't you?" He paused. "I've decided that after what you did to my boys, death would be a blessing. I'm not going to give you that.

She felt him grab the back of her shirt and began to drag her across the floor. Although her body was broken and she was bleeding from the gash in her stomach, she still fought him. Neither one of them seemed to realize that something else was happening at the moment. Her stab wound was already beginning to heal.

The throb of the music made her broken bones ache and her head spin. She was dropped roughly onto the black painted concrete floor, in front of a ruby red couch. Amanda did not even have to look up to know where she was or whose feet she was now staring at. Over the concussive noise of the club, she made out one familiar voice.

"What do we have here?"

A dress boot slid under her, kicking her onto her back. There was a glass dangling loosely between two of his fingers and his free hand was resting on the shoulder of some young thing with long dark hair.

"See baby," He continued, pointing at Amanda. "this is what happens when you don't listen. Understand? So, be a good girl, yeah?" The Telepath said.

The woman nodded obediently, he was already in control of her mind. Amanda recognized the glazed over mindless look in her eyes. She glared at the Telepath and growled deep, she would kill him.

Chameleon leaned forward and started to reach for her. She did not care why or that his Master was standing right behind him. Amanda reached back and pulled the knife still tucked into her lower back and sliced deep into the side of his hand. He jerked back, holding his wounded appendage. Before the other two could touch her, she stabbed the blade deep into his foot, pinning one of his legs to the floor.

"Bitch!" The Shadowed One yelled, back handing her hard.

Amanda laughed through broken teeth and bloody lips, spitting her blood onto his shoes.

"You hit like a girl." She said.

"Hold her!"Chameleon screamed at them, pulling her knife from his foot.

She tried to fight back but a voice in her head, one that pushed past the iron safe hold she had in her pocket, commanded her down. The Telepath and Shadowed One, each put a boot on her wrists, keeping her there. Still, she growled and tried to push through the hold their Master had on her mind. The Chameleon stood from his place on the couch, moving over to her, he pulled two of his own knives.

"You wanna play with knives bitch?" He asked, tossing one around in his hand. "That's my department."

With that, he drove one each into her wrists, driving them down into the concrete floor so she could not move. Then he stepped back and straightened his suit before downing the rest of his drink. The Blood Kings stood back to survey their work, laughing at her predicament.

Their joy was short lived though. Amanda only heard the shattering of the glass skylight above and then a thud of heavy boots landing on the table. She turned to look at the Blood Kings reaction and saw even their Master stepping back. The mortals on the dance floor began to run for the exit, recognizing that something was about to happen.

While they were distracted, she began to pull at the knives holding her wrists. That same voice commanded her back down and she watched his head jerk back suddenly, dropping the hood of his cloak. He had an overly exaggerated jawline, reminded her of a stretched out Halloween mask and taught pale skin. His hair was long and black but stringy. There was a line of blood coming from one nostril, which he dabbed at before looking at the man responsible.

"Don't do that again. You'll not be touching her." A thick Scottish brogue echoed through the club.

Somehow Finn had managed to get out of the cabinet and right now, she was happy he did. She heard his boots hit the dance floor as he jumped from the table. He had their full attention and she was going to take advantage of it. Amanda began to pull at the daggers holding her wrists. She could feel them ripping muscle, slicing flesh, fracturing her wrists and cutting arteries. The lights around them began to flicker and all but her seemed to notice.

"Aah.." She screamed as she began to pull herself free.

With her hands freed, her body became suddenly vertical. She had not pushed herself up off the floor, but one foot rolled ankle to toe and she uprighted. Amanda turned to look at them, her eyes had become darker than the Shadowed One's. She turned her attention then, to the Master, shadows curling slowly around her even in the light of the club. Then she pointed at him and spoke one word.

"You."

Her voice was a booming phantom whisper, it seemed to come from no where and everywhere at once. Even their Master did not understand what was happening, he too looked around nervously. Finn only smiled silently to himself. The Master knew one thing, she had marked him for death.

Amanda started toward the Blood Kings, each light she walked under bursting in a shower of glass and sparks as she passed. The Shadowed One, turned toward her when she stepped into the darkness and summoned one of his own shadows to strike her. She waved her hand and it dissipated.

"That wasn't smart." She said, pausing in her movements.

"You don't get it do you bitch! You can't stop me! I am shadow, I will never die! So, there isn't anything you can do to me!" He shouted.

"You think you're dark?" She asked, cocking her head. "That you're a God, immortal? No, I am darkness. I am forever. Allow me to show you."

Amanda was calm in her movements, as if she had all the time in the world. The Blood Kings realized they were beat and turned to run.

"Where ya going lads? Parties only startin." Finn said, his brogue thick.

Then he turned his attention to the Master, leaping from the table and pulling the two silver knives he had strapped to his back.

"Hmm...I'm not going to waste my time with you child." He said to Finn

The air around him shifted and swirled. Smoke began to curl up around him and his form began to fade. Amanda felt the Shadow Realm began to move. She would not allow him to escape so easily. She grabbed one of the daggers from the floor, blood still coating the blades and threw it into the shadows forming around him. He made an attempt to wave it away but the dagger did not waver. It struck him in the upper shoulder and the shadows around him dropped.

He looked down at the blade in his shoulder and then back at her, shock evident on his face. The Blood Kings, paused in their movements, having heard their Masters grunt of pain.

"I'm not finished with you yet." She said moving toward him.

"Nae love. Go after the runts. I've got this one." He said, nodding toward the Master.

"Have it your way." The Master said to Finn.

Amanda turned and headed toward the back exit, leaving the Scotsman to deal with their leader. The Master pulled off his cloak, dropping it on the bar behind him and revealing the short sword he kept strapped to his back. He pulled it, moving slow at first and then quickly. He drew the sword down, attempting to cut Finn in two. However, he had underestimated his opponent. Finn side stepped, his daggers blocking the blade and throwing them off. Then, he kicked the Master in his stomach, hard enough to send him flying back through the thick wooden bar.

Then he stepped back and beckoned to the elder vampire to get up off the ground.

"Is that the best you got? After all these years, that's all you can do?" Finn questioned.

The Master growled and pushed himself off the ground, attempting this time to run Finn through. Again he weaved around his blade, slicing down into the soft flesh of the Master's spine, his other blade slicing into the side of his neck and his boot simultaneously slamming into his knee, shattering it.

The Master gasped in pain, dabbing at the gash in his back. When he looked up at Finn, his eyes had become black pools of hollow emptiness.

"You'll pay for that!" He roared.

"Then come make me." Finn challenged.

He was faster this time but not fast enough to hit the younger vampire. Spinning his short sword around his hand, he made an attempt to slice into the flesh of Finn's knees but Finn jumped out of the way and kneed him in the face, hard. Then he drove his elbow down into the Master's head before stabbing both daggers down into the meat of his shoulders and stepping back.

The floor was now glistening red from the amount of blood the Master was losing. He was weaving as he attempted to stand. His grip on the sword loosened and it fell to the floor. Then he pulled the knives out of his shoulders, glaring at the man who had put them there.

"Silver," The Master said, before dropping one of the blades.

"It doesn't work on me. So, if that's the best you got, then you've already lost. You can't kill me."

"We'll see about that." He said, his voice deepening.

Finn cocked his head to one side as he watched the vampire before him weaken. His attempts at weaponry had failed. He held up one of his massive, bloody hands and without saying a word, began to pull shadows into his palm.

Finn dropped his coat and prepared for what the Master was about to do. He knew it would hurt for a moment and then he would regret every minute of what he had done. An orb of shadow and crackling blue energy slammed into the side of Finn's face, rocking his head momentarily. When he slowly turned back to look at the Master, Finn's eyes had become empty white, iridescent pools.

"Ya shouldn't have done that mate." His voice was, distant.

The mere sound of it made the room feel several degrees colder. Now the Master could see his breath with every exhale. Finn, flexed his shoulders and from his back emerged two large black feathery wings.

"What are you?" He asked.

Suddenly, that arrogant, all powerful confidence had disappeared.

"Death." Was all Finn said.

Realizing that he was out of his league and that dealing with Amanda might be easier, he too, attempted to turn and run for the alley. Finn was blocking his exit before he could even take a step.

"Where ya going lad?" He asked, walking toward him.

The Master moved backwards away from the Angel of Death in front of him.

"I'm not finished with you yet." Finn said.

He balled his fist and it collided with the side of the Master's face hard enough to send him flying back through empty tables and the heavy metal railing that divided the dance floor. With a sigh, Finn's wings folded behind his back and he moved slowly toward the vampire lying on the floor.

When the Master pulled himself back to his feet, he noticed something was wrong. His jaw was not broken, the flesh on his face was not split from the impact or cut by the metal bars he had been thrown through. There were flakes of skin, rotten skin on his shirt and they were coming from him. He scrambled to a table and grabbed a napkin holder to look at himself in its reflection. Where Finn had hit him, was now rotting away faster than it could heal.

The Master turned to look at the angel still lounging by the bar, waiting for him to realize what had happened. He knew that there was no way even he could beat the Angel of Death, his best chance of survival was to run. So, again he tried to head for the rear exit.

Finn leapt up from his place at the bar, and spreading his wings, lifted the Master into the air, throwing him back down into the concrete. He collided with such force, the ground cracked around him and there was a snap as his spine broke. This time, Finn gave him no time to recover. He began punching him repeatedly, knocking out decaying teeth and turning his decaying jaw into dust. Finally, he slammed his boot into the Master's sternum, causing the broken bone to pierce his black heart.

"Stay down!" He yelled, his voice booming.

Moving back to the bar, he threw back a shot, his features fading back to that of the more human version of himself. With a sigh, he pulled up a chair and sat down. Finn was busy minding his drink when a fist came flying at him, hitting him in the jaw and knocking him out of his chair. Shaking his head, he slowly stood up.

The Master was standing only a few feet away. His features had changed, his eyes were red speckled with bits of black. There were large demonic claws at the end of his fingers and two large leathery wings at his back.

"What-" Finn Started to ask a question but was met with brute force, cutting of his question.

The Master had kicked him in the stomach, sending him flying into one of the brick walls of the club. He hit hard enough to knock him unconscious. Satisfied with what he had done, the Master finally headed outside to where the Blood Kings were fighting.

Chapter 41

Outside, behind the club, Amanda had been dealing with her own issues. The Blood Kings were attempting to get away and so far, had succeeded. She was following them through the shadowy doorways that littered Los Angeles. They had climbed into a black Escalade parked behind the club and were now speeding through the night. Why did the Shadowed One not run and hide in the realm? She wondered.

Her thoughts were quickly answered when they turned onto one of the main streets in the area. A few miles in front of the speeding Escalade, a gothic figure began to emerge. She walked off one of the side streets, stopping in the middle of the road they were heading down. Amanda watched her with curiosity.

The mysterious woman was dressed in a knee length lacy corset dress and mid-calf combat boots. Her fiery red locks waved around her as she moved, almost as if she was conjuring her own storm. There was blue lightning crackling in her eyes, circling around her hands and forearms. Amanda watched as the woman lifted her hands to her mid-section, waving them around each other. She brought her right hand up and slapped her palm on the pavement in front of her.

The car slammed into an invisible wall, several feet from the woman. Amanda had stopped moving, standing yards behind the Escalade. Who was this woman? What was she? Where did she come from? As she stepped toward them, he tapped her on the shoulder with the tip of her katana. She glanced down at the blade, slowly taking it from him she placed it back in its sheath. There was no question on his face, no worry in his brow, he knew what was happening. He knew even before she did, what she was about to do.

Amanda stood, waiting for them to exit the vehicle and as she waited, she pulled the scarf from her face and then dropped her hood. Shaking her hair from its restraints, she closed her eyes for a moment. The raven locks darkened and then shadow passed from head to tip, turning the once mortal strands into writhing serpents of shadow. When she opened her eyes, they appeared vacant. Darkness spread across her anatomy, swirling around her fingers with their every flex and turn.

The witch was growing impatient, again she brought her hands close together, curling her fingers as if they were claws of a rotting tree branch. Her electric gaze shot toward the car, and then she jerked her hands apart. What was left of the vehicle dissembled before her, the doors, and outer casing, flying off in every direction. Her hands fell back to her sides, resting, ready at her hips.

The Blood Kings climbed from the frame of the vehicle, stepping out onto the street to face her. Each of them pulled off the dress jacket they were wearing, unbuttoning their sleeves and rolling them up to the elbow.

Although they were moving in real time, Amanda saw their every move in slow motion. Her eyes scanning over every inch of their anatomy, watching every move of their muscles as they flexed beneath their pale flesh. The Chameleon pulled two large knives from the sheaths strapped at his hips, Telepath, unstrapped the cat of nine tails on his back, its leathery straps decorated with shards of silver. She smirked as they glimmered in the dim light, knowing somehow that they no longer affected her. The Shadowed One, reached over his shoulder and pulled a sword that had been hidden on his back.

"Do you know who the hell we are?!" Shadowed One shouted.

"We're Blood Kings! You can't stop us, you can't bring us down." Telepath added.

"We'll see about that." She said, her other hand beginning to gather more shadows.

"Come on boys, let's teach this bitch who she's messing with." Chameleon. declared.

"All right. Let's play." She said.

Amanda raised both hands suddenly, spreading her arms and the shadows she had been gathering, spread out around her. Every light on the street behind her burst in a hale of broken glass and sparks. She began to laugh excitedly. The sudden release of power, caused them to pause in their movements.

"Do you know who I am Blood Kings? I am the Goddess Shiva Ma, I own the Shadow Realm and everything in it. And my husband is the Angel of Death. You," She pointed at the Shadowed One. "have been meddling in things of which you have no right. And now, you're going to pay for that."

In that moment, her human memories of Sara swept over her. The deaths of the girls she swore she would protect and the pain they had put her through. Every minute of torment came rushing back to her. That anger she had worked so hard to kill was now fire, burning its way through her veins. A deep, ethereal growl clawed violently up through her chest. Amanda balled her hands into fists and turned her attention back to the men in front of her.

They stepped even further back away from her, sensing their death blowing in the wind. The air around them grew rapidly colder as her anger spread down every street in Los Angeles. The Blood Kings were about to learn what real death and immortality was like.

"What are you waiting for!? Kill her already?!" Shadowed One shouted at the other two.

"Yes . . .please do try." Amanda coaxed.

The Telepath and the Chameleon both charged her, one whipping his cat of nine tails through the air in a fruitless attempt to injure her. Amanda was quicker than even him. She punched the air before her and a ball of dark matter hit him in the sternum, sending him flying backwards. They would die on her terms. Chameleon, sliced at her torso first with the blade in his right hand and then with the one in his left. Amanda was faster than he and she did not need her katana anymore to kill him. She had become something more than a vampire. He was a creature of the darkness and as all things dark belonged to the Shadow Goddess, his life would be reclaimed. She blocked his attempts to lacerate her flesh, with each of her forearms. Then she kicked him in the stomach, hard enough to cause him to cough blood.

The Chameleon stumbled backwards and looked at her in shock. He had not expected this level of strength from her. This time, when he came at her, he flipped the blades under his fists, slashing at the soft tissue of her throat. She leaned back out of his reach, pushing his arm away from her and landing another kick, to his rib-cage There was a resounding crack as she shattered them, one of the jagged pieces of bone pierced his lung. Amanda had enough of his games, she owed him so much for the pain he had inflicted upon her.

"Is that the best you got?" She mocked.

There was a sound behind her, and she leapt into the air, flipping over the Telepath who had attempted to sneak up on her. She slammed her boot into his spine, snapping it on impact. He grunted in pain and fell forward. Then she stomped her boot on his throat, crushing his larynx. It would not kill him but it would incapacitate him for a moment.

"Wait your turn!" She shouted.

She felt the Shadowed One began to shift, he was trying to move into her realm. Amanda curled her fingers, closed her hand and pulled up a ball of crackling purple energy. She then threw it in his direction, sending him to the ground.

"Tsk tsk tsk. This is not Collins, we're not playing by your rules anymore. We're playing by mine now! You stay right where you are. I'll get to you." She warned.

As she was momentarily distracted, the Chameleon managed to leap from his place and drive one of his large knives down into the meat of her upper torso. Amanda turned on him, her black eyes now crackling with the same purple energy she had only a second ago, thrown at his leader. She glanced down at the blade that was sticking through her body. Her fingers wrapped slowly around the handle and she began to pull it out. The Chameleon was not going to give her the opportunity to remove it. He attempted to drive the other one into the other side of her.

She sensed his movements and her left hand caught his wrist, holding it effortlessly. Cocking her head, she watched the strain pass across his features as he fought to push the blade downward. With one quick push upward, she snapped his wrist and he dropped the knife, grunting in pain. Amanda was not finished punishing him for his insult, she jerked his arm sideways and heard his elbow snap. It's sharp point pushing through his flesh.

Satisfied that he had learned not to fight unfairly, she rotated her body and kicked him hard in the side simultaneously letting go of his arm. He flew backwards, hitting the brick wall of the building behind him and going through the wall.

With him out of her way for the moment, she gripped the handle of the knife and pulled it from her shoulder. Amanda dropped it on the ground, it clanked as it hit the pavement.

"That wasn't smart Patrick." She said.

Chameleon was just pulling himself up out of the brick ruble when he heard her say his real name. The Blood Kings looked at each other with shock.

"What did you just say?" He said, cocking his head as if he had heard her wrong.

"I know all your real names." She hissed.

There was suddenly a sound behind her and Amanda noticed the witch in front of her had shifted and the energy around her arms fading into a crimson. The Chameleon in front of her was grinning. She turned around to see what was going on.

Her eyes scanned from the street to the man on the rooftop. He had emerged but Finn had not. That meant, somehow, he had overcome Finn. The Master had hurt her, her best friend and now the man she loved. At first she said nothing and then, her hands began to shake but not with fear.

"Do you boys know what it means to be the Goddess of the Shadows?" She asked through grit teeth.

"Allow me to show you."

Her voice was calmer than it should have been. The shadows that were present, began to crawl into the light, listening to the command of their dark queen. Amanda turned her attention to the Chameleon. She had played with him enough. Now he would learn what it meant to suffer. There was no sound but she was suddenly a few inches from him, her eyes crackling with red and purple light.

She grabbed him by his broken arm and tossed him through another building. Then she turned on the Telepath, the energy in her eyes growing. She lowered her gaze and he grabbed the sides of his head, screaming in pain, blood began to run from his nose. That was not the worst pain she planned to cause him. Amanda ripped the whip from his hand, hard enough to snap every finger he had wrapped around its handle. She began hitting him with his own weapon, a warriors cry echoed from her lips and even the Master stepped back unsure.

The silver shards on the end of the whip, sliced through his flesh, and she knew its bite hurt. Not satisfied with the damage it was doing, she reached down, pulling shadows and dark energy into both her hands before punching him in the chest. Her hearing was now so acute she could hear his heart trying to stop beating.

"Oh no you don't. Stay with me." She said, her voice laced with power.

Grabbing him by his shirt, she pulled him forward, digging her fingers into the wounds the whip had created. He screamed, blood dripping down her hand, decorating the pavement. Their Master had hurt someone she loved, she would not let them die so easily. She would make them pay for what he had done. Amanda balled up her fist, energy crackling around it still and punched him in the throat before kicking his knee backwards and snapping it. She broke his other knee, her fist caved his rib-cage and then she hit his jaw until she shattered every bone in his face. Finally, she grabbed one of his wrists and yanked hard, pulling his left arm from its socket.

She was panting but she was in no way tired, she was excited, blood thirsty, craving revenge. The Telepath was semi conscious when she turned away from him, wrapping her right arm around his neck and pulling. She did not decapitate him but pulled his head from his body with one yank, taking his spine with it. Amanda held it up by the long bone that used to be his back, and let out a war cry. Then she turned and tossed the entire thing at the Shadowed One.

"Here's your shit back!" She growled.

Realizing he was beat, he tried to turn and run but she turned her palms upward and a wall of dark energy sprang up around them, blocking his path.

"Your Master hurt my husband. You're going to suffer the consequences."

The witch looked around, her eyes scanning over the dark wall behind her. Even she seemed surprise at the amount of power Amanda now held sway over. The Shadowed One would die soon enough, but she was not finished with the Chameleon.

"So," She said, holding up one palm. "You wanna play with knives."

Shadows swirled in her hand and then solidified into a solid silver blade.

"Hmm…this looks like fun. Wanna find out?" She asked, repeating the very same question he had asked her back in Collins.

"Can…can she just do that?" The Shadowed One asked no one in particular.

A smirk spread across her face and she looked at him,

winking. Then, without even a glance in the Chameleon's direction, she threw the knife. He had no time to dodge it, it pierced his chest. When Amanda turned back to him, she dropped her hands to the side and from the shadows she continued to pull a torrent of knives. Each one piercing his upper torso, his legs, his neck and groin. He knelt on the ground, slowly, with shaking hands began to pull them from his body.

"No no." She said, appearing in front of him.

She grabbed him by his hair, lifting his face to hers, another dagger in her hand. Amanda tossed it, handle to blade and back again.

"Are we having fun yet?" She asked, her eyes twinkling.

The Chameleon spit blood in her face, in retaliation of her assault. She blinked a few times before tucking away the other knife and twisting one that had impaled his stomach. He coughed, blood dribbling from his mouth. Amanda planned to shove the last one into his heart, but now she had a better idea. She began to grab each one of them and she did not pull them out but drug them through his flesh until they had no more flesh to cut and fell. Skin, muscle and tendons dangled from him, tassels of mortality. With a toothy grin, Amanda grabbed the one in his gut she had been twisting and pulled it up through his chest cavity, slicing through his lower intestine, stomach, lungs and then cutting his heart in two. She stared deep into his eyes, watching as the light drifted from them. To amuse herself, she pulled that knife out and then drove it down through the top of his skull.
Amanda let go of him, dropping his corpse to the ground. She had made a beautiful mess of the place. A majority of her outfit and her skin was covered in slick, hot blood. The pale asphalt was deep red with blood and entrails. Stepping over the body of the Chameleon, she moved back to the middle of the street. Shadowed One was not the one she wanted to kill at this moment.
Looking down at the man she loved, her eyes trailed up the side of the building to the Master, crouching there and watching in

amusement. Behind her, she heard the Shadowed One speak.

"Are you gonna just sit there while she tears us apart?" He asked his Master.

For a moment he said nothing. Being a man of few words, Amanda did not expect him to say anything at all. Then he spoke.

"You think you can do whatever you want and get away with it Amanda? You come into my town, your little *whore* burns our house down and now you're killing my boys." He said, jumping off the building and stepping over Finn.

"I don't take to kindly to that."

She began to laugh.

"You don't get it do you? I don't answer to you. I answer to no one. I am darkness. I am the definition of evil. You...you're just a pawn, a whelp...the disease that we tolerate."

Her grin widened when she saw a pair of hollow white eyes behind him.

"What's funny bitch?" Master asked.

"And you've managed to piss off the embodiment of death." She said, gesturing behind him.

The Master turned to look and before he could react, he was flying across the street.

"You lil shite." He growled.

Finn wanted to leave him to Amanda, to give her the revenge she so desperately deserved. His anger was becoming hard to control. Her dark pools met his and with a nod she said.

"Go get em love."

He turned away from her, his features becoming more skeletal with every move. Amanda turned to the Shadowed One, who was finally standing and facing her. She owed this main endless amounts of suffering, too bad she did not have time to make him relive the pain he caused her.

"Tell me something Amanda...did you miss me?" The Shadowed One dared ask.

A low growl crawled up from her diaphragm and before he could raise his sword, she had grabbed him by his throat and tossed him into the side of a building. All she could see right now, was not his suffering but the image of Sara burned into her memory. She could hear her voice in her head, crying for her name.

The Shadowed One was still powerful though, she had underestimated him. From the gaping hole in the building where he had landed, there came a tendril. It whipped out, catching her by the side of the face. Her head jerked from the impact and she jumped back momentarily.

When he stepped out to greet her, she noticed his skin had changed. What was once flawless caramel, was now a pale gray and his eyes were the color of oil. He had stripped off his dress shirt and she could now see the kinetic shadow tattoos that moved around his body. In his right hand, he held a weapon she had never seen before. It was a sword but the blade glowed iridescent purple and swirled with the same shadows that were now standing behind him.

Amanda dabbed the side of her face, licking her own blood off her finger. She lowered her head and glared at him.

"That's right bitch! I've still got power in the Shadow Realm. It belongs to me!" He shouted.

"We'll see about that. What you have...its stolen power. You want to see what a real creature of the Shadows can do?" She asked.

The shadows that surrounded them began to swirl up around her, changing her skin to that same gray color, decorating her in similar tattoos. However, they did not stop there, her oily black eyes thrummed with purple light, matching the glow of his sword. Her feet became talons, as if she were a bird of prey, from her fingertips grew long black claws and from her crown came horns of the deepest burgundy.

"Come get me Shadow Chaser." She mocked, beckoning to him with one claw.

He spun his sword and stepped from the ruins of the building. The Shadowed One brought his blade down, meaning to slice into the meat of her shoulder. She dodged, her claws slicing his mid-section. Then, as he was distracted by pain, Amanda moved behind him, kicking him. Her clawed feet sliced into the tender skin there as well but no sooner had she cut him, he was healing.

He turned to face her, the arrogant smirk she despised so much, plastered on his features. Amanda was so focused on him, she failed to notice the tendril of shadow sneaking up behind her. That was until, a ball of bright blue electric energy came flying past her head. It collided with the tendril, dissolving it on impact.

"You get him. I'll keep those at bay." She said.

It was the first move Amanda had seen her make in all this time. The Shadowed One turned toward her, lowing his sword for a moment.

"What the hell is that bitch doing here?" He asked.

"Never mind," He said to no one in particular before glancing over his shoulder at Amanda. "if you'll excuse me a moment. I'm gonna take care of her."

"You don't touch her!" Amanda yelled.

She stepped toward him and even with all her power, he

managed to move behind her, slicing through the tendons in the back of her knees as he did. Amanda had no control over her legs, they collapsed under her. The witch was powerful but Amanda could recognize the fear in her eyes as the Shadowed One started toward her. She had been one of their women at one time.

From her place on the ground, Amanda watched him move toward her. Her eyes staring into the slowly shrinking woman's. She squeezed them shut and when she opened them, all she could see was Sara's face. She was seeing Sara be murdered all over again.

The shadows around her drifted over her form, winding around the wounds on her legs and mending her flesh. Slowly she stood, her body surging with dark energy. Amanda moved behind him, grabbing him by his long locks and flinging him into the empty car frame. She was now standing over him, blood dripping down his face.

"You will not touch her again!" She warned.

He was smirking as he got to his feet. Just when he had managed to pull himself back up, a red crackling ball of energy hit him in the chest, sending him to the other side of the street. Amanda glanced over her shoulder to see the witch had regained her courage. There was a knowing look between the two of them and they started for him.

"All right," He said, getting up. "You wanna do it this way. Fine then."

The tendrils of shadow he had been controlling, swelled up around him, readying for attack. But they were greeted with the same energy he had been hit with only moments ago. Amanda quickly closed the gap between them, her fist colliding with his jaw hard enough to break it in one hit. She did not let him have a moment to breath. Her knee rammed into his rib-cage until she heard both of them shatter from the impact.

He was stumbling and gasping for air, making fruitless efforts to hit her with his sword. She was too fast for even him. Every move she made a blur.

Amanda landed a spinning kick to the side of his face, sending him stumbling to the ground. She yanked him back up, tossing him through the shell of the Escalade this time. Holding up both her palms, shadows and dark energy began to swirl, roll and twist. They bled from the side of her hands, winding until they formed into long metal chains, coated with pure silver.

"You remember these?" She said, cocking her head to the side, a gleam of insanity twinkling in her oily pools.

Spinning on her feet, she whipped the chains at him, one after another. She wanted him to know the same pain he had caused her. He managed to dodge her attempts a few times but she heard the end of the chain connect with the small of his back and one across the side of his face. With the flick of her wrist, she wound the chain around his neck and pulled hard, sending him flying into another building.

His flesh hissed in protest of the metal coiled around his neck and the lacerations of his body. The Shadowed One, rocked on the ground as pain coursed through his body. He grabbed the chain on his neck, unwinding it as it seared the flesh of his hands. Then he pushed himself to his feet, jerking one of his legs back into place before standing and spitting a mouthful of teeth and blood.

"Are we having fun yet?" She asked before cackling.

"Fuck you bitch! This doesn't change anything. Sara is dead! You failed to protect her..." He laughed. "and I still got to fuck that-"

Amanda had him by his throat and was slamming him into the ground before he could finish his sentence.

"You will not say her name!" She screamed, he voice almost demonic.

It was time to end this, she had, had her fun. The claws on

583

her right hand extended and she began to rip at his face, tearing chunks of and muscle from his chest. Amanda tore at the tendons in his arms, ripped the skin clean off his legs, punching her bloody fists into his bare muscle. She tossed her head back and let out a banshee scream before sinking a mouthful of razor sharp black teeth into his throat, ripping it out. As he lay bleeding to death, she continued to tear into his body, tossing organs as she went. Until there was nothing left but skeleton and she was dripping with blood and chunks of human matter.

Amanda was panting when she stood. It was over, the Blood Kings were finally dead. So why then did she not feel a sense of closure. Why did she feel that there was something she was missing? Something was not right. She should feel elated, happy, anything. Instead, she felt a sense of doom. Almost as if killing them released something worse into the world, something darker.

Chapter 42

The Master recovered quickly from the blow Finn had landed and now he stood, ripping off the shirt he was wearing to reveal the black veins that decorated his body. The wings he had displayed in the nightclub now spread to their full length, two large horns curled back from his crown, a long tail whipped around behind him and his teeth extended to long sharp points. It was astounding how he managed to fit them in his mouth. Now, the distorted muscle structure made sense. Although Finn had not wanted to believe it, he knew this demon. He and the rest of his brothers and sisters knew him. Finn regretted getting Amanda involved in the fight with the Blood Kings because he knew it would not end unless their Master was taken down as well. The problem was, he did not know if even the three of them would be strong enough to take him out. To put him back where he belonged.

If he could buy Amanda some time, she could escape from this fight unscathed, he would not lose her again. He ripped open the black shirt he was wearing, buttons flying in every direction. His long black feathered wings spread out behind him and from between his shoulders, he pulled a blade he had not used in a long time. It resonated with dark light, shifting somewhere between angelic and demonic. Finn cracked his neck, rolled his shoulders and prepared to face the king of lies once more.

"You think you're enough to put me back in the pit Gabriel?" He asked, using the angels real name.

"Nae, but you won't leave here in one piece." He replied, spinning his sword.

They collided with the force of a thousand storms, sparks flying off Finn's sword as it hit the claws on the Master's large hands. Finn slammed his foot into the Master's knee as they fought for control, the blade pushing against the claws. It made the Master waver for a moment but he regained composure quickly.

The skin on one of Finn's hand's peeled back, revealing his

more skeletal form and with that hand he hit the Master in the side of the face, causing the skin to fall off. His head reeled back and then he pushed hard against Finn's blade, causing him to stumble backwards. Touching the rotting skin, the Master glared up at Finn.

"You'll pay for that angel." He threatened.

Finn smirked, spinning his sword again before beckoning to him with his skeletal hand. The Master grinned an unnerving grin and before Finn could move, he had him by the throat and was tossing him into a light pole. There was a crack as he fractured a lung from the impact, bending the metal when he hit. Finn shook his head and pushed himself to his feet. But the Master was on him before he could fully stand, grabbing him by his jaw and squeezing hard enough to crack his teeth.

Finn's eyes caught sight of Amanda slaughtering the Blood Kings and he found the strength to work through the pain. He drove his sword through the Master's stomach, all the way to the hilt. There was an audible roar as hundreds of years of angelic power pierced the flesh of tainted one. It was enough to make him let go of Finn, dropping him hard to the concrete. With the Master distracted by the sword in his stomach, Finn went to work. Both hands becoming skeletal, his eyes turning that empty iridescent white. He punched one knee and then another before jumping up and kicking his sword deeper into his torso.

The Master stumbled backwards, but not far. He grabbed the sword and began to pull it out, his flesh burning as it gripped the handle. Then he held it in both hands, snapping the blade over one large knee. With a demonic roar he headed for Finn.

Finn was not entirely out of weapons, he flapped his large wings and from them came a cloud of ash. When it hit the Master's flesh, it caused it to decay down to the muscle. However, he healed nearly as quickly as it hit.

There was a scream from Amanda and both of them turned to look. The Master gave Finn a side glance and he could see a twinkle in his eyes. He would not let that monster touch her. Finn knew what he was about to do would hurt but he had no other choice. Crouching down, he flapped his large wings again and this time he tackled the demon into one of the buildings. Hitting him was the equivalent of colliding with a titanium wall, there was not mercy. Finn felt his shoulders break, muscles tear and his rib-cage fracture from the impact.

As he was pulling himself up out of the rubble and iron hand grabbed the back of his neck, dragging him out of the building. Finn tried to fight but every time he did, the Master would punch him in the side of the face, hitting with his full power. The Scotsman had been in a lot of fights before with quite a number of evil things but he had never felt anything hit as hard as he could.

"For all your efforts, all your fight…you're still going to watch her die." He said, his voice demonic.

Amanda had finished dispatching the Blood Kings and now she turned her attention to the Master. She saw him dragging Finn out of the building, leathery wings on his back. It did not matter what he was, she did not care. The only thing she could see was he had hurt the man she loved and he was responsible for much more than that. Picking up the silver chains (not knowing if they would work or not) she cracked one on the cement, creating sparks as she did.

The next time she whipped one of the chains, it wrapped around the Masters neck. He looked up in surprise, he had been so focused on Finn that he did not see it coming.

"You get the hell away from him!"

She screamed before yanking with both hands and sending him flying against her wall of shadows. Even through broken bloody teeth, Finn grinned. His love had found her strength again, she was whole and he knew she would be a force to be reckoned with now.

As the Master was pulling himself to his feet, a ball of hot white, electric energy hit him square in the chest. It burned his flesh, creating a spiderweb of bloody cracks all across his body. Amanda glanced over her shoulder to see the witch standing just behind her, there was white lightning coursing over her entire body.

"Stay down!" The witch screamed.

"Finn are you all right?" She asked, keeping her eyes on the Master.

"Aye love. I'm fine now." He replied, pushing slowly to his feet.

"You hurt my love. Tsk tsk tsk." She said before growling.

Amanda coiled the chain around each wrist and began to hit him repeatedly, lashing it around his neck several times and tossing him around. The witch continued to hit him as he was flying through the air. Although they never let up, he managed to pick himself back up and make an attempt to fight back. As the chain neared him the last time, he stuck his hand up, catching it around his fist and pulling. She was sent flying, but the shadows around her caught her in mid air and she gently glided back down to the ground.

He began to pull himself back up and the witch tried to strike him again but he was too fast this time. He countered with his own ball of dark energy. It hit her and sent her backwards into the wall of shadows.

"No!" Amanda screamed.

The Goddess ran to her side and found her conscious, startled and her ribs broken but she was still with them. Amanda helped her to her feet. The witch held up a hand.

"I'm fine. I'm fine." She reassured.

Finn had managed to limp over to where they were now standing, he was holding his ribs and one of his wings was hanging low. Amanda turned to him.

"What the hell is he?" She asked.

"At there…the father of lies, the deceiver…the lil shite as I call em'" He answered.

"Not-" She stared to ask.

"The devil bitch!" The Master said.

They all turned to look at him, Finn and Amanda putting the witch behind her to protect her. There was a knowing glance between Amanda and Finn before she whispered to the witch.

"Can you open a doorway?" She asked.

"If you can buy me some time." The Witch replied.

Straightening themselves, Amanda and Finn moved toward the Master. Holding out his hands Finn began to pull swirling dark energy and the pale fleshy color of decay. Amanda followed suit, pulling into hers the dripping oily energy of her shadow realm. The witch only needed a few minutes, they could give that to her.

Finn closed his hands, the energy continuing to move around his fists and he sped behind the master, hitting him in the spine. The skin on his back began to decay, healing as soon as it rotted. Amanda threw one ball at the side of his face, the other one toward his torso.

The energy hit him in the jaw, whipping his head back violently and cracking his skin. On his chest where the other one hit a small hole formed. Together they continued to hit him from every side. Finn straightened one hand and with his skeletal fingers, sliced off one of his leathery wings. The Master roared and spun, hitting Finn in the side of the face. Amanda did not give him the chance to do any more, grabbing up one of the chains she had dropped, she hit him in the other side of his jaw. He gave her a sideways glare, slowly turning to look at her.

There was a moment where they stood staring at one another, neither one knowing what they wanted to do. He opened his wide mouth and roared. Amanda responded, opening hers and let out a banshee shriek. The Master blinked, momentarily stunned at what just happened. He did not stand still for long.

She could see the muscles in his powerful thighs began to tense and she knew what he was thinking. He never had a chance to move because behind him, Finn moved, slicing through his other wing before driving his skeletal hand through his back and out his front. Finn pulled his hand out with a resounding pop, jumping out of his reach. The Master collapsed to his knees, holding the hole in his stomach.

Glancing behind him, Amanda could see the glowing red crack that had formed a few feet away. The Witch stood just behind her, chanting something in Latin, her eyes bright red, her body glowing with an orange light. Amanda opened her mouth wide, spreading her arms as she began to pull in every shadow around her. Her flesh turned a black, her nails grew slick with the same color and when she was finished, she was nearly invisible against the darkness. She would need all the power she had for what she was about to do.

"You don't get it do you? You cannot kill me. I am forever, I will be here long after you die. I am Legion and Lucifer in the flesh. This is my Earthly realm. I rule this place."

The Goddess smirked, stepping closer to him. He towered over her, smirking with the same arrogance the Shadowed One had shown so many times.

"Not anymore you don't" She replied.

Then, she leapt into the air and slammed both of her feet into his chest, sending him flying back into the glowing red pit behind him. The Witch did not hesitate, she clapped her hands together and the open doorway slammed shut with a thundering clap.

No one moved, they all stood staring at the place the Master had been only a second ago. Amanda blinked staring in disbelief. He was gone, they were all gone. After all the hell, after everything, it was over. There would be no more Blood Kings, no more suffering. Sara could finally be at peace and Amanda could go on with life. She could have an entirely new life.

The black faded slowly from her skin and Finn reached down to help her up. There were tears in her eyes as she looked into his deep brown pools. She could not believe it. She half expected him to spring back out of the ground and kill them all. There was nothing, only silence.

"They're gone," Her voice cracked. "it's over." She said, shocked.

"Aye love, it's over." Finn whispered.

He wrapped his arms around her waist and pulling her close, kissed her hard. She welcomed his touch, his embrace and whatever he could give her. Amanda was now looking forward to whatever the future meant. She might be a Goddess of Shadows but the horizon seemed brighter. Nothing had turned out the way she expected it and she knew she would miss Sara for the rest of her life, she had someone to help her.

Chapter 43

Amanda had been so enamored with her victory, that everything else around her became muffled. She never noticed the Witch moving behind her or felt the fluctuation in her energy. The world suddenly seemed to explode as a white fireball hit the center of Finn's chest. It sent him flying back into one of the brick buildings behind him. Brick and mortar crumbled from the impact. Amanda turned to the Witch.

"He's not who he claims to be." She explained.

Amanda looked from the Witch to the figure emerging from the building. Slowly, she backed away from him. As he stepped over the ruble, he began to laugh. It rumbled through his chest and echoed off the buildings.

"I couldn't have done this without ye lasses." He smirked.

"No no." Amanda shook her head.

Finn started toward her.

"Oh yea girlie. I've been waiting for decades to kick that lil shite back into his dungeon. Ye helped me do it. Believe me, I am grateful. For that reason, I will nae kill ye. But yer lil whore of Babylon there," He said pointing at the Witch."she'll have tae go."

"Heh, then come get me." The Witch said, beckoning to him.

He laughed, turning away momentarily.

"Ye think ye can take me on? Remember lass, ye tried that once. Ye could nae handle me."

She opened her mouth to respond but he cut her off.

"Ye couldn't handle a few inches of me," He said, grabbing his groin. "what makes ye thing ye can handle the rest of me? Best ye step off love before ye get hurt."

His words cut deep. The Witch was strong but Amanda recognized the look in her eyes. They flashed red and a long tendril of energy, whipped the side of his face. It seared and fractured the flash, revealing the white bone of his jaw. His head snapped to the side and he slowly turned back to glare at her.

Amanda stood stunned, watching the entire thing play out before her. She had trusted him with her life. Her stomach churned at the realization she had made love to him. She snapped back to reality as she heard Finn growl. The voice that came out was something between demonic and god-like. Whatever he was, his true self was something worse than the Blood Kings. The hairs on her arm stiffened and rose with the goosebumps now tingling across her skin. With Finn distracted, she moved further away. He pointed at the Witch, his voice booming.

"Ye hoor of Babylon, bastard child of the occult! Shut yer mouth before I shut if for ye!" He threatened.

His eyes shifted quickly to Amanda.

"Where ye going lass? I'm nae finished with ye."
He was next to her before she could blink.

The Witch shifted but before she could move, he waved his hand and she was sent flying into a shadowy wall.

"That's enough of that now." He was nonchalant.

"You're not gonna touch me! Never again! I can't believe I trusted you! Sara trusted you! You son of a bitch!" Amanda screamed, her eyes welling with tears.

Finn rolled his eyes, rubbing his bottom lip.

"Ye girls were so easy. Ye wanted to hop my knob the minute ye met me. It was nothing to convince ye I loved ye. Did ye never wonder how I knew everything about ye? How I knew what would kill em? Why I wanted em dead?" He asked.

"You're wife-" She started to say.

"Nae, never existed. I didn't even hav' tae say a name. Just play the sorrowful husband and ye bought into it." His voice dripped with amusement.

"You'll pay for that! For everything! I promise you will!" She threatened.

Finn laughed. Her anger entertained him.

"What's funny asshole?" She asked.

"Ye think ye can kill me? I'm the reason ye could nae get to Sara in time. I needed th' lil runt killed off. She was gettin in th' way. If ye couldn't beat me then, why do ye think ye can beat me now? Huh?" He replied, smirking.

Amanda felt cold pass through every cell of her body. Her hands began to tremble and she clinched her fists to make it stop. The images of Sara's final moments, filled her mind as his words replayed. She hated him, she hated herself more for trusting him. Here she thought she could trust him and he too was lying to her. Amanda realized she had been so caught up in what he said, she forgot to answer him. Summoning her courage, digging for her anger, she turned to him with fury in her eyes.

"I don't care who or what you are. So, you pulled one over on me. Good for you, I'm impressed, really. But you forgot one thing, I'm still a Goddess." She growled.

"Oh ho ho," He clapped his hands, walking a few paces before turning and beginning to move back toward her. "Good for ye lass. Ye almost had me convinced. Tell me something, *Goddess*," He made air quotes as he spoke her title. "how exactly do ye expect to beat me when ye are so afraid ye cannae summon real anger? Hm?"

When he was only a few inches away from her, she slammed her fist into his jaw, hard enough to send him into a metal light pole. It dented on impact and groaned with the threat of collapse. The bulb shattered, raining down sparks and glass.

"Real enough for you?" She asked arrogantly.

Finn shook his head before pushing to his feet. She even heard a groan escape his lips. As he raised his head, fragments of skin began to drip from his jaw. Amanda expected to see bone and muscle but instead she saw leathery flesh. There was a noise behind her and she glanced over her shoulder to see the Witch making her way back to the fight. How long had she been unconscious? Or had she been waiting? The Witch was the no name element. Her motives, he reason for being here was a mystery. Although the longer she was around the more Amanda had a feeling she wanted Finn's head. He was cracking his neck and fingering the hole in his face.

"Damned slappers the both of ye. Never good for nothing but feckin and killin'. I've tried tae be reasonable with the both of ye. But I see now that's nae gonna happen. So, I'll give ye yer way." He said, warning in his voice.

The screams of a million souls could be heard as his humanistic features began to chip away and his body slowly changed. It was horrific watching him peel off his flesh as if a snake shedding.

The skin of his face peeled away, revealing protruding cheekbones. His nose broadened, becoming more defined. His forehead jutted out, becoming more pronounced and rigid. Finn's flesh paled to the color of bone, giving his face the characteristics of a demonic skull. The hazel pools, once vibrant, rolled back into his head and disappeared, leaving hollow sockets. His lower jaw expanded and elongated to accommodate his mouthful of long, sharp teeth. The upper and lower canines became more evident, overlapping as they grew into curved daggers.

Finn's legs expanded and stretched, making him grow to over eight feet tall when the change was over. Their muscle mass increased, creating a thick bulging veins that pressed under the skin. His legs were adorned in armor up to the thigh. The metal of which was the color of a starless sky and thick as a human arm. His shoulders broadened, the bones shifting as his muscle mass increased, becoming more defined. A valley of luminescent, fire red veins spread from his shoulders to the rest of his anatomy. They appeared to throb with a life of their own, as if writing serpents. It seemed they would break free of his body at any moment.

The entirety of his torso was covered in a similar armor as his legs. It was comprised of a foreign metal. It was harder than the hardest tungsten, forged in the fires of Hell, down in the darkest pit. His pauldrons were decorated with large spikes, their points stained with old blood. His now deadly hands, were dressed in heavily clawed gauntlets.

In the pockets of his back, birthed oily, feathery wings. Their bottom feathers stained red with the blood constantly oozing from between their layers of down. Where the red fell, tendrils of crimson spread across the ground. There was not way of knowing what it would do to flesh. His wing span was large enough to block out the moon.

His once beautiful hair, disappeared, replaced by hard bone, from which two horns waved back into sharp points. There were cracks of hell fire burning bright within his obsidian tines. His flesh darkened into a black she had never seen before but his face remained skeletal white.

Amanda stepped back, looking him over. Her eyes widened as they scrolled over the apex of his thighs. The cloth covering that hung between his powerful legs, left nothing to the imagination. He would not be allowed to touch her again.

As he exhaled, coal black breath flowed from his mouth. It was almost as if his insides were on fire. When he finally spoke, the Scottish accent was gone. Every word echoed off the buildings, booming loud enough to make the ears bleed if one was mortal. It shattered invisible car windows and triggered alarms. There was the agony of tortured souls to accompany his words.

"Death will not come easily for you. Decide now if you still want to do this Amanda." He said.

She cocked her head slightly, was he afraid he would not win? Is that his reason for negotiating?

"Dying, no matter how long it takes, is better than standing at your side. Quit stalling you over-sized troll and fight me!"

Although she was afraid, she refused to let it control her actions. She had no way of knowing what he could do to her. Of course, that never stopped her before.

"Fine then, have it your way." He replied.

He reached over his shoulder with one of his massive hands, the muscles in his arms bulging with the bend of his elbow. There was the sound of metal scraping metal and from his back, he produced a large sword. The pommel was made from the lower jaw bone of a lesser demon. Its thick bone handle was wrapped in living human tissue and with every move of his hand, a voice cried out for mercy. A long jagged blade protruded from the grip. It was made of the same metal as his armor. Amanda could only estimate its girth. It had to be nearly two inches thick, almost a foot wide and nearly six feet long.

Overhead, they heard the distinct flapping of large wings. They looked skyward and saw the silhouettes of uncountable demonic figures circling the street. The figures wore no clothes, knowing not the shame of nudity. The Witch moved to stand beside Amanda, both women readying for an enemy they were unprepared to engage. Turning to the Witch, Amanda spoke.

"Who or what is he?" She asked.

"That...that's venenum Dei. The poison of God, the accuser, the destroyer, the seducer. The Chief of Satans,Prince of devils. He is Bechira. To you, he is Samael and he's here to take over the Earthly realm." The Witch said.

"We'll see about that." Amanda replied.

Amanda was not unfamiliar with one of the most prolific demons of the Bible. However, no text had described his true form in int entirety. His powerful voice drew her attention.

"Understand, there are worse things than death. I can grant you true immortality and use your flesh, bones and organs as I see fit. You will feel every agonizing moment of pain. Are you prepared for that?" He asked.

"Is that it?" She asked, pulling shadows into her hand. "You plan to kill me by talking me to death? Or is this how you seduce? Because, I gotta tell ya, not very seductive."

"I already did that. All I had to do to get in your knickers was play the heartbroken husband and pretend to give a shit about little Sara." He said with a chuckle.

"You son of a bitch!" She screamed.

That coaxed a toothy grin from him. The shadows Amanda had been manipulating, wound into a cylindrical shape in her hand. Then suddenly fell away and dissipated. Amanda now held a weapon of her own. Its pommel was an orb of shadow and deep purple energy, fluctuating from black, to purple, and deep magenta. The blade was the color of the moon, and the grip was intricately carved from an unknown material, with sigils burning bright on its surface. Her Goddess features had returned but her courage remained shaken. Doubt began to enter her mind as she raised her sword. She knew she had to fight him but she was unsure if she could defeat him. Amanda would rather die trying, then not face him.

Samael exhaled a black, smoky sigh as he sniffed the air.

"I can smell your fear." He said.

"Yeah, well smell this!" The Witch screamed.

A whip of white energy struck his chest, scouring his armor, and creating sparks as it made contact. She spun on her toes, lashing at his armor feudally. The last strike cut into one of his massive wings, feathers drifted to the ground. From his dark flesh trickled bright orange blood. He turned to look at the wound she created and then at the Witch. Samael smirked and raised his hand to toss her again. She threw her hands in front of her, palms facing outward.

"Et disperdet te malum." She said, her voice polyphonic.

He jerked his hand back and hissed between his teeth. She had hurt him.

"You'll pay for that witch!" He growled.

Samael raised his massive sword to swing at her, but was blocked by Amanda. Her blade connected with his and she shoved upwards, throwing it off. The feat took all of her strength to perform. His sword was heavy without having force behind it. With him pressing down, it was equivalent of stopping a falling tower.

"Is that all?" He mocked. "All your power and that's the best you can do?"

Amanda seemed to glide across the ground as she moved toward him, her sword slicing deep into his left wing. Then she spun on her toes, and drew her sword up between his shoulders, severing the tendons holding his wings in position. Samael stumbled slightly, wings drooping as blood ran down his spine.

She slid away from him, moving back to stand beside the Witch. His blood dripped off the tip of her sword as she watched him struggle.

"Is that better?" She asked, rather catty.

A growl emanated from his throat and he turned toward her.

"You'll pay for that." He warned.

Samael lifted his sword, and drove it deep into the concrete, creating large cracks. Amanda took the opportunity to strike. She tightened her grip and swung with all her might. Sparks flew as her sword struck his gauntlet and was ripped from her hands. His free hand caught her by the throat, lifting her and backhanding her with one of his metal gauntlets.

It felt as if she was hit by a train. All the bones of her skull shattered and she spit teeth. The Witch reacted too late, her electric whip lashed through the air. He caught it with one of his massive hands, allowing it to wind around the gauntlet. She had never known anyone to do that.

"Wait your turn witch!" He growled.

The demon pulled, sending her through the air, and she collided with the building behind him. There was a wince and then she fell silent. Amanda was clinging to consciousness, the world around her blurred and wavered. Blood dribbled from the corner of her mouth as she stared up at him.

"What's the matter Goddess? Too much for you?" He smirked.

She only now realized that he had a growing hard on beneath the thin strip of fabric covering his genitals.

"Fuck you." She slurred.

"Not yet." He replied.

Then he kicked her in the stomach, letting go of her as he did. Her back slammed into a light pole before she fell to the ground.

Every breath she took felt as if she had daggers in her lungs. She knew her ribs were broken, that her sternum was shattered, and several of her internal organs were ruptured. A weak breath left her lips as she attempted to push to her feet. Her arms collapsed beneath her and she fell.

Samael turned on his feet and headed for the Witch (who was only beginning to wake). He lifted her by the back of her head, shocking her into consciousness. She kicked helplessly as she dangled in the air.

"Angelus gratia-" She started to say.

He slapped her hard enough to break her teeth.

"Tsk tsk tsk...None of that now. Tell me witch, have you ever been sodomized by a demon?" He asked.

"No...no." She said, her eyes wide with shock.

"Oh, yeah. By the time I'm done with you, you'll never want anyone but me. You may never be able to walk   again either. All that magic crap, will be gone." He replied.

Then, he pulled aside his loin cloth to reveal his still hard throbbing cock. He began to stroke his length, fiery orange precum dripped off the head, creating small puddles at his feet.

"You're not gonna touch me! Not again!" She screamed.

"But I am. Besides Althea, you enjoyed every minute of it before." He said, smirking.

"I wasn't given a choice! You never gave me a choice! But now my mind is my own! You won't do that to me again!" She replied.

"We'll see." He said.

Then he hooked a claw under the bottom of her skirt and began to draw it upward.

"Let's see what you're hiding under that little dress."

Althea tried to kick him, to draw up energy, anything to stop this from happening but she could do nothing. His grip was binding her. So, she tried to telepathically reach Amanda, to rouse her from her comatose state. There was only static in her mind, as if she could get no signal. So the Witch tried screaming at her.

"Amanda! Wake up! Amanda!"

Amanda twitched, moving her head slightly but that was all. The Witch continued to scream. But there was no other movement from her. In the darkness, Amanda began to hear a familiar voice. It was not Sara's but another voice.

'*Amanda...Amanda...I need you to wake up.*' He said.

"Mmm...James?" She whispered weakly.

'*Yes honey, its me.*' He replied.

It was the man she had fallen in love with. The real James and not the tainted version the Chameleon had pretended to be. With the Shadow Realm so close and Samael in the flesh, she could only assume it had opened a doorway to the spirit world.

"Help me James." She whimpered as she began to cry.

'*I can't, I'm sorry sweetie. I need you to listen to me. It's the only thing I can do.*' He said.

She winced in desperation.

'*I know hun. Amanda you are stronger than him. You are darkness incarnate. Older than Lucifer. Older than God.*

But you have to let the darkness take over. Truly become the Goddess. Then you can kill him.' James replied.

"How? I don't know how." She mumbled.

'You have to invite it in.' He replied.

Silence blanketed her mind and she moaned again. Then, with soft bloody lips, she whispered to the shadows. It was as if she suddenly knew what she needed to say.

"Ego accipere ad tenebris
Ego invocare in tenebris
Ego Cactus quod dea
Ego sum Shiva Ma." She whispered.

The wall of shadows began to vibrate as a stream of them snaked across the ground, pouring into her mouth and nose. She gasped as if new life had been thrust into her. There was a sound as she inhaled, a sort of growl. She slowly pushed to her feet, rolling her body upright. Another growl, several octaves deeper, tickled her throat. It was enough to pull Samael's attention from Althea.

A droplet of blood fell from Amanda's bottom lip and crashed into the cracked pavement. It splashed in its own segregated puddle. It was so small that its significance went unnoticed. But it was important. A physical declaration, it would be the last blood she ever shed at the hands of monsters like him.

With a ragged voice, she spoke. She named him. Althea had already done that but something in her screamed furiously for her to do the same.

"Samael." She uttered.

It solidified reality, gave her power over him. In his name, she discovered his weaknesses, she knew how to kill him. Within her belly, she felt something happening, a sort of birth of a new her. The power had shifted in her favor.

Slowly, glowing purple veins of shadow energy, spread through her grey skin, highlighting her eyes with ancient sigils. The phosphorescent energy sunk into her hollow pools, replacing them with amethyst gems. It spread through her long locks, transforming them into shadows before weaving together and creating two electric violet horns that curled above her crowns.

Amanda smiled a toothy smile, revealing three rows of shark like teeth. A long forked tongue flicked mockingly at Samael, taunting and teasing him. Even now she knew he wished to bed her again. Her long oily claws now replaced the end of her fingertips. They dripped a deep maroon poison, its effects unknown. Her feet transformed, becoming canine in nature, its four front claws and due claw, mirrored the others. Above her tailbone she felt something push violently through her gray flesh and then could feel its extension. It whipped about behind her, and with it she struck the ground, cracking the pavement. She had grown a tail.

The shadows swirled up around her torso before dropping to the ground. On her chest she wore a metallic chest plate with matching shoulder armor. Her clothes now consisted of nothing more than a short gray corset dress. The skirt of which was slit seductively up the side.

A legion of crawling, howling figures moved through the shadows around them. The Goddess had brought her own army. Their purple glowing eyes pierced the darkness. The real battle was about to begin. She stood glaring at Samael, watching him violate the Witch. He would pay for every crime he has committed up to this point.

Chapter 44

The Goddess made her way over to the demon, her moves silent. He was unaware of her presence until she grabbed the forearm of his violating hand. By the time he meant to react, she yanked the arm completely from the socket. A roar emanated from his lips and he dropped the Witch. Bright orange blood poured from the hole in his torso and bits of flesh and mahogany muscle dangled from the hole.

As Samael pressed his free hand to the wound and stumbled around, she turned his arm over in her hand, examining the dark appendage. Then she threw it down, arched her back and tossed her head back. Opening wide her tooth maw, she roared something between a banshee scream and lioness roar. It caused the shadowy wall around her to rattle, as if it was made of glass. She lowered her head and glared at the massive demon before her, her black lips twitching. Saliva dripped from her bottom lip as her hunger for his flesh increased. The Witch was cautious as she approached.

"Amanda?" She asked.

Two piercing purple gems flickered her way.

"Not anymore." She whispered.

"Aman-" She started to say.

"You should hide. This fight...it no longer concerns you." She warned.

The Witch glanced between the Goddess and Samael, then slowly began backing away. When she was certain, that the demon was not going to make a move toward her, she scurried off to hide in one of the buildings.

"I'm impressed." Samael said.

"I'm not here to entertain you demon. I'm here to assist you in returning to your proper place. Or...and I most hope for this...to kill you if you do not wish to comply. Please...don't comply...I so want the latter." She almost moaned.

"Then-" He was interrupted.

The Goddess was a blur as one hand ripped half of his injured wing off and the other, sliced deep into his leg. Her magenta poison quickly invaded his skin. The results were something of an acid. His leg began to steadily dissolve from the inside out, dripping onto the pavement as a black goop. Samael roared in pain, causing the tortured souls he held sway over, to scream in agony. He then began to laugh.

"Every time you hurt me, you hurt them." He laughed.

"Hmm...that's none of my concern. You must have me mistaken for Amanda. She is...was the bleeding heart. Me...I don't care about human souls or human suffering. I'd kill the Witch if it helped to put you back in your cage." She said coolly.

The laugh in his voice faded. It was the last time she would ever see him smile. A sudden silence blanketed the Earth as if Gaia knew something profound was about to happen. The demons above seem to slow in their movements, the shadow creatures behind her stopped slithering so quickly and her breathing ceased. All the world paused momentarily.

Then, the Goddess moved. She burst from her position with such speed that Samael had no time to react. With one hand, she ripped his other arm from its socket before poisoning his remaining limb. The Goddess ripped flesh from his other leg, tossing it down into the black puddle under him. She had shifted the scales and brought him down to her level.

The Goddess could have stopped there and killed him quickly but she had promised to make him suffer. To help him understand pain in ways he never had before. She shoved her claws up through the bottom of his head and wrapped her hand around his bottom jaw.

With one pull, she ripped his jaw off, splattering herself in his vibrant blood. Her flesh was beginning to look almost a burnt sienna, with the mixture of vampiric and demonic blood.

His long pointed tongue flapped about helplessly as blood and saliva ran down the front of his chest. The demon looked more horrific, and in a way, pathetic. He made incoherent sounds as he thrashed around, trying anything to move away from her. There was nothing he could do. He had no appendages to defend himself, no mouth to speak his nasty words. There was nothing he could do to hurt her, or anyone else, anymore.

"It's not fun is it...having no power...no control over your own body. Having someone rape you of your freedom...all the while, never knowing if or when you're gonna die. Who knows, I could have the Witch patch you up, so I can keep doing this. So...when are you going to die? Ask yourself that." She whispered to him.

The Goddess stepped back and thrust her claws deep into his gut, sending his entrails spilling out onto the pavement. For her final act, the piece de resistance, she grabbed both his massive horns and with a powerful pull, ripped off the entire top of his skull.

When she had finished dismembering him, he was little more than a stump. His body continued to dissolve under the onslaught of poison. She stood watching him melt into the dark oily puddle.

In an act of dominance, she threw her head back and roared. The creatures of her realm responded, yipping and scattering through the Shadow Realm.

As she lowered her head, her more human features began to return. The horns on the top of her head, wafting away in a gust of wind and shadow. In place of her battle ready dress, she wore a long black cloak that shifted around her as if it too was a living shadow. Her feet, once demonic in nature, were now bare. She seemed to glide across the ground, rather than walk. She headed for one of the dark walls that surrounded the street.

The Witch had come out from her hiding place and was watching her as she began to pass into the realm that was now her home. Sensing her presence, she turned and smiled at the Witch before fading into the dark ether...

Chapter 45

The town of Collins and the events that occurred within its boundaries remained forever a secret. There was nothing about the fire, nothing about the factory and the skeletons stacked outside. No one but the Goddess, a Witch with no name, and the dead, knew. Amanda McNabb was never heard from again. They continued to search for signs of her but could find nothing. She seemed to have disappeared off the face of the planet.

There were theories and stories about some dark woman with glowing purple eyes. Nothing could be validated. After that day, the death of the Blood Kings, she was never seen. Even the Witch could not summon her, no matter how hard she tried.

Los Angeles Police Department continue to investigate the massacre on Doheny Road and the accounts of a fight in Club Bootsy. Rumors had it that an angel had killed a man at the bar. They found fingerprints and some blood but none of them matched in the database. Mysteriously, that same night, three well known actors disappeared without a trace. Some wondered if the angel killed them. The case eventually went cold and was all but forgotten about.

On the same day Nathan Reilly, Shane Finley and Colin Caine went missing, someone dropped Shane's wife off at the hospital. News reports said she was bloody, bruised and with signs of malnutrition. Someone at the hospital leaked to the press that she had severe signs of sexual assault as well. No one else at the hospital would validate these claims.

The Goddess never discovered the Witch's true identity or her reason for coming to Amanda's aide. Rather than push the subject, Shiva Ma, chose to leave it alone. She understood that the woman's reasons were her own and she would respect that. Still, she did check in on her from time to time.

Afterward

So, what do you do when you discover a secret so terrible that your mind cannot comprehend it? If you knew something evil was going on, something beyond human, would you do something about it? Or would you run from the fight? What Amanda and Sara did, would make them enemies among the fans for years to come. If they ever knew their names. Sometimes you have to do what is right and be willing to accept whatever may come.

Always remember, in **every** work of fiction is a little **truth**.

Raven Black

Raven Black was raised in Spencerville, Indiana. She grew up, spending a vast majority of her time, playing by herself. So, she began to cultivate a vivid imagination. Growing up poor meant having very little money to do anything. However, her mother took advantage of the local libraries free services, such as checking out books.

Raven would get a stack of books, overtime she went to the library and would spend the rest of her summer reading. When she was not doing that, her mother came up with various art projects. Raven will tell you that it was because of her mother that she began to gain a passion for writing and art. It did not stop there, when Raven picked up her first set of acrylics, her mother encouraged her hobby. She would get her art supplies for Christmas or her birthday and her father bought her first book, which was published under a different publisher.

Often misunderstood, she prefers to spend her time with the people who get to know her and understand her. She would rather be at home with her fiancé or spending time with her family.

www.ingramcontent.com/pod-product-compliance
Lightning Source LLC
Chambersburg PA
CBHW020452020726
47493CB00001B/4